APOCALYPSE SOCIETY BOOK THREE

# WICKED DECEIT

## ALY BECK

© 2022 Aly Beck

All rights reserved. No part of this book may be reproduced in any form or by any electronic or mechanical means, including information storage and retrieval systems, without written permission from the author. This is a work of fiction. Names, characters, organizations, places, events, and incidents are either products of the author's imagination or used fictitiously. Any resemblance to actual persons, living or dead, or actual events is purely coincidental. If you're reading this anywhere other than Amazon then, you're a pirate, and your soul now belongs to me. Bend at the knee and praise your new queen! BWHAHA. You're to do my bidding from now on, and my bidding states: don't fucking pirate books, asshat!

**Cover by:**

**Editing and proofreading by: Jenni Gauntt**

**Formatting by: Pretty in Ink Creations**

*May your batteries be strong when the spicy hide and seek comes, so you can too.*

# WELCOMES & WARNINGS

Hello and welcome to the final book in the Apocalypse Society series! I'm so excited for you all to be here. But first, please take a close look at the warnings provided before going in!

**This is the DARKEST book of the series and I always take these warnings very seriously. Please read these so you know what you're about to walk into.**

**This book is set in a prep school/high school setting but is recommended for people 18+ due to the mature material within these pages. All characters depicted in this book ARE 18+ and consenting adults. This is a <u>dark reverse harem</u> romance with some scenes you need to be aware of. Please follow THIS LINK to view ALL the warnings about this book.**

**All in all, this book was meant for a mature audience. <u>This book WILL end in a HEA!</u>**

Also note, that my characters are *not* me. They don't hold my beliefs or feelings and are fictional. My characters say and do things I don't condone, but again, they're fictional. They'll say politically incorrect phrases, curse, and fight. *But they're still not me.*

**If you find ANY mistakes within this book, please email me a screenshot:** *alybeck2988@gmail.com*

# PART ONE

# ONE

## CHASE

Twelve miserable hours and counting since Zepp and Seger took off with my girlfriend to their mansion on a hill. They practically kidnapped her from under my nose. One second, she was in my arms, and the next, she was in their backseat, begging me to save her from her evil twin kidnappers. I can still see the fear in her eyes and hear her screams of protest as they drove away manically laughing.

Okay, well—she didn't need the saving part. And she didn't really do the screaming and protesting parts, either. Shit. Fine. Kaycee went willingly, with a dopey smile on her face when they promised her a twin sandwich. She didn't even put up a fight. It's driving me bonkers because I'm fucking jealous. My Sunshine, who lights up my entire existence, hasn't been in my vicinity in twelve hours, fifty-five minutes, and three seconds. Instead, I was stuck with my sister. Who I love dearly, by the way. But... but... My Sunshine!

It was their idea to leave me here with my sister, Ainsley. Don't get me wrong, I know we needed time to deal with the fallout from my dad's arrest. The fact that the FBI didn't really have him, and he was in the grasp of a secret government agency, Veritas. And that we had lost everything since the wonderful government had frozen all our assets and taken our home. Yeah, okay. We needed time to bond and heal.

But I miss Kaycee.

Shit. I think I'm going through withdrawals. Does that happen when you miss someone? Kaycee's like football—kind of. No, not really. Shit! I forget what her voice sounds like or her laugh. I need to hug her ASAP and hold her in my arms. Or I might die a painful Kaycee-induced death. Dramatic? Absolutely! But they should be back from their field trip from Casa West by now.

My eyes scan my phone, hoping for a call or a text or something. For shit's sake. I scan the time and date: Saturday, 11:59 P.M. It's a minute away from being another day, and I'm about to experience it without her. Shit! The last text they sent me was a picture of their enormous pool, with a hidden cave and waterfall. Oh, and Seger's bare ass cheek. Thanks, bro—just what I wanted to see. From there, I can only guess they went skinny-dipping. And dare I say, I bet they had hot, pool sex! WITHOUT ME! The audacity of my boyfriends-in-law! I should make a new rule: no sexy time unless we're all included. Is that too much to ask?

Apparently, my Sunshine's thing is breaking and entering to find clues of her best friend's murder… oh and the psycho cult that's after her. I may have missed out on the first time when they broke into Shaw's office. You know, that time they left me sleeping on the couch, and went off and had fun without me. I whined enough that they finally decided to include me in the Crowe break in. Shit, my heart was in my throat as I sat in the car listening in through the earpiece to everything Kaycee was experiencing–then when she was caught, I thought we'd all be in a shit load of trouble. Thank fuck Kayce is a good actress… and a god damn phone thief–can't forget that. She never misses an opportunity to sneak her sticky fingers into someone's pocket and take their phone. But thanks to her sticky fingers, we got into Crowe's secure computer–which turned up jack shit–through Carter's crazy spy disc thingy and got to mirror his phone. Shit. What a senior year....

We have to do it again, anyway. One spy disc in Carter's dad's office and one super spy disc in Shaw's before the Christmas charity event we all somehow got invited to. I still can't believe Carter got his hands on those cool discs AND is a damn genius. How many geniuses does one boyfriend-in-law group need? Two, apparently. So, where does that leave me? The jock? The cool one? The.... shit, what am I to this group?

I heave a sigh, working myself out of my frantic thoughts. Blinking rapidly at the white ceiling of the Maze House, I let the darkness of the room settle on me. The wind howls between the bushes of the maze, making finger-like shadows dance along the ceiling. Shivers dance down my spine, and unexpected goosebumps prickle my skin.

An unexplained douse of anxiety churns in the pit of my stomach, sending an uneasy feeling through my tingling limbs. I've tried to sleep for the past two hours, promising Ainsley when I walked her home that I'd sleep. But something is nagging at me in the back of my mind. Like an itch I can't scratch, and it's driving me batty.

I blink at the ceiling again. What the shit is going on? I reach for my phone again on the table and unlock it. The bright light illuminates my face, almost blinding me. But shit, there are no messages and no phone calls—still. I swallow hard, my heart beating against my ribs. It's almost one in the morning on a Sunday. They never mentioned staying over, and they're never this late. So, where the hell is my girlfriend? Oh, and Seger and Zepp—yeah, them too. I swear to God after this, they sure as shit aren't allowed to leave me out of their group activities. No Chase left behind, damn it! Especially when they pull this whole, I'm disappearing until late into the night. Shit. It's stupid because now I'm here wallowing away in my stupid self-pity with anxiety that makes me want to claw out my own damn eyes. Shit, I think they're twitching. Do eyeballs twitch?

My stomach turns, and anxiety blares warning sirens inside my head. It's one in the morning, Chase. They're dead on the side of the road in an unavoidable accident. Shit! They got abducted by aliens, and they're harvesting their organs and probing their unsuspecting buttholes as we speak. Oh, well, shit... no, not that one.

Although, I think aliens could definitely exist up there. But that's beside the point. Maybe they were kidnapped this time, and they're missing... Or they—I close my eyes and take a deep breath. Shit. I can't go down this spiraling road of bullshit. This happens every time my anxiety spikes, I end up thinking the worst of every situation, and then I panic. Or fall deep into the depths of my depression and barely make it out alive.

The only way this anxiety will go the hell away is when my Sunshine is back in my arms and cuddling into my chest to ease this tension mounting inside of me. The moment she walks through that door, I'm scooping her up and locking us in Zepp's room. Screw them for leaving me here. Alone. I don't need Chase time right now; I need Kaycee time. My bottom lip juts out. and I'm fucking pouting again.

I grind my teeth, pulling up Zepp's contact information. I haven't called anyone in years. Am I still doing it right? I mean, who calls people anymore? Old people, that's who. Sorry, Grandma, I don't want to have a thirty-minute conversation about the gators you caught, or whatever they do down there in Louisiana.

I take a deep breath and hit the call button. Out of the three of them, Zepp's the one who is responsible and answers a phone call. Putting my phone up to my ear, I frown when it rings and rings and then goes to voicemail. My bottom lip sticks out again. Fine, shithead, I'll try Seger. Except I get the same response. Nothing. Nada. Shit!

The anxiety in my gut explodes when I pull up Kaycee's contact information, and her picture stares back at me. She doesn't know I took it. Shit, she'd probably kill me if she knew I used it. But I can't help the ease it brings me just looking at the smile lighting up her face. Crinkles form around her eyes, and her head is thrown back in laughter at something Seger said. She looks so damn beautiful in her oversized sweater and leggings. This girl, man. I don't know what she's done to me, but she's done something. She's infected me with her entire being, and I never want to be without her.

I dial her number and curse under my breath when it rings and rings and rings and then finally goes to voicemail. I try again and get the same response.

What the shit is happening right now? Are they breaking up with me? Is this a twinsome now, and they're fucking me over? I should tell Grumpy! He'll go kidnap her with me. Us against them. And then... Nah. They wouldn't. Wait, would they?

Shit. I look around the room, praying they'll come through the front door. Come on, come on! I mentally will them to come through the door in: five, four, three, two, one. Shit, I'm not magic. And this only means one thing, I have to call him. At one-something in the morning. He's grumpy on the best of days. But if I interrupt his sleep? He'll bury me under a hedge, and I'll never be heard from again. Here lies the body of Chase, torn apart by a grumpy asshole whose sleep was interrupted.

I frown, staring at the number I don't want to call but dial it anyway.

"Fuck you want?" he barks into the phone with so much damn authority, I swear my balls shrivel into nothing, and my dick ceases to exist.

I look down and lightly tap my balls. It's okay, boys. He won't take you away today.

"Jesus, Man, is that the way you always answer the phone?" I gasp, jumping to my feet.

Between his grumpy voice and everyone else missing, I can't help but move around the room.

"When it's you calling, and it's one thirty in the morning, yeah. That's exactly how I answer the fucking phone. So, I repeat. What the fuck do you want, Elf Ears?"

I wrinkle my nose and touch my offended ears. "Why Elf Ears? Seriously? That's offensive to the elf community, asshole."

"I am not having a fucking conversation with you about elves and their fucking feelings!" He huffs out curses, and then silence greets me.

I take the phone away from my ear and stare at my brightly lit background with a frown and scoff.

"Shithead hung up on me," I growl, with my heart pounding against my ribs. "Asshole!" I shout to the ceiling, tempted to throw my phone across the room and smash it to pieces. But I stop my arm mid-throw because violence never solves anything. Unless you're Seger and Carter who think their fist solves everything. With a heavy sigh rocking through my chest, I call the dickbag back. Crawling back to him on my fucking knees.

"Fuck off, Benoit!" Carter growls and then hangs up. A-fucking-gain.

"Shit-eating dick hole!" I hiss, trying to call him back, but it immediately goes to voicemail. Again and again, he ignores my calls like I'm a needy girlfriend or something.

For real, who invited this dick to the harem? Huh? I look down at the floor and nod. Right. We insisted. I think I'm regretting our decision now. Is it too late to call an island meeting and take a vote?

> Me: You grumpy asshole. This is about Kaycee not being back!
>
> Me: Is everyone in the stupid chat ignoring me? Where are you?
>
> Me: If you decided to stay at Casa West from a sex coma then you should have told me!
>
> Me: And included me in the sexcipades!
>
> Me: Answer me! Anyone?
>
> Me: ANYONE SERIOUSLY!!!
>
> Me: I'm inserting trackers up your asses! Make it happen, Grumpy!

I pace the room, pulling at the ends of my hair. Shit. Double shit! Where the hell is everyone? I call and call, but no one answers. Either they're ignoring my annoying ass, or they're dead. Or they're caught by the Apocalypse. Shit! Or caught by Veritas. Or maybe… Abducted. Aliens. Butthole probes. Shit. No.

Think more logically, Chase. They're probably sleeping. They had way too much wild cave sex, and now they're exhausted. Yeah, yeah. That's it. They're exhausted and unable to come to the damn phone. They'll call me in the morning. But shit! It's already two in the morning—fourteen hours later. Have I been pacing for two hours? Have I lost my fucking mind? Yeah, yeah, I have.

Worry courses through me like a damn wave, tripling my anxiety. Something happened, and I can't put my damn finger on it. I heave a breath and force myself to sit on the edge of the couch and pick up my phone again. Assholes better answer this time, or I'm serious about the trackers up their buttholes. If they thought the aliens were bad, I'm worse.

I hold my breath as the phone dials out and rings, and rings, and rings.

"Chase," Seger says in a groggy voice, and my breath leaves my lungs.

"Asshole!" I shout. "Where the hell are you? I've been calling forever and—"

"Shut the fuck up and listen to me," Seger grunts.

My face falls when the chaos in the background explodes through the phone. And I hear it all. My fucking heart shatters in my chest when frantic cries and loud orders erupt around Seger. Beeps and yells and scuffing shoes.

"Seger," I say in a deep voice, jumping to my feet. "Wha—"

"We were in a fucking car accident that we'll have to talk about later," he gasps out, trying to catch his breath.

"Is… is everyone okay?" I worry my lip to the point blood gushes into my mouth.

"Get to the fucking hospital. We're at East Point Memorial," he says through shuddering breaths.

"You fucking tell me right now!" I shout, searching everywhere for my fucking shoes.

"I don't fucking know. Zepp's gone. She's gone. And they won't tell me shit!" Seger curses and then cries out. "Get the fuck here, man, I can't do this shit alone." Tears burn in the back of my eyes when I sink my teeth into my bottom lip to keep it from quivering more.

"What the hell happened?" My breaths completely leave my lungs when I bend at the waist, sucking in air.

"Fucking get here, and I'll tell you," he rasps out, emotions clogging his voice. "Just fucking get here," he barks out with more authority.

"Yeah, Man, I'm coming as fast as I can! I'll be there in like an hour," I ramble off, shoving my feet into my shoes and shouldering my phone. I push out the front door, jogging towards the maze.

"Thank fuck," he mumbles, sleep creeping into his voice. "Oh, and Chase?" His words slur together, but I catch what he says, even though my heart is pounding in my ears blocking out everything but his voice.

"Yeah?"

"Don't forget to bring Grumpy," he whispers, hanging up the phone.

I wrinkle my nose, standing in the middle of the front yard. A cool draft blows across my legs, and when I look down, I'm standing in my damn boxers.

"Shit!" I curse, storming back into the Maze House, shoving off my shoes, and putting on a pair of jeans. Once I'm satisfied I've put myself together enough to make it to the hospital, I grab my keys and high tail it to Grumpy's apartment, despite the time of night and the fact I'm about to not have an asshole. He's going to murder me.

---

My heart hammers in my chest when I stand outside his apartment door, pounding on it like my fucking life depends on it. Because it does. Accident. Hospital. Seger's words replay in my mind over and over. Shit! What about Kaycee? Zepp? Where are they? Are they there? They have to be!

"Open up, you dickless fucker!" I hiss through the wood, trying to keep my voice low enough not to draw attention to me. But I also want this asshole to hear me.

"You and I both know I'm not fucking dickless," Carter growls, grabbing me by the collar of my shirt and tossing me inside his messy ass apartment.

I grunt, rolling on the floor and landing on my back with an oomph.

"Fuck you want, Elf Ears? I thought I made it pretty fucking clear I didn't want to speak to you," Carter grunts, standing above me.

I grind my teeth when he pushes his foot into my chest with enough pressure to knock the air from my lungs. Jesus, is this what it's like to die from suffocation?

"Seger's in the hospital. And Zepp and Kaycee are missing." I gasp out, relieved when his foot leaves my chest. My head falls back onto his sticky floor, and I secretly hope I'm not laying in leftover spooge he forgot to clean up.

"The what?" He growls, reaching down to grab me by the shirt again. He pulls us nose to nose, forcing our faces together as he snarls at me. "THE WHAT?" He shouts, shaking me in his fist.

Well, if I thought suffocation by his foot on my chest was bad. This is fucking worse. I grunt, throwing a weak fist into his temple to get him the hell off me. He stumbles back, dropping me to my feet. Sheesh, finally. I straighten my shirt and throw him my best scowl as I right my damn hair and smooth it back into place.

"The hell do you think I was calling you for? Shit! They've been missing all night. I finally got a hold of Seger ten seconds ago. I've been in fucking limbo! And now we need to get to the damn hospital," I shout, getting into his snarling face, poking a finger into his hard as hell chest.

Could this asshole rip me in half with his hands? Yes. Yes, he could. But I don't care. I'm tired of him shoving me around. I lift weights damn it! I should be able to take him on.

His nostrils flare as he stares me down, his fists clenching. "Anything else? She fucking okay? Did you fucking talk to her?"

"Just Seger. He doesn't know anything. So, I came straight here to get you since you wouldn't answer your fucking phone," I say through clenched teeth. "Can we go yet?"

"Let's get the fuck out of here and go find our fucking girl," Carter says, swiping a trembling hand down his face.

He walks toward his desk and shuts his computer down.

Paperwork is strewn across the surface, and he pushes it together and shoves it into a locked drawer.

"What the hell were you doing?" I ask, wrinkling my brow when he looks back at me with a fallen face.

"More research," he mumbles, grabbing his jacket and putting it on. "Now, stop asking me stupid fucking questions, and let's get out of here." He mumbles something else beneath his breath, but I don't catch it.

What I do catch is the emotions he's trying to suppress to the back of his throat. But he can't fool me. Cruel Carter feels, and I've seen it on more than one occasion. When he does though, it always involves our Kaycee.

# TWO

## SEGER

Everything hurts, and I'm fucking dying, and no one will tell me anything. I'm going to jam my fist down someone's throat in two seconds if I don't get some goddamn answers. I check the clock on the wall, grinding my teeth at the incessant fucking ticking. 2:30 A.M. Why the fuck can't I get any answers?!

"WHERE THE FUCK ARE THEY?" I shout again, pounding against the stupid hospital bed I'm bound to with IVs and a heart monitor. I'm ten fucking seconds away from pulling these fuckers out of my arm and walking the fuck out of here! "It's been hours!" I shout again in a pained voice. I've been here unconscious for what felt like hours on end, and when I finally woke up, I was way too out of it to make any decisions.

A frazzled nurse, tired of my shit, peeks into the room with a frown, shaking her head for the millionth time. It's only been a few hours since they brought me here—apparently unconscious. From the moment my eyes popped open, and I registered where I was and what the fuck happened to me, I've been a terrible patient.

"Mr. West," she sighs, pulling the curtain back to reveal herself. "You were in a serious car accident. You need to calm down before you rip your stitches open. Again," she growls the last part, tsking at me like a child. She shoves her hands into latex gloves and examines the stitches on my forehead, making sure to poke harder than necessary. Fair enough, I fucking guess. I've been one shithead of a patient. But if they told me shit, then maybe I wouldn't be yelling like a banshee. Shaking her head, she backs away, muttering something under her breath. Probably about how excited she is that I'll be discharged soon.

"I won't stop until I know my brother and girlfriend are okay. Are they here? Will you tell me anything? You have to understand," I plead, turning on all the charm.

I bat my eyelashes and fold my hands together, but she doesn't buy it. Damn it, where's Benoit and his charm when you need him? He could talk her out of her damn old woman panties and get her to tell me anything I wanted to know. But no, he's not here, and I have no fucking way to get her to open up.

"You know I can't tell you anything about her," she says, moving toward my IV bag, hanging from a metal arm above me. The machine it's attached to beeps an obnoxious song, making my damn ears ache. I groan, rocking my head from side to side, trying to drown it out.

"But my brother?" I ask, watching her punch the buttons with a heavy sigh.

"I'm right here." My damn heart leaps from my chest when that pale mother fucker walks through the curtain with bloodstained clothes. He grimaces, limping into the room with a groan. "I could hear your screams down the hall," he hisses between clenched teeth, pain shooting through his face when he takes another step. Squeezing his eyes shut, he takes several deep breaths and freezes.

"You're not supposed to be out of bed," the nurse gasps, hurrying towards him. Curses slip from her lips, mumbling about him being up and walking around before he's ready. But he waves her off, sending a scowl in her direction, making her huff in annoyance. She narrows her eyes between the two of us and places her hands on her hips like she's about to rip both of us new assholes.

"I'm checking myself out," he grumbles, coming to sit on the edge of my bed, doing something he hasn't done in a long time. He grabs my hand, squeezes my fingers, and sighs in relief from the contact. His entire body relaxes simultaneously as mine does, and our shoulders sag.

"Mr. West!" The nurse hisses. And just like I thought, she's ripping us new assholes, but my brain hurts too much for this kind of verbal assault. "You are to be in this hospital until we can clear you to go home. You both probably have concussions, and who knows what else. Stay put in this room until we can confirm you're okay," she says, narrowing her eyes at us like we're up to something.

"You and your dislike of hospitals will catch up to you one day," I murmur, shaking my aching head. I don't blame him for his dislike of this fucking place in particular. It brings back memories I don't want to relive. Fuck. The world fucking swims, and my vision blurs. "Ugh. My head," I groan, pushing my palms into my eyes to relieve the building pressure.

"Here, this will help," the nurse says, softening her features. Sympathy roars through her eyes when she steps up and injects something amazing into my IV, relieving me of some of my pain. Instantly, it hits me, and my muscles relax. But my damn brain still hurts and throbs. "You boys need to be careful. I'll turn down the lights, but you need to take it easy. And you, other Mr. West, you need to be incredibly careful. I'll allow you to stay here if you stay put. No leaving until we get your test results back," she says, placing a hand on his shoulder, backtracking when he flinches. "I suggest staying right here. For now, you're still under our care." She gives him a pointed look until he reluctantly nods in agreement.

Zepp bites his cut lip, watching her pull the curtain back

around us. The lights fade, bathing us in the faint glow from the hallway. The constant pressure twisting inside my skull finally eases a bit, and I relax back into the bed with a small sigh.

"Where is she?" He asks, turning his misty eyes towards mine. "Where's Kace?"

"Believe me, brother, I've tried for fucking hours to get answers. And the assholes around here won't tell me a damn thing," I swallow hard, trying to keep the damn tears from leaking down my face. "They won't tell me anything." My voice breaks when I think of Kaycee lying injured somewhere in this hospital with no one familiar around her. Is she here? Is she somewhere else? Is she even fucking alive? What is she feeling right now? Is she scared? Looking for us? Fuck, we need to find her, so she knows we are okay. And I need to lay my hands on her and make sure she's okay. I won't believe a fucking word until my eyes are on her.

"What the hell happened?" Zepp breathes, widening his eyes on me.

I shake my head. "I... I don't remember." Swallowing the hard lump forming in my throat, I try conjuring up the memories of our trip home. But it's all dark spots and static movies playing on repeat with no end in sight and definitely no fucking answers.

Zepp's shoulders shake with emotions, and he hangs his head. "Whatever happened.... It was my fault. I was driving."

Hands gripping the wheel. Knuckles turning white. Zepp's emotions blasted through his eyes. Shit. Pain roars through the front of my mind, and I wince when flashes of our trip speed through my mind. Fuck, if I could just remember the whole thing.

"Zepp," I croak, squeezing his hand again. "There's no fucking way it was your fault." I squint, trying to fight my damn headache off.

"How do you know?" Zepp murmurs, looking to me for answers. But I just shake my head.

A throat clearing draws our attention to a lone figure standing just inside our room, hovering near the drawn-back curtain. More light pours in from the hallway, painting him in a faint glow. His silhouette alone makes my heart skip frantically inside my chest when he enters the room. A suffocating aura of authority comes off him in waves. We're practically choking on it. No wonder this dickbag oversees a deadly cult.

My chest tightens when he stands off to the side, watching us with intense eyes. Much like Zepp, he's cataloging everything about us. From the freckles on our noses to the damn moles on our toes. Masked glee breaks through his deadly eyes when they finally settle on the multitude of bruises lining our bodies.

"Zeppelin and Seger West," he says matter-of-factly with a small amount of glee laced in his tone. The edge of his lip ticks up in what looks like a satisfied smirk, sending shivers down my back. He's a fucking shark on the attack. An ominous, uneasy feeling settles over me, sending goosebumps pebbling across my flesh, and the hairs on the back of my neck stand on end. Whatever he has to say won't be fucking good or nice.

"Mr. Cunningham." When Zepp says his name, his voice dips low, to a vicious growl. His spine snaps straight, only wincing once when he's at full height, but he doesn't let it stop him from trying to intimidate the predator before us.

Carter's dad scowls. "It's Detective Cunningham to you, son. And I just have a few questions for you boys regarding the accident."

Out of the corner of my eye, Zepp gives me a discreet nod and squeezes my hand again. Yeah, we fucking got this. We can take this asshole on and answer his questions as honestly as possible because we don't know shit about fuck.

"What about it?" I ask, trying to keep the snarl out of my

voice. "And at two in the morning? Can't this wait?" I narrow my eyes expecting him to answer, but instead, he ignores my complaint completely, pursing his lips.

"Who was driving the vehicle?" Cushing Cunningham asks, eyes darting between us.

His fingers reach into his pocket, and he pulls out a small notepad from his pants. Flipping it open, he taps the end of his pen against it and waits for our answer in the blistering silence. Sweat forms on my brow from the intensity of his stare, and I swear he can see right through us, and knows every answer. Fuck. He probably does and wants us to admit what happened. But it wasn't our fault. Was it?

Zepp clears his throat, and all the guilt inside him displays like a fucking movie on his drooping face, showcasing every amount of guilt he feels. Exhaustion sweeps over him, and I can tell he's about to spill his guilty guts and confide in this asshole about everything he knows.

Zepp's mouth pops open, but before he can get any words out, a glaring woman steps inside our room and marches toward Cushing. She shakes her head with a scowl that could put the fear of God in the Pope. Shit.

I squint my eyes when she walks through the dark and stands before a baffled Mr.—oh my bad—Detective Cunningham. The realization hits me square in the chest and I sputter, choking on my spit. Standing before us is an older, darker-eyed, darker-haired version of the woman we love. And holy fuck, I thought Kaycee was scary when she was angry–well sometimes, just don't tell her. Her angry voice grabs us by the balls every time she scowls at us, or snarks at us, and now I see where she gets it from. The woman snarling at the detective like he's a pesky fly is Kaycee's mother.

"No, no, and no," she demands in a sharp voice, smoothing out her shirt. Stepping up to Detective Cunningham, she gives him the meanest scowl and snarl I've ever seen. "This is not happening right now, Sir."

I nearly choke on my spit again when she repeatedly pokes a finger into his chest, forcing him to stumble back over his feet. I swear a stupefied expression passes over his face when he looks her over from head to toe. He even looks to us for help, but we offer him none.

His face reddens in anger, and a familiar vein bursts on his forehead, and when he goes to open his mouth again, she cuts him off.

"These children were just involved in a horrific accident. And by the report, your officers submitted two hours ago, the investigation is over. It was a hit and run. Isn't that correct, Detective?" She raises a pointed brow, exuding so much confidence it fills the room, and suffocates us.

Cushing swipes at his nose and stands tall. "We may have deemed the investigation a hit-and-run, but we still like to talk to the people involved."

"And you're more than welcome to speak with them when an adult is present and when the sun is up. It's currently almost three in the morning, and you're wanting to speak with them now? Yeah, I don't think so. They are on pain medications and are still in the hospital. I can have my lawyer assist me with this if you'd like?" She asks, crossing her arms over her chest after backing him into a corner—literally. I've never wanted to fucking whoop so loud in my damn life when his face falls, and he sees he has no other choices but to comply to the crazy fucking woman standing in front of him.

His back presses against the corner of the room, and he frowns, looking down at her in confusion. I don't think anyone has ever taken him on like this or challenged his authority. I'd love to warn her to back off because he's a psychopath. But I have a feeling she'd win every challenge against him.

"Take care, boys. We'll be in touch very soon," he says through gritted teeth and saunters out of the room with anger radiating off him. Uh, that's a fuck no from me. We will not be in contact, and he can shove his questions up his tight ass. Fuck.

Obviously, he didn't get what he came for. Thanks to our guardian angel, who watches him walk down the hallway until he disappears. Once he's out of sight, she turns to face us, and her hardened expression falls into despair. Her big brown eyes well up with tears as she takes in our injuries. Her teeth sink into her quivering lower lip until she takes a big breath and calms herself.

"Zeppelin and Seger West?" She asks in a small voice, taking a step forward.

Shit. She didn't know if it was us for sure. I furrow my brows, but now in awe of this crazy ass...

"I'm Mercy Cole, Kaycee's mom," she says, offering us a warm smile. "I wanted to check on you boys. They told me you were in the car too, and I wanted to see you and make sure you were okay." I furrow my brows wondering how the hell she knew it was us and how the hell she got our information. Those bastards wouldn't tell me a fucking thing about anything. "Well, I may have bribed them for information," she says sheepishly, running a hand down her shirt. "I needed to know who was in the car with my baby, and what had happened." My eyes widen at the bribing part, and I rear back. Yeah, that's definitely Kaycee's fucking mom. And now it all makes sense where Kaycee gets her spunk from.

Zepp straightens, and his bruising face lights up. "And Kaycee?" He asks desperately.

"Please," I gasp, forcing myself to sit up. "Tell us she's okay."

"Please," Zepp echoes my plea again.

My breath hitches in my already aching chest when Mercy nods her head, and she grimaces—fucking grimaces. God, my heart falls into my ass, and I squeeze Zepp's hand so tight, I might pop his fingers off. I hang on for dear life because I'd die if something happened to Kace. Fuck life.

"Kace is fine, ish," she says through a sigh, and her shoulders sag.

"Ish? Ish? What the f—" I scowl when Zepp covers my mouth with his palm, and I breathe heavily through my nose. He raises a stern brow and gives me a subtle nod, ensuring I watch my tongue.

Right—fuck. Impress the mom, not turn her away using my favorite word. Fuck. I've never had to worry about it before. Dad never cared enough to fucking stop me, and the teachers all turned a blind eye. So, no more slips of the tongue. This could be like my future mother-in-law or something. Be a good fucking boy, Seger, and don't fuck this up. I internally cringe because I fuck everything up. Like this, being here. We wouldn't be here if we had just stayed at the mansion instead of going home, and Kace wouldn't be in the hospital.

He lets go, and we turn our attention back to Mercy who hides her mouth behind her hand. She clears her throat and nods.

"Kaycee is in surgery right now."

"What?"

"Why? Surgery?" I yelp from moving so quickly, pushing myself up out of bed, but grunt when the IV holds me back and lifts underneath my skin. I frown, yanking it out, and throw it aside, much to the horror of Kaycee's mom, staring at me like I've gone mad. Blood splashes down my fingers but fuck it. The need to run to Kaycee overrides everything inside of me. Even if the pain splitting my damn head in half knocks me back. Pain explodes everywhere from the quick movements, and my vision dances with bright stars. I groan, sitting back down and holding my head. Mercy gently hands me a paper towel from beside the sink, and I hold it to the wound on my wrist. The blood soaks through, but thankfully fucking stops before she speaks next.

She holds up a placating hand. "The doctors say she'll be fine. She sustained several injuries from when she was tossed from the car."

"T-tossed?" Zepp gasps, a bead of sweat pouring down his temple.

Before my eyes, the color drains from Zepp's face and washes him out. His fingers tremble when he swipes his cheek, and I know exactly where his fucking genius brain has gone to. He's thinking this is all his fault and he's going to stew over it for the next few days until he fucking bursts.

"What do you mean, tossed?" He gasps out the word, clutching his chest and heaving breaths.

I grab his hand again, squeezing his fingers, and he squeezes back, side-eyeing me. Gratitude bleeds through him, but I know he won't settle the fuck down until Kaycee is in our arms.

"I can tell from here you were the one in the driver's seat," she says in a stern but thoughtful tone, lightly placing a hand on his shoulder. She forces my brother to focus on her. "But it wasn't your fault. You understand that, right? From the investigation, a drunk driver rear-ended you at around 11:00 P.M. They forced you off the road and into a light pole, nearly throwing you over the cliff. Boys, it's a miracle you all came out alive. It could have been so much worse." As the words leave her lips, her breaths shudder. Confirming to me, this entire situation could have killed us. By some fucking miracle, we are all alive—injured and in surgery—but alive.

The tension in my body leaves at the soothing and caring tone she gives us. Love sits in her eyes for our well-being, and she doesn't even know us. Yet—at least. All she knows so far is we were the ones in the car with her daughter. We were the ones who put her in danger. And we were the ones who caused this entire fucking mess. Maybe? Fuck, I don't know.

My brows furrow, much to my bruise's screaming protests. "We don't remember," I whisper in horror, eyes moving all around the room to avoid her stare.

Why can't we remember? I squeeze my protesting eyes shut and take a deep breath, bringing back the only memories I can remember, and trying with all my might to figure out our last steps. Mentally, I retrace everything we did last night before we piled into the car and left. We had a nice dinner with our little brother and then watched a movie in the theater room. Vaguely, I remember cuddling with Kaycee on the couch until her clothes were dry enough to wear home. Fuck. I blow out a breath, remembering when we showed Kaycee the pool, we kept alive in honor of our mother, and then the moment we jumped in. I suppress the snort lodged in my nose, thinking about her angry face when she resurfaced after we had jumped in. And then.... the faint memories of Kaycee's echoing moans drift through my mind on repeat. Images of her sitting on the rocks with her legs spread, and my brother and I taking her together slams into me. Fuck. We had mind-blowing cave sex right before ending our night at Casa West. It's something I'll never forget.

A smile blooms on my face when my little brother, Hendrix's happy little face, pops into my head. He had been so excited to see us, squealing when we had dinner with him after our swim. But after that? After our dinner and the movie? It's nothing but darkness. Like a damn black hole living in my brain and sucking up all the memories. Why is it so damn fuzzy? We had to have left in Zepp's Porsche, obviously; we crashed the mother fucker, and now we're here. But getting into the car and driving off? The car ride until we crashed? Yeah, I can't remember shit.

"I wouldn't think so, Boys. You—you came in unconscious and very battered. At least, that's what they're saying." Emotions clog her voice when she waves a hand, trying to bat them away. "I'm so sorry you don't remember. They mentioned calling home to inform your parents of the accident." She takes a quick look around the room, seeking any sort of personal items that might belong to our parents. Fuck. She must have bribed them well if they gave up that kind of information.

She won't find any personal belongings around this room. Not from our parents. Even if they called the step monster, she wouldn't leave her mansion on the hill or call us to make sure we're okay. The only thing her greedy fucking ass would have done is check the death certificates to see if she's a billionaire, but that's the extent of her worry.

"Kaycee," Zepp says, desperately searching Mercy's eyes. "What is she in surgery for? How long? Is she going to be okay? I..." He cuts himself off, sucking in another frantic breath.

She holds up a hand. "She'll be fine, I promise. After being ejected from the vehicle, she fractured her elbow and had minor scratches, bruising on her face, and a broken nose." I cringe thinking back to the bruising on her face after Hadley beat her ass a few months ago. Unfairly as fuck too. Thank Fuck for Zepp and his crazy bruising cream, we were able to help the swelling and bruising go down. Maybe we can do that this time, too. I shake my aching head, groaning through all this new information, and tune back into her words at the worst fucking moment.

"It's a very minor surgery. They just need to put in a metal plate and some pins to hold her bones back together." She gives a sharp and reassuring nod and starts talking more. But my mind can only focus on the so, totally, not fucking okay details she gave.

Pins? A metal plate? In the realm of everything that's fucking okay, that's not fucking included. A flush works its way up my neck and sweat coats my palms. My stomach turns at the thought of them drilling into her bone, and I swear a green tint takes over my face. I'm two seconds away from hurling until I hear my brother yacking into the vomit bowl the nurse left us as just in case. My stomach protests and twists from the sound of his heaves, threatening to spill whatever the fuck is in my stomach.

"I'm fine," Zepp gasps, shaking an arm in the air.

Yeah, so totally fucking fine, my ass. I blow out a breath and get my fucking stomach under control. When the bile settles back down and my mouth no longer waters with the urge to purge, I turn my attention back to Mercy, who watches us with a keen eye.

"Pay him no attention," I grumble, holding my stomach. "Him and hospitals don't mix." Her brows furrow in concern as she watches him with a close motherly eye.

Zepp's eyes peer around the room again, as he takes in heavy breaths. A glaze falls over his eyes, probably taking him back to the moments of our mother's death in this very hospital. Since being here every day during her cancer treatments, and then watching her die at the incompetent hands of the hospital, Zepp hasn't stepped foot in here since. And I feel him, I really fucking do. The last place I want to be is here, where my mom took her last damn breath because they couldn't figure out she had cancer for months.

Walking over to the mini sink, Mercy wets a paper towel and gingerly hands it to him, watching his every move. He wipes his mouth, hovering above the bowl in case anything else decides to spew. Heaving a few more times, his body finally slumps in defeat, and wild breaths pour from his parted lips.

Her brown eyes look between the two of us as a knowing smirk twitches the edge of her lips. Something clicks into place in her eyes, and she nods.

"I have a feeling my daughter has been keeping some big secrets from me," she murmurs with a warm, knowing smile.

At that moment, I know we're truly fucking made—she knows about us. Well, two of us, at least. Fuck. Thankfully, she doesn't seem like the type of mom to blow a gasket on her kid for having two boyfriends. Not with the way she's affectionately looking at us with warm love in her eyes. But how the hell will she react when she realizes there's four of us, not two. Fuck. We're in so much damn trouble. I swallow hard when I think about the rest of her family. Met her sister, she was cool. But Body Slammer? Fuck. He'll spike us into next week. And isn't her dad a big, scary guy? I've seen pictures of him. He will murder us, tear us into tiny pieces, and dispose of us where no one could find us.

I swallow hard, and my eyes widen. "I'm innocent," I blurt before I can think.

She barks out a laugh, much like Kaycee's, and shakes her head. "Okay, Boys, here's my phone number. Call me whenever you're out and want to come to her room. She's going to be here for a few days, at least until Wednesday, so they can observe her injuries. They said she'd be out of it for a while after the surgery. So, we'll be playing the waiting game."

Mercy waves her goodbye and waltzes out of the room with a slight backward glance. Her eyes sparkle with knowing, and I slump back into the hospital bed.

"Well, shit. We've been made," I say, lightly running my fingers down my bruised-up face.

Zepp straightens over the bowl, blowing out a breath. When he stands to dispose of it, he turns an ugly shade of green, stopping in his tracks. When he finally gets himself under control, he disposes of the vomit and wipes his face off with the paper towel again.

"She's......"

"Intimidating, for fucking sure," I sigh, pulling the blanket higher up my body and check the clock. 3:00 A.M. Fuck. They better let us leave soon, or I'll throw a bigger fit than before. I'm about to yell out when the curtain yanks to the side, and our very relieved looking nurse waltzes in.

"Alright, Mr. West and Mr. West," the nurse announces

with a bright smile. "The doctors have made an exception and cleared both of you for discharge. You're mainly bruised, but you'll both live. They recommend some ibuprofen, antibiotics in case of infection, and rest for you to heal." She raises a brow, turning to Zepp, who looks more uncomfortable than I've ever seen him in the corner of the room, hovering around the garbage can. "This goes for both of you. You boys are extremely lucky you don't have more injuries than a slight concussion and abrasions. So, get some rest and take your anti-inflammatories, and you'll be okay. Luckily for you two, you were seat belted in." The nurse works around us, clucking her tongue at me for pulling out my IV and places gauze on my wound. She cleans me up, removing everything I was hooked up to, and says her gleeful goodbyes.

"Thank you," Zepp says with a polite nod, shoving his hands into his pockets.

As soon as the nurse walks out, I heave my aching legs over the edge of the bed with a groan. Fuck. Pain ricochets everywhere, bouncing off every damn muscle. I don't think the fucking pain meds did a damn thing for me long term. They worked for a fucking minute, but the moment she stepped away, it came back with a vengeance. My nerves fire off in a display of fucking fireworks. I grip the edge of the bed with bruising force, white-knuckling until I pull myself to my feet.

"Fuck," I growl, balancing myself with the edge of the bed again. Zepp stands awkwardly in the corner of the room, staring straight ahead with big eyes, zoning out to who the hell knows where. "Hey, man," I say, snapping my fingers to gain his attention. His eyes widen, and he shakes his head a bit, knocking himself out of the horror show playing in his mind. "We'll call her mom and get up there as soon as possible, okay?" He nods again, taking a deep breath.

My fucking brother, man. He can look the devil in the eye and march through hell to get there, but he can't stand to be in the hospital. I don't blame him. This is where our mom went in her moment of need, and they fucked her over with a cancer diagnosis. She was in and out complaining of stomach pains for months, and they did nothing to help her. It wasn't until she was on her deathbed, that they finally had an answer for her. So, our trust in this hospital and its doctors is minimal at fucking best.

"Yeah," he says in a small voice, hanging his head. "Seg," he mumbles, shrinking back into the damn corner. Fuck me. I need to get him out of here.

"Zeppelin Dominic West, you ugly bastard," I gripe, stumbling toward him on baby deer legs. I clasp his good cheek, forcing him to look at me. "Stop thinking those stupid fucking thoughts. You got me? We don't know what the fuck happened. If it was a drunk driver, which I highly fucking doubt, then that's what happened. If it was that asshole who shall not be fucking named, then it wasn't your fault. You feel me, Zepp? You fucking got that?" With every passionate word I speak, my grip gets tighter and tighter, until I'm squeezing him hard enough to make him flinch.

I want him to know that this shit wasn't my fault or his fault, or our girlfriend's fault. It's no one's fault, but those fucking Apocalypse bastards—it has to be them.

"If it was them," Zepp says, swallowing hard. "Then they've upped their game." His voice dips so low that I feel all the emotions coming from him when he says it.

"Yeah," I breathe, leaning my forehead against his. "They've upped their shit, and it's turned very fucking physical." We close our eyes, soaking in the presence of each other, taking in our strength together. Our twin connection has always been something we've depended on. Now more than ever.

"We knew they were capable of so much, but this?" Zepp murmurs, pressing harder into my forehead. "What will they do next?"

"If they broke her fucking arm and crashed our car, then it can only worsen from here."

"We're putting Kaycee on a tight leash," Zepp murmurs. "I'll fashion one myself if I need to. She doesn't leave our sight. She can't go pee without one of us standing outside the stall. We need to be everywhere, so they can't get to her." Tears fall from his closed eyes, pooling on his long lashes, and cascade down his cheeks.

"We got this. We've got fucking Grumpy to figure this out, too," I say, through the emotions bubbling up in my throat.

"Yeah?" Zepp's voice cracks when he says the word. "And where was he tonight?" he whispers so low that my entire body locks up.

"We'll figure this out," I say, licking my lips, not wanting to believe what he said. My mind screams accusations left and right. If the Apocalypse did this, then where the hell was their Beta? And how much did he fucking know? Was he there again like he was before?

I pull away from Zepp and march around the room. My legs find their strength, but my head swims with dizziness, turning my stomach until the urge to hurl overwhelms me. I hold back the gag sitting in the back of my throat, forcing myself to find some clothes to wear. I don't have fucking time to get sick or be away from Kaycee any longer.

"Jesus," I murmur, picking up my shirt and jeans out of a small container left by the hospital staff.

Holding it up, my blood freezes in my veins at the carnage displayed on my favorite damn shirt. Fuck! This was something my mom gave me years ago, knowing it was way too fucking big. And now look at it. There's dirt and dark red blood staining every inch of the fabric. To some, it would be ruined, but for me—it's a damn treasure I'll keep forever. I hold back my cringe when I redress in the bloody and ruined clothes, opting to ignore the stains and continue. I don't have time to whine about my favorite shirt getting ruined. I don't have time to complain about my revolting stomach or the band playing a loud and annoying drum beat in my damn head. There's only one person on my mind right now, and that's Kaycee. She's somewhere in this hospital under the knife, and we need to get to her.

"I don't think she was thrown from the car," Zepp mumbles, bending down to tie my shoe when I hold my spinning head. Those deep, green, all-knowing eyes of his peer up at me from his knelt position, and he frowns. "Something happened there. But I don't know what."

"You think she'd remember?" I say with desperation. "God, whatever they did to her, I fucking hope not. If they broke her arm, Zepp...."

"I know," he says, sadness taking over his voice. "I know, bro," he whispers, slowly getting to his feet.

"Let's go find our girlfriend," I say, pushing open the curtain to our room, revealing the busy hallway of the emergency room.

# THREE

## SEGER

THE SECOND we step out together and look around, we stop dead in our tracks. Two figures haul ass toward us with varying degrees of pain crossing their faces. Their eyes dart around like they haven't spotted us yet, but they're barreling this way, pushing nurses and doctors out of their way. Well, Grumpy is scaring them with his snarl—I should say. Chase bites his lips, extending his neck to look through the crowd while following behind the maniac pushing through the fucking crowd. Note to self, If I ever need someone to lead the way, Carter's my dude.

I cock my head, focusing on Carter's twisted and sour expression. The intensity wafting off him smacks me in the chest so hard, it's like a damn omen of danger telling me to get the fuck out. Looking around the crowded corridor, I think other people can feel his anger, too. Every doctor and nurse in the vicinity takes a step back, refusing to move until he passes by. By the look on his twisted face, he'd probably throw a damn doctor at this point just to find out answers. But when he makes eye contact with one male doctor five feet away, the doctor scurries away, clutching a file to his chest. Shit. Someone needs to loosen old Cruel Carter up or he's going to die of an aneurysm or something.

Chase's expression mimics Carter's, but there's no cruelty

on his face—only concern. His brows furrow when he spots us, and he taps Carter on the chest twice, nearly losing his damn fingers in the process. Carter scowls, picking him up by the scruff of his shirt until he points us out again with a squeak. If my head wasn't hurting so bad, I'd laugh at the faces of the nurses, picking up their phones to call security. I'm pretty sure they'd have to tranquilize Carter at this point and put him down for a little nap.

Carter growls, putting him back on his feet, and then leaves him in the damn dust. In what seems like four long strides he stands before me, I raise a brow in waiting. He huffs and puffs like a damn angry wolf but doesn't speak a fucking word. Finally, Chase comes up in front of us and scowls in Carter's direction.

"Dick!" He hisses, crossing his arms.

"Where the fuck is Kaycee?" Grumpy asks, looking grumpier than ever with a scowl and wrinkled clothes.

Right. He's getting right to the point asking about his obsession, and not us. We're in this relationship, too. Dickbag.

"We're fucking fine, too. Thanks for asking, assholes," I mumble, trying not to talk too loudly. Every word I speak sends pain zapping through my damn brain and I just want to lay down. No matter how bad I want to yell at the dickbag before me, I can't.

Zepp shakes his head, putting an arm across my chest. "Not here. Not now. Let's talk somewhere else," he says, with all his usual wisdom returning. Thank God, because I can't navigate shit right now.

Zepp nods his head, and we all follow in silence. He pulls out his phone and quickly calls Kaycee's mom, asking where her surgery is happening. He gets the information, but instead of heading directly upstairs, we take a detour and find ourselves in the hospital's parking lot at three something on Sunday morning.

"You better fucking tell me what the FUCK is going on

before I jam my fist so far down your throat it comes out of your asshole," Carter barks, standing rigid with wild fucking eyes. Jesus, someone needs to put him out of his misery already or he's going to kill us.

"Now, hold on, Grumpy," Chase says with narrowed eyes. "We don't know what the shit is going on."

"Yeah, don't take your fucking grumpy, dick head routine out on us. Because we don't fucking know either," I shout, wanting to lunge toward him and knock his shitty attitude out of him.

But my legs wobble, and my head fucking spins, sending my damn stomach into a tilt a whirl. I still feel like I might upchuck on his damn shirt. Maybe that would make him fuck off. Or piss him off more. I can't decide which solution is better.

Zepp licks his lips, pacing a tiny spot in front of us like he wasn't just sick ten minutes ago. He shakes his head, biting at his nails.

"We were at the mansion," he says in a small voice, looking around to ensure no one else had followed us. "We got into the car, and then nothing."

"Fucking nothing?" Carter growls. "What the fuck do you mean?" He asks, clenching his fists, just twitching to knock someone in the face. Jesus, if we don't get him to Kaycee ASAP, he might disembowel us before we get the actual answers. And I fucking like my insides, so I want them to stay, you know, inside my fucking body.

"He means, we can't remember what the hell happened. It's like a dark fucking spot in our memories," I say in a small voice, a deep breath rocking through my bruised chest.

"What the hell does that mean? How can you not remember?" Chase asks in confusion, shaking his head. "Maybe you guys hit your heads too hard?"

I narrow my eyes at him until the blinding pain takes over my brain, and I grunt, "We have concussions, you dick," I hiss, holding my aching head, and trying to keep the vomit churning in my stomach again down in my gut. I need a fucking bed, ibuprofen, and my fucking girl.

"Oh," Chase's face falls and he grimaces, rubbing the back of his neck. "Shit. Sorry, dude," he mumbles his apology, looking us over like he just saw us for the first time.

Carter's assessing eyes take in our bloodied appearance, glancing at us from head to toe. He snarls at us, taking off in the opposite direction. I sigh, watching his massive form disappear into the shadows of the parking lot, wondering what the hell he's going to do. It isn't until I hear the growl, shout, and thunk do I fully understand he's gone to battle against a large tree in the distance. I pray the tree says uncle before Carter beats it to a pulp and knocks it over with his bare hands. I wouldn't put it past him to bite the damn thing, either.

"That guy really needs to sort out his shit," Chase says, swiping a hand over his brow. "He's been a ball of tension since I had to drag his ass out of his apartment. He almost fucking attacked me!" Chase exclaims with wide eyes, holding his hand over his chest. "Psycho," he mutters under his breath.

"He was at his apartment?" Zepp asks, attempting to straighten his spine, but winces when he's at full height. He groans, taking a deep breath, and works through the pain obviously working through him.

I snort to myself at the sight of him. You'd never know he was hunched in a darkened corner of the emergency room, shaking like a damn leaf two seconds ago. Now he's standing here like the same old Zepp, oozing confidence despite the pain roaring through his body. Most likely coming up with a Zepp-like plan. And thank fuck for that. My brain hurts way too goddamn much to put anything useful into this conversation.

"Yeah," Chase says, waving. "And he sure as shit was NOT happy to see me. I can tell you that."

"I had no fucking involvement in whatever the fuck happened," Carter says through clenched teeth, with blood dripping from his knuckles onto the pavement.

I cock my head, staring at his psycho ass standing in front of us all bloodied, and crazy looking. His chest heaves rapidly going in and out as he stares at us with a wildness in his eyes. He's two seconds away from pouncing and wailing on us until we give him the answers he wants to hear. Even if it's the wrong damn answers. There's no fucking way I could get him to Kaycee right now. For one, he'd scare the living shit out of everyone in the hospital looking like a damn serial killer on the loose. And for two, she's in surgery and we won't be able to see her for a long time. I know how that shit works. She'll go to recovery afterward and we won't be able to see her if she's in ICU.

"What happened? Where's Kaycee? God, she isn't dying, is she?" The color drains from Chase's face when he turns to me, pleading with his eyes for answers.

"Her mom says she's going to be okay. She's in surgery right now. They had to put fucking—" I trail off, covering my mouth at the thought of pins and plates and whatever shit they're putting into her elbow. I shiver at the thought of that shit going inside her body and staying inside of her.

"They had to put pins in her elbow. She broke her arm. Her mom said she had been thrown from the vehicle...." Zepp says, shaking his head. "But something isn't adding up. I don't understand what happened and why she'd be thrown from the car. Her mom said something about them finding her on the road after being ejected." Zepp swallows hard, turning to look away from us.

"Surgery? There's some fucking doctor opening her the fuck up?" Carter gasps, and I think he's petrified for the first time in his life. Fuck. If I was an asshole—which I totally am—I'd memorialize this moment with a picture.

Every ounce of color drains from Carter's face and he turns a sickly shade of white, turning him into a ghost. The only sign he's alive is the blood caked on his knuckles from fucking up the tree a few minutes ago. With a shaky and whole body shakes, he swipes at his face. His dark eyes dance around the parking lot, looking for who knows. His sanity? His fucking thoughts?

"Shit," Chase says, shaking his head.

"We talked to her mom," Zepp says, through a deep breath, continuing his pacing. "She said we could come up there when everything was done, and Kace had a room. It'll be hours, though. We should probably go home and get some rest until then," he says, looking at me with a grimace, knowing the answer to what he said.

"Fuck that," I spit, moving too quickly. "We can't leave! What if she wakes up?" Panic overtakes me, as the images of her waking up alone and scared run through my fucking mind. What if she needs us? What if she's scared or in pain and we're not there? Fuck!

"Dude," Chase says, pointing to the blood on my shirt. "You need to go home and change and shower. If you walk into Kace's room looking like *The Walking Dead* extras, she'll throw a fit. Don't make Sunshine throw a fit after all this." His voice trails off and he swallows the lump in his throat. Running a hand through his hair, he shakes his head.

I growl, looking down at my bloodied clothes. "Fucking fine!" I shout, reluctantly agreeing to this stupid as fuck plan, even though I know it needs to happen. I don't want to scare her by walking in with all this blood and dirt all over me.

"We'll go home, grab a shower, change, and get some rest. Then come back after," Zepp says with a nod, getting out his phone. "I'll text Mercy and let her know we're headed home."

"Beg her to tell us when Kaycee is out," Chase says,

hovering over Zepp's shoulder, reading every word. "Tell her, man!" He gripes as Zepp swats him away like a pesky fly and sends him a scathing look.

"I told her," he says with a resigned look, gazing down at the screen.

"Okay, let's go home," I say as Chase points us toward his vehicle. "Get some rest and then we can come back and be annoying boyfriends."

"Fuck that!" Carter hisses, knocking his shoulder into Chase's, making him stumble back. Chase scowls in his direction as he rights himself, following Carter with his eyes until he stops completely, shaking his head. "I'm fucking staying here tonight until I hear something. I'll sleep in the fucking waiting room, but I need to be here," Carter says with an unsure voice, his tough exterior falling away for the first time. He winces when he rubs his knuckles and checks his wounds. "I can't leave knowing someone has their hands inside her fucking elbow and that she isn't okay. I'll be a fucking bear until I know." Vulnerability leaks from his voice when he turns to look at us and heaves a breath. Every ounce of fight leaves him, and his shoulders slump forward as he waits to hear what we have to say.

"Fucking go man," I say, waving a hand without care. We make our way toward Chase's car with slow strides, waiting for Carter to either leave with us or go inside.

Zepp blows out a breath, lingering near the passenger door. He stares down at his phone, typing out another reply, and sighs. "She said it's on the eighth floor, they're in the waiting room if you want to go make nice." Carter straightens, giving us a tight nod and marches into the hospital with determination. I pray for the people inside and hope they don't cross that asshole before he sees Kaycee.

"He really needs to loosen up," Chase murmurs from the driver's seat when Zepp and I climb in.

"The only person who will loosen him up is the person

lying in a hospital bed right now," Zepp says, buckling himself in.

"Touché," Chase says, backs out of the parking space and heads toward the school.

Dread sits in the pit of my stomach during the drive back to school. I know it can only go up from here with the idle conversation around me and the vow we made to keep Kaycee safe. We won't let anyone fuck with her again. And she won't like it because we'll be up her ass further than we've ever been. She'll get over it and hopefully appreciate it.

"So, it's settled," Zepp says as we pull into the school's parking lot. He stares down, squinting at his phone, and types out a message to Carter. "She's out of surgery," he says, and we all let out a collective sigh of relief. "But he can't see her for a while. Her mom is in there with her right now, and he swears he'll give us some updates."

A pink tint takes over the sky as the sun breaks through the darkness. Today is a new day. My baby is out of surgery. She'll be fine, and we'll move her ass into our damn house for her own protection. Never again will she wander campus alone or go from class to class by herself. She'll always have us around. Whether she likes it or fucking not, it's going to happen. Even if I have to put a collar around her throat and drag her from point A to B. Then, I'll know she's fucking safe and with us.

# FOUR

## KAYCEE

*"We killed the rabbit! We killed the rabbit!"*

My heart hammers against my chest as the darkness pulls me under. My mouth falls open in a silent scream, begging for any noise to come through. Help! I want to scream for someone to save me from this eternal cloud of darkness circling me.

My body sparks to life with aches and throbs, pounding through every inch of my body. It consumes me through a revolving door of pain. The pressure pushes against my ribs, creeping up toward my aching throat. I desperately try to claw my way out of the numbing darkness, but my limbs won't cooperate again. In the middle of the road, I'm back there, with the voices dancing around me.

"We killed the rabbit! We killed the rabbit!" That voice sings, again and again, echoing through the depths of the endless darkness. It bounces around in my brain, and I desperately want to claw it out.

My elbow snaps in half, and my throat burns when my cries of pain fly from my parted lips. I'm fucking dying, and there's no one here to save me. Only me. I groan, rolling around on the hard road they left me on, staring into the bright rainbows dancing across the sky.

"We killed the rabbit!" The voice sings again, giggling the

whole time they prance around my body in a happy dance of my demise.

Death—my heart sinks into my stomach, swallowing it whole. Am I dead? My breath picks up rapidly, squeezing through the tender ache in my nose. I try to focus on the surrounding sounds instead of the manic taunts echoing in my mind. My entire body stings until a soft murmur from above me soothes the pain instantly. I whimper when a hand lightly brushes through my hair, tucking it behind my ear.

"We're all here for you, Kace," my mother's voice rings through the damn nightmare, settling my aching bones. "She'll be okay," she murmurs in a soft voice, talking to someone else in the distance. "Why don't you boys get some coffee or something, okay? Don't make me kick you out to get some rest," she says in a clear, stern voice. "It's been over a day of you boys watching her sleep. You need to take care of yourselves, too."

The pain evaporates, and everything settles inside of me, snapping in place. The nightmare voice rings in my head like a constant reminder of what happened to us. But it slowly fades to the background, chased away by the familiar touch running through my hair. Safety seems to wrap itself around me like a security blanket, and then and only then does darkness take over my brain, falling into a dreamless sleep.

---

My brain rouses again, drifting through a deep and hazy fog. Silence clings to the static filling my ears instead of the incessant voice singing about my death. Pain rips at my eyelashes when I try to peel them open, breaking through to a bright light pouring in from somewhere. I squint, blinking as sandpaper settles on my eyeballs, and I quickly squeeze them shut.

What the hell happened to me? And why is it so hard to stay awake and open my eyes?

A metronome of beeps breaks through the static, invading my ears. *Beep. Beep. Beep.* Ugh. Make it stop. I peel my chapped lips apart, ready to tell Zepp to turn his alarm off. But nothing comes out except a garbled demand for him to make it stop. The alarm pierces through my ears, and I furrow my brows in agitation. And why isn't Zepp turning it off?

I grunt, trying to lift my arms to wipe my eyes so I can open them again, but fail when they stay limp at my sides. Panic roars through me when the feeling of concrete sits heavy on top of my body. I take a panicked breath, sucking in as much air as possible, and try to move my arms again. I lift them an inch, but they fall back down, refusing to cooperate with me.

Panic fully sets in, heaving my heavy chest, and I cry out. Why can't I move? Where the hell am I?

Vicious memories assault my brain, taking me through various distorted visuals, flashing by in rapid succession. One after the other they never stop swirling together in a mishmash of images I can't quite make out. Again and again they run through my mind until they come in clearer and clearer, and I partially understand what the hell happened to me. It's still fuzzy and distorted, but it's there.

The car. The crash. A slight hint at the psychos. Their masks. The giggle. They injected something into my throbbing neck, causing my world to turn to colors. God. My arm, my aching arm. *Snap.*

My boys! Where are they? What happened to them? Are they safe? Breaths force through my burning nose until my lips pop open, gulping for air, and bringing it to my aching lungs. Everything inside me burns with every breath and rubber bands constrict my chest, making it harder and harder to suck in oxygen.

My eyes finally snap open again, greeting the brightly lit

room. I don't bother shutting them and blink until I can adjust. I'm too amped up with my heart speeding out of control and I need the fucking answers to my questions. My eyes dart around the small white room, taking in the small TV mounted on the wall and the drop ceiling staring back at me. As the beeping picks up, I turn my head and spy the heart rate monitor beside my bed.

My hospital bed.

My breaths pick up at a frantic pace, burning and whistling through my aching nose. I will my muscles to move, finally getting them to cooperate, except for one arm. Cringing, I try to pick it up off the bed I'm in, but it refuses to budge, weighed down by an enormous blue cast.

A lone whimper fills the room as I try to escape wherever I'm at until a shadow breaks through the light. My mom's soft smile calms my nerves, and her fingers brush against my good arm. I swallow hard when a new pair of hands rests on my legs, looking down at me with such concern that it takes my breath away.

"Baby, shh," she coos, getting some hair out of my face.

"Mom?" I gasp out in a deep rasp, a heat searing through my scratchy throat.

She nods, a sadness sitting in her eyes. "Yeah, Sweet Pea, you gave us a hell of a scare. Do you remember what happened? You want some water?"

My cracked lips part as the barrage of broken pictures and voices flash through my mind again, flickering like an old movie sputtering to life. The throbbing in my head increases more when I clamp my eyes shut, shaking the images away. I don't want to think about them or listen to the demented voice repeating what they said through a manic giggle. I don't want to think about the fact that they tried to fucking kill me —I think. I don't know what the hell happened or what their intentions were. But I'm still here and not six feet in the dirt.

So, either they fucked up and didn't complete the mission, or they want me alive.

Cool water flows over my dry and heavy tongue and down my throat, chilling my empty stomach. I suck it down, gulp after gulp, through the straw between my lips.

"My boys," I whisper through the heavy emotions clogging my throat.

I squeeze my eyes shut so hard that pain blooms behind my eyes. They were in the car after those assholes attacked me. Their heads were limp and lifeless, and their eyes weren't open. What the hell happened to them?

"I'm right here, Angel," a familiar deep, emotion-filled voice responds from a few inches away, startling me out of my wicked nightmare.

Relief washes through me at the sight of him alive and well. Bruises linger around his neck, dipping down onto his chest, hidden by his shirt. A large cut over his right clavicle with blackish-bluish color tints his beautifully tattooed skin. His fingers gently squeeze my leg, reassuring me of his presence again, and my body melts into the bed. One of them is safe—hurt—but alive, and I sag in relief.

"Seger," I gasp, looking him up and down. He locks eyes with my mom, and she pecks my cheek, taking a step back.

Tears fall down my face when he leans over the bed, gently pressing his face into my bruised neck. His shoulders shake, jolting his entire body, and warm tears fall onto my skin.

"We were so fucking worried," he mutters into my throbbing neck through violent sobs. "So—fucking—" he gasps out, lightly clinging to me like he'll never see me again.

I cling to him like a lifeline. I almost lost him—them. My fingers clutch his t-shirt, begging him never to leave my side again. I never want to feel the helplessness I felt inside the car.

"Where's Zepp?" I ask, moving my aching free hand

through his brown locks, soothing every ounce of sadness from his body. He lifts his head, resting his forehead lightly against mine, only pulling back when I wince from the pain of his skin against mine. I must have bruises everywhere with the amount of aches throbbing through every inch of me.

"He stepped out an hour ago with your other boyfriends to grab some food." My eyes widen when I look at my smug-looking mother uttering a phrase I never thought I'd hear her say.

She smirks, looking down at her phone, undoubtedly conducting business from my bedside. "It's been almost two days since your accident, Sweet Pea. We've gotten to know each other very well. Plus, you had some very interesting facts to catch me up on while you're all hopped up on truth serum."

"Almost t-two days ago?" I swallow hard, thinking back to my last memory. How could two days disappear without a trace? The last thing I remember is....... The wreck and some staticy images coming through. And that voice... God that voice. But two days? I've been in and out for two days with no recollection?

I look back at Seger's grimacing face, and he nods. "You had some pretty interesting things to say while on pain medication," Seger mutters, looking away from me as quickly as he can. Pain medicine? I can't remember. And two whole fucking days of my loose lips without a filter? Fuck. I'm so fucked.

Every ounce of color I possess fades away, leaving me an empty, pale ghost. Even the bruises lining my flesh evacuate, running as fast as they can away from here. Dear God, where's a hole in the ground when you need one? Because I could use it to swallow me whole.

"What—Oh, God! What did I say?" I mutter in a shrill, frantic voice, looking between the two of them. Forget what happened to me and why my arm is suddenly in a bright blue, clunky cast. I need to know I didn't utter all the damn secrets I've kept from them.

"You're lucky I like them," my mother says again, setting her phone down. "They seem like good boys. I had to shove them out a few times and remind them to eat and bathe. They were starting to stink." She snorts, rubbing her temples.

"I'll tell you later," Seger whispers, shaking his head. A small smile forms on his lips like he's thinking about what I said, and he can't help himself.

I really, really hope I didn't go into detail. Like *DETAIL-detail*! Shit! The last thing I need is to tell my mom about—gulp—my five ways. Or the backdoor sex I seem to enjoy. I look at Seger with desperate eyes, but he shakes his head, covering his mouth so I can't see him laughing at me. He's laughing at me now, turning his back with shaking shoulders. I frown. Whatever I said was funny or incredibly embarrassing. I'm leaning more toward the embarrassing side of things, considering Seger can't look at me now without snickering.

"I'm so glad you're okay. I don't—I don't remember what happened. There's some things, but nothing......" I say in a small voice, forcing Seger to turn back to me. He clasps my good hand in his, leaning down carefully to kiss my knuckles. His warm breaths blow across my skin, and I slump into the bed. "What day is it?"

The urge to spill what happened after the accident, at least the things I can remember, sits on the tip of my tongue. But if my mom finds out, she'll pull me from school to protect me. Even with my life on the line, I can't back out now. Maggie needs me to solve this, and so do all the others that these psychos have killed. They're depending on me to serve them justice because they don't have a voice anymore. No one can do this but me and my guys. Even if it kills me, I'll solve this once and for all. That's what I came here for, and I'm so close to bringing these dickbags down, I can taste it.

"Neither do we," he whispers with sadness, running a

careful finger down my aching cheek. "And it's Monday afternoon."

"From the way they found the accident, Sweet Pea—" My mom's lips roll together in a tight line. Tension fills her face, but she lets it all go with a long sigh. "It was a hit and run, possibly a drunk driver. By the look of the damage to the car, someone did a number on you guys." She shakes her head, rubbing a hand across her forehead. "They called me late and a state police officer drove by the site and immediately called an ambulance. Oh, baby—" A lone tear falls on her cheek. "They found you thrown outside the car, broken, and your arm. You had surgery two days ago to put it back into place." She nods toward the cast on my arm, confirming my fears.

I was riding in the Porsche with the twins in the darkness of the windy roads, coming back from the West mansion. The waves crashed below us, and a car rammed into the back of our vehicle like a crazy person. They shoved us off the road, and then…. Shivers work up my spine, remembering how creepy the dark, deserted road was. But after that? It's bits and pieces. I barely remember what they did to me. Their murmured voices. Shadows in the rainbow clouds. Masks glaring down at me. But what happened?

"You've been in and out for almost two days," my mom states with a tired, tight smile. "I'm glad you're awake now. Your dad would be here, too, but he's on a job in New York. He sends his love, and wants to Facetime as soon as you wake up."

"Two days?" I breathe again, still baffled that it's been almost two whole days lost to nothing but darkness and muttered confessions.

"Yeah," Seger winces. "Angel, you have a concussion and a broken arm. It looked like someone beat you up with the bruising on your face and your fu-friggin nose." A hiccup in his voice breaks my heart in half. He clears his throat, wiping away the evidence of his emotions. Tears swim in his eyes again as he leans down to peck my cheek, lingering against my flesh.

"I love you, Angel," he murmurs against my cheek, reluctant to pull away.

"Love you, too," I breathe, snuggling into his palm. I close my eyes, reveling in the comfort of his touch, finally breathing for the first time since I opened my eyes.

I shiver when rogue images of the boys in the front seats, held captive by the masked assailant, flash through my mind. Their evil faces stared back at me, sneering in my direction. Their taunts and laughs echo in my mind in splintered and broken images, leaving me to wonder if it was real. Or if my mind is making up all these crazy images because I can't fully remember what happened. And why am I remembering this so well and the Seger can't? What the hell is happening?

My breath shudders in my chest, and bile burns at the back of my throat. It seeps onto my tongue, distorting my taste. My mouth fills with saliva, my stomach twisting and writhing in knots. Vomit forces itself up my esophagus, burning my nose, and watering my eyes.

"Oh, no," my mother gasps, jumping up to grab a bucket from my bedside. As soon as it's under my mouth, I spew bile everywhere, choking on the water I had taken in.

Seger gently helps me sit up, holding back my hair. His hand rubs up and down my back gently, avoiding the painful spots. He helps me through a few more heaves, and when it's done, he grabs a Kleenex and wipes my lips. Mom walks across the room, discarding my vomit, and stands in the bathroom for a minute, leaving Seger and me to ourselves.

"I'm so sorry, Angel. This is so fucked up," he rasps, helping me settle back onto the bed. He fluffs my pillow, swallowing hard when he meets my eyes.

"They did this," I whisper, letting his warmth wrap around me in a gentle hug. His arm wraps around my shoulder, nose in my hair.

"I know they fucking did. They are going to pay for what they did to you. I promise you, and we will find the answers we need," he mumbles into my neck, carefully squeezing his arms around my body.

"Sunshine." My body jumps at the sound of Chase's broken whisper from the doorway.

I swallow hard, squinting to take in his haggard appearance. Every piece of clothing on his body is riddled with wrinkles and food stains. His blonde hair sticks up in every direction, looking greasy and unkempt. His eyes crinkle when he stares at me, hope filling his eyes at the sight of me sitting up and talking.

"Chase," I murmur desperately, reaching my good hand for him while clinging to Seger. I need them all surrounding me before I go insane with all the craziness running through my brain.

Chase stands frozen in the doorway, eyes gliding up and down my body. His brows furrow, and he takes a step forward, revealing the other two frozen figures standing behind him. Their eyes meet mine and drink down my body, checking to see if I'm really awake or not. Standing stock still, they don't move a muscle.

Zepp's sad eyes meet mine, glancing away quickly. I lick my lips when my eyes scan him, just like he had done mine. Similar bruises and wounds line his body, starting where his seatbelt had dug into his shoulder and clavicle to the bruises lining his cheekbone and below his eye. He shutters with nerves, and in a way that is so unlike himself, he fiddles with his fingers and avoids my eyes. Gone is the confident man I have grown to love and trust. Replaced by a man so unsure of himself, he let Carter step around him and take his place.

Carter stands stoic, blocking Zepp out completely. He shoves his hands into his pockets, staring me over with no expression lining his face. When his eyes connect with mine, a fire brews in the depths of his soul. It's promising me swift retribution against the people who did this to me.

Finally, Carter breaks free from Zepp and Chase, making his way across the room with determination. Scowling, he stands beside Seger, who raises a brow at me, and then smirks. Seger steps aside with a huff, letting Carter hover above me with the intensity of a fucking madman. I swallow hard when a vibrating growl erupts from his chest. He takes me gently into his arms and pushes his forehead against mine. Warm breaths brush over my nose and down my cheeks when he sucks in my scent and squeezes me gently. I ignore the pain, reminding my aching body that I was in a car crash, but I can't bring myself to care. The pain registers, almost blinding me with its intensity, but his touch grounds me to the spot. I could happily die here in his arms. Chase and Zepp slowly trickle in, coming to my bedside with wide eyes.

"Don't you ever fucking do that again; you fucking hear me?" Carter says, squeezing his arms around me tighter. "Don't you ever fucking scare me like that," he breathes heavily into my neck, and I swear a tear hits my skin, disappearing into my hospital gown.

"I promise," I murmur through the tears pooling in my eyes. "I promise I'll never leave you." And I do. I mentally swear to myself and my boys that I'll never leave them. Not like this, and not now. Maybe when I'm eighty, and my body is done dealing with these four idiots daily, but not right now.

"I'm going to step out for a minute and speak with your doctor," my mother says from beyond, near the doorway, but Carter squeezes me harder, not letting me go.

"Okay," I say in a muffled voice, waving my good hand at her.

Carter reluctantly pulls away, narrowing his eyes at me again. "Never fucking again," he snarls, brushing his lips against mine in a gentle but meaningful kiss. "Never again,"

Carter says against my lips, forcing his tongue into my mouth. He groans, overtaking me in such a passionate kiss I forget where I am. He sucks the soul from my body until I remember that I just vomited my guts out. If my tongue tastes like day-old lasagna mixed with bile, he doesn't pull back. His tongue swirls with mine in a possessive manner, leaving everyone in a hundred-mile vicinity with the knowledge I am his.

"Jesus, man, you're hogging our girl!" Chase whines, pulling my eyes to him. He gives me a tight smile, forcing Carter off my body with a shove.

Carter stumbles back and rights himself, squaring his shoulders. A deep snarl emanates from his throat, and he looks like he's two seconds away from peeing on me. Jesus. Talk about a protective asshole marking his territory when, in reality, it's all their territory. But I really hope they don't all pee on me. Double checking, I make sure he's not pulling out his massive dong. And nope! Thank fuck. The last thing I need is a wet hospital gown.

"Grumpy," I mumble when he takes a step toward Chase, cracking his knuckles. Maybe they need to fight it out one day and learn to get along, but today is not the day. Especially not here. "We need to get you guys a get-along t-shirt," I hum, thinking aloud and then laughing, imagining their grumpy faces when I force an oversized shirt over their heads and force them to do everything together. Go to the bathroom. Play football. The possibilities are endless, and they'd hate every second of it. If they can share in the bedroom, then they can share a t-shirt—simple logic.

"Focus, Angel. You're giggling at nothing," Seger says with an amused grin, snapping his fingers in front of my face. I swear my eyes cross when I force myself to focus on his smiling face.

"Is it the pain meds?" Chase asks with his eyebrows into his hairline. He nods then, looking over my doped-up face.

"Yeah, it definitely has to be the pain meds. You good, Sunshine?" He snorts when he asks, laughing when I stick my tongue out at him.

Carter grunts and turns to me, pointing his fingers in my face. If he's not careful, I'll bite it off. "Never fucking again," he growls and then storms away with his arms crossed over his chest.

"Yeah, never again," I mutter, mocking his grumpy, deep voice. Instantly, I regret the moment I roll my eyes and wince when the pain in my entire body hits me.

"See, you selfish prick, you hurt her," Chase says with a frown, pressing his lips onto my forehead. "I love you, My Sunshine," he murmurs against my head. "Please don't scare us like that again. I know you couldn't help it, but I've had to babysit two grumpy dicks, and a third who is drowning in guilt." Setting his forehead against mine, he gazes deep into my eyes.

"Sorry about that," I whisper, caressing the tension from his face with my good hand. I run my fingers through his greasy hair and dig my nails into his scalp until all the tension in his body leaves him at once, and he sighs in satisfaction.

"I've missed you a lot, Sunshine. I hope we can get you out of here soon," Chase whispers, lightly brushing his lips against mine again. He pulls back, looking over to Zepp, who stands back, still fiddling with his fingers. "I've told him over and over again, Sunshine. But he won't believe me." Chase claps Zepp on the shoulder, shoving him toward the bed, where he hovers just above me, avoiding my eyes once again.

"I'm sorry, Baby Girl." Zepp swallows hard, taking another step back. His swollen eyes cast down, counting the dots on the floor like they're the best thing he's ever seen.

Seger sighs from right behind him, forcing Zepp to stay where he is. He shakes his head, grimacing at his brother. "I've tried to fucking tell him it's not his fault," Seger says softly, putting his hand on Zepp's shoulder.

"We've all fucking told him repeatedly, but he's such a bleeding-heart pussy, he won't hear our words. So, fucking tell him, Sweetheart, before I throw him over a cliff for his pouting," Carter growls from the windowsill, not bothering to look over at us. Instead, he keeps his eyes on the skyline outside.

"Wow, dickhead, way to be a supportive boyfriend-in-law. We're supposed to cheer each other on, not threaten to throw each other off a cliff," Chase murmurs through disgust, sending scathing looks toward Carter, who scoffs, waving a hand. He mumbles something else about them all being idiots, and grunts, never taking his eyes off the blue sky.

I shake my head, regretting the damn movement again as pain invades my stiff neck. Sheesh, when will this end? I don't know how much more of this pain I can take in one sitting. I look back to Zepp, who stands awkwardly before me, fiddling with the hem of his shirt now. Seger stands behind him, keeping him from running away from the guilt clouding around him.

"Why would you think it's your fault?" I ask hoarsely, reaching a desperate hand out for him so I can feel the warmth of his hand wrapping around mine.

With reluctance, he wraps his fingers around mine, letting me pull him toward the edge of the bed. But he keeps his distance, not getting too close. His worried eyes roam over my body until he connects his misty gaze with mine, and the guilt slams into me with the force of a wrecking ball.

"I didn't fucking know it would happen," Carter blurts out of nowhere, pulling my attention away from Zepp. "I had no fucking idea. They were radio silent. I didn't fucking think…. I didn't think anything of it." Carter hangs his head, swallowing hard, as he swims in massive amounts of guilt. "If I were closer to the inside, I would have warned you if they had fucking said something. There's no way in fuck I would have stood by and let something like this happen to you. I never would." He shakes his head, running a hand through his hair, pulling at the strands. "Sweetheart," he says with such vulnerability rising in his voice, it chokes me.

"No," I whisper, taking a deep breath. "You two listen to me. It wasn't anyone's fault but the assholes who did this to me. Got it? It wasn't you or you," I say, gesturing toward the two guilt-ridden idiots looking towards the ground in shame. "All of you, none of this is your fault...."

It's my fault—all of it. If I didn't know the boys, they wouldn't have been involved if I didn't associate with them. They wouldn't be crowded around my hospital bed with sadness clouding their eyes or wrinkles on their foreheads. All of this is on me. I knew better than getting involved with anyone while investigating Magnolia's murder. I should have kept my distance and never mingled with them.

"Don't you dare say it, Sunshine," Chase whispers in desperation, dropping to his knees beside the bed. He crawls toward me, shoving his hand into mine, and intertwining our fingers. He squeezes, looking deep into my eyes. "Don't even think what you're thinking."

"But it is," I whisper back through a shattered voice, breaking into a million pieces. "All of this is my fault."

All this guilt is crushing, breaking my ribs, and splintering my heart—knowing I put them in danger. *ME!* I did this to Zepp and Seger. Until now, the Apocalypse hadn't injured us to this extent. Not like this. It was getting thrown into dumpsters, having goo shoved down my shirt, but not bodily harm —well, maybe the violent diarrhea from the stupid laxative sprinkles, that was definitely bodily harm. I swear my soul left my body that day in the depths of the toilet at school and in my apartment.

"Fucking no," Carter growls. "It's their fault, Sweetheart. They're the ones who hit you... It's not like you jumped in front of their fucking car and asked for it. None of this is your fucking fault. Don't make me fuck it out of you, I swear to all things holy," he growls his entire speech, jumping to his feet and waving his arms around until he stops abruptly. "If it's anyone's fault, it's fucking mine. I should have fucking known they were up to something. I could have warned you.." he trails off, running a hand over his face, showing off his scabbed knuckles.

"They drugged you and me, I think. I vaguely remember them pushing needles into your necks and then mine." I grimace, running my fingers over the throbbing spots on my neck, confirming to myself that that's where the puncture wound is, when I feel the raised up skin beneath my fingers. "And then they beat my face in and dragged me out of the car and fucking broke my arm. I think….." I scrunch my nose out of instinct, instantly regretting the action when the excruciating pain explodes through my face. I wince, trying to hold back the hiss of pain escaping through my clenched teeth.

"I'm sorry, back the fuck up. They fucking drugged you? THE FUCK?" Carter's angry shouts echo off the walls, hopefully not drawing any attention to us. Carter's chest heaves, and his fingers curl into tight fists, white-knuckling from the force. He stomps toward me with wicked intent gleaming in his eyes.

I've seen Carter angry—at the world or the boys. Or hell, I've seen him furious at me, too. But this Carter? This Carter is a whole hell of a lot scarier. And okay, sexier, too. Who knew the whole touch-her-and-die sentiment would be so damn invigorating? His brown eyes scream, 'I will murder a mother fucker for you.' And I believe it. In fact, it's kind of hot to have someone on my side who could take someone down just for me.

"Yeah," I say, looking over the clunky cast gripping my right arm. "I vaguely remember needles. My neck burned, and God, it hurt, but I can't be sure. There must be a reason I can't remember so much, right?"

Carter sits down on my other side, clamping his eyes shut.

Deep calming breaths pour from his nose, and he nods, likely counting in his head. "Could be a sedative or something," he confirms with a sharp head nod.

"They wore creepy masks—that part I remember—just not how many there were or who they were for sure. I can't remember much." I lean my head against Chase when he squeezes my fingers in his.

"It's not your fault, Baby Girl." Zepp sighs, rubbing a hand down his face, wincing from the pain. I give him a sharp nod, swallowing all this guilt down into the pit of my stomach. If he can't feel guilty, then neither can I.

"Come here," I say, waggling a finger at him. He nods again, moving in closer. "Now kiss me so you know there's nothing to feel guilty over, okay?" I whisper when he leans in, gently touching my face.

Gently, he rests his lips on mine, avoiding the bruises lining my face and his. We finally part, staring into the depths of each other's eyes. His hurting soul stares back at me, and I get it. We're all raw and exposed right now. Paper-thin. Bruised and battered, rattled around. But we'll make it through this. We have to. We have a big bad villain to defeat, and I won't rest until they've gone down.

"Alright!" My mom's loud voice echoes through the hospital room, announcing her arrival before entering through the door. The boys jump back, rushing to find a spot as far away from me as possible. "I've got good news!" Clapping her hands in a golf clap, she walks toward my hospital bed with a grin. Her eyes light up as she watches the boys one by one, a knowing look letting me know she knew what they had been doing. And it wasn't standing back from me.

"Have a seat, boys. Get comfortable for the rest of the day. I know now that she's awake, you definitely won't leave." She snickers at them as they awkwardly maneuver themselves into the sparse furnishings.

"What's the news?" I ask, hoping she says we can

leave now.

"We're breaking you out of here on Wednesday. Dr. Spencer says he'd like to keep you here for two full nights since you were out of it for so long, and wants to take extra precautions with your concussion. They'd like to run more tests tomorrow. And after that, I can take you home." She gives me a tight smile.

"Home, home?" Swallowing hard, I look at the boys watching us with rapt attention.

Seger bounces his leg in anticipation. Chase chews on his bottom lip, plucking nonexistent lint from his wrinkled clothes. Carter stares out the window, a vacant expression darkening his unshaven face. And Zepp stares with wide, glossy eyes, barely keeping his guilt from consuming him.

Mom's mouth tightens further, her eyes surveying the scene. "I just thought that after what you went through, you'd be more comfortable at home. Besides, Thanksgiving is next week. You'll be coming home on Sunday, anyway."

"No," I blurt louder than necessary. A heavy pressure sits on my heaving chest as the panic digs its claws into me and takes hold. The mere thought of leaving the boys behind while I go home to heal sends my head into a spinning mess, swirling the room into a mass of colors. "Please, Mom, I need to get my things from my apartment, and… and… I don't want to leave, not yet," I gasp out, unable to get the rest of my words past my heavy tongue.

The only reassurance I get is when I look at her sympathetic face, and her eyes move from each boy, finally landing on me. A laugh bubbles from her throat as she runs a hand along her forehead and rolls her eyes toward the ceiling with a defeated huff.

"I never won arguments against you," she mutters, causing one boy to snicker. "Fine, you want to go back to campus?" I nod, and she throws her hands up in defeat, muttering fine.

Mom is not a pushover by any means, but this fight? I think she knew she wouldn't win. Not only from my arguments. She'd have four boys to argue with, too. By the desperate look in their eyes, they won't let me out of their sight for an exceptionally long time. I can already envision the leash around my throat or a tracker in my ass or something. I know they'll decide on something drastic. I shudder at the thought of them slamming me into a cage and hiding me under the bed. No, that's way too drastic for even them. Or is it? Shit! They better not lock me away or I'll bite them, because we have a shit ton of investigating to do. And I can't be locked away for any of it. I'll need them more now than ever. Especially with the Apocalypse dicks not fighting fair anymore. I mean, who uses drugs and big vehicles to mow down their victims, but not kill them? Whatever. I'm glad to be alive, but I can't get these thoughts out of my chaotic brain.

Time flies in my tiny hospital bed. The sun moves in the sky, almost sinking into the winter horizon. After hours of being awake, getting checked out by Dr. Spencer—who gives me the all-clear for now, but insists I still need to stay until Wednesday—my mom orders pizza for all of us. I watch in horror/fascination as the boys devour three pizzas on their own. They don't utter a word as they stuff their faces, only grunting when someone tries to steal a piece from their box. And as for me? Lead sits in the pits of my stomach, knotting around the bland-tasting food. I know I need to eat each bite to get my strength back, but it's hard when someone has set out to endanger my life. Or hell, trying to kill me.

The next few months will challenge my mental, emotional, and physical strength, testing everything I have left in me. I have a fractured face and a broken arm from what they've done to me. But the one thing I don't have is a broken spirit. I'm Kaycee fucking Cole, and nothing will stop me in my quest for justice for those who can't speak out for themselves.

# FIVE

**ZEPPELIN**

"Go home," Mrs. Cole says for the millionth time with a smile tugging at her lips. "You boys have been here all day. You're starting to stink up the room. Go home, shower, rest, and then come back tomorrow morning. But not before ten a.m. Do you boys understand?" She places her hands on her hips, hardening her eyes on us as we all nod in agreement.

We've barely left Kaycee's side since we were discharged on early Sunday morning. Monday came and went when she had woken up, and we spent every moment with her until Mercy kicked us out. And now here we are again on a Tuesday night, getting kicked out. Hell, we've barely been to class throughout this whole ordeal. It's not like we'd be able to concentrate, anyway. So, why go? All four of us have settled into the routine of getting out of bed in a hurry and heading up here by nine in the morning.

I shiver from her stern voice and give her a sharp nod. "Yes, we understand. Thank you for letting us stay for so long."

Her face falls, softening when she comes forward. I stand rigid when she wraps her motherly arms around me, swiping up and down my bruised back. I don't complain when the pain throbs against my insides, and instead, I gently hug her back. It's been years since I've had a mother to embrace, and this feels too good to pass up. It warms me from the inside out that she's taken such diligent care of us and barely knows us.

"You boys are more than welcome back. I want you four to take care of yourselves, too. Kaycee is…"

"Stubborn?" Chase snorts, earning a small laugh from Mercy.

"One hundred percent her father," she says, raising a brow. "You know, after this hospital stay is all said and done, we need to have a very long discussion. I support whatever you all have going on because I can see how much you care for her. Tomorrow, I'm leaving my baby in your hands," she says softly, wringing her hands together after she pulls back from our embrace. "For a few days, you'll have to care for her because I know there's no way I can drag her home now. Understood?"

We all nod our stiff acknowledgments at the tiny threat she threw in there, and she smiles. "Now, go home before I have them call security," she barks in a demanding voice, shooing us away with a hand gesture. We say our goodbyes, kissing Kaycee's forehead as she sleeps, and make our way out of the room.

"I think she likes us," Chase beams when we enter the elevator.

The elevator doors close, leaving the four of us in stiff silence. We've been cooped up in Kaycee's hospital room all day, and now we can finally talk about how we're going to keep Kace safe after she comes home. As the elevator descends to the lobby floor, my mind works overtime on the list of things we need to do before she comes home in the next few days. And then, an idea hits me. One I've never thought of before, but it would work for us.

"Yeah, she may like us, but what about her dad?" Seger gripes, running a hand down his face. He leans back against the elevator wall, resting his head. "He'll probably kill us or something."

"Imagine being related to her brother, Body Slammer, though!" Chase says through an excited grin.

Seger barks out a laugh. "We could ask him to body slam us into the dirt."

Raising a brow at his comment, I can't help but shake my aching head. Getting body-slammed by the man nicknamed Body Slammer is not on my list of things to do. Besides, he sent some guy to the hospital because he slams so hard. Ugh. I need more ibuprofen and a shit ton of rest. I've loved every second of being by Kaycee's side while she's slowly recovered, but it has taken its toll on my body since the crash.

"You guys are fucking idiots," Carter grumbles through a tired sigh, shutting his eyes. "He'd probably break our fucking necks the moment he met us."

A smile tugs at my lips at the mere mention of meeting her family. If they're anything like her sister Callie or her mom, I can't wait to shake their hands. Seger and I have only had each other and Chase these last few years. It's nice to think Kaycee's family might be our family one day.

The elevator beeps, bringing us to the ground floor, and we exit as a group. Exhaustion pulls at my limbs. My eyes threaten to close until we walk out into the cool night air, heading towards Chase's car. Anxiety hits me square in the chest when Seger and I squish into the backseat, sitting shoulder to shoulder. Getting into a car will never feel the same after our car crash. How we are always roped into the back, I'll never know. Possibly because Carter is bigger than the three of us combined and wouldn't fit back here, or he won shotgun. I smirk when he grunts in the front seat, shifting around uncomfortably, trying to work the seatbelt over his shoulder. Soon enough, we're taking off back to school.

"I have an idea," I say, leaning my head against the

window of the backseat, fighting through the anxiety bubbling in my gut. No one tells you once you're in a car accident, the moment you step back into another metal death trap, you panic.

"Dude, go on," Chase says, slowly pulling into the packed parking lot at school.

"Kaycee's going to hate it," I grumble, reaching for the door handle and getting out. "Even more than our vow to never let her out of our sight."

The others follow as we make our way back to the Maze House. We weave through the clearing surrounded by the tall hedges and finally step inside the darkened house. Contentment settles over me when I sink into the depths of my couch, cradling my aching head. Dear Lord, I need that ibuprofen and a long nap with Kaycee in my arms.

Seger makes a beeline toward the kitchen, fetching four beer bottles, and hands them out. Even though I'm positive we aren't allowed to have these, I open it anyway—anything to take away the dull ache throbbing through my entire body and mind.

"So, what exactly is Kaycee going to fucking hate? You know, I'd really like to go home to my place and sleep," Carter says without heat sitting behind his words.

I sigh, gulping down a few mouthfuls, and nod. "We agreed Kace won't be allowed to walk around without one of us present."

"Yeah, we discussed that," Seger says, slumping into the couch and kicking his feet up. "So, what are you trying to get at? You're the worst when it comes to this," he grumbles, cursing me out.

I roll my eyes when Chase sniggers, agreeing with Seger's statement. I reach into my pocket, pulling out a set of keys I stole from a certain backpack before its owner took it back. Thankfully, the Apocalypse hadn't messed with Carter's computer and left the backpack in my car untouched. Even when they had towed it to the junkyard, we could go through it and find our things.

The keys dangle from my fingers. "We have a B and E to do, and our girlfriend will not be happy when she realizes what we've done."

Carter leans forward, resting his elbows on his knees. "I see," he says in a deep voice, downing the rest of his beer. "So, you're suggesting that we break into our girlfriend's apartment, take all her shit out, and...." He raises a brow, placing his empty bottle on the ground.

"We move her in here, where we can monitor her. We can sleep beside her, make sure she gets to class safely, and do anything she needs. And we'll know where she is at all times," I say with a sigh, looking around the room.

Seger rests his head against the back of the couch with his eyes closed, almost looking dead. And the only sign he's alive is the thumb he thrusts in the air, giving me the thumbs up. "Sounds good to me," he says in a sleepy voice.

"We can get a gigantic bed!" Chase says, his face lighting up with the possibility. "All of us can fit on it. That'd be friggin' sweet!" He grins, pulls out his phone, and taps on it.

"You won't be able to get that fucking thing here in time. That shit takes weeks," Carter grumbles, staring daggers at the phone in Chase's hands. "Besides, you're fucking poor, Elf Ears," he hisses, earning a scowl from Chase, who waves a hand in his direction.

"Watch me," Chase says through a frown, tapping on his phone again.

"You'll get used to Benoit charm," Seger says through a yawn.. "He can get anything he wants with that smile and those puppy dog eyes."

Chase stands, dragging his phone to his ear, and steps out onto the porch. His shadow paces back and forth as he animatedly talks to whoever is on the other side.

"I need some fucking sleep," Carter mumbles, standing up. "I'll see you assholes in the morning."

"Be here bright and early," I say, shoving the keys into my pocket. "We're going to get her shit and set her up there," I say, pointing to my bedroom. "All before we get her from the hospital."

Carter nods, waving us off, and heads toward the door. "It's a good fucking plan, West. If they fucking hit you guys with a car, then who knows what the fuck else they have up their sleeves."

"You still haven't heard anything?" I ask, and he shakes his head.

"No, not fucking yet. It's been too fucking silent," Carter mumbles, running a hand down his face. "I keep checking back into Crowe's fucking computer, and there's nothing there either. He's gotten a few emails here and there mentioning his investments, but that's it." He stares off toward the wall, finally bringing his eyes to mine. "Over Thanksgiving, I'm fucking breaking into Shaw's and my dad's office. I'm setting the next disc, no matter what."

I raise a brow at how forthcoming he is with this information, and he sighs again. "Don't look so fucking surprised, West. I'm trying to fucking... I'm trying to fucking be open and fucking..."

I hold up a hand and nod. "I get it, Cunningham."

He blows out a breath. "It wasn't fucking me, okay?" It's something he's repeatedly said, and no matter how often we say we believe him, he's still skeptical of us, begging us to believe him. "I was in my apartment doing work." Without another word, he leaves through the front door, disappearing into the shadows of the maze. Going where I can only assume is to bed and not having a secret meeting with the enemy. But by the look in his eyes and how they pleaded with me to believe him, I fucking do. Carter's never given me any reason not to believe him, and until he does, I'll continue to trust him.

Chase waltzes back into the front room with a grin on his face. He waggles his brows at me and digs into a sleeping Seger's jeans.

"What are you doing?" I ask, leaning back and watching his every move. His tongue pokes out from between his lips as his hand digs into the depths of Seger's back jean pocket, really searching for something.

"Ah-ha! I got it," he says with a fist pump, holding Seger's leather wallet. He looks through it, pulls out our black card, and rattles the numbers off into the phone. He paces around the living room again, rattling off our address here, and even gives the instructions to make it through the maze. He snorts when he has to tell them again, reassures them that we live in a maze, and then hangs up.

"What was that?" I ask when he shoves his phone into his pocket.

He shrugs, puts the black card back into Seger's wallet, and gracefully puts it back into his pocket. I raise a brow, not even remotely concerned he just used our card to pay for the giant bed he proposed.

"I ordered us a bed and all the bedding needed to sleep in it tonight," he says with a grin. "It's huge, dude, but it'll fit. Plus, it'll be here in two hours."

My face falls. "Two hours? What the hell did you do? Offer them a blow job? It's like ten o'clock on a Tuesday night." My jaw falls open at the prospect of someone delivering anything at this time of night.

He shrugs, plopping onto the couch next to me, leaning his head back. "Nothing a few extra hundreds won't do. Plus, it's a local business, and apparently, they love the West's. I even managed to get them to add in the sheets in Kaycee's favorite color, too."

I snort, squeezing the bridge of my nose. "Wonderful," I murmur through a sigh.

"So, she'll have a massive bed to come back to. It's one we can tie her to when she's being bad, and we'll always know where to find her," Chase says with pride.

"Great," I say. "Now we just need to magically get her stuff here; then we'll really be ready for her."

Chase holds out his fist, and I lightly pound it with mine. "Everything will be all right, man. We'll never let her out of our sight, ever."

# SIX

## KAYCEE

"Up you go, Baby Girl," Zepp says, settling his hands on my waist. Carefully, like I'm a breakable trinket, he pulls me to my feet, leaving the wheelchair I rode out on in the dust.

Pain explodes through my body after lying in bed for a few days with minimal movements. But today, I'm finally out of here with light restrictions: no video games, computer, or TV for the next twenty-four hours. And even after the twenty-four-hour period, I need to be careful. Watching a screen for too long could cause more issues down the road. Each restriction the doctor listed is an arrow to my tech-loving heart. After trying to watch TV and getting the worst headache of my life, I understood its necessity. He cut me off from everything I love. Twenty-four hours, that's it. I can survive without technology, right? I'll sleep, mostly. Laying down and sleeping sounds like the best medicine. I can't wait to lie down next to the boys and snuggle my pain away.

With my forehead resting against Zepp's chest, I take a few sharp breaths through my mouth. Four days after the accident, my body still hasn't fully recovered. Not by a long shot. The bruising and swelling on my face have gotten a little better. But not a lot. It throbs and makes me want to vomit when I accidentally scratch across the blues and purples. The severity of the break will cause more tenderness and prolonged bruising, but it'll heal without any other medical interventions. Eventually. But for now, I'll look like a walking, talking bruise. And with my previous nose break, it was bound to happen again. So, hurray, I'll have a crooked nose for the rest of my life, but thankfully, they didn't have to do surgery or set it. So, I win some and lose some. I have to remind myself day in and day out that I'm alive. They are alive.

Dr. Spencer swears my nose will heal in four weeks, and I can only hope it's the truth. Antibiotics and another doctor's visit are in my future, thanks to my arm. I'm thankful to get out of the sterile environment they subjected me to for the past few days. I just want to go to the Maze House, relax, and forget this entire situation happened.

Chase and Zeppelin stay close to my side, worry lines wrinkling their handsome faces. I lean into them, taking full advantage of their support and warmth. I wouldn't want to be anywhere else but here in their grasps. With their arms resting around me, keeping me upright, my muscles loosen. Instantly around these boys, my body relaxes, knowing they're my safety net, catching me when I fall.

My mom's white BMW pulls up to the curb of the hospital with a smooth stop. Her eyes dance as she watches the boys assist me towards the vehicle. I don't know what's going through her mind, but I can tell that she's up to something by her evil-mother grin. And I hate it when she's up to something. It means I'm going to suffer more than I already am.

I look behind me once, a twinge squeezing my aching muscles. The tall building soars into the sky, with eight floors and a thousand windows overlooking East Point Bluff. Swallowing hard, I mentally pray to God that I never have to return. So long, East Point Hospital. I won't miss you—ever.

The boys walk me to the car, open the door, and help me settle into the passenger's seat. Zepp even reaches over me and clicks the seat belt tight, pulling a few times to ensure the belt is secure.

"What gentlemen you boys are." The devilish grin on my mom's face says it all. I'm so screwed. This car ride is going to be hell on wheels. Is it too late to back out and escape to Chase's car?

Chase grins back, kissing my cheek. "Anything for her, Mrs. C."

She scoffs, waving a hand. "It's Mercy, please."

Chase nods, confirming he heard her but doesn't utter another word. He shoves his hands in his pockets and rocks on his feet.

"Look at the time, boys. It's Wednesday at noon, and you boys are playing hooky. How about you all meet us at Ruby's for lunch?" My mom raises a brow.

Zepp's eyebrows raise in surprise as his head jerks back from her request. Chase's eyes light up, and a grin takes over his face. He practically jumps up and down with glee at her invitation. I'm not sure who is enjoying this more, my mom or Chase.

"Absolutely! That place is the shit—err—I mean, we love that place. It's delicious." He grins again, nervously bobbing his head.

"Thank you for the invite. We'd love to have lunch with you." Zepp gives her a small polite smile, stepping back from the car. I notice the wince he tries to hide, but I can tell he and Seger are still in pain from the crash, too. Although, I don't think they'd admit it to me. Not with the severe pain I'm in. They're always looking out for me instead of themselves.

"Then we'll meet you there. Just have to stop by and get my baby's prescriptions." My cheeks heat, burning down my neck and to the tip of my ears.

Ducking my head, I avoid their eyes. God, this is so embarrassing. Can I hide now? Can the world swallow me up before she embarrasses me so much? This insane woman even goes as far as lightly pinching my cheeks with affection, babbling at me like I'm her cute baby until I swat her away. If she's not careful, she'll lose an eye. I'm not above maiming my mom for embarrassing the hell out of me.

To their credit, the boys try to hide their snickers at my expense, but I see the laughter in the traitors' eyes. I narrow my eyes at them, promising a swift death when they shut the car door for me. Fuckers. They're leaving me alone with this maniac I call my mother. And they're getting off scot-free, walking back to Chase's car with each other. Despite the pain, I turn in my seat and watch them with pleading eyes. Take me with you, please.

My mother snorts, driving off the hospital's campus toward the pharmacy down the road. Pins and needles prickle at my skin as the world flashes by. Anxiety creeps tension into my muscles, locking them up. It starts with my shoulders and kinking my neck, and makes its way down to my curling toes. Relax, breathe deep. Just relax. Your mother is driving, and no one is following you. I swallow the lump in my throat and lean against the headrest.

Flashes of our accident pour into my mind with stupid, intrusive thoughts detailing the SUV plowing down into the back of us. When the sound of the impact echoes in my ears, I jump and look around. Heavy breaths pour from my parted lips until I realize we're still safely driving down the road, going the speed limit. There's no accident. Again. I lived through Hell. I'm safe now.

My heart pumps at a rapid speed, pounding against my bruised ribs. My fingers curl around my mom's hand, squeezing the life out of her, turning her fingers white. The heat of her gaze spears through me. Ten. Nine. Eight. Breathing through this stupid panic bubbling in the depths of my gut, I blow out a breath and count again. Seven. Six. Five. Four. The world beside me flashes by in a blur as I settle myself, looking out the window. Three. Two. One. My head clears, and the panic subsides—for now.

"You'll be okay, baby," she whispers, squeezing my hand again. "I promise riding in a car will get better." She swears it will, but my body doesn't respond to her coos of comfort. Instead, my muscles bunch and contract, refusing to believe her soothing words.

"Okay," I murmur, blowing out a breath again.

Get a hold of yourself, Kace. Mom wouldn't crash. I thought that with the boys, too, but the Apocalypse had other fun ideas. Shit. I'm never going to get away from this anxiety chasing me wherever I go. It'll follow me until I die, and hopefully, that's not soon.

"So," my mom says, breaking through my mini freak-out. I don't have to look at her to hear the amusement in her voice. Or the vicious smirk on her lips. Here we go. This is it. The final interrogation. Shit. "Four boyfriends, huh?" I press my head against the headrest, fighting a war with myself, taking a deep breath.

*It's okay. It's okay. I am safe. My mom is driving. This car won't crash. We won't die.*

"Yup," I offer through a tight breath and gritted teeth.

My mom hums under her breath when we pull into the pharmacy's parking lot. She guides us towards a lengthy line of cars waiting in the drive-through, prolonging this nightmare of a conversation. My eyes dart out the window, my hand inching towards the door handle, eager to escape. I could jump out and run like Hell anywhere but here, but I think she'd come and find me. Maybe the boys would come and save me?

"Give me more than that, Kaycee Addison. There are four of them. Four. That's... That's insane. I mean—don't get me wrong, Sweet Pea. They're lovely. I can tell by how they look at you how much they care about you," she rambles without taking a breath between her words. "But how does that even work? There's only one of you and four of them. And, well, I don't want to know..." she trails off, shaking her head.

I bite my lip, heat crawling up my face at her implication. Yeah, there's no way I'm telling my mom the specifics of our sexy time. There are four of them, one of me, and only three holes to fill. I shudder, refusing to look at her. I imagine she'd see the guilt and answers written all over my face. So, like a coward, I hide. Call me whatever you'd like, but my mom is like a human lie detector. I clam up, letting her use her imagination and figure it out. Oh, on second thought. That's worse. Please, don't let her use her imagination. If she figures out how we conduct our relationship, she'll keep driving until I'm safely at home—locking me in my room until I'm thirty-five and throwing away the key.

The car lurches forward, stopping again in the line as a breath blows from between my lips. How do I explain this to her without going into detail? Talk about awkward. Where are those weird aliens when you need them? Like, please abduct me now. I won't mind the probes or exams as long as they take me away from her prying eyes. Lock me in an alien prison and call it a day.

I roll my lips together and carefully set my head back. The truth is what she wants, so I guess that's all I have now.

"I love them," I whisper, staring down at the dark blue cast encasing my right arm. Tiny stick figure doodles and each boy's signatures line the rough exterior, bringing my mind back to earlier at the hospital.

They stayed with me every second they could. Sitting with me and entertaining me everyday I was there. Unless they had a class or went to sleep, they were by my side. And when they had to leave, a pained look crossed their faces. They looked two seconds away from kidnapping me or hiding in the bathroom. Half of me believes they were hiding out in the parking lot, waiting for visiting hours to begin so they could be there the second it started.

"You love them?" she asks without skepticism. I swallow hard, connecting our gazes. Nodding, I confirm her answer.

Her lips tremble, immediately stopping it with one finger resting against her top lip. "Wow, you love them. I just— you've come so far, Pumpkin. So, so far. It's incredible to think we could barely hug you before this, and now? Now you're—" Her nose scrunches, and her eyes widen. "Are you safe, at least?" *Shit! God, not this conversation.*

"Mom!" I groan, covering my eyes with my good hand, refusing to look at her. Heat blooms on my cheeks, and I swear I'm going to be a tomato by the time we make it to lunch.

"It's a perfectly appropriate question, Kace. There are four teenage boys following you around like you're a goddess. You're four times more likely to—well, get pregnant or—God forbid—get an STD. Are you safe? Are you the only one? Explain this to me before we get to lunch, or I will ask them." Heat takes over my face again when I think about our future lunch. Great. More time for her to interrogate them, and she will, too.

"Fine," I grumble when the car moves forward again. "We are all in a committed relationship together. They're it for me, and I am it for them. We are safe. I'm on birth control. I got it a few months ago." My mom's eyes narrow in on me, but my answer sates her curiosity for now.

"Birth control? That's very reasonable of you. Did you do it alone?" She watches my reaction again, and I throw my sister under the bus with a pained glance. Sorry, Cals. It was you or me, and I chose you.

"Ah, Callie, huh?" She snorts, shaking her head. "Well, I'm proud of you," she whispers, looking at me with glossy eyes. "Most teenagers think they're invincible. But you, my love, made a wise decision."

"Thanks, Mom," I say through a breath, hoping this terrible conversation is over.

We finally make it to the pharmacy window, getting my new pain medications and antibiotics for the next month. With instructions on how to take them in hand, we finally head toward what is sure to be a tasty lunch, sprinkled with massive amounts of interrogation and embarrassment. I hope those idiots I call my boyfriends are prepared.

"Please don't interrogate them," I plead, jutting my bottom lip.

I curl my fingers together in prayer—well, attempt to with my cast. And she scoffs—friggin' scoffs—at me. Welcome to the biggest disaster of the century, where my boys are the tiny town about to get hammered by the eye of the friggin' hurricane—aka my mother. She's all calm and proper, but soon, she'll unleash her hellish ways on the boys, scaring them away with her words. Does anyone have any duct tape? Please? Rope? A kidnap kit? Please take her away from here.

Turning the car's steering wheel, she settles us into a parking spot next to Chase's orange sports car. Switching the car off, she practically cackles like the evil witch, and my stomach knots more than it already was.

"Interrogate? No, no. I won't do that. We are going to have a nice, civil conversation." She offers me a not-so reassuring smile. My stomach flips, and I know this will be the most awful lunch hour of my life.

# SEVEN

## KAYCEE

With a grin a mile wide, my mother marches towards the front door of the café, throwing it open. A cacophony of voices echoes through the brightly lit, well-decorated restaurant. Several patrons sit at various booths and tables, talking and laughing. Every time I walk through these doors, my jaw falls to the floor—bright colors pep up the place. No one could have a bad time here, especially with the beautiful paintings lining the walls. All the mythological creatures staring down at us eases some of my pain. But then I remember why we're here and why my mother insisted on taking them to lunch.

Despite being locked in a hospital room with them for the last three days, my mother hasn't broken the *get to know you* barrier. I see it gleaming in her eye as we make our way to a large booth in the back. Her chin raises with confidence as if she's on an important job, meeting with a client. She rests her purse in the crook of her elbow, strolling towards the boys with deadly intent. Honestly, she looks as fresh as a daisy. No trace of the hospital lingers. But for me? I look like I got my ass kicked, and a car ran over me to finish the job. Technically, I was, I guess. But I still hate the fact it's written on my face.

The further I get into the café, the more eyes I feel on me. They try to use discretion when looking me up and down but fail miserably when their eyes widen at my appearance. Yeah. Yeah. I've got bruises on my face and a cast on my arm, making me look like hammered shit. I understand the stares, but I wish they'd stop before my flesh goes up in flames. The patrons shrink back in horror, while others whisper to their friends, pointing in my direction like I'm a freak-circus show on display for their entertainment. I huff a breath, keeping my eyes glued to the boys in the big booth at the back. Screw the mean girls giggling behind their hands at my wounds.

The boys murmur as we approach, snapping their heads up and away from each other. Their eyes dart around, scooting in their seats, breaking up their conversation. Guilt twists their faces, and I can tell they are plotting something behind my back. What it is, I don't know. But I have a feeling I'll find out later. Or I'll drag it out of them.

The boys stare between my mom and me, swallowing hard when she motions for me to sit on the empty booth seat across from the four of them squished together. Taking her time, she settles next to me, smiling at each of the boys like a predator ready to sink her teeth into them.

'I'm sorry,' I mouth across the table.

Chase smirks, shrugging off my attempt with indifference. Seger and Zepp glance at one another but shrug, too. And Carter. That smug, fucking bastard sits there with no worries at all. Seriously. He—just—doesn't react at all. He's neutral with his hands folded in his lap and ease in his shoulders. There's no tick to his tense jaw. Just... What the fuck? I'm in an alternate universe. That's all there is to it. Be afraid, assholes. Be very afraid!

Isn't this a big deal to them, meeting my mom at a restaurant? My mom! They should shake in their boots. But no, they're not. They radiate confidence and cockiness, not knowing what the hell they've gotten themselves into. Staring at her, they have stars in their eyes and awe on their faces.

They look at her as if she's the fucking queen. Not someone who's about to tear them apart with scathing questions.

You're the blood in the water, boys. And my mom? She's the circling shark, inhaling the scent, waiting to attack at the right time. Welcome to the right time, you bumbling idiots.

Our server comes by, and thankfully it's not Espie this time. In fact, I haven't seen her around much lately. Only in the halls here and there, but not here. Since she served us that one time, I don't think she works here anymore. As far as I'm aware, her only job now is working for the stupid cult who put me into this mess. I'd rather her be here, as our server, eyeing Seger like she wants to eat him again, than have her roaming the halls with psychopaths. Hell, who knows? Maybe she's a psycho, too. But she must be if she's hanging with them and carrying out their cruel orders.

The new server takes our drink and food orders. Thankfully, she doesn't ogle Seger or any of the boys as she does, and then she walks away. She quickly comes back, hands us our glasses, and asks if we're okay. I scowl, taking out my phone, which is complicated considering my right hand is my dominant hand. Now I'll have to figure out how to type, write, bathe, and use the bathroom with my left hand—just another thing to add to my shitlist against the Apocalypse.

I maneuver my phone under the table with as much discretion as possible, away from my mom's prying eyes.

**MY CUTIES:**

> Me: She is going to interrogate the hell out of you! I'm sorry.

Their phones buzz in their pockets, and I know they do. Each of their eyes gazes at me, and then they stare up at the ceiling, pretending this is nothing to be concerned about.

Discreetly, I try to motion for them to answer their damn texts. I plead with them with my best puppy dog eyes. And yeah, nothing. They don't flinch or look at me. Bastard-coated bastards. They're going to regret the day they agreed to lunch with my mother, Mercy Cole.

> Me: I hate you all. You asked for it.

Buzzing sounds again, and still, nothing. I narrow my eyes at each of them. Chase smiles. Carter winks. And the twins grin in unison. Fine. Let the battle begin.

"So, boys, tell me a little about yourselves. We've been cooped up in that tiny hospital room, and I feel we've barely scratched the surface of getting to know one another. So, let's start over." She takes a sip of her drink, eyeing the boys critically. "You know I'm Mercy. So, tell me more about yourselves."

Chase's eyes light up, smiling back at her. "I'm Chase Benoit," he says, holding out his hand. She takes it, shaking it up and down.

She cocks a brow. "Benoit? Like…"

"Yeah." He beams, nodding his head. "He's my dad." He swallows hard, fighting to keep the smile on his face. Ghosts cloud his eyes, taking him back to the day they hauled his father off to jail, and my heart hurts for him. He's trying so hard not to slip back into bed and never get out.

"How's he holding up? I met him years ago. You know he collaborated with my husband?" My mom asks carefully with a mother-like precision. She must see the hurt on his twisting face.

Chase nods again. "He-he's doing okay," he sighs, rubbing the back of his neck. "Hanging in there the best he can." He plasters a smile back on his face, adjusting his posture. "But, oh yeah, I remember that! Dad brought me to the set. I even had eyes for a cute blonde girl." A pink tint takes over his cheeks when he slips a glance my way, driving his teeth into his bottom lip.

"Oh, I think I heard about you. You two were the best of friends on set. My husband, Cam, and your father, Tate, always joked that you'd marry each other one day." My mother flashes a grin so bright that I go blind. Friggin' blind and taken aback at where this conversation is going.

"Yeah," Chase says with way too much enthusiasm. "One of these days!" He winks at me again and—

What circle of hell am I in?

Why are they torturing me? Together? Was this a planned Kaycee torture session? I frown, bringing up the group chat. Fuck! Typing with my left hand is so much harder than I thought it would be.

> Me: Stop panfering to hger

I peer around the table when I hit send, only noticing then that I fucked up almost every word. This left handed thing is going to suck for the next few months until I can get this cast off and have a healed arm.

Seger snorts from across the table, tucking his phone back into his pocket. Mischief swims in his moss-green eyes as he leans his elbows on the table. *Set. On. Fire.* I hum in my mind, wishing I'd never agreed to this. Who knew going to lunch with my mom would turn on me.

"And how about you two?" my mom says, resting her chin on her palm, staring at the twins.

"I'm Zeppelin West," he says, extending his hand.

Didn't we spend three days in the hospital together? Wouldn't they have talked without me alert and present? Ugh. I need to fake an injury and lay down. This is... too much. I need to leave this restaurant ASAP. I need to get away from here.

"I'm Seger West." He also shakes my mom's hand, falling

into a conversation about their father and how my mom grew up on his music.

"And you?" she asks Carter.

"Carter Cunningham," he says as politely as I've ever heard him. He shakes her hand, smiles, and jokes with her

What the hell? Where's Grumpy gone? Impressing my mom? Ugh. My head hurts.

I rub my hand along my forehead, silently pleading for a bed.

"You, okay?" Mom asks, patting my legs.

"Yeah," I breathe. "Just ready for food and bed." She taps my leg again as our food comes.

The guys dig in like animals, devouring their cheeseburgers. I blink as silence finally settles around the table. Even my mother digs into her salad with zest. Thank goodness. Someone needed to shut her up. And if it had to be rabbit food, then by the grace of God, bless the lettuce for its sacrifice.

"So, boys," my mother begins again, swiping a napkin across her lips. "What are your intentions with my daughter?"

The boys stop mid-bite, suspending their burgers in the air. A piece of meat falls from Chase's mouth before he can swallow the lump of food in his cheeks.

"I—uh—we love her," Chase says, setting his burger down. "We just want to, you know, grow together. Nothing but good intentions, Ma'am." The other boys nod in agreement.

"Hmm. I'm so glad we can have this conversation. So—you are all with her?" This fork in front of me is pretty tempting. Do you think she'd be concerned if I gouged my eyeballs out right here and now? Maybe it'd stop the ridiculous questions falling from her lips.

"Yes, Mrs. Cole," Zepp says, folding his hands on the table. Adjusting his posture, he leans in, ready for business.

"It's along the lines of a polyamorous relationship. We're all in this together and exclusive to one another." My mother nods, mulling his words over.

"Of course, there are many ways to explore a relationship besides traditional monogamy in this day and age. Men love men, women love women, and obviously, four men love one woman," Mom says, taking a sip of her iced tea, soaking in the information they're feeding her, even though we went over this in the car. And as much as I hate my mom asking these questions and embarrassing the ever-living shit out of me, I'm glad I have her in my corner. Most parents would run for the hills or disown their daughter, but my family is different.

"Exactly," Seger pipes up. "We've always been a little untraditional." He shrugs nonchalantly, sitting back in the booth, pride puffing out his chest.

"And you four?" My mom waggles her finger between the four of them.

"Fuck no," Carter spits out and then sighs, swiping a hand down his face. "Respectfully speaking, I'm as straight as an arrow. I don't get my jollies off from another man. Not that there's anything wrong with that. To each their own." He clears his throat, looking down at the table. "Just not for me," he mumbles, drawing circles on the table.

"Pfft, speak for yourself." Seger grins. Jesus. What a weird conversation to have with my mother. Are we traveling down this road? This whole, are you bi, road? I mean, I'm good with that, but with my mother present? She's too nosy for her own good.

"Mom," I hiss, thumping her leg under the table. But she brushes me off, listening to Seger as he speaks.

"I'm not saying I'm against it or anything. It's just never happened. But if it does, I won't stop it." Seger shrugs, grinning over at me.

Images of him and Chase rolling around on the floor with

Seger's hand down his pants, making out with their tongues tangling together and their hands pulling at each other's clothes and hair. Hands disappearing below the belt, stroking one another, and getting off together rapidly flash through my mind. Hmm. It is kind of hot—sort of. Well, wow... Okay, really hot imagining my boyfriend's enjoying each other. My thighs clench together. It is hot. He gives me a knowing grin, winking. The bastard knew what he did there. I huff, taking a bite of my cheeseburger, hoping the sound of my loud chewing will drown out her questions.

"Very interesting. I hope I'm not making you boys uncomfortable. I'm simply asking to understand your relationship more for my daughter's sake." The boys shake their heads, giving my nosy mom more fuel to add to her fire.

"I've been in the book business a long time, editing manuscripts mostly. I'm the head of my publishing company now." she muses, resting her hand under her chin. A sly grin takes over her lips when she tilts her head, undoubtedly reminiscing about a previous client's work. "I've had book after book slide over my desk. Romances, contemporaries, even long-drawn-out fantasy novels, but my absolute favorites are reverse harems," she says, tapping a manicured nail against her chin.

"Reverse harems?" Chase asks, dipping his brow.

"One girl, multiple men in a committed and loving relationship," she says while taking another drink.

"So, like us? Oh my God, Sunshine, we are your harem." Chase snorts with glee, fist bumping Seger.

Am I in a coma? And this is all some weird hallucination my mind has made up about my mom finding out about this and being okay with it? Or did I transport to some bizarre dimension?

"My absolute favorite book was—" A grin takes over her face as she thinks about it. "Oh goodness, those boys, phew. They made the books worth it." She fans herself. "It was seven boys, each unique in their way, much like your relationship, and one girl. Those boys loved her dearly. Every single one of them. Even if they started as enemies, each boy had a different aspect they brought to the relationship, and I think that's why it sucked me in. Some had tattoos. Some had piercings, and one even had a Jacob's ladder..." she trails off, staring off with a whimsical grin.

I blink a few times as Carter, Seger, and Zeppelin stop what they're doing entirely, looking at my mom with wide eyes. I furrow my brows in confusion as the word repeats in my mind. Jacob's Ladder? Isn't that a place? A biblical reference?

"But in the end, it all works out. They save her, and she saves them. They end up all falling in love. A beautiful story," she whispers again, losing herself in the book she must have read many years before.

I'm so lost in my head when I look up at the boys. I raise a brow, baffled by their suddenly surprised expressions. With wide eyes, the boys each blink at my mom in surprise. A pink tint takes over Zepp's cheeks, and Seger breaks into a tiny snigger, hiding behind his hand. Carter hasn't moved for five minutes, staring at her with wide eyes. But Chase? Chase and I appear to be in the same confused boat.

"Oh, ah, excuse me a minute," my mom says, staring down at her ringing and buzzing phone. Getting up from the booth of doom, she heads towards the bathroom in the back.

"What is it?" Chase says, looking toward the other guys for answers.

Carter gives a small huff, shaking his head. "No, no way, I'm not fucking telling you." He says, biting into his burger again. He shakes his head, completely ignoring Chase's pleas.

Chase whips his head toward the twins. Seger sniggers in response, hiding his lips behind his palm. "Oh man, no fucking way. I can't believe your mom said that. At the fucking lunch table. Damn a Jacob's ladder? Oh my God!" He snorts, shaking with laughter.

"Ugh! What the hell does it mean?" Chase asks a nasal whine slipping into his voice.

As they argue, I take my phone out again and bring up Google.

*'What is a Jacob's Ladder?'*

Oh.

My.

God.

So not a biblical reference, although it could probably take me to heaven. My eyes widen, and I hide my phone from the prying eyes around me. I shouldn't have looked it up in public. The other people behind me could have seen the piercing on my phone. I need a safe search next time I'm in public, especially looking *THAT* up.

I whip my head towards Carter, immediately seeing it on him first. But does his baseball bat need that many bars in it? Yes. The answer is yes. The perfectly placed bars form bumps, providing the ultimate pleasure. Holy fuck. It's the crème de la crème of dick piercings. Fuck the Prince Albert, give me a—

"Holy shit, no!" Chase hisses, bringing his hands to cover junk. "No way in hell is someone spiking little Chase with—" His eyebrows furrow as Zepp sighs, leaning in again and whispering more. "Shit! Twelve studs? Seriously?" His gray eyes widen. "Who does that?" he hisses, clutching himself again.

"Eh, wouldn't be too bad," Seger shrugs, devouring the rest of his food in one bite. Bits of mayo, ketchup, and mustard sit on his smug-looking lips as he licks his fingers. I'd be impressed with his skills if it weren't for the exhaustion pulling at my muscles. "Besides, think of how it'd feel for Kaycee," he says, extending his tongue out to lick his finger again—exaggerating the movement to pull my eyes towards his lapping tongue.

On second thought, yeah, think of how it would feel for me! So, Carter can get a vibrating tongue ring. And Seger can provide the extra pleasure with a new dick piercing. I blink, looking between the boys, and nod.

"If you're so brave, you do it," Chase says with a taunting look, leaning against the table.

"Fine," Seger says with a shrug. "Let's do it."

"Fine," Carter says through an evil-looking grin. "I have an appointment on Saturday for a touch-up on my sword. I'll pull some strings and get you an appointment, too."

Seger freezes, biting into his lower lip. A faint flash of fear spears through his eyes, but he shakes it off and shrugs.

"Cool," he says, taking a drink, and then flashes a grin at me. "Angel, will you hold my hand?"

I raise a brow, and my lips pop open. "Uh, sure," I huff.

"Will you hold my hand too, Vixen?" Carter rumbles, rubbing his foot against mine under the table.

My cheeks heat at the thought of both their dicks getting worked on simultaneously, and a whimper falls from my throat.

"Yes," I rasp.

"You're seriously going to let some strange dude put a needle through your dick? Multiple times? Like, impale it over and over?" Chase asks again with wide eyes, imagining the picture. He shakes his head, looking down at the food on his plate. Instantly, he shoves it away with a frown, turning a sickly shade of green.

"Pain is pleasure or something like that," Seger waves off his comment like it's nothing, not even cringing at the thought of needles piercing through his most sensitive area and... Wow. All his fear is gone and replaced with his usual cocky confidence. We'll see how confident he is come Saturday.

We all straighten and pretend to talk about school when my mother stiffly returns to the booth and shoves her phone back into her purse. She picks at her salad, staring intensely into the green leaves, before shaking her head.

"What are you boys up to for Thanksgiving next week?" She asks in a soft voice, looking at each of the boys.

Chase swallows hard, turning to look in the other direction. "Ah, I usually have a big meal with my dad and sister, Ainsley, but not this year." He clears his throat, shuffling in his seat. "We're traveling to my grandparents' house in Louisiana."

My mother gives him a small smile, reaching over to clasp his hand. "They will love to see you. Whatever is going on with your dad, I know he's a good guy. Keep the faith, okay?" She says, squeezing his hand, and he brightens up.

"Thanks, Mrs. C," he whispers when she retracts her hand, and his shoulders sag with small amounts of relief.

"And you?" She asks Carter, whose eyes dart to me and back to her.

He swallows hard. "Dad and my stepmom are throwing a big dinner for the police department." He shifts uncomfortably in his seat, adjusting his posture.

I raise a brow, tilting my head when our eyes meet, and he quickly darts his eyes away. Yeah, I'll revisit that scenario later and see what he has to say for himself.

"We rarely do anything," Seger says, leaning his chin on his hand.

"Yeah, usually low-key. Our chef makes an enormous meal, and we come and go as we wish. But our stepmom rarely celebrates," Zepp adds.

My mom smirks. "Then join us," she says, just as I take a drink.

The pop I just drank splashes up my nose, and I gag and cough.

Seger snorts. "You sure? I mean, it's really nice of you, Mrs. C, but..."

"Nonsense," she says, waving a hand. "If I didn't want

you boys there, I wouldn't have extended an invitation. And don't worry, I'll keep my husband in check. You'll be fine."

Seger pales, eyes widening as he stares at me silently begging for help.

"Yeah, fun for sure," I murmur with sarcasm.

"Then it's settled! If your family plans fall through, you boys are more than welcome to join the fun!" She says through a smile, but I see the evil in her eyes. Sure, Callie knows about the boys and enjoyed them. But my father? My brother? He will have some things to say as well, even if the boys idolize him.

# EIGHT

## KAYCEE

"All right, boys," my mom says with a smile as we exit the diner. Walking through the parking lot, we make our way towards our cars. "It was lovely to meet you all, but why don't you head back to school? I'd like to have a word with my daughter, and then I'll bring her back to you." The boys exchange glances but don't argue with her. Because there's no arguing with this woman. Crap. That means I'm going to have to ride in a car with her again. I look at her, blinking rapidly as she soaks in the love from the boys who beam back at her. Even Carter grins a genuine smile, nodding in agreement with her statement.

"Thanks for lunch, Mrs. C," Chase beams, barely containing the hug he wants to wrap her in. He bounces on his toes in excitement, and finally settles, leaning against his car.

"Thanks for lunch, it was fu—friggin' amazing!" Seger snickers under his breath, holding back his smile. I narrow my eyes at their antics, secretly hoping this was all a bad dream and I'd wake up soon. Seriously, am I in some sort of weird coma? Because that's what it feels like. Maybe I should pinch myself–and nope—that didn't work either.

"Thank you for lunch, Mercy. It was nice to sit down with

you again, and not in the hospital," Zepp says cordially with a grin, tipping his head respectfully in her direction. I sneak a peek at the woman in question, and her grin once again reflects the sun.

"Thank you," Carter says without gruffness in his voice. Instead, it's full of respect and gratitude. And he smiles, like really smiles at her with all his teeth. Which should be frightening, like the big bad wolf or something, but he looks pleasant and completely at ease.

And I'm so fucking lost with how this conversation is going. I need a damn nap and some good pain medication to sleep off this whole experience. My heart skips a beat when one by one, they eye me, and settle into Chase's car. They take off down the highway, and I swear a little piece of my heart goes with them.

Once in my mom's BMW, she smiles over at me. "That was fun," she titters a laugh.

"Fun?" I grumble, "You basically interrogated them and then talked about a dick piercing." She snorts at that.

"Yes, well, you know me. When it comes to good books, I get carried away." She reaches between the seats as she speaks, pulling out a large yellow envelope. Breaths seep from my nose when she finally hands it over, displaying the CaliState logo stamped on the outside.

My eyes widen at the label sitting on the corner of the envelope, and it can only mean one thing.

"CaliState," I squeak in shock, staring in disbelief. Never in a million years, since Parkford denied my scholarship, did I think I'd get into another college on such short notice. Especially somewhere like this, where my boys will attend, too.

Mom pats my leg, urging me to open it. "It came a day before your accident. I was going to surprise you and bring it, but well, here I am. Now open it! I didn't know you applied there!" She says through a smile, squealing with excitement.

I grin, tearing into the envelope with shaky hands. Tears burn my eyes when I pull the packet out, and my breaths leave me. A miracle in golden writing has me wiping tears from my cheeks, and I hiccup, hugging the papers to my chest. My salvation sits in my hands and gives me another chance at college. Something I didn't think I'd get to do when the Apocalypse swooped in and took my dream college, Parkford, away from me. And now, I have another chance to do this right and live my college dream.

"I got in," I whisper in awe through a quivering voice.

Pulling the papers away from my frantic heartbeat, I stare at the acceptance letter. Scanning the words repeatedly, my heart flutters in my chest with excitement. Someone pinch me into reality. This can't be happening. Holy shit. I got into Cali-State. I fucking got in!

My mom's face explodes with emotions spewing down her cheeks. "I'm so proud of you!" Leaning over, she captures me in the biggest hug and squeezes me against her, and pours her love into me. Pride puffs through her chest when she snuggles into me. She pulls back, wiping the happy tears from her eyes, smiling so wide she can't hide her happiness.

"I got in." I breathe again, leaning my head against the headrest. My eyes close on their own accord as the possibilities run through my mind. Next year will be a fantasy come true, and I can't wait to leave this place and move on to my future.

Our future.

My boys. They are attending there, too. We'll all be together on the same campus. All of us, except for Carter. He'll be—well—wherever *CC Tech* is, I guess. He isn't going to college. Would he follow? How would it all work? Ugh. I have to make it through this year. Even so, I fucking got into a college! It might not be Parkford and all its expensive glory, but I've come to accept they took away my scholarship because of the Apocalypse. Does it suck balls? Absolutely. Parkford was a dream—a place Magnolia and I had dreamed about attending together. She was taken away, and so was it. In the grand scheme of things, my future holds something more exciting now. Plans change, and I'm okay with that now. Change is terrifying, but if I have my boys by my side, I'll be okay.

My mom and I talk a little more about the boys on the way back to school. I can tell she's hesitant to ask a lot of questions, specifically about the logistics of our relationship. So, we keep the conversation light and fluffy as she pulls into the school's parking lot.

The boys lean against Chase's car, anxiety, and tension lining their muscles. Once the car parks, they eagerly wait for me to exit the vehicle, but my mom holds up a hand. They nod in understanding, staying by Chase's vehicle. But they never take their searing gazes away from me.

"I don't want to upset you, but I need to discuss with you the phone call I received at lunch." Her throat clears, bobbing under the emotions bubbling to the surface. She heaves a sigh, twiddling her fingers together in her lap. Alarm slams through me at her motions. This isn't like her. My mother is always confident and sure with her movements. She's not one to twiddle her fingers and prolong a hard conversation. Something serious must have happened for her to curl in on herself.

"What's wrong?" I ask, furrowing my brows, watching her every move.

She sighs heavily, running a hand along her forehead. "I—you remember Addison Shepherd? Magnolia's mom? She was a good friend for so long, and then—" She cuts herself off with a deep breath, reeling her tears back in. "Of course you remember her. She was my best friend for years," she mutters, chastising herself with the wave of her hand.

"Yeah, you two were close, and then I never saw her again

unless she dropped Mags off to play." My mom shakes her head, swiping at tears running down her face.

My heart drops into my churning stomach and blends to smithereens when she looks at me with tear-filled eyes. I know before she opens her mouth what she's about to say. Guilt slams into me at a rapid pace, and I want to punch myself in the face and drop off the face of the earth. I was there. Someone could have come and saved her if I had just called for help. I could have saved her from the fate that Crowe handed her when she lay in that hospital bed and weakly yelled for him to save her. When I close my eyes, soaking in the car's silence, I see Addison's face flash in my mind. Weak, pale, and pathetically coughing. I was so close, but yet so far away. Crowe wouldn't have let me do anything, though. If I had called the cops or the hospital to come and save her, he would have stopped it. I swallow the bile in my throat when my mother's voice rings through the car, cementing Addison's fate.

"I got the news at lunch that she'd been sick for a few months. Her slimy husband, Victor Crowe, said he had her transferred to the hospital, and she...." She hiccups through the words, holding her fingers to her trembling lips.

"What happened to her, Mom?" My stomach knots and twists, threatening to send my lunch right back out.

"Her heart gave out." Her lips roll together when frantic breaths soar through her nose.

"Mom." I lean over again, quickly taking her into a hug. Her body relaxes in my touch, and she happily soothes a hand up and down my back.

"Sorry, Sweet Pea," she whispers. "I know you just got out of the hospital, but I didn't want to keep this from you and have you hear about this later. I've sent Crowe some flowers and... I can't imagine how he's holding up. First Magnolia and now his wife. It's been a hard two years for him." She takes a deep breath, kissing the top of my head. "I'll be fine. She and I drifted apart many years ago."

"But why?" I blurt, hoping she'll give me answers. As heart-wrenching as this is, I need to understand how two best friends suddenly drifted apart.

Addison was a staple in our home, and her daughter, Magnolia, was my best friend. Everything we did was together. Outings, playdates, and shopping adventures (that I hated), but being with her and having Addison there was familiar. Until she pulled away. Magnolia still came around, spent the night, and played with me. But Addison retreated, leaving my mom, her best friend, in the dust. The last time I saw Addison was when I sat in Magnolia's room. She looked so sick and pale in her hospital bed. She could barely lift her arms when she had called for Crowe, her husband. And now, she's another name on the list of their victims—another person whose death I need to rectify.

My mom worries her bottom lip between her teeth, blinking back tears, sighing. "Addison—I loved her dearly, but she didn't like me nagging about her love life. I was not and am not a fan of Crowe." Her head turns to look at me as I nod. "There's just something about him, deep in my gut, telling me he's...I don't have an appropriate word to describe it. She didn't want to argue with me anymore about my concerns and walked away from the friendship. And now the woman who helped me through a lot in life is dead." Tears spill over her cheeks again, but she plays it off.

"I'm so sorry about all that happened. I didn't realize—" Mom snorts, adjusting her posture.

"You were a kid, too young to understand the dynamic. Now, your boyfriends look like they're about to devour this car to make sure you're okay. So go on, go back to school, and get some rest. And I mean rest, Kaycee. You need to take it easy for the next few days until you come home for Thanksgiving. Stay in your apartment, lay in bed, and make those boys cater to you. There are four of them, after all. You're excused from school for the rest of the week. Call me if you need anything. Otherwise, I'll see you when you get home." Leaning over, she kisses my forehead and hands me my pain pills. "And take these if you need to." I nod and grab them.

"Thanks, Mom," I whisper, clinging to her in a desperate hug. For some reason, this feels like a critical moment for us, and I don't want to let her go. I've never felt comfortable enough to rest in her arms without my skin wanting to peel away from my bones. But here and now, I've never felt more secure and loved in her embrace.

"You're welcome, Sweet Pea. I'm thrilled for you. You've grown so damn much in the few months you've been away. Oh God, I'm going to cry again," she murmurs the last part, wiping a hand across her moist cheeks. I snort, pulling away. "Your brother will be here to escort you home on Sunday afternoon. I'll tell him to behave, but I'd be careful with how many boys you bring around." A smirk pulls at the edge of her lips when she eyes the boys who step away from Chase's vehicle with determination.

"I don't know, and they're kinda super fans. It's weird," I mumble, looking out the window toward them.

I swallow hard at the intensity of their glares. They cross their arms across their broad chests, anticipating my exit. They're ready to swoop in whenever my mom is done with me. Or they might drag me out of this car before she's ready to let me go.

"Go on before they start circling the car like blood-thirsty sharks." She barks a laugh, shooing me away from the car with a hand wave.

I stand in the middle of the parking lot with my meds and a college acceptance letter in hand, watching as my mom slowly leaves. She puts a hand out the window, waving like crazy, and then she disappears down the main road leading out of East Point Bluff. My mind turns to all the possibilities, but my body begs for bed more than anything. Despite laying in a hospital bed for three days doing nothing, I'm fucking exhausted. I'm beat—between the meal, the badgering, and the humiliation. I want them to carry me through the maze and cuddle me forever until I fall into a dreamless sleep. I scrunch my nose, looking up at the sun high in the sky. It's only four in the afternoon but fuck the time of day.

"You good, Sunshine?" Chase whispers, trailing a finger down my swollen and bruised cheek.

"Yeah," I rasp, leaning into his touch, despite the pain spearing through me from the mere touch of his fingertip.

"Here," Seger murmurs, pulling the things from my hands and stuffing them under his arms. "Let's get you home."

Home.

That glorious word sends butterflies swooping in my belly, and warmth spreads throughout my limbs. I sigh with realization. My home doesn't have walls or a roof. Home is where my heart is. The arms I fall into when I'm having a dreadful day and the eyes I look into when I need reassurance. Home is where the spankings and teasing hands are. It's where my boys are. And right now, with all their eyes on me and their hands on my body, I am home, and I never want to leave them again.

"Home," I rasp, with emotions thickening my throat.

My eyes grow heavy the longer we stand here, staring at one another. The boys can't take their eyes off me as they, once again, catalog my injuries from head to toe. With a gentleness I haven't seen before, Chase scoops me up into his arms. He allows me the comfort of burying my face in his neck carefully, avoiding my bumps and bruises. Once I'm settled, we set off toward our home with four walls and a protective maze surrounding it.

"I'm tying you to the bed, Baby Girl," Zepp mumbles from Chase's side. "We won't leave your side, ever. Anything you need, we'll do it." I smile against Chase's neck, inhaling his crisp scent.

Every inch of my body aches and throbs, so I don't argue with Zepp. If they want to keep me in bed and watch over me, for once, I'll let them. I need my strength for what's about to come, and if my princes want to coddle me, I'm down. Just tie me to the bed and feed me cupcakes. I won't complain. Not today, at least.

My eyes close against Chase, my brain barely hanging onto the moment. With the sharp turns Chase makes, I can tell we've made it into the depths of the maze. The cool air rustles the surrounding evergreens, encasing us in its protective hedges. The breeze brushes through my hair, and goosebumps form along my skin. I sigh into Chase's neck again, reveling in his warmth. His arms tighten around me when sleep slowly takes me under its spell, and I fall into the abyss of darkness, barely clinging to reality. It isn't until Chase whispers in my ear that my brain comes back online and registers what he says.

"We have a surprise for you, Sunshine," Chase whispers, gently squeezing my ass.

"You didn't have to get me anything," I mumble sleepily, dragging my eyes open, but they refuse. Even though I was out of it for two whole days after the accident, my mind and body still get exhausted so damn easily.

"Ah, you'll like this surprise, Angel," Seger says, rubbing his hands together. I don't have to look up at the joyful smile lining his face because the giddy laugh says it all. They're up to something, and I don't know if I'll like it.

My eyes stay closed as Chase walks up the stairs to the porch, through the front door, and across the hardwood floors. Without looking, I hear the other boys behind us until we all come to a stop.

"Open your eyes, Sweetheart," Carter mumbles against my hair, kissing my head.

"Can't we just go to sleep?" I ask through a yawn, forcing my eyes open.

"Nope! Gotta see this, Sunshine." I grunt when Chase's deft fingers poke into my aching sides, and I lift my head to glare at him. He smiles, revealing all his teeth that I want to punch for interrupting my sleep.

"Turn around, Sunshine. I can't wait for you to see this," Chase whispers, lowering my feet to the floor. His hands stay on my hips when my wobbly legs gain strength and I turn around.

My jaw falls open, and my breaths evade me. Light gray decorates the once white walls, lit up by fairy lights hanging from every corner of the room. A bed fit for a king—or eight kings—sits in the middle of the room. A fluffy dark gray comforter and a million fluffy pillows line the headboard. It's so large, over the top, and nothing else fits around it. A large closet sits to the right of the bed. It's open and displays a large built-in dresser and what suspiciously looks like my clothes neatly hanging from plastic hangers. The only other objects sitting in the room are my computers and a new desk tucked into the corner.

"You like it?" Chase asks with a grin. "It's the biggest fucking bed we could find. I swear you could get five more boyfriends, and we'd still have room for you."

Carter grunts, "No more boyfriends." I swear I hear his teeth crack when I sleepily snicker at him.

"Not even three more? There's definitely room for them," I say through a playful grin, and he narrows his eyes.

"No fucking more. I'm the last fucking one. I'll kill any man who tries to enter this fucking harem. You hear me, Little Troll?" He growls the last part, pointing a finger in my direction. I frown at the stupid nickname, bringing a wave of old memories from when I first started at this school.

I bite at him and shake my head. "I'm not a troll, damn it.

But, fine. No more boyfriends. I'd hate to put someone else's life in danger because you're a psycho." I fake a huff.

He scoffs at the psycho part, but his chest puffs out. "Damn right," he murmurs. "Now pay attention to the fucking work we put together in a night."

"So romantic," I mumble but shake it away.

Chase snorts. "Look at what we did for you, Sunshine."

The full effect of what they've put together for not only me but us hits me right in the feels when I look at the room again. "It's beautiful," I whisper, stepping into the room. Every detail, everything I've ever wanted, sits in this room. And the bed is a perk. No longer will we have to squish into my tiny bed or create a pallet on the floor. We will all fit together and have room to space out or cuddle.

"We, uh, well—" Zepp stutters, rubbing the back of his neck, nervously looking at the other boys out of the corner of his eyes.

I raise a brow, turning to look at each of them. Suspicions immediately have my hackles raised, and my arms' hair stands on end. I cock my head when Zepp actually sputters to find the words he wants to say.

"We moved you out of your fucking apartment," Carter blurts, a deep, possessive growl emanating from the back of his throat. "You can't live by yourself anymore. We can't let that fucking happen."

"You moved me out?" I ask in a deep voice, attempting to put my hands on my hips. But with only one bendable arm, I look lopsided and uncoordinated. Narrowing my eyes, I assess my men standing before me.

They firm their stances, puffing their chests like alpha beasts, crossing their arms, and tightening their jaws, creating a wall of sexy man-meat. They came into this argument thinking there would be a fight with me, and they were ready to take me down. Half of me is pissed–no, not pissed. I'm hurt that they did this without asking and didn't communicate with me. They moved my things without my permission. Don't get me wrong. I get their reasoning. Their protective instincts are kicking into high gear. Magnolia is dead. Addison is dead. We got in a car crash, and they injured the three of us. So, I knew it wouldn't be too long before they hauled my ass into this house and didn't let me go. Next, they'll want to insert a tracker under my skin to follow where I go. Annoying? Yes, but it's necessary for my safety.

"We... we can't function with you constantly sleeping somewhere else," Chase pleads, lowering his voice. Keeping his passion-filled eyes planted on me, he firms his stance again, making himself ten-feet tall.

"We need you protected and under this fucking roof. With them, you'll be safe here," Carter adds through gritted teeth, clenching and unclenching his fists at his side.

"And you?" I ask, raising a brow.

"He can't move in yet," Zepp says, rubbing his chin.

"Not fucking yet. Not with all these fucking eyes on me around campus. It was a fucking risk going to the hospital with you so damn much and out for fucking lunch. But I couldn't fucking say no when you were in pain. But I can stay over," Carter growls with sweat beading at his furrowed brow. He takes a deep breath through his flaring nostrils, trying to regain his composure. I'm convinced he's ready to fight me or fuck me. Or both—I'm not sure.

"What they said, Baby Girl," Zepp says, taking a tentative step towards me, demanding my eyes on him. Authority wafts off him in waves, forcing me to stand at attention and focus only on him. "With how callous they've become regarding your life, we need you here to protect you and keep our eyes on you," Zeppelin demands again, pointing a finger towards the floor for added effect.

"Don't make me shackle you to the fucking bed," Seger's firm voice sends shivers down my spine.

*Well, don't threaten me with a good time.*

Staring at the boys with unblinking eyes, I wait for them to continue pleading their case. They are all in. Fighting the good fight. Good vs. Evil, and all that. This is what my life has become and will be for many years, God willing. I've shackled myself to four protective, ruthless boys who won't take no for an answer. This time, at least. And you know what, I'll let them win this. If they want to shackle me to this massive bed and keep me safe and occupied, who am I to stop them?

"Okay." I shrug, walking towards the bed and sitting on the edge.

I let the exhaustion I've felt since leaving the hospital take over, and one by one, my limbs tingle and beg for rest, falling limp at my side like I am a pliable rag doll made of dough.

A small smile pulls at the corners of my lips, watching the boys stare at one another with furrowed brows. Hands wave, eyebrows wiggle, and tiny mumbled words escape their lips as they succumb to a silent conversation about what to do with me.

They, too, expected a bigger fight than this. I can tell. Their bodies stand tense and rigid, but slowly, they relax with realization. I'm not fighting them on this. I'd rather be here with them any night of the week than in my stuffy apartment, constantly looking over my shoulder. Besides, I haven't slept in my apartment in a while. I'm always here with them, anyway. So, now it's official; I live here.

"Okay? O-fucking-kay?" Seger gapes, shaking his head in disbelief. "That's it?"

"That's it," I confirm through a sigh, and they all relax.

"Do you want a shower before we lay down?" Chase asks, coming to kneel in front of me.

His large palms rub up and down my thighs, soothing the tension in my muscles away. And those eyes, those beautiful gray eyes, fill to the brim with concern at the sight of me. He catalogs every bruise lining my face, moving down to the cast again with sorrow in his eyes.

"A shower sounds good," I rasp through a tired sigh.

Leaning into Chase's warm and inviting embrace, he picks me up with ease. Maneuvering me into his arms bridal style, he shifts me through the doorway to the bathroom.

Zepp comes into the bathroom with his shirt off and a garbage bag. Together, they wrap my broken arm, securing it from the water. Our clothes disappear from our bodies, and we jump into the warmth of the shower. My body shivers, adjusting to the heat boiling over my body, but ever so slowly, every ounce of tension leaves me.

Chase stands behind me, holding me upright with his hands under my armpits. I lean back into him, resting my head on his shoulder, and shut my eyes. A shudder runs through me when Zepp's warm hands roam all over my body, making sure the water washes away everything. A hint of his manly soap hits my nose when a soft washcloth slowly glides over every inch of my flesh. I hum in satisfaction when he washes every bit of me, not leaving anything out of his perusal. But it's not sexual, it's caring and loving. And I know when my eyes grow heavy and my head feels like a boulder, I'm well cared for.

I'm barely awake when the four of them maneuver my tired as hell body out of the shower. I lean on one, burying my face in their chest, and the others surround us, running warm towels over my body–unleashing my arm from its bag prison–and through my hair. A firm set of arms picks me up and slowly carries me into the bedroom. They lay me flat on the cushy bed and get me dressed. Soft pants encase my legs, and a loose T-shirt hangs from my body when they wrap me in their warmth and the comforter.

I sigh in satisfaction, burying my face in whoever rests in front of me. They curl their fingers carefully in my hair and leave a lingering kiss on my head. This is the damn life, having all my boys surrounding me as I fall asleep in this gigantic bed meant for us.

"Goodnight, baby," Seger whispers against my head, leaving another soft kiss.

"Sleep well, Sunshine," Chase whispers, curled up tightly to my other side.

"Sweet dreams, Baby Girl," Zepp says from above me in a soft voice, running his fingers through my damp hair.

Carter squeezes my calf from below. "Night, Sweetheart," he mumbles, shifting closer to my legs.

"Goodnight, boys," I whisper, closing my eyes and curling into Seger more.

They mumble another goodnight, and that should be my cue to sleep. Really, it should be. But my brain roars like a hurricane barreling through, constantly reminding me of what happened just a few days ago. Our car wreck. The singing voice. Everything that we went through that I can remember. My entire body tenses in my boys' grasps, and my breaths pick up as I'm hit with a barrage of images playing on repeat.

The cherry on top? What the hell did I say on pain medication when I was passed out? It should be my last concern, considering I almost died. But it's the best worry to focus on because I can get an answer to it.

"What the hell did I tell my mom on drugs?" I mumble against Seger's bare chest. He stiffens his hold on me, and then his chest shakes with laughter. Great, this can't be a good sign. He's laughing at me.

"Oh, Sunshine, I don't think you want to know," Chase mutters sleepily from the other side, tightening his fingers on my waist.

"Tell me," I huff. "But please don't tell me I told her everything."

Zepp snorts, muttering incoherently from above, moving his fingers through my hair again.

"Not everything," Seger confirms through a tired sigh.

"Just how much you needed us there and how much you loved us and our enormous dicks. It was flattering," Chase says, smiling against me and holding back his laugh.

Seger's chest vibrates more when a full-on belly laugh explodes from him. "Really fucking flattering, especially when she went into detail. Every. Little. Detail." He punctuates each word dramatically for an added effect.

My heart stops inside my chest. Like dead. Not moving. At least, that's what I want. Rip it from my chest and bury me below the house. I never want to face my mom again or them. Maybe I'll become a nun and stow away in the nunnery, hiding behind black robes. Then they'll never find me.

"I said what?!" I hiss, eyes widening. "I did not!" Dear God, I sat in a car with her for over thirty minutes, and she didn't mention a thing. Not letting on that she knew, she drove me around asking me all kinds of questions, and she knew all the answers. What the fuck?

"Go back to sleep, Baby Girl. Your mom just waved it off and laughed about it. She thought you were hallucinating," Zepp says through a yawn, playing with my hair again.

"I seriously said that?" I hiss again, swallowing hard.

How could they have looked my mother in the eyes after I said that about their dicks? Oh my God, no wonder my mom had the sex safety talk with me! She knew I knew.

"Apparently, I have a fucking baseball bat for a dick?" Carter says, lifting his head off the bed to meet my horrified eyes. "Very flattering, Vixen," he murmurs, rubbing my leg.

Fuckity fuck. Kill me now.

"I know nothing," I mumble, hiding my blazing red cheeks from their snickers.

"Mmhmm," he hums, squeezing my calf.

"Shut it! And go to sleep," I hiss through my embarrassment, hoping sleep will claim me quickly before I die.

After the mortification settles in, I'm finally able to close my eyes. Whatever I said or didn't, be damned. Exhaustion has been a steady flowing feeling throughout the past four days, and I succumb to it without a second thought. Weird dreams plague my sleep, all featuring a certain giggle I can't get out of my head.

I jolted awake several times, covered in sweat and panting like I had just run a mile. My heart pounded against my chest, but thankfully after some coaxing from Chase, I could fall back to sleep and start the horrible process all over again.

# NINE

**KAYCEE**

As the morning sun rolls in, peeking through the windows of my new room, an alarm beside the bed goes off. Chase groans, rolling toward it and smashing it with a hand. He groans, pounding his fist into it a few times, but it doesn't do a damn thing. It still beeps an overly annoying sound.

"It's your phone," I mumble into the pillow, wishing the alarm would die a fiery death and burn in hell for waking me up. Even though I went to sleep yesterday at five o'clock, my body still doesn't feel rested.

"Shit," he curses, reaching for it again, and tosses it across the room. It hits the wall with a thump, still beeping its annoying song.

"Smooth move, Elf Ears," Carter grunts, rolling to sit on the edge of the bed. He runs a hand down his face and stands, thrusting his arms above his head. He groans when he stretches, even bending to touch his toes. "You didn't turn it fucking off. You just moved the fucking thing." Carter gripes, waltzing toward the phone on the ground. He picks it up, inspects it, and tosses it at Chase's head.

"Ouch, shithead!" Chase yelps when the phone hits him on the side of his temple. He frowns, rubbing at the spot, scowling at Carter's retreating back. "Asshole didn't have to throw it." Chase uses his index finger to peck at his phone screen, griping when it beeps all over again.

"Make it stop," Seger whines, burying his face in the crook of my neck. "I don't wanna, please, mommy," he whines again while squeezing my body.

"You have to," I rasp, peeking an eye open, and pushing against his body. "Go to school." Even though the boys sustained a few injuries from the accident, the doctor cleared them to return to normal activities, minus sports. Thankfully, football is over, and they're done for the year. Or I think the doctor would have had a fight on his hands.

"We can't miss any more days," Zepp says, waltzing out of the bathroom with a towel wrapped around his toned waist.

I raise a brow at the marvelous sight before me. Water dripping from the long strands on his hair and falling on his sculpted, yet bruised and battered chest. As I take in his gorgeous body, I suck in a breath noting the puke yellow bruise on his collarbone in the shape of a seatbelt. My stomach lurches as memories attack my brain. Shaking my head, I take in a few deep breaths when the bed moves from behind me, and Seger gets to his feet. Stretching his arms above his head, he doesn't hide the fact he's naked, and showing all his glory–and morning wood–to the entire room. I watch for an ungodly amount of time, thankful to have my mind off the bruises lining Zepp's chest. Although, it's short lived when Seger leans over me and kisses my cheek, begging through murmurs to let him stay, too. Bruises line his chest as well, in various states of healing.

"Go to school," I say through a yawn. "I'll be here when you get back." Seger sighs but nods in agreement, leaving the room to get dressed.

"They're better than they look," Zepp says, walking through the bedroom door. The sound of him rummaging through his dresser and getting dressed filters into the room.

"You fuckers will be late if you don't get a goddamn move on it," Carter shouts from the living room with a growl. "I'm going home!" he calls again before popping his head back into the doorway. "You," he says, pointing a finger at me with a snarl, tugging his lips over his teeth. He can try to be as intimidating as he wants, but he's not.

"Me?" I say with false innocence, placing my hand over my heart.

"Yes, Vixen. You, you stubborn ass woman, stay put today. No TV. No computer. And no fucking moving. Don't you dare answer the fucking door! Stay. The. Fuck. Put." He growls through gritted teeth, fingers digging into the wood of the door frame.

I scrunch my nose as an odd sensation trickles to my core. "Yes, Sir," I say with sarcasm, giving him a sloppy salute.

For a millisecond, Carter's eyes heat at the word Sir, but instead of commenting, he huffs and rolls his eyes. A frown takes over his lips, and then he walks away from us, stomping his feet. Moments later, the front door crashes open and slams shut with a thud, leaving us all stunned. Moody bastard. Sometimes I think he needs to vent some more of his frustrations. Either by pounding Seger's face in or pounding me into the mattress. Not until I'm healed, of course.

"I don't know why Grumpy is so worried. I'm staying with Sunshine today," Chase says with a lazy smile, tightening his hold on me. "Someone has to, and I volunteered," he mumbles with pride.

Seger grumbles, "No fucking, Benoit. She needs to heal, and the last thing she needs is for you to rearrange her insides with your sloppy thrusts."

Chase scoffs, shaking the bed when he sits up in a huff. "I do not have sloppy thrusts! My thrusts are fine, asshole."

"Right," Seger murmurs, poking the bear with his eye roll.

"Sunshine, tell them my thrusts are fine! You enjoy it when I rearrange your insides," he huffs, scrunching his nose.

I grab his arm, pull him back into bed, and snuggle into his bare chest. "Your dick is fine, and your thrusts are fine. Now, let's go back to bed," I mumble into his chest.

"See," Chase says, sticking his tongue out.

Seger snickers, leaning in to kiss my head. "Be a good girl today, Angel." Lightly he taps my ass and then turns to leave the room fully dressed in his uniform.

"Are you in any pain?" Chase asks, stroking his fingers up and down my back.

"Yeah," I murmur, nodding as a slight twinge from my neck makes me wince.

"Let me get breakfast. I'll bring you some in bed. I'll get your meds, and we can just lie here all day. Just the two of us," he whispers, kissing my temple.

"Okay," I say through a happy sigh as butterflies take flight in my belly.

Chase gets out of bed but leans back down, pulling the comforter to my chin. He kisses me again and walks out of the room. The sound of pots and pans echoes through the house, and I raise a brow at what he's doing. The only thing Seger keeps in the fridge is friggin' beer, so I have no idea what Chase is about to make me.

"Bye, Baby Girl," Zepp says as he strolls into the bedroom fully clothed for school. "Be a good girl," he says with a smirk, smoothing out his shirt. "We'll be back for lunch."

I snort. "Aye, aye, Captain! Have a good day," I say, pushing my lips into his and humming when he thrusts his controlling tongue into my mouth.

"Now I want to stay," he breathes but pulls away.

"No fucking, asshole!" Chase grunts from the kitchen in a warning.

"No fucking," Zepp says, raising a brow at me.

"Yeah, yeah. She gets it. Shit," Chase yells back, poking his head into the room with a frown. "Now, go away." He waves a hand, and I snort when Zepp adjusts himself in his pants and walks out the door, slapping Chase on the shoulder.

Before I know it, Chase comes in with two plates piled high with bacon and eggs, and I nearly spit out the water in my mouth. He smirks at me but doesn't say a damn thing when we eat his delicious food. The moment it hits my tongue, I have a mouthgasm. Who knew my man could cook so well? And why has he been holding out on me? What the hell?

After I'm full and he's removed the dishes, I take my pain meds and doze through the day with Chase happily cuddled against me. The twins come back for lunch, and Chase makes us all something, much to the boys' surprise, and they go back to school with full stomachs and smiles.

Chase and I cuddle on the couch, wrapped in a blanket. The TV plays some random show Chase turned on, but my eyes stay shut. The light peeking in through the windows and the light from the TV makes my head pound. Chase's fingers lightly drift over my good arm, puckering goosebumps along my skin. I sigh in relief when he rubs my temples and plays with my hair. I swear I could stay cocooned like this all day and let him treat me like a queen.

When a knock comes from the front door, my body jolts, and I look back at Chase.

"Expecting someone?" I whisper, and he shakes his head.

He shrugs, unwrapping himself from the confines of our comfy love nest. With caution, he walks to the door and looks out the peephole. On silent feet, I follow him. Even when a dizzy spell hits me with my first step away from the couch and the entire house swims in a blur, I stay behind him.

"Piper," Chase says in a confused voice, looking at me when I shrug.

"Open it, I guess," I whisper, gesturing for him to open the door. The quicker we see what she wants, the faster we can make her leave.

With a slight hesitation, Chase opens the door, revealing a grim-looking Piper, puckering her lips. Heavy emotions run through her blue eyes as tears fall, and she holds up my books. She sniffles, wiping her nose with her wrist.

"Poultry, pickles, and popcorn, Kaycee," she whispers, as her voice cracks from the emotions. Tears spring into her eyes as she takes me in, eyeing my injuries and cataloging them. "Oh, tater on my tots! I heard about your car accident, and I am so, so, so–oh, slimy sauerkraut." She hiccups, brings her fist to her mouth and lets out a demon shriek as more tears fall down her cheeks. "I'm so sorry someone left you on the side of the road!" She shrieks again with a trembling body, clinging to the side of the house until her knuckles turn white.

"It's okay. I'm okay." Which is the biggest lie I've told yet.

Am I okay? Hell no. Someone purposely broke my arm and smashed my face while hiding behind masks. Was it the Apocalypse? Hell yes, it was. But which ones? Was it the mysterious fourth member we've yet to figure out? And who the hell is Alpha? Is she staring me in the face right now? Or is it Hadley? Oscar? Zoe? Is it Trent? Any one of them could be the Alpha who gives out the horrendous orders to take me down.

Piper's water-filled eyes meet mine before she wipes her sniffling nose across her wrist again. With one last hiccup, she flicks the tears from her cheeks and straightens her spine. Chills spiral down my spine when she cocks her head, giving me the warmest smile she can muster. But it does anything but give me the warm and fuzzies, it makes me want to turn in the opposite direction and run away. How friggin' strange.

"Mr. Shaw asked me to bring you your homework assignments for the rest of the week." She swallows a lump in her throat, thrusting several heavy books in my direction. Dramatically, she looks away with another sad huff, erasing the creepy smile from her face. I remember when I first met her, I thought she was on some sort of drug, and every interaction I have with her seems to confirm my theory. I cock my head and wince, my injuries reminding me I shouldn't move too quickly or I'll give myself whiplash. Ugh.

"I went by your apartment, but I assumed the boys had locked you up when you weren't there." Her lips tremble as she gives me and Chase's protective hand in mine a tiny smile, and a knowing glint sparks to life in the depths of her crazy eyes. Goosebumps spread across my flesh when she looks me up and down, accessing me again.

I snort, wincing when the vibrations prickle my nose. "Yeah, sorry you went all the way over there. I'm here for a short time," I say with a sharp nod, instantly regretting the tiny detail I gave her.

Stupid, stupid, Kaycee! I mentally facepalm, sinking my teeth into my tongue. Maybe if I hold it down and suffer through the pain, it won't let anything else dumb slip through. I'm too exhausted, mentally and physically, to deal with Piper's crazy shenanigans. She could sit me down on the couch, engage in normal conversation, and I'd spill everything I know without meaning to. Fuck. I need to get out of this conversation asap. I wonder if I feigned near death, if she would walk away and leave us alone. All I want to do is snuggle into Chase's chest and sleep for the rest of the day.

Piper says a few more odd, food inspired words, and offers her prayers before wrapping an arm around me, and hugging the life out of me. I squeak from the pain, but she seems to hold me tighter, until I'm fighting for air. Seriously, what are her arms made of? Steel? Fuck, she's crushing my already crushed lungs, and I think this is how I'll die. Never mind the invisible ants crawling up my legs, begging me to scratch them away. She squeezes me another time, until Chase is peeling her damn arms away from me, and I land back on my feet with an umph. I blow out a breath when she waves her goodbye, skipping through the maze while singing a song. Her blonde hair swishes with every joyous step, until she completely disappears into the maze.

Chase and I exchange a look when he shuts the front door and locks it. Shaking my head, I put my books on the kitchen table and give them a dirty look. No matter how much I want to dive into my school work and catch up, I don't even want to think about it. Chase's warm hands knead at my shoulders, relaxing every inch of me into his touch. I sigh when he leads me back to the couch and cocoons us in a blanket, once again.

"That was suspicious," Chase mumbles as he pulls the blanket to my chin and settles behind me again. He presses play on his TV show and leans down, resting his head on mine. "She seemed more…Pipery than usual."

"More than suspicious, we'll have to monitor her," I say, as my eyes grow heavy once again, and I know sleep is on the horizon.

"Yup. Now, go to bed, Sunshine."

And so, I do.

# TEN

## KAYCEE

"I can't believe you're doing this," I mumble in shock from the backseat of Carter's sleek, blackened Tahoe. We idle in the parking lot of Soul's, our brightly lit up destination—one of the best tattoo shops in the state—Carter's words, not mine.

My fingers move against the leather of my seat, heated by the warmer underneath. I sigh into it, letting my butt warm, and thank God he didn't have a motorcycle.

When I met Carter, I always imagined him as more of a motorcycle type of guy. You know, that—I illegally race for money on the winding roads of East Point Bluff, and win every time— cliche type of bad boy. Much to my disappointment, he shoved me in the backseat of a SUV, instead of on the back of a sleek and sexy motorcycle. Although, there was a murmured promise that he'd take me on a motorcycle ride some time in the future when I wasn't so broken. My face is still healing from the trauma of my crash, and I wouldn't have been able to hang onto Carter's body anyway.

I shake my head, bringing myself back to the present, trailing my gaze over Seger's deep frown. He grimaces with tight muscles, locking him in place. Staring up at the shop in front of us, his eyes don't stray from the luminescent bulbs brightening the sidewalk. Lights pour from the tall windows of Soul's, giving us a peek at the people mingling inside.

Hanging between the passenger and driver's seats, I refocus my energy on my boys. My eyes bounce from the confident boyfriend leaning back in the driver's seat with his hands resting behind his head. And then to the pale boyfriend who looks like he's about to vomit his dinner all over the vehicle. He even holds his stomach, turning slightly green. I wrinkle my nose, scoot back an inch, and pat his shoulder. Nothing would console Seger right now, so the best I can do is run my fingers over his bare arm and offer my best.

Carter, my cocky as fuck boyfriend, silently taunts Seger with the wiggle of his brows, like an evil bastard. Moisture pours from the top of Seger's forehead, dripping down his cheeks and his jaw. His scowl deepens when he discreetly wipes it away with the back of his hand and shakes himself out of his morbid thoughts.

"This is dumb," he mutters to himself.

His wide, frantic eyes look over at Carter, begging for reassurance. My smug as fuck boyfriend smirks at Seger, offering him nothing but a laugh.

"Ready to get a needle or two in your dick?" Carter snarks with a chuckle, leaning back in the driver's seat without worry.

"Fuck," Seger grunts, pulling his hand to his mouth. He turns a darker shade of green at the mention of needles and dicks, and bends at the waist.

"Even if you yack, you're still getting a fucking needle through your dick, West. Man the fuck up," Carter goads, pounding a hand into Seger back. Seger grunts, giving Carter his best stink eye, and shoves him away. Carter barks out a laugh when his body connects with his door and rocks the vehicle.

You see this? Yeah, this is exactly what my entire Saturday has consisted of—him goading Seger, trying to push him, so he backs out of the dare Carter had laid down. From the moment we woke up and Carter came over, he harassed

Seger every second of the day. Even though Seger looks like he's about to shit his pants and run away, I don't think he will back down. He made a damn promise, and he's sticking to it.

"Grumpy," I chastise, thumping his shoulder with a stern look. "Be nice."

Carter scoffs, throwing a hand in the air. "What's the fun in bringing him to get a fucking dick piercing if I can't be a dick? What the fuck do you want me to do? Hold your hand?" He glares over at Seger, narrowing his eyes. "Besides you're still popping fucking pain meds like they're candy, and I'm going in all natural," he tacks on with a victorious grin.

"I don't need you to hold my hand, asshole. And thank fuck for the meds or I'd feel every fucking inch of that...that needle. Fuck," Seger grumbles, running a hand down his moist face. "I need Kaycee to hold my hand." Turning in his seat, he peers back at me with pleading puppy dog eyes with a trace of fear lingering near the surface.

Seger doesn't want me to know how terrified he really is. He's been psyching himself up for this entire experience, playing it off like it's nothing for the past week. *Nah, Angel. I'm fucking good*—that's what he'd say to me when I'd ask him if he really wanted to do this. And each time, that was his response. Up until now, I kind of believed him. That is until he started sweating bullets and turning green.

I shiver at the thought of getting my clit pierced. Err—no, thank you. That would be awful. Is that the equivalent of a dick piercing? Would it improve my orgasms? Oh, shit! I bet it would. But also, there'd be pain and—

"Focus," Carter murmurs, snapping his fingers in front of my face. "What the fuck were you thinking about this time?"

My eyes widen. Yeah, no. I can't admit that. Shit, think fast. Say something! Anything but what's on the tip of your tongue.

"Erm, nothing. I definitely wasn't thinking about orgasms with a clit piercing." *Smooth*, real smooth.

I mentally facepalm, cursing my damn tongue and brain for their lack of communication. Why do I always have to spout off what I'm really thinking? Ya know, one day, it'll get me hurt—or, shit—killed.

"Jesus, fuck," Carter grumbles again, shaking his head. "Of-fucking-course. That's where your brain went." I purse my lips when he mumbles more to himself, looking out the darkened window with a sigh.

So, I do the mature thing and flip him off, earning another scoff. Focusing on Seger, I answer his previous question with confidence. "Of course, I'll hold your hand," I say, leaving a lingering kiss on his cheek.

Melting under my lips, his entire body sags with momentary relief. His chest heaves a sigh, and he blows out a breath. Looking left and right, he bobs his head.

"Okay, let's do this," Seger proclaims, opening the car door and letting it swing wide.

The cool night air invades the car, sending shivers down my spine. I rub my hand over my arms and pull my coat closer to my body, wishing Seger would shut the door, but the man freezes with one leg out and the rest of his body in. Shit, I think he's broken. He's barely breathing with tight fists curled in his lap. A vacant look glazes his eyes, and I swear he's having a mini panic attack.

I swallow thickly, putting my hand on his shoulder. His muscles tense, feeling like rock beneath my fingers. But he still doesn't move. I look at Carter and frown when he erupts in a fit of laughter. Tears roll down his freckled cheeks, and he completely fucking loses it, doubling over with his entire body shaking. I watch in awe as he comes alive before my eyes. Gone is the angry man he presents for the world to see. In its place is a laugh so full of life and joy, my insides clench. If I could bottle up this man's laugh and save it in a jar, I would. I'd listen to it every night, filling myself up with his joy.

Butterflies flutter to life in my belly and I smile, watching him let it all go.

Carter wipes away his tears and gains his breaths. The utter joy lights up his face, chasing away the shadows that plague him. I don't realize I'm staring at him with a dopey, love-sick smile, until he raises a brow. In return, I give him a shrug and turn my attention back to the frozen, scowling man in the front seat. His leg dangles precariously out of the car, swinging in irritation. A fire burns in the depth of his moss-green eyes, staring daggers at Carter's amused face. If I'm not careful, these idiots will have a full on brawl in the parking lot and get arrested before they can go through with the piercings. Time to deflect and move shit along.

Clearing my throat, I ask the burning question on the tip of my tongue. "So, what exactly are you getting done again?" I cock my head to the side when Carter's grin grows across his lips, and he wiggles his brows.

"Gotta fix my sword, Vixen." My eyes follow his movements when he points towards his crotch, and visions of his damn sword swim in my mind. Oh, yes. Definitely a sword of epic proportions. My lips pop open and form an 'O' and amusement sparks in his eyes. "I never got it completed. Thought it might be about fucking time. Maybe a piercing too, as it'll be out of commission for a bit while I heal," he says with a nonchalant shrug. His eyes darken, and his pupils blow wide, dripping with lust.

An eager nod takes over my head without my consent. No matter where this man gets a piercing, I'm down. Balls. Dick. Nose. Eyebrow. Shit—anywhere. Maybe I could convince him to do all the above with incentive….

"Are you going to pierce your dick too?" Nibbling my bottom lip, I bat my eyelashes. Secretly hoping he says yes.

He shrugs again. "Depends on how I'm feeling. But what's a sword without extra ridges on it."

Extra fucking ridges? Yes. Yes. A million times yes. My

pussy weeps when I imagine the possibilities. Both of my boyfriends will be packing metal on their dicks. And my insides happily want to coax them into doing it several times. Too bad they aren't getting that delicious looking Jacob's Ladder. Is it too late to convince them?

"Do it," I moan.

Shit! I moaned. I straighten my back and check for drool on my lips. Nope. I'm good. I didn't drool—this time. But Hell, they're both looking at me like I'm the damn roast they want to devour or split. Now is not the time boys. I clear my throat, letting my eyes wander away from their heated gazes. Time to pretend my outburst never happened.

Carter smirks, slapping Seger on the shoulder. "Let's go," he barks out a demand, throwing open his door with zest. There's a pep in his step when he rounds the vehicle looking at Seger expectantly. "Move it or lose it, West. We ain't got all night," he barks out again, moving to throw Seger from the vehicle.

"Fuck off!" Seger growls, throwing a hand up. "I'm fucking coming."

Seger's back straightens, stepping out onto the pavement with tentative steps. He blows out a calming breath and shuts his door, moving to mine. Reaching a hand in, he helps me jump down from the vehicle like a gentleman. Interlocking our fingers together in a death grip, he pulls me along toward the shop, like I was the one hesitant to come. But now, some sort of confidence fills his chest, and he marches on with determination.

"You feeling okay today, Angel?" he asks, trying to distract himself from what he let Carter talk him into.

A few days have passed since I came home from the hospital. Aches and pains have become a daily reminder of the traumatic event we endured. Some days are better than others. Headaches come and go, some hurting more than others. Screen time is next to impossible, much to my disappointment. Talk about taking away my favorite things, minus the boys. They've been peaches through this whole experience, taking care of me when I needed them most.

Violent flashbacks frequently visit me in my sleep, waking me up in a pool of sweat with a startled gasp. The boys have been on edge, surrounding me in their support and love every time I jolt awake. Their reassurances are the only reason I agreed to get into Carter's death trap without a fight. Car rides continue to get easier each time I climb in, but my anxiety is in the back of my mind. Which is an improvement because tomorrow my brother is coming to collect me for Thanksgiving break, forcing me to buck up and ride in his car for three miserable hours.

"I'm okay today," I say, leaning into his body as we approach the front door.

"No turning back, West," Carter says with an amused smirk, pointing toward the door. "Once we walk through these doors, no pussing out." Seger scoffs.

I scrunch my nose in protest. "Why pussy?"

Carter's eyebrows furrow as his hand rests on the door handle, ready to open it. "That's just how it fucking goes, Sweetheart," he snarks with attitude, completely dismissing me. Bastard. His fingers tighten on the door about to throw it open, but I grab his shirt and drag him back.

"Well, my pussy does some pretty amazing things. It expands, contracts, and pushes out babies—or will in the future." The boys' eyebrows shoot up at that statement about babies, and I swear something odd flashes in their eyes. Shit. Do they even want children in the future? I shake it off, pointing a finger at his dick. "Your dangly bits are more sensitive than mine. Why isn't it called balling out? Or dicking out? Or..." I frown when Seger puts his hand over my mouth, silencing me from talking anymore. Asshole.

"Stop talking about your pussy, Angel," he says through an amused but pained grin. "I'm about to let some stranger touch my junk and stick a fucking needle through it for you. You can't get him all excited beforehand." I roll my eyes and lick his hand, which only makes him bark out a laugh and let go. He wipes it down his jeans, looking lighter than he has since we got here.

"Fucking fine," Carter grumbles with a roll of his eyes. "You can't ball out. Better, Sweetheart?" He makes sure to show that he thinks it's stupid and wants to use the disgusting word pussy but changes it anyway for me —swoon.

I smack my lips against his cheek, making a slight blush darken his cheeks. "Much better! Now let's get your dicks pierced and tattooed," I chortle, following Carter as he throws open the door with a head shake.

My heart unexpectedly pounds against my chest when I step into the tattoo shop. A heaviness creeps over me, and rubber bands constrict the airflow to my lungs. If this is Carter's happy place, then this is hell for me. Sure, I saw through the window how many people were there, but it didn't register that I would be in here too. People mill around, talking with one another and sharing loud laughs. Music pours from the speakers on the wall at a medium level, but mixed with the voices, it's overloading my entire mind. My skin crawls with invisible ants marching up my feet and legs. They dance across my skin until I reach down, scratching away their presence on my good arm. Swiftly, Seger grabs my hand, squeezing my wrist with his fingers. He stands before me, cupping my cheek in his palm with sympathy in his eyes. My eyes flutter to his, where they pull me into the depths of Seger—highlighting the massive amounts of concern swimming in their depths. I heave a breath and shake away my panic, letting it subside into nothing. It's just the two of us standing in the middle of a crowded room and no one else.

Carter steps away, looking over his shoulder with a scowl, eyeing my paling face. He stops at the front counter, leaning against it, and talks to the girl sitting behind it. They exchange a few words, and he quickly returns, shoving his hands into his pocket.

"Deep breaths, we can leave if you want," Seger murmurs, looking me over.

My damn heart soars. Forget the panic marching up my spine. This man recognized what I needed and immediately acted with no hesitation. It takes me back to the time he learned about grounding and tried to aid me out of a panic attack.

"No, I'm here for you both," I say with determination, looking deep into the vast green of his eyes, losing myself into a calming stupor.

Carter frowns, coming up beside me, running his fingers up my bare arm, eliciting goosebumps. I shudder under his scrutiny. "Good?" he asks softly, staring accusations at Seger like he did something to cause this.

"Overstimulation," I grumble, taking a deep breath and closing my eyes. Silently, I count to myself as I explain. "Too many people and mixed with music, it was just a little too much at first. But I'll be fine. It's calming down."

When I reopen my eyes, my boyfriends fill my vision. I cock my head at them having a silent, heated conversation with their eyebrows. Seriously? Them too? Why am I always out of the loop with their eyebrow dance conversations? First the twins, now Carter. It's bullshit. I frown, leaning in, and try to decipher what the hell they're saying with their intense eyes and the weird grunts. Simultaneously they stop, whipping their heads in my direction. Well, so much for getting answers today—that's for sure.

"We've got a private suite in the back, Sweetheart. That's where we'll be. No other people, and I'll ask them to turn this fucking shit down," Carter soothes, lightly kissing the side of my head. His warm lips linger, and I fucking melt into him when his chest brushes against my shoulder. Our fingers intertwine, and he pulls me closer to him in a possessive manner.

"They're ready for us," he grunts when his eyes look all around the room. He snarls at someone behind us like a psycho, making Seger snort at the poor unsuspecting sap. When I turn to look, the guy behind us stares at the ground with wide eyes and shakes his head.

Carter leads us to the backroom by my hand, following behind Lydia, the front desk girl. We weave through the shop, walking around tables filled with people in various stages of undress. Some people have their shirts or jeans off, with artists draped over them. Some get small pieces on their shoulders, and others get large, colorful pieces on their entire backside. I watch in awe, stupidly staring at them when they don't even flinch from the pain. One woman catches my eye and grins through the pain of the artist putting ink over her ribs. I swallow hard, pulling my eyes away from the mesmerizing art.

Lydia pulls open a large wooden door, gesturing for us to pile into the quiet room at the back of the establishment. The moment the door shuts behind her, the heaviness in my chest eases, and my breaths return to normal. The music cuts out, and the voices go entirely away, surrounding me in nothing but blissful silence.

"You finally came back to get it fixed, huh?" Lydia says with a small smile, looking down at her clipboard.

"Yeah," Carter grunts, leaning against the table pushed to one side of the room.

"And you?" The woman finally looks up, staring between them, and finally, her eyes settle on me. She smiles a genuine and friendly smile.

"My buddy here wants an ampallang piercing," Carter says with smug satisfaction. "He's super fucking thrilled if you can't tell." I try to cover up my snort when Seger glowers at him and tightens his fists.

Lydia snorts, looking Seger up and down with a watchful eye. She chuckles to herself, taking in his paling face and sweaty skin. She writes their requests and then looks up at Carter with a twinkle in her eye. I can tell she and Carter are on friendly terms because of his frequent visits, but nothing more.

"Okay, well, Matt and George will be here in just a second. I'm assuming George and you had a discussion on what specifics you wanted for your tattoo?" Carter nods, stroking his chin. "Good. Well, I'll have both of you take off your pants and underwear. Here are some covers to drape over yourselves until they come in. Just hang tight, and they'll be right with you," she says with a smile, looking at us as she instructs them on what to do. She swiftly leaves the room and closes the door behind her, leaving us to stew in silence.

Carter doesn't hesitate to pull his shirt over his head, revealing his delicious tattooed chest. I lick my lips, so desperate to lick cupcakes off his chest, that I miss him winding up to throw his shirt directly on top of my head. I grunt when it knocks me back a step. Fighting to get the hot fabric off my face, I finally win and pull it down with a pout.

A desert takes over my mouth, wiping all the moisture away when Carter undoes the buttons of his jeans. He doesn't give a shit when they roll over his muscular thighs, and he kicks them in my direction. I'm practically panting in the middle of the tattoo shop with one thing on my mind. Screw my aching muscles and broken arm, just fuck me silly until I can't see straight.

"Eyes up here, Vixen," he taunts with a smirk, pointing his finger toward his eyes. But fuck that, I don't want to look into his eyes. Well—not his top eyes, anyway. I could stare his snake in the eye all day long.

"Nope," I say, swallowing hard when he plays with the elastic of his boxers like a tease and then pulls them down his legs, too. Jesus, take the wheel. "The show is right there." I all but gasp out when he gives me a knowing grin, standing there completely naked with no shame. He stretches his arms above his head, exaggerating his movements so his monster baseball bat swings from side to side. How the hell does he carry that thing around all day? Or fit it in his damn jeans?

Carter snorts, sitting on the bed, pulling the cover-up over his lap, ending my show. I sigh.

"Yo, West," he barks, startling Seger out of his staring contest with the floor.

"Are you going to be, okay? I'm serious. You don't have to do this to prove anything," I mumble, running my free hand up his arm soothingly.

He shakes his head. "No way, Angel. I said I was going to do this, so I'm going to do this," he says, gritting his teeth.

He takes a deep, cleansing breath. With trembling hands, he pops the button of his jeans with less confidence than Carter had. Tentatively, he rolls them down his legs and kicks them toward his shoes, leaving them in a pile.

"This is for you, Angel," he chokes out. "All the pain I'm about to go through is for you." And then he drops his boxers into the same pile and clamors onto the second table. Quickly, he covers himself up and fidgets with the plastic cover-up.

I snort. "If that's what you want, I mean, I won't complain."

The other day, Seger and Carter sat down and discussed it. He figured out the piercing he wanted through a sweat-soaked face and a grimace. And ever since they showed me what he was going to get, I've been dreaming of what it could do when they slid in and out of me. The metal would feel orgasmic against my pussy walls as I came so hard. I close my eyes and hold back the groan, trying to escape the back of my throat. Wrong time to think this, Kace. You need to focus on your boyfriend, not rub your legs together like a horny hussy.

"Vixen," Carter's warning cuts through my mini fantasy,

and my body snaps straight. He raises a brow, pointing a finger toward my thighs rubbing together. "Don't fucking think about that right now."

Gasping in mock shock, I put my hand on my heart. "I would never!" I play it off like I have an itch or something. But by the look on Seger's face, he too thinks I'm thinking naughty thoughts. And he would be correct, but I have to keep my cool here.

"For once, Grumpy has the right idea," Seger says, frowning as he sits on the table, shifting around.

Just as I'm about to open my mouth to answer, a knock sounds at the door, and then two men covered in tattoos and piercings walk through the door with grins on their faces.

"Cunningham," the taller man says with a nod, coming forward to shake his hand.

"George," Carter says with a nod, clasping his hand. "Good to see you again," he says in a cordial tone, getting right down to business.

"And you must be..." the other man says, raising a brow at Seger as he shifts on the seat.

"Seger," he grunts, holding his hand out, and they shake.

The man snorts. "I'm Matt. You must be nervous?" He asks, wiping his hand down his black jeans with a grimace. I swallow my laugh for Seger's sake when he pales, staring at the man with wide eyes.

Seger licks his lips and gives a sharp nod. "A little," he grunts again, sitting up straight. "But this is something I've always wanted, so I said fuck it. Let's do this."

Matt gives him a respectable nod, grinning when he walks to a cabinet next to them. He pulls out a pair of latex gloves and puts them on. Once he secures them on his wrists, he puts sterilized instruments, still in their packages, onto the counter and spreads them out.

Behind me, Carter and George talk in hush whispers, and George gets his tattooing equipment set up on a counter near

Carter. Carter lays back and waves a hand for me to sit in the chair situated between him and Seger.

When I plop down, Carter twirls a piece of my hair as the buzzing of the tattoo machine goes off. Much to my amazement, George starts the tattoo free-handed like an expert. I don't know much about tattoos and stencils, but I'd say it's a huge feat to pull off what he's doing without any sort of guide. I peel my eyes away from Carter's tattoo and focus on my other poor boyfriend, who lays back on the table, sweating bullets. Seger's wide eyes stare up at the ceiling, and his fingers clutch the sides of the bed so hard that his fingers turn white from the pressure. All the color has drained from his entire body, and even the slightest movement makes him jump out of his skin.

I furrow my brows. "I think he's going to pass out," I say, getting to my feet. "Seger," I murmur, running a hand through his sweaty hair, trying to reassure him it will all be okay.

His frantic green eyes meet mine, and he nods. "I'm good, Angel," he says in a not-so-convincing tone, sounding more frantic than calm. "Seriously, so good," he murmurs, clutching onto my good hand with such a force I'm afraid he'll break it, too.

"Why don't you watch this?" George says from behind us, securing new gloves onto his hand. "I'm going to pierce him first, and then you can see it's no big deal." Seger swallows hard but turns his head in Carter's direction.

"It's a piece of fucking cake, West. So don't be a pussy," Carter says, putting his hands under his head. Carter takes a deep breath when George carefully places a clamp around his dick and holds it straight so Carter can't pull away from the needle about to come. I frown at his words, and he catches my eyes and rolls them toward the ceiling. "Fucking fine! Not pussy. Don't be a dangly bit, West! You fucking happy now?"

He snarks at me, settling back into his chair, when I hum happily under my breath at his correct usage.

"Jesus," Seger hisses, completely ignoring Carter's tirade. Instead, he watches the clamp in horror. His complexion goes from his normal color to bright green when George pushes one needle through the head of Carter's dick. "I'm going to die," Seger mumbles, tossing himself back onto the bed, but he can't peel his eyes off Carter. "I'm going to die by getting a fucking needle in my dick." I can't hold back the snort that slips out at his dramatics, and he glares at me.

Carter breathes through the procedure, getting not one, not two, but three separate piercings on his dick. One at the tip, another near the top, and one near the base. They all should have been painful, but he didn't bat an eye. In fact, through every separate needle going through his shaft, he laid there like it was nothing.

"Fucking see?" Carter growls, tossing his hand up in the air. "It was no big fucking deal. Now lay back and let Matt clamp your dick and fucking pierce it."

"Yes, Sir," Seger fake salutes him with his middle finger and lays back, trembling.

I raise a brow, looking back at Carter, who grins up at me. George cleans off the piercings and then tattoos Carter's pelvis, coloring in the handle of his sword. Every time I see it, I marvel at the beautiful artwork etched into his well-defined pelvis, followed by an intricate sword flowing down his entirety of his dick. It's beautiful and colorless, except for the swirls of color now getting added by George, who concentrates hard. When I first saw it, I thought it would have hurt like hell. By the look on his face, though, I don't think it does. Or, he's not letting on that it does.

Seger turns into a stiff board when Matt sterilizes the tip of his dick and then puts the clamp on.

"Fuck, fuck, fuck," he hisses, covering his eyes. "Tell me

when it's fucking over, Angel. I don't know if I'll survive this. Everything I have is yours."

"Now you're being dramatic," I say, holding tight to his hand.

He heaves a breath, not daring to look when Matt rips open the package to access a fresh needle.

"I'm going to die. Just make sure my grave says something fucking heroic. Like here lies Seger West, who sacrificed the end of his dick for a piece of metal so his girlfriend could have the ride of her life," he hisses, gripping me harder.

Matt snorts at Seger's declarations. "Bro, it won't be so bad. Just take several deep breaths and stay still. It'll be over in a minute, and then you can be on your way."

"Fucking cool, cool, yeah. I'm good. So, fucking good," Seger says through hyperventilating breaths. "I'm...." Seger's eyes widen, and his entire body locks up when Matt quickly puts the needle through the tip of his dick with precision.

My eyes pop wide when Seger's entire body slumps on the table, and his grip loosens on my hand, falling to the side. Matt quickly pushes the bar through without missing a beat and swipes away the blood, cleans the piercing, and then he's done.

"Oh, my fucking God, West!" Carter barks out, eyeing Seger and trying not to laugh at him. His artist peers up at Seger, chuckling under his breath. "Jesus fuck, I can't take him anywhere." Carter runs a hand down his face but continues to watch Seger, who hasn't moved an inch since he passed out.

"Be nice," I tsk, swatting my hand at Carter. He grins, catching my wrist, and kisses my knuckles.

"Always fucking am," Carter grunts, only showing his discomfort once as the artist continues to work along his pelvis, adding more designs and colors.

"Well, the worst is over. He might be a little light-headed when he comes to, but he'll survive," Matt says, standing and taking his gloves off. He tosses them into the trash and begins cleaning up his area by taking the needles and properly disposing of them into a red container. When Matt walks back over, he grins at me, gesturing toward the object in his hand. "This will wake him up," he says, breaking it and shoving it under Seger's nose.

Seger's hazy eyes pop open in a flash of confusion in a few sniffs. He looks between Matt and me, coughing his lungs out.

"What the fuck?" He wheezes, looking around with suspicion.

Carter can't contain himself any longer, letting out a loud, booming laugh. George backs off with a grin, shaking his head. "You passed the fuck out, you dingleberry," Carter wheezes, turning red, unable to catch his breath.

Seger scowls and scoffs. "He put a fucking needle through my fucking dick, you asshole," Seger says, turning bright red. Averting his eyes, he focuses on the papers Matt hands him, quickly explaining how to keep it clean and forbids sex for at least six weeks until it heals, and then condoms until after six months.

"You were a fucking champ, man. Just keep it clean and sanitary for at least six weeks, and you'll be good to go. The complete healing process could take up to six months, but you'll be good after that. And when you want more, you know where to find me," Matt says, shaking Seger's hand.

"Tattoos, yes. This?" He gripes, pointing down to his dick. "Give me a few fucking years. But, uh, thanks, man." Matt snorts at his response and steps out of the room, leaving George to finish.

Carter leans back in the seat, closing his eyes with deep breaths. His eager fingers reach for mine, intertwining them together. The only sign he experiences any discomfort is the twist of his mouth when George hits a few spots along his pelvic bone, and the gentle squeezes of his hand. Seger doesn't move an inch, using the extra time to groan about the pain stabbing at the tip of his dick, and then digs in his pocket for a few leftover pain pills from the accident and pops them. Which is probably a good thing because if he got up right now, he'd probably fall over again and pass out. I don't think I could pick his body off the ground, so it's better he rests with his eyes closed. After another hour of sitting there and watching the magic of Carter's tattoo getting finished, George wipes the area off, rattles off instructions, and then leaves the room after shaking Carter's hand and telling Seger to take care.

Carter cackles when he puts his clothes on, murmuring about Seger and how he can't wait to tell the others.

"This never leaves this fucking room!" Seger hisses when he buttons his pants, wincing and cursing under his breath. His fingers roam through his hair, tugging the ends with a grimace. "Why'd I let you talk me into this?" He grumbles, shaking his head.

"Yeah? And what the fuck are you going to give me if I keep my lips sealed?" Carter asks, cocking his head to the side. "And don't you dare offer me a fucking blow job or some shit. Our girl does that well enough. So, what will it be, West?" My cheeks heat at his words.

"I'll give you one thousand dollars to keep your lips sealed," Seger says, recoiling in pain when he pulls his shirt on. He bends at the waist, pulling in heavy breaths with his hands on his knees. His skin pales, draining him of any color, and I swear he's ten seconds away from passing out—again.

Carter snorts. "No fucking way. I can pull that out of my ass. I don't need your money. Give me something good, West. Or the video I took goes out for the world to see." Seger's eyes widen from his position, and with a trembling body, he lurches forward, trying to grab Carter's phone, but only catches air.

"Don't you fucking do it!" Seger gripes, trying to reach for it again. Carter shoves his phone into his pocket, protecting it with his hand.

"Gimme something good," he says through a playful smirk.

"We'll give you an entire day and night with Kaycee by yourself with no interruptions," Seger barks out, stepping back and grinding his teeth.

I frown, crossing my arms. "Why do I have to be the bargaining chip?" I huff.

"Because you're the only thing that psycho grumpy asshole wants," Seger says, keeping his eyes locked on Carter's.

I gape at him, ready to tell him off. But Carter beats me to it. "Fucking deal," he says, reaching his hand out, and they shake.

"What the hell? Do I not get any say in this?" I hiss, staring between the two.

"Aw, Sweetheart, you wound me. You don't want to spend a fucking day with just me?" Carter asks in a playful tone, reaching over to grab the back of my neck. I yelp when he pulls me forward, resting his forehead against mine.

"Well, of course, I want to spend time with you. I just don't enjoy being the bargaining chip," I grumble, pouting.

He chuckles, plucking my lip. "You're the best chip around, Sweetheart. Now, let's get West out of here before he passes out again."

"I heard that! You can't say it anymore. We shook on it," Seger gripes, stepping out into the shop. "And you better erase that video, asshole!"

Carter's chest rumbles when he puts his arm around my shoulders and guides me into the now emptied-out main shop. The music still blares, but everyone has gotten what they needed and left. We pay George and Matt their fees and walk out toward the car. Well, some of us walk. My face twists when Seger limps beside me, holding a protective hand over his junk.

"Angel," Seger hisses between clenched teeth, easing himself into the backseat with me and groaning the entire time. Gently, he closes the door and settles himself into the seat with agony written all over his face.

I snort, shaking my head in mock disappointment. "I told you, you didn't have to do it."

He groans, running a hand down his face. "Fuck, but it'll feel so damn good for you, Angel. Imagine the extra metal on both of us." He wiggles his brows playfully, and finally, the color returns to his cheeks.

Carter carefully gets into the driver's seat without complaint and turns on the car, and eases it out of the parking lot. "Now, let's get some fucking food at Ruby's. We need to feed Nancy back there."

Seger blanches. "You fucking dick. We are outside the room. OUTSIDE! You can't talk about it anymore. It's like fucking *Fight Club*. Whatever happens in the dick piercing room, stays in the dick piercing room, for fuck's sake. No more dick jokes."

Carter shrugs, turning onto the main highway. "It'll be okay, West. Your secret and the video will be safe with me. I won't tell a soul," he chuckles the entire way to Ruby's, giving me the slightest hint he's up to something. And it's all confirmed when Seger digs his phone out of his pocket and stares at the screen like it kicked his puppy.

Seger's eyes zone in on Carter when he parks the car, cackling into the steering wheel. "Asshole!" He shouts, shooting between the seats and pummels Carter with his fists.

I furrow my brows when the phone falls to the floor, and I pick it up, letting them beat the shit out of each other in the front. Thankfully, we're parked.

> Chase: Shit, dude! I can't believe it!
>
> Zepp: You seriously.... Did you pass out?...
>
> Chase: Oh my god, he passed out. He fucking passed out!
>
> Chase: Dude... that's... hilarious! I'm showing Ainsley. HA.
>
> Zepp: Bro, you, okay?
>
> Chase: Ainsley says you're an idiot HAAAH
>
> Zepp: Seg? Seriously....
>
> Me: He's fine... currently beating the shit out of Carter.
>
> Chase: Be extra good to him now, Sunshine.

I shake my head as they continue their conversation and bring myself back to the boys, punching each other so hard that the damn car is rocking with their movements. And it's not the whole... *if the car is rocking, don't come a-knocking type* of situation I want to be in. Seger grunts from the pain of Carter's fists honing in on the bruises still darkening Seger's chest and abdomen. For shit's sake, If they aren't careful, Seger is going to be in more pain. Time to call off the hounds and get some much needed food.

"Come on, you raging lunatics, let's go eat. And no dessert for you, Grumpy," I shout, trying to get between their massive bodies and pull them apart. Which is harder than you'd think, especially with a broken arm.

"What?" Carter hisses at me, whipping his head toward me with an angry glare.

The moment it registers I threaten to take away his dessert, his face twists into a pained expression.

Seger, panting and sweaty, lands in the passenger's seat

and winces when he covers his dick and groans. "Shouldn't have done that," Seger whines. "I might pass out again. Fuck," he murmurs, closing his eyes.

"Food, now," I groan, getting out of the backseat and heading toward the restaurant with or without them.

"But, Sweetheart, I need your dessert," Carter whines, wrapping his arm around my waist. He stops us in the middle of the dark parking lot, murmuring dirty things into my ear. I shiver when Seger walks up to us, a different shade of green from before.

"I fucked up," he heaves, wrapping his arms around his stomach. "I fucked up so hard. My dick is going to fall off."

Carter snorts and slaps him on the back. "Cheer up, West. Just think, in a week, you won't even notice it. And no comment on your dick," Carter says with a grin, pulling me towards the restaurant. "Now, stop your bitching, and let's fucking eat."

Seger huffs, stands straight, mutters under his breath, and stops dead when his phone rings.

"I swear to fuck, Grumpy! If you sent this to anyone else...." Seger frowns when he answers the phone, and then his expression blanks. "Uh, yeah. No, we'll be there," he grinds out, running a hand down his face.

"What is it?" I ask, taking a step away from Carter.

Seger swallows hard. "I gotta get back. My fucking dad wandered off, and the nurse we hired to stay with him, can't find him." He blows out a breath, and we pile back into the SUV, taking him straight to Zepp.

Our headlights beam off Zepp resting against Seger's Porsche with worry pulling down his brow. Thank God they still have Seger's car to get them around town and back home or we'd have to drive them everywhere. And by we, I mean Chase or Carter. Because my parents still won't give me back my car after those idiots keyed and totaled mine.

"Any word yet?" I ask when we step out of the car.

Zepp immediately shakes his head and sighs. "Nothing, but she's still looking. We should get going," he says with massive amounts of worry tinging his voice.

"Shit," Seger gripes, putting a hand over his dick with a grimace. "Now, I have to ride in the car again and then traipse through the fucking woods, when all I want to do is ice my dick."

"Ice your junk after we find dad," Zepp's lips roll together when Seger tosses him the keys.

"Yeah, yeah. Let's go find the old man so we can get back," Seger gripes before turning to me. "We'll be back after a while, Angel," he murmurs, stepping close and kissing my cheek. "Be a good girl."

Running my fingers through his hair relaxes his entire body against mine, and I nod. "I'm always good. Now, go find your dad, I bet he's so confused. But please be safe, especially—" I swallow hard, my eyes misting with the thoughts of the accident on the same road they're about to travel.

I don't know how they're so okay with getting into vehicles, and I'm such a mess every time I step foot into one. Worry gnaws at my insides when he steps away with a knowing look glinting in his eye.

"No bullshit," he whispers, cocking a brow. "I'm terrified, but I have to go, Angel. I promise we'll be safe. Okay?" It's like he read the thoughts directly from my mind, reading my worry, and knew exactly how I was feeling.

I nod, sucking in a breath. "No bullshit? I'll miss you. Please don't die." I try to give him a reassuring smile when he walks away, giving me a small wave before disappearing into the tiny death trap and pulling away with more waves out the window.

Carter doesn't utter a word when they drive off into the night and disappear down the long and windy highway. More anxiety spikes in my gut at the thought of them taking the same roads we did that fateful night we plummeted into the light pole at the hands of the Apocalypse. What if it happens again? What if they cut the break lines or something worse this time? I swallow hard, leaning into Carter's embrace when he wraps his arm around my shoulders. A heavy boulder sits in the pits of my gut, but I have to shake it off. There's nothing I can do but pray for their safe return and hope this wasn't a ploy to get them away from school grounds. Something doesn't sit right with me as we make our way through the maze and intrusive thoughts about them dying on the side of the road run through my mind. Or us dying inside the Maze House since we're finally alone.

"Earth to Vixen," Carter murmurs in my ear, stopping us outside the front door of the house.

I shake myself from my thoughts. "Sorry," I murmur, for once keeping my crazy thoughts to myself. So, that's a win for me, at least. For now, anyway. I can't be held accountable for what my tongue says before my brain can process what it really should say. Is it inappropriate at times? Okay, all the time? Most definitely. But thankfully for me, I got enough sleep last night. I can keep my worrying thoughts to myself and pretend like this isn't happening.

"Something is on your fucking mind. Now spill," he says in a low, demanding voice, forcing my eyes to his. His warm palms cup my face, holding me still.

I could try to pull out of his grasp and tell him to leave it alone, but when I look into the depths of his eyes, something makes my heart pitter patter with emotions. My tongue loosens, and all my worries come pouring out.

"The Apocalypse has been really silent since the car wreck a week ago. I'm just worried that something bad is about to happen," I say, swallowing the lump in my throat.

His dark eyes quickly dart around the maze before he leans in, sealing his lips over mine. His sharp teeth drag across my bottom lip, leaving me a shaking mess when he finally puts his tongue back in his mouth and keeps his claws to himself.

"It's fucking normal to feel that way. They've been silent all around. We'll make sure Tweedle Dee and Tweedle Dumb check in every hour." I wrinkle my nose at the name he calls them, but nod in response, licking my swollen lip.

"Now, let's go tell Elf Ears he's ordering us pizza–my treat, of course. And then we can give that asshole a proper goodbye before he has to leave tomorrow to swampville, USA," he says, as a smile tilts the edges of his lips.

"Seriously with the Elf Ears, Grumpy!" Chase harrumphs, crossing his arms over his–wait–his bare chest. "You're drooling, Sunshine. You act like you've never seen me half naked before," he says, waltzing forward with so much swagger in his step, his hips move, and his smile grows. "I think it's time to take advantage of the time we have left together. Don't you?" His thumb swipes over my swollen bottom lip, and I can't do anything but nod. Words? What are words when these two massively sexy men gang up on me and threaten me with sexy time? Plus, hello and goodbye sex are the best kind of sex.

"Pizza after?" I ask when Chase grabs me by the hand and drags me into the house with Carter eagerly trailing behind us. I peek at him when he lifts his shirt over his head and wipes his mouth off.

"Just cleaning off your fucking seat first," he says with a smirk. I swear every ounce of my blood rushes to my pussy, and all rational thought falls away. Images of my fingers curling over the thick headboard and riding his face into oblivion as Chase fucks me from behind rushes through. And yup, I'm a damn goner.

"Right, my dick is the only working dick in that house," Chase says, pumping a fist into the air, and we stumble into the bedroom and lock ourselves away into a passion filled bubble.

Once we're all sweaty and satisfied, Chase orders our pizza, giving the poor pizza delivery man the instructions to find us. After several texts back and forth, and Chase reassuring the man we weren't going to murder him, he finally found the Maze House. An hour later, we're sprawled out on the living room floor in nothing but our birthday suits, eating pizza, and waiting for the twins to come back from finding their father. Turns out, the nurse located him right before the boys arrived, giving them time to settle him into his room and spend time with him. We will be going through the whole goodbye experience tomorrow when my brother picks me up for Thanksgiving break and takes me home, away from my boys. But that's tomorrow Kaycee's problem. For now, I'll enjoy the cuddles and kisses until we have to leave each other's arms and head in different directions.

# ELEVEN

## KAYCEE

CHASE THROWS his arms around me, squeezing me until my breath seizes in my lungs. "Can't. Breathe." I hiss, trying to swat him away, but he only squeezes tighter. Oxygen? Who needs it? Certainly not me right now.

"A whole week, Sunshine," Chase murmurs, somehow tightening his grip, and I swear small sobs escape him when he buries his nose in my hair. Through a deep inhale, his body relaxes, and he rests his chin on my shoulder.

"Dude, it's just a week," Seger grumbles from beside us, leaning against his Porsche.

"A week without all of you!" Chase cries out in his dramatic fashion, clinging to me more. If that's possible. I swear we are about to mold into one person.

I sigh, letting him have his moment of neediness. The truth is, I'll miss him, too. Thanksgiving break is only for one week, starting today—Sunday— and then we're back to school for finals before East Point lets us out for a month for Christmas break. This week will be hard for him and me while he's in Louisiana visiting his grandparents because his father is still in Veritas' custody.

As we stand in the emptying parking lot of the school, more kids emerge with their bags thrown over their shoulders. Most kids head home to enjoy their break with their families, while a handful of students stay in their apartments for various reasons.

I catch my bullies, Trent and Oscar's, eyes as they meander towards their cars on the opposite side of the lot. Shivers work down my spine at the predatory look in their eyes. My heart pumps double time when Oscar licks his lips, locking his eyes on me—creepy bastard.

He's always looked at me like I was his next meal. They've avoided us since the accident, giving the group a wide berth. Thanks to my doctor's orders, I haven't been back to classes since I was let out of the hospital. Blissfully staying in the Maze House, I've soaked up the boys' attention. They've pampered me with breakfast in bed and lunch on the couch. Zepp reads to me every night. And Seger gives me a play-by-play when he plays Angel Warrior while I lay my head in his lap. We've made this whole—Kaycee can't touch technology—work.

"You'll have me," Ainsley protests from behind Chase with a frown.

My eyes connect with hers from over Chase's shoulder, silently pleading with her to pull him off me.

A smile works its way across Ainsley's lips, and she lights up. Her health has improved since she confessed Magnolia and her were an item and how much she loved her. Her long, dirty blonde waves sit just past her shoulders in the bright fall sun, and color fills her cheeks, replacing her once pale face and giving her a healthy appearance for the first time this year. But most notably, the fake smiles have vanished, replaced by genuine ones, full of love and life. Ainsley has grabbed life by the horns, and she's finally thriving again. I hope Magnolia is looking down from Heaven with a smile as she watches Ainsley come back to life and breathe for the first time since she was taken.

Chase blows out a breath and steps back from me—finally giving me room to breathe. The warmth of his fingertips bites into my shoulders as he holds me at arm's length and looks me over with sadness in his eyes.

"I'll miss you, Sunshine," he murmurs, leaning in to take my lips. "You'll Facetime me every day? Call me? Text me? Just don't forget about me." I furrow my brows at the last part and cock my head.

"I could never forget about you, dummy," I mumble with reassurance.

He gives me a sharp nod and kisses my cheek like he thought I'd really forget about him. I may have three other boyfriends to keep me company, but nobody compares to Chase Benoit. Not even them.

"Better not," he whispers.

"Dude," Seger whines, pushing off his car. "You sound like a needy girlfriend. It's only a week. She'll text you every day, and you'll live."

Chase wrinkles his nose and lets go. "Fine. I'll just... miss this. You'll be here, doing God knows what, and we'll be down in Louisiana with grandma and grandpa, sulking and not having any fun." Chase frowns, and his entire body deflates.

When his eyes fall to the ground in shame, I know exactly where his mind wanders off to. Like a never-ending loop, his thoughts stray back to his dad, who sits in prison on false embezzlement charges by the Apocalypse bastards. Although we verified the FBI isn't holding him and it's Veritas instead keeping him locked away, we still don't have many answers. I've investigated his paper trail online several times, trying to gauge when he'll be released or if Veritas has anything on him. And they don't—not really. They're either protecting him by hiding him, knowing everything there is to know about the case. Or they're in the dark, trying to figure everything out and keeping him safe. Either way, they locked Tate Benoit away for something. And it's still up to us to break him out and clear his name.

"It'll be okay. We'll text and Facetime," I say, rubbing my fingers along the scruff of his jaw, enjoying the roughness against my palms.

Humming under his breath, he leans into my hand and lays his on mine. His eyes light up, brightening his entire face. "Naked FaceTime?" He asks, bouncing on his toes with excitement. "Oh, Sunshine! They can lay you on the bed and—"

"Ew gross, Chase," Ainsley screeches in horror, slapping him across the back of the head. "I'm standing here, too." My cheeks heat when she shakes her head in disapproval and scrunches up her perfect face in disappointment. "I don't need to hear about your... your... God—your sex life!"

Chase frowns, rubbing his head. "Shit, Ains! I am going to miss my girlfriend. Is that such a damn crime?" He grumbles, scowling at her like he wants to push her away.

She huffs, but a playful smile crosses her lips. "No, it's not a crime. I like your girlfriend. I just wish you wouldn't, you know, announce to the world about your private FaceTime sessions." She playfully gags, sticking her finger down her throat and dry heaves toward the ground.

"What about private FaceTime sessions?" Zepp asks, blinking up from his phone like a zombie, coming into the conversation without a clue.

I don't blame his zoned out look though. Ever since his father made his great escape last night, he's been in constant contact with the home nurse trying to ensure it doesn't happen again. Unfortunately, the nurse informed the boys that it would probably happen on more than one occasion, and the only solution would be tying him to the bed. Which, yeah, they don't want to do that to him. They'd rather him have free roaming privileges and ride out the later parts of his dementia with him at peace and free. So, Zepp is currently looking into trackers he can place in his father's shoes so they always know where he is, ensuring that if he does escape, then he'll be found safely.

"We'll be having them. Lots of them!" Chase whoops, throwing a fist in the air. "And I won't miss a damn thing!" His face lights up at the thought of being included, and I'm so damn glad, too.

I'd hate for him to miss anything–not that he would. But still...where was I going with this? I cock my head, imagining all the many, many shenanigans we could get into over a video call and nearly moan on the spot. Fuck. I gotta focus on what's going on around me. I blink rapidly, catching the eye of Chase, and he winks at me–fucking winks. My cheeks heat. I must have been pretty transparent with my thoughts again. Shit.

"This has been nice and all, but we need to head out, Chase. Grandma already texted me asking if we were at the airport yet." Ainsley peers down at her phone and types out a reply.

"Don't have too much fun without me, Sunshine," Chase whispers, quickly placing his lips on mine.

Our tongues swirl rapidly together in a desperate goodbye filled with groans and moans. My fingers curl into the front of his shirt, pulling him impossibly close. I nearly gasp when a weird sensation trickles over me at the thought of Chase being across the country. For months now, I've had him by my side and gotten used to his fantastic cooking, cuddles, and laughs.

"We fucking won't. We'll be fucking working," Carter grunts, heaving a bag over his shoulder. He pops the back end of his Tahoe, throws his bags inside, and shuts it with a thud.

"Wait, work?" I frown. "What are you talking about? This is vacation, damn it," I pout at the prospect of work.

Zepp gives me a tight smile. "You are taking a field trip

over break. Ask him," he says, nodding his head toward a scowling Carter, who huffs.

"And fucking fighting lessons," Carter grunts, crossing his arms.

"F-fighting lessons?" I gape between him and Seger.

"Yeah, Angel! It'll be your dream come true. Your hot and sweaty boyfriends pummeling one another so you can learn to defend yourself." Seger wiggles his brow as those vivid images pop into my mind.

His words take me back to when I spied on Seger and Carter in the old abandoned gym, beating the shit out of one another. Then my mind jumps to when I stupidly went there and took care of Carter's wounds, and he told me off and called me dumb. Shit, he calls me names all the time. Now, they're endearing instead of insulting—if that's a thing. Who knew the word bitch could make butterflies erupt in my stomach? I fan myself at the thought of them all sweaty, hot, and furious, pounding their fists into each other's faces. Blood dripped down their jaws and eyes. Seger always got the worst of it, and Carter came out on top without injury. Well, except that one time in the gym when I cleaned his wounds after he kicked Seger's ass. But other times I think the man is a damn wizard with healing abilities. But damn, it made me feel things I hadn't felt before. So, if I got to experience that up close and personal—sign me the fuck up.

"We'll discuss it later," Zepp murmurs, nodding towards a familiar-looking car pulling into the lot.

Shit, fuck! My stomach drops out of my ass. I was so caught up in Chase's crushing embrace; I forgot who was picking me up and why I wanted my weird boyfriends as far away as possible.

"Holy shit," Chase squeaks, standing rigid by his sister. His eyes widen in glee or horror—I'm not sure. But I swear he turns blue from holding his breath for so long.

"Body Slammer," Seger gapes, dropping his arms to his

side. "It's fucking Body Slammer!" He squeals like a fangirl, looking excitedly at Chase while jumping up and down. My eyes widen at his fanboy ways, and I watch in horror, as my other boyfriends, sans Carter, join in. Are they going to start a Body Slammer Fan club? Seger would be the damn president, and Chase would be by his side.

"Fuck," I hiss when my gigantic football player brother climbs out of the driver's side of his car, followed by my sister from the passenger's side.

No. No. No. This couldn't get any worse. Why? Why did my mom insist my siblings come and get me? Why couldn't I have been given another car after mine was keyed and totaled? Then this wouldn't be an issue! I'm being punished, that has to be it. The big guy in the sky must be looking down at me and laughing at my pain. I groan at the sight of Bodhi meandering towards us with a shit-eating grin. He's up to no good, and I can already tell before he opens his stupid mouth, that he's about to torture me. Dear God, I hope he doesn't figure my relationship out. He'll either kill them or tell my dad—and I can't decide which is worse.

"Mom said you had made some interesting new friends, Squirt," Bodhi says through a smirk, tossing his heavy arm over my shoulders. I grunt at the weight of his arm, trying to bat him away, but he just pulls me closer and inspects the boys with narrowed eyes. That's the thing about my annoying brother, he's always putting his arm around me and holding me close. Even though I freaking hate every second of it, he doesn't care. Over the years, even though I fucking hate hugs and touch, I've gotten used to it from him.

"Friends, right," Callie murmurs, staring at the boys with a knowing grin. "Nice to see you boys again."

Bodhi cocks his head to the side and frowns. "Hold up, you've met her friends, and I haven't?"

"I'm special," Callie says, barking out a laugh. "You," she says, pointing to Carter. "You must be Grumpy."

Carter blanches, narrowing his eyes at Chase and Seger. "You introduced me as Grumpy? What the fuck?" He hisses between clenched teeth.

"I see it," Callie says, nodding her head in satisfaction.

"It's Carter," he grumbles, nodding his head to my brother and sister in greeting.

Bodhi stands rigid at my side, tightening me into his body. His eyes roam over the boys, taking them in. One by one, he does his brotherly inspection with a stone face without giving me any clue as to what's going through his brain. The last thing I need is for him to discover these are my boyfriends. And my boyfriends would be good to remember that, too. If my brother finds out right now, he might tear them apart and bury them in our backyard without leaving a trace.

"You're a fucking legend here at East Point, man. I'm Seger, Kaycee's bo—best friend," Seger says, tripping over his words, but he recovers gracefully without my brother noticing. The only words my brother heard were, *you're a legend*, and it went straight to his over-inflated head.

Seger holds out his hand with an infatuated grin, patiently waiting for my brother to return the favor. As soon as their hands clasp, I swear Seger falls more in love with my brother than he does with me. I can just see him proposing–he'd drop to his knees, proclaim his love, and swear to have Bodhi's children. I side eye my boyfriend with a frown.

"I had some good times here at East Point," Bodhi muses, staring off toward the direction of the football field with longing in his eyes. If there's one way to distract my brother, it's football.

"You're playing for Milligan, right?" Chase asks, stepping up despite Ainsley's protests. They need to head to the airport, so they don't miss their flight. "I'm Chase, Kaycee's other best friend." Learning from Seger's mistake, Chase doesn't fumble over his words. No, he only emphasizes the word "other" before moving on—the grin taking over Chase's face triples when Bodhi shakes his hand tight. Chase combusts with stars in his eyes, and I can mentally hear him saying he won't wash his hand for a week.

Is it wrong to want to stab my boyfriends over their weird obsession with my brother? No—okay—perfectly legal.

"Yeah, I'm in my last year," Bodhi says wistfully. "Close to finishing."

"Are you hopeful for the draft?" Seger asks, widening his eyes. "That'd be fucking epic, man. Getting into the draft and the NFL."

"Oh, believe me. Bodhi, the Body Slammer, has a lot of prospects. You should see how he fills the stands with all his adoring fans. I think you boys would fit right in," Callie says, looking over the campus with a wistful expression.

"Shit, yes!" Chase says with a whoop.

"That'd be so epic," Seger says, looking at me. "Can we?" He practically begs, intertwining his fingers together in prayer.

"You guys should come," Bodhi says with a smirk, watching Seger's reaction. "We play the day after Thanksgiving. I'm only here to pick up Squirt and take her home. After eating on Thursday, I'm back to Milligan to prepare."

"Shit, that's unfair," Chase whines, throwing his hands up. "The one Thanksgiving we're out of state."

"We have to go," Ainsley says, tugging at his sleeve. "Like, now, if we want to make our flight. Grandma will flip her shit if we don't get there," she grumbles, pulling him back.

Instinctively, Chase takes a step forward but thinks better of it and shakes his head. By the desperate look in his eye, I see he wants to say goodbye again. But with my brother standing right in front of us, Chase has no chance but to pretend he is the best friend he claimed he was.

"Have a good trip," I say, waving my free hand.

"Bye, Sunshine!" He shouts, climbing into his car. When

he and Ainsley take off out of the parking lot, he gives me one last longing look and speeds off toward the main road, heading to the East Point Bluff Airport.

Bodhi's jaw tightens as he watches the car disappear onto the highway, and then he narrows his eyes at me.

"I think that little shit likes you," he says loud enough for the remaining boys to hear. They all stand at attention, looking between one another until Callie's cackles echo through the lot.

"Something like that," she wheezes, bending at the waist.

"The hell is so funny?" Bodhi asks, wrinkling his nose.

"Nothing," I yelp, dislodging myself from his grip. "Let's go home," I grunt, pushing his massive body towards his car. "But give me a minute."

"Aw, does my Squirt need to say goodbye to her besties?" Bodhi goads with a grin.

Ugh. Jackass. If he only knew.

"Get in the car, Bodhi," Callie sings. "And goodbye, boys. I'll see you two on Thursday." She points to Seger and Zepp, who nod their acknowledgment and wave a hand in my direction.

Their faces fall when they realize they won't be able to kiss me goodbye. But we'll see each other again in a few days over Thanksgiving dinner and then after. My mother already gave them the okay to spend the night—in separate beds—so they wouldn't have to make the drive back after a big dinner.

My siblings jump into Bodhi's car, and relief slams into me. This is such a mess. I know my brother and dad will eventually find out I'm in a five-way relationship, but I'd rather it not be right now. Give it a few years until I'm an adult living on my own. Then I could take their disapproving faces. At least my mom and sister know, and hopefully, they haven't spilled the beans. But knowing my mom and her big mouth, my overprotective father already knows every single thing about our relationship. Hurray! Thanksgiving dinner will be another level of shit-show.

"Well, I guess I'll see you soon," I say with sadness in my voice, staring at the twins and Carter with longing. I wish I could march over there and kiss them like I did Chase and give them a proper goodbye.

"Wednesday, to be exact," Zepp says with a sharp nod.

"And are you going to explain what we're doing?" I ask, raising a brow.

Carter snorts. "Yeah, I don't fucking know if we should tell you this time." And then he sighs, running a hand down his face. "I'm coming to pick you up on Wednesday morning. My dad will be out of the office, and I need your help getting into his computer. Hopefully, we'll set the last fucking disc in and get some more insight into what he's doing."

"Just us?" I ask, looking at Seger and Zepp.

"Just us, Sweetheart," Carter murmurs. "I won alone time with you, remember?" He adds with a wink and saunters away toward his vehicle with an extra pep in his step. It's almost as if he has something planned for his special time with me.

"Okay, I'll see you then." Carter nods at my words and gets into his SUV. His car roars to life and then leaves us in the dust.

"See you guys on Thursday. Get ready to be investigated like criminals," I grumble with a roll of my eyes.

"It'll be fine, Angel," Seger says with a grin.

"We'll be fine, Baby Girl," Zepp says, shoving his phone in his pocket. "No worries."

I wave to them as they get into Seger's Porsche and drive off, leaving me standing alone in the empty parking lot. My brother honks the horn, knocking me out of my damn thoughts, and I swiftly flip him off while he barks out a laugh at my jumpy reaction. Fucker. Finally, I climb into the car and settle into the backseat after putting my bags into the trunk.

Bodhi turns in his seat, looking me up and down with suspicion. "Those are your new friends?" He asks, raising a suspicious brow.

A blush heats the back of my neck and spreads toward my cheeks, but before I can defend my damn honor, my phone beeps in my lap. Bodhi yaps on in the front seat as I read over Carter's words, quickly tuning out my brother.

> Grumpy: Me and you. Wednesday. I'm picking you up.

> Me: Grumpy.......

> Grumpy: Be fucking ready for me bright and early, Vixen.

> Me: Fine....

# TWELVE

## KAYCEE

CARTER'S FINGERS tighten around the steering wheel, cracking under the pressure when he maneuvers the large SUV through the crazy turns. My stomach turns when we round a sharp curve, riding the white line. My body shifts closer to the window with every swerve, and I swear I'm ten seconds away from jumping out the window and taking my chances on the side of the road. Would road rash hurt that bad? Probably. But it'd be better than dying at the hands of my crazy boyfriend's driving skills. Seriously. What the hell? The weeds outside look inviting, and they'd probably cushion my fall, too.

I scowl in his direction, taking in the deep frown lines marring his gorgeous face. Dark freckles pop over the bridge of his nose, trailing a line over his cheeks, and disappear into his hairline. Have I ever noticed how many there are before? Have I taken the time to count them one by one with the tips of my fingers? I sigh away the distraction my mind is trying to fascinate me with. Maybe it's the stress of what we're about to do. Or maybe it's the fact Thanksgiving is tomorrow, and Seger and Zepp are coming to dinner with my entire family. My. Entire. Family. Like the first meeting with my brother in the parking lot went swimmingly… Not. Dinner will be the epitome of torturous Hell with a cherry on top for good measure. My brother already promised all kinds of bullshit with threatening promises. Hell, when Carter came and got me for this adventure, my brother eyed him the whole time with suspicion. Just, fuck my life, seriously.

Something big is nagging at Carter and making him curl his fingers tighter around the steering wheel, quickening our speed to eighty-seven. Shit! I'm going to die in this tomb he calls a vehicle, and no one will find us in the depths of the sea below. This is my crash a few weeks ago, all over again. I eye his foot as he brakes for a turn, and thankfully the car complies. But God, my heart pounds against my ribs, and sweat wets my palms when I dig my fingernails into the supple leather. The sound of my nails scratching against the surface fills the quiet vehicle. Once again, I assumed he'd blare some sort of screamo, rock type of music as we make our way to cause chaos. And, I was proven wrong. Hence the stifling silence filling the air.

I squeak when he takes another sharp turn, forcing my body into the door once again. My seatbelt tightens across my chest and squeezes me to the seat. I've held my tongue for the past two hours since he picked me up at my parent's house, and took off like a fucking psycho stealing a car, and jumped on the curvy highway. He shifts again, throwing me back towards him, and I can't pretend I feel normal anymore. Every turn he makes, every time he puts the pedal to the metal, my heart flutters in my chest. And not the good kind of flutter either. It's the *'I'm about to shit my pants because Carter is driving like a maniac, getting us to our destination a whole hour earlier than he should have'* kind of driving.

"Carter," I gasp out, clutching onto the oh-shit bar above my head.

I heave out a breath when the car slows to a more acceptable speed, and he leans back in his seat. Unpeeling his fingers from around the steering wheel he was intent on choking, he focuses on me. Again, so not safe, but I'm thankful to be in our lane and going the speed limit. It's an improvement. And that's all I can ask for.

"Fuck. Shit! Sorry, Sweetheart." His palm bounces off the steering wheel in frustration before smoothing down his out-of-control blonde hair. He peers over at me, setting his hand on my thigh, and gives it a small squeeze. My hand finds its way, resting on top of his for comfort.

Like any other time I'm around the boys and touching them, a calmness takes over my entire body, and my muscles finally unbunch from the stress of his driving. Remind me to never step into a vehicle with him when he's worried—or maybe ever again. I mean, in a getaway situation, this would be ideal. We could rob a bank, and then we'd get away from the cops chasing us. But no one is chasing us right now, well, except for his demons, or whatever is eating away at him.

"It's okay, Grumpy," I mumble, tapping his hand.

I feel his glare of death before he opens his big mouth.

"Fucking no it's not," he growls through clenched teeth, returning to his previous gesture of strangling the steering wheel until it begs for mercy. Use me, damn it. Not the steering wheel. But he doesn't listen. His knuckles turn white, and his body is as rigid as a board. "There's so many fucking unknowns. You could open your fucking mouth and get yourself hurt or kidnapped or shoved into a basement. Or whatever... everything could go wrong."

I blanch, my lips popping open. "Well that's just rude automatically assuming I'll mess it up," I grumble, crossing my arms over my chest. Note to self, my boyfriend is extremely rude when he's upset. Or that could possibly be his normal demeanor. Who knows. "But you said he won't be home, right?" I side-eye him as his features deflate, and guilt slams into him.

"Fuck," he growls with remorse. A deep breath rocks through him, and he once again relaxes. Let's see how long it lasts for this time. "I tracked my dad downtown at a homeless shelter getting everything ready for the charity Thanksgiving dinner tomorrow. He should be tangled up in his fake charity shit until after eight. We have all fucking day to do our thing," he says, blowing out a breath.

The soothing beat of the turn signal clicks until he pulls onto a long blacktopped driveway surrounded by trees. Their shadows dance along the car as we make our way down the long road, making me wonder where the hell we are. Carter rarely talks about home. Unless it's a comment about how hellish it is or how his step mom is a gold digging whore hiding away here.

Pulling myself from the beautiful scenery, I frown at Carter's rigid posture. Shit. His relaxation didn't last long at all. A twitch forms in his jaw from his teeth clenching, and all his confidence drains away. It's not reassuring in the slightest that he's this nervous to step foot inside his home. He's supposed to be the confident one in this situation since we're going behind enemy lines and into the monster's den.

"Be confident, Grumpy! You're the one leading us into this," I mutter, shaking my head. My eyes land back out into the forest, and he huffs.

"What did you say?" He grinds out, clamping down on the damn steering wheel again. He's either going to kill it or make it come from the pleasure of his choking. He cocks a brow, looking at me with an unreadable expression.

And shit, I said all of that out loud. Time to change the subject before I really set him off.

"And you've checked the cameras and looped them?" I ask, attempting to continue our conversation before I went off the rails into Kaycee land and crashed.

This whole, Kaycee not sleeping very well last night because she tossed and turned without her boyfriends next to her bullshit, is not good for my detective skills. I'm supposed to be bright eyed and bushy tailed, ready for action. Instead,

I'm getting stuck in my head and saying the first shit that comes to mind. Speaking of... I peek at Carter who smirks in amusement, trying to hide his laughter.

"Did I say that all out loud again?" I grumble, my cheeks turning pink. His grin grows wider. "Of course I did. Back on track, Grumpy!" I clap my hands, forcing him to put his eyes back on the impossibly long driveway.

Focus, Kace. Get your mind back in the game! Mentally, I go through the steps he pounded into me—and not the sexy way, either—last night over our planning session on video chat. Loop the cameras so his dad won't know we are there—check. Make sure his dad is occupied so he won't find us snooping in his office—check. His father and stepmother, Francesca, are down at the soup kitchen with the state police offering Thanksgiving meals. And according to him, Piper should be gone, too. Doing whatever it is Piper does in her spare time. Hopefully not her damn bio father either. God, gross. I have to stop thinking about the time we spied on them and the nightmares that ensued after their very public displays of grossness.

"Yeah," he says, holding the word out.

"Then we'll be fine," I say with a shrug.

Fine, yeah. We'll be totally fine like that time we walked into Crowe's house, and I got caught. But then I got my revenge and stole his phone. Which, well, damn, I got in trouble for that, too. I mean, it wasn't really that much of a punishment letting my boyfriends tie me up with silk and have their wicked way with me. A shiver works through me at the thought of both situations—half good—half bad. Crowe was at least as decent as he could be when he caught us. He played it off like the hero, grieving guy he wanted to present. Now, Cushing Cunningham? I have no idea what kind of Hell we'd pay if he caught us snooping in his office. Carter seems to think his father has more in his office than Crowe would, and that's why this is so important to do.

"Don't fucking jinx us," he mumbles, rubbing a hand down his face. "Well, Sweetheart. Welcome to Hell," Carter grumbles, throwing the SUV into park near the four car garage at the end of the long driveway.

I peek back out the back window, realizing that the main road isn't visible from here. It's nothing but gigantic trees swaying in the cool wind and a long driveway leading to a house of horrors. Or whatever Carter says about this house. Shit. If he was playing me and didn't love me like I know he does, even though he won't say it, he could murder me. Hell. He could bury me in the woods and no one would know. Peeking at Carter, I watch his grinning face, almost like he's finally relaxed with what we're about to do.

"You need more fucking sleep," he gripes playfully. "Come on. Let's get this fucking over with."

"Hell is huge," I say with awe, cocking my head at the sight.

My jaw drops from the money oozing from the ridiculously large structure erected in front of me. It could probably poop one hundred dollar bills out of its gutters and dispense dollar coins from chimneys like waterfalls. I hold back my snort at the imagery running through my mind and lean back to stare up at it. I swear it looks like a tall skyscraper swaying in the wind because of its height. The house—no, scratch that, it's not even a house, it's a damn mansion nestled deep in the woods. Only accessible through a mile-long driveway. It's hidden so well from the road you'd never guess this was here. Perfect place for a psycho murdering cult leader. I wonder if there's a secret room inside where he stores all his victims?

Growing up, my parents had money. Expensive vacation homes. Cruises. Out of country visits. I've been through them all, and I've seen my fair share of rich buildings. But this is way more than I expected. Especially for a state police detective, whose salary could definitely not afford all this. Pretty damn suspect, if you ask me. Sure he got money from Carter's mom's passing. But this? Jesus. This is made from blood money.

Everything about the house is immaculate. From the large rounded, second-story porch held up by marble pillars, to the massive windows letting the sunshine in, and finally to the beautifully polished wood siding without a speck of dirt. Several gardeners roam around with a variety of tools in their hands, bending at the waist to gather leaves, and prune the bushes. They don't spare us a second glance, opting to continue their work when we step out of the vehicle, slamming the doors loudly behind us.

"I expected more," I murmur jokingly, wrinkling my nose when I stare at the massive home Carter affectionately calls Hell. "Where are the fountains dripping in gold? Where are the statues and diamond door knobs?" Am I exaggerating? Yes. But it's not like I haven't seen it before at the twins' mansion. Now that was a ridiculous mansion.

Carter snorts. "We aren't the fucking West family, Vixen. This is fucking Hell with marble floors and elegant fucking ballrooms." Disdain glazes over his eyes, and his lip curls, showing off his pearly whites as he stares at the house in question.

"Well, you could jazz it up a little. It looks sad and neglected," I say with sarcasm, snorting when he clutches my waist, pulling my body back against his.

"Keep up the sass, Vixen," His hot breath blows in my ear as his fingers slowly move south. A loud yelp escapes my throat when his hot fingers grab tightly to my ass cheek, sinking hard into my flesh. "And I'll show you what happens to sassy girlfriends. I have a million and one ideas."

There's a pussy-clenching threat lining his words, and I'm not complaining. And neither is my hussy of a vagina, desperate for him to make good on those lovely threats. It's been too long since he's fucked me speechless, but that's his own damn fault. Leaning back, I rest my head on his shoulder and boop his nose. His eyes pop wide when he stares down at me and squeezes my ass harder, snarling at me. Carter likes to think he's scary or something, but I've got news for him. I laugh, booping him again, and pull away from his embrace.

"Oh, I will. Now, let's do the damn thing." I look back at him over my shoulder, and he rolls his eyes toward the sky, grumbling to himself about how weird I am. Or something along those lines.

"Be fucking good," he mumbles in my ear when he catches up to me and swats my ass. I shriek when my body falls forward, stumbling over my wobbly legs, narrowly missing kissing the ground. I huff, righting myself ready to tear him apart, but I'm greeted by his fine retreating ass. Hate to see them go, but I love to watch them leave.

I frown, crossing my arms. "What is it with you guys and that phrase? I'm always good," I mumble, making mean faces behind his back. Be good, Kace. I swear I hear that on repeat day in and day out. What do they take me for?

He smirks, some of his earlier stress melting away from him when he approaches the beautiful set of French doors. Seeming happier now that we're here and no other cars or signs of life exist. Opening the front door, he gestures for me to enter.

"Welcome to the seventh circle of Hell. Please keep your mouth shut and hands to yourself at all times. Or punishments await," he says in his best mocking announcer voice when we enter the echoey entryway.

I scoff. "Oh ye of little faith," I accuse, pointing a stern finger at him and giving him my best stink eye.

Unfortunately, it only makes him grunt like a caveman and roll his eyes, confirming he has little confidence in my abilities to keep my mouth shut. Or not take things I shouldn't. Okay. His worry is warranted. I'm a hot mess when it comes to focusing and….

Shit.

His meaty fingers wrap around my wrist, jostling me down the hall and knocking me out of my nonstop thoughts. Stupid random throughs always carrying me away. So much so, I miss half the house when my caveman drags me like a damn sheep down a long hallway, herding me somewhere.

Before me an inconspicuous, large wooden door, stands taller than any door I've ever seen. I crane my neck until I finally find where the door meets the tall ceilings. Peering around, I notice another tall door down the way with similar features. So, if this is the office door we are in search of, then it doesn't immediately scream open me or search me. Eh, well —except for the weird looking eyes carved into the wood grain, making it look possessed. Is this a warning sign that evil awaits behind this door? I cock my head, searching the wood again and note several pairs of eyes looking back at me. The door is watching my every move, reporting back to the head dick in charge and…

I freeze when Carter's hand disappears into the depths of my coat pocket, rustling around. His breath rolls across my ear as he crowds behind me. Seductively, he nips at my lobe, dragging it between his teeth and distracting me as he searches for my prize possession. My eyes roll into the back of my head when his entire body presses against me, making me wish he could just throw me down. Once he finds whatever he's looking for, he kisses my cheek, murmuring sweet nothings—or maybe those are curses. My cheeks heat as my pick lock kit comes into view and I stare dreamily at it, imagining the possibilities.

Nothing is off limits now. Office drawers. Hidden closets. Secret rooms. I cross my fingers for the secret rooms. You can't hide anything from me, Cushing Cunningham. Especially with this in my grasp.

Who knows what treasures he hides in the depths of his drawers? Office drawers. Ew. Not drawers as in his underwear and… shit. Now I'm thinking of the wrong Cunningham's underwear. Carter's dick piercings. Carter's sword. Carter's—

"Jesus Christ. How much sleep did you get last night?" Carter whispers harshly in my ear, tapping the kit in his fingers. "Get a fucking move on, Vixen. We need to do this as quickly as possible." He thrusts his hips into mine, knocking me into action. Jerk. That's at least one way to get me going.

I pick the lock one handed, something I've been training to do since the doctors sealed my arm into a damn itchy cast. Writing, typing, and anything in between has been one handed, and it fucking sucks. I'll rejoice the day they saw this thing off of me, and I can finally scratch my arm. It'll feel better than two consecutive orgasms and a cupcake reward afterward.

Shit.

Now, I'm thinking about cupcakes and licking them off the boys, and….. I shake my head, focusing on my task. I can't prove my boyfriend right. Ignoring his dig about my sleep schedule, I victoriously thrust the office door open with ease, letting it smack into the wall. Ta-da! Or by the scowl in his face, not so ta-da. Oops–I cringe. If there's one thing we should be doing, it's not leaving any trace that we were here. And that's exactly what I did. I'll just play it off like I did nothing wrong and spread my arms wide, displaying my crime. Smugly, I look over my shoulder at him, earning more eye rolls and scoffs. Seriously. Where's the appreciation? The gratitude? I was a good fucking girl, damn it. I want my cake…wait, I really do want some cake now. I wonder if he'll really reward me for being a good girl after this with frosting and… Oh, fuck.

Carter pulls me into the office with greater force than necessary and swivels me around. I grunt when he slams my back into the wall, and my breath leaves my lungs in one long exhale when my casted arm almost bangs into the wall. Pain stings every inch of my arm like tiny knives poking into my skin. Bastard. I scowl at him, but he doesn't notice through the twisted expression on his face.

Fury eats at his face but softens when my fingers run through his hair, and he melts. Every ounce of whatever he was feeling fades away into vulnerabilities shining through his wide eyes. His long lashes move rapidly as he blinks, coming back to himself. Almost as if he were lost in a weird fog, and I was his lighthouse leading him back.

"I'm fucking terrified," he murmurs his confession through one long, emotion-filled breath, clearly not wanting to admit his feelings.

My heart skips a beat when he leans into my touch, relaxing in the comfort of my presence, instead of pushing me away. Piece by piece, I'm prying him open with my crowbar, until he always tells me what's going through his mind.

"I know," I whisper through a heavy tongue. "And no, I was up all night tossing and turning. This whole thing…. It's a reminder of what we did before." I swallow hard, focusing on the acknowledgement in his twinkling eyes. Fine, I proved him right, okay? But, I have to use my own logic against me, too. If he needs to open up to me about his feelings, then I can do the same. Even if it bruises my poor pride just a smidge.

Last night, as I lay in my lonely bed at my parents' with the lights off, the nerves blossomed in my gut. Only growing stronger. I don't think I slept a wink, knowing in a matter of twelve hours we'd be walking into the lion's den without an actual clue what we were getting into. My only reassurance was Carter had told me more than once that he had everything under control. And I believed him and still do. He assured me everyone would be preoccupied and out of the house.

All I know is, there's a ticking time bomb looming over my head. It's counting down the days I have left on earth before the Apocalypse decides to strike me down. So, we have to get this done and spy on him like we did with Shaw and Crowe. Cushing Cunningham is the last brother on our list to look into. Last night without any help, Carter broke into Shaw's office and his apartment and placed the discs in his computers. Only time will tell until we see the results of that.

Carter leans his forehead against mine, taking heaving breaths and grounding himself. The whole world falls away, leaving just the two of us to revel in each other. My eyes flutter shut when the heavy pounding of his heart rattles against my palm as it glides over his sculpted chest. With everything I have, I focus on the feel of his life force pounding against it. His fear comes through in waves. He doesn't have to utter a word for me to see it written all over his face. I shiver when he puts his hand over mine, holding me there against his heart.

"Okay," he murmurs, leaning in to brush his lips against mine in a gentle kiss. His soft lips remain against mine for a solid three seconds before he pulls back. "Let's get to work." He nods his head and steps back.

Taking the discs out of his pocket, along with the ice pack he had shoved in there, he holds them up to the light again. My heart kicks up at their beauty. The same mesmerizing feeling washes over me when the specks glint in the light. After handling them when we put them in Crowe's office to spy on him, I'm still amazed at what they can do. How can two little discs spy so much? Just by taking a computer apart and placing one in there, we can see everything the person on the other side does.

"Let's do the damn thing," he mutters, heading to his father's large and shiny wooden desk near the open window.

Sunshine leaks in, shining a spotlight on every corner of the large room. Now that his gigantic form isn't hovering above me and blocking my view, I take in the room. Bookshelves line the walls, filled to the brim with different types of books. Old ones. New ones. Even ancient ones with peeling spines. I breathe in the familiar smell of books, and my shoulders sag. Nothing beats the scent of books, no matter how old they are. If we weren't standing in a psychopath's office, I might be impressed. I twirl in place, peeking at every corner.

Visions of a secret room hiding behind these walls, concealing whatever he doesn't want the world to see, come to life in my wandering mind. As I peer around the room, running my fingers over the worn spines of books, Carter gets to work taking apart Cushing's desktop tower and putting the disc next to the motherboard. He grunts and curses, but everything goes as smoothly as we could have hoped in under two minutes. This time, we didn't need to be super quick, just efficient. He quietly puts the computer back together as I tug on every book, making sure there are no hidden cabinets or rooms behind them.

"The fuck you doing?" Carter barks, making me jump out of my damn skin. Scowling in his direction, I continue my perusal of the books, poking the tip of my tongue out in concentration.

I shrug, pulling on another book and holding my breath. I yearn to hear the whorls of mechanical mechanisms, but it doesn't happen. My shoulders sag. Damn it. No secret room with this one. Maybe there's something on the walls that opens it instead. I peek at the wood paneling, knocking my knuckles against it, and shake my head in utter disappointment. Every villain has a secret place they hide the bodies or treasures—I'm hoping for gold coins or something.

"Checking for hidden rooms," I mumble, running my finger down the next spine and pulling it out. "Every evil character has their own secret lair where they take the victims. I just figured, maybe it's here in the most unsuspecting place." I check the next book again, pulling it out and putting it back. Repeatedly, I check, until I've made it to the end of the aisle of books.

Carter leans against his father's desk with his arms crossed over his chest and snorts in amusement at my antics. He marches toward me with something mischievous shining in his dark, brooding eyes. Curling his fingers around my hips, he pulls me against him, rolling his devious tongue over my pulse point. I swear to God whenever he does that, my panties melt into nothing and completely disintegrate into dust. What I wouldn't give to have more alone time with him in this office or in his bed. Too bad he's still forbidden from having sex or his dick might fall off. But Seger's sweet words pour through my mind, 'You can still ride my face, Angel.'

"We need to keep moving, Vixen. Before I'm tempted to say fuck my father and fuck my aching dick and fuck you over his desk. Then we'd sure as fuck get caught because I wouldn't stop myself from coming all over his shit to fuck with him," he murmurs in my ear as his meaty fingers drop into the waistband of my leggings and swirl around the sensitive skin. My muscles bunch beneath his touch, egging him on to keep going. Yes! Yes! I mean No…No…. We can't do this right now!

Turning around, I let him cage me in between his muscly arms and the bookcase behind me. I cock my head to the side, taking in his features like I love to do. It'll never get old, tracing the freckles dotting his nose and cheeks, which get duller the more winter sets in and the sun doesn't heat the earth as much.

"How about this," he growls, swooping in to take my lips prisoner with such passion, I swear my soul leaves my body and now floats, observing from above. His tongue invades my mouth, sending shivers down my spine. I moan when the warm metal of his tongue ring thrashes with my tongue. Breathlessly he pulls away, forcing his giant hand to cover my face. Ack! What the hell? This was sexy time! Albeit sexy time we didn't necessarily have time for, but still!

"What the hell?" I whine, trying to slap his hand away

from squishing my poor nose back into my face. Pain erupts, making my eyes water from the stupid bruising still present and lining my face.

"You're a fucking temptress, I swear to all things holy," he groans, adjusting his dick. "You made him wake up," he curses more, taking a step back away from me like I'm the plague.

Asshole.

I frown, marching toward Cushing's desk, and plop in his cushy chair. "Yeah, and you're the asshole who cornered me and stuck his tongue down my throat. Don't blame me for your baseball bat reawakening at the worst time ready to hit a home run." I shake my head in fake fury, pointing a haughty finger in his direction. "You're the dumb dumb who got a dick piercing," I gently remind him, pursing my lips.

He huffs, but that cocky smile crosses his lips. "You know, we never had that fucking discussion about my baseball bat dick." My smile falls into the depths of my churning stomach.

No. No. We do not need to talk about it. Not one bit. Shit. I bite my lips when he saunters over, leaning over the other side. He stares me down when his palms lay flat on the desk's surface, and he smirks when I follow his movements with lusty, hussy eyes. Damn him and his delicious arms and baseball bat.

"Tell me, Vixen. What's so great about my baseball bat? And why is it referred to as that of all fucking things?"

No. There's no way in hell I'm telling him it's because his dick is huge, and I was afraid it wouldn't fit inside me, resembling a baseball bat standing at attention. Sometimes I'm still frightened it might not fit and tear me in two. But yeah, so not telling him the truth. Deny. Deny. Deny.

I blink a few times and bring my pick lock kit out from my pocket again, and search for drawers with my good hand. Anything to get away from this awkward as hell conversation. I can only imagine the look on his face. If I told him the truth, it'd only boost his already enormous ego, and we can't afford that.

"How about the office files, huh?" I ask, picking the lock of the top drawer until I feel his heat glaring down from behind me. Shit. Double shit!

His fingers wrap around my ponytail, and he yanks my head back until my eyes stare deep into his brown, honey eyes. The same eyes I could get lost in for days. They darken with a fire blazing in them when he tilts his head and leans over me so his mouth is level with mine.

"Vixen," he murmurs, brushing his lips against mine. "Tell me now before I bend you over my knee and smack your ass red. You won't be able to sit down for a week, and I won't even have to use my fucking baseball bat of a dick to inflict that type of pain." I shiver at his words, puckering my lips and pressing them into his Spiderman style. I grunt when he tightens his hold on my ponytail, yanking my hairs by the roots. I press harder, hoping this distraction works wonders, but all it does is fuck me over because he won't leave it alone.

"Can't we discuss this later when we're not in danger of getting caught?" I mumble, fiddling with my picklock, which is currently protruding from the lock of the desk drawer.

He smirks, shaking his head when I sigh in defeat because we stay like that for a minute straight, sitting in silence and staring into each other's eyes. He doesn't waver or let loose of my ponytail, keeping it tight in his grip. A clock in the distance ticks away, filling the dreadful silence, and the reminder time is not on our side. Shit. I hate silence. It makes an awkward ringing in my ears and sends my nerves into a frenzy. The clock strikes again, and finally I heave a sigh.

"Fine," I huff, glaring at his smug as fuck face knowing he won. This round, that is. And that's it. I won't let him win anything again. "You have a big dick. Is that what you wanted to hear? Or should I talk to the fella myself?" I grumble when he snorts in my face, kissing my cheek in victory.

"He might fucking like it," he says, stepping back and unwinding his fingers from my hair. "Maybe you should tell him all about how fucking big he is." The smirk that grows on his face makes me want to slap him.

"Maybe I'll talk to Big Carter later. For now, I need to search," I hum when I pull the drawer open and find it empty, much to my disappointment. I pout, slumping my shoulders, and continue my search.

I repeat the same thing with every drawer in his desk, but again, we come up empty-handed like with everything we've done. I'm not sure what I expected when he said we should check out the drawers. Evidence that the Apocalypse was up to something? Proof of what they were up to? Hell, maybe an address to their main place of operations would be helpful at this point.

Just like last time when we wasted a whole day going into Crowe's office, under the guise of me needing alone time in Magnolia's room. Returning to her room was like a slap in the face. Since coming to East Point, I haven't lost sight of who I wanted to avenge, but it has shifted slightly. Magnolia isn't the only person's death I want the authorities to look into. I want justice for every single person they have wronged and for them to go to prison and rot. They don't deserve to walk this earth with all the bullshit they've pulled.

He snorts again, murmuring about Big Carter and a baseball bat. But he lets me do my thing while he stands guard. Occasionally, he walks around the office, checking between books. Even though I already know there's no secret room within these walls. It still makes me wonder where the hell they take these people for five days at a time, and no one has a clue. So, hopefully, with our computer invasion, we can find some information without Cushing being any wiser. Like where they do this, why they do this, and how they make money? I have so many questions to ask, and I want all the answers to them.

"All right," I groan, standing from my spot. I make sure each desk drawer is back in its proper place and locked once again.

"Done?" he asks, raising a brow and walking toward me.

"Mhmm, your father doesn't have any juicy secrets hidden in here. Such a shame," I mumble when he grabs my good hand and pulls me away.

"Well, let's get the fuck out of this house before he comes home. I'll come back later and look in his room for a safe or any-fucking-thing that catches my eye. But for now, let's go back to my apartment." A wide grin splits his face when he turns to face me, forcing my body into his. "I like what West fucking said," he murmurs, licking his way down my jawline.

"Carter," I groan, trying to shove at his chest. "You're going to…"

"Fuck!" He howls, taking in several breaths. His hand slips between us, and he covers his junk, forcing his raging hard on down. Pain etches his face, forcing him to take several deep breaths before he could release his hand over his dick.

Looking down, I gently pat his dick, and he winces. "I'll kiss it better," I whisper with a devious smile, making him recoil.

His scowl could scare children away and make flowers wilt on the spot. "You're fucking enjoying this too much."

I shrug. "Maybe, maybe not. I told you, idiots, you didn't have to do that," I tsk, marching toward the closed door separating us from the rest of the house.

I wonder if he'd take me to his bedroom here and show me around. What exactly would Carter's room look like? Like his apartment? Probably. It'd have trees growing out of it by now with wildlife creating their own habitat. I hesitate in front of the office door and look behind me. Carter lazily strolls toward me with his hands in his pocket and fiery blaze burning in his eyes. He settles behind me, clutching my hip. I feel every plane of his body and melt into him.

"You won't be saying that when I fuck you with these new additions in a few weeks. You think my fucking tongue ring makes you see stars? Wait until my dick with these piercings hits your pussy walls. You won't know what to fucking do with yourself, but fuck it. And then when you come, you had better scream my name, and Jesus Christ," he hisses the last word, taking a step back from me, cupping himself. He doubles over at the waist, sucking in several breaths. A redness takes over his face, and his veins protrude from his neck from the pain of his boner.

"Poor, poor pierced baseball bat," I murmur, tapping his hand that lays over his dick. I earn myself a death glare that would make any other person back up and run for their lives, but not me. I simply tap it again and snicker when he snatches my wrist.

"Wait!" He hisses, wrapping an arm around my waist and my mouth. He silences my movements. "Listen," he murmurs directly in my ear, staring at the door with blooming terror in his eyes.

A murmured voice slips through the cracks of the closed office door, sounding too faint to hear what she's saying. But it's enough to give us confirmation that Francesca is back and moving around. Several thuds happen right outside the door and move further away quickly. My ears ring when silence finally takes over the corridor outside the room, and we hold our breaths. His palm tightens around my mouth. I trace the tip of my tongue along his calloused hand, earning a grunt in return.

"Vixen, I'm going to need you to fucking stop that now. Seems we've run into a fucking problem, and that drugged up, gold digging bitch my dad likes to keep around just stumbled home from the soup kitchen early." I stop moving my tongue along his palm.

"So, what do we do?" I murmur into his palm, and he sighs, pressing his ear to the door.

"It's quiet now," he grunts, taking his hand away, and wipes it down his jeans. "We might be able to sneak out without anyone noticing. I didn't hear my fucking dad, just her. Hopefully she's fucking passed out by now and drooling." The clock in the room ticks through another few minutes as we stand rigidly against the door, not daring to move a muscle or leave the room.

Grabbing me by the wrist again, he opens the door. We step out one by one, with me looking directly into his back, and we stop suddenly. The aching tip of my nose squishes into his hard back, reverberating pain through my whole face. You know, the doctor said my broken nose would heal in four weeks, but I anticipated maybe a quicker recovery. It's only been a week since I got out of the hospital, but it feels like a lifetime of suffering. It's been so damn slow and painful. I can't wait for a time when my nose doesn't hurt at the slightest touch. It's so damn sensitive. Every time I scratch it, I want to cry from the overwhelming pain. Whoever beat my ass at the wreck site and took it out on my nose, should burn in the deepest depths of Hell. If this doesn't heal properly, I'm tracking them down and shoving my foot up their ass.

I peek around his broad shoulders, and my entire body stiffens. Shit. You know, we could have been caught by Bigfoot himself, and it would have been better. He may have eaten us, leaving no evidence behind. But it would have been better than this situation. Hell, I would have taken Crowe again. At least I charmed my way out of that potential catastrophe. Instead, we get the worst person possible. I sneak back behind Carter, making myself look as small as possible.

"Carter!" Her over excited squeals echo through the small hallway, shattering my ear drums.

"Piper," he growls, backing up. My back bangs into the closed door, forcing an oomph from my throat. I swear his foot moves to stomp on mine, but if he values his life, he won't. His foot stops mid air, hovering above mine before he puts it back on the ground. Good, he values his life. "The fuck are you doing here?" he asks her through gritted teeth.

She scoffs, pulling me out of my weird thoughts. Jesus, I need to sleep better tonight so I can focus at our dinner tomorrow. I need to be tip top to endure my brother's weird protective bull shit he's no doubt going to pull. He already threatened their balls if they fucked me over. But, shh. I haven't told them that detail yet. They'd probably crap their pants in front of their football idol and whither away from the embarrassment.

I cringe at the sound of her nails hitting the screen of her phone. "Oh silly, you act like I don't live here," she says through fake cheer, setting my teeth on edge.

Every time I'm in her presence, something in the back of my mind sends off warning bells. Maybe it's the overly sweet personality or the weird food references she gives. But what really stands out is the way she can go off in a matter of minutes. Like that one time in the cafeteria when I told her I didn't need a tour, that Chase had already stepped up. She lost her shit at me. If it hadn't been for Seger, I think she would have carved my heart out with her bare hands and sacrificed it to the macaroni gods.

"Yeah, but that's the fucking point. You usually don't fucking live here," he growls again, and his fists tighten to almost white at his sides. Note to self, call Seger so they can punch the shit out of each other.

"Oh, sugar on my toast! You'd think me coming home to visit my mother wouldn't be greeted by such hostility," she gasped but still typed on her phone through the entire exchange. "Besides, I was the one down at the soup kitchen helping until mother fell ill with a headache. I had to bring her back, you grouchy gnocchi." I wrinkle my nose at the new reference she made. Where the hell does she get these ideas?

I lean into the warmth of Carter's back, praying in the back of my mind the tiny psycho doesn't see me standing here. If she looked up from her phone for a second, she would. So, I'm hoping her texting or whatever she's doing keeps her distracted for long enough that she won't catch a glimpse of me in hiding. For the love of God, please don't see me.

"Oh, cheese curds! Kaycee?" She gasps again, and I sigh into Carter's stiff back, mentally slamming my manifestation. If I had just kept my brain quiet, maybe she wouldn't have looked up. But now, her beady blue eyes sear into me hiding behind Carter's back, and she grins.

"Heya, Piper," I murmur, timidly peeking around Carter's big back.

Her brows furrow, but something in her eyes hardens when she looks at Carter and then at me.

"We were just…" I trail off when Carter jumps in and steals the words from my mouth.

"Leaving," Carter snarls, clutching my hand. "Don't say a fucking word," he growls in my ear, sending sharp shivers down my spine.

"So damn bossy," I yelp, forcefully pulled toward the front door we came through. My little legs barely keep up with his long strides as he rushes us down the hall and into the living room I never got to inspect. My eyes dart around, cataloging the simple decorations, matching the rest of the house.

"So soon?" Piper asks, running behind us with furrowed brows. "Daddy will be home soon!"

Carter stops dead, forcing me into his back again. You know, I love his strong back and his tattoos. And all the yummy hot muscles. My tongue aches to trace the outlines of every single piece of ink lining his body. Hell, I even love to sink my damn nails into his flesh when he fucks me hard. But I've had enough of running into it every five seconds and crushing my nose when he decides to just stop while we are walking. I scowl when his hand tightens on my wrist, and I swear the bastard is relaying some sort of message. Probably shut the fuck up and don't engage with the psycho. Yeah, that's probably it. I don't have to be a mind reader to know that's exactly what Carter wants to tell me. If I could read the grumpy man's thoughts, it'd probably consist of: Shut the fuck up, Kaycee. Be a good girl, Kaycee. Don't say or steal things, Kaycee. Sheesh. You'd think he'd be more grateful to me for all the crazy things I've done. It brought us together, now didn't it?

"Daddy?" He growls, swinging back to face her smiling, blissful face. If serenity had a facial expression, it would be Piper's. She dreamily stares into the sky, clutching her hands in prayer, and she nods.

With a scowl that could tame the devil, I expect him to pounce on her crazy ass and knock the word daddy out of her mouth with one punch. Clutching his fist tight, and tightening his grip on me, he remains stock still. Not moving a muscle. Well, except the one ticking in his jaw, and the vein throbbing over his eyebrow. I inspect closer, zoning in on the twitch on his right eye. Okay, so he is moving somewhat, but he's not pouncing on her to shut her up. In my book, that's an improvement.

"Yes! Of course, Silly! He's my daddy, too," she says, twisting a lock of her blonde hair with a girlish grin that doesn't sit right with me.

Carter grits his teeth and blows out an angry breath, getting himself under control. By the way his hand flexes around my wrist, I can tell he's working on a plan to ditch her and get us back to the SUV without subjecting ourselves to anymore of her torture.

"Right," he finally says through a heavy breath. "Your stepdad." He purses his lips like the words burn his tongue, and his face pinches.

She giggles and nods her head, staring at the two of us. "Oh, pickled pears! You two could stay! We could all have such a wonderful dinner together!" She practically jumps up and down at the prospect of having me there. "I have an entire meal planned for tonight! Ham, potatoes, corn, and lots of yummy desserts!" She giggles again, golf clapping to herself in satisfaction.

I recoil from her invitation, trying not to visibly show how uncomfortable I'm getting.

"Erm, thanks for the invite, Piper. But my parents are expecting me home," I say with a grimace when her face falls into a thunderstorm of brewing emotions.

She narrows her eyes. "Then why are you here? Why can't you stay? I want you to stay here!" She stomps her foot, and her voice booms through the living room.

"Piper?" Francesca asks in a quiet voice, rubbing at her eyes from the corner of the couch.

I jump hearing her voice, not having realized she had been here throughout this entire conversation. She must have laid down when they got home while we were in the office and dozed off for a bit.

"I want them to stay for dinner," Piper whines, turning to her mother with red cheeks. Her foot stomps into the ground a few times, rocking some of the pictures on the wall.

Francesca swallows hard, putting her hands up in a placating manner. Her red hair sticks up in every direction while her beautiful dinner dress clings to her curves. And I swear, there's something about Francesca Hurst that seems so familiar. Like the shape of her eyes or the curve of her nose. It's almost as if I should know her from somewhere with the level of familiarity I feel. But I can't place it because aside from her name, I've never met her before. I've researched the hell out of her and her ex-husband, but this woman is a stranger to me.

"It's okay, Piper. They have to go. They can come back some other time and have dinner with us," she coos in a soft voice, tucking a piece of hair behind Piper's ear.

Piper's hands tighten into fists when her eyes find mine again and harden. In two seconds, I swear she's about to rip my throat out, but she loosens her stance and shakes her head. Cocking her head to the side, her easy smile spreads across her face, and she jumps again.

"Yes, yes! We'll get together very soon! All of us will! It'll be so much fun!" she giggles again, sounding a little more unhinged than normal.

"I won't be back for Thanksgiving," Carter blurts out of nowhere, tightening his hold on my wrist.

"And where will you be, big brother?" Piper says with a manic grin, again something sparking deep in the depths of her crazy ass eyes.

All the hairs on my arm stand on end when she stares directly into my eyes as Carter answers her. Her head cocks, swishing her blonde hair with the movement. I swallow hard, transfixed in her crazy gaze. I don't know what she's thinking. Her smile grows, showing off her pearly white teeth.

"None of your fucking business. I have shit to do," he hisses, sending Francesca back a step. I look up at him with wide eyes, noting the reddening of his face. I'd back up too, if I were them. He's ten seconds away from exploding and leaving his body parts scattered across the room, and blood splattered on the walls. "And I'm not your fucking brother or your fucking son. You. Are. Not. My. Fucking. Family."

I am—I think to myself. I'm this man's family. My boys are his brothers. Together we are the... wait. What do people in these types of relationships do when marriage comes about? If I want to, that is. I've always thought I wasn't the marrying type because of who I am and how my body reacts to others.

Each and every day, my boys prove me wrong. But what if they're my people, my family, and I want to marry them? Each of them? Is it possible to take on four guys at once? Am I Kaycee Cole-West-Cunningham-Benoit? No, wait. I'll make them take my last name. I mean, if they wanted to get married. Do they? Wait shit.... I shake myself out of those weird swirling thoughts and focus on the psycho twirling her hair.

Piper grins more. "No need for the brash behavior, you prickly pickle," Piper says her insult with such a pep in her voice that you almost wouldn't hear it. But I did. Every word she's spoken since we got caught has made my chest tighten. Now, there's nothing stopping her from running back to Cushing and telling him everything. How's Carter going to explain us being here together? Will he say it's all part of the act he has to put on?

I'm on the edge of my seat with her false positivity and weird food references. There's something about her that sets off alarm bells inside my head, now more than ever. What the hell is she up to? Everything is my guess. Murderer? Plotter? Psychopath?

"Then we'll see you in a few weeks for Christmas break," Francesca says in a tight voice, holding a hand over her heart.

"And then the Christmas charity event!" Piper says through another giggle. "Oh, it'll be so much fun to dress up and bid on new items up for auction! I can't wait!"

I blink a few times and nod. "It'll be a lot of fun," I say in a monotone voice, keeping every emotion at bay.

"It will be. I can't wait to see you there, Kace! It'll be your first, and you'll have so much fun," she giggles again, reverting to the Piper I knew from before by jumping up and down, swishing her hair.

I give her a tight smile and tug on Carter's wrist, trying to be discreet. But I'm not careful enough when we catch Piper's eye.

"We should go," I say with a fake sense of sadness.

"Aw, Carter! Did you two finally hook up?" Piper asks, her voice dipping low.

"I was helping him study," I say, lying through my damn teeth. "With finals next week, he needed a little help. He was embarrassed to ask, but I offered." Once again, Carter's hand grips my wrist so tight, that I swear the bones are breaking from the force of his warning.

"So fucking embarrassed," he growls, clenching his teeth more. How are they still hanging in there and not falling out? I need to have a serious talk to him about his aggression and anger issues.

Piper tilts her head and nods. "Well, that's so sweet of you, Kaycee. I know you're so smart and to help my dumb, dumb brother! You must be working miracles."

"That's fucking it, we're out. Happy fucking Thanksgiving!" Carter snarls, practically throwing me out of the house and dragging me toward the car.

My feet drag across the driveway as my short stubby legs try to keep up with his long strides. God, why does he have to have such long ass legs, and I'm stuck with these short, non-bendy things that can't keep up with him. Keeping up with these tall bastards and their fast walking is almost impossible. Especially when his fingers tighten around my arm, and he speeds up. Great. This is fantastic.. I'd inform him of this little difficulty I'm going through, if he wasn't so damn angry from our interaction with crazy Piper. He's likely to lash out and say mean things if I open my mouth. So, like a good girl, I keep my damn lips sealed and carry on across the driveway.

Eyes burn into my damn skull when he forces me into the passenger's seat and violently slams the door shut on my scrunched up face. He really needs to sort out his anger. As he rounds the front of his SUV, I peek out the blacked-out window to find Piper staring at me from the large picture window of the house. Her grin stays in place even when Carter jumps in the car and starts it with a roar.

"I'm buying you a fucking gag, and I'm sticking it down your throat. When I say don't fucking say anything stupid, I fucking mean it!" Carter growls, throwing the car into drive, and races down the driveway and onto the road at breakneck speeds.

Anxiety prickles at the back of my neck when he speeds down the road. The only sounds floating through the car are the changing gears and my frantic, uneven breaths. One. Two. Three. Four. I count to myself, leaning back in the leather seat, trying to find comfort in the things around me. Panic takes hold, squeezing my chest tight. Five. Six. Seven. Eight. My lips pop open when he takes a curve too quickly, and I slide in my seat.

I yelp, tightening my seatbelt. "No need to be so rude," I say, crossing my arms over my chest. I grunt when my cast digs in through my shirt. I can't wait to get this stupid thing off.

"I swear to fucking Christ, I'm going to kill that fucking woman with my bare hands," he snarls, slamming his hand into the steering wheel. "But first," he shouts, whipping the car into an almost vacant parking lot, and slams the brakes. The SUV skids in the rock parking lot, but finally comes to a stop.

I want to ask him what the Hell he thinks he's doing by going so fast, but I get distracted by the nondescript white building with cracking paint and a fucking XXX painted on the wall.

"What is this place?" I ask with wide eyes.

"Here's what's going to fucking happen," Carter says, evening his voice out. Every ounce of anger dissipates when he heaves a calming breath. "Since I can't fuck you into submission, I'm going to buy something that can." Ah, so that's his issue. He needs to be laid. Wait, what?

My cheeks heat, and my eyes widen. "What?" I gasp when he points a finger at me.

"My dick fucking hurts every time I get hard, and I can't fuck you yet. So, I'm going to walk into the shady as fuck sex shop and buy something. And you're going to be a good fucking girl and shut your mouth. In fact, maybe I'll buy a fucking gag while I'm in there, too." He rubs his chin, letting his eyes linger on the building, and then that evil smile he loves to wear crosses his lips.

I want to jerk back when he takes my jaw in his hand and squeezes it until I'm looking into his unhinged eyes. And he calls Piper the psycho. They may not be family, but I think it's in the water in that house. He sinks his teeth into his bottom lip.

"Will you be a good fucking girl?" He asks, raising a brow. I try to nod, but he squeezes harder. It's never to hurt me, just to show me who is in charge. "Use your words," he growls, barely in control.

I narrow my eyes but attempt to nod. "Yeah," I mutter.

"Good fucking girl," he murmurs, leaning in until his lips brush against mine. "Now don't move from this spot or I'll fucking spank you." With his parting words, he jumps out of the SUV and beelines it into the shady as hell sex shop.

How the hell did he know about this place, and why is he bringing me here? What is he buying to torture me with now? Jesus, would he seriously get me a gag? I don't think I'd like that. Fuck. I nervously twiddle my thumbs together, watching the time tick by. I could have played a round of Angel Warrior with Seger by now, but instead, I'm stuck here in his warm Tahoe with my thumbs up my ass while he cruises the aisles of a sex shop, looking for God knows what. Something to fuck me with? I startle, thinking about the large dildos I've accidentally come across online. He wouldn't....would he?

After another ten minutes, Carter walks out of the store with determination all over his face and a solid black bag filled with things inside. My stomach flips when he gets into the SUV and turns to me.

"We're going back to my fucking apartment on campus to look over the disc I put in my father's computer. And then, this," he says, tapping the bag a few times but never opening it. "Will serve its purpose." I gulp when he turns on the car and heads toward campus. My heart hammers in my chest. "You better text your mommy and daddy and let them know you'll be fucking indisposed for the next forty-eight hours." A wicked grin lights up his face when I pull out my phone and do as he says. Whatever he has planned for me is either sexy or evil. Maybe both?

# THIRTEEN

## CARTER

I LICK MY LIPS, looking back at Kaycee on my bed. My heart fucking flutters—*flutters*—at the sight of her legs swishing in the air. She smiles down at her phone, flipping through Flash-Gram without a care in the world.

What the fuck is she doing to me?

I grunt, turning back to my computer. Crowe's computer was fucking cut and dry with jack shit on it. But this? My father's computer is riddled with fucking codes, and my disc is having a hell of a time cutting through. It will, but it's straining under pressure. Fucking prototypes. This is my failing ear communication device all over again. The moment we needed it at Crowe's AKA Lucas Van Buren's house to investigate, it failed and left my fucking girl stranded at arm's length from a monster. My computer makes loud whirring noises like it's about to fucking die on me.

Shit.

I run my hand through my hair, looking back at the object of my fucking downfall. She's shattered every fucking wall around me, and she does it with the tilt of her innocent fucking head and a beautiful smile—a smile that could melt the devil's resolve. Hell, maybe it has because my resolve is at fucking zero with her. She could ask me anything, and I'd tell her to fuck off. But she'd persist, and I'd cave to her will. Like

I always fucking do. It's like she's a damn magical center, and I'm her piece forced to do whatever she says. I lift a brow. Is my bitch ass vixen a witch in disguise? That'd explain a whole hell of a lot. I shake my head at the weird fucking thoughts.

I blow out a breath, trying to think of anything but her. But my brain is in a constant loop of fucking worry about her safety. The moment my dick touched her, he couldn't get enough. Like a fucking pussy addict for the most infuriating woman on the planet. She's my drug of choice, running through my veins twenty-four-seven, and I never want to leave this damn high. Deep in my gut, I know the other shoe is about to drop at any given time. It could be tomorrow or the next fucking day, but it's going to happen, and it's going to involve her.

I growl, looking down at the offending appendage standing tall inside my jeans and straining against the constricting fabric. Go the fuck down, you dick! We can't do anything about it because we just had to show fucking West how painless a piercing would be. Cocky fucking dickbag, mother fucker. This hurts worse than the needle puncturing my cock for a tattoo. This hurts worse than when Kaycee kneed me in the damn balls. Fuck me. Fuck. Pain shoots up my abdomen. I curl my fists, getting harder at the thought of her defiance. Our relationship is a push and pull. She says stupid shit to push my buttons, and I push back with a snarl, and it always ends with my tongue in her mouth and my dick in her pussy. Shit. Sometimes, I want to tame her and put her in a cage where only I can see her. But that's the thing about my Vixen. You can't tame her or tell her what to fucking do. She doesn't follow commands like a good fucking girl.

Don't steal from murderers—check, she's done that. Don't steal from the psycho asshole, me—check, and she's done that, too. She's done everything to get herself killed since coming here, and I'm not done protecting her yet. Over my dead body, will anyone harm the hair on her head. They'll meet the end of my fucking fist to their throat if they do. And that's a promise.

I glare at my stupid dick with a snarl peeling back my lips. I didn't think about the whole abstaining from sex bullshit when I laid down the dare. Hell, I didn't fucking think I'd get a piercing, let alone three. Shit. More pain ricochets, knotting my stomach. Fuck. Need, swirling with dripping desire, courses through me with the urge to sink inside her. Fuck the pain it's causing me. I need her. Now. My dick throbs, and I curse my fucking luck. Two weeks — I have to last two fucking weeks before I can touch myself and two more after that to fuck her with it. Denying myself this one pleasure will be worth it. I'll be damned if the next time I get off it will be by my own hand instead of using her perfect pussy. No, fuck that, I'll wait. Even if it pisses me the fuck off. I'm counting down the fucking days until the Christmas Charity event. By then, me and my dick will be good to go. I can't wait to see the look on her face when we walk into the presidential suite of the ritzy-ass hotel where my father hosts his events.

I grit my teeth and curl my fists against the computer chair. I will fuck her, but there won't be any relief for me. It'll all be for her. Everything is for her. This. That. And everything in between.

I plug in a few more codes on my computer, slowly breaking through to the other side.

"Find anything?" She asks, sprawled out on my bed on her back. Her eyes dance around the room, taking it in, and she huffs when they land on the mysterious black bag I refuse to show her. She wants a peek so bad, and it's eating her up from the inside out and killing her. But I sure as shit won't tell her. Not yet, at least.

I smirk, turning back to the computer with massive green and red codes running across the screen.

"Not fucking yet," I grunt, daring her to defy me. She has

that look in her eye. I can see it from here—the one where she wants to disregard anything I say and do what she wants.

The vast blue of her eyes sucks me in every time I stare at her. They project so much on what is going through her head, and she doesn't even know it. I can read her like an open book, but I'd never tell her that. Her brows furrow, her eyes dart back to the bag, and she sticks her fucking bottom lip out.

"What's in the bag?" She asks for the millionth time, batting her eyelashes in my direction like it'll make me fucking open it. I'm tempted. But I'll let her continue being a brat and punish her later. "Grumpy. Tell me what's in the bag, please?" She pouts, folding her fingers together in a pleading gesture when she sits up.

I grin, chuckling to myself. "What's in the bag?" I hum, mocking her, and turn back toward my computer. I grunt when a pillow catches the side of my head. She crosses her arms and sticks her tongue out at me. "Soon, Vixen. You'll find out soon enough. Now sit fucking still and let me fucking work," I grunt, throwing the pillow back to my bed.

"Or what?" she asks in a breathy voice, making my stupid dick jerk again. Down, asshole.

"Or I'll fucking spank you so hard; you'll have welts for Thanksgiving dinner. And how fucking awkward would that be?" I raise a brow, and she throws herself back, muttering under her breath. Goddamn brat—my brat.

Taking out my phone, I navigate to our boys' group chat. Which is fucking ridiculous, if you ask me. But Elf Ears insisted on it, claiming we needed a boyfriend in-laws only group so we could plan shit without her knowing.

> Grumpy: Twiddles Dumbs, you almost here?

I scowl at my nickname on the screen. I swear to all things

fucking holy, I'm going to drown Elf Ears in his fucking drool. Do you think she'd miss him?

> West#1: Yeah, almost fucking there, you impatient bastard!
>
> West#1: Huh… look at that. I am boyfriend #1
>
> TheBestBoyfriendinlaw: Rethink that!

I scowl again, rubbing a hand down my face. I'm surrounded by juvenile assholes who make stupid nicknames on group chats. Well, two can play at that game.

**TheBestBoyfriendinlaw's name has been changed to ElfEars by Grumpy.**

There. Take that dickface.

> ElfEars: GRUMPYY! WHYYYY?? The elf population is going to track you down now! You're so insensitive to their kind.
>
> Grumpy: Shut the fuck up, Benoit.
>
> West#2: Wait… why am I number 2?
>
> ElfEars: There's two of you…..
>
> Grumpy: Not this shit again! Are you fucking here or not? We've got something to do.
>
> ElfEars: Why am I always left out of the fun? I'm stuck in humidity, which is giving me swamp ass..
>
> West#1: Swamp ass…..Jesus, I'm so fucking glad I didn't have to go to Louisiana.
>
> Grumpy: JUST GET HERE!
>
> West#2: Walking into your building, dick.

I shake my head and look back at Kaycee, who inspects me through narrowed eyes. She sits back on my bed and folds her arms. Again.

"You assholes have a group chat without me?" She huffs with accusation just as my apartment door bursts open and stifles a yelp.

"Heya, Angel," Seger rumbles, sweeping her into his arms. He frowns when she sits stiffly in his lap, glaring at me until I throw my hands in the air. "Why is she pouting? What did you do to her?" He raises a brow, eyeing me like I fucking did something.

"You guys have a group chat without me, and he won't tell me what's in the bag," she says, cocking her head to the side and examining the bag like she might glimpse through it and see what I'm hiding.

I curse under my breath when her pleading eyes turn to me again, and she bats her long eyelashes. I'm so fucking whipped. It's ridiculous.

"You told her about the boyfriend-in-laws group chat?" Seger fake accuses with a gasp, making our girlfriend pout even more.

What the fuck is this life?

I turn toward the other West, who stands stock still in the doorway of my apartment. His eye twitches when his eyes wander, taking in my entire apartment. A horrified expression passes over his ghostly white face, devoid of any color.

I frown. What the fuck is he looking at? I wrinkle my nose at the piles of dirty clothes and dirty plates and a half-eaten sandwich on the kitchen counter. When the fuck did I leave that there? I scratch my chin but shrug. Maybe I can still eat it.

"You got a fucking problem, West number two?" I goad when he directs his eyes toward me and slams my apartment door shut with a thud, shaking the walls.

Thank God none of the other students are around for our

small group meeting in my apartment. To the Apocalypse, I hope it seems like I'm doing my fucking job by getting close to these assholes and her. But for what I have planned next, I'm glad no dickbags are left on campus. Even the security guards are scarce but usually flee when I'm in the vicinity. The out-of-country students left to be with their friends' families, and the staff traveled home to enjoy Thanksgiving with their families tomorrow. Even Shaw, thank fuck. So tonight, it's just us here. I've entirely blocked any ounce of technology from working on this campus besides my computer and their phones.

"Don't fucking mind him, Grumpy. Your apartment is going to give him a coronary. He'll be fine," Seger says, antagonizing his damn brother to the point Zepp marches forward and sits next to a still pouting Kaycee. "Maybe," he murmurs.

I huff in fake annoyance at the stupid fucking nickname they gave me. So what if I'm goddamn grumpy? I have a right to be a downright asshole to everyone around me. Maybe. Or maybe I'm just an insufferable dick who has been through a shit ton in my life to fill the depths of hell up with my anguish. Perhaps that's it. Or I'm just a dick. I'll go with that.

"What did you find?" Zepp asks, sweat running down his forehead, and refuses to meet my eyes.

I eye Seger as he cradles my girlfriend, and I shake my head. At one point in my life, I could have taken the West twins out with the snap of my fingers, but now I can't. Because the woman I'm attached to is fucking in love with them, too. And—okay. They're all right—I fucking guess.

"Piper caught us coming out of Cushing's office," Kaycee says with a disgusted look, bringing back the memories of our encounter with Piper.

Fuck my life. That Piper bitch was sent from hell to fuck everything up. Our parents aren't even fucking married.

Francesca just showed up one day with the little psycho in tow. My father proclaimed they were together, and that was that. But now that Piper saw Kaycee there, I know she'll tell him. And if she realized we were coming out of his office—well—I'm fucking dead. He'll have my ass somehow.

"She what?" Zepp hisses, jumping to his feet.

"She fucking caught you?" Seger asks, tightening his grip on Kace.

"Why was she even there?" Zepp asks with an undercurrent of accusation, narrowing his beady little eyes at me.

I grind my teeth, jumping to my feet so I can see eye to eye with West number two.

"What? Do you think I fucking invited that psycho ass bitch to my house where her mom lives and fucks my dad? You think I said, "Oh, hey, Pipes! Come to my fucking house while I ransack my dad's office and hope to catch him in a bunch of fucking lies?" Heat encases my cheeks as my hands tighten into fists. The same fists I want to sink into West number two's face. I push my nose into his, and he pushes back, never missing a beat.

"Whoa!" Kaycee yelps, jumping to her feet. She bravely pushes us apart, keeping her back to Zepp, who snarls at her and then at me. Her fingers run the length of my heaving chest as she squishes in between us and tilts her head.

"She was there unexpectedly. She invited me to her Thanksgiving dinner tonight…." Kaycee's nose crinkles when she recounts Piper's terrible invitation.

"But I said no fucking thanks, and we hightailed it out of there before Piper could get any more suspicious. I don't think she realized what we were doing, but yeah, she fucking saw Kace," I growl, running my hand through my hair twice, and then look back up at Zepp and snarl my next words. "You think I'd bring that psycho fucking bitch to my house, too? She fucking lives there, very fucking rarely, but she does. And so does her drugged-up whore of a mom. I got Kaycee into that fucking office undetected. We did our damn thing and fucked off afterward. Plus, we got what we needed, or hopefully will." I grind my teeth together at the thought of all our hard work not fucking working. Who the hell does my father have working for him that aids in his tech bullshit? They're almost as good as me—almost being the keyword. Whoever it is, they can't compete with me and my company. They're good, but I'm fucking better—I'm fucking Carter Cunningham.

If Piper mentions that Kaycee was there to my fucking father, it could go one of two ways. He could be furious that I brought her to our home and inside his forbidden office. Or, he could be delighted I'm making headway with her, considering he is, in fact, the asshole who demanded it. I'm leaning more in that fucking direction than anything. Or fucking hoping, anyway.

Zepp sighs, wiping his hand down his jeans. "So, what did you find out?" He swallows hard, turning green. I swear to fuck. He's about to lose his shit on my floor if I don't get his ass out of here.

"Nothing fucking yet. He must have something big on his end. It's throwing up all kinds of walls and fighting against the disc that should just easily breakthrough to see what the fuck he's doing. So, I have another program working on cutting through the tape. It'll take some time." I run a hand through my hair, heaving a sigh.

My eyes linger on my computer screen for a split second, knowing it will take a few more hours to break through.

"So, we have a few hours to kill? We're staying at the damn maze house tonight," Seger groans. "I'm so fucking tired of my stepmom and her weird looks. Ever since Kace hacked her shit and set her straight, she won't meet our eyes." He shakes his head in disgust, and I raise a brow as Zepp mutters an agreement.

Ah, right. All three of them took my fucking computer

and hacked that bitch's shit before they got into the car wreck. I crack a smile, thinking about the website they found their stepmom on. And then it falls thinking that the Apocalypse got to her, too, threatening her life if she didn't provide them with fifty grand a month. God, these fucks need to go down.

"Well then, how about we play a fucking game?" I ask, trying to settle my damn heart rate down when Kaycee perks up.

"Are you finally going to show me what's in the bag?" She asks, crossing the room to the bag. Before she can pick it up and take a peek, I snatch it off the table and hold it in the air. I smirk, dangling it just above her head, and she frowns, reaching for it again.

"Sit the fuck down," I bark, holding it way above her head.

She swallows hard, wanting to defy my orders, but huffs instead. Fucking little brat. I swear one day I'll spank the defiance out of her ass. But until then, I have a better fucking plan to execute. Sitting on the edge of my bed between the twins, she eyes my every move. I lick my lips when I set the bag down and slowly open it, secretly loving the little noises she makes when I'm too slow.

I pull the box out of the bag with deliberate movements and set it on my desk, turning to Kaycee, who examines the box with furrowed brows.

"Hide and seek," I say, popping the box's tabs and pulling out our newest toy.

"Hide and seek?" She asks, eyes focusing on the pink contraption in my hand.

"Hide and fucking seek," Seger grins and then pales, looking down at his crotch. "Fuck, man," he gasps, grabbing my shoulder when he folds forward, heaving breaths. He groans, cupping his aching dick like a whiny fucking baby.

"Suck it up, West number one," I say, trying not to laugh at him because as soon as my thoughts drift to Kaycee moaning and writhing, I bite my fist, keeping away the pain of my fucking cock.

"You suck it up, dickface! This hurts," he grumbles again, running a hand over his dick.

"So, hide and seek. I'm assuming that has something to do with it?" Zepp asks, stepping forward with that clinical eye he always holds. Even fucking better, he's not staring around at the mess in my apartment anymore or turning green. Such a fucking baby.

As if we fucking planned it with one brain between us, we turn to the woman sitting on my bed with wide inquisitive eyes. I can't tell if she's staring at her new pussy toy with awe, fear, or lust. But whatever the look is, I'll fucking take it.

"What do you mean, hide and seek?" She asks in a breathy voice, going straight to my fucking aching dick. She swallows hard again, looking nervously at the pink toy resting in my hands. "With that?"

"Listen carefully," I say in a deep, authoritative voice, stepping toward her. "You're going to lie back on the bed." She raises a defiant brow, not budging like I thought she would.

"Baby girl, do as he says, or else you'll get punished," Zepp rasps, clearly on the same fucking page as me. Maybe he should be West number one instead, because he knows what the fuck is going on.

She swallows hard again but hardens her eyes. "You know I don't like surprises," she murmurs, but she lays flat on her back like the good fucking girl she is. Breaths pour in and out of her nose rapidly as she eases onto the bed and stares at the ceiling. When we don't make a move forward, her eyes dart back and forth with suspicion. It's like she's waiting on us to descend on her like a hungry pack of wolves, ready to devour every inch of her. And fuck, do I fucking wish I could.

"Take off her fucking pants and panties," I bark out, gesturing for Seger to move forward.

"Again with the bossing around in the bedroom, asshole," he grumbles, but like the obedient fuckwipe he is, he carefully shimmies her leggings and panties to her ankles and tosses them over his shoulder. He raises her legs onto the bed, opening her glistening pussy up to all three of us. Shit! Fuck! Why did I think this was a good idea?

"Damn fucking no sex bullshit," Seger gripes, holding her lips open with two fingers and exposing every inch of her arousal.

My eyes transfix on her wetness, coating his fingers and making them glisten. Drool pools in my mouth like a starving man, and I drop to my knees at the alter of the goddess I'm about to fucking worship. I'll show her every inch of her worth with my tongue and fingers until the day I can sink my fat dick inside her and fill her with my cum again. Fuck. Shit. I take a deep breath, ignoring the pain searing through my aching dick. No matter the pain, I'd crawl through a field of shards of glass to get a taste of her one last time.

"This is fucking torture," I murmur, brushing my lips along her thigh.

My dick fucking bounces, sending pain through my whole body when I blow on her pussy, and she shivers, stifling a moan.

"Then why do it?" She asks in a breathy voice, reaching to run her fingers through my hair.

"Because, Angel, this isn't about us," Seger says, swallowing hard. Lust blows his pupils wide as he looks down at her.

"This is all about you," Zepp says, laying beside her on the bed. He swipes her hair off her forehead and smiles.

"For your fucking pleasure, we get pleasure. We may not be able to fuck you yet," I mumble into her, blowing more air over her clit and pussy. I narrow my eyes at Zepp when he clears his throat with a smug smile.

"They may not be able to fuck you, but I sure can," he

practically purrs, running his fingers down her jaw with a possessive gleam coming to life in his eyes.

"You have to win to be able to fuck her," I growl, swiping my tongue over her clit. Her hips buck. Chasing my tongue, I grin, biting into her thigh until she's thrashing and trying to punch me in the head. She pants, losing her breath when Zepp restrains her arms at her sides, carefully avoiding any further pain to her broken arm. Her eyes dilate to almost black when she gazes back at me, silently begging for me to do her in. And who am I to deny my Vixen anything but pleasure. Of course, she's in for a real treat for the next hour or so. Because what I have in mind is going to blow her fucking panties off.

"Win?" She pants. "How do you win?"

I raise my head from between her thighs, admiring the red mark on her porcelain skin. It's red and angry, with my teeth indents branded into her skin. Marking her as fucking mine. If it were up to me, she'd have these everywhere so everyone saw who the fuck she belonged to. Me. Them. Chase. She'd have all our marks, and no one would ever fuck with her again. Looking down, I admire the glistening pussy juices leaking from her and run the flat of my tongue along her opening. Pulling back, I smack my lips together in satisfaction, letting her wetness coat my lips.

"Fucking hell, Vixen. You taste so fucking good." I collect spit in my mouth, reveling in her taste, and then spit on her pussy. Every inch of her shivers when my fingers work inside of her, creating more and more wetness, until it's dripping toward her ass. At the sight of it, my dick pleads with me to say fuck it and fuck her hard and fast.

"Now," I say, teasing the thick head of the vibrator against her opening. "This will go inside you, and this part will rest against your clit." Her dilated eyes watch me from above, and she nods her approval. I slip it snugly inside her, wiggling it more until her hips raise off the bed, and then step away before I do something fucking stupid. "Put on your pants, Vixen." I see the hesitation in the twins' eyes when I gesture for them to follow me and leave her side. Not that I don't fucking blame them, but they do it anyway, throwing her clothes at her.

She huffs, pulling up her pants and panties, muttering obscenities. Her nose scrunches when she sits on the edge of the bed, staring up at us with wild eyes. She scoots around, obviously feeling the intrusion of the toy seated inside of her.

"So, what's next?" She rasps, clearing her throat. Her eyes skim between the three of us but land on me, awaiting my instructions like the eager little bitch she is. I close my eyes and blow out a breath. Fuck. This next part is going to throw me over the fucking edge.

My heart fucking pumps in my chest when I pull my phone from my pocket and pull up the app in charge of the vibrator. I smirk when I hit a few buttons, but it falls from my face when she gasps. My dick swells more the moment the vibrator buzzes to life against her clit, and she yelps, curling her fingers into my comforter. Her eyes roll into the back of her head, and her lips pop open, moving her hips back and forth, grinding herself into the mattress.

"Death, this is what fucking death feels like," Seger hisses, biting into his fist again. His other hand works to push his dick down, and I can't help the laugh that escapes me.

Zepp swallows hard, watching her work herself up against the vibrator and nearly fucking comes undone when she moans so loud, I'm sure the next fucking town heard her. I grin again, shutting the damn thing down, and her eyes pop open in protest.

"I was almost there," she whines through her heaving breaths. "Please," she begs, biting into her bottom lip.

"Rule number one," I say, holding up a finger. "No fucking coming until we find you." She blinks up at me and gestures for me to go on. I can see the desperation and excitement sparkling in the depths of her beautiful baby blues. "Rule number two, we'll give you a three-minute head start, but the moment the fucking timer goes off, it's game on, Vixen. You hide anywhere in the maze and the maze only. Anywhere but the goddamn house, and we'll find you. But the vibrator is under my control. So you hide, and we find. Whoever finds you gets first dibs on fucking."

"What about you two?" she says through a heavy breath, getting to her wobbly feet.

I grin more, taking a step back toward the bag, and pull out the next toy. "I'll fuck you with this and that," I say, pointing to the vibrator in her. "I don't need my dick to fuck you, Vixen. I just need creativity to get the fucking job done. Now," I say, resting the tip of the thick dildo under her chin and raising it. "Run and hide, Little Vixen." Her eyes blow wide, and she takes off out of my apartment door and bursts outside.

"Is it safe to let her do that?" Zepp asks, taking a step toward the door with concern etching onto his face.

"No one is fucking here. The staff is gone, and I'm sure as shit positive the Apocalypse doesn't have anything up their sleeve right now," I say, watching the time on my phone.

"How can you be so fucking sure?" Seger grumbles, looking back over at my computer.

"I fucking can't be," I say, running a hand down my face. "But there's no one here. I turned off the fucking cameras to this place before bringing her back here. We're safe," I say with a convincing nod.

"For now," Zepp says, stepping toward the door.

"Has it been three fucking minutes yet?" Seger grumbles, bouncing from foot to foot. "I want to fucking taste her while I can."

I smirk as my timer goes off, and we all head toward the door. "Let's get to the fucking maze and find our girlfriend so we can fuck the shit out of her."

"You're on, fucking losers," Seger shouts, pushing us out of the way. His fast footfalls echo down the shitty stairwell and into the fresh air.

I look at Zepp and smirk, taking off down the hallway with an excited whoop, tossing my fist in the air. Nothing but life bleeds through me, and I feel so fucking free for once. No dad is looking over my shoulder, ordering me to do shit. No Alpha telling me more bullshit. Just me and my damn brothers hunting our girlfriend in a fucking maze full of so many hiding spots. I thank the fucking creator for his paranoia. This is life.

I growl when Zepp's big ass head passes me instantly, jumping down the stairs and heading off outside with a loud laugh. Fuck, when the hell did he get so fast? Fucking football players and their graceful movements.

My chest tightens when I pause in the doorway with a smirk, watching those idiots race to the maze. Reaching into my pocket, I pull out my phone and bring up the intensity of her vibrator before stepping out the door into the night air.

"We're coming for you, Sweetheart," I mumble, shoving the enormous dick-shaped toy into my back pocket. If anyone saw me now, they wouldn't even fucking recognize me. Because I don't even recognize myself. One day, we'll all be free, but we have to make a few more sacrifices to get there for now.

# FOURTEEN

**KAYCEE**

I BITE into my fist the moment the vibrator buzzes to life inside my pussy and on my aching clit. The tease Carter gave me earlier with his tongue did nothing to soothe the need. Bastard. Of course, that was his plan all along. Get me all worked up, so I'd run around with a damn vibrator up my hoo-ha. All so they could chase me.

Heat pools in my pussy at the thought of them wildly looking around for me, trying to get a glimpse of me. All so they could fuck me in the dirt, a reward for finding me first. A shiver runs through me, and my legs shake from the thought. Sweat forms on my forehead as I sink deeper into my hiding spot, hoping someone finds me soon. The way this thing moves against my clit and hits that spot deep inside drives me wild. All I want is for one of them to find me and fuck me silly. But another half of me wants to play the damn game and hide from them forever. I wonder what prize I'll get if they never find me.

My heart pounds when I take a step back from the bushes concealing me, and my knees buckle when the vibrations pick up to an alarming speed. My breaths pour out rapidly, and I try to hide the little whimpers escaping my throat. But there's no stopping the loud moan escaping through my parted lips.

My greedy hips work against the damn vibrator again, begging for more friction.

Frustration builds inside me, and I mentally beg for my orgasm to come. But it's like I have a direct mental link with the asshole in charge of making the vibrations. As soon as I get closer and closer to the peak, it shuts off and makes my insides tingle.

Shit! Fuck. Gah!

I mentally chant curse words when my fingers dig into the dying grass beneath me, and my head leans against the decaying fountain that probably hasn't worked since the school opened. My eyes roll into the back of my head when goosebumps prickle along my skin as the vibrations start up again, more intense this time, buzzing in a rhythmic beat. My pussy clenches around the toy nestled inside me, snuggling it close and begging for the release building deep in my core.

White stars brighten under my lids when I throw my head back and silently howl toward the stars with my jaw ajar and my eyes squeezing shut. My toes crack under the pressure of curling them so hard in my slip-on shoes. Slapping a hand over my open mouth, I force back the noises daring to escape. Loud footfalls sound a yard away from my hiding spot, and their voices ring out in a taunting tone. Mentally, I count down in my head and ease my breathing to a minimum, trying to cover up the frantic breaths sawing through my nose. I swallow hard, holding my breath when a voice drifts through the light breeze of the cool night.

"Where are you, Angel?" Seger sings from a distance with a laughing taunt. "Come out, Angel! We won't hurt you." He pauses for a second, not making a sound, and it's only then that I hear his muttered curse.

I blow out a quiet breath. Fuck. This is exhilarating torture. The thought of them searching through the maze for me so they could properly fuck me, only finding me by my moans and whimpers. My breath shudders when my pussy clenches around the toy again.

"Come out, come out, wherever you fucking are," Carter sings, his voice carrying through the winds, sending shivers down my spine.

My muscles lock up, and I throw my head back, sinking my teeth into my bottom lip. The metallic tinge of blood fills my mouth, but I hold in the scream lodged in my throat when the vibrations kick up at different speeds and patterns, and I want to go over the damn cliff.

"Marco!" Seger yells, getting closer and closer to the little pocket of bushes I'm hidden behind.

'Polo,' I mentally say, tempted to respond to his call, and let someone easily win. But my stupid competitive side kicks, silencing my cries and forcing me to hunker down in the bushes. Even when I'm half delirious and high on the impending orgasm, it still won't let me call out to them and end my suffering. They have to earn their reward, even if it fucks me over.

I crawl on my hands and knees to the back edge of the pocket on shaky legs and sigh when I lay flat on my back. I can't help the cry that leaves my lips when the vibrations start again and again. Over and over, it buzzes inside of me, going from one extreme to the other. My hips lift off the ground, chasing my elusive orgasm, hellbent on getting away from me. But it stops again, and I thrust my fists into the ground with all my might with a thunk. Pain bounces up my fist and arm, and I wince, glaring up at the sky.

"Mother fucker," I gasp for air.

A ringing comes to life in my ears when I try to listen for the guys wandering around the maze with heavy steps, but they don't bother hiding their presence. Their low voices carry through the wind, not hiding the fact they're getting closer and closer to the spot concealing me. As the minutes go by, I wonder if they're ever going to find me, and give me the relief I need.

I strain my ears, and panic sets in when everything around me goes quiet. Only the tiny rustling of the branches blowing in the wind and the faint sound of birds chirping in the distance, until that too quiets. I swallow hard, eyes darting all around when silence encases me in an embrace. As quietly as I can, I breathe through my nose trying not to huff and puff like I had before. Because that'd definitely give my spot away. Every muscle inside my body tenses, waiting for the next moment the vibrator decides to buzz to life and give me away.

"Here, Little Vixen, where are you?" Carter sings out, stopping just outside my hiding spot. God, he has to know I'm in here somewhere and that I wouldn't hide in plain sight. After all this time, I've caught onto all the little nooks and crannies of the sex maze. Not that I've participated in any fun inside these hedges like I'm sure the boys have in the past. I frown. Yeah, now is not the time to start thinking about them rolling around in the throes of passion with other girls.

I hold my breath, tensing every muscle in my body in preparation for what he's about to do. If he starts the vibrator now, he'll hear the faint buzz and thump of it working inside me. He'd hear my pathetic screams, and I'd beg him to fuck me. Shit! I shudder when he turns the vibrator on with more intensity than before. I want to cry out. I want to scream for the vibrations to give me what I want and for someone to take me. But I hold my breath, counting down the seconds until he goes back the other way.

"Fuck, where are you?" He growls like a predator and is so close I swear I can hear him sigh with frustration before he marches off in the opposite direction. For a man who knew this maze so intimately, he sure hasn't checked my little hidey-hole. More power to me—AH!

I cover my mouth with my hand when my hips lift in the

air, seeking any form of friction I can find. The vibrations take over, and my eyes roll into my head, and goosebumps pimple across my skin when my fingers dig into the grass, pulling it between my fingers. I don't even flinch when a warm body presses into mine and his deep voice, pulling me out of my lust-filled fog.

"Shh." I whimper when Zepp replaces his hand with mine and grins. "I win," he murmurs, leaning down to press his tongue along my jawline, leaving marks all over my skin.

"Please," I choke out when the vibrations intensify. My pussy flutters around the vibrator on the verge of falling over the cliff into oblivion.

Zepp grunts, thrusting his tongue into my mouth and grinds his hardening cock against my aching core. I moan into his mouth, gripping the back of his head and forcing him harder against me.

"You win," I pant when I undo his pants. "I've waited long enough. Please," I beg, reaching into his boxers and pumping his hard length into my hand.

He moans, thrusts into my hand and retakes my mouth. "Hurry, baby girl. If I want to claim my prize, we need to be quick," he grunts, pulling down my leggings and panties and tossing them aside with his jeans and t-shirt. I quickly remove my sweater and bra, refusing to have any barrier between us. He palms my breasts, squeezing them as tight as he can.

His warm mouth peppers kisses along my ankle, calf, and thigh. Gripping his hair hard, I force him to the spot that's been craving his attention. My head lolls back hard into the ground when his tongue glides over my pussy and wiggles against the vibrator. I howl when the tip of his tongue brushes my clit, and he swirls around it, slowly removing the vibrator from my cunt. My breaths heave frantically when he sits up, my wetness glistening in the moonlight, and eyes the vibrator with a lust glinting in his almost black eyes. I nearly combust when he seals his mouth over the toy and sucks down all my wetness onto his tongue, groaning loudly at the taste of my arousal.

"My prize," he rasps, gripping his hard shaft and gently stroking.

Precum glistens on the tip of his dick, leaking from his slit. Veins bulge from the sides of his swollen dick as it bobs in place. He leans over me, stares into my eyes, and thrusts hard into me. My entire body bounces up when he fills me, and we groan together.

"So good, baby girl," he mutters, thrusting in and out again. "You feel like heaven wrapped around my cock." He nips down my jawline, sucking my skin between his teeth. "I want you to come around my cock and do it now." Birds take flight when my screams echo off the surrounding building a mile away, penetrating through the bushes and alerting anyone in a mile radius. I just came with the force of a hurricane. Black dots swim in my vision, halting my breaths altogether. My pussy clenches around Zepp's dick, pulling him deeper inside. With a grunt, he ruts into me, pounding our hips together. The sound of smacking flesh fills the air, alerting the others to the winner of the game, and footfalls sound running toward us.

Through my sex-filled fog, I hear the distinct sound of Seger's angry voice from above me and more footsteps following behind him.

"Fuck you!" Seger barks out, folding his arms over his chest. His features twist into a pained expression, pushing at the tip of his dick through his jeans.

"Why did I think this was a good fucking idea?" Carter gripes, standing next to Seger.

"What were you two going to do about it?" Zepp grunts, backing out of my pussy completely. Swiveling his hips, he drags his moist tip against my clit, and then pounds again with such force I cry out from the intrusion.

"I have my fucking ways," Carter grits back as pain envelops his entire face.

Zepp pulls out teasingly, brushing his tip along my clit, and rubs it in circles. I groan, babbling for him to fuck me more, but he only chuckles in response. His hands reach down and grip my hips, flipping me onto my stomach, knocking the air from my lungs. Pushing between my shoulder blades, he forces my cheek to rest on the cool, moist grass, but takes care to ensure my broken arm is in a safe position. When a breeze blows by my wet pussy and a shiver spreads through me, I close my eyes. Who knew, I'd end up being the hussy in the bushes asking her boyfriends to rail her after a game of hide and seek. Oh, to know what these poor bushes have had to see. Probably way too much, and now I'm a part of the crowd hooking up in the bushes.

"I have a tongue, asshole! My dick may not work, but we have this, too," Seger gripes, tossing his arms in the air. His eyes dart around until they land on something in Carter's pocket, dragging a huge flesh-colored dildo out, and hoists it in the air with triumph.

"My toy," Carter grunts, reaching for the dildo, but Seger grabs it harder, yanking it toward him.

"You snooze, you lose, dickbag," Seger quips, trying to pull the dick from Carter's grasp.

Carter grunts. "Fuck that. I paid for it, it's my dick, and I'll use it." I huff, not focusing on their ridiculous banter and instead focus on the impending orgasm blossoming deep in my stomach. I want to chant to the sky and sing my praises when more and more pressure builds deep in my gut, and my pussy flutters around Zepp.

As Carter and Seger continue to argue, Zepp tunes them out, continuing his deliciously deep thrusts. I swear I meet Jesus when his lips brush my ear, and he whispers dirty as hell words into my ear. 'I'm going to take your ass so hard. You'll be squirming in your seat tomorrow when we eat with your family.' That one sent white-hot shivers through my entire body and a moan from my lips.

The tip of the vibrator brushes my clit, coming out of nowhere again. A moan slips free again when he pulls it to my pussy, going back and forth, working me up again. I don't know where the hell he got it from again, but thank God. This orgasm is two seconds away from making me shout "boom goes the dynamite". I whine when it's pulled away from my clit, and Zepp's fingers take over, diving inside my pussy and creating more wetness.

"Would you two idiots stop fighting and help me screw our girlfriend?" Zepp barks out in a husky but demanding voice.

Seger and Carter fall to their knees in silence. Ah, music to my damn, horny ears. I sigh. Finally, they're getting with the program. *Let's get this show on the road*. They share a look and nod, turning their lustful gazes to me, melting me into a puddle of goo. "And video call Chase. Make sure he's in on this, too," Zepp demands with authority, working his fingers along my slit and clit. My toes curl, but he never gives me enough to shatter, and always keeps me on the edge.

My breath catches in my throat when the pop of a top happens and ice cold lube drips down my crack. Zepp soaks his fingers in the lube, swirling it around my ass, until he sticks the tip of his fingers in and brings it back out.

"I'm surrounded by a bunch of bossy dickweeds," Seger grumbles, plucking his phone from his pocket and dialing it.

"Dude!" Chase's cheerful voice sings through the line. "Shit! I'm so happy to see your ugly face. I've been bored as shit here. How's everything going?" Chase's happy-go-lucky voice breezes through the air.

Zepp slowly works his slick-coated fingers in my ass, loosening me up to take him. Everything ceases to exist around us when his knuckles sink into me, and I finally relax and loosen up. Goosebumps spread everywhere, and I cry out when more pressure works against my ass. One finger. Two fingers. And finally three disappear deep inside me, driving me mad when he plunges them in and out. Shudders erupt throughout my entire body when he slides himself inside of me with ease, erasing every thought but one. Where the hell did he get lube? From his pocket? From the bushes? Did Carter bring it with? Was it in the damn bag?

His clean hand covers my mouth when his dick is fully seated and pulls me to my knees. I shiver, feeling like a sacrificial lamb spread out before them in my nude state, when my back meets Zepp's front. He securely locks an arm around my abdomen, keeping me close to him as he lightly thrusts. My chest heaves when I lock eyes with Seger, who bites his lips, perusing my body with lust-filled blackened eyes. His head falls back, and he groans into the sky, covering his aching dick again with his hand.

"You fucking alone, Elf Ears? West number one is tongue-tied at the moment," Carter grunts, finally prying the dildo from Seger's hands when he sits frozen, panting at my nakedness.

"Uh, yeah?" Chase responds. "I'm hiding from my friggin Grandparents right now in my bedroom."

Carter takes the phone from Seger's grip and points the dildo at the camera with a menacing look. "Lock the fucking door, and put on some headphones, Elf Ears. I have a feeling you're going to like this fucking show."

"Shit? What are you holding? Is that—" Chase chokes when Carter turns the camera toward me, and Chase's stunned-looking face comes into view, and his eyes widen. "Holy shitballs," he rasps, scrambling away from the phone, leaving us with a picture of the ceiling. The sound of the lock clicks through the phone, and he's back in front of the camera with his shirt off, showing his golden skin.

"Ya fucking good?" Carter gripes, turning the phone back

to himself. He raises a brow at Chase, choking over the phone.

"Don't show me your ugly mug, Grumpy! Turn it back to my girlfriend. And Zepp," Chase shouts, earning himself a grunt. Carter turns the screen back to me, showcasing Chase's face full on the screen, and then hands it off to Seger. "Heya, Sunshine," he murmurs, reaching below the camera and sighing when his hand works up and down. "Fuck her good, Zepp. Don't let our girlfriend down."

Zepp grunts, thrusting in and out of my ass. My mouth pops open when my entire body tingles, starting at the top of my spine and slowly inches down, until my pussy clamps around nothing. I'm ten seconds away from detonating like a fucking bomb about to go off. And I swear if it doesn't happen soon, I'm doing it myself.

My breaths shudder in my chest when Carter crawls my way with a wicked glint in his eye, stopping right in front of me. His hot breath glides over my flesh, and his tongue flicks out in snake-like movements. The warmth of Carter's tongue wets down my chest until he's encasing my nipple with his heat. A strangled cry leaves my lips when he clamps down on my nipple and soothes it with his wicked tongue.

"You're going to fuck her ass," he says glancing at Zepp, "and I'm going to fuck your pussy with this," he says, holding the thick flesh-colored dildo up to my face. I nod my approval, and he tweaks my nipple again. "That's my good fucking girl," he hums, rubbing the tip of the fake dick along my lips. "Wet it with your tongue," he demands with a manic look in his eye like he's as desperate as I am.

I don't waste any time as Zepp slowly pumps in and out of me, wetting the thick tip of the rubber dick about to go inside of me. I clench around nothing, making Zepp moan in my ear.

"Torture, this is fucking torture. My dick hurts so fucking

bad," Seger grumbles, dragging his knees across the ground, crawling toward me.

"Suck it the fuck up," Carter growls, popping the tip of the dildo out of my mouth. Saliva spills from my lips and drips down my chin and onto my heaving chest. And four sets of eyes are all on me, watching me with such intent, I clench around Zepp again.

"Shit! Do it already," Chase's raspy voice comes through the phone, displaying only his reddened face. His teeth sink into his lips as his hand works harder and harder on his length.

Carter captures my mouth, forcing his tongue to glide against mine. The toy's tip runs through my wet lower lips and plunges deep inside of me. Just like Carter would have done if his dick wasn't forbidden from touching me right now.

"Jesus Christ, run the...." I peek an eye open to Chase.

A glazed-over expression takes over his eyes when he grunts, throwing his head back in ecstasy. Ropes of stringy cum release all over the camera, distorting his image into nothing but swirls. Throaty moans spill through the phone as he continues to work himself up and down, finally stopping.

"That's it, baby girl. Come all over my cock, and squeeze me. Make me come in your ass," Zepp pants in my hair, clamping his teeth down and sucking my earlobe into his mouth.

I cry out when Seger's lips suck the skin of my neck, and his hands squeeze my tits into a vise grip. In the grass, Chase's protests from the now-thrown phone echo through the maze, but we are too much into a lustful haze to pay attention to his demands to see what we're doing.

I come on a silent scream, squeezing Zepp until he comes in my ass and slumps against me. Carter grunts, taking the toy from my pussy. My eyes bug out at the sight of Carter and

Seger twisting their tongues around the thick shaft to get a taste of my wetness together but never touch tongues.

"You taste like a damn cupcake I never want to fucking give up," Seger moans, popping the end of the toy into his mouth. His cheeks hollow out as he stares at me, then roll back when he pops it out with a loud smack. "I can't fucking wait until the charity event. No matter-fucking-what, I'm fucking you. Piercings be damned," Seger gripes, handing the toy back to Carter.

Carter stares at it and scowls, muttering something about cleaning it properly and storing it by our bed at the Maze House.

"Assholes! Don't forget about me! You left me looking at the dirt! Helllloooo, over here on the phone!" Chase gripes until Seger finally picks up his phone. "Finally," he huffs in annoyance and pouts.

I wrinkle my nose when Zepp carefully pulls out, running his hands along my body. He puts my bra back in place, and Seger grabs my sweater. Together, they put me back in one piece, even putting my pants on. I kiss them on wobbly legs and take the phone, leaning into Seger's embrace. Seger grunts when his raging hard-on pokes me in the back but doesn't whine when he wraps his arm around me. Chase must have wiped off the screen because his beautiful smiling face greets me.

"How's Louisiana?" I rasp in a tired voice.

Chase beams, recounting how happy his grandparents seem to have them there. They even got a call from his dad, wishing them the best. Everything seems to be on the up and up, and the joy is evident on Chase's face. We end the call, promising a repeat tomorrow.

"Take her back to the fucking house. I need to check the progress of the disc," Carter grumbles, leaning over to kiss my lips. "Be a good fucking girl and get some rest now. I'll be there in a few." Carter's retreating form sets my teeth on edge as he leaves the maze and heads to his apartment. Something in my gut tells me we are about to find out what the Apocalypse is all about, but we won't know until Carter spills the beans.

"Should we go with him?" I ask, looking between the twins as Seger puts his phone away.

Zepp eyes the spot Carter slipped between the bushes and shakes his head.

"He'll meet us at the house," he says with a sharp nod. But there's something there, something like unease fluttering through his eyes.

Seger grunts and throws me over his shoulder. "Time for bed, Angel. And it's time for me to start thinking about sexy grandmas or baseball or rats because my dick won't disappear. Jesus, this was a terrible idea for Seger Jr. He's suffering...." Seger mumbles more about his aching dick as I punch him in the kidneys, only earning a swat to the ass.

After a few hours of laying around in bed, Seger sits up and looks down at his phone.

"Well looks like my dick will go away. Grumpy wants me to meet him in the gym, right fucking now, as he says," Seger gripes, pulls on some loose basketball shorts and ties his shoes. "Don't wait up for me, Angel." He presses one last kiss to my head and heads out the door to beat the shit out of the other man I love. "Shit!" He curses looking down at his phone again, shaking his head. "What is it?" I ask, raising a brow when he shakes his head.

"Fuck," he murmurs, running his hand down his face. "Zepp!" He shouts, gaining his brother's attention from the other room.

"Yeah?" Zepp asks, popping his head into the bedroom.

"The fucking nurse is calling again," he says, putting phone to his ear. He nods, talking to the woman, and curses under his breath. "Yeah, one of us will be there." He hangs up the phone and groans. "Dad's missing again," he mutters.

"I'll go," Zepp says, grabbing his keys. "You go do whatever Carter needs you to do." Zepp kisses my head and heads out the door to take care of his father.

I sigh, resting my head on the pillow. "You're going to have to come, Angel face," Seger says, grinning above my head. "We'll teach ya how to punch." He grins, pulling me to my feet. "That way no one ever fucks with you again."

"And getting to see you two pummel each other?" I ask, putting my shoes on despite my body protesting. Excitement pours through me as the mental images run through my mind of blood, sweat, and lots of action.

"Abso-fucking-lutely," Seger says through a grin, barking out a laugh.

Without hesitation, Seger drags me to the abandoned gym, where Carter and him focus on teaching me what I need to know. Even with my cast on my arm, I learn how to block and punch so I can protect myself when I need to—if I need to. In the back of my mind, I know I'm not learning much, but it'll help in case of an emergency. Afterwards, we clean up and all cuddle into bed when Zepp comes strolling in after rounding up his father.

"All good?" I ask, peeking an eye open and taking in Zepp's haggard appearance.

He grunts, running a hand down his face. Standing stock still he eventually nods and peels off his clothes, climbing into bed with us. Resting himself above me, he runs his fingers through my hair, and I sigh with relaxation.

"Bro?" Seger murmurs, shifting in front of me. "Is he good?"

"He was naked in the woods. I don't really want to talk about it," he grumbles in response, earning a chuckle from Seger before we all drift off to sleep. Well, everyone but me.

My mind whirls as I stare up at the ceiling, listening to the lullabies of their snores and sleepy murmurs. I cringe when memories assault me, sinking their fangs in deep and holding me hostage.

Swallowing hard, I push the images away with a hammering heart, wishing every memory from the crash would disappear. I know they won't. They'll always be with me, especially since the Christmas Charity event is right around the corner. Every nightmare I've had will greet me with smiles when my family and I waltz into the extravagant party three weeks away.

Magnolia perished in the midst of a wild party with her girlfriend at her side. She was ripped from this world with a crowd of people surrounding her, and no one noticed a thing.

So, what waits for me when I enter the lion's den with nothing but a pretty dress and anxiety? Death? Kidnapping? Anything? Perpetually teetering on the edge of unknowing is going to push me over the edge.

"Shh, Angel," Seger mumbles, pulling me closer. "What's wrong?"

I swallow the bile swimming in my throat and snuggle deep into his bare chest, taking in his scent.

"The Christmas Charity event is in three weeks. What are we going to walk into?" I whisper, trying to quiet the rampant anxiety choking the air from my lungs.

"It'll be okay, Angel. We'll come up with a plan. Chase is your date, and we'll all be there to keep an eye on you. Okay?" His voice is rough with sleep, and his fingers work through my hair.

I understand what he's saying and what reassurances he's trying to give me. But I can't help the nagging feeling that the other shoe is about to drop, and we're in for a world of fucking hurt.

# FIFTEEN

## KAYCEE

It's been three weeks since Carter, Seger, and Zepp accompanied me to Thanksgiving dinner, and I swore my brother was done fucking with them. He poked and prodded and antagonized the boys until they were squirming in their seats with grimaces on their faces. Talk about a fucking awkward experience. They should just be thankful my father wasn't there to scare the shit out of them, too. We ended up making it through and had a nice dinner. The boys and I came up with a plan for tonight that night, discussing where we'd meet inside the event, and what we'd do. They promised to never leave my side, but we'll see because tonight is the night of hell, and I don't know if I'm ready.

Chase should thank his lucky stars he was in Louisiana throughout Thanksgiving break and wasn't here. But now that he is, he's in for a hell of a bumpy ride tonight. And by hell of a ride, I mean he's in for literal hell. Not only at the event itself, but here in the rental house my parents found in East Point to make our drive easier to the hotel where the charity event is being held.

My brother's eyes twinkle with delight at the terror etched onto Chase's face. "So, you're one of the shits who has been shacking up with my little sister?" Bodhi chortles, placing his forearms on the kitchen island's countertop we're all surrounding. He sips his second glass of whiskey, rolling the ice in his glass like some mob boss awaiting the snitch's answer.

Frowning, I glare at the oversized prick I call my brother. Disowning is a thing, right? If it is, his ass is out—forever. Never mind, he changed his prickish ways over the past year. But he'll be dead to me if he continues down this I'm-your-big-brother-I must-protect-you path. Now, he's intentionally being a jerk to make Chase squirm.

"You've met. We've been over this," I say through clenched teeth, ten seconds away from punching him in the face.

His beady brown eyes eat away at Chase, looking him over from head to toe. He's eating his very existence apart. Stiffening his muscles, he puffs up his chest, looking at Chase like he's about to grab a steak knife and stab him through the heart. Fuck my life.

"Yeah, but this one wasn't at Thanksgiving dinner," Bodhi says through a big, toothy grin, pointing a finger in Chase's direction. "I interrogated the other three over dinner, and we came to an agreement. But this one?" He cocks a brow, stepping toward Chase's trembling body.

Bodhi may be their football idol, but right now, he's looking at Bodhi with terror in his eyes and the urge to run. His fingers twitch at his side, and I can tell he's plotting his escape routes.

"Don't listen to him," I say, grasping Chase's shaking and sweaty hand. "He's a bully." I narrow my eyes on my stupid brother's smirking face. He's loving every second of making my poor boyfriend sweat bullets.

"I'm not a bully, just a concerned brother," Bodhi retorts without missing a beat.

"He was in the parking lot. You met," I say, trying to count to ten in my head.

One, don't stab my brother. Two, don't maim my brother.

Three, don't trip him over a cliff. I puff out a breath once I make it to ten, and I'm certain I won't smack some sense into him. He's come a long way since he first met all of them and finally wrapped his head around my happiness, but it doesn't stop him from puffing out his chest and acting like a damn caveman. Brotherly duties, my ass. He just wants to be a jerk.

"Mhm, but he wasn't at Thanksgiving," Callie retorts, leaning against the island with a manic grin spreading across her traitorous face.

"See?" Bodhi says, swirling his drink again. "He wasn't at Thanksgiving," he mimics Callie's voice, leaning forward.

I throw my head back, staring up at the ceiling. Please, send down a lightning bolt and blast my brother away. Set him on fire. Cut off his damn tongue before he scares Chase away for good. I groan when it doesn't happen and sigh, looking at Chase. We're going to have to endure this Hell for a short time more.

"Oh my gosh, don't you kids look amazing!" I breathe a sigh of relief when my mother's voice shuts Bodhi's bullying down. He frowns, slicing his finger across his neck, promising a world of hurt later. Chase sputters, shaking like a damn leaf. Pfft. Fuck that. I'll hide all my boyfriends from my brother from here on out.

Mom sashays into the kitchen with a megawatt grin, lighting up the room. Her dark, sparkling brown eyes light up at the sight of all of us standing around the kitchen island. A pleased hum of satisfaction slips from her throat when she sees my hand in Chase's and gives him an approving nod.

His hand squeezes mine when my father's eyes glide across the room, briefly narrowing at Chase with suspicion. Complete and utter panic sweeps across Chase's face when he looks at me white as a sheet, and his hand squeezes mine even harder to the point it feels like my bones will crack.

"It'll be okay," I murmur, squeezing his hand back and trying to sound reassuring.

"You say that now," he mumbles through a shaky breath, stiffening his spine. "He looks like he wants to eat me." His gray eyes stray to my father once more, who stands across the room with deadly intent settling over his face. Shit. My father might murder every single one of my boyfriends.

"RIP, boys. I'll stand by your graves every day and weep, remembering the good times we had," I mumble, shaking my head. Chase's body jolts, and he barely stifles his yelp. I furrow my brows. "What?" I ask, cocking my head to the side.

"You said that out loud," he frantically hisses at me, darting his eyes around the room. "You don't think?" He trails off, heaving a breath. "I'm going to die," he whines in a soft voice, trying not to draw my brother's attention to him.

"Oh," I say, biting my bottom lip, trying to hide the smile threatening to emerge. "You won't die." I pat his arm, and he glares at me, obviously not convinced about his safety. Whatever, I won't let my brother or my father tear him limb from limb.

"And look at you," my mother says, looking at Chase with a warm, motherly smile. "It's so wonderful to see you again." The tension drops from Chase's shoulders, as they slide back into their normal position and away from his ears. He sighs with burning cheeks when my mother steps in front of him, squeezing his shoulders in a small embrace.

"It's good to see you again too, Mrs. C," he says, clearing his throat and focusing on her.

The joyful smile on my mom's face lights up the whole damn world right now. If only she knew what we were about to walk into. If only *I* knew what we were about to walk into. It's still a fucking mystery to me. The boys have reassured me over and over that it's just a normal rich person event. But I don't think it is. Something about this entire charity event stinks like fish, but we haven't been able to figure out why. We dug through Cushing's computer and found nothing.

We've dug through Shaw's computer and found jackshit. We've come up empty handed in every area we've searched. Yeah, shits about to go down. If only I knew what kind of shit.

"I told you before," she says through a grin, squeezing his shoulders again. "Call me Mercy," she chastises him, looking his suit up and down with approval.

Chase wears a black suit, looking handsome as ever. I even batted my eyelashes and somehow convinced him to choose the baby blue bow tie to match my lace dress.

It took a whole Saturday of miserable, anxiety induced shopping to find the perfect dress for this event. My sister snickered at me when my mom had fussed over every dress and begged me to put them on. But every piece of fabric scratched against my skin, and I practically broke out in hives until we found the right one. And it was perfect, not a scratchy piece of fabric found anywhere. Soft blue powders the dress, mixing with the sparse floral design and transparent lace. The back buttons up from my waist and tightens around the base of my throat but offers enough coverage.

A deep throat clears from behind us, far too close for comfort. My heart leaps from my chest when Chase scrambles to look at me with wide eyes, flaring with panic.

"Oh! I'd like to introduce you to my husband." My mom's chipper voice echoes through the room like a death bell.

I frown when imagery of Chase's bloodied head on a table after a meeting with a guillotine comes to mind. Shit! I can't think like that right now. My father would never murder my boyfriend like that. Would he?

Chase's hand tightens around mine, and his eyes go wide, giving Bodhi and Dex a full look at the terror he's feeling. My brother raises his glass with a chuckle, and Dex's face pales in sympathy.

Almost in slow motion, we turn around, still clutching to one another. My father eyes Chase's hand with narrowed eyes and purses his lips in disapproval. His face tightens into a predatory smile. Dear God, my family is enjoying this torture way too much.

My handsome boyfriend shrinks back from his gaze, and his eyes dart toward the front door, looking to make his escape. His focus strays from the predator lurking in front of us. His trembling hand clasps tightly onto mine, cutting off my blood supply.

"It's nice to meet you, Sir." Any trace of my fun-loving, charismatic boyfriend vanishes. Instead, he is replaced by the trembling puppy dog standing beside me, hanging onto me like I might help him stay afloat in the river he's about to drown in.

My father eyes Chase, stopping at his feet and meticulously making his way back up to his pale face. Internally, I see him picking him apart, piece by piece. Sniggers sound behind us from our very amused audience, who don't hide their merriment. I side-eye the laughing buffoons, and they laugh harder, turning red and doubling over. Ugh. Why was I blessed with these people? Couldn't I have been an only child? My mother croons at them to hush, but it's useless. Chase gulps again as my father moves in on him.

"So, you're the boyfriend?" he asks in a gravelly voice.

Chase straightens his back, jutting his chin up. And with one last big breath, he finally calms his nerves and shakes them away.

"Yes, Sir," he says with a nod. "I'm Chase Benoit. You worked with my dad years ago. Amazing work, by the way. The writing, Sir, is fantastic." My dad raises a brow, amusement sparkling in his ocean eyes.

"So you read my books?" His voice dips dangerously low, and only I can tell he's preparing to fuck with Chase.

Chase's eyes widen, panic spiking the throbbing vein in his neck. "I—uh—er, maybe," he sputters out, panting for air.

My dad cracks a grin, slapping a rough hand on Chase's

shoulder. "I remember you, kid," Dad says, slapping him again, jostling Chase's stacked body straight into mine. "You were a good boy back then. Always polite on set—hell, you even entertained Kaycee."

"Ah, yeah—I—uh—thanks!" Chase beams with a smile. His voice comes out in breathy relief, and every muscle in his body relaxes as he stares up at my father, eagerly awaiting his next words.

A devious smirk pulls at the edges of my father's lips, and he steps forward again, bringing them chest to chest. Chase swallows so hard it's heard all around the now silent room. My eyes widen when my massive father, who stands at 6'4, looks Chase directly in the eyes and puts on his meanest scowl.

"But remember this—" My father's voice drops low, seizing Chase's shoulder in his massive grip. "Kaycee is my baby. Treat her with respect and treat her right or…" A wolfish grin takes over his face when he affectionately slaps Chase on the shoulder. Stepping back, my father nods to everyone else, taking off toward the front door. My mother giggles at him with so much love in her eyes I want to puke. As she passes to follow my father outside, she glides her fingers over Chase's pale face.

"I think he likes you," she coos and exits the house.

The moment my parents are outside, the house erupts in so much laughter I can't help but crack a smile.

Chase nods mutely at no one, staring at the front door in shock. His rigid muscles don't relax, and his breaths pick up before he turns to me and shakes his head.

"Likes me? A-and what the shit does *or* mean?" he squeaks, grasping my hand again. He turns to me with wild eyes, searching me over in his frantic state. "Sunshine, seriously! Don't laugh at me! What does he mean by 'or'?" he hisses, walking us toward the front door.

I snort, trying to cover it with my hand, but I can't help

myself when a full-blown giggle attack takes over, and my face turns red from the lack of oxygen.

"I officially hate you all!" Chase gripes, pulling me toward the front door.

"Welcome to the family, Little Benoit," Bodhi says through a massive grin, slapping Chase on the back. "You'll fit right in. But I can't wait to see the look on my father's face when he realizes you're not the only one!" Bodhi cackles out the front door, leaving us in the dust where Chase abruptly stops.

He grins as my sister, and her boyfriend pass us by, leaving us alone in the large, rented house.

"I know tonight is something we've all been afraid of. We don't know what's going to come," Chase swallows hard, tucking a stray strand of hair behind my ear. "But you look beautiful, Sunshine. Like, beyond my wildest dreams. I love you. I'll protect you," he murmurs the last part, a hiccup escaping him when he looks me over.

"I love you too," I whisper, stepping up and planting my lips on his. His fingers dig into my waist, dragging me forward to deepen the kiss. The tip of his tongue rubs along the seam of my lips, begging for entrance. I give him one small taste before a familiar, deep voice breaks us apart in a hurry.

"Ahem," A throat clears from behind us, and I stumble back when Chase pushes me away with an inhuman squeak.

I blink a few times, righting myself, and glare at my boyfriend standing rigidly before my father. He wipes his lips off like he wasn't just sucking my tongue into his mouth. With a hard swallow, he puts his hands in the air in surrender.

My father smirks. "How about we get into the limo? We have a worthy charity to attend to," Dad says, gesturing toward the door. His ice blue eyes sparkle with mischief when Chase flounders over his words, turning a deep shade of red.

"Yes, Sir. Sorry, Sir. I was just.." Chase stumbles over his words and feet, tripping toward my father. The only reason he doesn't hit the ground is because my father catches him by the scruff of his suit and holds him up.

"I heard what you said, Son," my father murmurs, and I finally see the admiration. "Keep up the good work. Or else…." Again with the threats that turn Chase paler than a ghost and a slight hint of green. His cheeks expand like he's about to blow chunks all over my father's shoes. Which would not sit well with the man still holding him up. A smile plays at the edges of my father's lips when he puts Chase back onto his feet and wipes down the arms of his suit. "Yeah, son, or else…." His words trail off again in some sort of threat that I can't comprehend.

What would my father do to Chase? Or all the boys for that matter? Bury them? Make them disappear like some sort of mafia boss? Shit, I've been reading way too many books for that. When my morbid thoughts fall away, the only sign my father was there is the gloomy, crestfallen face of my boyfriend staring at my father's retreating back as he slips through the front door.

"Shit," Chase hisses and frantically grabs my hand. "Note to self, Sunshine. Don't kiss you when your family is around." Shaking his head, he pulls me outside into the cool December air, which nips at my exposed skin.

Chase and I pile into the sleek black limo my mother insisted we arrive all together in and settle into our seats. All around us my family laughs with one another, passing around a bottle of expensive champagne, and fills tall glasses. Once we're all settled, the limo takes off down the long driveway of the rented house and heads down the darkened highway. Familiar dark streets surround us as my family's idle chatter fills the car, and they slowly sip at their drinks.

Old anxiety creeps in when I clutch Chase's hand, and he looks at me, furrowing his brows. I give him a tight smile, trying to reassure him I'm okay. But he instinctively knows and squeezes my hand in reassurance. The anxiety creeps up my spine and tingles through my body. I take a deep breath, working through the bone crushing feeling weighing me down.

"It's okay, Sunshine," he murmurs in my ear. Despite his promise to keep his lips to himself, he leans in and leaves a lingering kiss on my cheek. All the while his eyes never stray from my parents.

I swallow the heavy lump of anxiety and try to force it back into the depths of where it came from. Not daring to speak through the emotions tightening my throat, I nod my head, clutching him for support. The day will come when I ride in a car and no longer feel like my chest will cave in from the pressure. But today is not the day, and my fear continues to chase me through the duration of the drive.

Bright white lights sway through the night sky, illuminating the way to our destination. Like the damn bat call in the sky, I can't take my eyes off the mess we are most likely about to walk into. I feel it deep in my gut that after tonight, everything will change.

An ominous sensation flows through me, and alarm bells ring in my head. Violent shivers run down my spine, and my whole body shakes from the aftermath. The usually bright, full moon is covered in dark clouds, causing the towering hotel in the distance to be illuminated by only a speckling of street lights and various lit windows.

As we pull up to the front side of the prestigious hotel, my heart sinks into my ass. People mingle outside on a makeshift red carpet, posing for the flashing cameras. They smile with diamonds dripping from the women's necks and ears, decked out in the highest end fashionable dresses. More trepidation races through me at the sight of the growing crowd. Lines and lines of people wait to get in and smile more for the camera.

I've been so focused on the Apocalypse's next move, I didn't take into account there would be so many damn people here and that I would be out there with them, too. I swallow hard, counting in my head to ground myself, and turn to Chase, memorizing the specks hidden in the depths of his gray eyes. Never wanting to forget the way his bushy blonde brows dip when he's concerned or the way he bites his lip when he's excited, I take him all in. Right now he looks at me like I'm the most precious treasure he'll ever have, and he never wants to lose me.

As the doors open from the outside, I look at the brightly lit, beautiful hotel soaring into the sky. Apprehension sits like a heavy stone in my gut when I come face to face with the very event I've been fretting over for the past few months. Chase grips my hand tightly and helps me out of the car, guiding me toward the mouth of the monster.

On the outside, the illustrious East Point Hotel presents itself as this beautiful and welcoming gem, beckoning people inside with rich promises. But on the inside, the structure fills with rot, but not from the wooden structure holding it up or the plaster lining its walls. It's rotting from the occupants entering its doors who are about to walk across its marble floors and stand by its grand staircase.

Our prime suspects will drink, be merry, and schmooze unsuspecting people under the guise that their money will go to needy foster kids throughout the county. Who knows? Maybe that's precisely where it will go. Or it'll go to line their pockets, like everything else they do. From experience, they're greedy beyond measure, killing their wives and children to get their grubby hands on any sort of money, damning the consequences.

All we have to do is figure out how the rest of the town plays into all this. Are they contributors? We know they willingly cover up the crimes of the Apocalypse, so what do they get? The money? The satisfaction?

Tonight, we continue our investigation.

# SIXTEEN

## KAYCEE

People chatter in small groups around the massive ballroom of the East Point Hotel, decked out in beautiful ball gowns and sleek tuxedos. Waiters carry trays of champagne and fancy finger snacks around the room, delivering them to people who raise a hand. Multiple tables of silent auction items are spread throughout, with places for names and bidding amounts. Sailboats, condos, and even a date with several women who volunteered are up for auction. All in the name of charity.

The Christmas charity event disguises itself as a ploy to raise money for the foster kids in the county. Explaining they're trying to give these kids a better life with new clothes, laptops, and even college funds to help further their education. From the research the boys and I have done, some money finds its way to the children who need it most, and the other fraction of the money goes to line the pockets of the man or organization putting on this front. Or so we think. There's no evidence to show it does, but deep in my gut, I know Cushing Cunningham is up to no good when it comes to a wealthy event like this.

My eyes dart around the room, taking in the scene. Everything is lavish, sparing no expense in setting it up with diamonds and expensive drinks. Not only is everyone dressed for a Hollywood red carpet, but they also decorated the entire room to match. Several men and women, including Piper, come and go from a guarded room, smirking when they come out. Their eyes trail across the crowd with triumph, and pride puffs out their suit-lined chests. I wrinkle my brow, noting several guards standing outside, checking IDs and signaling them to enter, making me wonder why someone would have to show an ID to enter. What are they hiding in there?

"You look so beautiful," Chase whispers, dragging me from my thoughts about the forbidden room.

I eye it, narrowing my eyes from the dark corner we're hiding in when Cushing comes waltzing out with a smarmy grin. He shakes several hands of the men waiting outside and engages in quiet conversation, leaning in to whisper in their ears. What the hell are they saying? And what are they doing? And why is it hidden? Do they have these mysterious investments that Crowe had talked about on the phone when we spied on him?

What....

"Oh, Sunshine," Chase sing-songs, cupping my cheek. He smirks when he forces my face to his and stares adoringly at me. He tilts his head and taps on the side of my temple. "What's going through your mind?"

I swallow hard and shake my head. "Something is off with that room," I say, moving my eyes and begging him to follow my gaze.

He quickly peeks, taking in the slew of men and women coming and going, and nods. "Yeah, it seems fishy. When we find the others we'll investigate, okay?" I give him a small smile and pull him close, reveling in the heat of his embrace. "They should be meeting us here soon," he promises, holding me tight.

Our bodies meet, pressing into one another like a puzzle piece clicking into place. His warmth seeps through his suit, filling my stomach with swarming butterflies. Like Carter had promised a few weeks ago when we went to his apartment after the icky goo, he got us a big hotel suite tonight.

"Before," he murmurs in my ear, leaning down so his lips brush my skin. "I said you look so beautiful tonight."

My cheeks heat at his words, and I reach up for him, letting my fingers trail over the smooth skin of his jaw.

"Well, you don't look half-bad yourself," I murmur, kissing the underside of his chin, admiring how his broad shoulders and chest fit into the confines of his tux.

My hand runs the length of his chest, plucking at the matching blue bowtie I convinced him to wear. Okay, well—convince isn't the right word. Chase didn't bat an eye when I held it up, and I told him it matched my lace blue dress. He jumped at the chance to wear it and put it on with a grin.

He sighs, pulling me closer, and we sway to nonexistent music, only the tune in our minds. "Well, shit," he murmurs, pulling his face out of the crook of my neck. "Here comes Grumpy. You might cream your panties at the sight of him, Sunshine." He kisses my cheek one last time, and I shiver when his heat disappears, but someone else replaces him from behind.

A warmth presses at my backside, wrapping an arm around my waist. "You look so fucking delectable, Sweetheart. I could lick you," Carter mumbles against my ear and pushes himself harder against me. I feel every plane of muscle contracting when his fingers glide over my abdomen. Thank God we're hiding from prying eyes in a dark alcove, separating us from the enormous crowd pouring into the room, or he'd be caught feeling me up. And I might just let him do all kinds of dirty things to me here in the shadows.

Chase snorts, looking Carter up and down. "I'll get us some drinks. Think I can sneak some champagne?" His blonde eyebrows wiggle up and down, walking backward toward the mahogany bar in a brightly lit part of the ballroom.

Warm kisses trail down my jaw, moving slowly toward my ear. I hum, closing my eyes and leaning my back into Carter's embrace. If I could stay in his arms forever, I would. I heave a breath, feeling the prying eyes of everyone in the room. Being in public, especially with my family and a set of murderers running around, puts a damper on that feeling simmering low in my gut. A constant worry gnaws at my insides when Carter touches the skin of my thigh, trailing up toward my panty line, and then he pulls away. The Apocalypse is always watching, and they're everywhere inside this building.

"I never thought I'd miss someone as much as I fucking missed you," he whispers into my ear, hugging me tighter, his muscles relaxing as he holds me close.

"It's only been a few weeks since we left school," I snort, turning myself around to face him, and wrap my arms around his neck, careful not to get my cast caught. Talk about clashing with my beautiful designer dress, too. His meaty fingers wrap around my neck with an intense grip, pulling my forehead to his.

His breaths pick up, and his fingers dig into my hip. But I let him have this moment. Sure, we've texted like crazy from our respective homes and have video chatted almost every night preparing for this event, but not being in each other's arms has been hard. For all of us, not just me.

"And tonight." Trailing a finger over his suited chest, my finger circles his nipple ring, poking through his dress shirt. Lust sparkles through his brown, hooded eyes when I tug the ring through his shirt—warmth pools in my belly when he shivers, grasping my wrist to stop me.

"Tonight, I take you to the presidential suite and make up for when I was stuck without you," he rumbles softly, moving his hand under the back of my dress. "And I can't wait to show you what my new hardware can do. I'm going to beat your pussy so hard. You'll be screaming my name." He punctuates his words by dragging me closer.

I melt into him when his fingertips dance across the bare flesh of my thigh, inching closer and closer to my ass. His breath skates across my skin, tickling ever so slightly as he takes a firm grip, one cheek in each hand. His muted groans are music to my ears when he squeezes hard, rolling my hips into his, proving how hard he missed me. And I do mean hard. Phew. How will we make it through this whole event without sneaking off to do some naughty things in the elevators? Wait…the elevators–no, they have cameras in those, so that's a no go. We need to go to this mysterious room Carter booked us so we can say fuck it all and enjoy our evening together.

"For the first time in my life, I've found a bad habit I don't want to kick. I want to fucking consume you every chance I get. Being away from you was the hardest thing I've ever fucking felt. And I've never felt like this before," he breathes in my ear, nipping at my lobe.

Breathing? What's breathing? There's no such thing as oxygen in this room. After his confession, I tug him impossibly closer. The hard planes of his body press into mine, and I fucking turn into goo in his arms with a pleasurable sigh.

From the boy whose mother never hugged him or told him she loved him to the man standing in front of me with his heart on display. He's turned into more than what I ever thought he could be. His tongue won't let him say the words, but his heart is on his sleeve, spewing the feelings he shoves down into the pit of his stomach.

"I love you, too," I mutter under the approving vibrations rumbling from his chest.

He kisses the top of my head, lingering for longer than necessary. "What can I say? You make me this way," he mutters back, ignoring my declaration of love like he always does. But I'll take it for now because it's as good as I'm going to get. He'll say it one day when he's comfortable, but I know it'll be a while, and that's okay.

I'm so carried away with him in my arms in our hidden spot, that I forget we are in enemy territory. And in a very public place—filled with nosy rich people, eager for more gossip. Or, you know, my parents and siblings.

"Is there a reason your hand is up my daughter's skirt?" My father's growl fills the tiny space we thought we hid in.

And just like that, I'm dropped like a hot potato and pushed back, nearly falling over my shoes. My father catches my shoulder, stopping my fall, but clings on and steps forward.

Carter's brown eyes widen in panic, sizing up my pissed-off father. Fire burns in the depths of my father's pupils, and the death grip on his champagne flute tightens, whitening his knuckles.

"I, um—" For the first time since I've met him, Carter clams up, and the cat has caught his tongue. He has no snarky comment to offer or swagger in his stance. Carter's lips flop like a fish out of water, gaping at me and back at my father with an unreadable face. "I'm her boyfriend," he exclaims—a deep red rushes across his cheeks and down his neck. Even the tips of his ears turn a tomato color, and I'm sure if I examined the rest of his extremities, they'd be the same.

I mentally facepalm and groan at the way this whole thing has turned out. This is not how I envisioned introducing my boyfriends to my dad. I wanted to take it slow, not throw them all into the ring at once and watch as they flounder. Maybe it's better to rip the Bandaid off in public. At least then, he can't murder all of us.

My father takes a casual sip of his drink, humming angrily under the bubbles. He finally removes his fingers from my shoulder, taking a deep, calming breath. Tension finally eases from his face, forcing himself back from the cliff of anger he was teetering on. Well, for now at least. My eyes widen, and I try to signal a finger across my throat when my adorable, golden retriever boyfriend shows up with drinks in his hands and a glorious smile on his face. Poor, poor oblivious bastard.

"Hey!" Chase shouts in an excited greeting, utterly oblivious to the man standing in our circle. He struts up with three drinks in his hand and a goofy grin. "I got us—" Chase's eyes widen in panic, his lips pop open, and every word he is about to say drops off into a strangled squeak.

Tension rises as my father inspects Chase with a critical eye–or maybe a twitching eye. I lean forward, taking a close look at my red-faced father. And, yup! There it is, the tell-tale twitch of his eye signifying he's about to blow a damn gasket. Could this night get any worse? Famous last words…

Chase's eyes turn into saucers staring at Carter's pale face and back to my father. Quickly he hides the drinks behind his back like my father hadn't caught the move.

Carter runs a shaky hand through his blonde hair and blows out a heavy breath. The color returns to his face, but his eyes drift left and right, plotting his escape. I don't blame him for wanting to run, because I kind of want to run, too. Do you think they'd notice if I slowly backed away and let them meet their fate by themselves? Yeah, I think they'd notice. Especially with the way they eye me, pleading for me to jump in and save their skin.

"Does the other one know about that?" My father asks, tilting his head toward Chase.

"Know about what?" Chase asks with suspicion, cocking his head to the side. He finally looks at my father in the face and winces under the scrutiny of his penetrating stare. "Oh," he squeaks like a mouse again.

"Dad—" I breathe through irritation, putting a hand up.

"No worries, Mr. Cole," Chase says, lifting his chin with confidence–something he shouldn't have right now. My father will chew them up and spit them out before they can blink. "We're cool." He nods toward a sweating Carter and grins, playing the tension down like the mediator he thinks he is. "So, totally cool," he murmurs, side-eyeing Carter who is so totally not cool with this situation.

Dad frowns, staring at the three of us and blinking rapidly. The wheels visibly turn in his brain as he thinks it over. And dear God, I hope he doesn't think it over too much. He'll drag my ass out of this event and out of this town before I can utter a word. Shit, this was a dumbass idea to think I could pull one over on him. Taking another sip, I see the moment a light clicks in his brain when he rears back and really takes a look at the three of us. And I mean really looks at us with bright, wide, knowing eyes. Fuck. We're dead. Just bury us now because there won't be anything left when he's through with us. He scowls and opens his mouth, but whatever he was going to say falls to the wayside. Instead, he runs a hand down his reddened face and huffs.

"You keep your hands to yourself for the rest of the evening," he growls at Carter, stepping up to his trembling body. "If I catch you feeling up my daughter again, I'll cut your hands off myself."

My heart drops into my stomach at the sound of my father's violent threat. Would he really? I mean, he's good with his hands and a creative writer, but to saw off my boyfriend's wandering hands? Would he? Or....

"Of course, Sir," he gasps out, taking a step back.

"And you..." he growls at Chase, pointing a finger. Chase visibly swallows, staring down the beast in the eyes.

"Dad," I say again, a little more forcefully. His eyes snap to mine, shaking his head.

"Any more boyfriends you need to tell me about?" He asks through clenched teeth, looking around the room with a fire in his eyes. Okay, so I give my mom and sister credit. They didn't utter a word to my unsuspecting father. Although, right now, it might have been nice to have him in the know. Then he wouldn't be hunting down my other potential boyfriends he does not know about.

I swear my heart falls to the floor when my favorite twins saunter up to us. Seger wears an impressive grin, fingers wrapped around a champagne flute. Zepp creases his brow, examining the scene unfolding. His fingers glide over his freshly shaved chin, freezing in place. He darts his eyes from the four of us to his brother and back again. Before he can stop Seger by the wrist in warning, Seger opens his cocky as hell mouth, spouting the stupidest thing he could.

"Ah, cool, Angel! You told him?"

Swallow me whole. Jesus, take me now. I'm ready to die an early death and forget this all happened. If this continues, I'm as good as gone, and he'll lock me in my room until I'm thirty-five. Okay, maybe not that dramatic. But my father is so protective. He's probably seeing red by now, and we're all in grave danger. I dart my eyes across the room. We should probably run.

I send daggers in Seger's direction when he steps up to my father with a grin on his face. "Hey, Mr. Cole, I'm Seger." He extends his hand with a grin, fully expecting a friendly handshake. But what he gets drops the grin from his face and makes his Adam's apple bob.

My father blinks rapidly, staring down at Seger's suspended hand and back up to his face. Zepp stands beside Seger with a huff, observing the scene unfolding. Shaking his head, he leans over and quickly whispers in Seger's ear. Seger's eyes widen, and his muscles stiffen. Slowly, Zepp lowers his brother's arm back to his side. And they, too, stand like the rest of my boyfriends: petrified and motionless before the damn predator about to devour them whole. Goodbye boyfriends, it was nice knowing you. I won't ever forget you.

"Dad," I beg again, turning on my puppy dog eyes.

He eyes the five of us with suspicion boiling in his eyes, only stopping to look each guy over like he's making a mental hit list. Shit. He probably is. He's never been the shotgun type of dad. But now? Yeah, now I'm thinking we will walk in on him cleaning his gun and throwing out threats.

His frown deepens, wrinkling his face, and he narrows his eyes. "I need to have a word with your mother," he mutters, eyeing us all again. "And then we'll have a very long conversation together." He stares at each boy in the eyes and then stomps off in my mother's direction, muttering curse words under his breath.

My mom's twinkling eye takes us all in from a distance, and when my father approaches, she coos at him, running her fingers over his cheeks and talking in a hushed tone. I have no doubts now she's detailing everything to my father by the way their eyes keep slicing at us. My father's veins bulge, and his entire face turns red.

"Shit," Seger gasps in horror, finally able to move. He tries to make a run for it, but Zepp stops him by the scruff of his shirt.

"Yeah, shit." Chase scowls, handing us our drinks once hidden behind his back.

Carter grasps the flute and, in one gulp, drinks the entire contents of his glass. He marches out into the open with a frantic scowl and shoves the glass onto a drink tray passing by, grabbing two more. At first, I think he's brought me another, but I quickly realize he's drowning his fears away with two champagne glasses at a time.

"You fuckheads didn't get caught groping—" Carter groans through a full-body shiver, draining the third drink in a second.

"Groping?" Seger gasps, turning toward Carter with his mouth open wide. "You fucking didn't," he says, letting his laughter boil over.

"Shut the fuck up, West," Carter snarls, gulping down another drink from a full glass.

Wait... where did he get it? He just had two empty ones, and now he has two full ones again. I peek around the room, but we are back in our hidden space, and the crowd has thinned out. Even my parents have disappeared, and hopefully, they weren't dragged somewhere nefarious. But I shake that thought away. They held the event in three rooms of the hotel, each with different possibilities for patrons to enjoy. There are bands, auctions, and even a donation room. So people wander around aimlessly, moving from room to room.

Just when I think I can have some time to myself, my hair rises on my neck. I curse, looking behind me. Only to find the tick that never leaves me waltzing forward.

"He's not too bad, boys," Bodhi says through a cocky grin. I wish the world would swallow me whole, spit me out in a new region, give me a new name, and let me live in peace.

Seger's mouth falls open. "Body Slammer," he practically squeals, clutching Zepp's arm. "It's fucking Body Slammer," he hisses again, breaths heaving in his chest.

Bodhi tosses his head back and laughs. "We've been through this, West. Whichever one you are." Bodhi rolls his eyes, but secretly I think he likes the attention my fanboy boyfriends give him.

I frown when Seger stares at my brother like he stares at me—with stars in his eyes and hearts above his head. Shit. Is he going to leave me for my brother? After the torturous events at Thanksgiving dinner, I wouldn't think he'd want to. But he still stares at him like he's the light of his damn life, and I'm... well... I'm chopped liver now.

A heavy arm rests on my shoulders, pulling me into his bulky side. "My dear, sweet little sister. So, this is all of them. All together and in one place," he says with a mischievous grin, lighting up his stupid face.

"Please don't start this now," I groan, wrestling against his hold, but he grips me tighter. "You've already met them all," I hiss.

There were two very effective ways to get my brother away from me when I was a kid. Bite him or kick him in the nuts. He'd stagger away, yelling at dad because I hit him. Eyeing his arm on my shoulder, I weigh my options. Bite or nuts? Which will hurt more?

"No, this should be fun," he says, pulling me closer until my face is practically in his armpit.

Biting it is.

"Don't make me bite you," I growl, heaving a fist into his gut, and I recoil. Pain shoots up my left arm, my only good arm, and I cringe.

Seger, Carter, and I are going to have a serious conversation about more self-defense lessons. The one time in the gym wasn't enough. I barely learned how to swing my arm. Not to mention after twenty minutes of hopping around the old boxing ring, I died from lack of oxygen. I should have made them take me jogging or something because my endurance is shit. I need to learn how to punch better, harder, and faster. How the hell am I supposed to succeed against the enemy when my brother doesn't even flinch when I beat him?

"You're like a fly," Bodhi teases, ruffling my perfectly styled hair.

"Bodhi!" Shoving my good hand into his side, I knock him away from me. And he laughs and laughs, heaving breaths and knee-slapping himself.

"Alright, alright," he says, swatting at me again. His eyes linger on my very tense boyfriends and then back to me. "How'd you pull that off?" he asks through a smirk, waving toward the guys.

"I've been asking myself that very question since I met them. Nice to see you boys again," my sister Callie says with a grin. "If you ever need support, just ask Dex." Dex lifts a hand, waving to them with a grin. "He's been through it all before." A reassuring smile forms on her lips with sympathy forming in her eyes. As if to say, 'sorry boys, we have a scary father who will tear you apart.'

"And I thought I had it hard. There are four of you. I can't imagine." His hand wipes invisible sweat from his forehead, grimacing. "Prepare yourself. He's super scary and protective."

"True story." Chase swallows hard, taking a sip of his stolen champagne. "Shit's scary by yourself and the threats...." His body shivers, remembering the threat my father gave him before.

"He threatened you?" Zepp asks, flattening his palms against his tux pants.

"More or less." Chase scoffs, drinking the rest of his drink.

"That's fucking great," Seger murmurs, shaking his head. "Are we even going to survive this, Angel?" His moss-green eyes plead with me.

"Stop scaring them," I huff, walking toward Seger. I cup his face into my palm, pulling his tall form towards mine. "You'll be fine, big guy. I won't let my dad hurt you."

He smiles down at me. "I missed you," he murmurs again, rubbing his nose against mine. I sigh in relief.

Having them so far away, tied to family obligations, was hard. My pieces were scattered across the map. And me? I barely breathed through the whole thing. Thank God they're here now, flanking my sides and protecting me from whatever evil lurks in the ballroom, or I'd be dead. Literally. We still don't understand why we are here or why my family was invited to attend. Talk about suspicious behavior. The only thing I can think of is that my parents can contribute to the charity because of their wealth.

"Yuck, gross, don't do that to my little sister." Callie fake gags, sticking her finger down her throat.

"Shut up. I've seen Dex's tongue down your throat more times than I care to." I shoot back over my shoulder.

"Little sisters are so annoying. Why did we beg Mom for one?" She snorts, looking at Bodhi's smirk.

"So, do your boyfriends know about your little online friend? What was his name? I mean—if he was a guy." Bodhi snaps his fingers.

"Tristan!" my sister shouts with a grin. "That's what his name is!"

I sigh. Why did I have to be put in this family? I could have been an only child with loving parents. Instead, I get these two idiots giggling over Tristan, who they still think doesn't exist. Hmmm. This could be fun.

"You haven't told them?" Zepp whispers, boldly brushing his lips across my cheek in greeting.

"Haven't had the chance," I whisper back, running my fingers over his cheek. Humming, he closes his eyes.

"Well, this should be fucking fun," Seger mutters through an evil grin, rubbing his hands together.

"Yeah, we know about him," Chase says, casually taking a sip.

My brother's eyebrows raise, looking over at my equally confused sister. They gape at one another, and my sister waves a hand.

"She's told you about him? Like, she has no idea who he is, you know that, right?" Callie says, scrunching up her face. "God, don't tell me you added him to all this." I wrinkle my nose at her judgmental statement.

Seger shrugs. "He's actually here tonight."

Bless these boys. Bless them so hard. I could kiss each one of them. Once this event is over, when my parents leave, I'm going to rock their worlds, showing them exactly how much I love them.

"What?" Bodhi's deep voice fills our small circle, dipped in concern.

"Oh, Kace, is he... like, stalking you or something?" Callie asks in a hushed tone, staring around the massive ballroom full of people.

"Eh, kind of. He never leaves." I snort, bringing her attention back to me. "Follows me around like a lost little puppy dog."

"I fucking do not," Seger huffs in fake outrage.

"What?" Callie whispers, staring at Seger with wide eyes.

"Right," I say through a grin. "So, I accidentally met Tristan this year. They go to East Point, too."

"They?" Bodhi asks, frowning.

"Accidentally?" Callie breathes, staring at me like I'm insane. "You mean—he's not some sixty-year-old pervert living in his mom's basement?"

"Not by a long shot," Zepp says, stepping forward. "My brother and I were going through a rough time a few years ago. We stumbled upon Kaycee in an online battle of Angel Warrior and quickly became friends. Because of our dad's fame, we vowed to stay anonymous. And well…. fate had other funny ideas." The tips of his fingers brush against the small of my back, forcing shivers down my spine.

"The two of you?" Bodhi wiggles a finger between the twins. "Seriously?"

"You'll catch flies, jerk," I mumble, forcing my brother's jaw closed. "It's all true." I nod, ignoring his glare.

"Fuck, I need more to drink," he mutters, taking a step and stopping. "Listen here, you little shits. I love my sister, even when she's a pain in the ass. So don't break her heart. You think my dad is scary? Well, you've got another thing coming. And for fuck's sake, wear condoms, and be safe!" he cringes at his last remark, shaking his head. "And just… be good. Treat her with respect. Don't hurt her, or I hurt you. Got it?"

All the boys nod, not wanting to argue with Bodhi before he stomps off toward the other end of the room towards the bar. His threatening gaze never leaves us as he grabs multiple drinks and downs them one after the other, and slams the glasses down with a scowl. Nothing puts the fear of God into someone's boyfriends like having their idol tell them to wear condoms.

"Huh, never thought he'd resort to that," Callie says through a smirk, watching him closely.

"All right, Cals, let's leave these kids alone and go drink or something." Dex's arm wraps around Callie's shoulders, pulling her into his side.

"I can't believe Tristan is real and is….them," my sister huffs out while walking away. Peeking over her shoulder, she examines the boys and me again, finally giving into Dex's tugging.

Callie and Dex join Bodhi at the bar and then disappear, walking into an adjoining room to mingle. People in elegant clothes surround them, laughing and talking to one another. The once quiet ballroom fills with their small murmurs, belly laughs and soft giggles. Small groups of women draped in expensive ball gowns and men in ridiculous tuxedos loiter, filling the space with their private tales and gossiping about who-did-what. Or who is doing who? Or whatever the uber-rich talk about. I pull my thoughts away from my siblings, peek toward the exclusive room, and frown. It once had two guards standing outside it, but now it's abandoned. And the long lines have vanished.

"Well, that went well," Zepp says sarcastically with a scoff.

"Ah, yeah, not too bad. I think they like me," Chase beams delusionally, rocking back on his heels with a huge grin.

"Your father is going to fucking murder me," Carter hisses, running a hand down his sweating face. Worry lines form on his forehead as his eyes move back and forth, surveying the room.

We all turn toward Carter, who has another full drink in

his trembling hand. His eyes scan the room again with a nervous tic forming in his jaw.

I wrap my hand around his wrist, stopping him from drinking again. "It'll be fine," I whisper, running my manicured nail down the side of his moist face, trying to soothe away the discomfort my father left behind. Of course, I'm lying through my damn teeth. He got caught with his hand up my damn skirt, for shit's sake. He might as well have bent me over and screwed me right there. I'm not excited for the talk my father wants to have later.

"Yeah, man, it'll be fine. A few years down the road, he'll jokingly say, you're the kid who couldn't keep his hands to himself," Seger laughs, discreetly drinking champagne.

"Shit, I can't wait," Chase chuckles, downing the rest of his drink.

Carter's eyes blow wide during his perusal of the ballroom. His back snaps ramrod straight, and his jaw clenches incredibly tight His beautiful brown eyes glaze over, turning him into an unreadable stone structure. My brows furrow when an impenetrable mask I've never seen shifts into place, and Carter is no longer the Carter I know.

"You guys need to get the fuck back," he growls, pointing toward the wall. "Stand there and shut the fuck up. Don't move," he hisses.

The three of them share a concerned look, but they take a few steps back without argument, much to my surprise. They disappear into the shadows and lean against the wall, keeping their eyes on the two of us.

My heart pounds when the hairs on the back of my neck stand on end, alerting me to the danger making his way toward us. Carter gazes down at me with those ruthless, frigid eyes. His entire expression tightens, and when he stares at me, he looks right through me. At the moment, I am nothing to him when he wears this mask: nothing but a warm body in front of him. I'm not his girlfriend or lover. I am the scum beneath his shoes, and I don't know what scares me more: the look in his eyes or how easily he can turn himself off like this. A sharp shiver rolls through my body at the feel of eyes roaming over me.

"Do you trust me, Sweetheart?" he mumbles, not moving his lips. I nod. "Good, then keep your pretty fucking mouth shut, and I fucking mean it this time. Don't make me silence you." I nod again, swallowing hard at his words.

"Hello, son," a deep voice says from behind us. Carter guides me by turning me around and placing my back against his front. His heavy hand rests on my waist, locking me in place with his grip.

"Father." Carter's voice dips so low that it's almost impossible to hear through his rumble.

Cushing Cunningham stands before us, dressed in a suit easily more expensive than a house. His slicked-back blonde hair lies on his head, not a piece out of place. A smarmy smile spreads on his lips at the sight of us two. His eyes hone in on Carter's hand, squeezing my waist, and he grins more. His arm tightens around the dazed woman on his arm, and she leans into him.

I nearly gasp at the vacant look on her face. Her eyes don't focus on anyone, just like when I saw her at Carter's house. It's like she's there, but the lights have dimmed on the inside, and she's no longer home. Her piercing dead blue eyes catch sight of us, and she smiles widely, looking plastic and fake.

"Francesca, say hello," Cushing coos, tightening his grip on her waist. When his fingers dig deep into the fabric of her dress, most likely pinching her, her entire body jumps.

"Oh, yes! Hello, Carter. It's lovely to see you tonight." Her sickly sweet voice comes out like a melody.

Piper's mother, who I assumed was happily married to Carter's father, seems anything but happy. She's been on my mind since we saw her slumped over, sleeping on the couch. With those weird marks on her wrist and a glazed look in her eyes, Francesca stands like a mannequin, perfectly put together in a tight red dress that dips toward her navel. Her surgically enhanced breasts barely stay contained with the stretched fabric. A large diamond necklace sits around her neck, and expensive bracelets hang from her wrists.

"And who is this?" Cushing purrs, stepping out of Francesca's embrace, leaving her to stare off into space.

Cushing's eyes eat every inch of my flesh. My long baby blue gown can't protect me from his prowling gaze. Starting with the flats on my feet and slowly bringing his gaze up, he lingers on my light removable cast, encasing my right arm with a manic grin across his face.

"I'm Kaycee," I say, trying not to squirm under his watchful eyes.

I lean back into Carter's chest more, seeking his protection. What is Cushing's game? And why is he staring at me like he wants to tie me up and devour me?

Carter stiffens behind me, squeezing my waist in a warning. I can tell he wants to whisper, 'Shut up' in my ear. But when have I ever listened to him, or anyone for that matter?

"Well, Kaycee, it's so wonderful to meet you. You must have been the girl my son snuck home when I was away. Forgive me for being out and not being able to introduce myself properly." He grins further when the effects his words have on me show all over my face. Carter gives my waist another squeeze, this time for reassurance instead of threatening. How the hell did he know we were there? Shit. Fucking Piper! She must have reported back to him. Not that I thought she'd keep that secret to herself. But still, she could have kept her crazy mouth shut. I heave a breath when he continues to ramble and force myself to listen to him again.

"I've heard so many beautiful things about you. My boy talks nonstop about your wonderful friendship. But seeing you in person doesn't do his words justice." He smirks, stepping forward to take my free hand in his. Warm lips press against my wrist, lingering more than necessary, until he pulls back with a seductive grin.

Carter's chest vibrates against my back, holding back the growl trapped in his throat. Cushing smirks, pulling back from my hand. But I keep my promise this time and zip my lips, so I say nothing stupid. Why hasn't he done anything yet if he knows we were over? Or has he? Does he know what we were up to? Probably. Shit. My heart rate spikes at the possibility of him being onto us and figuring out what we're doing.

"I was so sorry to hear about your car accident," he says, nodding his head toward my right arm still snug in its cast. "It was quite the scene to come across." A solemn expression passes over his face as he shakes his head.

"You were the cop?" I ask, swallowing hard again.

"Indeed." Something odd passes over his face, almost like pride, and then it drops into a frown. "To see three young souls stranded on the side of the road and you—" He leans in slightly. "And you were on the ground, so broken. It was a shame... you poor, poor girl." He tuts, clicking his tongue as his dirty eyes roam over my body. Shivers spike all over my body until I'm trembling in fear in Carter's arms.

Every hair on my body stands on end as he speaks. He was there. In the aftermath of it all, he stood there. And why stop there? Maybe he was the one to dole out my injuries as well? Goosebumps break out over my skin at the thought of him standing over me and breaking my arm.

"Cushing," Francesca whispers. "I'm sure she doesn't want to relive it all." Her hand pats his shoulder, curling around it.

In that single move, her diamond bracelets fall from her wrists, moving up her forearms and revealing the strange, angry, and blistering marks completely encompassing her wrists. I cock my head, and my breath stalls in my lungs from the depth of the wounds. She doesn't wince when they slide back over the marks, and she smiles.

His jaw ticks as he glances back at her and stands to full height. "Of course. Sorry, dear. It's a night that will live in my memories forever." I blink as he stares at me with pools of evil flashing across his face.

He's a devil in disguise, hidden in plain sight, presented on a platform to the world as a good samaritan. A leader in the police force, promising his citizens he's there to help. But he's not. He makes Carter look like a sparkling saint as everyone worships him for their good deeds. Cushing embodies evil, which wafts off of him in waves, spreading around the room and taking victims.

Stepping back into Carter's embrace again, I ground myself in his presence. I soak in the heat of his body and the cologne marking his skin. Breathe in. Breathe out. Calmness rushes over me, blanketing me in the fresh air. No matter the situation, Carter wouldn't let anything happen to me. Ever. Even with his mask in place, I know the real Carter. He's nestled deep inside, full of compassion, kindness, and, dare I say it, love.

"Mr. Cunningham! So wonderful to see you again!" The man speaking doesn't look at him as he approaches our group. His beady hazel eyes stare at me while shaking Cushing's hand.

Breathe in. Breathe out, damn it. I swallow hard, stomping out the panic swirling in my gut.

The man beside Cushing doesn't look like his picture. He's the one I wanted to stab for changing everything about Magnolia's autopsy. And now, here he is in the flesh, looking plumper and happier than before, with diamond rings sitting on his grubby fingers and gold teeth in his mouth. He leers over at me with a predatory smile, cranking up my anxiety. He says something, but my ears fill with loud static.

One by one, each of my nightmares waltz by, greeting Cushing like an old friend. The mayor, the judge, the coroner, the district attorney, Mr. Shaw, and finally, Victor Crowe. Each more glamorous than the next. Diamonds, beautiful women, gold teeth, and expensive suits. They are all flashy billboards of wealth and excess.

The three brothers stand together in solidarity, joking and laughing while side-eyeing me and sizing me up.

More people from East Point come up to them, shaking their hands with smiles. Everyone thanks them for this beautiful evening of giving back to the community and thanks them for giving to the foster kids in need around our area. And all the while, they peer over at me with curiosity. Some make it obvious. But some? Some are coy about it, looking from under their fake eyelashes or hiding behind their hair.

Tiny ants crawl up my flesh, nipping at me, crawling inside me. My nails scratch at my arms and stomach. With every swipe, I want to tear my flesh off until familiar hands grab at me. They pull me away from Carter, and out of the prying eyes of my enemies, until we're slowly walking around the edge of the room. People continue to chatter and laugh, looking away from me. No one seems to notice when we slip through the crowd now. Once their eyes were on me, but they must have gotten their fill.

My mind drifts, dissociating me from the world around me. I shiver, watching the women around the room blinking their fake eyelashes. They're huge and beautiful, but all I can think about is that video I watched on FlashGram explaining their origins, and I swallow a snort.

"Cumbrellas," I blurted in a whisper, unable to hold my damn tongue from the thoughts endlessly swirling inside my frantic mind. This earns me stares from the guys, mixed with confusion.

"Jesus Christ," Seger murmurs, clutching my hand, pulling me toward the exit.

My guards surround me with solemn faces and darting eyes. Chase takes position behind me with his hands lazily in his suit pockets, but he remains alert. Like the leader he is,

Zepp stands proud in front of me with rigid shoulders and his chest puffed out. He scans the entire room with a sharp eye, taking in the surroundings like he usually does.

"Come again?" Seger chokes out, pulling me through the crowd with force. I hold him tight, almost falling over my feet.

"Fake eyelashes," I say in a daze, looking at the fancy women to our right and examining the clumpy spiders hanging off their eyelids. Imagine if they just jumped off their faces and made a run for it across the floor, causing everyone to panic. Attack of the fake eyelashes!

"That's what they used to be called." I scrunch my nose when one woman looks at me, and her eyelashes move from their spot and sit askew on her eye. Gross. Doesn't the glue make them stick better? How does that work?

Seger stiffens, his chest vibrating with laughter when he side-eyes me. "Right, Angel. Cumbrellas, mhmm. We'll have to test that theory out sometime." He says it so offhandedly I almost don't catch the heat sitting behind his words when he struggles to get them out.

I recoil and stare up at him. "I don't have fake eyelashes." Never have and never will. Not with a name like cumbrellas. But it makes a girl wonder if the cum really slides off the eyelashes to protect the eyeballs. Because, I don't think I'd want their salty swimmers in my eyes causing all kinds of problems.

"We can get you some, Sunshine," Chase says, hiding his smile behind his hand. He chuckles a few times and then focuses on our surroundings.

"I don't think that's true, baby girl," Zepp mumbles, looking over his shoulder.

His teeth sink into his bottom lip, fighting off a smile. What the hell? It's not that funny. It's history, damn it! Doubt seeps in when I look around, remembering the video I watched.

"But I watched a video of it on FlashGram," I say in defense. "The lady said that's what they were called." I frown. She wouldn't lie would she? Fuck, she probably made it up to get views. Shit.

A hot breath nips at my earlobe, and I jump, nearly yelping when he pulls me into him. "Well, we can test the fucking theory," Carter says and then leans into me more, resting his lips against my ear. "We're going to take turns coming all over your pretty fucking face. You better hope your eyelashes can handle it." My face heats at Carter's brash words, but a pleasurable tingle starts at the tip of my toes.

"Oh, yes," I mumble before I can stop myself.

Deep down my pussy approves, squeezing air. Heat pools in my center, and wetness seeps out when the visions swim through my head. Like a damn movie, I can see it now. Me dropping to my knees, letting them form a circle around me with their hard dicks out. They'd pump themselves in their hands, and I'd be waiting with an open mouth and fake eyelashes to protect my eyes from their salty sperm. They'd come all over my face, and then my damn eyes would burn because shit, cumbrellas are totally worthless–at least that's what fantasy me would think. I'd spit and sputter, and curse at them for getting cum all over my face, and then I'd choke and die. Dramatic? Yes.

"Come on, Angel," Seger whispers, tugging me harder toward the exit a few steps away. A smirk graces his lips, and lust darkens his deep green eyes, knowing exactly where my mind went to.

"They won't work," I grumble, earning a chuckle from Zepp.

"That's why we have to try, right, baby girl?" Zepp asks in a low, gravelly voice.

My pussy perks up again at the sound of his voice. But then my imagination takes over. I really don't want to look like a dripping glazed donut. Or do I? Hmm. They might win this one.

"For science!" Chase snickers, slapping my butt and making me yelp.

I glare back at him, giving him my meanest scowl. But he just grins at me with the most innocent face. Looking behind him, I watch Carter drop away from us and dip into the crowd. He blends in, in his snug suit, heading in the opposite direction toward his father. I narrow my eyes, following his every agonizing step separating us. A burn spreads across my chest and aches with the distance he puts between us. His eyes never dart back to our group. Instead, he keeps his eyes locked on his father, who mingles with his brothers. Probably gossiping about all the menacing things they're going to do tonight after this sham of a charity event. Maybe we should put a tracker on their asses?

I purse my lips when Carter finally stops next to his father. That frightening, unreadable mask drops like a curtain over his face, hiding the true man beneath. A coldness glazes over his eyes, giving him the air of indifference. From here, he doesn't look like my Carter. He looks like the Carter I met the first week of school. Cruel, snarly, and completely uncaring.

"Why is Carter staying?" I croak, peeling my eyes away from him. All I want to do is grab his arm, flip off his dad, and ride off into the sunset together. But we can't. Not yet. Carter still has to play this role, and I still have to be me.

"He has to take care of that. It's a fragile situation, but we needed to move you, baby girl." Zepp says, eyes looking all around us for any potential threats.

"I know," I sigh with disappointment.

As we step into the adjoining room, I catch my mother's eye. She excuses herself from a couple she's chatting with and walks toward us with her eyebrows raised. Suspicion lines her frowning face when she steps up in front of me, and examines my face.

"Sweet Pea," she says, narrowing her eyes. "You okay?"

*Don't be suspicious. Don't be suspicious.* My eyes widen as the song plays through my head, and I'm ten seconds away from singing out loud and definitely alerting my mom something is wrong. So instead, I go the safe route and shake my head. Yup, everything's fine here. Nothing to see here.

I swallow hard. "Just need some fresh air. I'm okay." Smooth—I pat myself on the back. For once, I didn't blurt the real reason my heart is pounding against my chest and feels like it's about to fall out of my ass. But shit, judging by her tight smile, I don't think she believes me.

She raises a brow. "Are you leaving?" Her eyes dart to the boys when they conveniently look at the ceiling and avoid her gaze.

So, how the hell do I tell my mom? Like hey mom, I'm staying in a huge hotel room with my four massive boyfriends. We'll probably bone at least twice tonight and once tomorrow when the sun comes up. Yeah, that'll go over well. She already had to intervene when my dad had a mini stroke at the sight of them.

"Oh, so it's like that?" She says in a playful tone, putting her hands on her hips. Great—explanation it is. Alright, I can do this.

"Mom, I..." she holds up a hand, silencing me. I snap my lips shut, eyeing her with my biggest puppy dog eyes. Silently I'm begging her to let this slide. And not to tell dad—that's the most important one. He'll force a chastity belt on me and lock me away in my room until I'm thirty-two.

"I never thought I'd have to worry about you in my life. But I trust you. You're a grownup now, Kace. And you boys are loving, responsible men. If I hadn't spent three days with you and seen how much you truly care about her, I'd put my foot down, but I'm not going to. I'm going to walk back to your father and distract him as you four do whatever you're going to do. When should I expect to see you again?" She asks, taking a step back.

"Umm, I..... a few days?" I squeak out with uncertainty.

Who knows how long these boys will keep me? Could be four days or it could be two.

She blows out a breath. "Be good. Be responsible. And have fun. I love you," she says, chugging down the rest of her drink.

"Love you, too," I mumble, stepping in and hugging her. She stiffens and then wraps her arms around me in a loving hug, squeezing me tight.

"Now go before your father catches wind. He's already threatened their balls," she hisses, waving us along.

"Not the balls," Chase yelps, putting a hand over his junk as we walk away from my mother as a group and head toward the main elevators. "Shit! Not the balls," he murmurs again, further protecting his junk until we're out of the room.

A fountain splashes water in the middle of the lobby entryway, echoing off the swanky marble walls. The front desk staff mills around, conducting traffic to the large ballroom. More elegant couples arrive by limos and escorts, wandering through the front doors.

"It's the entire town," I whisper as the doors close us into the mirrored elevator. Three sets of eyes burn through me. "They all—they all wear it like a prize. Whatever money they're making from killing these kids... goes into their pockets. Did you see the coroner? He had gold teeth... diamonds everywhere...." I trail off, thinking about their overly expensive suits and plastic smiles.

"But how?" Chase asks, clutching onto my arm.

"How are they making it?" Zepp asks, rubbing at his chin.

"Fuck if I know. Can't we just have one sane night? Like, is that too much to ask?" Seger waves his arms around, staring up at the ceiling.

"Did anyone else find that odd?" Chase asks, scrunching

his adorable nose. "It's like they were lining up to meet her." His gray eyes, filled to the brim with concern, connect with mine.

"I think they were," I whisper, curling into him. "Did you see the secret room? People were coming and going, and it had security outside of it. But before I could investigate, it was gone." I shake my head, a pounding developing behind my watery eyes.

"Gone?" Zepp asks.

"Fucking secret room?" Seger barks out in outrage.

"Yeah, security had disappeared, and the lines vanished. The doors were closed, and the room behind it was dark. It's like it never existed." I swallow hard, cementing the room to memory. I will never forget the faces of the guards or the faces of the people walking into that room. Whoever they are and whatever they're doing was terrible. I can feel it deep in my swirling gut.

We got off the elevator on the sixteenth floor with a collective sigh of relief. The boys place themselves around me, and we walk down the quiet hallway. The cushy carpet sinks beneath our footsteps, hiding our approach to the room at the end of the hall.

"Wow, Grumpy went all out." Seger whistles under his breath, patting at his pockets for the key.

"The Presidential Suite," Zepp says, running his finger over the golden plaque beside the door.

"Let's see what Grumpy got us," Seger says, sliding the key over the large black pad with a huge grin. I almost hold my breath until the indicator light turns green and our door beeps, granting us access.

# SEVENTEEN

## KAYCEE

Chase grabs my hand and leads me into the breathtaking room, fit for a damn king and queen. I stop dead two steps into the room, taking it all in with wide eyes and a pounding heart. Moving my eyes to every corner of the opulent room, I savor what we have here. This moment will forever live in our memories for years to come. The uninterrupted time we get to spend together in luxury. Even if the enemy is downstairs and crawling over every inch of the large hotel.

The door softly shuts behind us when we're all inside. Silence engulfs the room. No one breathes or dares to move. Together, we take in the space with awe and wonder, soaking in the luxurious suite.

Throughout my life, I've lived comfortably with my parents' wealth. They made sure our home and belongings were modest but never flashy, teaching us the value of a dollar. My father flew commercial instead of first-class, even with his fame. My clothes were from Target or Kohl's unless my mother found something she just had to get at a cute boutique. We splurged on a vacation here and there, but we never had a room like this. If we went to New York, we stayed with my Grandma Kay or my Aunt Cece. But this room? Hell, the word room doesn't even describe it. Most hotels are one room with two beds. This has a full kitchen in view with a bar full of booze, a baby grand piano, a bed big enough for all of us, and a spiral staircase leading to an upper floor.

My jaw drops. "This isn't a hotel room. It's a damn luxury apartment," I mutter in awe.

Seger chuckles, resting his hand on my lower back. Gently, he urges me forward, and we walk through the gorgeous living room. Overhead lights bathe the baby grand piano sitting in the middle of the room like a spotlight, drawing us to it. Large picture windows display the sparkling stars as the background, letting the whole world glimpse whoever plays here.

A nonsense song plays through the piano as my fingers brush along the white keys. I glimpse outside, having to stop myself from pressing my nose against the glass. Everything below looks so small and insignificant from way up here. Like all our worries don't matter as long as we're locked up in this room and in each other's arms. I never want to let this feeling of security go.

"Is that a fucking spiral staircase?" Chase gapes, drawing my attention back to him. His fingers brush against the cool metal, and a grin spreads across his lips. Happiness rings in his eyes, and he whoops, throwing his fist into the air. "Shit! This place is like an adult playground." His loud footfalls smack against the black-painted metal as he marches up the stairs, echoing through the giant suite. I giggle at his happiness, looking up when he leans over. His blonde locks encase his face from the gravity, when he looks down at us. "Holy shit! This tub holds like ten people! It's a damn swimming pool. Sunshine! I need you naked and in this tub in like five seconds," he demands, waving a hand for us to join. He eagerly steps away, and the sound of water flows from the faucets upstairs.

Every feeling I had waltzing out of the charity event washes away. And I haven't made it into the bath yet.

Serenity takes over my muscles, and I finally relax, taking a peek out the tall window again. The stars call me tonight, twinkling from above, and beg me to stare at them. As a child, I counted the stars in the sky. I never got past one-hundred before I had to start again, but I've always felt them by my side, guiding me to wherever I needed to go.

I'm thrown out of my thoughts when two strong arms wrap around my waist and throw me over their shoulder. I squeal when their shoulder digs into my abdomen, and I drive my fist into their kidney.

"Jesus, baby girl," Zepp huffs, clueing me in to who has me staring at their fine ass. I mean, damn. I knew they looked hot in their suit jackets, but these pants really cling to his assets like a glove. I'd be lying if I said this was a bad position to be in. It's glorious.

Zepp marches up the stairs with Seger on our heels. Their footfalls pound against the metal stairs, loudly echoing through the room. Finally, he plops me back to my feet, and I grunt when I land on shaky legs. Too much blood must have rushed to my head while I was upside down and hypnotized by his ass cheeks. My body sways back and forth with disorientation, finally getting a good look around the top floor.

"Wow," I whisper, looking around the lofted bathroom.

My lips pop open taking in the second story, and seriously, it's like a fantasy room. Large floor-to-ceiling windows make up the entire wall, giving way to the night sky, twinkling with golden stars from the heavens. I relax, once again feeling one with the stars.

"This fucking tub," Seger mutters in awe. His fingers work desperately at the knot keeping his tie around his neck, loosening it. Once it's off, he throws it over the railing, letting it land on the first floor.

"I hate wearing these suits," Chase grumbles, pulling at his cute bowtie and snapping it off with one swipe. He throws it to the floor without care and unbuttons his shirt, leaving me with one half-naked boyfriend. He shimmies out of his pants, leaving him in a pair of tight boxer-briefs, clinging to his package.

I try not to lick my lips or drool when Zepp's fingers brush against my chin. He takes hold and slowly forces me to look deep into his moss-green eyes. I shiver from the intensity, falling deep into the abyss of his gaze. The way he stares at me is like I'm the sun to his universe—the most important thing he revolves around.

"You look beautiful tonight, baby girl," Leaning in, Zepp brushes the flat of his tongue up my neck and swirls it around. My flesh sucks between his teeth, and I turn to jello in his grasp. My fingers curl around his shirt, pulling him impossibly closer to me. Until our chests meet and we share a breath.

"You look pretty handsome, too," I say through a breathless moan, running my fingers up the back of his neck, and through his hair. I pull his mouth closer to my skin, letting him mark me for the world to see.

His fingers brush the back of my neck, working through my blonde spiral curls and letting them fall over my shoulder. Zeppelin's fingers work the clasps on the back of my dress, undoing them one by one. The fabric loosens against my chest and stomach, and cool air breezes by my lower back, soon replaced by warm fingertips swirling across my flesh. My eyes close on instinct, letting his touch consume me. It takes me over, letting every burden fall to the wayside. I lean into him, craning my neck when his lips find their way back to my jaw.

"Are you feeling better?" he whispers as his warm fingers dance along my sides, finally swirling across my abdomen. My muscles bunch and flutter when he begins his descent, practically egging him on to continue down south.

"Yes, now that we are away from the crowd." Is what I think I mumble, but who knows. Every ounce of moisture on my tongue disappears when his finger thumps against my aching clit.

"We'll figure it out, baby girl. I promise. We'll sort all this out and keep you safe." I hum in agreement, mentally begging him to continue the circles he's started. Zepp leaves one last lingering kiss against my lips with a grin a mile wide, and then steps back.

I sigh, knowing pleasure would be drawn out. My eyes pop open when he cups my face and gently inserts his finger, bright with my wetness, into my mouth. Holding eye contact, I suck it in and hollow out my cheeks. A blackness takes over his eyes when his pupils dilate, and I'm pretty sure I could convince him to take me right here, right now. His teeth sink into his bottom lip, and just for a moment, it's just the two of us.

"Look at this. We can put lavender scent in," Chase says, breaking the spell holding us captive. Chase holds up two small, scented bags for us to see. Our eyes dart to him, and he grins, ripping open the packages, and dumps them all in. The heavenly scent of lavender and relaxation pulses through the room, carried by the billowing steam of the hot bath running into the large tub.

We're jolted out of relaxation when Grumpy storms through the front door of the hotel room with a loud bang. His curses ring throughout the entire hotel room on incoherent mutters, but I still know what he's saying. Fuck this and fuck that and fuck my dad. The list goes on. The click of the lock mechanism locks into place, making this room feel ten times more secure. We all share a look when his loud footfalls sound up the metal staircase with more explicit curses pouring from his lips. If this is any indication to how the rest of his night went when we left, then it can only mean bad things are brewing.

Carter doesn't stop when he makes it up the stairs into the lofted bathroom carrying three large bottles. One whiskey, one dark wine, and one bubbly wine in a pink bottle. He sets them down on the ground with care, grabbing me from the spot I stand in with force. I fall into his arms, yelping my protests. He pulls me up his body, forcing me to wrap my legs around his waist, trusting him. He doesn't stop when he gets to the edge of the tub to remove his clothes or mine. Instead, like the madman he is, he climbs into the hot water and sinks into it. Only when we're fully seated and the water rests against my belly, does he finally blow out a breath. His fingers intertwine in my hair, wrapping it around his fist. Our foreheads rest together, breathing the same air. His hold tightens around me impossibly tight. I don't dare move a muscle or breathe in fear of what he'll say next. Whatever prompted this move was one of desperation. He's grounding himself to me and protecting me in his grip. Even though everyone present in this room would never harm me.

"She goes nowhere fucking alone, from here on out," Carter growls, looking at each of the boys.

The boys don't utter a word when they strip to their boxers, joining us in the tub's warmth. Someone activates the jets, swirling the salts even more. The relaxing lavender spills into every part of the tub and room. My body relaxes in his embrace, but his muscles don't seem to get the message. He tenses around me, breathing hard. Finally he sits back, staring deep into my eyes. And I, once again, get lost in the vastness of his telling eyes. His are truly the windows to his soul, showing his vulnerabilities, and everything he's feeling.

"Did anything happen after we left?" Zepp asks with caution, keeping his distance from the clingy monster holding me tighter.

"Nothing between my father and me, but Alpha made a fucking reappearance and texted me," Carter says through labored breaths. His chest expands and deflates at an alarming rate.

"What did they say?" I ask, wrapping my broken arm around the back of his neck.

My stomach turns in knots at the sight of fear resting deep in the depths of his expressive brown eyes.

"They said, 'Only a little while longer. Stay true to the course.'" His muscles melt under my touch, releasing an ounce of tension, but something more lingers in his eyes, giving me the illusion he's not telling me everything. Any trace of his anger disappears before my eyes as he looks up at me, memorizing my face at this moment.

"You think they're closing in?" Seger asks, moving his fingers through the warm water.

"Time is running out," Zepp says, nodding his head.

"Yeah," Carter huffs, "Time is not on our side. Their fucking ears and eyes are everywhere."

"You don't think they'd try anything here. Do you?" Chase asks, worry lines creasing his forehead.

His eyes dart over the railing, almost as if he suspects someone will beat down the door to get to me. I mean, they could. Everyone in this town is obviously in on whatever they do. They could probably steal me in broad daylight, slit my throat, and leave me for dead. No one would bat an eye. I swallow hard at that imagery, hoping it never comes to that. I know time is not on my side, but I don't want to think about what they want from me. Could I last five days in their grasp, if that's what it came down to?

"With the entire town here, I don't think they'd lift a finger tonight. But only tonight," Zepp trails off, staring out the darkened windows. I can tell the moment his thoughts pull him in and consume him, his jaw begins to tick.

"So the question is, when do they strike? And how?" Seger asks, trying to keep the anger out of his voice.

"Again, with the fucking questions we have no answers to," Carter says through clenched teeth.

"You think they'll tell you? Bring you in on whatever?"

Chase asks, slipping down into the water, submerging his chin into the heat.

"I don't fucking know," Carter says through a defeated sigh and closes his eyes. "They haven't so far. I never know what the fuck they're up to. Like tonight, why the hell was she invited? Why did my father look at her like a prized possession? Just why?" I wrap him tighter in my arms, resting my forehead against his. He blinks a few times, losing himself in my eyes, and I let him. He needs to step out of reality and into whatever world he can find inside me.

"We will figure it out," I mumble with reassurance. "But for now," I sigh, sitting up and cupping his cheeks. "Take my mind off of tonight?"

His brown eyes quickly spark to life, transforming from dull to hooded at my request. His fingers tighten around my waist. "You really want that, Sweetheart?" His deep voice cracks in a husky whisper. I know it's the moment he and Seger have been waiting for over the past month. Tonight is the night they finally get to use their pierced dicks.

Three sets of eyes stare us down with volcanic levels of heat. Their breaths stall inside their chests—growing, desperate heat brews between the five of us. Tensions rise to a fever pitch, so palpable we could grasp it. Every inch of me trembles with anticipation. The boys move in, encompassing us in a circle, intent on worshiping every inch of me.

"Yes, please," I whisper, sinking my teeth into my bottom lip.

# EIGHTEEN

### KAYCEE

"Let's get this dress off." Light as feather touches dance along my shoulder, pulling the sleeves of my dress down my arms. Shivers trickle up and down my spine despite the heat steaming off the water, and goosebumps line my arms.

"And this," Seger mumbles, reaching for my removable cast, but waiting for my approval.

I give him a sharp nod, and we work together, undoing the Velcro straps holding my arm in. Once he slides the hard plastic cast off, he sets it in a dry area and sets my under-sleeve with it, too. I groan, stretching my fingers and slowly moving my arm straight. It's been over a month since my surgery, and I'm allowed to move it around slowly. Other than sleeping and bathing, I'm supposed to wear my cast. I'm just thankful they took the hard plaster one off, and gave me one I could take off after Thanksgiving.

I sigh when the fingers roam over my body, and it hits me hard. I'll never get over how much they affect me, how one simple touch sends my body into bliss instead of turmoil.

I lean my head back against Seger's shoulder. Multiple fingers pull at my soaked dress, sticking to every inch of my skin. Yanking and tearing it down my body with several grunts, the fabric falls away, leaving me bare—exposed to the room. Their eyes feast on me like a delicious dinner presented to them on a platter for them to consume. I don't have to look up to feel the fiery heat roaring in their eyes.

"Fuck," Seger mutters, running his fingers down the slope of my breast.

The brush of his fingertips circles my nipple until it buds painfully tight and stiff. The same gentle fingers flick it and then the other, moving back to their delicate swirls. It's delicious torture I want them to repeat over and over again.

"No underwear? No bra?" Zepp asks in a husky voice, dropping low with need.

Warm breaths pass across my nipple, followed by the warmth of a moist tongue. Circling. Nipping. Sucking. Over and over again, driving me to insanity. I try to reply with words. I really do. But my tongue sticks to the roof of my mouth, and a desert appears, drying everything out. I moan when he cups my pussy.

They all work together in tandem to work me up but don't allow me to go over the edge. Bastards. The peak of my orgasm blossoms in my abdomen, and then they all back off as one. They're like-minded, reading each other so easily when it comes to torturing me with expert hands.

A finger lightly brushes against my clit in feather-like strokes, going in tiny circles. I arch my back, trying to force myself down on it. But whoever it is chuckles at my desperation for more. I throw my head back, moaning to the ceiling when lightning bolts blast through my body, tightening my nipples to hard buds again.

Someone finally has mercy on their poor girlfriend when heavy circles push against my aching clit. Stars form in my eyes, and I grind heavily against them. Mentally, I beg someone to screw my brains out in a hurry before I explode around nothing when all I want to do is come around someone's cock. I suck in a breath, and everything stalls around me. In all different directions, four fingers enter me one by one. Together, like a damn dream team, they work their fingers in and out. I babble incoherent moans, half begging them to stop and half begging them never to stop. My brain can't decide when my nerve endings ignite, taking over my rational thoughts.

"Fuck, Angel," Seger hisses from behind me, poking my ass with his excitement.

His new metal accessory on the tip of his dick slides against my skin, eliciting more moans and sharp shivers. Thankfully, it's been a month, and both boys were cleared to engage in sexual activity. And it just so happened that today was the day they got the green light.

I cry out in frustration when they pull their fingers away, leaving only one.

"Sunshine," Chase whispers. "You're so wet," he groans, running his fingers through my wetness and coating his fingers.

"So fucking ready for us," Carter grunts, fisting himself in hard strokes.

I'm again dickmatized by his length, shiny with his newly-healed piercings. I swallow hard, imagining what it will feel like deep inside me. We've waited so long to do this, and tonight is the night we try them out. It's been a hard month of not coming for them.

Precum drips from his throbbing red tip as he stalks toward me, completely nude through the water. As Carter parts the water with his steps, he makes his intentions perfectly clear. It's written all over his determined, snarly face. Carter is the predator swimming in the depths of the water, and I'm the willing prey, standing stock still and waiting for him.

Seger kisses my cheek. "I think Grumpy needs you more than me right now," he murmurs, not taking his eyes off the predator standing before me. Before stepping out of the tub, he kisses me and sits behind Chase, who lounges in the water.

Carter's rough grip wraps around my hips, bending me, and wrapping himself around me. The heavy beat of his heart pounds against my back and his bent knees split around me, forcing me to my tippy toes. His arm wraps around my waist once he has me where he wants me and only stops to put on a condom. And then—then he slams home, jamming himself completely inside with a loud grunt, nearly knocking me forward.

My arms reach out, clinging to the outside of the tub to anchor myself when he thrusts again and again, knocking his hips into mine with such force, I sputter a breath, gasping for air when he pounds into me, not waiting for me to adjust or ask me if I'm okay this time. He fucks me—hard, harder than he's ever fucked before. His breaths wheeze in his chest with every heavy pound he gives, and our skin slapping echoes through the room. My eyes roll into my head when his grip tightens, and I swear his dick swells to a bigger size. His piercings rub against my pussy walls, and my toes curl from the sensations. They always said it'd be worth the wait, and boy, were they right.

"Fuck," he grunts again, picking up speed and pounding into me until my ass jiggles and tingles.

Carter's aching heart pounds against my back as he stops to catch his frantic breaths, tightening his hold across my waist. His chest heaves, slick with sweat again.

"It'll be okay," I whisper in a strained voice. My fingers brush his hand, interlocking our fingers together, trying to reassure him I won't slip away from him.

"It'll be fucking okay when I roast those sick mother fuckers trying to hurt you. Until then—until then, I won't rest...."

"We'll all protect her," Zepp says quietly, earning head nods from the other two.

"All for one, and one for all, or some shit," Chase says, dropping to his knees.

The water in the tub barely skims his pecs, hitting my upper thighs. Even if it went over his head, I don't think he'd mind drowning at my feet. Lust swims in the depths of his gray eyes when he peers up at me, licking his lips.

Seger snorts, rolling his eyes. "We aren't the damn musketeers."

"We're the Kayceeteers." Chase snorts, fist-pumping to his stupid joke and splashing water everywhere with a silly grin.

"You guys are stupid," I breathe a laugh, running my fingers through Chase's shaggy blonde locks from where he looks up at me on his knees.

Carter groans as I squeeze around him. "Fuckity fuck, shut up," he says, pulling out and slamming back in.

Every thought taking up real estate inside my mind evaporates into thin air, fucked to the darkest part of my mind. It's locked away with the key thrown into the abyss by the big dick screwing me so hard I don't remember my name anymore. Who am I? No one. Who is after me? No one right now.

His breaths become manic and wild with every thrust—growling and snarling at anyone who looks at me, marking his damn territory. He owns me now, possessing me in every sense of the word, while the others stand back and watch with hooded eyes. It's weird to think three guys can sit around watching their girlfriend getting railed by a man who was once their biggest enemy. A man they warned me to stay away from so many times. But here he is, locking eyes with them, fucking me however he wants.

Carter slows his thrusts, coming to a stop, leaving himself buried deep inside me. Again. Reaching between my legs, his fingers spread me like a damn dessert and revealing my clit for a feast.

"Make her come, Elf Ears," Carter grunts, reaching around to grab Chase's head.

I expect a protest for the use of that ridiculous nickname. Instead, I get exactly what I want without him uttering a word. *Oh, God. Yes.* My lips pop open at the sensation of Chase's warm tongue lapping at my clit and moan toward the ceiling, throwing my head back onto Carter's chest. A shiver works down my spine when Chase grins against my flesh teasingly like he's secretly up to no good. When the tip of his tongue curls against my clit, I finally catch on to the words he's spelling out with the tip of his tongue like a pencil.

*Chase Tate Benoit.*

He does it again and again, tracing his name. Then he moves on to Seger's full name—middle name in-friggin-cluded. Fuck. I'm going to die of orgasms, if that's even possible.

Lapping away, his tongue puts more and more pressure on my throbbing clit. I beg and pant for a quick release, reaching to rest my fingers in his hair. But the only response I receive is a vibrating chuckle. He's teasing me. Fucking teasing me. He knows I'm close, but he holds back. He swirls his tongue, circling, taking the pressure away, and drawing out Seger's full name.

*Seger Dominic West.*

Oh, God. Swirl. Swirl. Letter. Another damn letter. Another, and another—oh hell. I'm going to combust before he does everyone else's name. But he backs off again, trailing kisses on my inner thighs. I briefly thought of slamming my thighs closed and forcing him back again, but he must have read my mind. He dives back in, this time spelling Zeppelin's full name.

*Zeppelin Declan West.*

Fuck. My head lolls back on its own, no longer able to keep it upright.

*Carter James Cunningham*

"Mmm, Sunshine," Chase's muffled voice says between licks. "You taste delicious as always." Twisted words slip from my weighted tongue, making little sense if any.

If you ran the alphabet together, you'd get aklsdjfak; lsdjf; aklsdjflajds. And that's what I sound like, panting like a dog.

And then, Carter opens his smooth mouth, incapacitating me more—smooth fucker.

"I'm claiming your ass today," Carter whispers, nipping at my ear. Goosebumps erupt on every piece of my naked flesh. My pussy flutters around him, nearly coming on the spot, but Chase keeps holding off on the pressure. Writing their names as soft as possible on my clit.

"Mmhmm," he whispers again. "I thought you might like that. I'm going to shove my baseball bat dick so far up your ass, and you'll remember who you belong to. You're mine. You're theirs. You'll remember that, won't you? You won't go wandering off doing stupid shit and hurt yourself, will you? No. You're. Fucking. Ours." Words are unattainable right now, no matter if I could get my tongue to work, I can't make a sound.

"Words, baby girl." Zepp's warm breaths flutter against my breast, sucking my hardened nipple into his mouth. The slickness of his tongue rolls over the tip, shuddering my body.

"She's so close," Carter grits out, running a hand through my hair. He grabs hold, angling my head to expose my neck.

His thrusts start up again, slow and steady. He's holding back with every ounce of willpower he possesses. He wants to ram into me to keep claiming me until I'm a mess.

"Faster," he hisses, shoving his fingers into Chase's hair, shoving his face further into me.

Without protest, Chase's tongue works double-time, sweeping back and forth. Up and down. Spinning in circles until his whole mouth suctions around my clit. Forget the names he's etching onto my clit; he's driving this whole thing home in one flick of his tongue.

I detonate with a sharp cry, exploding into oblivion and calling out their names in raspy chants. I curl my fingers tighter in Chase's hair. Shit. I'm a goner, sinking further and further into the abyss of my blinding orgasm. White takes over my vision, and my muscles seize, spasming and contracting without my consent.

"Holy shit," Chase rasps, climbing to his shaky feet.

My blurry eyes open on his glistening face. He leans in, forcing his tongue into my mouth, letting me taste myself on his wicked tongue.

Carter grunts, pulling himself out of my pussy. His fingers dance in my come, collecting it. I moan into Chase's mouth, grabbing the sides of his face. Carter preps me with his fingers, loosening my ass slowly.

My limbs wobble like limp noodles in Carter's arms. When they promised to take my chaotic thoughts away, they delivered. My breaths shudder in my chest: my heart pounds, a desperate drumbeat against my ribs.

"Come here," Chase whispers, guiding my body onto him. His dick throbs, looking angry and purple from holding back for so long. He enters my pussy in one agonizingly slow thrust. Groaning his name, I lean forward, capturing his lips with mine.

Carter settles behind me, patiently pushing himself into my ass. He takes his time, shoving his gigantic dick into me with the help of lube, and I'm thankful. My body would have rejected him if he had gone too quickly. He's thicker and longer than the other three. I was always too scared to take him there, but that fear evades me right now.

Every inch of my body bursts into flames as they work together, thrusting in tandem. One in, one out. Over and over. Fingers brush my sensitive clit, sending shivers down my spine. I clench around them, making them groan together, picking up their speed.

Hands glide through my hair, grabbing hold. I don't care who it is or what they want me to do. I'll do anything right now. Zepp stands beside Chase outside the tub, stroking himself from base to tip, rolling his thumb over his leaking slit. He stares down at me with a raw, longing hunger swimming in his eyes.

And who am I to deny him anything?

My tongue swirls over his tip, humming with appreciation. Hollowing out my cheeks, I suck his throbbing dick into my mouth the rest of the way. I bob my head and take him into the back of my relaxed throat, receiving his moans and mumbled words of praise.

"Fuck shit," Carter grunts. His hips slap heavily against mine, moving my entire body forward, forcing me up and down on Chase.

Chase's face twists as he grunts, lifting his hips, meeting me thrust-for-thrust. He throbs harder, bouncing off my fluttering walls. Fingers dig into my flesh, leaving bruises behind in their wake. Three distinctive grunts echo throughout the bathroom. Carter's deep growly whines. Chase's wheezing grunts. And Zepp's breathless murmurs. They're a symphony playing in harmony with each other—strings whining in tune, orchestrating a single prayer of worship to my body.

When I open my watery eyes, Zepp takes a step back. His chest heaves, glistening with a sheen of sweat. "Later, baby girl," he murmurs, running a finger down my aching jaw. "If I keep this up, I'll come down your throat." I arch a brow at him, and he grins. "I want to bury myself deep in your ass before coming." I shiver at his words. Yeah, okay. That works, too.

Carter bites into the crook of my neck, grunting my name. His hips sputter with uneven thrusts. Every muscle in his body tightens, getting more rigid and out of control.

"Ahh, fuck!" He grunts, stilling inside of me. The warmth of his come spills into me as he holds my flesh tight between his teeth. Clamping down harder and harder until I think he's going to break through the flesh and spill blood.

"Jesus, Kaycee," Chase moans, clutching onto me.

Watching Chase's expressive face contort and twist into ecstasy is a fantastic sight that sets off another explosion of my own. With his head thrown back, beautiful gray eyes screwed shut, and his mouth hanging open—it's a true sight of beauty. I could stare at it all day.

As we sit in the tub fused together, catching our breaths, no one makes a move to disentangle. No one utters a word. We simply take our time coming back to the moment while our chaotic breaths mingle together.

"I love you," I whisper, looking at both of them. "So much," I say, catching each of their eyes.

Chase's smile takes over his entire face, lighting up his eyes and wrinkling his nose. Kissing my lips, he returns the words in a murmur and expresses all of his love.

Carter sighs, kissing my cheek, and nods. Huh, well then. He's still in denial about our love, but that's okay. I'll give him time to figure it out. After everything with his parents, I don't blame him. Not at all. So I'll be patient and let him come to me when he's ready to say it. But I secretly feel it with every interaction and every small touch. Carter loves me. He can't get it past his tight lips, yet. Whatever, I've managed to tame him a little, which counts to me.

Carter and Chase move to the other side of the tub, leaning back with dopey grins on their face.

"Oh, baby, this isn't going to last long," Seger groans, grabbing me by the hips.

"You never fucking last long, you two-pump chump," Carter says from across the tub, earning himself a scathing stare.

"So fucking what? My girlfriend has an amazing pussy. So,

fuck off," Seger retorts, peppering kisses along my neck until he's a breath away from my lips. "It may not last long, but you always feel so damn good," he murmurs right before he softly plants his lips against mine.

Our tongues glide against each other in a wild dance when he urgently brings me forward onto his lap. He moans, moving my hips back and forth just enough for his tip to brush against my pussy. Reaching down, I pump his length in my hand a few times, reveling in the feel of his new piercing against my palm. Seger swats my hand away, adding a condom on, and then I line myself up. We groan in unison with relief when I sink onto him, and he stretches my aching pussy, using Chase's dripping cum to guide him further in.

My hips roll forward, encouraged by his hands on my waist. He moans my name, only stopping to lean me against him. My forehead rests against his, peering into the depth of his eyes full of love and lust.

Zeppelin works himself into my ass, carefully spreading me wide without discomfort. I heave a breath when his tip pushes through my tight hole, and he slips the rest of the way in with a muted curse.

"Fuck yes," Seger whispers, weaving his fingers through my hair. He yanks my lips down to his with force, and his tongue invades my mouth. He swallows my moans, thrusting himself up into me.

"See, baby girl, " Zepp whispers, holding tight to my hips. "This is exactly where I wanted to be," he groans, burying himself to the hilt. His entire body trembles when he pulls out and pushes back in, almost succumbing to his impending orgasm.

Seger curses beneath his breath when he begins to move with Zepp's thrusts, and my pussy tightens around him. I cry out when fingers pinch my nipples and twist them until they're throbbing. But just as quickly as the pain comes, a warm tongue wraps around it and soothes out the sharp pain.

Stiff fingers circle my clit, overwhelming every inch of me. The pressure builds deep in my abdomen, setting everything inside me on fire.

"Yes," I moan, leaning my head back on Zepp's shoulder. "Yes, yes, yes." My raspy chant echoes through the entire hotel room, amplified by the echoey bathroom.

"Come, Angel. Come. You're killing me," Seger begs in a strained voice, brushing his tongue along the seams of my lips. I moan into his mouth, grinding my hips on his, earning moans from the twins.

"Baby girl, come," Zepp whispers, dragging his teeth on my neck.

Another orgasm wreaks havoc on my body—shivering and moaning, I'm panting their names. The boys go over the edge with me, joining me in ecstasy and emptying themselves inside of me. We slump as one, murmuring our love to one another.

I heave a sigh, resting my forehead against Seger's shoulder when Zepp pulls out. His warm fingers move up and down my back, splashing water and cleaning me up. Seger lifts me from his embrace and sets me beside him.

"Did we distract you enough?" Seger murmurs, kissing the edge of my lips.

"Mmhmmm," I murmur when my eyes flutter, fighting off the overwhelming need to fall asleep.

"Let's get you to bed, baby girl." Zepp reaches down and picks me up like I'm a damn feather.

I don't bother to open my eyes when two towels dry me off, put my cast back on, and deposit me onto the softness of the big bed. The boys murmur around me, probably telling secrets to each other, but eventually settle into bed.

Seger and Chase encase me in their body heat, one on each side of me. Carter's head rests on my stomach with his arms winding around my body, holding me tight. Zeppelin takes his usual spot above me, threading his fingers through my hair, massaging and softly pulling the roots in a relaxing way.

We fall asleep in each other's arms, drifting away with the distant memory of the danger lurking in the shadows, waiting to pounce. Whatever tonight was or whatever they were trying to achieve, we still don't know. To me, it was a show. But for who or what, I'm stumped.

Why would the whole town line up get a glimpse of me?

# NINETEEN

## CHASE

Carter looms over my girl, weaving his fingers through her long hair, and yanks her head back. Her sexy gasp goes straight to my balls, and little Chase perks up inside my basketball shorts. Not now, fella. We have to wait until this giant takes his damn leave before we can act.

Shit! Come on, Grumpy! Leave already so I can hog my girl to myself. Mentally I whine, throwing my limbs all around like a child in the midst of a tantrum. I'm half tempted to throw myself on the ground, kicking and screaming so he fucks off already. He'd give me a weird look, or shit, he'd probably kick me in the head and kidnap her. I frown. That would be counterproductive on my part. I'm trying to get her alone so I can have my wicked way with her, not get her kidnapped by her other boyfriend who insists he needs to leave.

I throw my head back and stare up at the ceiling. Shit, is that too much to ask for one on one time with my girl? I never get time to get my hands on her all by myself. Sharing is caring and all that shit, but I need my girl tonight. She's mine. I called dibs. Plus, I have lots and lots of plans which include her pussy, my dick, and maybe a movie or two. I'd love to shove my tongue down her throat and–shit, calm down, dude. I purse my lips, trying to think about football or my damn grandma in a bathing suit, and discreetly put my hand over my aching junk. The last thing I need to do is salute Grumpy with my dick before he leaves.

"Be a good fucking girl," he says in that low, demanding voice he loves to use on her.

And...my dick bounces, too. You, sir, are getting way too comfortable with his bossy ways–I think, looking down at the offending appendage with a stern eye. We can't get turned on by Grumpy's gruff commands...not here anyway. When I look up from my dick that won't go down, I catch Kaycee's eyes, and she raises a brow. So, back to the ceiling my eyes go. I whistle in my mind like I wasn't doing anything at all.

"I'll be back later after checking on my dad's computer for something."

Something? Something? What the hell does that mean, exactly? Grumpy hasn't been very forthcoming with information lately, and I'm starting to suspect he's up to something. But what could that something be? Hmmm? I don't want to say I'm suspicious as hell, but shit, I'm suspicious as hell about how tight his lips have been. Ever since he broke into his dad's office and ran into Piper, he's been keeping something from us. Question is, what is that something? I never want to think the worst of Grumpy; especially now that he's weaseled his way into this relationship–which again, is my fault. Well, I'll blame Seger, too. Zepp was resistant at first, but we all know who holds the balls in this five-way relationship. It sure as shit isn't any of us. It's my little lady who is currently staring daggers into the Grumpy man clinging to her hair. Shoo, boy! Go! But I know we'll be here in this standoff for awhile, judging by the defiant look she's giving him. I cross my arms over my chest in irritation, letting little Chase fly high. Fuck it. Maybe my dick will scare him away.

"I'm always good," she mumbles, fiddling with the diamond bracelet we got her, or should I say, my rich ass friends, got her as a Christmas present. It's a beautiful piece we all picked out together and planned for. My only contribution was talking the sales lady into giving it to us at a lower price and expediting the process.

One of these days my dad will be out of Veritas' hold, and then we'll be back to normal once they clear his name. That's all I want. I want my dad to be out of custody and back with us. My stomach churns at him being stuck there forever, but Kaycee and Carter have assured me he'll be out before I know it. I sure hope so. I know they wouldn't lie to me. They've seen the evidence and shown me, but still. It hurts to know he's stuck there for now, and there's nothing I can do about it. Shit, we can't even visit him yet. I haven't seen him since the start of school.

I lick my lips and check my phone. He should call me soon since I didn't get to say hello on Christmas a few days ago. My heart sinks thinking about Ainsley and me spending Christmas alone in my apartment. If it weren't for my found family coming to our rescue this morning and bringing us to this Christmas Wonderland in the Maze House, we probably would have had a shitty Christmas.

My brows furrow when I refocus on my surroundings, and Kaycee and Carter are gone. Shit! Maybe he did kidnap her, afterall. And then left me by myself! Can't he see the desperation standing at attention in my damn shorts? What a dick. I huff, moving to stare out the window, and look for their shadows in the bushes. But I don't have to stare long when I feel Carter's presence looming behind me. Good, he didn't take her. Before I turn around to face him, I put my hand over my stupid dick and turn around. He eyes my hand, but thankfully doesn't make any of his usual Grumpy comments. I'm, instead, greeted by the most serious face I've ever come across. Or he needs to poop—maybe that's why he's going home.

"Keep her safe, Elf Ears. Don't fucking make me regret

having to leave," he hisses with an unmistakable threat in his voice. His eyes dart to the object of our affection sitting on the couch, staring down at her phone with a grin.

"You think I'd let her get hurt?" I ask, grinding my teeth.

The asshole always thinks the worst of me and my poor ears. I mean, they aren't even elfish. And even if they were, girls dig that! More specifically, my girl. Especially when she nibbles on them and–shit...my dick throbs again, and I squeeze the tip to make this damn boner go away. You'd think I never got laid by the way he's acting.

He sighs, running a hand down his face. Thank fuck he can't read my mind. He'd know I was thinking about his ass to make my boner go away, and...yeah, it's not working. Grandma in a bathing suit! Grandpa in a bathing suit! Fuck. My mom in a bathing suit? Oh, shit. Relief spears through me, okay. That did it. From now on if I'm horny and I don't want to be, it'll be mom on my brain.

"Fuck, I know you wouldn't. But with the twins gone on some weird emergency again, I'm just on fucking edge right now. I can't fucking place it, but something feels off. Just stay inside, okay?" Carter's eyes always tell a true story to us, and right now, I see the genuine worry resting in them when he looks at me.

Right. The new nurse Zepp and Seger hired called them back home for an emergency. Again. This seems to happen more now. Something about Corbin trying to burn the house down or wander into the woods in his damn birthday suit. Maybe it was him walking naked outside in the middle of winter with his wrinkly ass on display. Shit, maybe he took another wife, and he's run away with her. Anything is a possibility with that old bastard—especially the nudity part. Who the hell knows?

"You think something is about to go down?" I ask as my skin prickles with anxiety, and my gut rolls.

"I don't fucking know. I know that she better be fucking safe by the time tomorrow rolls around, Elf Ears." He says, squeezing my shoulder in his massive grip. Shit. He's going to squeeze my damn shoulder right out of the socket if he doesn't take his monster hand off me. I peer down at his hands again. Shit, they're huge. You know, I think Kace was right. The bigger the hands, the bigger the…..No. Nope. Gotta stop these thoughts right here and now or little Chase will spring back to life.

Mom in a bathing suit! And focus, dickbag. I take a deep breath and fucking ground myself to the situation. Carter is about to leave, and there's a possible threat lurking in the damn shadows.

"Is… is campus secure?" My insecurities gnaw at my rolling insides, and I peek at Kaycee, hoping I can keep her safe while everyone else is away.

"Last I checked before we came, no one else was on fucking campus. The parking lots are empty. The school is a ghost town because of Christmas. Fuck, even the security guards are gone. They shut the school down," he says in a gruff tone, grinding his teeth together. "But I just got a fucking notification and have a hit on that fucking website I've been looking into. I need to get back and see what the fuck they're up to before it's too late." Sincerity bleeds into his eyes when he cocks his head and narrows his eyes. "I ain't fucking lying," he adds through a grumble.

Yeah, I believe him. I'd never doubt Grumpy for a second. All I know is he's been keeping something from us, but it must not be important. Or maybe it's too scary for us to handle. Shit! Why can't he just tell me? Momentary relief rocks through me at the prospect of being completely alone on campus. If he hasn't spotted anyone on the cameras during his surveillance, then I know we're good. But I still have that weird, nagging feeling in the back of my mind. The stupid cult has been way too silent since their car crash over a month ago. In fact, we haven't heard a damn thing from them since the charity event. Maybe a few stares here and there, but nothing major. So, what the shit is about to happen? It's the calm before the storm. Shit, so much for my relief.

"Yeah. Shit. I know, but you're freaking me the fuck out," I grumble when he squeezes my shoulder one last time–almost affectionately. I stare down at his massive hand again and sigh. "Whatever happens tonight, I'll keep her as safe as possible. Now, get the hell out of here," I say in a light tone, shooing him away.

He raises a brow and frowns, but does as he's told and stalks off like a psycho on some sort of psycho mission. Shit, maybe I should warn the townsfolk. Psycho on the loose! Warn the entire world before he burns it down! I'm thrown out of my weird thoughts when the door slams behind him, shaking the walls and rattling the decorations almost off the wall. I wonder how pissed the twins would be if he broke their precious decorations?

A sinking sensation tugs at my lower gut, and my face falls when I turn back towards the window, looking through the pitch-black night. Shit, maybe we should have gone with him for safety purposes and then boned Kaycee long and hard in his bed. How pissed would he be when I fucked her while he worked? Probably a shit ton. We'd be safe, at least. Well maybe. He might resort to violence if I did that.

I think back to his words as I stare out the window–the entire campus is dark, and no one is here. It's just me, Grumpy, and Kaycee on site. So, I have to trust his words. We should be safely nestled inside the Maze House until everyone comes back. Shit, what could go wrong in a matter of hours? Yeah, famous last words every murder victim in the horror movies ever spoke. I mentally facepalm. Whatever, we'll stay here, enjoy each other's company, have some eggnog, and then sleep cuddled on our massive bed. Shit, yeah. That's the life. And nothing, I repeat, nothing will go wrong! Dream it til you believe it, right?

Carter's enormous silhouette disappears through the maze until the darkness swallows him whole. Even the stars refuse to show themselves through the ominous clouds, brewing a crisp winter wind. It knocks against the bushes, and their finger-like branches sway in the breeze, looking like they're about to break through the windows and grab us. Shaking my head, I knock the thoughts from my mind. We're fine. Everything's a-okay! Nothing to see here. I need to knock this shit off and focus on my girl. Tonight is fine; everything is fucking fine. Nothing but me and my sexy as hell girlfriend alone in the Maze House—all good here.

I relax my tense body when a set of small arms wraps around my waist, and her head nuzzles into my back. I regain my breath, thinking of the here and now, not what could come.

"Did you have a good day?" She whispers, kissing my back through my t-shirt.

A grin takes over when I spin to face her and cradle her face in my palms. The excitement we had surprising her with our own little Christmas in the Maze House was something out of a fucking movie. Her eyes lit up when we revealed the Christmas tree by the window and the twins' sparse decorations from when their mom was alive. It's been the best fucking day, plus we gave her our special present—a diamond bracelet. It's something we've planned for weeks now, and finally, it's sitting on her wrist.

"The best day, Sunshine. But I think it's about to get even better," I murmur, kissing along her jawline, tracking every hitch of her breath and the low whines in her throat. "Wanna watch a movie and snuggle?" I ask, licking my way down her smooth neck.

My dick presses against my gym shorts, begging to be seen by the one woman he adores. And okay, I love her too. This time though, I let myself imagine her standing naked before me. I swear to shit I'm going to drop to my knees, worship her cunt, and then beg her to marry me. Shit—is it too soon for a marriage proposal? Nah. I may be eighteen, but I know what I want in my life. And it's her–it has been since the moment I laid eyes on her. I think that's why when she got marked, and we were blackmailed into stepping away from her that it hurt so bad. When I look to the future, I see Kaycee standing in the sun. Like my own literal sunshine.

"Yes," she gasps out, clinging to the front of my shirt, pulling me close.

Our bodies fuse, and I grin when I nip her flesh between my teeth, pulling more moans out of her beautiful fucking throat. It's like music to my little elf ears, hearing her beg for me to do more with tiny noises. Moving my hand down to her ass, I squeeze it in my hands, rolling her hips towards me. I'm sure by now my dick is poking her in the middle of her stomach, and I'm even more positive she feels it when her fingers wrap around it. Ugh. Fuck. I shutter, almost coming undone when she pumps my dick through my shorts. Yeah–there's a marriage proposal in the future I can feel it in my… well my dick.

My eyes bug out when she drops to her knees in the kitchen and stares up at me with those big blue eyes full of wonder. I swallow hard.

"Sunshine," I murmur, brushing my fingers through her hair and moving it away from her eyes.

Every time she stares at me like that, I fall apart on the inside. Hell, even the outside. My Sunshine knows exactly what she does to me.

I suck in a breath when she unties the strings of my basketball shorts and pulls them down my thighs with vigor. Her painted red fingernails brush over my skin when she reaches up, freeing my cock from the constricting confines of my boxers. Pre-cum leaks from my slit when she wets her lips and looks at him head-on with determination in her eyes. My eyes roll back when all the blood rushes from one head to the other, gathering at the tip of my raging hard-on once again. Pillow soft lips brush against my mushroom head, laying soft kisses, and barely touching my heated flesh.

Goddamn. Shitballs.

I heave a breath when the warmth of her tongue leaves a trail of spit over my tip. And when my eyes peer down at her, they fill with lust when my sticky pre-cum leaves a line from her lips to my dick. I almost come from the sight but hold back when her entire warm mouth encases my tip and sucks it in.

Don't hip thrust. Don't hump her gorgeous face. Shit. This is harder than my dick.

"You've had a hard few days," she says in a sultry voice.

Will. Not. Hump. *Yet*.

I swallow hard, looking down at the girl I'm lucky to have in my life. I often think about what would have happened if I hadn't pursued her when she first showed up. That image plays in my mind repeatedly. She was standing by the parking lot, looking over at all of us, with her sister by her side. Shit, she even distracted Seger enough that he threw the football her way instead of to me. If she hadn't handed it back…. If she hadn't been so damn elusive with her name, we might not all be here. But for some reason, she intrigued me, and I always go after what I want. I'm the luckiest son of a bitch on the planet.

"Yeah," I breathe, "it's been a weird few days." My fingers run through her hair, gathering it in my grasp. "And I have a feeling… Oh, god, Sunshine," I gasp, trying hard not to buck my hips and shove my cock down her throat when she takes me entirely into her mouth.

I groan when my tip hits the back of her throat, and she

gags around me, pulling me out. She rests my tip along her lips, rubbing it along them like she's putting on chapstick, and slathers them with the mixture of spit and pre-cum. Her tongue pokes out, tracing my slit, and then she takes me back into her warm and inviting mouth.

Shit!

I lean my head back, reveling in the feeling of having her all to myself and wrapped around me like I've been fantasizing about all day. It's times like this I crave. Don't get me wrong, sharing her with my two best friends and that overprotective dick is fine. But I enjoy these times when I get to hold my Sunshine and cuddle her to my chest. And she's all mine.

"Jesus, Sunshine," I rasp when my balls tighten and forcefully hold her against me. I want to capture this feeling, put it in a jar, and keep it forever in my grasp.

She hums her approval, running her tongue on the underside of my dick. Tricky woman. She knows all the little buttons to push to make me cum faster than lightning. Shit! I come undone completely when her fingernails lightly scratch at my balls, and I explode into her mouth like I haven't come in months. My fingers tighten in her hair, holding her against me until I've emptied every ounce of cum from my balls into her mouth.

My body completely deflates, slumping forward, as I try to catch my breath. As she comes up off her knees, she stares at me with a small smile, running her fingers over my heaving chest. Running my thumb over her swollen lips, I gather the cum sitting at the edge of them, and shove it back into her mouth. Little Chase reawakens the moment her tongue laps at the cum on the tip of my thumb with a satisfied hum.

*Not now, dude. We just got off.* I mentally chastise my dick saluting us again. Which doesn't go unnoticed by Kaycee when she grins at me.

"Better?" she rasps with lust swimming in her eyes.

I bring her salty lips to mine, not fucking caring my cum was just on her tongue. "You spoil me."

I want to leave her breathless and with legs full of jelly, and I won't stop until she does. Shit, maybe I can convince her to smother me with her pussy and ride my face while screaming yeehaw, Chase! Damn, what a visual that is. You think I could convince her to get cowboy boots and a hat? Oh, oh! Maybe some assless chaps, too. We gotta work on our roleplay someday because I have so many fantasies I want to reenact. I should make a list... Damn it, dude. I groan, forcing my dick back into my boxers, and pull up my shorts. If I keep thinking like this I might have to bend her over the damn countertops and fuck her raw.

"Yeah, now let's go watch that movie! What time was your dad supposed to call?" She asks, moving towards the fridge for two sodas. She turns and looks at me, tilting her head when I can't take my eyes off her.

"I love ya, Sunshine," I say, grabbing my drink and her free hand. I drag her to the couch, pulling her beside me. Everything feels right when she snuggles into my side and lets out one of those perfect little content sighs I love.

"He should call soon," I say with a sigh, twisting her hair between my fingers.

"It'll be a nice call," she says with a grin, looking up at me with so much love my fucking heart bursts.

"It will be. Shit. I'm always so scared...." I whisper, running a hand down my face. "I'm always so scared he's going to tell me they're locking him up for good or some shit."

"They won't," she says with confidence. "I check every week, Chase. They're just holding him through this investigation, but it's not going anywhere. They have nothing on him." I swallow when she says that and lean down to press my lips to hers.

"Thank you, Sunshine," I murmur through the kisses and then settle back.

I'm not sure I pay attention to the movie as much as she does, but it's nice to have the noise distracting from the upcoming phone call with my dad. He doesn't get to do it very often since he's in custody. Here and there, I get a few letters and the occasional call. But it seems today will be a good day to hear from him.

Twirling Kaycee's hair between my fingers, I massage her scalp, soaking up her content moans. Her body relaxes under my touch, giving me damn butterflies. Butterflies! Who knew a girl could do this shit to me? Butterflies? Not knowing what to say? She turns me into a bumbling idiot. But a good idiot. At least, I think I'm a good idiot. She never seems to complain. The only one who seems to complain is Grumpy, but he's, well—grumpy all the time.

Since the stupid charity event, we've been hiding out and keeping our heads down. Heads down, get it? My head has been fucking down. Down in the depths of my beautiful girlfriend's thighs. Just me—and her—and moans, tongues, and fuck, where was I going with this again?

Shit.

Right.

We've kept ourselves busy with the holiday break, trying to keep Kaycee safe and out of the Apocalypse's grasp. The way they watched her at the charity event was pure psycho-status, making my stomach tighten with anxiety. From what we've found, it doesn't surprise me that they're all creepy assholes. Creepy-as-shit bastards are trying to get their hands on my gal for who-knows-what. That'll never happen, bro. Never. She's mine to protect and keep, and I'll fucking watch her like a hawk until school starts again. But Carter is correct. Something feels weird—off. Maybe after my dad calls, I'll take her away from here to a hotel or something. I don't have a house to go to, and I can't take her home where her big scary dad is.

"I love you, Sunshine," my voice pierces through the silence again, movie be damned. "Maybe after the movie, we could go for a drive?" Yeah, a drive far away from here, and maybe out of town. Thank God I still have Seger's credit card saved on my phone. He'll never know until he gets the bill.

She rolls over, looking up at me with those magnificent blue eyes resembling the middle of the ocean. Dark. Deep. Blue. They're full of everything she's thinking, even when trying to keep a blank slate. The most beautiful smile graces her face, lighting up the entire room, and my heart picks up speed. Every time she smiles, my heart flutters with an overwhelming sense of love and warmth. Shit, I'm so pussy-whipped it's ridiculous. But I don't give a shit anymore. She's mine, and I'm hers—along with three other dudes.

"I love you too," she whispers back. "And that sounds nice. Maybe some ice cream?" She grins at that, and my mind goes to very dirty, sticky places. I nod my head in agreement, continuing to run my fingers through her hair.

The moment I saw her, I knew she'd be special. I guess that's why I tried and failed to catch her attention so many times. It's strange and arrogant to say, but I've never had to work so hard with a girl in my entire damn life. Like seriously, all I had to say was my last name, and they'd fall to their knees. Literally, I've gotten so many blowjobs like that.

Name drop. Boom! Blowjob.

I don't play like that now, though. That was the old Chase. And the guy right here holding his girlfriend, so she feels comfortable? He's the new and improved me—the guy I actually like. I went through the motions back then, trying to find happiness in mouths and pussy. You know, typical guy shit. It wasn't that many girls, I guess. Me and the twins have shared a few times—always have. Our greatest mistake was letting

Hadley Lacey take a ride on the twin, Chase express. I shiver at the thought. Years ago, she was okay. But now she's a goddamn nightmare wrapped in pretty clothes. If I could erase our sexual encounter, I would. Too bad she recorded the twins and her in the throes of passion as blackmail. That turned them away, and they dropped her faster than you can say *twin sandwich*. Shit. Even thinking about her makes my stomach turn, especially after learning she's in the Apocalypse cult doing all their dirty work and hurting my girlfriend.

"What are you thinking about?" Her voice drips like sweet honey, staring straight into my soul. She shifts, straddling my lap in one movement.

Her limber fingers roam through my hair. I'd never cut it now—ever. I'll keep it shaggy until I'm ninety years old to feel her fingers run through it every day. Tingles run down my spine at the touch of a strand of hair, and my mind goes blank with relaxation—this woman, she's going to put me in an early grave.

"How you'll be the death of me," I murmur through gritted teeth when she grinds against me.

She hums when she tugs my hair and forces my neck to snap back. I swallow hard, completely falling to her mercy when her lips suction, and her teeth drag across my flesh. And yup, there's all the blood running away from my thinking head and heading straight south to my sex-obsessed head, raising like a giant flag. Oh shit, and she notices too when she whimpers, grinding harder against my lap. Don't come in your damn pants, just hold it together until you can flip her over and fuck her raw.

"Grumpy is right. You're a temptress, Sunshine." Shivers roll up and down my spine, sprouting goosebumps everywhere.

"Mmm, how so?" she whispers, trailing her lips across my jawline, slowly moving toward my lips.

Shit. We're doing this again.

The sweetest scent fills my nose—mangos and vanilla. Mmm, my Sunshine must have used a new body wash or shampoo. I groan, aching to nibble her, eat her, and consume her pleasure on every surface of this house. No chair, couch, counter, bed, or floor will go untouched before those assholes get home.

Hell yes, I can't wait to have her screaming beneath me. I'll try that new move I learned from the sex book I stole from the library. There's a move called *The Salty Pretzel*, calling my damn name. All I need is some rope, a sturdy bedpost, and one willing girlfriend. Shit. My dick jerks in my shorts again. Yeah, we're doing this shit again. I groan, imagining Kaycee tied up, bare, and ready to take me from behind.

"You smell delicious. I could eat you," I moan into her lips, wrapping my arms around her body. My hands grasp her perfect petite ass, squeezing and shifting her forward.

"Then why don't you?" See? Killing me.

Grinding her hips down, she moans the softest little moan. It's almost comparable to the little noises she makes when she eats. Mmm, cupcakes. I need to get her more of those. Making my Sunshine smile back at me swirls butterflies in my belly. More. Damn. Butterflies.

My hands halt her hips from rolling, and I flip the tables on her with little effort. She yelps as my body presses down on hers. My fingers work up and down her sides. A smile crosses my lips when she breaks out in hysterical laughter, trying to prevent my fingers from digging into her sides.

"Chase!" she squeals, laughing until water pours from her eyes, and finally, I give in, sealing my mouth over the flesh of her neck. She giggles more, breathy moans trickling from her throat.

"Repeat it, Sunshine." I brush my lips against her flesh, nipping and sucking, marking my ray of sunshine as mine.

My hips move on their own, grinding hers, and I'm hard as a rock again. Little Chase doesn't care that we just came not even an hour ago. He's calling the shots now, and he says, we fuck now. Joy lights up her face with laugh lines, and she's breathless, wheezing and begging for breath when my fingers continue their journey. But I don't relent. I pounce on her, enjoying how her breaths brush against my skin. Tangling her fingers through my hair, she pulls my lips away from her neck.

"You're a little devil," she whispers, tugging my hair again. Shivers force themselves down my spine, jerking my body, and I swear I come in my shorts. Shit, that's not supposed to happen with the pull of my hair. She's supposed to pull my cock.

"Would a little devil do this?" I mock with a grin, rolling my hard dick on her center, eliciting the best raspy, horny sounds from her throat.

She throws her head back into the couch, body arching into mine. No words have to leave her lips—only the feel of her body against mine, begging for more.

"Yes, the devil would do that," she moans with a raspy voice, coming out in breathy pants.

I swivel my hips so my dick rubs right along her clothed crease. Her moans fill the room. Shit, my groans fill the room in unison with hers. Like we're singing a sexy song of lust and need, begging each other for the release we desperately need. My balls tingle again, pulling towards my abdomen. Hot fire spears down my spine, and fuck, if I'm not careful, I'll come from this. A-freaking-gain. While dry humping, nonetheless. And how could I, an eighteen-year-old dude, explain I came in my pants from dry humping?

"Is your phone vibrating? Or are you just overly excited right now?" I snort at her words. Leaning down, I rest my forehead on hers, staring into the depths of her eyes.

Shit. I want to sink inside of her, but I've been waiting to hear from my dad all day. I close my eyes, breathing in her frantic breaths. Later—I'll sink inside her later and fuck her brains out after we get a hotel room and get far away from here.

"Worst buzz kill," I mutter, fishing for my phone and pulling it out—a random number flashes across it. Usually, when my dad calls, it's from the prison. But this one is new. It's our area code, so it's from Cali.

My brows furrow when I answer with hesitation, hoping it's my dad on the other end. My reluctance is short-lived when I hear my dad's soothing voice on the other side, sending all my worries away. My dad has always been my rock and my voice of reason. He's the man who raised Ainsley and me on his own after my mom tucked tail and left us. He was a superstar juggling a budding movie career, two kids, and a production company. Hell, he still is. He's my idol.

Climbing off Kaycee is the hardest thing I've done today. And the second? My dick. But it slowly deflates as I pace the room, especially with the seriousness in my dad's tone tonight. My gut churns again with an uneasy feeling. Something is off again, even with him. My dad speaks in a soft voice, catching up on what I've been up to. I hold up a finger to Kace, letting her know I'm going to the guys' room to pace and talk in private so she can enjoy the rest of the movie still playing on the big screen. She nods, and as I'm about to leave the room, her phone buzzes loudly on the table, and it makes me pause.

Concern washes over me as I watch all the color draining from her face. I swallow hard, something again nagging at me when I hold her shut-off gaze. A strange burning sensation flares through my chest when she brushes me off.

She slaps the phone back down, leaving it on the table with a grimace and a head shake. Meeting me in the middle of the room, she kisses my cheek, lingering for more than a second. Her entire body trembles, and when I go to throw my arm around her body, she shakes her head, motioning she'll be in her room. A knot forms in the pit of my stomach when she sits at her computer with her fingers working like lightning over the keys. Everything inside me is telling me something is off, screaming in a loud warning siren inside my brain. It tells me to scoop her up and get the fuck out of here before it all goes to shit.

"Son, did you hear me?" My dad's voice booms through the phone, grabbing my attention back to him.

I pace the living room, biting my nails. I keep a close watch on the woman who eyes me wearily, eventually shooing me away with a flick of her wrist. I sigh, nodding, and make my way towards the front door, clicking the lock in place and ensuring everything is secure before I march towards the other bedroom, giving her the privacy she wants. But my chest still feels heavy with every step I take into the bedroom away from her.

"Uh, yeah, sorry, Dad," I say, wrinkling my nose when I enter the room.

Half the room has dirty clothes on the floor, and the other half is clean as a whistle. They don't even sleep in here anymore, opting to sleep in the big bed with the rest of us. So, how the shit is it so damn dirty? Since Kaycee moved in here with us, we have stayed in her room every night and cuddled in bed. Well, the three of us, at least. Carter, not so much. Only when he can get away. I guess. He tries to carefully sneak around, keeping up the weird charade he's in with us, but not with us. Which makes this whole relationship complicated in public.

"Where are you?" I ask as a cool winter breeze lifts the hair on my arms, and I freeze on the spot.

What the shit? I whip my head toward the window at the far end of the room—my brows furrow. I didn't open it. Did I? Fuck no, I didn't. I lean closer to it as my heart pounds against my ribs and follow the broken glass on the ground. My mouth pops open in shock as glass crunches beneath my feet. My father continues to speak as I take a picture and forward it to Grumpy, asking him what the fuck? I swallow my panic looking all around the room for any sign someone is in here. But the hole in the glass is only as small as the rock lying in the debris. I pick it up and inspect it as my father continues to speak.

"Ah, that's what I wanted to talk to you about real fast, bud. They've taken me into a secured location," he says, lowering his voice and catching my attention again.

"Really? Why?" I breathe, stumbling back from the mess. My mind moves a million miles a minute, trying to process everything–his words, the broken window, and the safety of my girl. I need to get her out of here now before it escalates into something we can't come back from.

I stalk back out of the room and peek at Kaycee, who stares at the computer with wide, glossy eyes. My eyes dart across the house, listening for any noises that might be out of place. But nothing seems to be wrong. Everything is in order. Shit. Maybe one of the twins accidentally broke it before they left? But that seems unlikely. I stand guard, looking at Kaycee when I send a text to the twins asking if they broke the fucking window.

The phone muffles, and a crackling noise comes through from my dad's end. "Yes," he whispers into the phone. "A week ago, Special Agent Seven came and took me from prison. She gave me my clothes and a private room at some compound." Compound? Agent Seven? What the hell?

My poor heart pounds frantically. Running my free hand through my hair, I can't help the laugh that bubbles out with relief. Maybe everything will be fine if they've let him out. Maybe they're tracking these Apocalypse bastards right now, and we have nothing to worry about. I pace back towards the twins' room with a new reassurance that we'll be okay. And that I have nothing to fear with Kaycee on the other side of the house.

"So, does this mean…?"

"Not so fast, bud," he sighs, deflating my momentary happy bubble. "I'm not out of the woods yet. I'm still in their custody, whoever they are. I just wanted to give you and Ains a heads up. Everything seems to be looking up for me. They're figuring it all out." Hearing the crack in my dad's voice tightens my throat with renewed worries.

"I love you, Dad. I'm glad everything is looking up. Maybe you'll be home before New Year's," I say before we talk a little more and say our goodbyes.

Hanging up the phone, I take a few steps towards the bedroom door with the intent to check on Kaycee. Whatever is happening here, I need to get Kace out and to safety. I'll take her to a hotel far, far away from here. But we need to do it now. I didn't want to freak my dad out or get off the phone with him, but I know something is about to happen in my gut. And that creepy feeling I've had all day settles in my gut —time to leave.

Just as I'm about to leave the twins' bedroom, ready to tell Kace the excellent news and check on her again, my phone dings in my hand, stopping me in my tracks.

> Seger: Dude…we didn't break the window…..

Shit! If he didn't break the damn window. Then who did? Fuck! Kaycee! I swallow a gasp when the lights in the entire house blink out, blanketing me in black, except for my phone. As I light up the screen, searching for the damn flashlight, a familiar voice halts me in my tracks.

"I don't think so," says a giggly voice and then pounces before I can get a good look at her or defend myself.

A cold metal whacks me in the temple several times, knocking me over. I stumble over my feet, grunting from the force of the hit, and smack into the floor. My vision blurs, spotting white, and finally, the fight leaves my body. My limbs tingle with pins and needles. My fingers curl, but I can't move them to defend myself. I grunt when a second, larger fist collides with my head.

And lights out. That's all, folks.

The end.

# TWENTY

## CHASE

One moment a crazy person attacks me, and the next? Next, I'm sucking in nonexistent oxygen into my burning lungs. I hack, trying to pull in air, but every breath I draw in constricts my throat, and I swear it burns like fire. Rubber bands pulling tightly around my chest, like an elephant, tap dancing on top of me and not allowing me to breathe. Shit! What happened? I shake my aching head, feeling the remnants of blood trickling down my face. I wince when I touch my temple. Red lines my fingertips when I bring them into the moonbeams peering through the window. Right, someone used my head for punching practice. I groan. My damn aching body pulsates whenever I move, throbbing with my heartbeat.

Groaning, I roll over to my aching belly, heaving onto the carpet. The room spins, and I'm forced to put my forehead on the carpet, taking deep, burning breaths before climbing to my hands and knees. Every ounce of energy I try to expel burns out—poof. Actually—everything burns. *Really* fucking burns. My skin bubbles, feeling like someone holds a damn torch under it.

My eyes blink open in a foggy haze, making the contents of the twin's room disappear before my eyes. Am I outside? I wipe my eyes, hissing from the pain exploding through my face. For a moment, I fucking forgot some crazy psycho chick jumped me. A chick! I'm not saying chicks can't be badass. Look at my girl—

My girl! Fuck. Shit. My Kaycee!

"Kaycee!" I croak, forcing myself onto my stumbling feet.

Before I can take a step, the damn room spins out of control, swirling the contents of my stomach. I bend at the waist, hacking out a powerful, breath-stealing cough. A gag works its way up my throat, and the taste of bile hits my tongue. Shit. I don't have time for this! I need to get to Kaycee because something is fucking wrong here. It's all confirmed when the smell smacks me in the face and buckles my knees, and sends me to the ground.

The smell works its way up my nose, making me pause. What is that? With a shaky breath, I take another deep inhale, and it hits me again. It's like a campfire in the middle of our house. Crackling. Popping. Hissing. And heat. Sweat bubbles down my forehead, mingling with the blood dripping from my head wound. It's so damn hot in here, and it's getting harder to breathe.

I force myself to my weak Bambi legs, rushing towards the bedroom door, taking one final look around the twin's room before I place my hand on the doorknob. I stop dead, dread building in the pits of my soul. Shit. This....this can't be good.

A fiery warmth meets my palms. I know doors shouldn't be this warm, and neither should doorknobs. Our heat doesn't work that well. Fear takes hold of me when it warms under my palm again, searing my fingers. I back off, staring at the wooden door in shock. My limbs freeze, and my mind rolls through the possibilities. Taking a staggering step back, I finally see the whole shitty, fucked up picture. The room fills with more nauseating billows of smoke coming from beneath the closed door. Shit. I didn't shut that before I came in here, did I? My head pounds as more blackness pours in, floating in the air. Last I checked, however long ago, the house was fine. And now... There's a goddamn fire in the house–the same house that was occupied by just Kaycee and me.

My heart speeds up. Kaycee. Oh, shit. Is this their end game? Burn us like fucking popcorn?

I run for the door. Fuck my safety. Fuck it all! If they got to her... If they fucking took her away from us, I'll kill them with my bare hands.

Images of her lifeless body on the ground run through my mind. It's a fucking nightmare come true. We never knew what they would do, but I never expected this. Tears burn in my eyes when I picture her tiny body engulfed in flames, begging for someone to save her.

Opening the bedroom door a crack, I try to be as careful as possible. Everything inside my body freezes despite the hellfire spreading throughout the living room. Flames eat the rafters and my favorite damn couch. It's everywhere, burning everything in its path—panic bubbles in my gut. There isn't a speck of the front room or kitchen untouched from the blaze. But Kaycee. Her door. It's shut, and the flames are knocking, asking for permission. Well, permission not granted, you fucking fire!

Adrenaline pours through my veins, pumping my heart at double the speed and knocking against my aching chest. I swallow down reason, preparing myself for the hell I'm about to walk through. Kaycee is worth everything, and I'll be damned if I let her lie there and die because I was too chicken to save her. I'm coming, Sunshine. Hang on!

I ignore my protesting brain with a shaky breath. It's desperately pleading with me to jump out the window and save myself from the hot as fuck fire roaring in front of my eyes. I ignore it, sizing up the best path to her room. Carter's in the fucking wind. I'm the only one left on campus who can save her.

I cry out from the heat the moment I rush from the bedroom. Sweat drips from every orifice, and my nerves tingle from the pain of the inferno licking my skin. But fuck it. Fuck all the pain. I'll run through hell to save my girl, even if it means I get burned in the process.

Through my frantic steps toward the bedroom, I scan the rest of the room, hoping deep in my gut she isn't lying on the ground in the midst of the fire. I search and search, looking for her anywhere. But there's no sign of her in the living room. Thank fuckity, fuck for that. It's too far gone to examine more. I thrust her bedroom door open with my aching shoulder, slamming the door shut behind me.

I lean against her bedroom closet, noting the holes in the wood while taking deep breaths. I try sucking in the fleeting oxygen back into my lungs. The fire hasn't touched the room yet. But the smoke is fucking impossible to see through. I could open a window to clear it, but even an idiot like me knows adding any amount of oxygen will blow this place to the ground, and I'll be fried fucking chicken.

A deep cough rocks through my lungs when I look around again. Back in elementary school, they drilled fire safety into us every year. When smoke hits, get on your hands and knees. I drop to my hands and knees, feeling around on the carpet for my girlfriend. The air in front of me clears out, and I can see through the burning smoke. My eyes dry out, and my lungs burn when I feel around. Relief slams through me when she isn't here, but panic rises again. Because if Kaycee isn't here, then where the hell is she? If the smoke hadn't stolen my tears, I'd sob hysterically from the relief and worry. I need to get the fuck out of here before the whole house burns to the damn ground with me inside.

My body freezes again for the second time in the last ten minutes, my mind reeling. I heave a breath running the tip of my finger over tiny red droplets lining the carpet. I squish it between my fingertips, gagging when it spreads over my fingerprint. My stomach rolls when I follow the perfect red splatters towards the bedroom door, watching the spots disappear under the door and out into the inferno. Shit! No. No. What the hell? I tear her room apart, looking for anything else. But there's nothing. She's not here. And I don't know what scares me more? That she's not here, or who made her bleed?

The flesh on my arms blisters and burns—actually, everywhere, burns and blisters rise off the left side of my body. I have no choice but to leave the house. It creaks and snaps—smoke billows in from beneath the door.

I open Kaycee's window and jump out onto the wet grass, running towards the front of the house with my last bits of energy. Heat pours from the flames shooting out the front room and front door windows. The entire front porch drops to the ground, burning so hot the wood bends and breaks to its new master. Choked coughs expel from my wheezing lungs, but I carry forward. I have to. I can't stop now. If I stop, I die. And if I die, then no one will know what happened to me. Or Kaycee.

My Kaycee.

Shit. Shit. Shit.

A shadow sits where my heart was, pounding against my battered and aching ribs. Blood exists inside of me, but it's gone cold. I'm ice without her, and I won't thaw until she's back in my arms. I won't sleep until she's back home where she belongs.

Red and orange flames illuminate the night sky like the sun coming up for the day. But it's only shining down on the destruction in front of me, shimmering from the inferno. Thick black smoke snuffs the stars gleaming from the sky. The heavy scent of gasoline is pungent in the air and fills my nose. Whoever did this—the Apocalypse bastards—did it on purpose. They knew I was there, and they tried to end my life. Shit—I run my aching hand through my singed hair and pull, inflicting more pain. Shit. Fuck! I almost died! But I fucking….I fucking lost Kaycee. Pain swells everywhere. But my heart breaks inside my chest at the realization. My Sunshine is gone. The Maze House is on fire. And someone tried to end me.

My knees buckle beneath me, unable to hold my weight any longer. Sweat pours down my face and chest, burning the singed skin on my body. It all burns and aches with every move I make. I want to cry out. I want to move and call for more help, but I'm frozen, staring up at the thick flames, eating everything like a hungry monster. A second later, I wouldn't be here. A second later, I'd be burned. A second later—

"Chase!" someone shouts from afar, but the flames eat their voice, too. It's muffled, consumed by the constant snapping sound of the wood buckling under the blaze.

But I can't. I can't stop my heart from splintering in two. I can't stop the vomit churning or the pain searing my body. I burn. I ache. But fuck my skin, it'll heal. If we don't find her, she'll die. She'll die. She'll die. She'll die! SHIT!

"They took her," I mutter, voice thick and low.

"No," Seger croaks, dropping to his knees. The wild, desperate look in his eyes examines me, looking me over from head to toe, taking in every burn and scrape. But he can't see on the inside. He can't see the pain eating me alive.

"I looked everywhere," I whisper again, shaking my head. "She wasn't there. They took her," I repeat.

His hand rests on my cheeks, thumbs swiping at the angry red skin blistering. Tears erupt from his eyes, boiling over the edge and dropping to his chin. He shakes his head in disbelief.

"No," he whispers. "Please," he says again, grabbing harder onto my face. I flinch at the pain erupting from his touch.

But I deserve it. I let her go and did this to her. If we hadn't separated, this wouldn't have happened. If I had protected her better, then she would still be here. If Kaycee dies, it's my fault. They should stay away from me. I'm nothing but an anchor dragging them down to the ocean's depths. Soon they'll be drowning like I am.

"He needs an ambulance," Zepp whispers, voice dipping low. He's trying hard to be the calm one. But he's losing his battle, too.

Our eyes never leave the flames dancing in the night sky.

"You can't blame yourself, you fucking hear me?" Seger says, bringing my eyes to his.

The flames in his eyes match the fire from the sky. He is monstrous, ready to destroy whatever he has to, to avenge his girl. Like a match, he sparks me, too.

"What happened?" Zepp asks, dropping down into the wet grass. "Chase? Tell me, please." His assessing eyes check me over, too. He covers his mouth, shaking his head.

I explain everything—the phone call—the look on Kaycee's face when she tried to play it off—and finally, getting hit on the head by a giggling asshole and being out for what felt like hours.

"We won't settle until she's back in our arms," Zepp says in an eerily calm voice, clenching his fist so tight, I swear he's going to puncture his skin.

"They fucking planned this!" Seger shouts, throwing his fist into the hard ground with a grunt of pain. "Dad was fucking fine when we went home. There wasn't an emergency, they were just trying to get us to leave, and they fucking won!" He growls the last part, punching the ground repeatedly until blood seeps from his knuckles.

"Now we are coming for them," Zepp says, staring at the fire roaring through the sky. "We need to call 911." Seger nods, digs out his phone and makes the call explaining about the fire and our missing girlfriend.

Zepp shifts his hand into his pocket, pulling out his phone. I watch from the ground as his brows furrow and then widen in horror. Seger shifts next to me, plopping down into the grass. His hands work through his hair with tension filling every muscle in his body.

"They're supposed to be coming to put the fire out. I told them about Kace. I told them everything," Seger mutters, sounding utterly defeated.

Zepp's eyes blink rapidly at his phone and the fire.

"Holy fuck," Seger says, staring down at his phone.

Fuck I don't even know where my phone went. I run my aching hand down over my gym shorts and find nothing until I hit a piece of paper that wasn't there before I was knocked out cold. I grunt, crying out in pain when I unfold the paper and hold it in the air. When I read the barely legible words scrawled across the page, all the air leaves my lungs. Tears fill my eyes as I lay helplessly on the lawn, half-burnt to a crisp like a fucking marshmallow. Pain erupts everywhere, setting my nerves on fire. All I want is something to cool this burn off, but I won't rest until we find Kaycee and bring her back to us.

Zeppelin looks up with more determination than I've ever seen before in his eyes. "We have a plan," is all he says, helping me to my aching feet.

"We have a fucking plan," Seger rasps to confirm some phantom plan I'm in the dark about. All I know is what the note says:

*I'll fucking save her. Save yourself.*

I grunt, biting my tongue when pain encompasses my entire left side. Seger mutters how sorry he is under his breath when he helps me to my feet with Zepp on the other side. Together, they drag me out of the maze, pulling me to the beginning. The fire rages on, burning a piece of history down to the ground. By the time help arrives, our Maze House will be no more.

"Oh my god!" Ainsley cries, dropping to her knees in front of me. "Are you okay?" She chokes out, looking me up and down. "I saw the fire from my apartment!"

"Stay with him, Ains. Right the fuck here," Seger says through clenched teeth, pointing toward the hedges.

"Okay," she whispers, sitting beside me. "Ambulance?" Her fingers tremble when she takes in the extent of my injuries.

"They're on their way. So are the cops. We've got big fucking problems right now, Ains. We need to keep you safe, him safe, and find Kaycee." Seger paces in front of us, biting his nails.

"We've got a plan," Zepp reiterates, staring at the rising flames of the house.

Sirens blast in the distance, getting closer to our destination until blue and red lights cut through the pitch-black night.

Zepp and Seger peer down at their phones again and look at each other. They give a nod, turning back to Ains and me.

"We're going to get Kaycee back. When the ambulance gets here, you have to go with them. Get help," Zepp demands, and I nod.

With that, the twins rush from the maze into the darkness, disappearing out of view. Lead sits heavily in the pit of my stomach when I stare up at Ainsley. Tears leak down her face, and her sobs fill the air. Ainsley yelps when an explosion of people in uniforms converges on the maze. EMTs and firefighters rush to the scene, and head through the maze to the house. An EMT stops and looks me over.

"We'll get you to the hospital now, okay? We need to get these burns looked at," she whispers, looking over my injuries.

# TWENTY-ONE

### KAYCEE

"Is your phone vibrating? Or are you just overly excited right now?" I ask Chase through a giggle, feeling the buzz vibrating against my thigh.

"Worst buzz kill," Chase mutters, fishing out his phone and pulling it out of his pocket.

Crinkles form across his forehead when he reads the number flashing across the screen. His eyes dart to mine when he answers the call on the third ring with hesitation, giving a soft, cautious hello. His cute eyebrows dance up and down with excitement, and his shoulders slump in relief.

Every inch of him has been in a constant state of stress for the past few days and only intensified when he knew his dad would call. I know he's been excited yet nervous to talk to his dad. And by the radiant look of admiration sparkling in his eyes and the easy smile crossing his face, I can tell it's the phone call he's been anxiously awaiting all day. Every few minutes, he'd look at the clock with a dopey look on his face, counting down the hours until he got to hear from his father. It's not often he gets to these days, so he takes what he can get.

My eyes track Chase as he crosses the room, pacing back and forth in true Chase fashion. When Chase suggested we watch a film, I was thankful for the distraction. Since the charity event a few weeks ago and everything surrounding it, I've needed something to take my mind off our situation. Something completely mind-numbing and unimportant did the trick; I never once thought about the event, snuggled into Chase's arms. His embrace took away every bit of stress that had been pent up.

Chase nods, barely getting a word into the conversation. My phone vibrates on the table as he paces around the living room. My heart skips a beat inside my chest, fluttering with the hope that it's one of the boys reaching out. The twins have been MIA almost all night. Their nurse texted them close to dinner time, explaining that their father had escaped again, and she needed their help finding him. I haven't heard a peep from either one of them since they took off. But they're probably so busy searching the woods for their father, like last time, I haven't bugged them. It hasn't stopped me from eyeing my phone since they left, aching to hear from them.

Carter said he needed to check something on his computer again. Something about a website that he didn't explain very well. I'm still in the dark about what he found on his dad's computer from that time we broke in and placed the disc there. He's kept a tight lip about it. And I'm not sure if it was for my benefit or if he found something horrible. Whatever it is, he's bit his tongue on the subject, and it's done nothing but piss me off. It's like the black bag full of sex toys all over again. I want to know what he's hiding. So, naturally, me being me, I tried to hack it myself. But of course, I couldn't find a damn thing on his computer through mine. It was sealed too tight, and I didn't have enough power to break through—what a shame. I can easily hack into AntiEyes and break into the Pentagon like it's nothing. But Carter's computer? It's locked up tighter than Fort Knox, the only place I couldn't break into.

A deep ache forms in my gut from the separation, which sounds completely insane because it's only been a few hours, but I feel it manifesting inside me. Physical symptoms have already started to take hold through body aches and anxiety. My body longs to hold them again or hear their voices again, and it makes me feel pitiful. How can I survive this world if I can't function without them for more than five seconds? Seriously. I survived Thanksgiving break and Christmas break without physically being near them, but here I am, whimpering on the couch like a baby because the other three took off. I'll have to reconnect with my therapist about these new developments and discuss why I'm being so weird.

I sigh, almost in heartbreak, when it isn't a text from one of them. I cock my head in confusion at the single notification sitting on my home screen, taunting me to open it. I shouldn't. It's too impossible to be real. There's no way in Hell it could be. Whoever sent it must know my curiosity always wins. One day, it'll be the cause of my death, too.

My fingers shake when I swipe it open, and my heart thrashes inside of me. Dizziness takes over, and the world sways around me. Closing my eyes, I take a deep breath and force myself to look at the message sent to me. It's inconspicuous and innocent. But mostly, it's completely impossible. The color drains from my face, and my fingers tremble as they hover above the screen. Every part of me freezes, and a bucket of cold water splashes over my head, rereading the words taunting me.

Chase stops at the corner of the room, making his way back toward me. Worry sits on every inch of his face at the sight of my frozen state. He holds my gaze and looks me over.

"You okay?" He asks in a soft voice, gesturing with his hand.

"Yeah," I croak, barely getting the words out. Am I convincing? Probably not. I'm a walking, talking ghost sitting in front of him. His eyebrows scrunch, narrowing his eyes in disbelief of my statement. "I'm fine," I tack on with the wave of my hand, sounding more confident than before.

I will be okay because I will survive. No matter what these assholes have thrown at me, I've survived to tell the tale. And I'll continue to do so, no matter what. Goo down my shirt—I survived. A car crash and broken arm—I survived. Laxative sprinkles on my pancakes—I survived. Okay, well, that one I barely made it through. I think my soul left through my ass that day I ate those delicious pancakes, but you know what? I survived, damn it. And they can't take that away from me.

Devastation clouds my mind all over again. Memories of the first night my mom sat me down and told me Magnolia was gone rushed back in a whirlwind of grief and anguish twisting my gut. Everything I've endured over the past year feels raw and at the surface. Tears burn the back of my eyes, but I swallow them down. This grief has to hang on for another few months so I can finally find more answers. Until then, I have to shove everything down into the box in my mind and forget it all. Mission first, grief last.

Ripping my eyes away from my phone, I slap it back down, leaving it on the table. To ease the worry wrinkling Chase's forehead, I kiss his cheek, lingering for a second, basking in his warmth. Whispering, I tell him I'll be in my room and head in its direction. When I look over my shoulder at his lingering stare, I see conflict brewing deep in his eyes. He wants to follow and make sure I'm alright, but I can't let him.

I sit down at my computer and type a few things, gaining access to the innocent-looking message I received. Eyes burn into the side of my head, and I can feel his stress and worry from here. Looking up from the screen, I give him a reassuring wave. His face contorts, grimacing with indecision. I wave him on again, trying to get him to leave my sight so I can get into it. Chase finally waves, pointing toward the twins' room. Albeit reluctantly, he walks out of view with one last dejected sigh.

A burning lump sits in my throat when I bring up my email. There sitting in my inbox is something I never thought I'd see again. Every week I waited on pins and needles to hear what Magnolia had to say. The good, the bad, and the incredibly ugly rested in her words. Back then, I tried to be as supportive as I could be, but I was far away. She was here, and there wasn't anything I could do about it. I tried getting into the cameras, but it wasn't possible from home. She repeatedly told me to stay out of it, that she had it handled. So many nights, I sat up wishing I hadn't listened to her and had gone ahead with protecting her. But she refused to let me, even threatening me if I showed up.

Regrets rush through me and pin me in place with the overwhelming what-ifs of life. What if I was here the whole time she was? I could have helped her more and done more to protect her. She'd still be alive and happy with Ainsley. But I wasn't here. I was at home, going to our old school, living my own life in a bubble. Magnolia was here, suffering at the hands of the Apocalypse and their minions, and it eventually got her killed. I could have—I would have—I wanted to do more. I suppose that's why I'm here now. Sure, I met the loves of my life. But I came here to find answers, and that's what I've found.

So now, staring at her words on my screen once again raises the hairs on the back of my neck.

My mouth dries out, and my heart skips a beat when I open the email that will likely change my life.

*Subject: Kaycee! I miss you so much. I wish you were here. See you soon!*

*To: KAC48@yohoo61.com*

*From: MagsColette@yohoo61.com*

*Kaycee,*
*It's been so long. Everywhere I look is dark and scary. Isn't death supposed to be peaceful and nice? Isn't heaven supposed to have lights and angels? I wish I had been there with you. But I'm not. And I know you've been looking into things you shouldn't have...things that'll get you killed. I have one last piece of evidence for you to see. It's the answers to your burning questions. <u>CLICK</u> the link and find out.*
*Love you,*
*Magnolia xoxoxo*
*P.S. I'll see you soon!*

TEARS SPILL over the brim of my eyes, run down my cheeks and fall on my computer desk. This isn't possible. Not at all. And I know it. There's no way she's sending me emails from the grave. No. Way. In. Hell. This has to be a play to get at me or another form of bullying.

I should get Chase and show him—make him see what I'm seeing so I know I'm not going crazy. But my finger has other ideas, clicking the link provided. I need to see what they sent me for myself first.

The sound of waves rushes through the speakers, drowning out any other sounds. The camera pans, showing a shoreline I don't recognize, and creeps alongside a sizable white vessel—a yacht. My heart drops into my ass when muffled music blasts from the ship.

A darkened skyline sits over the large yacht. Stars dot the sky, twinkling down on the party, raging as shadowed figures dance and grind on the large deck up top, tangling with laser lights beaming on them. They laugh and drunkenly sing with muffled words.

Some figures stumble in the shadows, never revealing their faces. Only one face is visible through the darkness on the deck below. A spotlight seems to shine down on her dopey-looking face. She smiles at the woman beside her, staring at her like she hung the stars in the sky, caressing her cheek. Her fingers rest in the girl's long brown hair, and she leans in, sharing a torrid kiss that would make nuns blush and quiver.

"Hell yes, here it goes!" A familiar male voice whispers from behind the camera. I sit rigidly in my chair when it registers whose voice continues to speak. I'm helplessly stuck staring as the camera jostles, zooming in on the kissing pair. Trent, the cameraman, mumbles a few words behind the lens, but I don't know what he says. I lean in, wishing I could make out his words, hoping it would give me more clues about what will happen.

Like a train wreck exploding in front of me, I can't take my eyes off her. A slow, sad smile spreads across my lips, tears burning tracks down my face. There she is, Magnolia in the flesh. Forever immortalized in video form, loving life and kissing the woman she pledged to spend her life with. They envisioned college together and coming out together. Their future was brighter than the damn stars sparkling above them and illuminating them in their essence. For as long as I live, I'll replay this moment repeatedly to remember what she had while she was away. She may have succumbed to an awful fate. But this right here? It's special.

Magnolia's curly auburn hair blows in the wild wind. The beautiful party dress wraps around her body like a glove, displaying the curves she always hid beneath her t-shirts and jeans. The most beautiful and serene smile spreads across her face as she stares into Ainsley's crystal blue eyes, emanating her love for her. Their lips collide again in a heated kiss with wandering hands, grabbing for anything they can get ahold of. They claw at one another, groping and pressing their bodies together with such passion that I squirm in my seat. The love they shared was something truly out of a fairytale and made for them. If only they had gotten their happily ever after in a palace made for them.

"I'll meet you downstairs?" Ainsley's muffled voice asks her, staring intensely into Magnolia's eyes.

Magnolia nods with that dopey, love-sick grin, taking in Ainsley. "Of course. I'll meet you down there in a minute. Thank you, babe, for keeping me safe tonight, for having me here. This has been the best night in a long time," Magnolia says with sincerity, meaning every word she spoke.

"Anything for you," Ainsley replies in a soft voice, running the tips of her fingers down Magnolia's jaw. "You're the best thing that's ever happened to me. After this is all over, we'll be free."

"Freedom," Magnolia smiles, leaning in for one more sweet kiss before parting ways.

"I love you, Maggie," Ainsley whispers again. "To the moon and back."

"Forever and ever, to infinity. I love you, too," Magnolia whispers.

Ainsley walks away, peering over her shoulder one last time. Her eyelashes flutter, and she blows Magnolia one last kiss before disappearing into the yacht's cabin with a coy smile. Leaving Magnolia alone on the darkened deck where she stands, she looks over the water, grinning in contemplation. There she was, happy for once in her life. Not like she hadn't been before, but she had finally found that one person who completed her. I run my hand over my aching heart, thinking about all the pieces in my life. They leave me with the same butterflies in my stomach, kisses that complete me, and a meaning to walk this earth. She had that with Ainsley, too. She was her missing piece, the one person who didn't judge her for who she was.

Movement catches my eye on the screen, like a shadow

moving through the darkness, sneaking up behind my best friend—a gleam beams off the sharp edge of something in the shadow's hand.

"No," I croak in desperation, reaching for the screen, hoping I can reach right through and grab Magnolia before her life ends. But I'm only met with the distorted image when my fist connects with the monitor, sending shockwaves of color over Magnolia's tortured face.

Magnolia's beautiful face contorts in pain. Deep anguish and betrayal pour out of her face through a silent scream from her open mouth, quickly covered by a black-gloved hand. Blood rushes as the person repeatedly stabs in different areas of Maggie's body, using her like a pin cushion. The offender uses every ounce of effort, grunting when the knife slices through her flesh like butter. Whoever they are, they stay behind her, stuck in the shadows, grunting their rage into Magnolia's body. I cry out when the unique knife in their hand reflects the laser lights from high above, dangling in the air before stabbing once again in Magnolia's chest. She gasps, begging with her eyes for anyone to notice she's being murdered in front of hundreds of people. But no one cares. No one sees what's happening right under their noses. They simply dance and sway, drinking the night away without a care in the world. But why would they care? They tortured her for months on end without remorse. Simply doing what they were told through text message. So, why would they look down from the upper deck and call out someone's being murdered when they could turn a blind eye and dance.

"God, no," I shriek again, covering my mouth with my hand. Desperate sobs leak through my fingers, and the screen turns fuzzy from the tears blurring my eyes and falling down my cheeks.

Her attacker reaches her arm around, slicing through her wrists with a manic giggle bubbling from their throat. My heart turns to ice when my distorted mind goes back to the memories of the car crash. That horrible fucking laugh. It's the same one that danced around my aching body, singing of my death.

The attacker's face lights up with glee as she finally comes into the light, and the camera focuses on her laughing form—blonde hair, blue eyes, and jumping with joy at her carnage with golf claps. Blood soaks through her black clothes, splatters line her face, and she smiles, licking her lips in pure ecstasy at what she had done. No remorse lines her smile when she looks directly into the camera and giggles again, giving a thumbs up.

Magnolia's stricken face says it all as she's pushed over the railing, splashing into the water, barely registering over the sound of the party raging behind her. Screams of laughter, dancing, and drinking continue around the evil standing on the deck below, laughing maniacally at the carnage she caused. I peel my eyes away, heaving frantic breaths. The camera never pans back to Magnolia's body falling into the restless sea. It simply fades to black with the sound of the waves eating a body and crashing onto the shore. Through quivery lips and shaking fingers, I exit the video, vowing to burn it, and never look at it again. Whoever sent this did so to taunt me. Or—

"It's a thing of beauty, isn't it?" A cool metal sits against my neck, nicking at my skin. It burns as the edges slice, parting my flesh like butter. Warm blood trickles down towards my clavicle, pooling in the crease.

"It was you the entire time." My voice leaks out as cracked and pain-stricken, earning nothing but snickers in return.

Shock sits like lead in the depths of my turning stomach, threatening to spill my delicious Christmas dinner. Am I dumbfounded by the turn of events? Yes, I fucking am. I can't wrap my brain around the fact it was her the entire time. Sure, she was shady as shit. But I never in my life suspected she was the one to murder my best friend. But why?

"Well, duh," she says, rolling her blue eyes toward the ceiling in exasperation. "Did you think anyone else could do it? Huh? No. My daddy entrusted me with the task, and I did it. She was mine to have, and I finally had her. It's just too bad it wasn't the way I wanted her," she growls the last part through clenched teeth as darkness shifts through her eyes.

"But why, Piper?" I whisper, turning my neck to look her in the eyes, pleading with any ounce of humanity she might have.

Her eyes roll again, shaking her head and letting me know she has none. She murdered my best friend for no reason and displayed no ounce of humanity. No soul is lying in the depths of her eyes now. In fact, there's nothing at all but a monster staring back at me with no emotions. Months and months of memories flash through my mind, replaying every interaction we've had together. The laughs and how she talks bring me to a screeching realization. She was pretending to fit in and seem normal. But right now? Piper no longer has to pretend that she cares or possesses any feelings in front of me. The jig is up, and my time has run out. Our only audience is the other two standing off to the side in the shadows of my room, looking on with grins.

"You want to know why? Because that bitch you called your best friend rejected me. REJECTED ME!" She hisses in my face, pressing the knife harder into my skin. More warm blood rolls down my neck and stains the edges of my shirt. "I loved her first! ME! And then she left me for that bitch. So, Daddy let me make her pay. I made her pay so good, didn't I? Did you see her face? Huh? Did you see it? It was so beautiful. So, so fucking beautiful. So beautiful. I want to do it again." She sighs dreamily, looking toward the ceiling with ill intent in her eyes. It's like she's going through the memories of her kill and reliving them.

"Calm your tits, Piper." My body jumps as a hand grabs my shirt, pulling me to my wobbly feet. "You aren't supposed to damage the merchandise. Which is too bad." Oscar's hand wraps around my throat, toying with the blood pouring from the wound and coating his fingers. His fingers dip towards my collar bone, groaning as the blood soaks his fingertips. "Maybe we could play first? Death will never know," he purrs, running his nose up and down my neck with sick intent.

I swallow hard, trying to erase the feeling of his fingers touching parts he shouldn't touch—panic bubbles in my chest. If I don't deescalate this situation, I'm in trouble. They could do anything to me without anyone knowing, and I'd be defenseless. Despite the boys teaching me how to kick and punch to defend myself, I'm not able to. No one tells you how bad you freeze up when you're pulled into situations like this. My mind stalls, but I know I need to make a move and keep them talking. They're the ones with the answers to everything.

"So Magnolia was yours to kill?" I ask, ignoring the burning hand running up and down my body, taking his fill of what he's always wanted—me.

It could be worse. They could stab me. They could kill me. Stay fucking calm. I repeat the phrase in my head over and over. If I do, maybe I'll believe it. Stay calm so I don't hyperventilate. Stay calm so I don't cry and miss important information. Focus. Ignore the burning tears in your eyes. Ignore everything except the answers you need.

"Oscar!" Piper hisses, hitting him on the side of the head. "Knock that shit off. She is not yours." Oscar stops, growling against my flesh. His fingers flex around my neck, tightening and loosening.

"She fucking could have been!" He hisses back, bringing my body flush against his like a possessive freak. "She could have been. And then things would have been different."

"Next time." Piper grins. "This one is his." She runs a finger down my jaw. "Yes, Magnolia was mine. Mine to fuck, mine to kill. And it was beautiful, so fucking beautiful."

Calm down. Breathe. Don't panic—please don't panic now. I need to keep them talking and give me answers. My chest burns with breaths I'm desperate to take, and I gasp for air.

"Why her? Why did it happen?" I ask in a breathy whisper, begging her for answers.

Piper's giggles explode through the room again as she does a gleeful happy dance. If I weren't in a chokehold, threatened by these two psychos, I'd throat punch her. I plan to do that later. You know, when I'm not on the verge of dying.

"You ask a lot of nosey little questions for a dead girl walking." She boops my damn nose with the tip of the large knife in her hands, nicking the end with a burn.

Close up; the knife has jewels adorning the handle. They glimmer in the lights of the room. Her hand barely fits around the handle. Something about it seems familiar. I've seen it before—before it stabbed my best friend—but I can't place it. And I can't get lost in my head right now. My life depends on it. And Chase. Chase! He's here, too. Crap. My sunshine! Where the hell is he? Have they hurt him?

"It happened because it had to happen. She deserved to die. Daddy said so, so it happened. Whatever Daddy says goes," she babbles on, making my stomach churn more.

Taking a deep breath, I blow out my bubbling panic. If I can keep her talking and distracting her, maybe I can get away. Maybe I can escape their clutches because I have a gut-wrenching feeling that a death sentence awaits me if I let them take me to a second location. I'll become what so many of their victims have become—dead. I have to keep myself safe to keep Chase alive—wherever he is.

"And what? The daddy you screw says it's time for me to die? For what?" I spit, trying to antagonize her into more confessions. I want her emotions so high that she makes a mistake and slips up so I can escape Oscar's wandering hands and grab Chase, wherever he is. My heart drops again and sorrow takes over. Chase. My poor Chase.

Piper's crazed grin spreads her lips so wide. Her pupils dilate as she giggles more. I cringe from the sound, and more flashbacks bring me back to the crazy voice at the car crash.

'We killed the rabbit!' And that giggle sets my teeth on edge, and more panic bubbles in my gut. My breaths heave, but I force myself to calm down.

One breath in. One breath out.

Piper steps forward, running the blade down my cheek. "Daddy says it's time for you to meet your end. It'll be slow and painful, and I'll enjoy watching every minute. You're a big hot-ticket item. More than Magnolia. More than all those other idiots. After your sweet, sweet death, I'll roll around in my money, fucking my daddy, and won't think twice about it." With every word she speaks, my stomach twists and rolls.

I wince, backing away from the tip of the knife cutting into the flesh of my cheek. Piper's words bounce around my head —big-ticket item? What the hell is that supposed to mean? More blood trickles down my cheek as the pad of her tongue runs along my flesh, lapping away at it. Her pleasure-filled moans fill the room as she swallows every drop. Bile turns in my stomach when she wipes her lips and grins more.

"God, you're so delicious. I bet he can't wait to taste you like this." She giggles again, giddily hopping in place with excitement.

"Who? Who do you keep talking about?" I ask, trying to keep the desperation out of my voice. They keep mentioning him. I'm almost afraid to know.

"The fourth horseman, of course! I bet you've been so curious about who he is! It's someone you know and love! Ahh! When you see him, you'll know! But until then, you're ours. Now, be a good little bitch and get in the trunk." Her face tightens with every word as she speaks, and any ounce of her peppy self disappears.

The knife in her hand points toward a large, old-fashioned traveling trunk, carried into the room by a smug-looking Trent. Great. This asshole again. Hasn't he fallen off a building yet?

Trent grins, setting the trunk on the floor with a thud. "It's done." He smiles more, opening the small chest.

"Mmm, good," Piper purrs, running a hand down his chest. "You're a good boy, Trent. Maybe I'll recommend you next. Once January comes, someone else will take her place."

"Fuck that!" Oscar yells, gripping me harder. "I've been in this longer than he has. I've killed more than he has. I'm next, Alpha!" My eyes widen when Piper smiles at her call name, and I nearly sputter. Alpha. It was her all along delivering the tasks the others inflicted on me.

Closing her eyes, she sighs. "Indeed you have, Delta," she purrs again, sauntering toward him with the sway of her hips. "I'll recommend you both. Delta and Panty Licker." She giggles at Trent's code name, making him frown.

"You lick panties one time—" he groans, covering his face. "No offense, Alpha, but we need to get a move on. The gasoline is soaking into the wood." A wicked grin spreads across his face when he steps up to me, getting too close for comfort. I try to wiggle out of the way, but Oscar holds me tighter to his body, and my anxiety spikes. Between my boyfriends, I'm fine sandwiched between them. But these two? The ants crawl up my legs, and my skin sears like fire with every touch they give.

Grabbing hold of my chin, Trent forces my eyes to his. "Heya, Stupid. Benoit is currently drowning in gasoline. I slathered it all over his unconscious body. When he wakes—if he wakes—he'll have a hell of a time getting out of here. The moment the flames meet his body, poof! Your precious lover boy will go up in smoke. And then I'll track down your precious twins and do the same." He grins more when tears cloud my vision, blurring the room into nothing but dark swirls.

Images of each of them dying at the hands of these assholes run through my mind. If they get hurt, it's all my fault. I befriended them and brought them into what I know. If it weren't for me, they'd be okay. But now, Trent will hunt them down and obliterate them for their knowledge.

"Leave them alone," I cry out in desperation, stomping my foot into his.

A satisfying crunch happens beneath my stomp, sending a short-lived thrill through me. It doesn't last long when he retaliates tenfold. He curses, throwing a punch into my gut, landing a solid hit on my abdomen. All the air evacuates my lungs, leaving me gasping and sputtering for precious oxygen I can't seem to pull in. No matter how much I try, pain radiates through my stomach. Acid burns my throat, bubbling up my throat from the pain of the hit. The acidic taste boils over onto my tongue, and I spit it out into Trent's grinning face, which falls the moment my spit hits him. Slowly with a scowl, he runs his hand down his face, flicking the spit off with one swish of his wrist.

Oscar holds me upright as I gasp, begging for the breath Trent stole from me. "They have nothing to do with this." I hiss again. "They're innocent! Leave them alone!" I do something I never thought I'd do. I beg for their lives.

"Oh, precious little Kaycee, they have everything to do with this. They intervened when they were told to back the fuck off..."

"Yeah, because I saved them," I hiss back, breathless from the punch. "I saved them from your torment and blackmail. You're all pieces of shit."

Piper smiles sadly. "It's too bad you weren't on our side. Your skills are remarkable," she coos like I'm a child, nodding her head once.

"I'd start saying your prayers. Better yet, start begging. Although, it won't do much, babe." Oscar growls in my ear, forcing my neck to the side.

"There's nowhere for you to run, rabbit. Nowhere to hide..." Trent grins, bringing a large capped syringe out of his pocket. Flicking the cap off the tip, it surges towards the floor, quickly picked up by a giggling Piper.

I kick and scream until my throat burns. Nothing I do makes them stop. The last vision I have before they plunge the needle into my throat is their faces, smiling with evil dwelling in their eyes. The devils surround me.

As the poison works through my veins, I think of happy thoughts. My parents. My siblings. Chase. Seger. Zeppelin. Carter. Their words. Their love. It holds me together. Will I die tonight? Maybe. But I'll die knowing I found the answers to my questions. Do I want to die? No. No, I don't. I'll fight tooth and nail no matter what.

I finally found out who killed Magnolia. Now I have to find out why.

My world blurs. Voices fall silent, and darkness takes me entirely as they stuff my body into the traveling trunk, and the lid closes over me.

Then nothing.

# PART TWO

# TWENTY-TWO

**KAYCEE**

I JOLT UPRIGHT, crying out in pain when my forehead connects with something hard, cracking like a whip inside my skull—a sharp ringing blasts in my ears from the impact. Deep pain ricochets through my cheeks and forehead, and I try to bring my hands up towards my face to inspect the damage, but the only thing I'm met with is resistance.

I grunt, pulling again, but nothing happens. The only sound greeting my ears is the clink of whatever holds my hands in place and a cool metal biting into the skin of my wrists. I twist them around, wincing when pain rocks through me again. Bile sits in the back of my throat when my hands won't move an inch, restrained by metal digging into me. If I can't move my hands, I can't move my body from whatever Hell I'm in. Goosebumps pucker on every inch of my flesh, raising the hairs on end. Every muscle turns to stone, and I sit stock-still. My breaths catch in the back of my throat. For some reason, I'm bound—handcuffed—chained to something. And my cast is magically gone. But where the hell am I? And what the hell happened to bring me here?

Agony hits me when I try to peel open my aching eyes. Blinking rapidly, I scan the brightly lit room. Heated spotlights point directly at me. I wince, momentarily blinded from the brightness after being unconscious for who the hell knows how long. I wince from the intensity of bulbs, trying to cover my eyes. Tears fill my eyes when blood seeps from around the metal cuffs encasing my wrists and drips onto the see-through glass beneath me.

My eyes screw closed, and I suck in frantic breaths, reeling myself in. Right now, I'm held together by safety pins and loose thread, threatening to unravel at any second. Everything hits me all at once, bashing heavily against my skull. Images break free, running through my mind rapidly. One after the other, without mercy. Piper. Magnolia's e-mail. Trent laughing after he soaked Chase in gasoline and left him to die in a blazing inferno. My heart hammers in my chest at the thought of Chase going up in smoke and being nothing but ashes to mourn by tomorrow. More tears leak down my face, and hopelessness settles in. My head swims in a fog, and my lungs burn from lack of oxygen, but I have to get myself together and assess the severity of my situation.

One breath in. One breath out. Count to ten and do it again. I mentally chant to myself repeatedly as my bravery returns, and I turn to face my new Hell. No matter how hopeless I feel right now, I have to keep pushing through and fighting with all my might. I do this for the snuffed-out voices of the people who can't speak up for themselves and tell the world what happened.

My eyes flutter open with hesitation, and I peer around the room. Gingerly, I pull at my restraints again, secretly hoping they'll break despite my weak attempt at getting free. I knew they wouldn't, deep in my gut, but I had to try one last time. If I'm stuck, then there's no way I'll get free. Deep aches form in every bone of my body, and my muscles contract in pain. Grunting, my nostrils flare, and I pull at my restraints with all my might. But it's no use. I strain and strain, but nothing breaks through the sturdy handcuffs chained to a long pole in the center of the glass enclosure I'm in.

The handcuffs clink around the skinny metal bar, running up the human-sized glass enclosure they put me in. It reaches through the mesh lid of the enclosure into the ceiling and goes out the bottom into the ground.

Goosebumps pucker along my skin when I lean back into the cold glass of the human-sized fish tank they've stuffed me in. Reveling in the feel of the icy glass against my skin, I savor the cold penetrating my clothes rather than the pain ricocheting through my body. I need to take stock of where I am and look for any possible escape routes. If I had my pick lock kit I'd be out of here in no time, like a super spy. But it seems they took everything from me except my clothes.

From my viewpoint inside the glass prison, several television monitors with my face and body line the edge of the room. Every move I make, every sound and whimper plays back in front of me like crazy stalker shit. I can only imagine who watches on the other side, taking pleasure in my pain. I bet they're laughing and soaking up the miserable expression lining my hollow-looking face. The only positive takeaway from this experience is they haven't undressed me completely. They've left my t-shirt and leggings on. But they took my cast, white sleeve, and my socks.

My body folds over, gagging into the empty tank. A violent shudder runs through me at the thought of their unwanted hands on me—touching me and removing things from my body. I hold back my tears at the idea of them touching me anywhere they liked while I was knocked out cold.

My breaths pick up, my chest tightening with a million rubber bands constricting my chest. Air escapes me, and darkness creeps into my vision. No! Do not do this to me right now. Just focus on staying alive and here. Stay calm—one breath in. One breath out.

I force myself into happier memories, scanning through mental images of the boys floating through my mind, encouraging words spilling from them. *You got this, Sunshine. Don't fucking give up, Sweetheart. Fight like a warrior, Angel. Come on, baby girl. Don't. Fall. Apart. Yet.*

I crack my eyes open and look around again, focusing on my surroundings. The room I'm in is in deplorable condition. For people making so much money off their dead wives, they don't invest it here. Peeling mid-century flowery wallpaper peels from the walls to my left and right, and old plaster crumbles have fallen to the corner of the room, with cracks on the walls left behind. Brown water stains rest on the ceiling from where I can see, but the weirdest part is the thick black curtains hanging close to the fish tank I'm in. There should be another wall there, or windows or something. Right?

"Oh, good." I leap out of my skin at the smooth voice coming over a speaker nestled somewhere in the tank. His voice seems like it's coming directly into my ear. "You're awake!" He exclaims with a strange, rumbly giggle.

"Where am I?" I ask with hesitation, darting my eyes around my enclosure, but no speaker comes into view.

The deep voice chuckles. "You all always ask the same questions. Where am I? Why are you doing this? Blah, blah, blah. And my answer is always the same, Pumpkin. Welcome to your last seconds on Earth."

Shutting my eyes tight, I fight the tears burning, begging to release down my cheeks. I could cry, pray, and plead until I was blue in the face, but they won't stop. Whatever they're doing, they've succeeded for this long, and they won't stop with me. They'll keep going with whatever game they're playing until they die. And even then, they'll have more assholes to carry on their legacy in other places for years to come. The Apocalypse Society needs to be stopped now, cut off at the head of their operation before they can grow anymore.

I shake my head. I could say so many cliche things: 'Please don't do this,' 'I'm innocent,' 'Why're you doing this to me?!'

But what's the point in pleading with psychopaths? They don't have souls. Much like Piper's blank eyes from the night—wait, hours before? Days before? I don't know how long it's been since they took me. But what I do know is that they won't listen. They'll laugh and get off on my pain. I've seen it plenty of times before.

"Get ready, Sugar, you're about to be famous. Smile at your customers! They've invested so much into this. You're on camera for millions to see. Actually, on second thought, don't! Scream your tits off. The audience likes it." Another distorted voice breaks through the speakers, sending dread into the pit of my turning stomach.

"Welcome investors and bidders to lot number 226," the creepy voice comes from the speakers again, sounding distorted like they're sitting deep underwater. "It's the night you've all been waiting for. Your last bids have been placed!" The voice booms with excitement, much like a movie announcer.

Cheerful music plays through the speakers, only interrupted by another, deep distorted voice. Sounding more distinct than the last one who spoke.

"Over the past few months, you've watched lot 226 through your screens. You've selected her torture, her embarrassments, and punishments." The voice pulls away from the speaker, clearing his throat before continuing. "You've watched her cry and yell. You've watched her pain, frustrations, and sadness. Now—welcome one and all for your final viewing of lot 226 as she endures your last requests and bids us farewell. You've spoken, and you shall receive." The music and voice cut away, giving me nothing more to go on.

Bidding? My embarrassment? My pain? What the hell did he mean by that? Is that what the cameras were for all-around school? They watched me. They. Recorded. It. All. And laughed at every ounce of torture. The goo. The laxative sprinkles. Hadley beating my ass. The camera they had placed in my room. Everything. And viewers decided on my punishments? The torture I went through at the hands of each and every student of this school. But what about Magnolia? Did they do the same? They filmed her murder, but it wasn't in a setting like this. She was killed out in the open and discarded afterward like human trash. The more I think about it, the more I realize just how amateur they were when she was killed. They've grown since then and expanded their kingdom.

My eyes drift toward the television screen, where my horrified face stares back at me—wide eyes, mouth parted, and pale as ever. Dried blood soaked into my t-shirt from the cut Piper inflicted and smeared across my face.

To my horror, icy water blasts into the tank from below, pouring in and rising higher and higher until it's up to my chin in seconds. My breaths pick up, and panic roars through my tightened chest, constricting tighter and tighter. Gasping desperately for air, I pull at my hands again, wishing I could break through the pipe or the metal of the handcuffs. They clink below the cold water, echoing through my death chamber like a death bell. There's no time to plot or think or plead. There's only enough time to gather my breaths and hope for the best. Because before I know it, that water will rise above my head and drown me before I can scream.

White-hot panic spears through me when water fills the tank more. Shit! If I were some sort of badass, I'd have picked it already and freed myself. I'd push through the top of the tank and take everyone out with my fists as the feds burst in and save the day. But I'm not a badass. And the feds don't know what's going on. Well—maybe Veritas. They seem to be onto something, even if they don't have a paper trail backing my claims. They know something, and they have Chase's dad. But they aren't here to save the day. No one is—only me. So, I can't depend on anyone else to get me out of this and survive. I'm all on my own.

Raising my chin, I gulp for air greedily, filling and refilling my lungs while I can suck it in. Oxygen eases the flaring panic warring inside my brain. I try to remind myself by chanting—don't panic—repeatedly inside my head, but it does little to ease the rising terror. Pfft. Yeah, fucking right. How can I not panic? I'm not fucking prepared for this. I can't swim or hold my breath or survive this. As proven by the twins forcing me into their pool, I hate swimming. I've never been good at it, but here I am. I'm stuck in a tank filled with cold water and have no way to escape.

Water rushes into my ears, sloshing and churning. The ends of my hair float in the rushing waters, soaking the ends and finally soaking every inch. I throw my head back, letting the water fill my ears, sucking in my oxygen.

"How long will she last, folks? Five minutes? Three minutes? The jury is still out! Let's watch and see." The voice says with giddy excitement, distorted by the rush of the water.

My heart thunders in my chest, pounding until it echoes in my ears, like a drum beating a frantic beat repeatedly.

Growing up, I never learned to swim. It terrified me. Getting in the pool with the twins was a big feat for me. I mean—the promise of sex in a water lagoon made it more enticing. So I did it. I swam, and they helped me. But the feeling of water over my head and unable to open my eyes isn't a party to me. The pressure sinks into me as the ice water covers my mouth. Shifting my legs, I shove my mouth above water one last time, taking the deepest breath I can muster before the water level rises above my head.

The eerie swishing and splashing of the water echoes in my ears like the death sentence it is. I kick at the glass, trying with all my might to break it down, to do anything to get this water away from me. My lungs burn with a deep ache, begging for fresh air. The voice of the speaker talks, but their words wash away.

I kick at the glass with my bare feet, pounding my heel into the thick, secure glass. The reverberation shoots up my legs like fire searing through my veins. My teeth grit together from the pain, but I refuse to cry out and give the water any more of my oxygen. The glass doesn't budge or bend. No matter how hard I kick, it doesn't crack or break. Panic sets in, and I frantically look around the cloudy water, looking for another escape route. All their victims' names repeatedly run through my mind, reminding me why I started this investigation. It may have started with my best friend, but it ended with more than her. So many people have died this exact way or worse. They've tortured people for too long, and it's time it ended.

I may be their rabbit in a trap, but I'll be damned if I go down without a fight. I'll fight and kick, scream and bite—anything to save my life from their greedy hands.

A deep shiver works through my limbs, and goosebumps pimple across every inch of my skin. The cold water sets my bones on edge. Sharp shivers take over my whole body, trembling my limbs. The feeling in my hands and feet slips away, and a tingle takes over. My lungs beg for clean air, and black dots take over the edges of my vision, begging me to succumb to the darkness awaiting me if I stay under the water any longer. Desperation eats at me when I kick the glass some more, sloshing the water into waves—anything to stay awake and alert. If I can make it through these agonizing five minutes, I can survive whatever else they have in store.

I lean against the glass, staring out through my watery grave. It squiggles and moves with the waves I've created, splashing onto the floor. Looking above me, I notice a fish tank lid again—flimsy and moveable. Without second-guessing my actions, I move inside the tank back and forth, creating massive waves. Water seeps through the mesh material, splashing on the disgusting carpet and creating puddles. I mentally fist-bump myself and keep going, making more and more waves, and spilling more out of the tank. Exhaustion pulls at my tired muscles, and more black dots litter my vision. In seconds, I know the world will blur, and I'll no longer exist. I have to keep going and moving and thinking so I don't die.

My body slows, going with the waves inside the tank. It's been more than a minute, and I know it has. Time slows down before my eyes, a drowsy feeling encasing me in its grasp. A heaviness pulls at my eyelids, begging them to shut so my body can cease. I grunt, expelling bubbles through my mouth, and shake my head. I refuse to give in to this sick game and let them watch me succumb under their thumb. I will not give up. I'll fight till the last second of my life. Moving back and forth again, I continue to splash the water over the sides of the tank. Back and forth. Back and forth. The water splashes and splashes over the edge, greeting the disgusting green carpet and soaking it.

Looking up in desperation, I throttle my entire body, using my feet to the tiny air pocket above me. My handcuffed hands strain against the pull, staying below and cutting into my skin further. It can bleed me out for all I care. I need this air. It's a sliver of hope directly above me.

A tiny miracle of air sits above my head, bringing it straight into my burning lungs. It's oxygen to my heart, which pounds and pounds frantically against my chest. Huffing and puffing, I cough and sputter, clearing my lungs of the intruding water, and replacing it with cool, fresh air.

"Well, well, well, little rabbit, it looks like you've won this round. I have notified the bids for under ninety seconds! Your prize awaits! On to the next!" The distorted voice booms out, ringing in my aching ears.

I cough harder, sloshing more water. My thoughts move at snail's speed, unable to process what's happening around me. My brain aches from the lack of oxygen, and a hammer hacks away at my brain matter.

The water drains from the tank, scattering shivers through my exhausted body. Every muscle in my body strains and refuses to move when I want them to. All I can do is suck more oxygen into my burning lungs. I'm a fucking blob—a useless lump, sitting and waiting for her execution.

Two black-hooded figures float through the room, like the figures who keyed my car and painted my apartment door with red slashes. Now they stand before me. Black masks cover their faces, concealing their true identity from me. Their hands tuck into the enormous sleeves, hiding their skin tones and any identifying factors that could lead me to their identities.

A hiss releases a side of the tank, opening like a glass door on hinges. Their black-gloved hands paw at me, gripping my hair in their grasp. Someone unlocks my handcuffs, leaving them attached to the pipe and off my aching wrists. Dragging my weak body out of the tank, I can barely stand on my own two feet. One figure throws a dark hood over my head, silently leading me out of the disgusting room as the carpet squishes beneath my bare feet. Their hands rest on my waist, fingers wrapping around my side. I soak in the warmth of their body glued to my side, wishing I could keep their heat with me. Even their leather gloves on my skin feel warm and cozy.

A cry of pain tears from down the hall, jerking my body to a halt. I stiffen, listening to her wails of anguish. She doesn't have to utter a word to tell her story. Her pain is evident with every agonizing scream. The faint murmur of the distorted speaker's voice flitters through the air in a deep tone, mocking the poor soul, begging the psychopaths to save her.

The fingers on my waist gently squeeze my side three times and continue to drag me forward. I patiently wait for my dragging feet to catch up. The darkened hood on my head drowns out the world. Only the screams and the scuff of my feet break through the darkness. But my sight? It's broken, for now, lost in the darkness they submerged me in.

The person grabbing my waist turns me around and forces my back to an icy surface. It feels like a large metal pole against my back with the hood on. Stripper pole? A metal water pipe? Nothing can be as bad as the damn fish tank.

No one speaks. The tension and silence in the room are deafening to my ringing ears, only broken up by the shuffle of their feet. Static surrounds me. Silent and deadly.

My muscles tighten as one of the cloaked figures wraps tough ropes around my wrists. Starting with the right one, they tighten it with a rough yank, rubbing it against the wounds on my wrist. An involuntary whimper leaves my throat as they tie the other wrist off, yanking and pulling the rope. My breath rapidly pours in and out of my nose when the realization hits me. They didn't tie it as tight on my left wrist. With caution, I move my left wrist around, testing the bounds of the rope–like I did with the right one, finding less resistance—almost no resistance. It doesn't burn into my wrist with every movement. It's barely hanging on, and for that, I'm thankful as fuck.

A gloved hand squeezes my left elbow, stopping my movements. It almost feels like they're warning me. But why? Why would any of these people warn me? Is someone other than Carter on my side? Or is it... No. He wouldn't sit back and watch me die, would he? It wouldn't be him, would it? But he'd have to if he were here, wouldn't he? He wouldn't be able to march out of here with me in his arms. Comfort settles over me, thinking about his presence beside me, and I relax my muscles. If it is him, I have to trust in him. If he's leaving me a free hand to get loose, he's giving me an advantage in whatever is about to come.

All thoughts evaporate as the hood is torn from my head, and I wince from the lights blaring down on me once again. Three hooded figures stand before me with their arms crossed over their chests. Not giving me any clue as to who these people are. I study them for longer than necessary when two more figures walk into the room with their masked faces held high. The door clicks behind them, locking us together. They march forward, instead of standing in the straight line of the others, and stand before me.

"Heya, Stupid." The one says with a distorted voice, bringing a finger to the side of my face. "Remember me?" They ask in a deep voice, sending my mind reeling back to the night of the car crash where their distorted words ring through my mind on repeat. And then again in my bedroom right before they drugged me again and brought me here.

It was him.

"Trent," I grunt, trying to pull from his grasp. "You were there? You wrecked into us?" I grind my teeth when he pulls up his mask and grins at me with pride bleeding into his eyes.

"Ah, I never thought you'd remember. You were blitzed out of your mind, Slut," he says, leaning in to brush his lips against my cheek, leaving a wet mark on my flesh. "I could have taken you then, and I could take you now." I swallow hard at what he's implying and follow his gaze when he looks at one of the hooded figures standing rigid in the line watching with rapt attention as Trent's hand creeps over my breast and squeezes hard. "Perfect," Trent mumbles, trailing unwanted kisses down my jaw. I stiffen with every groan and squeeze he gives my tit, and float to another universe, hoping to block this whole experience from my mind.

"You fucking dick," The other masked figure hisses, punching Trent square in the jaw and knocking him back. "If anyone gets a piece, it's fucking me!" He roars, whipping off his mask, and throws it to the floor.

I lick my lips, trying to move out of Oscar's sleazy gaze, but he only latches on more. "I've had my eyes on you from the moment you walked on campus. It's a shame you aren't mine to bring to heel." His eyes dip to my chest, and I swear he's about to grope me, too, but his gaze dips to my right arm secured behind my back. A devilish grin takes over his face. "You gave quite a fight, though," he says, nodding to my arm. "It took me a few kicks." I stiffen again, and the color drains from my face as the memories of the pain exploding through my arm resurface.

"It was you? You broke my arm?" I ask in a small voice, shaking my head. "You two were there?" Trent snorts and rolls his eyes.

"What did you expect? Your lover boy?" He scoffs but keeps his gaze on the same figure as before, who stands stock still, watching the exchange.

"Delta and Panty Licker." A figure steps forward with a growl in their distorted voice and cocks their head. "You're interrupting a broadcasting bid with your assaults." They wave their hands around in irritation, earning nothing but huffs from the other two.

"You'll get yours," Oscar murmurs so low, it barely registers what he's saying while plucking his mask off the floor.

"It was sanctioned by the real bosses anyway, Alpha," Trent hisses, setting his mask back onto his face. "We'll be on our way. Enjoy your stay," he sing-songs, waving a hand in the air.

I finally let out a breath when they leave the room and close the door behind them. The ghost of his disgusting touch lingers on my chest, but I have a feeling his wandering hands are the least of my worries now. I was drowned, groped, and now I'm loosely tied to a pole. What more could they do to me now?

I take a quick scan of the similar-looking room and wrinkle my nose at its appearance. The disgusting wallpaper from the previous room fills this room, too. It's peeling, moldy, and downright awful. Orange carpet, from what looks like the seventies, sits under my feet with mushrooms growing tall in the damp, dark corners. The musky air is tinted with iron and sulfur, giving the room a fantastic atmosphere.

Bile brews in the back of my throat, burning its way up. My legs wobble beneath me, but I'm forced to stand before three black-hooded figures. Their blackened masks give me nothing to go on, which is a shame. I wish I could read their faces to know what I'm up against this time now.

They stand and stare as I catch my wheezing breath. My skin tightens under their unwavering glare. It wraps around me, nearly choking the air from my lungs again. I avert my eyes, refusing to look at them, and take stock of my fucked up situation.

Construction tools lie discarded around the room. Some near me and some far away. Hammers. Pipes. Saws and screwdrivers. It's almost as if they were redoing the house and decided not to finish. It would explain the peeling paper and missing pieces.

"Welcome back to lot two hundred and twenty-six! What a fighter she's turned out to be," the distorted voice chuckles through the menacing speakers again. "Boy, do we have a treat for you! It was a long and drawn-out bidding war between Battling Babes and Tantalizing Toenails." My back stiffens at the words 'tantalizing toenails'. Dear God. What in the hell would they do with toenails? And what makes them tantalizing? Oh, God. Pull them off? Eat them? Crush my feet? Watch me suffer? I cringe, hoping that's not the direction we're going in.

"But you asked for battling babes fight and battling babes fight you will get!" The distorted voice sounds way too giddy again, clapping in the microphone. "The bidding is open for the winner of this high ticket show. Place your bids now and see who wins this showdown! Let the game begin!"

I sigh, leaning my head back on the pole. "A fight, huh?" I ask the three unmoved figures in a raspy voice.

Their arms crossed over their chests, and they still haven't moved or spoken. My guess? It's either Hadley, Espie, Zoe, or... or Carter who has been here. Carter... Carter, my big, mean, grumpy man. I want him to rush to me, wrap his arms around me, and tell me I will be okay.

"Not very fair, is it?" I taunt, nodding toward my bound arms. I shake my head, huffing another breath.

The burning in my lungs spreads like wildfire, taking every inch of breathing room. With every deep huff or breath, it fans the flames more. So if I need to fight, I'm screwed. Not only will I not be able to breathe, but they also tied my hands behind my back.

"Who the fuck says it needs to be fair, dumbass freak?" Hadley Lacey says with a sneer behind her mask.

Ahh, as I suspected. My number one fan has shown up to beat my ass once and for all—hurray.

"Obviously not you," I mumble. "You never fight fair, though, do you? Poisoning me, beating me in the hall?" I don't have the energy to keep spouting off, so I heave a breath and prepare myself for the fight I'm about to receive.

This time, a hooded figure steps forward, whipping the robe and mask off, revealing herself to me. Hadley sports a cute bra and matching thong set. Well—I guess it's cute. Pink. Frilly. Puke-inducing. Gross. Whoever told her to put that on sucks. A girl fight in underwear? How cliche can they get?

Hadley saunters forward with confidence in every step and chin held high. A smug grin takes over her face, and her beady eyes eat me up. A bright twinkle of victory shines in her eyes like she's won some special prize. Hadley claps her hands together in a small golf-type clap, bouncing on the balls of her feet in excitement. I'm a sweet and tasty morsel strapped to a pole, ready for her to devour with her fists—helpless and vulnerable, the way she likes them.

"This is going to be so much fun," she giggles with too

much enthusiasm, channeling my least favorite psychopath —Piper.

A shrill buzzer sounds over the speaker, and my heart drops into my stomach when she charges forward.

Hadley doesn't waste any time hammering her fist into every available surface of my body. Ribs. Face. Shit—mostly the face. Pain blooms everywhere on my body, roaring like an inferno. I scream and cry out, but I never beg. I never plead for her to stop what she's doing. Instead, letting her pound her relentless fists into me. Over and over, she fractures bones and snaps cartilage, inflicting as much pain as possible. All the while, her shrieks of laughter and joy echo through the room.

Warmth leaks from my nose and ears, giving me the impression blood is seeping from them. The taste of iron invades my tongue when I lick over a split in my lips. More pain erupts when her knuckles connect with my eyebrow, and I feel the skin tear in half.

My body crumbles to the sodden floor, falling into a whimpering heap. "Fight me like a woman, Hadley!" I hiss from the ground, staring up at her smug face. She twists her fist in her palm, soothing the ache from her punches. "Untie me so I can kick your ass!" I yell, receiving a punishing foot to my jaw. Stars dance in my vision, and my head lolls to the side from the force and then again when a solid piece of metal smacks me in the face. I knock back onto my ass, staring at the sodden floor with blood rushing from my nose. Warm blood pools in my mouth, where I swear one of my teeth wiggles under my tongue. Pain spreads everywhere when I heave a breath, trying to make it subside.

Whatever she hits me with, falls to the floor with a thud. I follow the movement, groaning loudly in pain and hanging my head. Pain ricochets through my entire face with a pounding pain I can't soothe. My weakened heart pounds in my chest, filling my ears. Blood pours from my mouth, dripping onto the sodden carpet. My fists curl behind my back, still stuck to the stupid pole. But enough is enough—I growl to myself.

If she won't give me a fair fight, I'll make her wish she never stepped in this room. I wiggle my wrist in the loosened rope and slip it through. Hadley runs her mouth, pacing back and forth in front of me. I watch her pound her fist into her palm repeatedly through my lashes, babbling about how dead I am.

I ignore her tirade, mentally thanking my guardian angel in a black robe. They looked out for me and helped set me free, whoever they are. Keeping my hand nestled behind me, I search the area for a weapon with my eyes. I keep my head down, letting my limp, wet hair hang in my face. It shields my true intentions as I scan the area around me, looking for anything to get my violent revenge.

Like the board game Clue, I spot my possible weapons across the room. Lead pipe. Hand saw. Hammer. And a rusted wrench just in reach with my blood smeared on the metal. I narrow my swollen eyes at the stupid tools. Geez. Any weapon will do. A chainsaw would do for all I care. Just call this the California Chainsaw Massacre.

Or, we could, if there was a chainsaw in here, and if it wouldn't call the big men from down the hall, or wherever they are hiding. Right now, I fantasize about chopping her hand off and slapping her silly with it. Can you imagine? Hitting Hadley with her own damn hands. I snort—I must be delirious from the pain lashing through me. Since there doesn't seem to be any fun tool lying right next to me, the rusted wrench closest to me will have to do. It'll cause damage to her pretty face.

"I don't think so, freak. You're going to be so black and blue by the time they find your body. They won't even recognize you." I don't look up as she cackles some more, rambling about my impending death. That's right, crazy lady. Keep on talking so I can find something to pound into your face. I focus my eyes on the fiery orange carpet—deep breath in and a deep breath out, drowning out her whiny voice.

Hadley paces in front of me, waving her hands all around. She talks on and on about how stupid and worthless I am. Keeping my eyes on her pacing form and the other two hooded figures in the room, I reach for the wrench as carefully as possible with my left hand. Once it's secure beside me, I undo my right hand and free myself from the rope.

Now is the time to even the odds.

I wobble to my feet with as much strength as I can muster, swaying, and the room spins, forcing me to hold onto the bar with my free hand. Everything weaves in the room, bright dots take over my vision, and the whole room disappears.

"You never learn when to stay down, do you? You just keep getting up and up—"

"I did it," I say, shaking my head.

Pain pounds everywhere on my face, especially my jaw, where I can still feel the imprint of her black boot.

"Did what, freak?" She hisses, popping her knuckles.

The corner of my mouth stretches up. "I hacked into your FlashGram account and medical records and told the world what a disgusting vagina you have. It was me," I say, trying not to bite my swollen tongue.

"Holy shit!" A deep, manly voice exclaims from under one of the black masks, distorted and laughing.

"You bitch," she says through clenched teeth and steps forward. Her back straightens, and she rolls her eyes, throwing her brown curly hair over her shoulder. "Duh. We all knew it was you, anyway. You aren't as slick as you think you are." The other figure snorts, earning a glare from Hadley.

"Did you ever get that sorted out?" I slur, my tongue feeling like the size of a truck and as heavy as one, too. My legs shake beneath me, barely holding me up. But I press on, walking forward, weaving on my unsteady legs.

She snarls at me like a rabid dog, growling and spitting saliva. "Shut up!" She shouts, waving her hands. "Shut the fuck up!"

I manage a manic grin through ragged breaths, revealing my blood-soaked teeth, trying as I might to seem tough and put together while my reality is closing in faster and faster. Here and now are the last seconds I'll be on Earth.

"Make me," I growl. My throat aches. Everything aches. But I hold tight to the wrench, heavy in the palm of my sweaty, tingling hands.

Hadley's screech is the only sign she's coming for me. Her feet pound against the floor, fist rising above her head to strike, leaving her face vulnerable and primed for my ambush. She never questioned why I wasn't tied up.

None of them did. They simply faced me and took in our exchange with pleasure. It was all part of their plan.

I was sure it was, up until the wrench pounds into her cheek, crushing her teeth and jaw, sending her to the floor with a squeal of pain.

"Fuck!" the other hooded figure shouts, marching toward me.

"Theee hissttt meeee!" She wails on the ground, rocking back and forth, clutching her bloody cheek.

"I'll do it again, " I wheeze, clutching onto the pole for dear life. My knees knock together, my ankles weakening, and I know I'm about to go down.

The hooded figure closest to me wraps an arm around my neck, applying pressure to all the right areas. I laugh at Hadley's injuries.

"That's—what—you—get!" I cry out with all my might as darkness takes over my vision, plummeting me into oblivion.

# TWENTY-THREE

## KAYCEE

Silence greets me the moment my mind rouses. Pain sings a song of sorrow and defeat throughout my body, aching and throbbing with every slow heartbeat thumping in my chest. Static rings in both ears, drowning out any other sound. For a suspended moment, I forget where I am and what's happened to me over the course of—well, I don't know how long. I know I'm somewhere strange, locked with killers I want nothing to do with. But how did I get in this wooden chair digging into my butt? And why are my hands locked to each chair's armrest, secured with more rope digging into my previous wounds?

Keeping my breathing the same, I try to take stock of where I am without alerting my captors that I'm awake. I take several deep breaths, listening as hard as I can through the constant ringing in my ears. Silence greets me in every direction, giving me the impression I'm alone. But I know I'm not. I feel their heated stares from somewhere. Whether they're viewing me from their control room or standing across the room silently waiting for me to wake, I know their eyes are on me—their prey.

A gloved hand moves to my throat, lifting my chin from my chest. Agony spears through me from the movement, and

I swear I'm about to shatter into a million pieces. I cry out from the pain, unable to hold it back.

"Open your eyes, little rabbit," a distorted voice demands, prying my eyelids open with their fingers.

Pain pierces like a knife through my swollen-shut eye, feeling like broken glass sitting beneath my puffy lid, poking and scratching my eye. I cry out as water fills my eyes, leaking down my face. My cry reverberates through the small room as my eyelid slams back shut. I shake out of his hold as much as I can with the person holding my neck from behind, leaving me be.

A chuckle rumbles in front of me, pulling away from my body toward the other side of the room. "Wakey, wakey, rabbit. We have big plans for you." His distorted voice sends shivers down my spine, and dread pools in the depth of my belly.

This is my end.

Through ragged breaths, I peel my good eye open. Water continually pours from it, blurring the hellish room they've put me in. Slowly, it comes into focus. And God, I wish I was dead. I'm in yet another room decorated the same way: moldy orange carpet, peeling flowery wallpaper, holes in the plaster, and water stains on the ceiling. A long mahogany bar sits toward the edge of the room, wrapped in a worn black leather, ripped and torn from years of neglect. A large dirt-caked mirror with liquor shelves sits above it, empty, with smears swirling across the glass. Thick black curtains hang from poles attached to the worn ceiling, blocking any windows from view. How they attached it without bringing the place down baffles me.

Reservation settles over me, and my shoulders slump in defeat. A festering feeling deep in my gut lets me know my fate has been sealed. It's been sealed from the moment they brought me to this decrepit house and put me in that fish tank. From the moment they tied me to a pole, letting their minion beat the hell out of me. The clock is ticking on the last seconds of my life, and death is imminent. If a miracle doesn't happen, I'm leaving this place in a black body bag, and the authorities will find my body sometime later. A sad story will follow a small headline about another suicide victim being found, and that will be that. The Apocalypse Society will continue their reign of terror without any recourse to their actions, and I'll be in the dirt and forgotten.

Three red-hooded figures stand side-by-side in front of me with their arms crossed over their chests. Devious masks are sitting on their faces, much different from the masks of the others. These are intricate, making each individual in red stand out from the sea of black cloaks, giving me the impression that these are the leaders of the society, conducting the choir of chaos.

Their equally scary, black-cloaked minions fill the room with black masks covering their faces again. Even the slumped-over figure in the corner of the room, moaning and groaning with a hand near her face. Hadley—I recognize her instantly without seeing her face. Good—I hurt her and knocked her smug face down a notch. She deserves a million more wrenches to the face until she feels my wrath and pain for everything she made me endure. I'll even add a little boot kick to the jaw for good measure. Despite the situation, a warm, giddy feeling bubbles up my throat in the form of a giggle, thinking about the scars she'll wear for the rest of her life. Whenever Hadley Lacey looks at herself in the mirror, she'll see the reflection of someone who got bested by me. She'll never forget the day she broke me open, but she'll never forget that the rabbit fought back and got her small measure of justice.

"Welcome," a distorted voice booms through the room, still hidden behind the mask in place.

I narrow my eyes at the man standing before me, speaking through the mask.

"Coward," I hiss through my broken teeth with venom, eyeing the man who doesn't flinch at my words. They continue to stare, ignoring my outburst. I don't dare bite my tongue now because I know whatever they have up their sleeve will hurt. They'll torture me more until I'm a bleeding stump, and I'll have no chance of escape.

These villains are nothing more than cowards hiding behind false faces because they can't fathom facing me themselves. For months they've made my life agony. The least they could do is show me their true selves. Even from here, I can tell who they are. It doesn't take a genius to decipher the three Van Buren brothers, who hide behind false names given to them at their adoptions, standing tall before me.

"We have another exciting event for you this afternoon," says another voice, stepping forward towards a camera placed on a tripod in the middle of the room.

"One of our last events is lot four hundred and seventy-five!" The fingers around my throat flex, forcing my head to the side.

Muffled screams come from the doorway, a desperate woman pleading and begging for her life. Two black-hooded minions carry in another chair similar to mine, occupied by a very distraught and bloodied woman—a familiar woman—I've only seen on two occasions before. My aching heart falls into my ass at the sight of Francesca Hurst, Piper's mother. Cushing's girlfriend, or wife, or whatever she is. Carter mentioned before that they were never married, and I never found solid information about their union. So, what is she doing in my realm of Hell, almost as bloodied and bruised as me?

"For the first time, we are bringing our lots together. Give a round of applause to lots two hundred and twenty-six and four hundred and seventy-five! Facing off in a new game created for your viewing pleasure. Place your bets now on who our victor will be!" The red-robed figure continues speaking into the camera, throwing his arms around in excitement, talking with his hands, and moving his body for the show. He's perfect for this circus, the ringmaster of it all.

I close my eyes on this nightmare, imagining I'm in another place and time, away from these sadistic fucks. I pray to a God I barely ever pray to, asking him to protect the ones I love. My parents. My siblings. And my boys. They deserve divine intervention and safety after this is said and done.

I hope Chase survived whatever they did to him when they came for me. I pray the twins stayed with their father, making sure he was alright. And when they hear of my death, I pray they don't blame themselves. Somewhere in the back of my mind, I hope Carter is okay. I don't know if he was called to action and is standing before me in the sea of black robes. An ache forms in my heart with the betraying thought of him standing before me with that cruel smirk I met him with, laughing at my naivete and stupidity. Maybe his fists are tightened at his sides, waiting for the perfect time to spring me from this prison. Fleeting lights of hope spark in my chest at the thought of my savior hiding in plain sight. When I look at the masked faces staring back at me, I can only blink and pray some more that safety is coming soon.

I close my eyes, painting a beautiful picture of my future in my mind. There's no here and now. Only the brightness of my future calling to me and begging me to focus on what could be or what will be. Moving into CaliState will be fun. I'll have a roommate in a dorm, where I'll rarely be. The boys will share a four-room suite and sneak me in after hours. I'll rotate between their beds, and eventually, Carter will buy us a house my sophomore year. He'll work from home while the rest of us go to school, and then we'll graduate together. Visions of our forever home construct before my eyes in vivid color. Green grass with children playing with their fathers. Football games. Cookouts. Family meals. Dreams I didn't know I wanted before my boys showed up and slammed into my life. It's all there at the tip of my fingers, slipping through like a fine sand I can't grasp.

"No!" A loud shriek permeates through the air, jerking me out of my reprieve.

A bucket of cold water falls over me when Francesca's frantic blue eyes search mine, looking me up and down while shaking her head. My fantasy instantly falls away, and reality sets in, bringing me back to the Hell they've dragged me into. Our knees brush together, giving us an up close and personal view of the terror we're about to live—or die—through. Her lips pop open, tears filling her eyes at the sight of my smashed up face. Her brows furrow, and she begins pleading with them to have mercy on us. But, mercy won't come. Not with the Apocalypse running the show. We're in their hands now, and nothing else matters.

Her chair moves an inch off the ground as she thrashes in her seat. She pulls and yanks at her roughly bound hands, screeching and howling until a red hood steps forward, slapping the soul from her body.

"Shut up, bitch," he growls. "You brought this on yourself." Grabbing a fistful of her dull red hair, he forces her face forward. Her dead eyes stare straight at me, lips parting in shock. Horror crosses her face. She wants to scream, darting her eyes at the others. But she doesn't. Every limb on her body shakes uncontrollably in her chair.

"This, ladies and gentlemen, is a little game I like to call humanities," the man says again. Trailing his finger across a large metal tray, he runs a finger over shiny tools: a hammer, screwdriver, grapefruit spoon, a small pair of pliers, a large knife, a blow torch attached to propane, and a hot poker–glowing red, ready for use.

What a fucking party.

Dread fills every molecule inside of me. My empty stomach churns violently, thrashing against its walls, begging for me to spew. But I'm frozen—frozen at the sight of the blow torch inching its hot flame toward me. Orange and blue flames dance in front of my face—the heat cascades across my flesh, threatening to bubble under the intensity.

"No!" repeats Francesca. "Leave the child alone! How could you! How could you sit back and do this to an innocent child! You're all sick fucks!" she roars, thrashing in her chair again. "Sick! Sick! Bastards! Do it to me! Leave her alone!" She howls, gaining the attention of the sick bastard with the blowtorch.

I don't even get a word edgewise to stop him from harming her. For the next few minutes, unspeakable tortures fall upon Piper's mom. She screams and shouts, begging them to stop, and they do. They stop everything, giving in to her pleas. But instead of stopping it completely, they walk toward me. She begs again for them to spare me, and they only return to her, repeating the torture. They're manipulating her humanity—her soul. It's either her or me. If one of us isn't in pain, the other is.

Francesca pants as sweat pours from every orifice on her body. Blood pools on the floor beneath her, painting it a dark shade of red. Continually, it drips from her face and arms.

Her skin is burned, poked, prodded, and hammered. Pain pours from her eyes, and the most helpless feeling falls over me. I can't do anything about it. I can't save her unless I take on the pain myself. She refuses to let that happen. Any time I open my mouth to take the brunt of the torture, she directs them back to her.

"Why are you doing this, Vic?" she rasps, words making it out in a whisper. "Why did you do this to me? What did I ever do to you?"

"You know why," one of the red hoods whispers, reaching for a tool on the tray. "You know exactly why you're in this little predicament!" He shouts now, shoving his mask off and throwing it to the floor in rage. His fingers wrap around an ornate knife, shining in the bright spotlight.

Victor Crowe stands ramrod straight, gripping the large knife tight in his fist. Anger surges over his face, tightening his jaw and forming a vicious sneer on his lips.

"Explain it to me," she pleads in a dull voice.

He stalks forward with a grunt, ramming the knife into her thigh. A small, pained cry falls from her dry lips, but that's all she gives him.

"You stole my daughter," he yells, nose to nose with her bleeding face. "You stole my daughter, ran away with her, and changed her name. And then that asshole adopted her. I had to find out years later where you went!" He hisses, pressing his forehead angrily into hers. "And then you dared to get married to that-that fucking reject. YOU. LEFT. ME! YOU WERE MINE!" He shouts in her face, only getting a tiny smile in return.

"You've always had an overactive imagination, Vic," she whispers. "You were obsessed with me. You stalked me. You raped me and forced me to have her. I never wanted you. I never loved you. I took my daughter away to save her from you, and look where that got me. I married Thomas because he loved me and promised us a good life-or..." Crowe cackles at her words falling off.

"Oh yeah, he loved you so much. He left you and your daughter with nothing but the clothes on your back. Well, let's just say he didn't have a choice, Sugar. I'm a compelling man when I need to be. Hurst filed for divorce the moment I knew about Victoria. Very sneaky, too, marrying him. Him adopting my daughter and changing her name, the name I gave her! I bet you didn't think I'd ever find out, did you? Until I caught up to you and forced you into my brother's hands." Another red hood chuckles, throwing his mask onto the floor and revealing the face of Cushing Cunningham.

"She was a very pliant prisoner. Obedient. The bitch cooked me dinner every night. Until she had to be thrown back into the basement and locked up." Cushing laughs, making her wince.

"You left me," Crowe says again in a calmer, more soothing voice. "So I went after everything you held dear or would hold dear." A manic grin splits his face, turning the acid in my gut, sending bile up my throat.

"Looks like you won then, congratulations," she says in a very soft voice, giving all the sarcasm she can muster. If her finger hadn't been crushed beneath the hammer, she'd twirl it for him or flip him the bird.

"I won," he proclaims, spreading his arms out. "We won," he points to the other two red-robed men. "And we'll always win. This is just the beginning of our rule! And it all started with your sister and her bitch of a daughter." Francesca's body slumps, the shock of her injuries stepping forward. She shakes her head, trying to keep the festering shivers at bay.

"I don't have a sister, and you know that," she simply says.

"Ah!" he says, holding a finger up in the air, holding his grin. He spins, so the entire room takes him in. Pointing at the camera still filming, he continues. "But you did have a sister. See, after you ran from me, I caught a whiff of something. Something big. Something like a sister you never knew existed. You see, your mommy was a whore and a home-wrecker."

If Francesca could look shocked under all the blood on her face, she would. Her blue eyes widen, staring straight at Crowe. He does a happy dance for the camera.

"Ahh! See! This is what I wanted!" He chuckles to his brothers in red. They grin, too, stepping closer to Crowe.

"Who? What?" she begs in whispered sobs. "You…?"

"See, in college, I met this magnificent woman. I followed her around, asked her out, and we started dating. Red hair and beautiful eyes, and she was on track to become a doctor. Looking back, I see why I loved you so much. When we met, I realized how similar the two of you were. That button nose, eye shape, hell, even your tits were the same. But then, she fucking left me, too, after a few months of dating. We graduated, and then she married some old fucker, and rode off into the sunset, and had that bitch of a kid." My jaw grinds together at his words. That bitch was my best friend. The one person who got me and understood me.

"So this entire thing..." her head slumps more, words slurring as she speaks. She's been through so much that I don't know how much more she can take. They could blow a feather into her face, and I think she'd completely collapse under the pressure. Guilt slams into me like a heavy train colliding with my chest. She'd be in better shape if I could have taken some of the torture away from her. But she didn't allow them to. She made them focus on her instead of me.

"You left me and disappeared into the sunset. So the moment I put two and two together, I made my carefully orchestrated moves. Took your sister's husband—poor guy—and that left them for me. I waited and waited until it all fell into place. Your real daddy? Absolutely loaded! And thanks to their death, your niece's death, and your sister's death, I'm a multi-millionaire. Now, to close this dreadful chapter with your untimely death. Such a shame, but a long time coming. The entire website wanted to know what poor lot four hundred and seventy-five did to deserve such torment. And now they know. You left me, so I took all of your family and turned your poor crazy daughter against you. Good lay—" Vomit burns my esophagus from the imagery of him and Piper screwing around. They will forever be etched into my memories like a train wreck you can't look away from. But even more disturbing is the fact he just admitted to turning Piper against her mother and using her for his own personal gains.

"Victoria!" Crowe booms, reaching a hand out to a black-hooded figure who saunters toward him with confidence leaking from her posture. Tearing off her mask, he holds her cheeks in his palms, staring deep into her eyes like a precious jewel. "My sweet, sweet, Victoria. When I finally found you, I renamed you after me to show the world who you belonged to. To show them that you were a Van Buren and had finally found your rightful place. You're so beautiful, love," he purrs, peppering kisses down her jaw.

"Daddy," she whispers. "Is all that true?" Her head cocks to the side, water forming in her eyes.

"Is what true, Love?" he asks huskily.

Piper's brows furrow, looking back at her mother's dying body, slumping in the chair like a ragdoll. "You forced Daddy Hurst out? Made him leave Francesca?" He grins more, gripping tight to her jaw. He no longer kisses at her flesh but sinks his fingertips in, leaving indentations and bruises for later.

"And you see where that's gotten me? It's right in your words." He mocks with deep chuckles coming from his chest.

"My finest piece on the chessboard." He looks back over to Francesca, snorting with glee. "I broke your marriage and broke your daughter. So much so that she fell to her knees when I swooped in to save her from you. She was so grateful and well—she opened her legs for me. She did anything I wanted her to do. I was so good at manipulating her, and I even convinced her I loved her." He delivers his rant like a villain at the end of a movie. Complete with manic laughing from him and his brothers joining in, cracking like a whip straight through Piper's broken heart.

Her bottom lip quivers, and streams of tears fall down her cheeks, collecting in the spot where Crowe holds her fighting form. She tries and fails to pull away from his grasp in desperation, pounding a fist into his arm and pleading with him to let her go.

"For your final torture," Crowe growls, shoving Piper to the ground with a thud. She lands on her ass with a startled yelp, staring up at Crowe like he broke her heart and shit in her shoes all at once. Pitiful tears stream down her face, head shaking back and forth. "You will watch the only child you ever loved die." He gives the nod to the others standing guard in black cloaks with a grin, watching in awe as they descend into madness with sharp, shiny knives gripped in their hands. Only five hooded figures circle her like the sharks they are, leaning down as one to cover her prone body with their cloaks. The others watch from the wall they stand against with envy as they go in for the kill.

"DADDY, NO!" Piper screams in desperation, crying out in pained whimpers.

Nothing but the slices of flesh and grunts fill the silent space as they fulfill their sick duty to their leaders. Piper's helpless cries fall off into nothing, forever silenced by the sharp end of a knife. I heave breaths, gagging when the black figures stand tall and lazily return to where they once were with blood coating their black cloaks and dripping on the floor. With them out of the way, Piper's lifeless and bloodied body remains mutilated where she lays. The last image I see of her is her cold, glazed-over blue eyes staring at the ceiling, pleading one last time for help that will never come.

My heart pounds in my chest when Crowe claps his hands, congratulating the killers with a small handshake. Like a proud father, he murmurs words of encouragement and slaps their shoulders before returning to his spot in the middle of the room. With disdain, he looks down at a sobbing Francesca, who stares at her only child left brutalized on the ground and blood collecting around her in a large pool.

The hand around my neck squeezes, returning my gaze to the madman smiling mere feet in front of me. He looks pleased with himself, and so do his brothers, who clap him on the shoulder. It's like they played the Super Bowl and won, and now they get their trophy. True and utter fear takes hold of my pounding heart when he turns his attention back to Francesca, and I can only guess what's coming next. And I don't have to wait long. Crowe silences Francesca with a knife plunging deep into her chest, killing her instantly.

"All of you, take the bodies and prepare them for their final resting places. Poor, poor dears. They couldn't handle life anymore." He fake cries into his hand as the black figures scurry around the room, gathering the bodies and pulling them out. "Everyone else out. It's time for the final and private ceremony." He grins, side-eyeing me with a sadistic glint sparkling in the depths of his depraved eyes.

Nerves prickle at the back of my neck, making my hair stand on end. How could I have ever looked him in the eye and thought he was sane? There's clear insanity behind his blue eyes that I've never seen before. Maybe in the past, he held it in and pretended to be the man we thought he was. Although, there's always been a trickle of unease whenever I was around him. Like there was something I couldn't put my finger on. And now I know what it was. He's unhinged.

"You all are doing so well," the still-masked, red-hooded figure says with pride. "Keep doing as you're told, and your promotion will come." His head bobs up and down when the remaining black-robed people walk by him towards the exit. "Delta!" he shouts the name as Oscar steps forward, straightening his back.

"Yes, Sir," he says, facing the masked member.

"You're promoted to Alpha. Your instructions will come directly from me now. Keep an eye out. Our new game begins in ten days," he says, squeezing Oscar's shoulder with affection.

"Yes, Sir," he says with glee in his tone, waltzing off and out the door.

A deafening click hits my ringing ears the moment Oscar shuts the door behind him. One sane person remains in a room with three crazy psychos in red robes. Who will win? Certainly not me. I've always said I'd fight tooth and nail to preserve my life, and I still will, but I know the odds are not in my favor right now. Considering I'm still tied up like a helpless victim, and they're standing free with grins on their faces. Only time will tell if my knight in shining armor will show up, freeing me from this sick dungeon of Hell, or if I meet my end.

"Oh, Kaycee," Crowe coos, pulling me out of my macabre thoughts, waltzing toward me with a grin. It's the same grin that he's worn since the moment he whipped off his mask and revealed his face. Glee lights him up as he steps closer to me, trailing a bloodied finger across my swollen jaw, where the remnants of Hadley's boot print are indented in my skin. "You've grown up before my eyes." I cringe, trying to back away as his fingers descend my broken jawline. Hissing under his touch, he only grins more.

"Did you find out everything you wanted to know?" he asks, cocking his head to the side.

"Why me?" I finally ask, causing him and the others to chuckle to themselves.

"Why not you? You came here with that look in your eyes —all fiery. The moment I noticed someone hacked into the autopsy report of Magnolia before I could correct the mistake of the helper, I knew it was you. You've always been so smart. But this time, it came to bite you in the ass," Crowe coos, almost in awe at my skill set.

"Maybe we could use her?" Cushing says, stepping forward with disgusting intent in his eyes. He looks my body over, giving a grin of approval. "I do need a new toy, and she would be perfect. We could force her into the cause." Cushing hums, bobbing his head to nonexistent music rolling around in his mind.

Crowe rolls his eyes. "She has a family, you fucking dimwit. What do you think they will do when their sweet baby Kaycee goes missing? Huh? Fucking look for her. And those boys?" With those words, he looks directly into my eyes, narrowing them.

"They'll look, too. We have to give them a body to mourn, or they'll never stop looking. Or then, they'll be next, and we'd fetch a healthy ransom from the twins." He grins again, making the other two snicker with delight at his ultimatum.

"So what's it going to be, little beauty? Your life for theirs?" Principal Shaw finally takes off his creepy-looking mask, smiling down at my broken face.

The answer to me is easy. Could the boys live without me? Yes. They did fine before. Would they be devastated? Absolutely. I've always known that if push came to shove, I would give my life for them for their safety. I'd do anything to ensure they lived blissfully for the rest of their lives. Even if I was dead and buried. As long as dirt rested above my casket and they were safely living the lives they were supposed to live, I'd do anything to rectify my mistake of pulling them into this bullshit. I brought them into this mess when I told them about my investigation, and I'll get them out of this mess by laying down my life.

My throat clogs and tightens around my voice box. Tears swim in my only working eye. If I do this, I need answers first. I came all this way, after all. So, why not go out knowing everything I need to know?

"What is all this? Where am I?" I ask, twirling a finger. "What's the point of this?"

Crowe nods his head. "Of course, you have some questions. Naturally," he says, waving a hand. "Welcome to Grandma's house, where it all began. Nestled in the woods, hidden from view."

"Grandma's house?" I mutter, looking over the decrepit wallpaper and moldy carpet. An address bounces inside my head, one we've heard a million times before but never found. "Forty-Four Rosebud drive. But this doesn't exist."

"Ah, again—it pays to have people in high places, Sugar. So, yes. This is where dear old Grandma lived and died. Come to think of it, in this very space." His eyes travel the room's length, getting lost in a deep memory—I'm sure their first kill. "Right over there," he says in a dreamy voice, pointing toward the corner of the room. "Right in front of the window is where we took her, stabbing her over and over again for her cruelty." He doesn't elaborate any more on the subject of her death or her treatment of them. But I can only guess with the bitterness tinging his tone how upset he was that she got rid of the three of them and dumped them like they were nothing but trash.

"This is the future," Shaw says, taking the reins of the conversation, beaming with pride. Spreading his arms out wide, he smiles again, eyeing the kingdom he built with a sparkle in his eye. "This is where our viewers can look through the lens of crimes they want to commit but without getting their hands dirty. With each subject we bring here, they seal the fate of our subjects by voting on their activities and choosing from three or four forms of fun." He grins wider, rubbing his hands together like he's planning something more nefarious for the next event, and loses himself in thought.

"It was between you and that Benoit chick at first. But your look." Cushing bites his bottom lip, checking me from head to toe again with a disgusting smirk eating away at his lips. "You really captured them with your smile. And her? She was too blah. I mean, we could have put her out of her misery." He throws his head back and barks out a cruel laugh, mocking Ainsley's misery at the death of the one she loved—the death they caused.

My heart squeezes as the memories of Ainsley's anguish roll through my mind, vividly reminding me of how the loss of Magnolia made her weep and wither away. Maybe the boys won't survive without me. That would be them, after all. They'll mourn my loss every second of every day, blaming themselves that I'm here and that they weren't here to save me.

"From the moment you walked onto campus, the cameras saw. We were in our selection phases, and our viewers picked you out right away, bidding and bidding until we couldn't deny them you any longer. From there, they bid on your torment. What the student body did to you, or what the teachers said and did. Classic, really," Shaw says, stepping closer to my chair and hovering above me.

"And then some lined up to meet me at the charity event," I say through a heavy sigh, heaving my chest. Because I'm the snoop I am, and I promised Magnolia so deeply that I'd find out who did this to her. I put myself on their radar with a big, fat X marked on my back. Granted, they would have watched and found someone else to nominate if it wasn't me they had chosen.

"Ah, clever girl," Crowe says with a compliment, patting my head like a dog.

If I had more energy, I'd bite him like a dog, too. Or kick him in the nuts. Or anything but sit here and listen to them spout about all their dirty deeds. All I've done is managed to prolong the inevitable, which is saving my life for now.

The feeling of my body circling the drain and taking all my energy slams into me, and I'm fading quickly. A fuzzy static clings to my fading brain. A heaviness takes over my drooping eyelids, begging me to rest and sleep for my remaining time on earth. I ache to disappear from the hellish nightmare and wake up from this awful dream in a faraway land with my boys at my side. Maybe somewhere sunny and bright, with the sand beneath my toes and my boys surrounding me, feeding me grapes and sparkling grape juice. A desperate girl can dream, can't she?

"Now is your final bow, Sugar. Say bye-bye to the audience." Crowe's high-pitched, over-excited bullshit voice brings me back from my private island of naked boyfriends. Let me go back to the sunshine and warm weather.

"A bye-bye? What are you going to do now?" I manage to mutter through my thickening and heavy tongue.

Cushing grins, stepping forward with a small knife in his hands. "Now you meet your doom." He giggles, fucking giggles, sounding more like his deceased niece than himself.

Piper's death rings through my mind again, and I squeeze my eye shut. Oh, Piper. She may have been a looney toon, but she didn't deserve the manipulation from her own flesh and blood. He broke her because her mother ran and hid from him. He slept with her and used her to murder Magnolia. Well, I guess the apple doesn't fall far from the tree. She was obsessive, and so was he. But she could have gotten the help she needed through medication and a therapist.

Shit—I think, shaking my head as much as they'll allow. I'm losing myself at the worst possible time. Then again...My mind brings me back to the picture I found in his office of him and Addison at college graduation. He must have lost her after that when she went off to medical school and left him. So, Francesca was Addison's half-sister? I never encountered anything to point me in that direction in my research.

"How did you know they were sisters?" I croak, peeking my working eye at him.

They continue to stare at me, moving the camera around to face me and whispering to each other.

"You're thinking about it, huh?" He smiles, tilting his crazy big head to the side.

"Mmhmm. Just curious if you're right or just so obsessive, you're insane." I earn a snort from someone in the room.

"Insane? Yeah, maybe. But my obsession brought me to sealed court records, and thanks to my connections and my brother here, I found a settlement to Francesca's whore of a mother from a Mr. Winston Ford, Addison's father. He paid her off and got away with having a secret love child. Not to mention the various bank accounts he secured for her, just like Addison, throughout the country. Her beneficiary? Piper.

Which makes her precious Daddy a very happy multi-millionaire. Again." He straightens his robe with a grin. So happy for himself. He's murdered tons of people to earn that blood money to pay for whatever he's paying for. It's certainly not for a healthy torture house, that's for sure.

"So, her grandparents?" I ask as they settle in front of me.

"Nothing a slow-acting poison couldn't do."

"And Addison?" That one stung to ask, ripping my heart in two thinking about my mother's hurt after learning of Addison's death. Sure, they weren't close anymore. But at one point in their lives, they were best friends.

I see it so clearly now from the other side. Crowe expertly manipulated Addison, playing her like a fiddle. Much like a controlling husband would, he separated her from her friends. He forced her out of work so she'd solely depend on him, and then he slowly made her rely on him and left her bedridden.

"Again, poison. She went quickly, and it was excruciating. Like she deserved. She left me, too." His hand rubs down his face, groaning at his painful memories. Painful, though. Pfft. He's certifiable. "I ordered the hit on Magnolia and gathered bidders to decide her fate as an experiment. I convinced my beautiful fuck buddy to carry out her death in the form of initiation to our ranks. It turns out she was more than willing to help her daddy. Our business really took off and developed into what it is today. Who knew killing people on camera could be so much fun!" Clapping his hands together, he steps forward again. "But now, enough about me. Let's get back to you. You came to this school to what? Find out who killed your precious best friend?" He grins again, leaning down to look me in the eyes.

"Mmhmm. And I found out, too, amongst other things," I mutter, heaving a heavy breath which gets harder and harder to do with my tightening lungs.

"What did you find out?" Shaw asks, rubbing his stubby jaw.

"A lot of things," I grunt.

"You mean the things I gave my son to give to you?" Cushing asks, smirking at me. If my face weren't so swollen, it would fall—my heart stalls in my chest at his words, piercing through me like a knife inserting into my aching heart. "Yeah, that's what I thought. He told you all about us. Who we were. Who Piper was. Everything, right? It was at my orders. I gave him the words to say. I told him to. You know why?" He drops to his knees in front of me, playing with the intricate knife in his hands. "Because you are his." The tip of the knife runs down the good side of my face, dipping close to my watery eye.

"No," I whisper. "He wouldn't—" Deny, deny, deny. Carter wouldn't do that to me—to us. I saw it in his eyes. He protected me, and he confided in me. Nothing about this makes sense. Carter loves me. You can't fake that emotion from within. Sure, he can wear an amazing mask, not letting anyone in to see his vulnerabilities and emotions. But he never wore it around me. Carter is true to me and not to this dickbag.

"Afraid so, Pumpkin," Cushing murmurs, furrowing his brow. "He knew the entire time. Set you up and played you like a little fiddle. Perfectly, too. So now you are the promotion he's been working so hard at. He's so obedient and loyal to us. He infiltrated your fascinating relationship perfectly, I must say. This whole thing worked out just like we planned. And his role? He played it well." He grins more, eating me up with his beady eyes. "So, tell me. Did he get into that tight little pussy of yours? Is that how far you fell in love with him?"

"Now," Shaw says, tilting his head. "Let's move on to the ceremony." His eyes light up at the word ceremony.

They shuffle around again, get the camera into position, and surround me for one final blow.

"Thank you for your sacrifice," Cushing murmurs, running a hand through my hair

"The world will fall to its knees when they learn little Kaycee Cole committed suicide." Shaw shakes his head, a fake sadness taking over his face.

"Poor little Kaycee couldn't bear the thought of her best friend's death anymore. She slit her wrists, slid into her tub, and slowly died." Crowe muses.

"At least that's what the coroner's report will say." Shaw shrugs.

"And my real death?" I swallow hard.

The walls close around me, suffocating me, forcing a heavyweight on my heaving chest. My mortality hangs in the balance, and my life is in their hungry hands. They're eager to move forward with their plan. How much will they make off of my death? How much money did they make off my pain?

At eye level, Crowe holds a tiny knife. Its gold-tinted jewels line the handle, sparkling off the soft spotlights pointing toward me. I'm the main event, after all.

"Bring him in. His true test begins now," Crowe shouts, filling the room, but he never stops running the tip of the knife down my arm and chest.

The door slams open and shut, and my eyes glue to the smug-looking man in red robes walking through the door. A heavy mask of confidence falls over his face. His brown eyes take me in, his smile widening at the sight of me tied to a chair, bloodied and bruised, my eye swollen shut and crusted over.

"Carter…" I whisper with a stunned expression.

Everything fades away when he cocks his head and smirks at me with the smuggest expression I've ever seen. "Hello, Sweetheart. Did you miss me?" He purrs without missing a beat.

"Let me introduce you to the fourth horseman you've been wondering about, meet Famine," Cushing says, meeting his son in the middle. They clasp hands, shaking them together in a joyous celebration of murmured words and a whoop of excitement from Cushing. With one last tap on his son's back, he breaks away and marches back towards me with deadly intent ringing in his eyes.

"Fourth horseman?" I gasp out as the knife's tip slices through my abdomen like it's nothing at all, ripping into my skin and settling just the tip into my flesh. My body instinctively curls around it, trying to run away from the stab wound's pain. My hands pull at my restraints, but nothing makes them stop.

Even as the knife plunges into my abdomen further, Carter's face doesn't move an inch, remaining cut from stone. His deep brown eyes light up when a pain-filled scream wretches from my throat and fills the room with my misery, even laughing with the other psychos as they whisper to one another. My heart drops deep into the depths of my aching stomach and churns to dust when he takes a step closer, joining the other assholes.

The three horsemen take their time, getting their fill of my pain. Little by little, the knife inches further into my stomach, aided by the three of them alternating—Crowe pushes a little, then gives it to Shaw, and then to Cunningham. Carter watches from the spot he's glued to, taking it all in with a cocked head. The warm blood trickles from the wound they've created, soaking through my shirt and spilling down my legs. His eyes track every movement, cataloging the blood. And when his eyes finally snap back up to mine, I see an unusual hardness gleaming in his eyes. His smirk never leaves his lips.

*Carter is the fourth horseman. But has he been this whole time?*

Betrayal stings through my veins despite the pain of the knife sticking out of my gut. Blood slowly pools around the wound and drips into my lap. The red paints the floor in tiny drips, staining the disgusting carpet. My head swims with chaotic thoughts, and our relationship flashes before my eyes.

Was I naive enough to believe that this man could come to light like I had begged him to? Did I really think I could drag him from the depths of Hell and release him from the grasp of the Apocalypse, when in reality, he was them all along?

A heaviness prickles the back of my neck when I lift my head, staring deep into his unchanged brown eyes, devoid of any sort of emotion. A nothingness stares back at me. And maybe that's his father's doing after all these years. Cushing finally got the soldier he was so desperate to get through his manipulations and blackmailed Carter into submission. But when did Carter turn over and become his father's doggy?

Memories assault me, taking me away from the chair they've tied me to, and I drift off to a heavenly place I want to remain. Our time together flashes before my eyes: the good, the bad, and the ugly.

From the first time I met Carter, he put on a cruel act, taking his pain out on everyone around him. He lashed out, talking down to anyone to keep them away. Even me. He pushed and pushed, but I eventually pulled him into my orbit and never wanted to let him go. My heart stings worse than the knife continuing to plow through my skin like it's cutting butter. I revel in the softness his eyes once showed, remembering the pain in them, and the happiness. Carter was happy at one point, I know that for sure. So, what is this? Is Carter too caught up to leave? Or is Carter a willing participant in my imminent death?

A sharp shiver works its way down my spine when Carter's soft finger brushes against my swollen cheek, twisting his fingers into some of my blood. I watch in horror as he brings his fingers up to his mouth and sucks the blood off his fingers. My lips pop open from the deep pain it causes, and I suck in a breath.

"It's a thing of beauty isn't it, boy?" His father asks him, slapping him on the shoulder. "And to think, you got a front row seat to the whole event." Cushing smirks then and cocks his head when my eyes pop open, and my temporary heaven evaporates. All I'm left to stare at is the four of them looming over me with grins on their faces. No souls lie behind their eyes when they eat up my broken body.

"I told you, little rabbit," Cushing murmurs with fire in his eyes, squeezing Carter's shoulder with a puffed out chest. Pride roars through him when he peeks at Carter, and for the first time ever, I swear he looks at Carter with parental love. "He knew all along. Who do you think shoved you into the fish tank and watched from afar as you helplessly drowned?" My eyes flicker to Carter who smirks at me and nods, confirming my worst fears.

"For your final test," Cushing says, shoving a pair of pliers into Carter's willing hand. "You've passed everything with flying colors. Your deception. Your torture. Now, take from her what she owes us," he says with a wicked glint.

Carter stares down at the pliers and raises a brow. "And what does she owe us?" he rumbles with a grin and straightens his robes.

Crowe frowns, crossing his arms over his chest. "For everything she's stuck her little rabbit nose in. For the hacking, and breaking into my fucking office, and for stealing my phone. Sticking her nose where it shouldn't be," Crowe grumbles, counting off my offenses. "Pluck off the end of her nose," he growls, stepping forward to loom over me once again. He growls, gritting his teeth, and snarls at me.

"Maybe the eyeballs?" Shaw says flippantly, waving a hand. "She's seen more than she needs to. How was my office? I should have known it was you and your merry gang of assholes who broke in there." He raises a brow at me, expecting an answer.

"Maybe her tongue?" Cushing says with a grin, squeezing my jaw. "Snip off the end and watch as she drowns in her own blood without being able to call for help. Not like any would come. Take a good look around, Sugar. This is your final resting place. If only you'd have stayed away," he hums, tapping my injured cheek like this was all my fault.

"I couldn't have stayed away," I snarl, trying to shove his hand off my face with a headbutt. It does nothing but make the room spin. The more time they take to talk and laugh in my face, the more blood drains from my wound. Although, with where they've stabbed, I can't be certain I'll go any time soon. Maybe this is what they intend to do to every victim. Stab them and then talk them to death. "I knew some asshole stole my best friend's life, and I was going to find out who did it," I say in a quivering voice, but it feels so damn good to look her murderers in the eyes and know who they are. I successfully fulfilled my promise to my best friend and found the man responsible for taking her life. I watched the life drain from her killer's eyes as she was thrown to the ground and stabbed multiple times. Magnolia hasn't been vindicated just yet, if only I could get the fuck out of this chair and fight my way out of here.

I close my eyes again, dreaming of someone bursting through the door to save my life. For a small second, I could have sworn Carter was that man, and maybe he is. I look up into his dead eyes and heave a breath. I don't know how much more I can take or how much longer I can keep my eyes open. A heaviness takes over my lids, and I just want to sleep for days.

"Yeah?" Carter asks with that patronizing smirk again. "How'd that work out for you, Little Troll?" I swallow hard when he steps forward, opening and closing the pair of pliers in his hands with a glint in his eye. I try to curl my fingers against the wooden handle of the chair when the metal tip of the pliers rubs against the flesh of my index finger, circling around my nail. He continues the pattern over every finger, tracing the outline of my nail bed.

"Don't," I beg for the first time. "Please, don't do it," I whisper, looking up into his eyes when he hovers above me. I want to beg for my life. I want to beg him to go back to the Carter I had grown to love so quickly these past few months. Give me back my grumpy man who refused to say he loved me, but I knew he did. Give him back to me, damn it! Don't let the real Carter be this lifeless man parading around in a meat suit full of smirks and snarky words. "Come back to me," I beg with tears spilling from my good eye and down my cheek. "Please," I beg again, cracking at the stony exterior of the man inching closer to me. "This isn't you," I croak, earning nothing but laughs from the four of them in return.

He twists his head, saying something to the other three, but I can't hear what he says through the loud pounding in my skull. Nothing but the blood whooshing through my ears and drowning everything else out. That's all I hear. All I want to hear. Through tear-filled eyes the three brothers back away from my chair, murmuring words to one another with smiles on their faces. Whatever he says to them, takes their attention away from us, and they leave him to do as he pleases. A little voice in the back of my head begs me to see past the mask covering the real man beneath it. But it's hard to lift the veil when his dark eyes capture mine in his unwavering gaze, and I fall down the dreaded rabbit hole back into his lifelessness. How can one man turn off his emotions for the world to see with such precision?

As fast as lightning, he grabs my hand in his and cocks his head. A grin so malevolent crosses his face, I swear a demon resides inside him. The shadows of the room cower in fear, including me. My body trembles when his thumb rubs the top of my hand, and fear truly sets in.

"I think I'll take a finger," Carter muses, earning chuckles from the dickbags lounging against the opposite wall.

"Take them all," Cushing encourages, checking the time on his watch. "But make it snappy, Son. We've got to close this lot out soon and move on to bigger and better things. We've got a whole horseman ceremony laid out for you at home. Plenty of women to fuck and food to eat. A celebration of the century," he says with enthusiasm and then returns to his conversation with his brothers.

Carter growls, gritting his teeth at his father's command. "I'll take all the fucking time I need," he shouts, giving me his back. "I will do whatever I fucking please." I swallow hard when their hard faces light up at his unruly demand, and Cushing nods.

"You want time alone?" He asks, raising a brow. "To do?"

"Whatever the fuck I see fit. She's mine, isn't she?" His gloved fingers curl into fists around the pliers dangling from his grip. "Mine to fucking torture. Mine to fucking bleed. She is mine to do with as I please," he growls every word, and by the rigid stance of his body, he's trying not to run to them and put his fist through their throats. I've been with him day in and day out now for months, so I can read his body like a map.

From here I see the grin lighting up Cushing's face. "A finger it is then," he says, gesturing for Carter to continue without moving to exit the room. "But we stay put first."

"We want a front row seat for the screams," Shaw says nonchalantly again, leaning against the wall with his eyebrows raised. "It just isn't the same through a monitor," he sighs through disappointment and urges Carter to continue.

"Nail," Carter says with a huff, turning on his toes to face me again, and I'm greeted by the stone, emotionless expression of Carter.

Leaning over me, he examines my face, blocking out the entire room from view. A smirk placed on his lips when the tool in his hand runs across my good cheek, and he puts his forehead against mine. The heat of his body pushes through mine, and he gasps for air quietly, pushing his forehead into mine until the pressure forces my eyes to his.

My chest shutters when his warm breaths mingle with mine, and I swear my heart leaps from my chest with a joyous dance, seeing the real man behind the mask of indifference.

"I have to," he breaths so quiet that I almost miss the confessions spilling from his lips. "Please trust me," he breathes again: "I will fucking save you, Sweetheart." He pulls away without saying another word and takes my tension-filled hand into his. Three squeezes say it all. I love you. I'll save you. Do not worry.

Tension fills every molecule of my body when the pointed metal of the pliers rests just beneath my fingernail, resting there until I meet his eyes again. Worry lines set in and wrinkle his brow, but he continues to stare as he pulls at my fingernail with gentle pressure, until he knows I know the deception is not on me. The deception is on the three men quietly talking and laughing at the millions of dollars they've made in the last few hours or days, or however long I've been here.

Tears fill to the brim when his hand squeezes mine three times again in reassurance, and I finally see every emotion fluttering through the depths of his once dead brown eyes. He cocks his head, face twisting with indecision, as the pliers dig deeper under my nail. I gasp from the burning pain, but give him a subtle nod in the end to continue and just pull it off. My eyes squeeze shut when pain rocks through my finger, and a disgusting squish sound happens before the pressure pops off my nail.

My cheeks cover in wetness when I can't keep my tears at bay any longer. I stare at Carter's grimacing and green face until he wipes all his emotions away again. He turns to the other three, holding my fingernail up in the air, and they whoop in celebration. Darkness encroaches on my vision until I close my eyes. In the distance, their voices echo like they're under water, but I swear through my fucked up hearing, I hear the door click and their footsteps retreat.

My head spins and lolls to the side when black dots scatter across my vision, and I heave a breath. If this rescue doesn't happen soon, I'm going to die tied to a chair with a knife sticking out of my gut and a fingernail missing from its bed. A warmth encases my body, and I relax into the rough surface of the chair, letting the darkness take over my brain. Maybe if I just sleep for a little bit. Just a small nap.

"Fuck! Sweetheart, open your fucking eyes," Carter hisses so quiet, I almost don't hear him when he taps my good cheek, rousing me. "You cannot fucking leave me yet, do you fucking hear me?"

I swallow hard, letting the pain envelop me completely, and it buzzes around my body.

"I can't," I mumble through a heavy tongue. A weakness takes over my limbs when the rope falls away, and I'm carefully lifted into his arms.

"You can and you fucking will, Sweetheart. I'll be damned if you die because I couldn't fucking save you. You die. I die. You got that?" A growl rumbles through his chest when he pulls me close, careful to keep the knife from bumping into anything.

# TWENTY-FOUR

## CARTER

**A few weeks earlier**

My dick fucking hurts, and it's goddamn agony—worse than fucking Hell. I grunt, cupping myself through my jeans, begging the cocksucker to go down. But it doesn't fucking listen, growing angrier and more desperate for the pussy we left behind. Not today, asshole. We had to go and prove West wrong and get a damn dick piercing or three. Now we have to live with the consequences of our stupid as fuck actions.

After watching Kaycee get railed by Zepp in the maze not five fucking seconds ago, I think I'm fucking dying. Sure, I got to stick a big fat fake cock up her pussy and watch her come like fucking God himself was back on earth, but it wasn't me inside her. It was rubber and bullshit.

I almost said fuck it and fucked her anyway, despite it all. But I stopped myself from doing it, thinking about how my piercings needed to heal properly or my junk might fall off. And I need my fucking junk to continue to fuck her sweet pussy in the future.

Sweat drips down my back as I make it back to my apartment in record time. My fucking cock aches to be inside of her, but each of my piercings protests the movement. Only a few more weeks now until the Christmas Charity event, and then I'll be fucking golden.

Curiosity burns through me as I walk up the stairs to my apartment. Excitement thrums through my veins, eager to check the results from the disc we set up on my father's computer. It's been a few hours since we ran off to the maze and played hide and seek, so it should be ready by my calculations. And boy, do I fucking hope it is. I can't wait to get my grubby hands on whatever my father is hiding in the depths of his computer. It has to be fucking good with all the bells and whistles installed on his hard drive meant to keep me out. I wasn't lying when I said it had to run through tough security to get through. But I want to see the results in private, all for myself, before I run back and tell Kaycee everything. I know she'll have questions later, but she is satisfied and exhausted from our day together for now. First, we went to my dad's and broke in, getting caught by Piper's psycho ass and her mother. Then my anger drove me to the damn shady sex shop, where I spent at least two hundred bucks on toys to pleasure my girl, and then we played hide and seek.

Once I'm in my apartment and sitting in front of my computer, I feel the gravity of everything pushing down on us. Every muscle in my body stiffens when I run my eyes across the screen of my computer, gathering information from my father, and my teeth clench. I run a trembling hand over my face, trying to outrun the nerves flaying me open, but I can't. It sits on my chest like a fucking elephant, suffocating me.

What appears on the screen confirms everything I need to know. We are so beyond royally fucked. So fucked. That's all there is to it. Goddamnit!

I swallow the bile shooting up my throat, take my phone out, ignore the group texts, and hopefully dial this number for the last fucking time. One more time, and this will all be fucking over. One more fucking time–is what I tell myself every time I have to dial this dickwad's number. Then I'll be free. Then we'll all be fucking safe.

It rings two times before he decides to pick up and exhales into the phone in greeting.

"Kid, you and these late-night calls," he chastises with a tired huff.

"I did what you fucking couldn't," I growl into the phone. "A little appreciation would be nice. And this is the only goddamn time I can get away to call."

If Kaycee found out, God knows she'd be so hurt I didn't tell her what I was in on, but I can't. I swore allegiance and signed my life away when I brought all this to their attention. She has to stay in the dark to keep herself safe. No one can know what I've been in on for months now.

"So tell me, kid. What have you got for me today?" He says in a low voice, no longer irritated.

"I should be asking you the same fucking thing. What have you got for me? You always leave me in the fucking dark on everything. I do your damn dirty work," I shout, jumping to my feet and stalking around the room. I pull the longer strands of my hair with my fist, reveling in the pain it provides.

"You know the rules, kid. You signed up for this when you came to us. You relay the information, and we store it. You watch, and we listen. You act, and we act when we can." He goes on and on, reciting the same bullshit he spouts every time I call him.

I roll my eyes towards the ceiling and hold the phone away from my ear. I'm ten seconds away from throwing it against the wall, collecting Kaycee, and fucking off to the Caribbean for the remainder of Thanksgiving break. Hell, even into Christmas break. We won't ever come back.

"I found a website," I say, again swallowing my vomit.

"A website?" He asks again, clicking a pen in the background.

"You fucking heard me. A website..." I close my eyes because I have no fucking idea what it is. Nothing about it screams psychos or killers or anything.

I stare at the blank-looking website displaying the CrossBonesBids.death.com name and logo. The fucking skull taking up the majority of the page stares back at me and mocks me with its knowledge of what these fuckheads are doing.

"What is it?" He interjects, stopping everything.

"What I don't fucking understand is how you couldn't have known? How have you not found this before and found out what they're doing on the fucking Internet?" I heave a breath, anger building in the pit of my stomach.

My fist clenches because I can tell by the sound of his smug as fuck voice he knows precisely what I'm talking about, and they're keeping it from me. They keep everything from me and expect me to blindly follow their lead into Hell. I'm beginning to think Veritas isn't all it's cracked up to be. They may be a secret government agency, but they sure as fuck take their goddamn time with everything, no matter who it hurts.

"Because it's nothing but a blank page asking for a password that we can't break through on our side," he mutters with frustration in his tone. But he can't imagine the fucking frustration I feel because it's not his ass on the line. It's fucking mine, my brothers', and most importantly, my damn girl's life on the line.

I grind my teeth at his admission, and I want to reach through the phone and fucking strangle him with my bare hands. But that would be frowned upon. They know more about this cult than they let on, and I'm about to lose my shit on every fucking thing.

"What the fuck! You knew they had a website? And you didn't fucking ask me to break through? What happens when I get behind the magic fucking password, huh? What are they hiding? And what the fuck is going to happen to my girlfriend?" A low growl builds in my throat at the possibility of losing my girlfriend, and even those damn idiots I call my brothers, to these assholes.

"We'll extract you all before it gets to that point, Carter. We will not let them hurt anyone else, you hear me, kid?" I nod even though he can't see it, but doubt creeps in. "But the location," he mutters. "We need a location, Cunningham, or we can't do shit. We can swoop in now and arrest potential suspects, but what we've had you do isn't exactly legal. They'd be out on the streets doing the same shit but learn how to hide it better. And they're already hiding everything too well for my liking. Hang in there, kid. Hide your girlfriend and buddies, and we'll be there soon."

"You said you had someone on the inside before. Are they still relaying information?" My heart rate spikes at the fucking question because I can't be the only fucking one they're using to get the information.

He hums, "Veritas has an agent planted on the inside still. They're relaying everything they can. But within the cult ranks, you are the highest individual we have on call. You have access to almost everything."

Almost everything, I mock in my head. Yeah, I don't know shit about the Apocalypse bastards because I'm in the dark twenty-four seven. "So, they don't know fuck about shit either?" I growl, wanting to smash my phone with my fist.

"They're telling us as much as they can, as discreetly as possible. Members of the society constantly surround them, unlike you. You have a privilege they don't. I will call upon you again when we have more to go on, but keep your eyes peeled at the event you're attending in a few weeks. The clock is ticking on your girlfriend's life, Cunningham, and I'm getting a distinct feeling that you're the only one who can stop this shit because we've tried and failed to bring these assholes down. I want a report sent about the website and anything you can gather. Especially if you unlock the password. Until then, don't call me in the middle of the night again," he barks the last part with authority and then fucking hangs up on me.

I kneel, too dumbfounded to move from all the information swirling in my head. They don't know any more than I do. And they're a goddamn government agency actively looking for these sickos to bring down. I grind my teeth together, pulling at my hair. This whole situation is so fucking fucked. I need to throw my fists into someone's face and let go of all this burning anger deep inside me.

> Grumpy: Meet me in the gym. We need to talk.

> West#1: With our fists, right, Grumpy?

> Grumpy: GYM Right Fucking NOW!

> ElfEars: And you wonder why we call you grumpy...sheesh, bro.

> West#1: I'm coming...Jesus...I just got my dick to go away too.

I recoil and stare at the phone, blinking.

> Grumpy: Fuck is that supposed to mean West?...

No response. Fuck it. I slam my fist into my computer desk and turn off the website glaring back at me and taunting me with the unknown.

I don't know the full extent of what is going on, but I feel I'll be breaking into a website here soon. They may have hidden everything else from me, somehow, but they won't with this. I'll pull all my fucking resources together and find out what they're up to. I just hope I'm not too late.

# TWENTY-FIVE

## CARTER

**The Day Of Kaycee's kidnapping**

The moment I left Kaycee and Chase, something violent churned inside me. Starting at the tips of my toes, knotting my stomach, and clouding my mind—something wasn't right. So, why the fuck did I leave? Because I had to. My computer finally dinged back with something fucking useful for our investigation, forcing me to leave them and check it out.

Anxiety builds in the depths of my gut, bubbling up my burning throat as I sit in front of my computer. It's no longer littered with code breaking through the contents of my father's computer, instead displaying a website. Something I wish I could step back from and pretend I didn't fucking see. But I can't.

My teeth grind together as I click through the different pages displayed on the complex website. A live number appears at the side of the screen, counting down something—a place to put bids in for different types of ideas. As I watch, they rise in number going from one-hundred to five-hundred in seconds. And continues to grow higher and higher and never stops.

. . .

*Watery Grave vs. Six Feet Under*
  *Battling Babes vs. Tantalizing Toe Nails.*
  *Humanities vs. Survival.*

"The fuck is this?" I growl, clicking on Watery Grave in hopes it takes me to some kind of menu.

My heart drops when a description pops up, describing the individual being handcuffed to a pole, and left to drown unless they could displace enough water. A menu pops up on the side of the screen on the amount of money you'd like to bid to win this method over the other. A real-time bidding war is happening before my eyes, advertising a show about to happen tomorrow night. It was all coming to a head, and fuck me. Fuck.

I growled, dialing the same number I'd dialed a few times before.

"Kid," he growls his usual upbeat greeting.

"I got through to the website, and it's...." I run a hand over my lips, shaking my head.

"What is it, Cunningham?" He asks, perking up. A pen clicks in the background like an annoying habit, and I bite my tongue.

"I don't know, but it's on my computer. It's bids. It's something. It's—I don't fucking know! But you need to fucking see it," I grit my teeth through every word, pressure building in my head to the point of explosion.

"Patch me through," he demands, clicking his pen a few more times.

"Fucking fine, but I—" I pause when a text comes through, vibrating my cheek.

My heart sinks, beating a thousand beats per minute when I pull the lit-up screen away from my face. A million worrying thoughts pour through my mind, freezing my entire body like ice has taken hold of my joints, and I'm a statue.

"But what?" His muffled voice asks through the phone, bringing me out of my stunned state.

A heaviness weighs on my tongue as he continues to bark at me to resume my words. But I hold the phone away from my face and stare at the mocking words summoning me to what's sure to be Hell.

> Alpha: Delta. Panty Licker. Beta. Come to the Maze House immediately.
>
> Delta: Yes, Alpha
>
> Panty licker: Yes, Alpha

"Kid!" He shouts through a rough rasp.

I shake my head, bring the phone back to my ear and close my eyes. I've been summoned to places before. 'Check on this person, Beta.' 'Be at this party, Beta.' 'Follow them around, Beta, and report back to us.' But I've never been asked to come to a place with the others like this. Sure, I was told to meet them in the hall to slime Kaycee with that disgusting as fuck goo. But this? This is at the mother fucking Maze House.

"I just got fucking summoned," I breathe through quivering lips. Every word I speak comes out in a tremble, forcing me to clear my throat to remove it. If what the website says is true, then my gut feeling from before is coming to fucking fruition.

There are a million moments in my life I've lived to regret. But this? Leaving Beniot and Kaycee alone at the Maze House when I thought the campus was fucking dead, so I could look into what my computer found will always be. This will be number one on the list for as long as I live. And if they have Kaycee and Benoit, I'll fight tooth and fucking nail to get them to safety. No matter the fucking cost. Put a bullet in my goddamn chest, drown me in a fucking pool, but don't take two people who mean more to me than the breath in my fucking lungs.

My stomach knots and twists, and I grip my hair with my free hand. Tears burn my eyes and drip down my cheek, escaping the tight hold I have on them. Deep buried emotions leak from tight lips, and I heave another soul-cleansing breath to bring myself back to the here and now. I have to keep my shit together if I'm going to save her. And hell, they might not have her yet. Maybe they're surrounding the place, and I can choke them all out before they fucking touch her or Beniot. Get your shit together, Cunningham. You have fucking people to save and people to fucking murder.

"Listen to me," the agent on the phone says in a gruff voice, reeling me back in again. "You have to go."

The world fucking freezes at his words and spins all at once. My body stiffens at his request, feeling like a hand plunging in and squeezing my heart until pain throbs through my chest.

"Go?" I question with hesitation. "How can I fucking go?" I shout, slamming my fist into the desk. "How the fuck...."

"This is a dire situation. We've lost contact with our agent on the inside. We can't track their location, kid. Go to their summons, and be our inside agent," he barks out with urgency in his voice and something like fear tinging his words. If he's fucking scared, then how can I remain fucking calm?

"You...want me to fucking go and fucking...." I trail off and close my eyes.

"And report back. But now you need to patch us through to the website. If we can get in, we can track where you're going to be and stop this before it starts. Trust in us, kid."

I hit a few keys, open my computer to theirs, and say a prayer to whoever is listening above that this all works out without my girl getting fucking hurt.

"I don't trust any-fucking-body," I hiss, straightening up.

"And if you fuck me over, I'll fuck you over. I don't give a flying dick who you are or what agency you're involved with," I shout into the phone, flinging it across the room before he can answer my threats.

My fingers pull at the ends of my hair, and I pace around my room, pulling at the roots. Throwing my head back, I roar at the ceiling with all my might, letting every ounce of frustration that's about to come my way out.

Kneeling, I pick up my cracked phone and shove it into my jeans pocket, praying they can track my phone wherever I go. With one last look around the room, I try to fucking center my anger into a ball in my chest, and then I bolt out the door and out into the brightly lit hallway. I run like my ass is on fire, and the gates of hell have opened up, because they fucking have. Jesus Christ, this is a goddamn nightmare pushing down on me from all angles. I have psychos expecting me to be a fucking psycho, and I have Veritas expecting me to step up and pretend to be the psycho to get them the information they need. Fuck!

My shirt clings to my back as a panicked sweat sets in, and my blood boils like hot lava. It isn't until I push out of the doors of my apartment building that I find relief in the cool winter air brushing past me. Panic sets in, spinning my heart out of control. My mind blazes with scenario after scenario, getting worse and worse with every thought. By the time I make it to the maze, nothing can show on my face. Absolutely no emotions can be present inside me when I jump into this situation headfirst.

But I fucking swear to all things holy, and my mother's grave, if they harmed a hair on her body, I will murder them all. That's a goddamn promise.

I pause just outside my apartment building and hide in the shadows to collect myself, wiping every ounce of feelings off my face into a blank slate. I'm made of fucking stone, and I won't fucking crack.

Breathe deep, dumbass. Deep fucking breaths. Wipe the emotions from your fucking face and hide them in a fucking box from now until you know what the hell is going on. They'll kill her if you show them how much she means to you. Instantly. Then they'll make you watch or kill you, too. They won't play around. There's no pass with them. I won't collect two hundred fucking dollars. She'll die because I love her, and I should have fucking told her the damn truth.

I should have told her. A million fucking times. Over and over. I should never have held my tongue. Fuck my mom for giving me that hang-up, and fuck my dad for being a piece of shit, and fuck me for not protecting the only woman I've ever loved.

This must be a test. Something is wrong—so fucking wrong. My fingers desperately grab at my black t-shirt over the left side of my chest. A burning sensation tightens, like taut rubber bands constricting my air. If I had to guess, Kaycee and Benoit are in deep shit.

I should have camped out at that damn house. No. I should have duct-taped my damn girlfriend, forced her into my car, and put her up in an apartment somewhere far the fuck from here. Everyone had been too quiet after the charity event. The only shining light was my girl, the hot tub, and finally claiming every part of her; that was a plus, too, even if those other idiots were there. They say you can't choose your blood relatives, and that's a fucking fact, but you can build your own damn family, and that's what they are. Those fucknuts are my brothers, and I'll be damned if any of them die. Not on my watch.

Stomping my way across campus toward the maze, I scowl and hide my worry behind my heavy mask of disdain. Silence greets me in the eerie labyrinth when I step foot through its mouth. Usually, moans and groans greet my ears, but tonight the whole place is a ghost town—only the damn wind swishing through the creaking branches reaches my ears. I walk through the maze with my head held high like I've done many times before and charge toward the house. A scowl etches across my lips, and every damn emotion I let out sucks back into the back of my mind, where I lock it away like the trash it is. It thrashes in its cage, begging to rear its ugly head, but I hold it back and slap on my best cruel expression. I will not fucking break before their eyes.

I squint as I reach the front of the house, stopping in my tracks. Every light in the house is on, illuminating the front yard, and light bounces off the swaying bushes. The darkness eats at me the more I stare. I want to charge in there like a damn bull and see what the fuck they think they're doing. But I don't. I curl my fists and heave a breath, and that's when I smell gasoline. The pungent scent hits my nostrils, and a gag bubbles in my throat from how strong it floats in the air.

"Beta!" A shrill voice rings through the silent air.

I jerk my head in her direction, grinding my teeth. Keeping my crude scowl in place, I march toward the house. Piper grins back at me from the porch, bouncing on her damn toes. She claps her hands before launching herself at me, forcing me to stumble back. My skin burns when her arms wrap around my neck, legs curling around my waist. Squeezing me tight, she sighs with happiness.

"Oh, brother, I'm so excited for you!" I grunt, knocking her off of me. Who the fuck knows? She might spread her fucking crazy germs to me.

"Excited for what?" I say with a bored tone, discreetly looking through the windows of the house Piper shouldn't have access to. No one should have access to this house except five people.

I let the brother comment slide because fuck no. Our parents aren't married. The only time I see 'ole Franny roaming around the prison I call home is at dinner time. She's a fucking ghost, too doped up to even care about what's going on. I try not to spend too much time there. It's too depressing—too quiet—too many damn ghosts.

Piper's eyes blow wide, and she grins more if that's fucking possible. "Your initiation, of course, silly!" She shrieks, tilting her head to the side.

My black heart sputters inside my chest. Initiation? The fuck is that? I hope it's not what I think it is. Could my night get any worse?

"The fuck is that supposed to mean?" I growl, crossing my arms.

"It means your Alpha is trying to guide you on your journey. Now get in the fucking house, God." She huffs with an abrupt personality change, pointing toward the house. "Let's go!"

My eyebrows dip as her body transforms. The peppy, food-spouting, analogy-giving, looney toon becomes a cold-blooded killer in front of me with narrowed eyes. Alpha. Fucking Alpha! I should have known this incognito bitch was the one doling out the orders of destruction. Fuck. Me. Act normal, you tool.

"Well?" she hisses, shoving at my shoulder. I let her, and I repeat, fucking let her push me into the house.

The instant I walk through the door, it hits me and nearly knocks me over. I plug my nose, gasping for breath. The thick scent of gasoline settles on my taste buds. Instead of inhaling it, I'm fucking eating it. Everywhere I turn, puddles upon puddles of the liquid pool on the floor, soaking into the hardwood. The furniture drips it, and it flows off the paintings and decorations.

"What's the plan?" I ask in a growl, assessing the room more.

"Plan? Are you that thick? You're going to light a fucking match and burn this place to the ground," she snarls, roughly slamming a matchbook into my hand.

"Fucking fine. I'll burn this hideous piece of shit down," I spit in disgust, looking at one of my favorite places on earth for the last time.

Memories of my time here play like a damn movie around me. Raiding their fridge, holding my girl, and being with my fucking family. This was home. Not that other fucking place. I'd never tell those assholes how much I enjoyed coming here, or that for the first time I felt like I could drop my mask and smile—really fucking smile. Fuck that. I can see it now. Seger would find a way to rub it in any chance he got. Benoit would light up like a fucking Christmas tree. And Zeppelin, he'd give me those smug as fuck looks any chance he got. So, my lips are sealed.

A slow, malicious smile spreads across Piper's lips. "Good boy, Beta," she whispers, basically moaning my code name and tapping the side of my face.

"So what happens after I burn this shithole down?" I walk around, away from her, taking in the beauty of this house.

"You go onto the next step, Beta. Your destiny! I can't wait for Daddy to tell you!" she breathes, almost in a slow, drawn-out moan, obviously feeling pleasure from whatever awaits me in the future. Shit. Fuck. As I peer around, desperately searching for the love of my life, my heart fucking pounds against my ribs. I swallow hard, noting I can't fucking find her anywhere. I curl my fingers into a fist around the matches she laid in my palm and control the anger begging to come out in the form of violence.

"And what is my fucking destiny?" I snarl, putting on my nastiest face when I peer back at her smiling form. Piper jumps in place with a giggle.

"You'll see," she says, booping my damn nose. "Now, light the match, and let's fucking go. We've got work to do." Her face shifts into a scowl, furrowing her brows. The switch in personality is immediate. Her once smiling face drops into a tight smile, and her body stiffens with her shoulders rolling back in a confident power pose.

"Fucking fine," I huff, taking a step away again so she can't boop my fucking nose. I swear I'll bite her fucking finger off if she does it again.

"Oh, and to prove your loyalty, make sure you start there." I swallow a heavy lump in my throat, following her finger toward the twins' bedroom, where a blonde lump lies on the floor, sprawled out unconscious and unmoving.

Double fuckity, fuck. Benoit.

"And the bitch?" Implying Kaycee is a bitch sits like acid on my tongue, burning and sour. Sure, I've said it to her before to push her away and keep her out of my face. I wanted to deny how utterly attracted I was to her. And you see how well that's gone over. From the moment I saw her, I knew she'd be trouble with a capital fucking T. I just didn't know she'd be my perfect brand of trouble.

"Oh, Daddy wanted her at the house ASAP! And you, too, so get a move on!" She waves her hands again, trying to get me to move. But my brains stuck on where they fucking took her to.

"What fucking house?" I grumble, shuffling my feet toward the dripping couch. A familiar-looking phone lies on the ground, covered in gasoline, and catches my eye.

Piper huffs, crossing her damn arms like a haughty ass bitch. But while she's distracted by her little temper tantrum, I snatch Kaycee's discarded phone off the floor. Discreetly, I check to see if it's in good working order, clean off the gasoline, and shove it into the waistband of my jeans.

"You're taking too much fucking time. Burn the bitch down, and I'll meet you outside. I'd suggest exiting through a window or something. I don't need you burning your face off before you start tonight. You get that's what you're doing, right? Like, don't piss off the rest of the Apocalypse before you become one of them." She grumbles, walking toward the front door like she's going to fucking let me be in here alone.

"Wait," I snarl. "Become one of them? The fuck are you

going on about?"

She rolls her eyes. "What the hell do you think you've been doing for the past few years? Sunbathing? Fuck, Carter, you're not a dummy. Your daddy will explain it, but you were chosen a long time ago, and now your birthright is happening. So chop, chop! I need to text Daddy with updates." Her eyes narrow, strolling toward me. "Hand it over. No one walks into Grandma's house with a phone." I scowl more, swallowing the hard lump sliding down my throat at the mention of Grandma. Because what the fuck is she talking about?

"Grandma's house?" I ask, shoving her hand away.

"Yeah, Grandma's house. Now, give me your phone. It's the protocol now. No phones in or out of the house." She doesn't elaborate further, sticking her hand out and wiggling her fingers with impatience.

Finally, I lose my patience and shove my phone into her awaiting hands. She can have it. AntiEyes is my baby, so they'll never break through it like Kaycee did. And if they do? Everything's encrypted now. They won't find anything on there but more blank messages and emails. I've learned that fucking lesson once when I thought it was secure, and no one on their payroll is as smart as my Sweetheart.

"Good boy," she coos again, pulling her phone out of her pocket. "You've got two minutes before we need to leave. Get the fire started, and let's fucking go." Piper walks into the front yard without glancing back over her shoulder, giggling. Through the window, I see her eyes firmly on her phone as she prances around, pacing wildly.

As soon as her attention is on that screen for more than five seconds, I quickly move. Running to Benoit on the ground, I slam the door shut behind me and check him over.

"Fucking, Benoit!" I shout, shaking his body. "Wake the fuck up before you become ash!" I hiss, checking his neck for a pulse. It firmly pounds against my fingers, so that's good.

"I'm throwing you out the fucking window," I grunt, trying to heave his heavy ass onto my shoulders.

Heavy. Ass. Mother. Fucker. I can't lift his beefy ass from the ground. For fuck's sake! I've seen him naked. He shouldn't be this hard to move. What does he have? Bricks in his ass? For fuck's sake, I should have that weird adrenaline shit coursing through me, giving me superhuman strength, but it's not there. His dead weight is too heavy to fucking move.

I sit back on my ass, running my hands through my hair, pulling at the ends. How the fuck am I going to pull this off? How can I save him and Kaycee without sacrifice?

After filling a pitcher with water, I toss it onto Benoit's body and stand back. Fuck. He doesn't budge—not a damn inch. Not a finger or leg twitch. The only sign he's alive is the slight murmur. Shit—fuck me.

"Benoit, man," my voice cracks as I sit beside his knocked-out body. "You gotta wake up. I need you to get Tweedle-Dee and Tweedle-Dum! You. Have. To. Survive." I growl, shaking him again with all my might until every inch of him moves. But still, he gives me nothing but a few slurring words.

"Five more minutes," he murmurs again. "Just leave me alone," he slurs. Fuck. What did they do to him? Drug him? Knock him out with a blow to the head? I grunt, checking his temple, and sure as shit, there's a huge, bloody mark. Fuck!

"Can't do that, shit-brick!" I hiss, trying to keep my shaking voice low enough to not draw attention to the bitch pacing the front yard.

Benoit doesn't fucking stir, and I have no fucking choice. I tear the room apart. Picking up discarded clothes and fucking trash and upending everything until I find a pencil and a wad of used paper. And they turn their fucking nose up at my chaotic apartment. Fucking Seger's dirty ass saves the damn day. Scribbling six very important words onto the old piece of paper, I shove it into Elf Ear's shorts and pray to fucking God he finds it before he's a molten marshmallow. Since I can't wake his ass up or throw him out the window, he's left me with no other choice.

The words replay in my mind over and over again:

*I'll fucking save her. Save yourself.*

Taking stock of the room one last time, everything is in place, and I put my fucking game face on. This is it. I have to go back out there to that psycho. This is the moment I need a fucking Oscar for the performance I'm about to give.

I grunt, slamming the door as I walk out of the room, leaving Benoit on the ground with a bloody head and passed out. Piper still paces the length of the lawn, nose buried in her damn phone. Her giggles soar through the damn room, forcing a shiver down my spine. Whoever the fuck she's talking to, I hope they keep it up. They've kept her occupied and need to do it for longer. Thank fuck.

I heave a relieved breath, shaking the tension from my chest when I stand before Kaycee's room. The room where so many of our memories together linger in the back of my mind. If I close my fucking eyes, I can feel her fingertips brushing across my shoulders, urging me to enter and figure out what happened to her. Walking into Kaycee's room, I stop dead and take it in.

Everything is in its place. It's as if she was just here, lying in the unmade bed, and had just taken off her sweater, which lies on the ground. Walking around, I rush, listening for crazy pants on the lawn. When silence greets my ears, I walk to her computer and lean in. My eyes widen at the email sitting on the screen, still open from the last person who viewed it. I swallow hard, click the video and watch it in its entirety with my heart pounding so hard, it feels like it's about to shoot out of my chest. Watching Piper's crazy-ass stab Magnolia repeatedly and ditch her over the railing like trash makes bile rise in my throat, triggering my gag reflex. I bend at the waist, dry heaving several times, but nothing comes up. I just heave and heave until I can't fucking take it anymore, and my breaths strangle in my chest. Closing my eyes, I suck in several fresh breaths and clear my mind. When I stand straight up, the video starts over again, and I punch the desk, leaving the indent of my fist in the wood. Fuck! I knew Piper was a batshit crazy ass bitch, but this? This is fucking off the charts insane. She's the Alpha, and she's in way fucking deeper than we fucking thought.

Running a hand down my face, I try to regain my breaths and my fucking composure. My mind whirls with chaotic thoughts, and indecision strikes again. I need to hurry this entire operation along and get the fuck out of here so crazy-pants outside doesn't notice I haven't lit the fucking fire. Because, yeah, that's not going to fucking happen on my watch. He's going to wake up covered in gasoline and get the fuck out of here before anything bad can happen to him.

My foot stalls when I take a step towards the door, and a genius idea strikes out of nowhere. Something I should have thought about the moment I saw that sick as fuck video the first time. Instead of dry heaving like a ballsack, I should have jumped into action and presented Veritas with one more piece of evidence against these cocksuckers. Without a second thought, I quickly forward the email to my private server, preserving it forever, and breathe easier. I can only hope nothing happens to this fucking house while I distract Piper long enough to get her away from here.

So, what is Piper truly capable of? Killing Kaycee? Hurting Kaycee? Am I going to have to witness this shit as a fucking bystander unable to do anything about it? I'm so fucking fucked being tied up in the middle of this sick shit.

I shake my head out of those thoughts, looking around the room one last time. I wish Kaycee would jump out of the fucking closet and proclaim this was all a sick ass joke and laugh in my face. But I know it's not. Kaycee's gone, and I'm about to be her only fucking hope of escape. My eyes slip to the floor near the door, and my blood pressure soars, forcing me to see red. Taunting red speckles lead from her computer chair to the bedroom door and fall into the other room. Little innocent drippings, but it's not innocent. They fucking hurt her. They made her bleed, and I will return the favor tenfold when I get my hands on them. Red takes over my vision, and I completely fucking fall away from myself. Pain explodes through my fucking hand when I come back to reality. Apparently, I'm punching the fuck out of her closet door. It's too solid to collapse, but the pain clears my head instantly. I let her go once. Not again. I'm fucking coming, Sweetheart.

I shut the bedroom door, forming a quick plan in my mind. I jump out of Kaycee's bedroom window and race to the front yard, grabbing Piper's arm with more force than necessary. I drag her through the front yard, as far from the fucking house as possible. Hopefully, touching her will infect me with some of her crazy. Because I'm fucking going to need it to survive whatever hell I'm walking into.

"Finally," she huffs, placing her phone in her pocket.

"It's fucking done. Benoit's roasting as we speak," I grit through clenched teeth, hoping she doesn't sense the lie because I sure as fuck didn't set that fire. I need to get her the fuck out of here and away from this house before she clues in to my massive lie. Fuck me if she does.

"Mmhmm, good," she hums, shifting something in her pocket before bringing it out. "Well, since you already started it, I'm going to speed it up a bit!" She giggles, slamming her thumb onto a red button and then clapping her hands. A sharp boom happens behind us, the ground vibrating at our feet, stopping me in my tracks. For the millionth time tonight, the world has stopped turning. Everything fucking freezes. I plead in my head as I turn around, praying to fuck that it's not what I think it is. But, it is. My heart stops. A bright light paints the sky in orange and yellow, illuminating the path we just walked, like the sun has come out. Twirling around to stare at the carnage, Piper grins, slapping me on the shoulder. "Look, Brother, look at what I did! Isn't it beautiful!" She golf claps repeatedly, jumping up and down with excitement.

"I've always wanted to do that," Piper giggles, staring over the destruction with stars in her eyes and cocking her head with a sigh.

What starts as tiny flames grows higher and higher on the porch. It engulfs it, eating away at it until it breaks through the windows, invading the barriers of the house, licking up the facade, climbing higher and higher. It crackles and pops as the wood screams in pain from the heat of the flames. All I can imagine is Chase on fire, and my heart breaks in half at him lying there and fighting for his life. Or maybe, he's knocked out, and the smoke will get him first, and it's all I can fucking hope. I just... I fucking... I suppress the violence brewing in my pent-up fists and turn to look at Piper, who still looks at the blazing inferno like she wants to hump it and have its babies.

I could choke Piper to death, knock her out, and save Benoit. I could do a lot of things. Snap her in two. Break her damn neck. But—but Kaycee. They took her somewhere. Somewhere I'm walking to, and I don't know the way. Only Piper does. If I kill her, I'll never find Kaycee. But if I don't do something now, what am I supposed to do? Save my damn brother? Or save my girl? Whatever decision I make fucks me and them. Save one and not the other.

As much of a dick as it makes me, and as much as my heart fucking hurts to walk away, I leave and turn my back on the burning house. I don't look back. I walk beside Piper with a stone face, continuing to leave every ounce of my feelings behind. My feelings died in the fire engulfing my brother's body, and I can't fucking do anything about it. I pretend like nothing is wrong, like part of the family I built this year isn't lying inside that house and dying.

Fuck.

# TWENTY-SIX

## CARTER

Piper yaps on and on throughout our walk. What she says, I don't fucking know. I should probably pay attention, but my mind is a million miles away with Benoit, praying he's awake by now. Praying, he found my note and leapt out the window. If I could just get away from Psycho Suzy, I could text the others. Warn them about Kaycee. Warn them about everything going on and come up with some sort of fucking plan.

Piper leads me through the forest at the back of campus. Thick trees hover above us, shrouding us in complete darkness. The thick branches snuff out the stars and the moon, bathing us in the eerie shadows, barely letting us glimpse our hands in front of our faces. Sticks crunch beneath our feet as we walk along the narrowing path. Low-hanging branches brush across my clothes and slap me in the face.

A deadly silence falls between us when Piper finally shuts her fucking mouth. Only my heavy breathing and heartbeat pound in my ears. We continue our journey through the never-ending rows of trees, crossing a familiar path. The ghost of Kaycee's defiant face, telling me she wouldn't leave the school, comes to mind. This is the same forest—the same path—I kindly gave Kaycee her first warning to leave. She wrote me off, scoffed at me—fucking typical. I tried to get her to leave this hellhole. I knew what was coming. Her name had come up, and they were going to start her damn bullying campaign, just like Magnolia the year before. Of course, Kaycee wasn't having it.

Deep regret sits in my gut. I repeatedly tried, even if it was under the demand of Alpha, to get Kaycee to leave. Leaving her in the dumpster, I'd hoped she'd cry and beg to go, but she didn't. Shoving her gorgeous face into a piss-filled toilet didn't even do the trick. It pissed her off, but it didn't make her pack her bags and high-tail it out of here. Everything I tried to accomplish under the guise of the Apocalypse didn't work. After they told me to monitor her and become her friend, I finally said fuck it and gave in. I escaped in her. She was my fucking drug and my obsession.

Dear God, I know I'm not a good man. I know I don't pray enough. But today—today, I need you. I only ask that you save Benoit's life and help me find Kaycee. I'll pay for all my sins. Just help me find her. Could you help me save her? Or I won't live with myself.

"We're here!" she says, clapping her hands together in excitement, reanimating the conversation that had died between us.

I wrinkle my nose when we walk up behind a miserable-looking two-story shit hole of a house—a house that needs to be torn down or burnt to a crisp. Thick boards sit over every window in the back, blocking the view from the outside. The faded blue siding hangs down in several spots, waving in the wind and smacking the house in a rhythmic beat with every blow. Missing pieces reveal the original wood below, and mud cakes the rest of the exterior.

I survey the area discreetly as Piper takes her phone out again and buries her nose in it. We're out in the middle of nowhere with nothing but the chirps of the crickets and the crisp wind to keep us company. The hairs on the back of my neck stand on end at the feel of eyes searing through me. Goosebumps skitter across my flesh when I whip my head around, looking off into the distance. I narrow my eyes at the shadows playing tricks on me in the distance, and I fucking swear it moves with the wind. I shake my head and refocus on Piper, who puts her phone in her pocket and smiles at me expectantly.

"What the fuck is this place?" I ask through clenched teeth when she waves me past the house's side, and we walk toward a dilapidated porch barely hanging on by a thread.

The pitiful fucking porch once had a nice white railing protecting its occupants from falling over. But long ago, the paint chipped, and the nails gave, sending it to the decorative bushes in front. I take the two steps up with caution—rotten wood crunches under my feet, threatening to send me to the cold ground below. I make my way toward a black mailbox with a keen eye, half-hanging from the faded blue siding, taking in every detail I can muster. The window frames are peeling white paint, and the house fucking leans to the left. Jesus. What a fucking dump. How is it still standing?

"Grandma's house!" she squeals like I should know what the fuck that means.

I scowl again. Because it's my only fucking facial expression right now. I'm about to step foot into the hungry wolves' den, where all my demons hide. And I'm sure I will have to do something fucking awful.

Piper pulls me toward the red front door with excitement, practically vibrating with the damn emotion. I want to drop-kick her ass for every giggle she gives.

As she pulls me along, yacking about who the fuck knows, two numbers on the outside of the house catch my attention. They wouldn't mean anything to anyone else. But to me? To me, they mean a-fucking-lot. Forty-four. Forty-four Rosebud Drive. The address we've seen multiple times before and have tried to track down. I guess I fucking found it too little, too late.

As we step through the broken front door and into the

house, a scream pierces the musty air. My body tenses. Every. Fucking. Muscle. They lock tight, no matter how hard Piper tries to pull me in the other direction. I'm a damn statue. Torrent thoughts run a marathon inside my head. Anxiety spikes. My heart works double-time as the scream sounds again.

Play your part and play it well to save Kaycee from whatever nightmare she's enduring.

I grin, sighing into her touch like it's a comfort. Instead, I want to chop her hand into tiny pieces and feed them to fucking sharks for breakfast.

"Is that the bitch?" My voice dips deep, dripping with false want and lust. But inside? My gut rolls and bile rises in my throat.

Piper giggles, finally pulling me toward a closed door of what appears to be the disgusting living room. There are holes, stains, and missing wood flooring pieces throughout the room. No one has occupied this place for many years—the only sign someone has been here is the updated electrical. Cameras look down from every corner, recording our movements. Other than those added features, the room is decrepit.

"Welcome to the beginning!" Piper preens with a grin, shoving me through the door.

The lock sounds behind us, but I'm frozen in place. Again. Jesus. I need to get myself under control. I scowl, crossing my arms and taking in the surrounding room. It's updated. Monitors sit everywhere, showing at least seven rooms on camera. I'm not sure what's more terrifying: the torture equipment in each room or the woman covered in blood, screaming her lungs out on screen three. But it's not Kaycee. Thank fuck. She's nowhere to be seen on any monitor.

"Welcome," says a distorted voice.

I swallow hard, perfecting my damn demented mask of depravity. Pretend you like this, asshole. For Kaycee. For your fucking friends. To bring these dickwads down.

Three red-robed monsters sit at a long table side-by-side. They don't move a muscle with their hands tucked into their oversized sleeves. A firm brick wall of red robes, each gesturing for me to sit in front of them on the lone rolling chair opposite them.

I sit without question. I know who they are through our research, and all the sleuthing we did to uncover their secrets. So it's no surprise when they remove their masks and reveal the murderous Van Buren brothers with grins stretching their faces–way creepier than the faceless masks.

"Hello, Son," My father purrs at me with pride in his voice. His dark eyes sparkle at the sight of me sitting before them like a lamb ready for slaughter.

"Father." My muscles turn slack, loosening in the chair, giving the three monsters the illusion I'm fine.

"As you can see, Beta, your time has come." That piece of shit Crowe croons at me with a grin, spreading his arms wide.

"And what exactly is coming?" My fingers twitch on the arm of the chair, drumming against the cool material.

"Your time to shine, Beta," Shaw says, straightening his spine. The glint in his beady eyes sets me on edge, but I don't show it. I simply raise my brow and wave a hand, begging them to continue. "For the past year, we have tested you. Your loyalty to our cause," he continues coolly, looking at his brothers with pride.

"A cause I had no knowledge about," I say dryly, bored with their words.

"And yet, you passed with flying colors every time. Every anonymous demand you fulfilled. You are a soldier, Son, destined for greatness!" My father continues with excitement, throwing his arms into the air with dramatics fit for the stage. And as for me? I want to fucking puke.

He praises me for blindly following orders I had no choice but to follow. I never knew what happened to those few I befriended, only that they ended up dead. I turned a blind eye for a while, blaming it on coincidence. I met them, and then they died. It wasn't right away. Months, maybe. But it all ended the same. Death. Mysterious suicides. I couldn't ignore it anymore after Kaycee came, and they mentioned her name in their bully brigade. I didn't want to, for any of them. I never in my fucking life wanted to cause someone's death. Now it's time for me to take a stand. I'm no longer afraid of my father turning me in for my crimes; he thinks I'm with them. What I'm so afraid of is that they'll hurt Kaycee. So this whole interaction has to be plotted and executed with perfection.

"So, what do you say, Beta? Are you ready for the trials that await you? Are you ready to rule this world?" I want to snort. That sounds way too dramatic. So, I smirk instead.

"You bet your fucking ass I am." Leaning forward, I place my forearms on the table, giving them a good look into my eyes. Like flipping a damn switch, all my feelings evaporate, and I'm dead on the inside.

"Excellent," my father responds with the evilest, most putrid look in his eyes.

"You successfully infiltrated your trial's life," Crowe says, grinning, and my heart nearly drops into my ass. My trial's life. Kaycee. "You were in deep. Tell me, how did you do it this time? Before, you infiltrated beautifully, but this time was different. Well-planned—executed so well. So now, the real work begins."

"It was easy to carve my way into her heart." My lip curls up in disgust, but not at worming my way into her life, but the way I have to say it. My stomach heaves at the lies spewing from my lips, and I swallow it down.

It wasn't easy. Kaycee was stubborn, defiant, and a royal pain in my ass at all fucking times. She weaseled her way into my heart, not the other way around. I chased her like a fool. She avoided me. I should have scared her, but I didn't. She stole more than my wallet and phone. She stole my damn heart.

"You will prove your loyalty to us once and for all," Shaw says, nodding towards Piper—who, for once, was as quiet as a mouse, soaking in their praise with a grin.

"And how will I do that?" I ask nonchalantly, leaning back in my chair, eyeing every sicko in the room.

"Follow your Alpha, and she will show you," Cushing says, sweeping a hand toward Piper.

They put their masks back on without further prompting and sit there like faceless statues.

I quietly follow Piper out of the room like an obedient soldier. I jut my chin out, grinding my teeth when we make our way down the disgusting hallway. The only thing I'm thankful for is that Piper keeps her motor mouth shut.

We pass several closed doors down the never-ending corridor, and a chill spikes up my spine as we stop. Almost in slow motion, Piper turns to me with stars in her fucking eyes and then throws open the door, gesturing for me to follow her up a set of steep stairs. Warm air rushes across my face as we step up, heading into an unfinished attic filled with a musty scent.

Step by step, I feel the guillotine hanging over my head, ready to strike me down where I stand. The evil of their claws tear into me and bleed me dry. And when I see her lying helplessly on a metal slab, I want to explode. My fingers curl into a fist at my side, pressing into my palm. I fucking try to keep the snarl off my face at the sight of her tiny, helpless body.

Dried blood covers her chest, and a cut bleeds on her perfect face. The same face I've watched day in and day out with smiles and tears. The face I fucking adore. I've mapped the freckles, memorized her moans and spasms, and how she shouts my name when she comes. Or when she needs me. Or when she tells me how much she loves me in that husky voice and grounds me to this fucking earth. Her blonde hair lays like a halo around her head. She's an angel to me, and I'm not about to lose her.

Indecision swallows me whole. I want to throttle Piper through the damn window and run with Kaycee in my arms to safety. But I can't. Every scenario runs through my mind, leading to my and Kaycee's death.

Say I throw Piper out the window and listen to her glorious death gurgle from the top floor. Sounds nice in theory. I'd watch the darkness drain from her evil eyes with glee. But then what? They heavily monitor this house with top-of-the-line surveillance equipment. How far would I get? I could scoop Kace into my arms and jump from the window, but I'd break my legs, and we'd never escape. The goons would come and take care of me, and they'd take her anyway, and I wouldn't be able to protect her. That's what I have to do right now--protect her from their evilness until I can sneak her away. But I have to preserve my life and hers.

"You need to remove her socks and that hideous cast," Piper says, waving her hand over Kaycee's form.

If I jumped out the window with her, would we survive the fall?

"The fuck does she need to be changed for?" I say, pushing the growl out of my voice.

Piper snorts. "It puts on a better show. Duh! Now get to it!" She huffs the last part, heading down the stairs again with her nose in her phone.

Fuck. Fuck. Fuck.

A vise constricts my chest, forcing my breath into pants. I have to get myself under control before they witness my breakdown on camera. I'm sure they watch every move I make and scrutinize my loyalty to them. It baffles me that they think I would be loyal after years of blackmail and blindly forcing me into situations. The jokes on them, though. I'm here to bring them the fuck down.

"You have five minutes, and then we move her! I'm sure

Oscar would love to if you don't do it," she says from the bottom of the stairs. At the sound of his name and the implication of him touching my girl, I can't help the snarl I send in her direction, thanking fuck she can't see it.

"Fuck that," I growl, curling my fists once again, letting my fingernails dig into the sensitive skin of my palms. I revel in the pain when they slice into my flesh, leaving crescent moons behind. Taking a deep breath, I tamp down the rage swirling like fucking Godzilla inside of me. I can't afford to lose my shit right now, and maybe that's all this is —one final fucking test to see where my loyalty lies." He doesn't get to put his hands on what's mine! I put in the hard work, and now I get my reward." What leaves my lips is nothing but half-truths. She is mine, and I'll be damned if he touches a hair on her head without fucking consequence. After I save her, I'll put a fucking knife through his throat and watch the life drain from his beady, creepy eyes. He's always had a hard-on for her. Hell, maybe I'll cut off that, too.

Piper giggles magically from the staircase, echoing through the drafty room. "Oh, believe me, you'll get your reward at the end of this!"

"Piper," I start with hesitation, trying to sound eager. "What will be my end reward? Will I get more time with her?" Closing my eyes, I breathe through the desperation eating away at me. Time is not on my side right now, but I need so much of it to get her to safety.

"After the ceremony, she's all yours! You'll be the final blow, of course, only if you pass all these tests! Now chop, chop, brother!" I huff at the stupid fucking brother comment again and shake my head.

"Give me an extra minute to appreciate what's in front of me," I demand.

"Mmm, understandable! Carry on." Her voice sounds far away, like she's already mentally checked out from the conversation. Hopefully her fucking phone keeps her occupied like before.

The sound of the door closing deflates my chest, and I know I have to hurry. I only hope Kaycee can forgive me for everything I'm about to do. I don't have her consent, and she can't tell me no, and it makes my stomach ache to think I'm removing clothes from her body unwillingly. It may not be her damn pants or shirt, but it's still her clothes. And Kaycee's consent is every-fucking-thing to me.

Reaching down with shaky hands, I take her shoes off and carefully place them on the ground. Then her socks. My fingers brush against the skin of her feet, letting her warmth soak into me. Her chest rises and falls, her heart beating steadily against my fingers. She's warm—alive—and right here for the taking. Indecision rages inside of me again, and war battles inside my brain. Kaycee is at my fingertips right now. But I can't save her like this.

I want to fall to my knees. Break down. Scream into the mother fucking void and beg for her life. Something. Anything to get her out of here and to safety.

I remove her cast and sleeve as quickly as I can, planning out my next moves. I don't know what we're about to walk into. All I know is that I will have time alone with her near the end, which will be my chance to grab her and fucking go. Pain is inevitable for both of us, no matter what happens. If I know she's getting hurt, it'll hurt me. All I can hope is that Veritas finds this location and gets here as fast as possible before we die. If Kaycee dies, I die. End of fucking story. No matter what I choose to do, it's a lose-lose. My choices are limited, and I can only hope for the fucking best.

Making sure to step in front of the camera, I take the phone secured in my waistband and stare at the bright screen. Using Kaycee's thumbprint, I unlock her phone and go to her text messages. If I could call those idiots, I would, but I can't chance anyone seeing me or hearing me do this. I lean over

Kace and bury my nose in her hair, inhaling her scent one last time. I use the remaining time I have to begin planning our escape.

**MY CUTIES:**

> Kaycee: They've taken Kaycee. This is Carter. They took my fucking phone and me to some house at the back of campus. It's through the fucking woods.

I hold my breath seeing the messages delivered but not read—my heart rate spikes when footsteps sound below the attic door, getting closer and closer to check on me.

> Kaycee: We don't have much time. They're going to hurt her. BAD.

> Kaycee: I don't know what to do. I DON'T KNOW WHAT TO FUCKING DO.

I hang my head, inhaling her scent again to calm my nerves. I don't know what to do. I may be smart, but I feel so fucking useless and weak right now. My brain turns in a million directions trying to guide me to a decision.

> Kaycee: Is Benoit ok? Fuck. Fuck. TWEEDLE-DEE TWEEDLE-DUM, ANSWER MY FUCKING TEXTS.

I want to slam her phone onto the metal gurney holding Kaycee's body. I'm at a loss. I'm—stuck. They are the only way I can get her out of here if we could turn off the cameras.

> Zepp: Are you there with her? Where? Benoit's burned severely. There's an ambulance on the way along with the cops.... But he's fighting through it.

> Kaycee: Tell him...I'm fucking sorry. I tried, man. I wanted to get him out, but fucking Piper...she lit it. Not me.

> Zepp: He'll understand. Now tell me everything.

And so I do with burning guilt searing me from the inside out. I tell him everything that's happened, and we formulate a plan. It's not solid, and we could get hurt. But we have a fucking plan and the drive to complete it. And now I have to act my ass off to get through this for her protection. Until the cops or Veritas can make it to this location. It's only a matter of time before they bust down the doors and find this place. But until then, I have to keep going.

# TWENTY-SEVEN

## CARTER

Deep. Fucking. Breaths.

I tug at the black robe's sleeves with slick black leather gloves that conceal my hands. A dark black mask hides the scowl I'm still sporting. Even if they can't see me, I know their eyes are watching my every move. No matter what, I'm playing my fucking part. After leaving my fucking heart in the attic, they led me back to the central control room and dressed me in this robe. My heart beats out of control, sitting here and waiting for their instructions on what to do next.

Kaycee sits on their main monitor screen with her eyes shut tight and her body lax. From here, I can tell she's fighting tears. Not that I fucking blame her. At the sight of her emotions, my fists curl in the squeaky gloves. I try not to show how fucking pissed I am over the entire situation. They forced Piper and me to shove her into a fucking fish tank she barely fit into. And now, I'm being subjected to watching her fucking fight for her life. I don't know what they're up to. I fucking wish I did.

"Get ready, Sugar, you're about to be famous. Smile at your customers. They've invested so much into this. You're on camera for millions to see. Actually, on second thought, don't! Scream your tits off. The audience likes it." My father leans toward a microphone with his mask in place, distorting his voice.

"You see that?" Shaw lifts his mask, pointing toward a computer in front of us. Numbers build higher and higher, showcasing the number of sickos tuning in to watch the show. And the main attraction? Kaycee's pain. Everything I saw on the website makes sense now. Views. Bids. It's real-life people getting off on people's pain and death.

"It's almost 200k viewers!" Crowe says, puffing up with pride. A large grin takes over his entire face when he turns to me. "Now," he starts, putting his hands under his chin. "It's time for you to announce her lot for all our viewers." He raises a brow, nodding toward the microphone nearest me.

I eye it with suspicion, but I know what I have to do. They'll force me to say it or kill me on the spot, no matter what. I've seen the guns they're packing in their robe pockets. If someone disobeys them, they'll shoot first and ask questions later. No matter what, I've been backed into a corner and bent over without fucking lube. Throughout this entire situation, I will have to play a part that's eating away at my insides and chipping away at my fucking heart. But Kaycee would one-hundred percent die if I didn't. I play my part, and she has to play hers in whatever they make her do.

"Here," my father says, slipping a piece of paper toward me with neat handwriting. A script of bullshit lays before my eyes, and my heart falls into my fucking ass. "Say these exact words, and we'll do the rest." He arches a pointed brow at me, promising me a world of hurt in one look if I fuck up even an inch.

Play your fucking part---my mind plays those words repeatedly as I lean into the microphone an inch away from my lips. My heart pounds a steady beat against my ribs, and an ache forms in my head. I know this is so wrong in the back of my mind.

"Welcome investors and bidders to lot number two

hundred and twenty-six," my voice comes out distorted and deep, thankfully covering the quiver in my voice.

The dark mask covering my face hides the grimace—thank fuck. I know from experience that if I show an ounce of weakness in front of my father, he'll pistol whip and then kill me. Even worse, if I show them an ounce of favor toward Kaycee right now, they'll know my act wasn't an act.

As the lot number leaves my lips and the bids start rolling in on the screen, my breath leaves my lungs. That fucking number. Breaking into Crowe's house didn't warrant much information if little at all. We found out about Addison's health, and Kaycee got to sit in Maggie's bedroom for closure. But that fucking number he had said over the phone when we spied on him has run through my head since. Two hundred and twenty-six—it all makes sense now. Everything that's fucking perplexed me over the last year clicks into place. The cameras in the hallways. They always knew what I was up to and how to track these people I was supposed to keep an eye on. It was all for this. Kaycee's torture and torment were an investment for them—a money-making scheme. And fuck me if it isn't working in their favor.

"It's the night you've all been waiting for. Your last bids have been placed!" I try hard to add fake excitement to my voice as cheerful elevator music plays through a second microphone. My father urges me to continue my speech with an angry wrist wave. "Over the past few months, you've watched lot two hundred and twenty-six through your screens. You've selected her torture, her embarrassments, and punishments." Vomit churns as I say the words, but I remember their weapons holstered away in their robes and continue.

Several videos clipped together of every incident Kaycee has endured since she walked on campus flashes across a monitor in a montage of clips. It's like a tribute to their cruelty, and they're eating it up like a fucking ice cream sundae. Their laughter floats through the control room with glee, cackling at her misfortunes. I feel it from here, pounding into my chest, and it fucking disgusts me. My fingernails threaten to burst through the leather gloves. But I remain calm on the outside and finish what I'm supposed to do. If I could overpower them and kill them now, I would.

Leaning away from the speaker, I clear the emotions from my throat before I can continue. "You've watched her cry and yell. You've watched her pain, frustrations, and sadness. Now —welcome one and all for your final viewing of lot two hundred and twenty-six as she endures your last requests and bids us farewell! You've spoken, and you shall receive!" Once my horrific speech is finished, I sit back in my chair. My heart assaults my ribs from the inside. I'm serving my girlfriend up on a platter for these sickos with a pretty bow on top of her head.

On camera, her face pales, completely voiding her of color. She eyes the camera, staring into my broken soul. My skin tingles with awareness, raising the hairs on my arms. Can she see me? Does she know I'm suffering as much as she is—that my heart is splitting into two at the sight of her bound wrists and dried blood painting her flesh? No. She doesn't. I don't want her to know I'm sitting here in a chair while she's on display. But I can't move. Not with the three evil bastards across from me with guns in reach. If I made a move, they'd take their guns out and shoot me dead before I could grab her and run.

My spine straightens as I watch her fight for her fucking life. She's drowning in a human-sized fish tank because I had to cuff her. I put her there—me. Fuck. I did this. If my Sweetheart lives, I'll never be able to look her in the eyes again without the guilt consuming me. Eyeing the bastards across from me, I calculate the moment I'll be able to steal their gun and fucking kill them.

The psychos chuckle and point as her body sways in the

rising water. Crowe peers down at a stopwatch in his hands and nods his head.

"We have thirty seconds until it drains," he says, pursing his lips.

"You're not fucking killing her?" I ask, trying to clear the emotions from my voice.

Crowe barks a laugh and slaps a hand down on the table separating us. "What good would she be if she died so soon? She'll have time to displace the water and take a breath. She's a very smart girl. She'll figure it out," he says, raising a brow at me like I should have guessed their fucking plans.

"You see those numbers, boy?" My father asks in a rough voice, pointing toward the screen. I nod in response. "If we killed our main attraction, what good would it be? She has several trials to go through before she meets her end." He gives me a sick smile at the end of his speech, and it does little to tamp down the nerves bursting to life inside of me.

I sit on pins and fucking needles when the water goes entirely over her head. She struggles in the water, fighting against her cuffs to get to the top for fresh air. She tugs at her wrists several times and looks around. Come on, Sweetheart! Calculate and fucking move. You can do this.

"And that's thirty seconds," Crowe says, stopping the timer. He waves a hand, and I see the water go down just a little before she realizes she can make waves and displace the water onto the ground.

I force my leg to stay still beneath the table when she bursts through the water and desperately gasps for air. Fuck yes, that's my girl. Outwardly, I can't express my anxiety to them through leg bouncing or any physical forms. I hold it in. All of it. Soon it'll be too much, like an overfilled balloon, and I'll fucking pop. But for now, I know she's safe, and I know they're at least keeping her alive long enough to enact our plan of getting Kaycee the fuck out of here.

My father's eyes narrow in on me, eyeing my stiff body.

Thankfully, my face is still covered, or he'd see the multitude of swollen teardrops falling down my cheeks. I compose myself through a deep breath, pretending that I enjoy her torment as she struggles to breathe on screen. She coughs and sputters, splashing the retreating water around.

"Time to move on," Crowe directs with another twirl of his hand.

"Alpha," my father shouts, pounding his fist onto the table.

The door behind me pops open, and Piper walks in with the same dark outfit as me: mask, gloves, and a long robe. Her posture is perfect with her chest out, shoulders back, and hands resting at her sides.

"Yes, daddies?" She purrs from beneath the masks.

Fucking gag me with a goddamn spoon. This word, of course, makes their smiles wider. For fuck's sakes, did they rail her, too? Manipulate her so much she thinks they all care for her? I want to bang my head against the wall until it splits open as she giggles again and preens under their watchful eyes. They look at her like they want to tear her apart in the worst fucking way possible.

"Take Beta with you to release the prisoner. Black hood her, then take her into room three. It's battling babes, so you know what to do," Crowe purrs, standing beside her in two strides.

His fingers dip below the mask, tracing her jawline with love and affection. If I could see her eyes, she'd be full-on gaga for her damn father. She sighs, giggling a small laugh, and nods.

"Let's go, Beta," she says dreamily.

Crowe grins more at her, pleased with his little puppet prancing toward the door in a love-sick daze. Fuck. So gross.

# TWENTY-EIGHT

## CARTER

I FOLLOW beside Piper like the good little soldier I'm pretending to be. My head may be held high, but my fucking heart bursts through my ribs as my mind anticipates this meeting. Sweat drips down my neck and in between my shoulder blades. Kaycee won't see me, won't know it's me, but I'll be by her side for just a moment. Whatever happens next, I need to help her in any way to ensure she doesn't get hurt even worse.

"We go in," Piper says, pulling keys from her pocket. "Undo the cuffs and then put this over her head. Then we take her down the hall. Once we are in the room, tie her to the pole, hands together tightly." I nod in response without a word. Shoving a black sack into my hands, she twists the knob and walks in with a small giggle erupting from under her mask like she's done this a million times. Hell, I bet they all have from the get-go. I wonder how many people Piper has killed since she stuck that knife deep into Magnolia and tossed her?

I close my eyes beneath the mask, trying to keep my dinner down in the depths of my churning stomach. Watching Kace through a screen in pain is one thing, but fucking walking into the torture room she's in is another. And knowing I can't do anything about it yet is slowly killing me on the inside.

Drag me behind a truck, chain my fucking feet, or beat my face in with your fists, but fucking please, don't make me see my girl like this.

A throat clearing forces my feet to move into the room. Jesus—this room—the fish tank sits in the middle with three cameras discreetly hanging from the ceiling, pointed directly at it. Large monitors sit in front of the tank, displaying her wheezing form, begging for breaths. Her wet head leans against the glass, barely able to move from the exertion of trying to save her life.

My heart shatters at the sight of her bruised and shivering body. Wild breaths heave through her, jolting her body more. Her beautiful ocean eyes evaluate every move we make, yet she doesn't fight us when we open the tank to her freedom. She's so close, but so far away.

Piper motions with a wave for me to unlock her hands as she grips Kaycee's hair. My fingers itch to punch Piper in the face until she bleeds, but the timing is off. They'll shoot me if I make a move now while they're watching through the cameras—this is a test, after all.

Once Kaycee is in my arms, we secure a black hood over her head. In silence, we lead Kaycee out of the disgusting room. Her feet squish and squelch into the gross carpet. My fingers wrap around her waist, holding her as close as possible without giving myself away. Her shivers wrack through her, jolting her entire body against me. Relief shoots through me when she presses the side of her body into mine. That's right, sweetheart, soak up my heat. It's one thing I can do for her before I leave her again.

A cry of pain tears from down the hall, jerking her body to a halt. I wait it out with her, refusing to drag her shaky legs any further. She stiffens against my side as we both listen to the woman wail through whatever the fuck they are doing to her. Probably something horrific. God, I need to get time alone with Kaycee. I need it for our plan to work. Piper mentioned the ceremony, whatever that was. I need it to get here so I can help my Sweetheart. So I can tell her once and for all that I love her.

My fingers continue to rest on her waist. Feeling Piper's gaze burn into my skull, I gently squeeze her side three times. *I love you. I will help. Please, don't give up.* It could mean so many things at this point to her. I want her to feel it in her beating heart—that someone in this hell-hole is on her side and is plotting her escape... Even if I die trying, I'll lay down my life for her. No matter what.

Without further prompting, I drag her down the hall because I have two fucking jobs to do. Her legs wobble and threaten to give, but I hold her up, keeping a firm hand attached to her waist. Piper leads us into another disgusting excuse for a room. You know, you'd think they'd invest in their torture chambers with all this money they've stolen. Not that I fucking want them to, but still. This is supposedly their livelihood—yet it's moldy, smelly, and unkempt. There's an odd amount of hand tools lying around in this room: wrenches, hammers, copper pipes lining the far wall, and other sorts of pipes. It's like old Greta was fixing this place up and then abandoned it. Or, you know, they murdered her before she could finish. Fucking psychopaths.

I walk Kaycee into the room, eyeing the pole Piper had mentioned before we came in. It stands from floor to ceiling, bolted in place. Through my mask, it seems like an old water pipe, rusted but sturdy. A hand waves me forward, urging me to tie my girlfriend to the fucking pole. Thrusting a rope into my free hand, she motions me again to hurry.

Turning Kaycee around, I take her right wrist into my hand. Her knees knock together, body shivering from the water dripping from her shirt plastered to her body. I don't know how much longer she'll be able to stand at this pole without falling to the ground, and it pisses me the fuck off. Fuck these assholes for putting her through this, and fuck me for having to take part.

Another black-robed figure enters the room with their head held high. Whoever it is nods toward Piper, who nods in return. They are obviously privy to whatever the fuck is about to go down. I wrap Kaycee's right wrist with the burning rope and tighten it with a rough yank. A small whimper from beneath the black hood on Kaycee breaks my fucking heart. The skin beneath the rope reddens with my harsh treatment and from the treatment of the handcuffs before.

Fuck. Someone kick my ass before I have to do it myself.

I can't leave her defenseless, not again. I've already watched her drown. I can't watch whatever they're going to do to her without giving her a fighting chance, especially if they expect me to stand by and watch her pain.

The room falls to a deafening silence as the other two watch me work. I feel their stares taking in every move I make, burning me and assessing me. They're making sure I do my job, monitoring me for the rest of the Apocalypse. So, with that in the back of my mind, I make my next moves as carefully as possible. My foot hits an average-sized wrench, knocking it closer to Kaycee's pole. If her left hand is free, she can grab it in self-defense. Thankfully, it scoots across the moldy orange carpet, as silent as a mouse creeping through a church.

When I wrap Kaycee's left wrist in the rope, I tie it as loose as possible without falling off. Over exaggerating my movements, I give the fuckheads the illusion I'm tightening them down. In reality, I'm giving her a weapon to bring them to their knees.

Kaycee moves her wrist around, twisting and turning, attempting to check the resistance in her rope. Which—fuck—there isn't any. I tied it so loose around her wrist that if she moves anymore, it'll fall off. And if that happens, fuck me—they'll retie it and shoot me dead. Then she'll never have a chance.

I wrap my gloved hand around her elbow, squeezing it in a warning. 'Stop moving, or we are both dead.' With a deep breath, I pull my hand away and bury every emotion inside of me, pushing them down into the depths of the darkness dwelling inside of me. The same darkness Kaycee shed light on and replaced with happiness and sunshine and butterflies. But now—now I need my darkness to bleed my heart dry and make me numb, to submerge me in fucking ice water until we can escape.

The second figure waves an impatient hand, bouncing on her toes. Fuck me. I rip Kaycee's hood off, walking toward the other two. We stand in formation, shoulder-to-shoulder, with our arms crossed over our chests.

When I step back from Kaycee and take my spot in line with the other figures, two more unknown people in black robes walk into the room with their masked faces held high. The door clicks behind them, locking us all into this hell hole. I clench my fist tight when they march forward instead of standing in the straight line with us, and they beeline for Kaycee, who eyes them with suspicion. I run my tongue along my top teeth, gluing my fucking feet to the ground.

"Heya, Stupid." The one says with a distorted voice, bringing a finger to the side of her face. His voice sounds smug and really fucking familiar. If I had to guess it's either Trent or Oscar hiding behind mask number one and probably mask number two.

"Remember me?" They ask in a deep voice making my fucking teeth grind together. I thank whatever asshole insisted on these masks so these dicks can't see I want to rip them apart piece by piece. But we're surrounded here.

"Trent," she grunts, trying to pull from his grasp. "You were there? You wrecked into us?" Pride bleeds from every evil inch of Trent when he pulls his mask off and smiles down at her.

"Ah, I never thought you'd remember. You were blitzed out of your mind, Slut," he says, leaning in to brush his lips against her cheek.

"I could have taken you then, and I could take you now," he rasps through a throaty moan, leaning into her more and kissing down her jaw. "Perfect," Trent mumbles, trailing unwanted kisses down her jaw. Her entire body stiffens with every groan he gives.

Red slashes cross my vision, taking over when he leans into her grinning more. His body melts into hers, taking what the fuck he wants while groping her breasts and groaning. His eyes discreetly slip to me with a smarmy smirk lining his lips. And that's the moment I know. They're testing everything I do. Slowly, I uncurl my fists and shake them out, trying to block out whatever the fuck they say to her. I'm not sure how much more I can take without blacking out and choking them all. If I lose control now, they'll kill me, and she'll die in their hands regardless.

My fingernails curl into my palm, and if I didn't have gloves on, they'd puncture my skin. My chest heaves with every deep breath I take, forcing myself to stay put so I don't put my fist through his teeth and make him swallow them. I close my eyes, refusing to hear the words that they say. I feel it in my churning gut that this is nothing more than a way to fuck with me and test my loyalties. Everything about this situation screams this is a fucking test.

"It was you? You broke my arm?" she asks in a small voice, shaking her head. "You two were there?" Trent snorts and rolls his eyes. My mind reels from their confession. I knew it was someone in the school, and I should have suspected them. But fuck! To hear it from their lips that they were the dickbags to attack not only Kaycee but Tweedle Dee and Tweedle Dumb, too. Fuck.

"What did you expect? Your lover boy?" Trent scoffs, slipping his gaze to me once again. Jealousy sits behind his eyes when he looks me up and down and scoffs once again.

"Delta and Panty Licker." Piper finally steps forward with a growl in her distorted voice and cocks her head. "You're interrupting a broadcasting bid with your assaults." She waves her hands around in irritation, earning nothing but huffs from Oscar and Trent. But thank fuck she stopped their wandering hands from touching Kaycee again.

Oscar murmurs something and finally picks up his mask from the ground and puts it on.

"It was sanctioned by the real bosses anyway, Alpha," Trent hisses, setting his mask back onto his face. "We'll be on our way. Enjoy your stay," he sing-songs, waving a hand in the air.

Kaycee's breathtaking blue eyes fill with dread when she looks around the room, inspecting it. Once her eyes land on us, understanding dawns on her, and she deflates. Her chest heaves as she sucks in air. After being submerged underwater for that time, I can't imagine she's breathing well or feeling well.

"Welcome back to lot two hundred and twenty-six! And boy, do we have a treat for you! It was a long and drawn-out bidding war between Battling Babes and Tantalizing Toenails." Her back stiffens against the pole at her back, and worry takes over her crinkled face when the voice reads off those two choices...

Kaycee has a mean poker face when she's not tired. Or distracted. She's stood up to me more times than I can count. She stepped on my toes and knocked me in the balls, like the badass she is. But right now, every emotion shows on her tired face. Every. Damn. One. She's too injured and way too tired to hide the telling parts of herself.

"But you asked for battling babes and a battling babes fight you will get!" Fuck me. Whichever psycho is giving this shitty announcement has way too much pep in his damn voice. Distorted or not, he sounds like he's getting a Goldendoodle for Christmas and can't wait to put a bow on its collar. "The bidding is open for the winner of this high ticket show. Place your bids now and see who wins this showdown! At the sound of the buzzer, let the game begin!"

Kaycee heaves a heavy sigh full of defeat. Don't give up yet, sweetheart. She leans her soaking head back on the pole. "A fight, huh?" Her raspy voice sends shivers down my spine, and my fists curl at the hurt curling around her.

I take the lead of the other two, standing stock-still. Without movement, we ignore our sacrificial lamb and don't pander to her witty remarks. Deep breath in, deep breath out. I need to continue playing my shitty part. Even when every inch of me crawls in disgust. I want to reach out and wrap her in my arms, snuggle her close, and never fucking let her go. If I were a fucking badass, I'd have my own pistol. Hell, I'd have a fucking army behind me, and we'd take these pieces of shits out. Where the fuck is Veritas and their fucking promise to extract her before it came to this? I'm beginning to think the secret government agency I put my trust in is fucking me over harder than these fucking cult douchebags. Shit! Where the fuck are they?

"Not very fair, is it?" she bravely taunts, nodding toward her bound arms. Huffing a shaky breath, she shakes her head in disgust.

Anxiety builds in my gut as someone finally makes a move. I'm not sure how much more Kace can take. Another hit. Another drowning. What else do they have in store for her after this? They alluded to prolonging her life for the money, but will her body be up for it?

"Who the fuck says it needs to be fair, dumbass freak?" Hadley fucking Lacey snarls behind her mask. My eyes roll up toward the ceiling, and I heave a breath at the sound of her annoying voice. I knew she was a part of this whole group, and I'd given her name to fucking Veritas. But goddamn, her voice is like nails on a chalkboard.

"Obviously not you," Kaycee mumbles. "You never fight fair, though, do you? Poisoning me, beating me in the hall?" One of the hooded figures steps forward, whipping the robe and mask off, revealing herself to us.

She sports a form-fitting bra and matching thong. God damn. A vision I never wanted to see. Pink, frilly, and fucking disgusting. Hadley saunters around like she's hot shit. Confidence oozes off her, chin raised and her pointy witch nose in the air. Her smug grin could curdle milk with one look.

Her beady eyes devour Kaycee like the true predator she is—a wolf on the prowl, waiting to pounce on her tiny rabbit in the woods. Bouncing on the balls of her feet, she claps her hands together in a small golf-type clap. Hadley rejoices in the fear emanating out of Kaycee's eyes. She'd bathe in it and soak it up if she could. What is happening isn't a disgusting act to her. She's getting off on Kaycee's pain and torment. But what the fuck do these assholes get out of this? All I know is they're recruits, not full members. Like me, except they weren't fucking blackmailed into this.

"This is going to be so much fun." Hadley's high-pitched giggles break through the tension of the room.

A shrill buzzer sounds over the intercom, marking the beginning of Kaycee's doom.

Hadley races toward her tied-up body like a freight train barreling at full speed, letting her anger and hatred billow steam out of her ears. It takes every ounce of my restraint to hold myself still—not running to her side like I desperately want. Fuck. Hadley pounds her fists into Kaycee's face. One cheek, then the next. Over and over. Kaycee's head whips back and forth from the force, crying in pain with every blow. Blood seeps from her twisted nose, painting her lips and chin in dark red when her fragile body crumbles to the sodden floor, falling into a whimpering heap.

"Fight me like a woman, Hadley!" she hisses, spitting venom between clenched, bloodied teeth.

Fuck yes. Keep strong, sweetheart. Keep your head up and keep that fire burning deep, Vixen. It's the same fire she used against me and anyone else who stood in her way. Fight, Kaycee. Don't. Fucking. Give. Up. Use your free damn hand!

"Untie me so I can kick your ass!" she yells through a slur, receiving a punishing foot to her jaw.

My body bounces, ready to swoop in and take her into my arms, when she falls back, thumping her head off the floor. And for one brief moment, she doesn't move or react to the punishing blow. She simply lays there, staring with unblinking eyes. I hold my breath, counting down the seconds until a soft groan slips between her lips. That's my fucking girl. Get up and kick some ass.

My jaw ticks, phantom pains prickling through my teeth. Watching the one I love lying on the floor defenseless is driving me fucking mad. I dart my eyes to the other assholes in the room, contemplating my actions. Once again, I could take them all out and fucking grab Kaycee, but I always come to the same conclusion. If I make a move, I die. And that strands Kace. Fuck!

Kaycee groans, letting her hair fall in front of her face. It curtains her features and blocks us from her eyes. I see the moment she discovers the wrench close by, and my heart skips a beat. This is fucking it. Her fingers inch toward it, but Piper isn't looking. She's distracted, staring up at the ceiling. And fucking Hadley won't shut her fucking trap, pacing around the room and threatening Kaycee more. The other figure just stands there with their arms folded, staring forward. They could fucking be asleep under their masks, and we'd have no idea.

"I don't think so, freak. You're going to be so black and blue by the time they find your body. They won't even recognize you," Hadley spits, throwing her head back in an evil cackle. God, someone needs to put her out of her fucking misery.

I hold my breath when Kaycee gets the wrench in her grasp and stumbles to her feet. She weaves back and forth on shaky knees but stands as tall as possible, balancing herself on the pole with her free hand to steady her swaying body. Her glazed eyes fog over more as her fight for survival continues. Just a little fucking longer, sweetheart. Keep your fighting spirit up.

"You never learn when to stay down, do you? You just keep getting up and up—" Hadley gapes, staring at Kaycee with shock.

Most of her victims must go down easily because she's staring at Kaycee like she's a zombie coming back to life. I swear she even pales a little. Hadley has always been a brutal, malicious bully since I met her, tearing down other girls. Jealousy ran through her veins like the very blood inside of her. Spiteful ass wench. If Kaycee uses that wrench in her hand to get her revenge on Hadley, I might cum in my pants. And cheer, of course, on the inside. Fuck—I'm so fucked up.

"I did it," Kaycee says confidently, even with a painful expression twisting her broken face. Blood drips everywhere now, dripping at her feet and soaking into the gross carpet.

"Did what, freak?" Hadley hisses, popping her knuckles and preparing for another attack.

I swallow the chuckle in my throat, imagining what Kaycee's next words will be. By the look on her face, I know exactly what she will say before she says it. And yup, there it is. She let it slip that she was the one to hack into Hadley's FlashGram and spill the beans on her infected vagina.

"Holy shit!" I sputter through the laughter I can't fucking contain, earning a scathing glare from Hadley. Her face glows red, seething with anger. God, this is priceless. She's like Rudolph, the red-faced cunt.

My girl won't back down. Fuck no. She's strong as hell, even with a swollen face and blood dripping down her face. She smiles at Hadley, exposing her bloody teeth. My body shudders, fighting the urge to help. Then she says, what is my undoing.

"Make me," she growls in retaliation for Hadley, telling her to shut up.

And all hell breaks loose before Piper and I can calm the situation down. The wrench connects with Hadley's face in a flash, knocking her to the ground. She spits and sputters, tossing a blood-curdling scream out. I stare down at her, grinning behind my mask.

"Fuck!" Piper shouts, marching toward Kaycee before I can stop her. Wrapping an arm around her neck, she applies enough pressure to take her down. But not before Kaycee gets the last word in on a squirming Hadley. Kaycee's eyes droop and her body slumps, succumbing to the darkness, begging to take her. At least there, her pain won't exist.

Piper scowls as she lifts her mask, keeping Kaycee pressed against her. "You failed to keep her secured!" She hisses, pointing a finger at me with accusation.

I scoff, lifting my mask. "You seriously think that's a good fight?" I roll my eyes, tossing a hand out. "You seriously think our viewers would want to see some bitch tied up while another wails on her? Fuck that. I made it interesting. Intriguing. They didn't know who was going to win." I shake my head, walking toward Piper, still clinging to Kaycee.

"To me, it looked like you helped her. You didn't, did you?" she barks, shoving Kaycee's body into mine before turning to help Hadley. I catch her immediately, trying not to relax with her in my arms. Her head lulls on my shoulder as I growl at Piper more.

"The fuck I look like?" I growl.

"Bravo! Bravo!" A loud voice rings through the room, and hands clap, gaining all of our attention.

I grunt at the figures moving into the room with their red

robes shining in the dull light. Their masks sit on top of their heads, giving us a disgusting view of their faces. Crowe smiles at us, pride lighting up his face.

"But Daddy, he—" Piper's lip pouts when Crowe holds a hand in her direction.

"No, no, Love, he did exactly what a leader would do," He coos at her, rubbing a finger down her jaw. Her face sags, and the same love-sick dopey expression takes over her face. She looks at him like he hung the moon, and to her, he did. Their deep kisses and groping session repeat in my mind every time I look at them together, and I want to gag on reflex.

"Besides, that stunt made the bids soar through the roof," Shaw says with a smirk, clapping his hands. "She's a money-maker, and when that wrench hit your poor face, it drove the bidders crazy," he cackles, looking down at Hadley as she holds her face, still bleeding everywhere.

The fuck is wrong with these fuckers? Everything. Everything is wrong with these assholes. They need serious help or a bullet to the fucking brain.

"And that's why, Son, it's time for you to earn your robe," my father says with a sickening proud smile, making my stomach drop into my ass. He cocks his head. "You've proven your worth to us. You improved the game, and now I think you're ready," he says smoothly, folding his hands together. But whatever words he uses makes my heart beat double time. The fuck does that mean?

"Delta, Panty Licker, take our hostage to the last room." He snaps his fingers in Trent and Oscar's direction, and they step forward.

Fuck. Fuck. I have her in my arms. She's here with me, yet I have to let her go. Especially with the silver peeking out from the split in the psycho's robes, taunting me if I fuck up and run with her. They'll shoot me on sight. Even with his words ringing in my head about trusting me and how I've proven myself, the time still isn't right.

Reigning in the boiling anger brewing inside me, I take a deep breath. In and out. Deep into my lungs. I let her go. Trent takes her lifeless form into his arms with a wicked grin. I immediately follow him with clenched fists, ready to punch his stupid fucking face.

"Son," my father's authoritative voice stops me in my tracks. After all these years, he still has this pull on me. It's conditioned me to obey his orders, fall to my knees, and do as he asks. Or at least, that's what he thinks. For now, I'm doing what I have to do to survive—for Kaycee.

"Father," I say, turning to look at the wall of crazies lining up in their red robes. Piper stands beside her father, staring up at him, smiling. It's sickly sweet and downright perverse.

"For this next round, you will sit out and watch from the office. Once the ceremony is complete, we'll invite you back in." His head tilts, watching my reaction.

"And then I get to do whatever I want?" I ask, slipping my evil smile back into place.

They chuckle at my response, and my blood boils in my veins.

"Oh, yes, whatever you want. She is your trial, after all. Much like the bitch before was hers," Shaw says, pointing toward Piper.

"And I got her good!" Piper giggles, clapping her hands.

I'd like to get her good—really fucking good. Maybe a throat punch and a trip to the bottom of the ocean in pieces would do her some good.

The crazies lead me back to the viewing room—the first room I saw them in—and sit me down. They don't say a word, leaving with only one instruction. Don't leave this room. I know this is another fucking test. And God damn do I need to fucking pass to save her.

# TWENTY-NINE

## CARTER

Every room in the house sits on the monitors in front of me: the empty fish tank, the empty pole, and the woman whose scream fills the hallway, begging in another empty room. They bound her hands, and blood drips from her chest where red welts are. Leaning forward, I scrunch my eyebrows at fucking Francesca Hurst when she throws her head back, begging them to stop the torture and set her free. My lips pop open as I watch her struggling against her restraints like a wild animal caught in a cage, thrashing her whole body around. It looks like my father let her out of his damn prison and led her straight to fucking Hell.

Moving my eyes, I finally spot Kaycee slumped over in a chair with two black figures tying her hands to the armrests. I grind my teeth in frustration. At least they aren't hurting her—yet. Fuck!

I pound my fist into the desk with a heavy thud. Knick-knacks, pencil holders, and a fucking folder lift into the air from the force of my frustration. Anger settles into the pits of my black heart and threatens to bubble over. A twitch forms in my right eye, and I heave a breath to straighten myself the fuck out. I should fucking be there with her, softening whatever they have up their sleeves.

Please, god, help me do the right fucking thing.

The door behind me clicks open and shuts swiftly, and my body stiffens. I sit rigidly in my chair and watch the black-robed figure march toward me with determination. Whoever the fuck it is, their mask obscures their face, not giving me any clues. Fuck, they could be here to kill me or take me to Kaycee.

Heavy breaths echo from beneath the mask, sounding scared and frantic. My breath hitches when she lifts it, and I'm greeted by a pair of familiar big brown eyes. I curl my fists in my lap, examining the face staring back at me. The shock takes over when she leans over the desk with frantic movements. From here, I can count the angry scars lining her face, giving me the impression she's already been through one Hell of a battle at one point in her life.

"I don't have much time," she whispers, holding out her hand. "Hand me your phone, call the number I dial, and ask for Agent Zero. Tell him Agent Seven is incapacitated and to send in the forces to the location at the back of the school grounds. Tell him it's nowhere we looked." Her voice quivers when she relays the information to my shocked ears. "Carter!" she barks again, snapping me back to her. "We have to move quickly!" she hisses, curling her fingers and gesturing for the phone still hidden in my waistband.

Shock grabs hold of me, and I'm frozen to the chair. Even my blood turns cold as it pumps through my veins. Not when she mentioned him—Agent Zero—the same agent that has been on my ass for the past few months for information. The same fucking agent I contacted at the beginning of all this, trying to find a solution before someone else got hurt. And look at that, someone is getting hurt.

"What the fuck?" I growl, staring at her extended hand like it might strike me.

"You called us, but you weren't the only one. I know you have her phone. They took mine. If I run for help, if I leave...." Fear grabs her by the neck, strangling her voice.

Espie, the newest student and Apocalypse recruit, is the Veritas insider Agent Zero spoke of before. She's the reason I'm sitting in this chair, waiting this out for Veritas or my time to escape with Kaycee.

She shakes her head. "I can't blow my cover. I've worked too long and too hard to blow it now. They'll kill me if I'm gone any longer. They literally let me go because I said I had to pee," she hisses, rolling her eyes toward the ceiling at that one, and shakes her head. "For a controlling cult, they're the most trusting group of psychopaths I have ever seen, but they're still deadly. Now, give me her phone so that you can call him." Her teeth grit, but I sense the urgency.

"Fucking bring them here now! Before she dies!" I jump to my feet, getting into her face. "How could you stand back and let all this happen right under your nose?! Where's the rest of Veritas?" I growl, fisting her robe in my hand, and pull her nose to mine. She doesn't flinch when my nostrils flare, and she again rolls her eyes at me.

"Carter Cunningham, owner and operator of CC Tech. You were involved in a car accident, killing a family of four, including two children. Your father has used this accident against you from the beginning to bend you to his will, and now he thinks he can trust you. And if our records and research have been any indication, your father also set the whole incident up. If you call my superior, we can end this right now. Veritas is on standby, waiting for my word. But we need to move." My fist unclenches from her robes, and she falls away from me, stumbling over her feet. Quickly, she rights herself but stares back at me with compassion.

"I will call them if you promise to protect her. You keep her under your damn nose! Because I can't fucking be in there right now," I snarl, beating my fist into the desk again, letting the pain I inflict on myself ground me to the spot.

A slow smile spreads across her face. "I knew you were one of the innocent ones, a good guy with a good heart. I promise to protect her within my abilities. But I cannot out myself as an agent, and you have to understand that. Just like you couldn't tell them you've been protecting her this entire time."

Staring down at the phone, she hands it back. A single local phone number sits on the screen, and she nods.

"Who called you before?" I ask, raising my eyes to hers. She smiles, lowering her black mask to blend in.

"A fellow student in desperate need. She, too, was coerced in by unfortunate circumstances and forced into submission by a heinous act, using her body against her. Know this, Carter Cunningham. You are not the only one who was used. Goodbye. Agent Zero is waiting for my call. Hurry now, before it's too late," she says in a soft but urgent voice.

Espie's retreating footsteps slip through the static of my ears. Of-fucking-course, this was the agent Veritas planted in the mix. Fuck. All our hard work is about to pay off. My heart rate skyrockets into oblivion at the prospect of getting us the fuck out of here.

I recheck the monitors, spying everyone's movements one last time. They're still in the room with Kaycee, talking, laughing, and just waiting for the event to start. The psychos whisper to each other, never taking their eyes off Kaycee. Thankfully, none of them notice when Espie walks into the room on silent feet. She moves like a trained assassin with precise, quiet, undetected footsteps. And it makes sense. Her association with Veritas makes her a deadly weapon. A breath of relief rocks my body when Espie saunters to Kaycee and picks her head up off her chest. Resting a hand under her chin, she keeps it there and allows her chest to expand more. Silently, I thank her for helping my girl breathe easier. But now, I have a phone call and an agent to make my bitch.

For one singular moment, the idea that this is another fucking fucked up test floats through my mind, and I quickly shake it off.

This is too damn urgent to question. Without any more thought about it, I dial the number while keeping a watchful eye on my passed-out girlfriend through the screen. After a few rings, the other line picks up in silence. No hello comes through, only a slight hissing. Clearing my throat, I pinch the bridge of my nose.

"Agent Zero, it's me," I rasp, forcing my voice to work. All these emotions—this rage boils like fucking water, ready to push the top off. "Agent Seven is incapacitated. She asked me to call and pass along the message. They took her phone and mine. I'm all that's fucking left. Send in the damn army! Send in, everyone! The love of my fucking life is about to die at their hands. We. Fucking. Need. You!" My heavy breaths pour from my nose, expanding my heaving chest. Sweat drips from my brow onto the table beneath me as I lean against it. Praying to a God I don't know exists. My love's life depends on these bastards right now.

"Jesus, kid," he replies in a gruff voice with the sounds of other agents swarming behind him. "I was beginning to think…." He trails off and sighs. "I was beginning to think we'd lost you and Agent Seven for good when you hadn't gotten back to me."

I frown, rechecking the cameras. They're moving all around the room, talking as Kaycee watches them. They use a blowtorch on Francesca's face and chest. I swallow hard at her screams of pain.

"Well, are you coming or not?" I shout as loud as I can without alerting the others in the room down the hall. "I'm in the woods, behind the school. It's on the school's grounds and has been this entire fucking time. Somewhere! Fuck! I don't know the exact location! A fucking psychotic ass bitch led me here," I growl, punching the table again. Fuck being quiet. Fuck all this. They need to get here now.

"Your location is impossible to locate," he says in a low voice, cracking with emotions. "We tried through the website, leading us to one address that does not exist. We've scoured everything to locate it."

He doesn't even have to fucking say the address for me to know. I've scoured the damn internet to break through, but I've never been able to find this shit hole. Forty-four Rosebud Drive. That's the fucking address no one can locate. It pings back to it repeatedly, but on the map, it's impossible.

"Impossible? Impossible to fucking locate? Are you deaf? Are you blind? Track this fucking phone! Ping off the damn towers!" He sighs through the phone at my antics, but he should be fucking used to it by now.

"The address is impossible and untraceable. Your phone's location pings to an address in Montana. I'm assuming, Carter, you are not in the mountains at a resort in Montana, correct?"

I swallow hard, taking a deep breath before I reach through this phone and suffocate Agent Zero. "No, Agent Zero. Does it sound like I'm in the mountains of fucking Montana? I'm at East Point Prep! In a fucking dilapidated house on the edge of the property! Please," I whisper the last part, losing hold of everything. "My..."

"Yes, kid. We've been trying to track the live stream for hours using your formulas, but nothing has led us there. You two aren't the only ones we need to retrieve. My agent and our informant are there as well. We are trying everything." He swallows hard, taking a deep breath. "We need you to continue doing what you are doing. Our agent is unarmed, stripped of her weapons, phone, and tracking devices." Vulnerability leaks into his voice, and my spine stiffens. "My agents are on their way. You said through the woods?"

That's just fucking great. A secret government agent is worried, and he's showing it. This whole thing is so fucked up.

"Yeah, we traveled through the woods for a good ten minutes before we came upon the fucking house. Trees and weeds are growing everywhere around it. You blink, and you fucking miss it. But I think that's all a part of their plans." I blow out a breath, trying to remember every detail of our walk.

"Continue to play your role," he says, gaining confidence. "And we'll continue to track your location. My scouts are on the grounds of the school now and heading your way. Someone will be there shortly to retrieve you all. Do not endanger anyone else's life."

"That's fine and dandy, but when it fucking comes time for my plan to happen, I'm saving my girlfriend first," I growl out. "No matter if I fucking die, I'm getting her out."

"Understandable," he says solemnly. "And your plan, Mr. Cunningham?"

"When the lights fade, we make our escape," I grit, rechecking the monitors with wide eyes.

Piper lies on the ground lifeless, and so does her mother. A black robe heads down the hall toward me.

"I've gotta go. I'll call this number back if there are any complications. For now, my rendezvous point is at the maze entrance with my brothers." Mentally, I go over the stupid-as-fuck plans only teenagers can make in the event of a disaster. And that's precisely what this is—a goddamn disaster.

He sighs. "Mr. Benoit was sent to the hospital the moment the ambulance arrived. We arrived shortly after, taking over for the police. He sustained burn injuries, and the extent is not known right now. The fire is being put out as we speak. Your friends are MIA, for obvious reasons, I surmise. Stay undercover, Mr. Cunningham. You know as well as I do— these are dangerous people. They've killed many times over and won't hesitate to put a bullet in your chest." With those ominous words, he hangs up, leaving me in the same fucked up spot as before.

I hang my head, stuffing Kaycee's phone back into my waistband. All this extra information floats around in my head. Kaycee. Veritas. Fucking psychos. I only have one option now because they may be on their way, but Veritas is no help to us. I'm on my own here, but if I can get her through the fucking boarded-up window, she'll be safe and in my brothers' arms.

I settle back into my seat and lean back, trying to look calmer than the storm brewing inside me. Determination pours through every ounce of my being when the door swings open, knocking into the wall behind it. Oscar rips off his mask, blood dripping down his black robes onto the floor, and he fucking grins. I don't flinch when I raise a brow at him, presenting myself as calmly as I can.

"God, that was exhilarating!" he beams, rubbing his hands together. "You're looking at the new Alpha. Did you see Piper's tears? I think I got hard. That bitch never saw it coming, and her death has been on the cards since Magnolia's bitch ass. Just one more piece of trash out of our way." On the inside, I recoil at his brash words because he's perfect for all this. Too bad Veritas is on their way, and they'll all fucking pay for this.

I raise my brow, a malicious smile in place. "Congratulations, brother, it seems you are moving up," I say, standing to clap his hand.

He snorts, pointing toward a closet near the back of the control room. "You too, brother. Your promotion waits for you. All you have to do is finish this last task. Man, you gonna... you know?" He thrusts his hips forward, biting his bottom lip. "The crowd would fucking love that with a knife in her, too. God. You got so fucking lucky." The world goes dark and closes in on me, focusing on the one word. I want to smash his face for insinuating bullshit while thrusting his hips into the air. But knife. He said fucking knife.

"Man, I don't fucking know anything that's going on. What knife?" I ask, popping my knuckles against my palm.

He tilts his head with a smirk and nods toward the

closet. All hope of getting answers disappears when he clams up, not uttering a fucking word when I follow him. Dread pools in my gut when he thrusts open a pair of closet doors. A red robe shines in the darkness of the dank closet, and my lips pop open. This is it. These are the same robes my father and his nitwit brothers had. This means….. I swallow the lump in my throat and force my breath into an even rhythm when the realization hits me square in the aching chest.

We've searched high and low, trying to figure out who the fourth horseman was. We've speculated frequently, thinking it was their dead brother who supposedly died in a car crash. Or some other mysterious person we didn't know of yet. But that's the thing about twists; you never see them coming. Because it's me. I'm the fourth horseman, and I just got my promotion within the ranks—so long recruit status and hello to all-powerful horseman status.

"Welcome to the fucking Apocalypse, Famine," Oscar whispers in awe, pulling out the red robe for me like it's the fucking king's. His eyes glimmer with respect and jealousy when he presents it to me with a bowed head. I see why these assholes let this power boost their egos. He's treating me like I'm his goddamn God and savior.

I take off my black robe and mask, throwing them to the floor in disgust. Staring at the red robe in fake awe, I widen my eyes. My breaths pick up as it's draped over my shoulders, laying heavy like bricks when I put my arms through the sleeves. This entire situation pushes down on me like I'm carrying the world on my back. And I have to keep pretending I'm okay and fucking excited to receive this.

Oscar reaches in, lifts the blood-red mask from its hook in the closet, and sets it in my trembling hands. I swallow hard, trying to tamp down my nerves. It stares back at me with white teeth and ominous black eyes with no soul behind it. It takes my breath away at what it represents. If I were in this completely, I'd be in genuine awe at the power this holds—at the power I would have within this organization.

"I'm the fourth horseman," I mumble, tracing my fingers over the soulless eyes of the mask.

"It was meant for you, man," Oscar whispers, looking down at the mask. Emotions burst through his stony exterior, proving that he has something deep inside of him that feels. Even if it's for the wrong cause. He should be concerned about the people around him, not the power these objects hold. "It was never meant for anyone else. They had to test your loyalty, and now this kingdom is yours, too." he whispers, gripping my shoulder in a tight squeeze. "But your last trial awaits," Oscar whispers, tracing his finger down the mask I refuse to put on my face. "We gotta get you in that room, man. I can't fucking wait until it's my turn."

"Is it the bitch?" I ask, straightening the robe, trying to dampen the worry brewing inside me.

Fuck—give me something, you psychotic tool. I try to peer over at the monitors displaying the rooms of the house. But I don't get a chance. That fuckface leads me toward the door, looking back at me with that insufferable smirk plastered on his bloody face. He leads me out of the control room, down the dilapidated hallway, and stops before a closed-door at the end. An eerie silence falls over us and the entire house, filling my ears with nothing but static. At one point, Francesca's screams were heard loud and clear from her torture, but now she's dead and gone. The only other person left to inflict pain on is the woman behind this door.

"Make the rabbit regret coming to this school," Oscar rasps with anticipation. Nodding toward the door, she sits behind. Resting a hand on my shoulder, he squeezes gently, and finally, my time comes.

"Bring him in. His test begins now," Crowe shouts through the closed door, and my skin crawls at his demand.

"It's your time to shine, Famine." Oscar grins, gesturing

for me to open the door and walk through. Walking through this door feels like a fucking trap, and my mind tells me to run for the hills, but my heart says the woman I love sits in there all alone and needs me. Whatever it takes to get her out of here, I will do it. "Welcome to the Ceremony." My breaths shutter, remembering what Piper told me. This is the ceremony where I'll have time with her alone. It's my fucking time to shine and my fucking time to drag her ass out of here before they kill her.

Whatever it fucking takes.

So many thoughts race through my mind as I stare at the disgusting mold-covered door. With a heaving breath and without an ounce of hesitation, I slam through the door like I own the fucking place. And I guess in their eyes, I do. This is my house now. My god damn kingdom, and they should bow down before me. So, I'm going to fucking own it now and save Kaycee. When the door slams behind me and clicks shut, my eyes glue to the broken and helpless face of the only girl I'll ever love.

I force a heavy mask of confidence on my face, smirking at her appearance. My smile widens at the sight of her tied to a chair, bloodied and bruised, and I cock my head. Tightness sears like a fucking knife tearing through my fucking chest at the sight of her eye swollen shut and crusted over with dried blood. I don't have to utter a word for the betrayal to smack her in the face, and a small light fades from the one eye she can open. All her hopes and dreams vanished the moment she saw me. And I want to kick my own ass.

"Carter..." she whispers with her lips popping open in shock.

What I wouldn't give to eradicate every person in this room with one look, throw her over my shoulder, and fucking save her. But at the sight of them and their smug faces, I know what hides beneath their robes, and one false move and we're dead.

I cock my head to the side, smirking the smuggest fucking smirk I can muster. I drop every ounce of emotion into a bottomless pit and fucking hide it there.

"Hello, Sweetheart. Did you miss me?" I purr, keeping the bubbling emotions from my voice. If I let them through, those assholes would hear the tremors taking over and would know I was still on her side.

"Let me introduce you to the fourth horseman you've been wondering about, meet Famine," my father comments, meeting me in two short strides from across the room. He clasps my hands with such pride I want to fucking puke. He shakes my hands with a sick and twisted celebration of murmured words about how proud of me he is that I passed all his tests tonight with flying colors, and now I only have to accomplish one more for my rank to be the highest it can be. He fucking whoops, tossing his fist in the air, and then beams at me. My father has never fucking beamed at me a day in his life. But now? Now I'm like the prodigal son who came home for the first time in years. With one last tap on my back, he breaks away and marches toward Kaycee with determination in his steps.

"Fourth horseman?" She gasps out in horror. Her finger nails dig into the wood of the chair, and I falter when the fucking knife in his hand disappears slowly into her flesh. She fights with all her might, curling forward to move away from the fucking weapon puncturing her, and pulls against the restraints. But nothing she does makes them stop, and there's nothing I can do either.

Pain erupts in my chest when I have to force myself not to react and push all those emotions back into the black hole they belong in. My feelings have no place here, not when our lives are on the line, and I'm waiting for the perfect moment to present itself. My stomach knots when I have to pretend to enjoy the pain pouring from her lips when her scream echoes through the room.

My father beckons me over with a discreet hand wave, forcing me to move closer to the destruction of my girl. Little by little, they push the knife into her. And little by little, I fucking die inside at the pain crossing her face. The scream erupting from her lips has my blood boiling over, but there's not a damn thing I can do to save her right now. All I can do is fucking hope that they'll leave before she bleeds out. And if they don't, I'll risk my fucking life to save her, no matter what. I'll let them shoot me over and over if it helps her escape.

I swallow down all the negative shit in my brain and fucking cock my head to the side like this is the most interesting thing I've ever seen. With rapt attention, I watch every fucking drip of blood spill down her legs and catalogue it for later when I murder my father and his sicko fuckhead brothers. Even though my heart is fucking breaking in half, I hold that sick smirk on my lips, staring into her eyes, really selling this whole fucking thing. Not only to the psychos side-eyeing me and making sure I'm paying attention, but to her. I have to make her think I've betrayed everything we've built so I can get close to her. Her every reaction has to be real. So, I can't fucking mess this up.

A pain pierces through me the moment I see the wheels turning in her head, and she begins to question our entire relationship from start to finish. It flashes across her face like a fucking movie for everyone to see, and I have to keep pretending I like this. So, when her eyes reconnect with mine I turn everything off again and go blank when I walk up to her. My trembling fingers caress her bloodied and swollen cheek. If I could wipe this away and take her pain away, I would. She sucks in a breath, trying to pull away from my fingers.

"It's a thing of beauty isn't it, boy?" My father asks, slapping me on the shoulder. "And to think, you got a front row seat to the whole event." My stomach sinks when he smirks and cocks his head, staring at Kaycee like she's his next juicy meal. "I told you, little rabbit," he murmurs with fire in his eyes, squeezing my shoulder with a puffed out chest. Pride roars through him when he peeks at me, and for the first time in my life, I think he loves me. "He knew all along. Who do you think shoved you into the fish tank and watched from afar as you helplessly drowned?" I continue with my blank stare, nodding to confirm what he said, and the light in her eyes dims. I fucking hate myself for what she's gone through and for my part in every single second of it. But I have to press on until I can get her alone, but it's fucking killing me to watch her lose faith in me with every second that passes. All I'm proving by standing here is that I'm the asshole she thought I was when we first met.

"For your final test," my father announces, shoving a pair of pliers into my hand. "You've passed everything with flying colors. Your deception. Your torture. Now, take from her what she owes us," he says with a wicked glint.

Bile swims in the back of my throat when I stare down at the pliers resting so easily in my hand and raise a brow. "And what does she owe us?" I rumble through a thickening throat, forcing a grin to split my lips, and straighten my robes as I stand tall.

Crowe frowns, crossing his arms over his chest. "For everything she's stuck her little rabbit nose in. For the hacking, and breaking into my fucking office, and for stealing my phone. Sticking her nose where it shouldn't be," Crowe grumbles, counting off her crimes one by one. "Pluck off the end of her nose," he growls, stepping forward to loom over her once again, knocking me slightly back. He growls, gritting his teeth, and snarls at her with menace in his eyes. I'll fucking pluck his nose off with my fist and shove the pliers down his throat before I let him touch her again.

"Maybe her eyeballs?" Shaw says flippantly, waving a hand. "She's seen more than she needs to. How was my office? I should have known it was you and your merry gang of assholes who broke in there." He raises a brow at her, expecting her to roll over and admit what she'd done so many months ago.

"Maybe her tongue?" My father says with a crooked as fuck grin, squeezing her aching jaw in his grip. He's fucking lucky I don't deck him right here and now and knock that fucking grin off his demented face. "Snip off the end and watch as she drowns in her own blood without being able to call for help. Not like any would come. Take a good look around, Sugar. This is your final resting place. If only you'd have stayed away," he hums, tapping her injured cheek. My fingers curl into a fist.

"I couldn't have stayed away," she snarls in retribution, setting my heart on fire. She tries to shove his hand off her face with a snarl and a headbutt, but it doesn't do anything to make him leave.

My stomach knots when more blood pours from her wound at a slow rate, dripping around her chair and bare feet. The more time these assholes take to laugh in her fucking face and brag about all the bullshit they've done, it's more likely she's going to die here. I need something fucking drastic to happen so they leave the room. Maybe I can have Zepp fucking send us into darkness right now, instead of later, and make them scatter. Fuck, I don't know what to do.

"I knew some asshole stole my best friend's life, and I was going to find out who did it," she says in a quivering voice and closes her eyes to regain her breath. But her body slumps further, curling in on herself, and I know the thoughts swirling in her fucking brain.

"Yeah?" I ask with a patronizing smirk again, stoking the fire from deep inside of her. "How'd that work out for you, Sweetheart?" The fire reignites in her eyes when I open and close the pliers in my hand, hopefully sending more adrenaline through her veins. I need something to perk her the fuck up until I can get her out of here. I can't have my Sweetheart fucking dying before my eyes. I'll go on a rampage and kill every mother fucker in this house before I let that happen. They can have me—all of me—before they get their hands on her again.

Her breaths quicken, and she tries to curl her fingers against the wooden armrest of the chair, trying to get away from me. But there's nowhere for her to go when I catch her. I take that opportunity to continue my torture, hoping to spark more strong words from her. I need to keep her talking and alive, and I need to stoke the fire extinguishing inside her. I turn the metal tip of the pliers, rubbing it against the flesh of her index finger, and continue to trace the outline of every finger.

"Don't." My heart fucking stops when she begs in a tiny whisper, chilling my fucking blood. Her plea rings in my head on repeat, and it's something I'll have to live with for the rest of my fucking life.

"Please, don't do it."

I want to fucking punch myself in the throat and throw myself into a pit of lava until I burn alive at the sound of her desperation leaking out in tiny whimpers. If there's one thing I know about Kaycee Cole, she isn't the type to beg. Even when she's backed into a corner, Kaycee keeps her lips sealed until her life is on the line. I swallow the lump in my throat, trying to retain the stony exterior I've built to fool them all into believing I'm the devil standing before her. But plea by plea, she's slowly chipping away at the character I'm playing. Her bloodshot eye searches mine, trying to find any hint of the man she fell in love with. She shudders when she digs deeper into my eyes, looking and looking. But Kaycee can't find the man she loves because I'm not him right now. The face looking back at her is a façade for all to see and hear.

"Come back to me," she croaks with tears spilling from her good eye, down her cheek and across her jaw. They fall to the floor, mingling with the blood dripping from her stab wound. And my fucking heart explodes in my chest when she utters her next words, pleading with me to give her any little sign that I'm still inside my fucking head and not some lunatic drawing patterns with the pliers.

"Please," she begs a-fucking-gain, and I swear I'm shattering before her. I don't know how much more I can force out of her without cracking completely. "This isn't you." Her voice breaks with conviction, and it's the final chink in my fucking armor. My body shudders, and I swallow hard, stiffening my muscles so I don't do anything fucking stupid.

Laughter sounds from behind me, and I grind my teeth at their mocking whispered words, but I laugh along, pretending this entire situation is something I'm involved with. Staring down at her, I see the glaze forming over her eye, and I know she's spiraling down the rabbit hole in her head, and it's threatening to pull her into the darkness if I don't fucking act.

I snarl, twisting my head to glare at the three fuckheads behind me, and straighten my posture, projecting my fucking authority on the three assholes.

"Would you three mind backing the fuck up? I have something to do and fucking say to this bitch," I hiss, twisting the pliers in the palm of my hand. "In fucking private." A cruel grin twists my lips, and even Crowe instinctively backs up with fear in his eyes. That's right, you dipshit, you will fucking fear me by the end of tonight when I slam your head so hard into the floor your brains splatter everywhere. Mark my words here and now, I will fucking end every single one of them. But first, my girl needs to be saved.

Shaw rolls his eyes like he can't be bothered with my attitude and backs up into Crowe, who in turn pushes him back. How they managed to build this fucking empire of murdering dirtbags is beyond me. They must have fumbled their way through this and had friends in high places to succeed.

I crack my neck and work the tension from my muscles before I turn back to her. The wheels in her mind are working at warp speed, sending her through every awful fucking scenario. Without thinking about anything else, I grab her hand, shaking her out of the darkness that is closing in on her. I cock my head, grinning like the god damned devil resides inside of me. My thumb gently swishes across the top of her hand, trying to lend some reassurances, but she only shrinks in on herself.

"I think I'll take a finger," I muse, earning chuckles from the dickbags lounging against the opposite wall.

"Take them all," Cushing encourages, checking the time on his watch. "But make it snappy, Son. We've got to close this lot out soon and move on to bigger and better things. We've got a whole horseman ceremony laid out for you at home. Plenty of women to fuck and food to eat. A celebration of the century," he says with enthusiasm and then returns to his conversation with his brothers. And my stomach fucking drops. A celebration? To what? Celebrate the death of three people tonight and my status as the last horseman. Yeah, I don't fucking think so. The only thing we'll be celebrating tonight is the beat-down the Apocalypse Society deserves.

An involuntary growl slips from my throat, and I grit my teeth so hard at my father's command that I might crack a damn tooth. "I'll take all the fucking time I need," I shout, giving Kaycee my back. "I will do whatever I fucking please."

"You want time alone?" He asks, raising a brow. "To do?"

"Whatever the fuck I see fit. She's mine, isn't she?" My gloved fingers curl into fists around the pliers dangling from my grip. "Mine to fucking torture. Mine to fucking bleed. She is mine to do with as I please," I growl every word, hiding the fucking tremor from my voice. Time is running out, and I need to get this show on the fucking road right the fuck now.

A grin lights up my cunt-father's face. "A finger it is then," he says, gesturing with a hand for me to continue without moving to exit the room. "But we stay put first."

"We want a front row seat for the screams," Shaw says nonchalantly again, leaning against the wall with his eyebrows raised. "It just isn't the same through a monitor," he sighs through disappointment and urges me to continue like he has somewhere more important to be.

"Nail," I proclaim with a huff, turning on my toes to face Kaycee again.

Her body shudders when I lean over her and examine the swelling on her face. Frantic breaths spear through me when I block out the entire room from view. A smirk places on my lips when the tool in my hand runs across her good cheek, tracing the freckles. I lick my lips, putting my forehead against her, and I finally fucking break. For a minuscule second, I revel in the feel of her. Her breaths brush over my parted lips. Quietly, I gasp for air, pushing my forehead into her until the pressure forces her good eye to pop open, and she peers deep into mine. To see what I've been hiding behind the mask I put in place the moment I walked into this house of horrors.

"I have to," I breathe the first words I can think of and convey what I need to convey as quickly and as quietly as possible. "Please trust me," I beg with all my might, trying to show her that I'm fucking trying. "I will fucking save you, Sweetheart." Before I can sit there for too much longer, I pull away without saying another word and take her tension-filled hand into mine. I swallow thickly, squeezing her hand three times telling her the words I could never say. I love you. I love you. I love you.

Tension fills every inch of my fucking body when the pointed metal of the pliers rests just beneath her fingernail, resting there until she meets my eyes again. Bitter bile rests in my throat, burning until I swallow it all down. I have no fucking choice in the matter. If I want to save her god damn life, then I have to yank her nail from its bed and fucking display it for the psychos waiting behind me. I keep my gaze on hers, letting every emotion out of the black box I put it in. It flickers across my eyes, showcasing everything to her and letting her see it all. A sharp cry falls from her lips when I gently pull the nail free, and I nearly barf when blood pools in its place.

Tears flow freely down her cheeks, covering her in wetness. She continues to watch me when I hold the stupid nail in the air, earning my place within the ranks of their fucked up club.

"Welcome to the club, kid," Crowe croons, staring behind me at the girl I'd tear my heart out for. He smirks, slapping me on the back.

"You made me proud, boy," My father says, cocking his head to the side. "You've earned your alone time with her. Never thought I'd see the day." He purses his lip, slapping me lightly on the face. "Get the job done." That is all he says before they exit the room, talking to one another.

My tongue runs the length of my bottom teeth, counting the steps they've taken down the hall. When I'm satisfied they won't come back in, I step into action, locking the door behind us, and shove a rickety old chair under the handle. It won't keep them out, but it'll slow them down. Strolling over to her at a quick pace, I keep the manic grin spread across my face for the cameras. As I pass each camera mounted on the wall, I eye them with narrowed eyes, turning them away from Kaycee, and kick down the tripods they had set up for their precious ceremony until I get to her. Now, no one will see what I'm truly up to until it's too fucking late. I kneel down in desperation, carefully palming her cheeks.

"Fuck! Sweetheart, open your fucking eyes," I hiss, tapping her good cheek to rouse her. "You cannot fucking leave me yet, do you fucking hear me? Now, give me a scream. Do something, Vixen, so they think I'm cooperating."

"I can't," she mumbles through a heavy tongue. I grunt, working the thick ropes from around her wrists holding her to the chair, and throw them behind me without a fucking care. All I care about right now is getting her the fuck out of here.

"You can, and you fucking will, Sweetheart. I'll be damned if you die because I couldn't fucking save you. You die. I die. You got that?" A growl rumbles through my chest when I pull her close, careful to keep the knife from bumping into anything.

# THIRTY

## CARTER

"I'm so sorry," I whisper, letting the tears I held for so long fall down my cheeks. I've been made of stone for way too long and all the feelings rush through me. "Give me a second, okay? I have a fucking plan, but you have to promise me something." I say, running a hand through her sweat-soaked hair.

"What?" she whispers in a small voice, barely registering over the whooshing in my ears.

"Do not give up. Do you fucking understand?" I bark out through gritted teeth. She nods once, looking my face over. "Sweetheart?" I whisper again as I pull her phone out of my waistband, typing a message to the group chat.

> Me: It's time!

> Zepp: On it!

"Yeah?" she asks, resting her forehead against my chest. My fingers run through her matted hair, carefully soothing her until it's time to move.

I close my eyes, letting the tears fall freely. My breaths shutter in my tightening chest, and I lick my lips. "I.... I.... fucking love you," I confess. "I'm so fucking sorry I couldn't say it, but I've known for a long time." My voice catches during my confession, and I close my eyes, reeling my emotions back in. I could break down now and fucking cry my eyes out. But I have shit to do and a woman to save.

"Me too," she whispers back, her voice trailing off.

"Stay with me, Sweetheart." I rasp, holding tight to her. At this point, I don't care what it looks like on camera to the assholes watching back in the viewing room.

"It was you, wasn't it? You left my hand out?" She asks with her warm breath brushing against my chest. Relief slams through me when the bright spotlights and the red lights from the cameras keeping watch blink out, bathing us in darkness.

I rest my lips on top of Kaycee's head, saying a brief prayer to once again save us and help us leave this hell together. The time has come to enact our plan and get this shitshow on the road.

"Yes, it was me," I whisper, lingering for a second longer. "And now it's time to go." Stepping back, I lift her frail body into my arms.

She doesn't utter a word when I move back the black curtains hanging from the ceiling, concealing the windows. My breaths rush out in victory when the lone window comes into view, blocked by multiple pieces of rotted two-by-fours—tiny slivers of moonlight leaking through the cracks of the wood. Tears burn the back of my eyes, and victory lifts the weight off my shoulders. This is fucking it. This is our way out, and it's within grabbing distance.

When Piper and I had rounded the back of the house, I took stock of every boarded-up window. I made a mental note where each one was, and finally, when they sat me in the control room, they gave me a view of the entire house. I knew there would be one in here and in every room along the way. It left no room for doubt.

Kaycee sits like a feather in my arms, light and unmoving,

but her blue eye stays on me. "I'm getting you out of here." A promise weaves its way through my words, making its mark.

A weak smile spreads on her cracking lips, and she nods, acknowledging my words. "The others?" Looking down at her, I nod in confirmation and kiss her forehead, never wanting to leave this embrace.

"They'll be here, Sweetheart. So, keep your promise, okay?" I kneel and set her lightly on the large window sill, where she rests, watching me as I tear through the boards and throw them to the ground, ripping through the flesh of my fingers.

I fish out Kaycee's phone and bring up the flashlight, shining it through the dirty glass. The bright light bursts through the window, flashing three times and signaling to the idiot outside that it's time to take our girl for help. I'm handing over my life through a window. Taking a shaky breath, relief finally shoots through me at the sight of a shadow running across the lawn at top speed. It's either him or Veritas, and my bets are on him. Veritas has been nothing but useless during this entire situation. Fuck them.

Seger's pale and sweaty face comes into view, standing right outside the window with fear beaming in his eyes. His gaze rakes over Kaycee's form as she sits in the window sill, looking half alive, and fucking bloodied all to hell. Thank fuck he found this place with my spotty directions because I wasn't sure he'd be able to. All I knew was we were in the middle of the woods, surrounded by tall fucking trees, and in a house that doesn't exist on paper. I gave my best guess, and this dickweed somehow found us before fucking Veritas.

"Son, hold off! Don't do anything until the lights come back on!" My father grunts from behind the locked door of the room. He pounds and pounds, threatening to send it off its old ass hinges. If he breaks through, we're screwed.

"Yeah, okay," I holler back with sarcasm, trying to get him to back off. But something in my gut tells me I need to hurry this along because my father isn't a fucking idiot, and he knows I've successfully fucked him over. I gently bring Kaycee back into my arms, avoiding the knife sticking out of her gut, and kiss her head again.

"It won't open!" I growl through the window at a pale Seger. Sweat pours off his face after his long run, and he huffs. His eyes narrow in on the lump in my arms. I hadn't prepared him—or any of them—for what he was about to see. Hell, I'm not fucking prepared either.

Seger whips his jacket off and wraps it around his fist. "Back the fuck up," he hisses, rearing his fist back. "I'm going to fucking break it." I cover Kaycee's ear with my hand and take a step back as the glass shatters all over the floor, exploding in a million different directions. He clears the rest of the shards, spraying more on the floor, and then throws his coat into the grass. My heart pounds violently as my father bangs his fist with more force, and the chair under the handle screeches on the floor.

"Take her to the maze. I've talked to an agent for Veritas, and they said something about a fucking ambulance." Tears stream down Seger's face, but he nods anyway. "I'm sorry, man, I'm so fucking sorry. I tried, but there—"

"Don't you be fucking sorry, you hear me? You were here, trying to find a way out. She'll understand," he pants as I place her into his awaiting arms.

I run a hand down my face and nod, but he can't be serious. I let her down so badly. She's hurt because I couldn't get her and run. She's in this condition, unable to fucking walk, knocking on death's door because of me. I left the fucking Maze House to talk to Veritas in secret. I fucking did this, and I'll never fucking forgive myself.

"Carter," she whispers, calling me out of my self-loathing. "None of this is your fault, Grumpy." I laugh a breath, shaking my head at that stupid fucking nickname they gave me. "I love you, and you remember that. Now come on," she says, waving a finger for me to join her.

I run a hand down my face again and shake my head. "Get her to safety. I have things I need to take care of." I peer over my shoulder as the hinges on the door finally break, and the bane of my existence barrels through like a damn bull, breaking everything in his angry path.

"Carter, man, no," Seger says through sadness. "You still have time to run. Come on." His head bobs toward the forest as he steps back, clutching Kaycee like a precious jewel. "Carter, brother," he pleads, tears forming in his eyes and running down his cheek.

"Go," I bark out. "Get the fuck out of here!" His body trembles with indecision, and his eyes dart from me to safety. "Take her to safety, man," I grit out, nodding at him to run and save her from the knife still sticking out of her stomach. A long time ago, someone told me that if I got stabbed, just to let it stay. I would not risk her life. Not again. If I can slow them down and harm them, I will.

"You don't have to!" Seger yells as he runs, only looking over his shoulder once.

"You, shit!" My father shouts, stomping toward me with rage contorting his reddened face, and his fingers curl into fists.

Well, our plan worked. The lights pulled the moment I had a chance alone with her, and Seger came to save her. Thankfully, they could find the house out of nowhere, unlike Veritas. But it seems like Veritas has finally found us by the sound of the sharp cries from outside. Everything I've done until this point was to save her. I don't fucking care about myself. If I can slow down these cult bastards, then so be it. I'll fucking do it.

I suck in one last breath, watching the dancing shadows in the forest until I know they're clear. Turning my body, I meet the barrel of a gun pointed directly at my chest. And three pissed-off assholes in red robes.

"What the fuck did you do?" My father asks, pulling the revolver's hammer back, and it clicks into place, putting a bullet into the chamber. I have no doubt that my father will pull the trigger and leave me for dead. In his eyes, I dished out the ultimate betrayal against him and his disgusting brothers.

Crowe steps forward, pushing up his sleeves like he's ready for a fight—which is fucking hilarious. "You played us good, didn't ya, boy?" He growls, pushing his nose into my face to provoke me. And well, I've waited long enough to enact my revenge on these fucking sickos.

I explode every ounce of anger into him, colliding my heavy fists with his face and crunching in his nose and cheeks. He cries out, falling to the floor with a thud. He tries to get up, but I straddle him, pounding his face over and over repeatedly until he's reduced to nothing more than a whimpering pool of blood.

"ENOUGH!" my father yells, still pointing the gun in my direction.

I heave myself off Crowe with heavy breaths, grinning as he remains on the floor, groaning and spouting curses. Blood pours from his crooked nose and paints his fingers. I spread my arms wide, silently asking who else wants a piece of me. If I'm going to die by the bullet in my father's gun, I might as well go out swinging.

I bark out a laugh when Shaw takes the bait and swings at me, but I weave and punch him in the gut. My fist lands hard and fast, knocking the air from his pathetic lungs. He wheezes, crumpling over, giving me the perfect opportunity to strike him in the temple. I send him flying right into Crowe, who lies on the ground, still groaning like a fucking baby.

"Sissy fucking assholes," I say, spitting on them as they lie there catching their breath. Reaching down, I intend to inflict more pain than they did to Kaycee, but my father has other plans.

"I said, enough!" My father yells again, shooting off his gun in my direction.

My breaths leave me, and a burn singes through the red robe I'm still wearing and through my t-shirt underneath. A warmth pools, bubbling from the wound going clean through my back, and I swallow hard. I knew he had no qualms about injuring me, and this fucking proves what an unfeeling bastard he is.

I face my father fully, holding my hand to the wound on my right shoulder. No one tells you about the burn a bullet causes as it enters and exits through your flesh, and let me fucking tell you, it doesn't feel good. Blood pours between my fingers, but I grin at him through it all and ignore the pain he inflicted on me. Images of Kaycee race through my mind and everything she's endured in this hell house all while I watched. I deserve this pain, but I fucking won.

"You didn't win." I hiss, taking a step toward him, intending to send my fist through his nose. "You will never win."

He cocks his head to the side and raises a brow. "I will win when my bastard son burns in Hell, you motherfucker," he says, cocking the hammer back and pulling the trigger again. Hitting me a second time through the right side of my chest. It burns as it exits through my back, and he laughs, cocking the gun one more time before emptying his weapon into my chest.

I throw my arms wide, letting the lead pierce through my flesh until I fall to my knees. I raise my chin, gasping for breath and tasting the unmistakable copper on my tongue. God has answered my prayers, after all.

These bullets will serve as retribution for my sins.

# THIRTY-ONE

## SEGER

Darkness covers us as we run from the house that we'd searched high and low for. Months of looking and, fuck, it was right under our noses, hidden in the trees at the back of campus.

Who would have fucking guessed there was a fucking house back here? I swallow hard, peering down at my fucking angel, bruised and bloody, in my arms. Whatever the fuck she went through had to be hell if she came out looking like this. In the back of my mind, I want to stay fucking ignorant about everything. If I don't, I'll fucking explode and lose my shit right here. We won't make it back to safety because I'll turn right the fuck around and murder them all. Kaycee needs me here, not fighting her fight.

"Angel—" I wheeze, sneaking a peek at the woman in my arms who has barely moved a muscle since I started sprinting through the dark forest.

I grunt when a branch whacks me in the fucking head and scratches my cheeks, leaving a burning wound behind, but I keep pushing myself harder and faster, pumping my legs like they've never pumped before. Let's fucking go; I chant in my head to keep up my motivation. I can't fall behind. Sticks and leaves crunch underfoot with every step I take, but no matter how dark it is in the center of the woods, I push forward trying not to trip over large roots until I can find a trail.

I readjust Kaycee in my grip, carefully lifting her higher to my chest. I try not to knock the fucking knife sticking out of her bloodied stomach. Kaycee's not heavy by any fucking means. She's like a hundred pounds soaking wet. As light as a fart in the fucking wind. But Jesus—after running the entire way here, through the woods at the edge of campus, I'm having difficulty keeping my legs pumping and oxygen in my lungs.

A burn works its way through my quads and hamstrings. My calves tighten so tight I think they'll explode like a fucking tire on its last leg.

"Fuck was that?" I gasp out, halting in the middle of the woods. Heavy breaths roll through my chest as I listen closely to the sounds around me. I strain my ears, greeted by nothing but an eerily silence.

Sweat pours down my forehead and drips onto my t-shirt. Every ache and pain in my body comes forward, screaming at me to sit down. My heart fucking shatters when a pain-filled whine falls from Kaycee's throat when she tries to lift an arm. Tears fill my eyes at the sound, tearing my damn soul into pieces, knowing she's in excruciating pain. She has to be delirious by now, from the damn knife sticking out of her stomach to the fucking bruises and swelling taking over her face. Fuck. This whole situation is a goddamn nightmare that never should have happened. I should have forced her to come with Zepp and me back to our house so we could check on our dad.

I swallow hard, searching the eternal darkness for any clue as to what the sound was. But only my heaving breaths fill the deafening silence. My body jolts when the sound booms again, breaking through the quiet of the trees and reverberating around us. My knees nearly buckle and collapse beneath me into the forest floor, but I stand tall, leaning against a tree. I look around, searching for the direction of the sound, hearing it pop again. I whip my head back in the direction I came from when it comes from behind me again.

My heart hammers heavily in my chest, and blood rushes to my ears. "Grumpy," I mumble, forcing my heavy tongue to move. Fear shoots through me when I step back toward the house, even with Kaycee in my arms. The unmistakable sound of gunshots pops through the air again, and then silence.

"Fuck," I hiss, taking another step in the wrong direction. I shake my head, looking down at the bundle in my arms. Her shallow breaths send my heart into a frenzy, beating like a crazy drum against my ribs. Fuck. She's pale—blood everywhere. She doesn't have long. If I go back to collect Carter's dumb ass, we'll all be dead. "Shit. Fuck. Damn it!" I shout into the nothingness, only hearing my small echo in return.

Pain pierces through me with every step away from the house. A war buzzes inside of me with indecision, but Carter's words repeat in my mind—get her to safety. He wanted me to get her to the hospital or in the cop's hands so we could end this. If I go back to him and save him, too, we'll all be dead. So, I fucking march on, picking up speed until I'm sprinting. Sticks snap beneath my pounding feet. Dirt and mud cake to my sneakers, but I push through the pain. I drive through nature, attempting to hold myself back from turning back around. Our mission was to save Kaycee from their grips, and that's what I'm going to do. Racing through the forest, I hold Kaycee tight against me, trying my best to avoid the fucking dagger sticking out of her stomach.

"Stop!" orders a deep, male voice, sending me tumbling to my knees in the mud.

Tears fall freely down my face when I look up into the dark masked face of a man holding a weapon aimed down at Kaycee and me. I quickly hold her closer to my chest, ensuring this man doesn't hurt her any more than she is. I swallow hard when he lifts his mask and examines my face and Kaycee's. A knowing look crosses his face, and he nods at us, extending a hand to pull me to my feet. He peers down at Kaycee's injuries again, cataloging every speck of blood, and meets my gaze again.

"Please," I beg, taking a step away. "I need to get her to the fucking ambulance."

He nods again, bringing his wrist up to his mouth. "Got her. Tell them to be prepared for a stab wound and multiple contusions to the face. She's losing a lot of blood, so prepare the doctors and the hospital. I'm Agent Thirteen with Veritas. Go to the maze. There are ambulances already here and ready for her," he says with a grim expression, nodding in the direction I was headed. "Be careful, son. This place is littered with those freaks. I'd escort you back, but we're headed that way." He points in the direction I came from, and I give a firm nod, giving him the confirmation they needed. Fuck. He didn't know where the hell he was going, and they were going in fucking blind. He doesn't spare me another glance before disappearing into the darkness with his weapon raised and ready to attack.

"Hang on, Angel. Don't you fucking dare give up on me." My voice catches in my throat as the emotions burn deep at the thought of losing her. Not just her, though. Everyone. If we lose her, we'll burst at the seams. We'll all fall apart. Kaycee is the glue that keeps us going and functioning. She keeps Chase out of bed and reminds him to take his meds. She helps me with my fucking homework and keeps my grades up. She keeps Grumpy fucking grounded and Zeppelin, well---she keeps him on his antsy ass toes. Fuck. We can't lose her. I fucking refuse.

Pushing harder than ever, I finally emerge from the woods, running into open acreage. Shit—why do the school grounds have to be so damn large? Why couldn't this have been a nice jog instead of a two-mile death run at a full sprint? I wheeze, gasping for breath in my tightening lungs. But fuck it, if I don't push harder. The moonlight does little to light my path when a dark cloud rolls in front of it. I can barely see what's in front of me as I frantically run at top speed.

Passing by the football field and the baseball field, the silent cheers from the ghost crowd cheer me on as if I were in a football game. Run faster. Try harder. Think of Kaycee as a football. Except don't spike her or lose your grip on her—fuck! My fingers tighten around her. Breaths pour harder from my nose. I pound the ground harder with my feet. I have to get my fucking girl to the maze.

The hedges come into view, waving in the wind. Their dried leaves wave me on, forcing me to the maze entrance that once led to our home on campus. Smoke still billows from the middle of the labyrinth, blowing in the wind. Zeppelin bites his damn nails, jerking his head toward me as I come into view.

I heave a breath, falling to my knees with Kaycee in my arms, looking around. She doesn't respond when I lay her gently on the grass. Dried blood paints every inch of her flesh, still dripping from underneath the knife protruding from her.

"Where the fuck is everyone?" I shout, looking around at the emptiness around me. "The fucking Veritas agent told me an ambulance would be here." My eyes dart around to the empty darkness, but no one is around to help us the fuck out. "Where....Where are they?" I cry out, holding Zepp's shirt in my fist.

"Fuck," Zepp hisses, running a finger down her jaw. Tears erupt from his eyes, falling down his cheeks. "The only ambulance that has been here was the one for Chase .."

"That's all fine and fucking dandy! But Kaycee needs a fucking ambulance. She needs the hospital!" Tears pour out, covering my cheeks in liquid. I jump to my feet, ready to race again towards the parking lot. If the fucking paramedics don't come to us, I'll drag them here kicking and screaming.

I take one step away from Zepp and Kaycee and stop dead in my tracks. Twenty pops happen in the woods behind us, and we jerk our heads in that direction. My mouth goes dry when Zepp and I look at each other, and I shake my head. Hope fills me, thinking of the agents taking down the sick fucks in the woods like hunters on the prowl.

"The Agents were in the woods," I murmur, praying to God above that Veritas takes out the evil shits responsible for this.

"Over here!" A woman's voice cries, startling us out of our stupor when she frantically runs past me and kneels over Kaycee. Relief works through me, and I swear I could fucking cry at the sight of her paramedic's uniform.

"No! It's not secure!" Another woman cries out from a distance in the shadows with panic spearing through her. Squinting, I barely see her from here, waving her arms and trying to pull back her coworker.

The paramedic looks Kaycee over, frantically checking her pulse, and nods. "Strong heartbeat despite the blood loss. The knife stopped a lot of the bleeding, but she's still in critical condition," she says confidently, looking between Zepp and me. Her mouth pops open once again to say something else, but she never gets the fucking chance.

I fall back onto my ass, hurrying back toward Zepp with wide eyes when a bullet lands right between her eyes. To my horror, she stays upright for half a second before falling backward and dying right in front of us with one last gurgle bubbling in her throat. And then, her body goes limp, draining the life from her.

A shrill scream echoes through the night from the direction of the paramedic who tried to warn her. My fucking heart breaks in half at another life so needlessly fucking lost at the hands of these dickbags. Her friend was just trying to help and do her duty by saving Kaycee's life, and she paid for it with her life. Fuck. Fuck! Could this get any fucking worse?

"No!" I shout in a frantic voice, leaning over Kaycee as best I can to protect her from whatever is stomping closer to us.

My breaths catch when I look up at Zepp's pale face, and he shakes his head at me. Fear rings through his eyes as he stands rigid, curling his fingers into his palm.

"Stay with her," he breathes out, not taking his eyes off the figures finally getting close to us.

"Don't be fucking stupid," I hiss, grabbing at the bottom of his shirt in desperation, trying to pull him to the ground before he gets shot, too.

In the blink of a fucking eye, more black-hooded figures surround us, forming a tight circle around us. My eyes move over the masks covering their faces, and fury bleeds through my veins.

"You're the cocksuckers who keyed my car!" I grit out, earning no response in return.

They simply stand in silence with their arms at their sides staring at us like prey while surrounding us, and there's nothing we can do. They don't move. Hell, it doesn't look like they're breathing either. Maybe they're zombie fucks who need a good fist to the brain, and I'm more than fucking happy to do it.

Suddenly, they split apart revealing the reason they haven't made a move. Three figures dressed in deep red robes approach us with disgusting and twisted masks covering their identities. But if I had to fucking guess, it's the three monsters in charge.

"No," I breathe, shaking my head in disbelief. They should be fucking dead and rotting in the woods by Veritas. Unless... "They... they fucking shot you!" I snarl, pointing at the minions and the red-cloak-wearing assholes.

All hope drains from me in one swoop when they enter the circle and loom over us. Their freaky masks lift from their faces, revealing the monsters they are. One by one, they rest them on top of their heads and give me a view of the real them. Their eyes shine at my misery when I scramble to my feet and stand in solidarity with Zepp. I grip his hand in mine, checking on Kaycee's breathing again. Her chest rapidly moves up and down, but she's fighting for her fucking breaths. The knife still sticks from her stomach, but the blood has dried. These assholes eat us alive with their gaze thinking they've found their next perfect targets. But we're far from that. I squeeze Zepp's hand letting him know I'm not going down without a fury of fists. And in return, he squeezes mine, letting me know he won't back down either. We're an impenetrable force, blocking them from taking Kaycee again.

Carter's dad looks at me with a grin, and a laugh spills from his lips. "You naïve little boy. Do you think I'd let some two-bit government agents ruin my plans? I have more firepower and have more men in place," he snarls, slamming his fist into my face.

Pain erupts in my mouth when my teeth bite down from the force, and blood floods my tongue. I grunt, falling onto my back next to Kaycee, giving him a view of the girl I'm trying to protect. I rub the heated spot on my cheek and jump to my feet again, spitting the blood on the ground. My jaw fucking aches from his hit, but if he thinks one measly hit is going to keep me down, he has another fucking thing coming to him.

Carter's dad's eyes glue to Kaycee's dying form, and he chuckles, admiring his dirty work. "It'll be my pleasure to eliminate you all. You've been a thorn in my fucking side since she walked on campus. I couldn't touch you two because your dear old step-mommy paid me off each month to keep you safe. But now? Fuck, now I want to take you back to my house and drive a screwdriver through each of your eyelids and watch as I get paid, and you fucking die like my disappointment of a son," he snarls the last part, looking way too similar to Carter, and my fucking heart drops and shrivels up into nothing.

I shake my head, fighting against the barrage of thoughts running rampant. That moment in the woods when the gunshots sounded into the night air, piercing the silence.

"You shot him?" I rasp, looking at Cushing with frantic eyes, looking for any sign of remorse. But I'm only met with pride and fucking happiness. "You... you fucking killed Carter?" Grumpy. Fuck. Our grumpy ass bear. He's... dead. No! I refuse to believe it until I see that fuckers body and bury him myself.

Tears burn my eyes, and I want to slump over and fucking grieve for my friend—fuck no—my goddamn family member. The same friend that we just gained not too long ago and brought out of the darkness. And now.....

Carter's father grins more, tilting his head. "Does it eat you up?" He coos, bending at the waist, talking to me like I'm a child. "Four bullets passed through his chest, and he fell to the ground like the wasted betrayal he was. He died almost instantly." My chest caves in at the thought, but I don't have fucking time to think when the crazies continue their speeches.

"What if..." Crowe says through a manic grin, looking between Zepp and me. I wrinkle my aching nose at his fucked up face, mentally high-fiving Carter for the punches he rained down on him. Or at least I hoped he did that before....before...the shots rang out. His beady eyes zero in on us, completely ignoring the dying girl he's already used as a punching bag. "This is fucking perfect," Crowe says, strolling forward with a cocky grin on his battered face. "Ransom," he says, pointing to Zepp and me, raising our hackles.

"Ransom?!" Zepp barks, jumping to his feet. He places himself between us and the red hoods, puffing out his chest.

"Of course." Shaw sneers. "You and your brother combined are worth more than that bitch. I can imagine getting millions out of your father for your safe return." He smirks, flicking his wrist at a few of the black robes.

And just like that, with that one fucking command, they descend on us—grabbing, pulling, trying to kick us to our knees. But we're the mother fucking Wests, and we don't go down that easily. We fight back, throwing punches, choke slamming, kicking, and grunting as our fists collide with their masked faces. We give as good as we get. All the while, we work around Kaycee, making sure these asshats don't fucking touch her again. The black-robed fucks yelp and curse through disguised voices, distorted by their creepy as fuck masks I recognize from our research. I grab the one in front of me and pound my knee into his nose, knocking his stupid fucking mask to the ground. My teeth grind when it reveals Oscar, sneering at me, throwing a fist into my already aching jaw. I wrap my arm around his head and fucking secure him in a headlock, repeatedly pounding my fist into his face. He struggles to break free, crying out like a goddamn ballsack when his nose cracks. And I fucking cackle with glee. Die, you asshole. Suffer for what you've done to Kaycee at the house, you sick fuck.

"Enough!" Cushing's voice echoes, forcing everyone to freeze. Our backs stiffen at the authoritative tone he uses, but I take my time keeping Oscar-fucking-Sanchez in a headlock. He tries to pry me off him, but I keep a good grip, slowly choking the air from his lungs with my arm secured around his throat.

The fight continues again as more black-robed dickbags come out of nowhere. I swear, they've tripled in thirty seconds surrounding us, waiting their turn to beat us down. Oscar wheezes, finally pushing away from me and stumbling away to catch his breath. He glares at me, baring his teeth, and returns for more. I gladly give him all I've got.

Zeppelin punches Trent in the ribs, hissing when he returns the favor. Surprise rocks through me when Zepp hits Trent right behind the ear and sends him flying to his back, knocking him out cold. Trent doesn't move an inch, and Zepp focuses his fists on another sucker jumping into the fight.

Another black-robed bastard tries to grab me from behind to stop my fists from finding Oscar again. Their hands wrap around my waist, giving me the best opportunity ever. Stars dance in my eyes after I ram the back of my skull into their face. Again and again, my head connects with their nose or cheek or whatever the fuck it is. It crunches. Satisfaction roars through my veins at the sound of her sissy ass shriek. I grunt, once again ramming my fist into Oscar's bloodied face.

"I fucking said enough!" Cushing roars, having enough of our defiance. A gun sounds, stopping all the commotions. The roughed up, black-robed dickbags stand rigid, watching their leader and awaiting further instructions.

As they're distracted, I fall to my knees, checking Kaycee's injuries. The paramedic said she was in critical condition before, and now it looks dire. She's barely taking in breaths, and her shirt has more blood sticking to her. If she doesn't get help now, she'll die on this miserable ground.

My heart drops when my head snaps up to the familiar grunt of my brother. He stumbles back in confusion, bringing his hand to his shoulder. His eyes widen, his face growing pale when his fingers return painted in red. He looks at me, and I fucking lose it. I swear my soul fucking fissures. Jumping to my feet, I take a few steps toward him, holding him up by his waist.

"I'll be fine," he grits. I swallow hard, eyeing the blood bubbling out of his bicep with panic in his tone. He doesn't want me to hear it, but I fucking hear it loud and clear. I don't think my brother could hide a damn thing from me.

"Motherfucker!" I shout, glaring daggers at Cushing's smug as fuck face.

He smirks, tilting his head at my reaction with glee. He fucking loves the tears falling from my face as I hold on to Zepp and drag him back to Kaycee. We sit beside her, guarding her body against the fuckers surrounding us again.

"You shot him!" I shout for all to hear, a crack of panic spearing through my voice. "You shot my fucking brother! You piece of unholy shit! I will beat you bloody. I will—"

I rear back as another gunshot rings through the air, and my instincts kick in. Throwing Zepp to the ground, I protect him with my entire body on top of his and Kaycee's. It might not be fucking effective, but I have to protect them both. He gasps as my weight presses in, but I'll be fucked on Sunday if I don't defend them both from crazies with guns. I can't have him getting fucking shot again.

Zepp grunts, pushing me into the sitting position and glaring at me. My eyes check him over, fingers brushing against his face and down his arms. But the only blood I see is from the wound on his arm. He bats me away, grabbing my wrist to stop my frantic search.

"I wasn't hit again, you psycho," he breathes in a shaky voice.

Massive amounts of sweat pours down his face, and his skin pales with every wince he gives. His left arm hangs limp by his side, a small hole visible straight through his arm. I whip my shirt off, pressing into his wound and using as much pressure as possible to stop the blood pooling into the grass. I tie it around him, letting my shirt soak up the blood. Looking down at Kaycee, I swallow hard when her breath grows dangerously slow. Maybe I should have fucking done this for her and stopped the bleeding with my shirt. But I don't....I don't fucking know. Guilt eats away at me, and hopelessness fills me up. I know fucking Veritas is here somewhere. So, where the fuck are their incompetent asses?

"Then who was shot?" I bark in desperation, checking Kaycee over again. But no new wounds pop up, thank fuck.

I sit up, whipping my head back and forth, checking the stiffened black-robes' postures. Not them. Kaycee's still passed out from her wounds. So yeah, not fucking good, but she didn't get shot. My breaths stall in my chest, eyes widening at the sight of the fucking ghost stumbling forward from behind the crazy assholes pointing guns in our direction. His knees wobble with every step, but determination sits in his dark eyes.

Every inch of him is pale except for the blood pouring from multiple holes in his chest. Sweat clings to his blonde hair, sticking to his scalp. A pained scowl etches onto his face with every staggering step he takes. But Carter Cunningham doesn't fucking care. He doesn't give a flying fuck. If this is his last breath, he'll do it fighting for us—for her. Carter propels himself forward on shaky feet, pointing his gun in Crowe's direction.

"Surprise, bitch," he growls, pulling the trigger before Crowe can defend himself. "I don't go down that easily," he slurs, slumping to his knees in the grass the moment the bullet fires from the barrel and hurls toward its target.

Vomit churns in my stomach, coming halfway up my throat at the carnage. Blood explodes from the gaping wound, taking half of Crowe's fucking face off, until his body falls forward without a sound. The only thing heard is the heavy thump of his body and the pathetic little gurgle bubbling from his throat. Death claims Crowe faster than I can let out a breath. It swoops in, grabs hold of his shirt, and drags his ass to Hell, where he belongs. I hope the devil pokes holes in every inch of his worthless soul to pay for his multitude of sins. He has a lot to atone for, and a lifetime in Hell won't amount to the lives he's taken in the name of greed.

Shit, I might hurl. Fuck. Clutching my stomach, I try to hold back the burning bile knocking against my teeth. I take a deep breath. Who knew getting shot could be so gruesome? Human matter splatters around Crowe. Shit—Carter killed Crowe. Fuck yes! I'd whoop for joy if the moment wasn't so stressful. And if I moved an inch, I'd throw up my empty stomach.

Looking around, I finally see where the first bullet went, and my eyes widen. Shit! My heart stalls in my chest, squeezing the air from my lungs. Cushing lies face down on the ground, convulsing with full-body movements from his toes to his head, knocking against the hard ground. Blood pours from the back of his head. Fuck. Carter. Jesus. He killed him, too.

"You slimy, traitorous fucker!" Shaw shrieks, jumping on Carter in the blink of an eye. "You killed my brothers, you limp-dicked, grimy noodle!" Shaw shrieks one last time, raising my eyebrows at the weird name-calling. Huh. Maybe ole Piper got it from her uncles. And, uh—gross. That's just fucking disgusting. I grunt, climbing to my feet when the others scatter, screeching at the sight of their precious leaders dead on the ground.

Shaw wrestles Carter to the ground without a fight, pounding fist after fist into Carter's face. Carter's body jumps with every hit, but he doesn't fight back. In fact, he doesn't make a fucking move to defend himself. Worry takes hold when Shaw gets more punches in, and I stumble in their direction, ready to help shake him off. I can't stand to see Carter get hurt any worse than he was when he was the one who had obviously received the gunshots from before.

"Move! Move!" a voice shouts from behind us, and I stop in my tracks at the authoritative tone.

My eyes widen as a tactical team dressed entirely in black approaches the epic shitshow happening. They move like fucking shadows in the night, toeing through the dark like they belong, making hand movements to each other. Two of them circle Shaw like sharks, baring their teeth and pointing their huge and terrifying guns directly into his temples, stopping him from throwing more punches.

I slink back, dropping next to Zepp and Kaycee, mentally begging for an ambulance to come and save them all. Frantically, my eyes dart around, trying to find their fucking rescue.

"Now, now, I suggest you stop right now before I blow your brains out," the guy says, pushing the tip of his long AR into Shaw's temple.

Shaw heaves breath after breath, putting his hands in the air. Damn, I kind of wish he'd try to run or fight, but he's too much of a fucking ballsack. Shaw looks above him with fury twisting his expression and takes in the face of the smiling guy, pointing his gun at him.

"You crazy-ass fucking psychos are done for," the man beside him says, pressing the tip of his AR into his other temple. "Get up, put your hands on your head, or Jordy here will blast your dick away in a freak accident." The blonde man beside him smiles, blue eyes twinkling with mischief.

"Hell yes, I will. These accidents happen all the time," Jordy says with a shrug, lowering his gun to Shaw's crotch. I swear, Shaw fucking squeaks like a little bitch at the thought of his dick getting blasted off. Not like he'll need it where he's going.

"Nice and easy now," the other guy says, helping Shaw's hands to his head, where he handcuffs them together and forces Shaw to stand. They eye Shaw like the piece of shit he is, wrinkling their noses at him. Jordy nods his head, ordering the other guy to take Shaw to the Hell he belongs in. He takes off with Shaw into the shadows where more figures lurk, pointing their guns at the other sick fucks crowding us.

Jordy waltzes toward Crowe and Cushing and kicks them with his boot. Rolling them to their backs, he grunts something to himself. Leaning down, he checks their pulses with his fingers and nods. Once he stands up, he straightens his back and grins at the carnage around him. All I can do is gape at the Veritas members hustling around and collecting the black-robed bastards and throwing them to the ground.

"Targets, dead. Threat neutralized. Scene clear! Make it rain!" he shouts, waving a hand without an ounce of urgency. I grind my teeth when he walks away from the dead bodies, almost reveling in the chaos consuming the area.

I whip my head when Hadley thumps to the ground with a man on top of her, forcing her hands behind her back. "Ow!" Hadley shrieks with green grass blades resting between her teeth. The man behind her presses a knee into her back, forcefully pulling her hands behind her. Cuffs clink into place as she slurs obscenities at them for touching her. "You can't do this! They manipulated me! It wasn't me!" she slurs out a cry as they bring her to her feet, exposing the bloody mark lining her cheek. I reel back at the carnage, only then noticing her broken teeth when she growls at me and bares her teeth.

"Save it," the man grunts, forcing her to walk forward on shaky legs. She shrieks and thrashes as he pushes her forward. "We all know about you, Hadley Lacey, and your disgusting family. It looks like rotting in prison is a new family trait." He grumbles, keeping her at bay with the barrel of his gun tucked between her shoulder blades. It's only then does she straighten up and shut her mouth, especially when someone mentions their lawyer.

I shake off the heavenly scene of her getting sat on the ground near an idling prison bus, and my breaths shudder. Thank fucking fuck these assholes showed up when they did. If they hadn't, we would all be as dead as a fucking doornail. I wipe a hand down my face, looking back to my pale brother, who stares at the craziness happening around us.

"Fuck," Zepp hisses, pressing his hand into the wound of his bicep. Tears leak down his cheeks, and he shakes his head trying as hard as he can to look reassuring to me. "I'll be fine," he rasps through a thick voice and wipes away his tears. "Worry about her and him, okay?" He asks with heavy emotions twisting his voice. "I'll be fine," he says one last time before leaning in and resting his forehead on my shoulder.

"Totally fucking fine," I murmur, wrapping my arm around him. My other fucking half, the man I shared a womb with, is not bleeding before me as we wait for an EMT.

We watch with tears in our eyes as a frantic medical team descends on Kaycee and begins to examine her. Through rough voices, they yell out to more paramedics who quickly bring a gurney and load her onto it. A paramedic hops up on top of her and begins chest compressions, yelling that they need to get her to surgery right away. I close my eyes when the whisper of one paramedic meets my ears saying the dreaded words I never want to hear.

"I don't think she's going to make it. She's lost too much blood." They could have said more. They could have said that they were wrong and that she'd live. But the blood rushed to my ears, drowning out the noise around me, and watched with longing in my frantically beating heart. My fucking life sped away with a knife in her fucking gut and an EMT pumping at her chest, frantically trying to bring her back to life.

"Carter," Zepp croaks, trying to climb to his feet, but he stumbles back and lands on his ass.

"Is he okay?" I shout to the EMTs loading his lifeless body onto a stretcher. "Is he fucking okay?" I shout, forcing my legs beneath me, and march toward their frantic voices. I push through the crowds of agents and criminals with their hands behind their backs until I run up to them and shove my way through.

My heart fucking stops at the sight of the blood pouring from his chest and beaten face, and my mouth pops open.

"Son," barks an EMT, grabbing me by the shoulder and pulling me back. I fucking let him as sobs rip through me, and the man I once deemed an evil bastard fights for his life in an ambulance destined for the hospital.

"Will he live?" I beg, turning to the lone EMT who stayed behind, and he pats my shoulder. Sympathy roars through his eyes, and his lips tighten.

"The truth?" He whispers softly, and I nod, urging him to continue. "It's a miracle he was still up and moving. His injuries are more than severe, they're life-threatening. If you believe in God, I'd start praying for that one." He taps my shoulder a few times and goes to walk away, but I pull him by the shirt.

"Don't say that shit!" I roar, getting in his face with tears pouring from my eyes. My vision blurs, and the world swirls together in one color. "Don't say it." My voice squeaks as the emotions grab me tight, and my entire body shakes.

"I'm so sorry, kid." he murmurs, peeling my hand away from his uniform, and turns away without another word.

I stand there in a sea of people running around like chickens with their heads cut off. Some black-robed fuckers try to escape through campus, thinking they're sneaky. Sharp cries sound in the distance as more and more of the Apocalypse Society falls to their knees at the hands of the government. I take a deep breath, moving once again to find my brother still in the grass holding his arm. I wipe the tears from my cheeks with my arm and march toward him, determined to get him to a doctor, too. He may not have been shot in the chest or stabbed, but he sure as hell will need someone to look at the gaping bullet wound on his bicep.

Chaos swirls around us when I drop to my knees in front of Zepp, grabbing his face.

"They're both at the hospital now. You doing okay?" I whisper, moving his head back and forth and examining every inch. He grunts, knocking my hands off him and knocking me onto my ass. For the first time tonight, I bark out a laugh, throwing my head back and looking at the innocent stars twinkling above us. Fuck.

"I'll be fine," he whispers in anguish, attempting to move but grunts more.

"You will be once you're looked at," I mutter through a deep breath, praying that everyone hurt gets the surgeries or whatever the fuck they need ASAP. I need to know what's going on, but first, I have to take care of my brother.

When I turn my head to look around the area, my eyes fall to the spot my love laid in for the longest time. Terror fills every inch of me when I lick my lips, and my limbs freeze at the sight of the blood pooling in the grass where she was laying. With trembling fingers, I run my fingers over the spot and bring them back to in front of my eyes. Her warm blood paints my fingers red, and I finally fucking lose my dinner. I heave and choke, pouring the contents of my stomach out onto the grass until there isn't anything else to purge. Sweat coats my forehead when I finally sit back and look at my sympathetic brother. His brows furrow when his good hand rubs up and down my back, and I grunt, throwing him off, and nod.

"I'm good," I breathe, tasting the aftereffects and cringe.

"Right," he hums through a pained expression, pushing into the wound on his arm again with my shirt.

"You need to go to the hospital," I say to Zepp, getting to my feet. I stumble slightly as the adrenaline ebbs out of my body and right myself. I reach down, pulling my brother to his feet too. He winces, tamping down the pained whine that escapes through his tight lips. He shakes his head, fear brewing in the back of his eyes.

Yeah, my scaredy-pants brother is about to go to the one place he fucking hates. But he has no damn choice in the matter. I'll drag him there kicking and screaming before I let him fucking die of infection.

"They fucking shot you," I grunt, throwing my arm

around his shoulders and directing him toward the flashing lights of the ambulances lining up in a neat row. His feet drag with every step, and I know if it were up to him, he'd hightail it to, well---I don't know where. Our home is nothing but ashes, and all our shit is gone. All our memories are lost because the Apocalypse tainted everything about this place.

I frown, turning my head toward the maze. This campus was once our reprieve from our shitty stepmom and her annoying ways. This was our home away from home, the one place we felt safe and secure. And in the blink of an eye, it's all gone. Tears form in my eyes at everything we've lost and everything we might lose in a matter of seconds. Life is so fucking precious, and we're still not safe.

Carter, Kaycee, and Chase are fighting for their lives. Our home may be gone and nothing more than ashes, but I can make another home as long as they're with us. Home isn't four walls built with nails and boards. Home is where your fucking heart resides—and that's what they are. They're my goddamn home, and I'll be damned if they fucking die.

He snorts at my words, nodding his head. "I know, brother. They shot me, and I'm going to get looked at," Zepp says in a weakened voice but gives me a thumbs up anyway with a grimace. Yeah, not so fucking convincing there, brother. I roll my eyes and drag him toward the nearest ambulance with an available paramedic.

Staring into the abyss of the unoccupied ambulance ties my stomach in knots, and my arm tightens around my brother. My emotions well up again, and I clamp my eyes shut, trying to force the horrific memories away. Memories of Kaycee secured in my arms and then of the paramedics taking off with her flow through my mind. Anything could happen to her right now. She could be…

"Fuck," I heave again, leaning my forehead on Zepp when we stop. "Is Kaycee going to be okay?" I whisper with desperation, clutching onto his shirt and pulling him closer.

We rest our foreheads against each other, blocking out everything. It's just me and him, standing together, and there's no one else around us.

My heart bounces against my ribs in a frantic beat, awaiting his answer. But he fucking pauses, closing his eyes, deep in thought. I don't know whether it's from the pain he's undergoing or if he's thinking about Kaycee and the others, too. His teeth sink into his bottom lip, and a ragged breath blows from his nose. His head shakes against mine, and his shoulders lift. No—fucking no. He can't say what I think he's about to say.

"I—don't know," he breathes, brushing my cheek with his warm breath. "I don't know if she'll…" he swallows hard, and I engulf him in a hug, clinging to him as tears pour from our eyes in mutual grief.

"Don't say that," I croak, pulling back and tapping his cheek. "Don't even fucking think it, okay? They'll all survive, or I'll go after them and drag them back. Got it?" He rolls his eyes in irritation but gives me a firm nod.

"Whatever you say, asshole," he mutters, stiffening when a paramedic comes into view, and spots the blood staining his arm. I swear he pales more and prepares to bolt in the other direction.

She rushes toward us, throwing gloves over her hands. "Got another one!" she shouts over her shoulders, getting two more men at her side. Their gloved hands inspect his bullet wound, and they wince. "Looks like you need to take a trip to the hospital with your friends." Zepp's worried eyes meet mine. I cup one cheek, putting my forehead on his. We rest like that for a split second as the paramedic urges Zepp to get a move on. He stalls, and his muscles tense.

"You got this," I whisper, bumping him. He swallows hard, wincing from the pain in his arm. "I'll come with you," I say, reassuring him. If there's one thing Zeppelin West doesn't like, it's hospitals.

Zepp clings to my hand when they work him over, putting an IV in his arm and an oxygen mask over his face. His frantic eyes tell me he's about to lose his shit until the paramedic smiles and informs us she's giving him some pain medicine. Zepp's body slumps when the drug hits his veins, and I sigh in relief. I know he's in pain, but the anxiety was riding him hard.

I sit back in the seat as they prepare to shut the doors and take us both to the hospital where Zepp will get better, and I'll pace around.

"Hold on!" Shouts a familiar out-of-breath voice from outside the ambulance. I gape when a familiar head pokes in, giving me a tight smile, and lifts a badge in the air. "Mr. West, I'm so sorry, but you need to come with me," Espie, the newest fucking student, says regretfully, motioning me to climb out.

I scowl, narrowing my eyes at the woman who is silently pleading with me to cooperate. But I don't want to fucking cooperate.

"The fuck?" I growl, cracking my knuckles and shaking my head. "Ain't no fucking way I'm leaving my brother," I snarl, taking a step forward to give her a piece of my damn mind.

"I'm sorry, Mr. West, but I must insist you come with me," she pleads again, gesturing for me to hop down.

I march toward her with a snarl on my lips and point a finger directly in her face because there's no fucking way I'm hopping out of here. "Fuck no. My girlfriend is fucking dying. Both of my brothers have been shot. My other brother is burned. Fuck that. I'm going with him." Rage storms inside of me, threatening to boil over. Where's Grumpy when you need to pound his face in? Oh, right. He's in the fucking hospital with gunshot wounds.

Desperation rushes through me, and I'm not above begging. I'll drop to my knees, plead my case, and fucking go to the hospital with my brother. There's no goddamn way they're going to drag me out of here and get their way. My family fucking needs me right now. I need to be at the hospital for all of them. Several deep breaths pass through my nose and out of my mouth to calm me the fuck down. I'm two seconds away from tearing someone into two pieces and going to jail myself. And I can't fucking afford that. If I don't calm my racing heart and the need to hurt someone, I'll do something I regret. And If I do that, I won't be able to be with everyone.

She nods in understanding. "I'm so sorry, Seger." When my eyes meet hers, she swallows hard. She almost shuts up—almost—but opens her fucking mouth again. "We need to talk to you, though. Get your side of things. My superior needs to speak to someone who was in the mix out here. He needs your story ASAP, and no, it can't wait." Her lips thin into a straight line, and she shakes her head when I open my mouth to protest. At this point, I don't think there's anything I could say to make her back the fuck up and leave me alone so I can see my family.

"And you, what? Were you there the whole fucking time to observe and not do shit?" I growl, hopping out of the ambulance with anger rushing through me at the thought of her being in the mix of everything and not stopping it. Proving to me, once again, Veritas is an incapable secret agency that needs to know their flaws. "Where were you when she was stabbed or bullied or beaten within an inch of her life? You see her fucking face?" I growl through clenched teeth, stepping up to her. Much to my surprise, Espie lifts her chin and tilts her head in acknowledgment. "Where the fuck was your organization? You failed us! You failed us all!" I heave a breath, tears leaking down my face. "You fucking failed the people you vowed to protect." I shake my head, wiping my nose with my fingers.

I dart my eyes to my brother, who rests on the gurney

with a blissed-out smile taking over his face. The paramedics have tears on their rosy cheeks when they look at me, nodding to acknowledge the pain spearing through me.

Zepp sighs loudly and waves a hand. "Go," he barks out in a high-pitched voice. "I'll be fine. I'll be perfectly fine." He smiles at me, the best one he can muster behind the oxygen mask over his mouth and nose.

"Fucking fine," I growl, staring back at the girl I want to tear limb from limb. "I'll fucking come to talk to them, but then your ass is taking me to the hospital ASAP. I will not be away from them any longer than I have to." My heart shudders when the doors of the ambulance close, closing off the view of my brother.

"He's in excellent hands, son." the woman paramedic says, slapping me on the shoulder as she rounds the vehicle and hops in. They're off the property in the blink of an eye, with their lights flashing and sirens blaring. Leaving me in the dark with two organizations I want to fucking murder with an ax.

Espie looks sheepish about it all as I scowl back at her. "I really am sorry. I know they all mean a lot to you, but he wants to speak to you before you leave." She waves me on, and I reluctantly follow behind her, shoving my hands into my pockets. The crisp night air blows across my chest, reminding me I'm standing around without a shirt. Which also reminds me every piece of my fucking heart is lying in a hospital bed. Everyone except me.

How the fuck did all this go so wrong? We were so careful. First, our house gets blown up with Chase inside, and then Kaycee gets taken right from under us. The only plus about this situation are the bodies lining the body bags. Crowe and Cushing lie side-by-side on the grass, deposited into black body bags, as people take pictures of their wounds and bodies. Fuckers deserved that. Rot in Hell, motherfuckers. I hope Satan fucks you up good.

Shaw sits handcuffed on the ground as a few Veritas agents repeatedly ask him questions. He scowls, tightening his lips, and shakes his head, refusing to talk. Let me fucking at him; I'll make him squeal like a damn pig and give up everything they want to know. He catches my eye as I walk behind Espie and grins at me like the psychopath he is.

"Mother fucker," I hiss, taking a step toward him, but Espie wraps her small hand around my bicep, stopping me. I huff a breath, looking back at her, and she motions for me to continue to follow her. "What will you do with Shaw?" I grit out, looking back at all the black robes lined up outside the hedge maze. Agents stand before them, writing their names and asking them questions.

I smirk at Oscar, who scowls at my freedom. His beady eyes follow me as I walk behind Espie. I grin at his bloodied and bruised face, knowing that I fucking did that to him. He growls at me, baring his teeth when I walk past, and I can't help the laugh that slips out. The agent behind him holds him down, hollering at him to stop. I wink at him, throwing him over the edge of his rage. He tries to get to his knees, and I mean, he tries hard. But the agent behind him throws out the F-bomb and fucking tases his ass.

"He'll go to prison and never get out," she murmurs with a sharp nod. "And so will all the other members online who were viewing. We're in the process of tracking them down. It could take months, but we'll get them." Something like reassurance settles within my rolling gut, and I crack a smile, imagining his ass in prison. All their asses are going to jail for the foreseeable future, and it's nice to finally have the fucking trash out of the way.

"Ah, Mr. West," A deep voice says in a grim greeting, gaining my attention. Turning away from Oscar's still body, I face the man in charge. He stands tall, posture straight, with graying hair mixed in with a deep brow, blowing in the wind. He holds out his hand, forcing me to shake his.

"And you are?" I grumble with urgency, trying to get the fucking show on the road.

"Right," he says, nodding his head. "I apologize for this having to happen right now. I know your brother and girlfriend were severely injured in this war, and my new team failed you on so many levels. I'm Agent Zero."

"Yeah, along with my other damn brothers. And apparently, you were here while she was getting hurt. What the Hell? Kaycee is going to fucking die…." I bring my fist to my lips, breathing deeply again. I might punch this fucker and send him to an early grave if I keep ranting.

He exchanges a heavy look with Espie, and she sighs. "Yes, I was here the entire time, but you have to understand, we had no evidence to put away those three in the middle of it all. All we had was circumstantial evidence and hearsay."

"No fucking evidence?!" I grit out, balling my fists. "How long have you been monitoring these psychopaths? Even I know they've been using a calling card at the end of their kills. Did you look at all their victims?"

The man swallows hard, running a hand through his hair. "My God, she really got into anything and everything, didn't she?" he whispers. "Your girlfriend is something else when it comes to computers. I'm assuming she got into our database as well?" I frown, holding his gaze. He chuckles. There's no way in Hell I'm implicating my girlfriend in front of his entire operation. "Smart," he says, nodding his head.

"Can we get on with this? They're all fucking at the hospital. My brother—everyone—I need to get there."

He holds up his hands. "I just need you to walk me through tonight. What you guys planned and how you executed it. Agent Seven has explained her end to me, involving Carter, but I need to hear your end."

I take a deep breath, reliving the last day of literal Hell. "We got a text from Carter from Kaycee's phone. He told us what happened and that he was trapped. He said he would have to play along so he didn't get himself killed or Kaycee. We made a plan and waited for a second text. We stationed Zepp to take out their power, and Carter would bring her to a window. I stood out in the woods, waiting for a sign. I saw him move the black curtain and flash his flashlight, and I took Kaycee and ran. Is that good-fucking-enough?" I growl as he exchanges another look with Espie.

"Agent Seven will escort you to the hospital. They have informed me they have rushed Kaycee to surgery to mend her injuries. Your brother is being patched up with non-life-threatening issues," he says tersely, dismissing me just like that.

"And the others? They're my family, too," I say with hope filling my chest. My brother is okay. Kaycee's getting the help she needs and will hopefully—no—Kace will survive this. They all will.

Agent Zero rolls his lips together, sighing. "Mr. Cunningham is in surgery as well to repair the damage. He's suffered major blood loss and critical injuries. They're doing the best they can. And Mr. Benoit is in recovery from his burns, getting fluids for now. But that's all I know," he says, eyes scanning the crowd. "Now, if you'll excuse me, I have many people to interrogate and paperwork to file." He pats my shoulder once, getting ready to retreat from this conversation. Yeah, that's not fucking happening.

"No," I growl, getting in his face. I don't give a shit if he is some big agent in some shitty company. "Where the fuck were you during this whole fight? Why the fuck didn't you protect that paramedic? Why the fuck did I get my ass kicked if you were here the whole time?" I growl, putting my nose against his. He holds his hands in the air as a few of his agents raise their guns.

"I get it, kid, you're upset right now. You've been through something no eighteen-year-old should go through. But we couldn't step in. It wasn't safe for us. Do you know how many agents they surrounded and murdered in the woods? I sent ten of my agents that way. There shouldn't have been a chance for them to sneak up on them, let alone shoot them. It wasn't safe for us to step out of the shadows until Carter took them out by surprise. You have to understand that your safety is important to us, but the safety of my agents is important, too. If I don't have them, I have no one to fight the good fight." My eyes bug out of my damn head at his admission. He just let us fucking fall on our asses while he watched. We could have fucking died, and he would have shrugged his shoulders all to protect his agents. Isn't that what cops and special forces are for? To step in when people are getting hurt instead of standing on the outside and not doing shit?

"My girlfriend was bleeding out. My brother got fucking shot for you! What the fuck!" I hiss, peeling my face away from his. I have to get my shit together if I want to live to see my family again. These assholes will probably go rogue and murder me for getting in their leader's face.

"When you calm down, kid, you'll understand why we did what we did. For the safety of all. Now, if you'll excuse me, I have shit to do and an investigation to wrap up." He raises a brow and walks away with his shoulders pulled back. Barking orders, he commands his people to take every black-robe toward a large bus with metal bars on the windows.

"Are they all going to prison?" I swallow hard, watching them march those bastards toward the bus.

One by one, they march them toward the bus with their hands secured behind their backs. They don't speak to the agents tugging them along. Their heads hang low, killing their protests.

Espie's gaze cuts into me again, and she nods. "Most of them. Our insider, Zoe," her eyes cut to me, and I swallow hard, thinking back to the time we caught Zoe and Principal Shaw together. And now it all hits me that maybe it wasn't exactly what she wanted. Maybe she was forced into doing whatever they made her do. "She'll be under our protection for the time being until all this is settled. We didn't have evidence before of their crimes. Not until I witnessed the murders." Her timid hand runs down her face with a drawn-out sigh. "This was my first case," she whispers, staring off at her team. "I've been with Veritas for two years training for this type of situation, but they don't prepare you for the real thing." She wipes away the sweat on her forehead and sighs again. "But let's get you to the hospital. I'm sure you're eager to get there."

# THIRTY-TWO

## SEGER

Nerves burst to life in my stomach, twisting it into knots. I gnaw on my lower lip, following Espie through the parking lot toward a blacked-out SUV. Exhaustion settled into my aching bones long ago, but there's no rest in sight for me. My brain is fucking alive with so many thoughts I don't think I'd be able to shut my eyes any time soon. Not that I could. There is too much to do and too many people to worry about. Half my fucking family is lying in hospital beds dying because of what they went through. And then there's me, alive and well, following my former classmate, who was an undercover agent this whole time.

"Get in," Espie says, gesturing toward the passenger side door when we approach the vehicle.

I blink several times, heave a breath, open the door, and climb in. I secure the seat belt over my chest and click it into place when she makes it around to the driver's side. Leaning my head back, I close my eyes, but I'm haunted by my rampant thoughts once again. Espie starts the SUV in my peripheral and messes with the radio, turning it down until silence is the only thing filling the car.

When I reopen my eyes and look around with a jolt, I realize Espie has driven us off the property, and we're coasting down the highway towards the hospital. Several cop cars plow toward the school, too little, too fucking late. Where the fuck were the authorities when all this was going down for the past year or so? Shit, who knows how long the Apocalypse has been up to this shit.

When I settle back in the seat and lean my head back, I feel her gaze again searing into me. It's like that time at the restaurant when she worked there. She couldn't take her eyes off me. I let it go for a few minutes, but every time we get stopped at a light, I feel it again, and I can't fucking take it anymore.

"Why are you looking at me like that?" I grunt, peeking an eye open to watch her. "You did it at the restaurant, too," I point out in a gruffer voice than normal. Exhaustion pulls at my limbs, and a heaviness takes over my mind, but the horror show plays in my mind every time I shut my eyes. I can't imagine what Kaycee fucking saw because what I saw was fucking terrifying.

She sucks in a breath, red brightening her cheeks and neck. The tips of her olive-skinned ears inflame. "I'm sorry. I don't mean to stare. You—uh, you remind me of someone I used to know." Her grip on the steering wheel tightens, white-knuckling as she presses on the gas pedal, speeding through town.

I raise a brow. "A good someone?" I gently probe, putting a teasing tilt to my voice. As harsh as it might sound, I don't give a fuck what she has to say. I just need a distraction to get me through this long and tense drive before I think myself into fucking oblivion. So many distinct possibilities ring through my mind: the good, the bad, and the very fucking ugly.

She snorts, running a finger across the top of her lip. "Not exactly." She shakes her head. "You remind me of the boy I once loved, then….." She swallows hard, blinking rapidly while staring ahead. Biting her lip, she sneaks a look at me and sighs. "His father killed me, and he let him," she whispers with so much raw hurt in her voice. I don't know how she's sitting here today telling me this. Grief flashes in her eyes until the vulnerabilities she had given me vanish into thin air. She grits her teeth, strangling the steering wheel until her knuckles turn white.

"He killed you?" I ask slowly, sitting straight up in my seat with furrowed brows. "Like fucking killed you?" I ask again, trying to understand whatever the fuck she's telling me. Killed her? I narrow my eyes on the scars lining her face when she brushes her fingers over them. Her fingers trail down toward a thicker-lined scar, running the distance across her throat and up to each ear.

I recoil, swallowing hard. How have I never noticed the scar before? Have we been too busy avoiding the new girl to notice she's lived a hellish life we couldn't imagine? Fuck. Why am I even thinking about this right now? I don't understand why this mysterious government agent is spilling her guts to me suddenly. Maybe it's because I look like this mysterious dude she was once in love with. But how the fuck can she stand to look at me if I look like the guy who aided in her—well—not so death? Well, fuck. Whatever she wants to tell me, she can. I'm invested now, and it's helping to take my mind off all the fucked up shit going on.

Her fingers work around the steering wheel and slowly loosen until she's completely relaxed in the driver's seat. She hums in response, nodding her head, and clears her throat. I lean forward, eyeing her as a glazed-over look takes over her eyes like she's lost deep in memory.

"I once had a relationship like you have," she whispers with such sadness I feel it in my tightening chest. She swallows hard, rubs at her eyes, and sighs. "Three boys. Mack, J.J., and Huxley," she murmurs their names with a heavy tongue and side-eyes me when we come to a complete stop at the next stoplight. "My mom immigrated from Chile when she was sixteen, met my dad shortly after, and then had me. We came from a large family up north, filled with, um—interesting people. My dad got transferred for his job to Southern California, working with this guy named Franco, and um, he was dangerous. But that's where I met them. They were his foster sons. They became my best friends, and then we became something more, and then, well... yeah," she murmurs the last part, blushing a little.

"And then they killed you? I don't understand?" I ask, sitting back in my seat again, readjusting my posture when the large, foreboding hospital comes into view a few blocks away.

"It's a long story and kind of complicated. Franco was a bad guy, raising them to be bad guys. One night, he..." a tear falls down her face, and she wipes it away quickly. "They burned my house down with me inside. All of them watched. That night, I died in their eyes, so here I am now. I'm tired of criminals getting away with shitty crimes and not paying for their actions. My name may be on a gravestone—" She rolls her lips in with a heavy sigh, pulling into a vacant parking spot near the hospital. "but I fight for people who can't fight for themselves. My Uncle Jonathan saved me after this." She points to the raised red marks on her face and neck. "And now I'm part of the best team in the country. And—shit." She gives a small laugh.

"I probably told you way too much information right now. Please don't tell anyone," she whispers, pleadingly looking at me. "I didn't mean to spill all that, but you look so much like him with the tattoos and everything. It's like my old best friend is sitting here again, and I kind of lost it the moment I saw you." She swallows a lump in her throat, and for some odd reason, I nod along. She's lived a life I can't imagine, betrayed by people she thought loved her. And here she is, standing taller and prouder and stronger than before, part of a team—albeit a shitty fucking team who shows up ten minutes late to the main event. Despite that, she's fucking here and standing tall, doing what she thinks is right.

"How can you even look at Zepp or me if they did that?" I ask, looking up toward the hospital's daunting height and then back to her.

"I guess my heart never stopped loving him," she murmurs, unbuckling her seat belt. "Come on, I'll help you find your brother. I'll flash my badge around." She jumps out of the car, with me not far behind her.

Without another word, we head into the vacant hospital, devoid of life except for the nurses and doctors milling around looking after their patients. Espie does as she said she would and flashes her badge at every nurse we encounter when looking for directions to Zepp's bed in the emergency department.

"Well," she says, playing with the badge hanging around her neck. "It was nice to meet you. Sorry about all this. Um— between you and me, if it were up to me, I would have arrested them when Carter told us about them a few months ago." My spine stiffens when she mentions Carter, but she keeps her big brown eyes pointed at the floor. I make a note to talk to Carter later because I will fucking speak to him later. There's no way he'll fucking die. He's too hard-headed to do something stupid like that.

"Um, well, good luck with everything," I say, running a hand across the back of my neck. What do you say to someone like this? I fucking hated her and the organization she works for thirty minutes ago, and now I feel bad for her and everything she's gone through.

"You, too," she says with a soft smile. "We'll be investigating more. So, I'll probably see you around. But here's my number if you ever have any questions," she says, handing me a slip of paper, and with that, Espie turns on her heel, muttering insults at herself, and marches out of the hospital.

I raise my eyebrows as she retreats, and my shoulders sag.

More exhaustion fights its way into my brain, but I have a few more missions to complete. I try to imagine I'm my Angel Warrior character battling through the last level against the Devil on a low life and forge on.

I close my eyes, standing outside my brother's room. It's the only damn room the nurses would let me go to since he's my family. I tried to explain to them that the others were my family, too, but they wouldn't fucking listen. I whip the curtain open, getting my first eyeful of Zepp and his room. He lies in the hospital bed, hooked up to several machines with his eyes closed, and a peaceful slumber has taken him over. He doesn't even twitch when I walk into the room and shut the loud curtain behind me. Darkness settles over the room, and finally, every inch of stress unfurls from my clenched muscles, and I sigh. My eyelids feel like cement is dragging them down, and I know a fitful sleep is right around the corner. I need to find Kaycee and Carter and Chase to find out something, but I literally can't move another inch without falling over.

I drag my feet across the dark room, looming over my other half. Kaycee may be my soul mate, but this man here was my womb mate. We've shared everything together—the darkest parts of our history. Suffering under our father's neglectful eye, losing our mom, and all the childhood shit we went through. We may fight and bicker, and sometimes I may want to bury him six feet deep in the backyard, but looming over him like this and letting my fingertips brush against his warm arm—it fucking kills me.

Tears fill my tired eyes, and I swear whenever I blink, sandpaper grits against my eyeballs. I look at the uncomfortable chair in the corner of the room and cringe. Right now, after everything I've witnessed tonight, I need to feel something real. He may kill me whenever he wakes up and discovers I'm spooning him, but he can suck it.

His warmth soaks into my side, and every ounce of

tension leaves my body in an instant. I snuggle into the bed next to my brother, who doesn't even stir. A buzz encases every inch of my body, and my mind whirls through everything that has transpired in the past forty-eight hours. Every scene plays in my mind, and I groan, begging sleep to take me so I can make sure everyone is okay. I snuggle into the side of Zepp's neck and fucking breathe for the first time tonight. Sleep tries taking me under its spell, but the wicked nightmares hold me captive and consume me, pulling me into the darkness of the Apocalypse and their merry band of fucking psychos.

Sometime later, I'm roused out of my sleep when measured footsteps walk into the room, peeling back the curtain separating us from the hallway. Peeking an eye open, a nurse stands before me with a glass of water.

"Here," she says with a small smile. "You've been here for a few hours, and I thought you might want this." I gulp down the glass of water with a muttered thanks and slump back into the bed.

"Is my brother going to be okay?" I watch him sleep out of the corner of my eye, steadily watching the rise and fall of his inhales and exhales.

"Oh, he's going to be fine. We were able to stitch up his wound without surgery. The bullet, thankfully, missed the important bits, including the bone. Everything is still intact, and his muscles and tendons should repair themselves on their own without us. He'll be on antibiotics for a while, but that's the extent of his injuries. He's just worn out now from the pain medicine we've given him, but we should release him in the next twelve hours." She smiles down at me as I nod my head at her words.

Okay, that's good. Zepp will be fine. My heart rate picks up, and I climb to my feet in front of the nurse, towering over her petite form.

"My girlfriend, Kaycee Cole," I start in a desperate voice,

basically pleading with this nurse to give me some answers. "She came in here a few hours ago. I need to know if she's okay. I need to see her, please. And... and.... Chase Benoit and Carter Cunningham are my damn brothers, too," I plead with the biggest puppy dog eyes I can muster, folding my hands together in a pleading gesture. "Can you, please, please, give me some answers? Are they okay? Did they...?" I trail off when she shakes her head and bites into her bottom lip. Sympathy weighs heavily in her eyes, and I can tell she knows something but can't say anything. My shoulders deflate.

She looks behind her for a brief second and then sighs. "I'm so sorry. I can't give you that information. I was able to tell you about him because he's your family. But they aren't. It's for patient privacy—I can't give out their information."

Before I can think about it, I'm on my knees, begging for a bread crumb of information. "Please. Please, give me something. She's the love of my life. If I lose her or my brothers, I won't be able to live with myself. Please, give me something," I whisper through quivering lips, holding back the tears threatening to spill from my aching eyes.

She sighs, checking behind her again. "I can't give you their information. But I can tell you the three you are looking for are on the eighth floor and their parents are here. If they feel like it, they can give you the information you need." My arms wrap around her with an oomph, squeezing her into an enormous hug. She stiffens and lightly pats my arm and peels herself away from me.

"Sorry," I mutter, rubbing a hand along my neck. "I just..."

"Go," she says with a nod. "I'll let your brother know you were here. He'll probably sleep for another few hours, anyway. I'll page you if he needs you, okay? Now go be with them too," she says, waving a wrist.

"Thank you," I whisper, taking off in a full-on sprint. My

muscles protest with every move, but I grit my teeth. Desperation soars through me when I jog down the hall, looking left and right for the elevators I need. Finally, I get on them and rub a hand down my chest—shit—my bare chest. No wonder everyone looked at me so damn funny. Not only was I running down their sacred halls, but I was also fucking shirtless. Shit, I bet they called security on my half-naked ass, but I don't give a shit. I'm on a fucking mission to get to the eighth floor. If only this elevator weren't so damn slow.

Finally, I get to the correct floor and take off down the hallways that twist and turn. Who knew a hospital could be so confusing? But I finally make it to my destination. Out of breath and exhausted, I rest my hands on my knees, sucking in breath after breath. Jesus. After that quick jog through the hospital, why was I so out of breath? Fuck. I ran like three miles with Kace in my arms last night, and here I am, hacking and sputtering.

Once I get my erratic breathing under control, I round the corner of a small waiting room and stop dead. The tension in the air is so thick that I'm choking on it. Kaycee's parents sit with long faces with their heads in their hands, muttering.

My heart leaps at the sight of Mr. Benoit sitting beside them, holding Ainsley as her head rests in his lap. His fingers brush through her hair, soothing her as she sleeps.

"How is she?" I blurt, startling them all out of their stupor.

Mrs. Cole immediately jumps to her feet, wrapping me in a tight hug. "We haven't heard anything yet. They're working to repair the damage of the stab wound," she gasps out through quivering lips, barely getting the word 'stab' out without breaking down. Tears fill her eyes when she looks at me and checks me over for any damage.

"And Chase?" I ask, looking at Mr. Benoit. He gives me a tight smile, stroking more of Ainsley's hair.

"He's in recovery and has several second-degree burns,

which will require skin grafts, but mostly, he'll be okay. He's in some pain, but it wasn't as bad as they had initially thought." he whispers.

My chest deflates—tiny amounts of tension leak off of me at their words. Half of them are okay, for now.

"There's nothing more we can do right now, but wait," Mrs. Cole says through a sigh, furrowing her brows. "Where is your shirt?" she asks, cocking her head to the side. Her eyes study the tattoos marking my chest and shoulders with furrowed brows, giving me her best motherly concern.

"Zepp was—they shot him—and I had to take it off. I—don't know." My fingertips run down my chest, and I shudder when goosebumps pucker my skin.

"Sit down," Mrs. Cole says, pulling me into a chair. "I'm going to the store," she whispers, grabbing her purse nearby.

"Mercy," Mr. Cole says through an exhausted sigh, running a hand down his face. He stands, making his way to her, cupping her face in his palms, looking deep into her eyes. It instantly hits me how he looks at her with hearts in his eyes and worries for her well-being in his heart.

"I have to. There's no sense in waiting around here. If I don't get out of here and stretch, I will pace a hole in the carpet. I just—" He kisses her cheek, pulling her close to his body. I know exactly how he feels as he wraps his arms around her waist and buries his nose into her hair.

The way he holds her. The way his love emanates off of him—I get it. It's how I feel about Kace and the others. Sure, I love her as my fucking future, but they are there, too. Chase will survive, maybe scarred. Kace will pull through without a fucking doubt, and so will Zepp, once he wakes up from his nap. But Carter? They shot him multiple times. Will our reluctant grumpy asshole make it out?

"Have you heard anything about Carter?" I ask, swallowing the growing lump in my throat.

"He's in surgery. That's all we know," Mr. Cole says softly.

"I'm sure we'll find out more information soon. They're all getting patched up, and they'll be okay." I swallow hard when he says the last phrase because it doesn't reach his eyes. He's saying it to make me feel better, but I hear the underlying words he's not saying.

No one is guaranteed tomorrow. No matter how hard you love them or need them in your life, they could still die. And that scares the shit out of me.

"Alright," Mrs. Cole whispers, clapping her hands softly together. "I'll be right back, okay? What size shirt do you wear? You need something. Oh dear, you need to shower," she says, shaking her head with the ghost of a smile on her lips. "You can't stay like that, not like last time. Remember? I had to kick you boys out to bathe and eat. You will not do that to yourself again, right? Take care of yourself, so when Kaycee recovers, her boyfriend is healthy. Okay?" Her motherly tone soothes me, and I nod in agreement.

I look down at my blood-stained hands and sigh. "Yes, Mrs. Cole. I'll do that." She grins again, lightly patting my cheek.

"Call me Mercy, and I hope you aren't lying. There are showers around here somewhere. I'll get you some supplies." With one last wave, she disappears, leaving down the hall on her mission to get me clothes.

"You good, kid?" Mr. Cole asks, sitting back in his chair with a tired groan. I give him another nod, settling back into the chair, too. Letting my eyes close for the second time tonight, I wait on pins and needles for news about my friends.

---

A HAND THUMPS MY CHEST, jolting me out of a nice fucking dream pertaining to a certain girl. But reality crashes down on me, bringing me back to the sounds of the hospital alive around me. I grunt, peeling my tired eyes open, and squint at the smug asshole beside me.

"Fucker," I hiss, wiping at my eyes. My heart squeezes in my chest at the sight of him up and moving and smiling at me.

"You were snoring, didn't think you'd want everyone to hear," Zepp says through a strained smile.

"They let you out?" My voice comes out as a husky rasp.

"About an hour ago." He nods toward the sling covering his right arm. "I have to wear this and try to keep it immobile." He frowns, slumping back into the seat. "Any word on the others?" As he asks his question, Kaycee's mom strolls back into the waiting room, looking as refreshed as ever with a small, satisfied smile. It's the same smile Kaycee gives when she's been up to something.

"Yes," she says, standing in front of us. "News on all of them. Kaycee's surgery was successful. They had to go in and fix her up around the knife wound." Her eyes well with tears at the mention of the knife, but she forges on, reining in her emotions. "Her body went through a lot of trauma, so they've placed her in a medically induced coma to help with the healing process and the brain swelling." She lays a hand on each of our arms, squeezing us in reassurance.

"A coma," I croak, running a hand through my hair. Tears prickle the back of my eyes, and a burn takes over the tip of my nose when the wetness coats my lashes and falls down my cheeks. "A coma?" I repeat, looking up at her for confirmation.

"Just for about two weeks," she whispers, rubbing over her heart. "She'll be fine," she says like she's trying to reassure everyone else that Kaycee will live through this.

"But she'll be okay?" Zepp asks, wincing when he accidentally jolts his arm.

"Not out of danger yet, boys. The next two weeks will be very vital. Kace lost a lot of blood." She swallows hard, clamping her eyes shut. "Her heart stopped on the table twice, and they didn't think..." I put my hand on hers without hesitation, still resting on my arm.

"She's a fighter," I rasp through a quivering lip.

"She never gives up," Zepp whispers, closing his eyes and giving a firm nod.

"The others?" I ask, trying to move the subject along.

"Chase is awake and being himself," Ainsley says from the other side of the room. "He's been asking about her, you guys, and Carter for the past hour. Yelling at anyone who walks by." She snorts, rubbing her tired eyes.

"Annoying asshole," I murmur, gaining a sly smile from Mr. Cole.

"So no change there," Zepp says, chuckling.

"Carter?" I ask with hope, eyeing the adults.

"He's in recovery," Mercy says, tapping my hand. "He has a long road ahead of him. I convinced a nurse—"

"More like bribed," Mr. Cole says with a grin.

"Fine," she huffs, "I bribed a nurse into giving me the details since no one came to see him. He was shot four times. His only saving grace was that it went straight through and didn't stay inside him. They repaired a lot of the damage, but he lost a lot of blood. They aren't sure if or when he'll wake up." A solemn look takes her over, and her shoulders sag. "I'm so sorry, boys. This is..... this is so much." Tears slip from her eyes, and Mr. Cole takes her into his strong arms, and she weeps into his chest.

"Shit," I curse, running a hand through my hair. "Shit," I murmur again as the world spins. Carter's grumpy ass could fucking die, and we never had time to tell him how fucking much he means to us.

For the rest of the day, we stayed tucked into the little waiting room. Mercy finds us a shower to use and gives me new clothes to wear, including new underwear. Not weird, right? She's basically my mother-in-law. So, I graciously take them, thanking her profusely for the fresh clothes since all of mine are nothing more than ash. We eat, sleep, and breathe in the small waiting room, taking up the space until we hear any news about any of our loved ones.

We wait. And wait. And wait some more on pins and needles until the call finally comes.

# THIRTY-THREE

## ZEPPELIN

"Two weeks ago, our newsroom buzzed to life with an unbelievable developing story out of East Point Bluff, California. It grew like wildfire as more and more town members were implicated in heinous and, quite frankly, unbelievable crimes that came to light. The town's top officials now sit behind bars as the FBI sifts through hours of falsified records, trying to determine fact from fiction." The blonde reporter's voice drifts through the TV, grabbing all of our attention. She stands rigid in front of the East Point Prep's main building, surrounded by multiple news outlets reporting the same story.

Yellow, 'do not cross,' tape drapes across every corner of the one-hundred-acre property, crawling with FBI agents. They're looking everywhere on campus, scouring through everyone's apartments, the classrooms, the computers, anything they can get their hands on. Their first stop was the house we rescued Kaycee from. They plastered pictures of the dingy torture rooms all over the news outlets and online. Part of me thinks they want the public to know the extent of what took place and how bad it was. No one will defend the scumbags who took children away from their families, tortured them for money, and forged suicide on their death certificates.

Reporters descended on East Point Bluff like rabid

zombies, looking for someone to bite. Only they didn't want to bite into a human. No—they wanted to bite into a juicy story. And we're the juicy story they've been waiting for.

From an outsider's perspective, it is a juicy story. It's not every day you hear a grown man got arrested for recruiting high schoolers to commit torture and murder with him to make millions of dollars with his brothers. Since his arrest, Shaw's sang like a bird, telling investigators everything they wanted to hear. Well, from what we've been told, anyway. Veritas hasn't been forthcoming with their information on what they've found. If Kaycee were awake, we'd have broken into their database already and watched his confession tapes. Of course, after seeing the love of my life's face and stab wound, I want to stay ignorant of the whole situation.

Much to our surprise, Shaw even implicated more officials from around town. The mayor, coroner, sheriff, and several state police officers have met the cold cells of justice in the past two weeks. Getting them thrown in jail is all fine and dandy because the streets of East Point Bluff needed a cleansing. The FBI has ripped every inch of this town up collecting evidence.

Thankfully, Shaw couldn't talk himself out of this situation or pay anyone to help him. Every asset he owns and every cent in his bank account is now in the hands of the FBI. Shaw was once a multi-millionaire from the murders he orchestrated, and now he's a penniless felon rotting away in jail. He'll never see the light of day, and that's all we could ask for.

Reporters have also moved in front of the hospital, camping out on the lawn and in the parking lot. The hospital staff has called the police on multiple occasions to get them under control. The sneaky reporters have tried it all, whether it's sneaking into the hospital trying to get a glimpse of us or getting information from our doctors. We're called 'The Surviving Five.' Hailed as heroes after saving our girl from the clutches of psychopaths while putting ourselves into harm's way.

"The vultures are still outside." Chase winces, moving the long red curtain back into place. He carefully sits back in his seat, setting his unbandaged elbow on the tiny round table between him and Seger.

Chase's recovery has been a lot faster than expected. He spent two days in intensive care and three in a standard room, and then they released him. Probably for the best, Chase was climbing the walls and yelling at anyone who would listen to him whine. Every time his doctor came out of his room, I swear he had aged ten years and grayed his hair.

Chase's burns weren't all second-degree like they initially suspected. He turned out okay despite walking through gasoline-soaked flames that covered every inch of our old home. He's a damn miracle. Several first-degree burns redden most of his left side, leaving painful swelling in its wake. Large blisters due to his second-degree burns line his arm and the left side of his abdomen and chest. So, having him walking around and talking normally is a damn miracle. His recovery baffles the doctors, claiming he should have been in the burn unit for weeks to work out his injuries. But he hasn't. Chase keeps his head held high and refuses to fall apart in anticipation of when Kaycee needs us. He may have gauze on his arms, stomach, and legs, but he's keeping a positive outlook on everything, unlike the old Chase.

"I don't think they'll ever leave," Seger grumbles, looking over his playing cards. "Got a four?" He asks Chase, raising a brow.

"Go fish, cocksucker," he sniggers.

Seger begrudgingly reaches into the pile for more cards with a scowl permanently fixed on his face. His hand overflows with cards, yet he still hasn't found a match. Half of me thinks Chase messed with the game to screw with him. Well, more than half. The way Chase's face lights up as Seger scowls more at the cards clues me in.

I smirk, pivoting back to the small TV mounted on the wall, and rub my chin. Images of East Point Bluff scroll across the screen again, highlighting the deceit of our lovely town for the millionth time.

The newscasters speculate about how all of this happened and for how long, going off on long tangents about the corrupt elite who run this town and what their crimes were. Murder. Violent acts. Abuse of a corpse. Corruption. Embezzlement. Illegal websites. And the list of their crimes goes on and on.

I shake my head. They've plastered this scandal on every news station, even globally. The day after Veritas saved our asses ten minutes too late, word spread like wildfire and only grew from there. First, reporters showed up for the FBI investigation outside East Point Prep. And then they camped out for the first glimpse of the press release. And now, they won't leave, especially since we're here.

Once they found out five students were involved somehow and brought the entire operation to its knees, they started stalking us. Day in and day out, Seger and I have had to watch our backs. But not only our backs, we also had to take care of our family lying helpless in the hospital. Two of them couldn't defend themselves. We've checked in on Carter, Chase, and Kaycee, making sure no one had snuck in to take pictures. Because, yeah—it almost happened. Thankfully, Mr. Cole was there to grab the reporter by the scruff of their collar and drag them out, cursing them every which way to Sunday and threatening them.

"Mr. Cunningham!" shouts a nurse from down the hall, earning a growl from the man himself.

I snort, darting my eyes toward the door. It's been the same thing every day since he woke up. They should have strapped him down to the rails to deter him from making a break for it every chance. But I'm sure he'd still find a way to chew through the straps if they did. Nothing has stopped him from coming in here and watching her rest with an eagle's protective eye. No matter how exhausted he is, he pushes through it and doesn't stop until Mrs. Cole forces him back to bed every night. It's the same routine day in and day out, so I'm not quite sure why the nurse continues to yell at him. They all know by now that he won't stay in his room, and they'll rejoice the day he gets discharged and probably throw a massive party.

I bark a laugh when Carter stumbles into the room with his hospital gown wide open at the back and a colorless face. He grunts breathlessly, leaning against his IV stand on wheels, gasping for air like he just broke out of his prison cell.

"Dude, did you forget your boxers again?" Chase asks mockingly, pointing toward his open gown before staring at his playing cards.

Carter frowns in a panic. His eyes widen when he twists his body, looking down at his ass. Relief slumps his rigid body, and he growls when his eyes land on his ass, flipping Chase the bird. He mutters a few colorful words in Chase's direction while attempting to catch his breath.

Flashbacks of Carter's first time running down the hallway after he had escaped his room come to mind, and I snicker to myself. Much to his horror, he had forgotten his boxers, giving the entire nursing staff a view of his ass. We didn't blink an eye when he waltzed in, completely naked under his open hospital gown, but the hospital staff threw an enormous fit, pointing their fingers at him and lecturing him.

"No," he huffs breathlessly, "I didn't forget my damn boxers."

"Again," Chase prods in a sing-song voice.

"For fuck's sakes, Elf Ears, that was one time," Carter grumbles, stumbling over his feet when he takes a step forward, eyeing the couch with longing. I roll my eyes at his stubbornness, tossing my good arm around his shoulders, and I help him inside the room.

"Leave him alone. They doped him up on some super fucking good pain meds. Remember, he told us he loved us." Seger smirks, earning the middle finger from Carter, who shoves his face into his hand with an exasperated sigh. He more than likely regrets his decision of coming down here so soon.

"Whatever I said, I didn't fucking mean." A pain-filled groan slips from his lips when he lowers himself onto the tiny couch and slumps breathless again.

"You love us, Grumpy. It's okay," Chase sniggers, looking over his handful of cards.

Carter runs a hand down his pale face, huffing a breath. "You think if I make him disappear anyone will notice?" Carter murmurs to me as his eyes lock on Kaycee.

Her blonde hair lays like a halo around her head like an earthly angel suspended in limbo, waiting for the moment she can return. Throughout her coma, she twitched and whimpered, making us wonder what was going through her mind. We've had countless one-sided conversations with her, trying to reassure her it was all over. Her nightmare was done, and she did it. She exposed the people responsible for Magnolia's death. She won. We won. And more importantly, we survived to tell the tale.

"I heard that, shithead," Chase mutters, getting back to his very heated game of go fish.

"Mr. Cunningham!" A red-faced nurse huffs, storming into the room. She glares down at Carter like he's the devil's spawn. "You can't walk out of your room whenever you want! You're supposed to be resting." She points her finger at him, waggling it in his irritated face. "They shot you four times in the chest, Mr. Cunningham. You need to stay in bed!"

Carter's recovery has been a little more intense. He laid in bed unconscious for four whole days after his surgery, and we weren't sure if he was going to survive at all. Although the four bullets that went straight through his chest didn't bounce around inside of him, he still had extensive damage and significant blood loss. He had laid on the house floor for several minutes before he could escape. Since he woke up, he has wanted to be here in Kaycee's room every day, especially today, because today is the day. The day we've all been waiting for—the two-week mark.

"Eleanor," Chase says in a soft voice, gaining the nurse's attention.

Her hand drops from its position as she fully turns to Chase. Every ounce of anger leaves her face, and her whole body relaxes. She smiles at him, making googly eyes like he's a damn angel sent from God. I swear, no matter how young or old women are, he charms the pants off them with a single look. It never fails when he turns on the Benoit Charm.

"Today's the day," he says softly, walking across the room with a pained swagger.

She sighs, nodding her head. She casts Kaycee a sad look, eyes brimming with tears. "Fine," she says in a small voice. "But you boys make sure he stays put! He needs to rest if he ever wants to get out of here." With one last firm nod, she stomps out of the room with a huff and shuts the door behind her.

"Smooth, man," I say, sitting down next to Carter and running a hand down my face. I stare forward, looking over at our girl and taking her in.

Sometimes, I half expected her to shoot up from the hospital bed with a grin, telling me she is joking. That this whole situation didn't end like this, and she's okay. It's wishful thinking. It never happens, but I need something to grasp onto right now or I'll lose my damn mind.

The past two weeks have been literal hell for us. Since the Maze House burnt to a crisp, we've been dealing with insurance and trying to get our shit in order. Our only option has been to stay with our dad. And between coming here every day, waiting on Carter's injuries, and Chase's, we've been going out of our minds with worry. Seger and I have been here every day, checking on them, although Mrs. Cole has pushed us out a few times for showers and took us to get dinner. It's been an odd bonding experience for us and Kace's parents. Her dad seems to like us now, which is good because once she's awake and better, I'm never taking my eyes off her.

"You think she'll be okay?" Carter murmurs.

"After everything she's been through, I think she'll wake up and be okay. She's so tough." Or I hope she will be.

We will have to deal with the fallout of this whole situation, but eventually, we'll have to testify in court and tell the feds all the information we gathered. Not to mention the mental and physical traumas, too. When a person goes through something like she did, it stays with them their whole life. Kaycee was almost beaten to death and stabbed, and so much more that hasn't been said, but Carter refuses to tell us everything. I can only assume the rest of what she endured was something out of a nightmare. I didn't go through as much as her. I was shot and watched everyone around me fall, and I still have night terrors. When she gets out of her coma, I can't imagine what she will go through.

"Boys."

My neck snaps toward Mrs. Cole as she floats into the room like an angel with a warm and inviting smile.

"Oh, honey, what on earth are you doing out of bed again?" She clucks her tongue at Carter, moving around the room to greet us with a small hug. Carter grumbles something unintelligible at her, but his eyes light up at the sight of her. He can pretend all day long he doesn't like the motherly attention she gives him, but it'd be a lie. Whenever she hugs him or chastises him for being out of bed, a small smile tilts his lips in appreciation.

"Leave him be, Mercy," Mr. Cole grumbles, walking

behind her. He gives us each a nod, moving straight to Kaycee's bedside and placing a kiss on her temple.

Every day it's the same routine for Mr. Cole. He walks in behind his wife with a tight smile and greets us with a slight nod before he goes to her bedside, whispering loving words. He then settles in the chair beside her bedside and reads a book while holding her hand.

"Are you boys ready?" Mercy asks with a small but hopeful grin.

"Today is the day!" Chase beams, throws his playing cards down on the table face down, and stands.

"Dude! We weren't done yet." Seger protests, throwing his arms in the air. "I still had a chance to come back and win!" He gripes, but I know there is no way in Hell he could have won with all those cards in his hand.

Chase tilts his head, giving Seger a lop-sided grin. "Are you sure about that?"

Seger's eyes narrow on him, frowning. "This is Go Fish! There's no way you could have rigged it!" He huffs, jumping to his feet. Realization falls over his crestfallen face as he blinks at Chase. "Wait—you can't, right? It's the world's easiest game." He frowns, looking between the cards discarded on the table and Chase.

Chase snorts, shrugging in response without uttering a word. Turning his back, he walks to Kaycee's other side, holding her hand as Seger continues glaring daggers at his back.

"I'm never playing a game with that cheating bastard again," Seger mumbles, standing by the couch.

"Oscar Sanchez, Hadley Lacey, and Trent Gallagher." I whip my head toward the television as they speak their names and gape at the photos lining the screen.

Hadley looks disheveled, with eyeliner running down her crying face and smudging black everywhere. You can tell by the sight of her mugshot that she's been crying for hours, and probably trying to talk her way out of the situation, but sorry, Hadley, there's no way out of this one. Oscar scowls at the camera with a bloodied and bruised face. I smirk when Seger sniggers beside me, taking pride in the punishment he gave him. Trent manically grins at the camera like a true psychopath, only sporting one bruise near his ear from yours truly.

"All three have been arrested for their vicious roles in the beating and the attempted murder of Kaycee Cole, and the death of countless other victims."

My heart sinks at the sound of her name. *Again*. They've done so many reports on Kaycee, highlighting her life like she's some sort of local celebrity. Some stations hail her as the true hero, but they'll never know how far she went to bat for her best friend. Not even her parents know why she came to East Point, and I doubt they will. It's something we've kept tight lipped about around them.

"When will they stop?" Seger groans as pictures of us and her float across the screen with the words, 'Surviving Five,' scrolling below on a constant loop.

"Not for a while, boys." Mr. Cole says, sighing. "You are all celebrities right now. It'll die down in a few weeks, rise again when the press gets more answers, and then it'll flair up yet again when their trials come. You're in for the long haul now."

"Don't let him worry you, boys. We have an excellent team of PR people working for us to keep you all safe," Mercy says, coming up beside us. Her eyes gaze at the screen with a frown, and finally, she shakes her head.

The pictures of all of us continue, mostly from our Flash-Gram accounts. Picture after picture of our smiling faces hanging off each other, and they even snagged private images from the day we put Kaycee's bedroom together. We are all huddled on the bed with smiles on our faces—selfie-style.

Thankfully, we have clothes on and haven't taken compromising photos together.

"This sucks," Chase mumbles, watching the screen with narrowed eyes.

We stand like that for a few more minutes, listening to the same reports over and over again. Sighing as our faces cross the screen again and then back to the brunette reporter standing in front of East Point Prep, still crawling with activity.

"Yes," she says into the microphone with a nod. "All students enrolled in East Point are now subjected to temporary virtual learning. No one is allowed in the buildings or on campus until the FBI can conduct its investigations. Everything is fairly tight-lipped at the moment. We presume everyone is a suspect at this time, including faculty and the student body."

"Ugh, turn it off! I don't even want to think about that virtual crap they have us doing," Chase groans, moving to sit by Carter, who by now is slumped over and snoring. The more rest he gets, the more color returns to his cheeks, and he looks better every day.

He blames himself for this entire situation. For Kaycee getting hurt under his nose and us getting shot and burned. He explained everything to us when he woke up with tears dripping down his cheeks. It's something we've never seen from him before. The three of us had a nice long discussion with him and reassured him we would have done the same if we were in his shoes. I know he'll live with the guilt for years to come because so will we. We all had a part in losing her that night, but we can't let it eat us alive.

"How is everyone doing this afternoon?" My heart rate spikes at the sight of her doctor walking through the door, several nurses trailing behind him.

Mrs. Cole smiles at him, shaking his hand. "Doing well today, Dr. Hana. We are all looking forward to Kaycee waking up." Dr. Hana grins, running his fingers through his thick black hair.

"Well then, I've got amazing news for all of you. As you know, we've been monitoring Kaycee's brain waves and her overall healing. Everything has gone according to plan. Her MRI shows decreased brain swelling, and her stab wound has healed wonderfully! Are you all ready?" His brown eyes meet each of our eyes as we nod in unison.

Dr. Hana nods at the two nurses standing beside Kaycee's bed, awaiting his instructions. The moment he nods his head, they inject something into her IV. We collectively hold our breaths as it mixes with her IV fluids and presumably goes into her veins, ready to start the wake-up process.

Hope blooms in my belly as we watch and wait for any sign of life.

"Now, we have started the slow process of waking her up. She may wake up in an hour, or she may wake up in twenty-four hours. Each patient is different. But she will come back sometime soon." he says with confidence, staring at his patient.

He exchanges a few more private words with her parents, shakes their hands, nods us goodbye, and slips out of the room. Leaving us all to stare at Kaycee's unmoving body with hope burning desperately in our eyes.

---

THE SUN GOES DOWN, plummeting the room into a comfortable darkness. No longer do the hospital hallways give me the creeps and make me want to run. I've been here for two weeks straight, and I'm finally used to all the extra noises. Even if the memories of my mother's death play on a constant loop in my head. This was the hospital she came to for help and the same hospital she perished in. I sigh, running a hand down my tired face. We've sat beside Kaycee's bedside on pins and needles, watching for the slightest movements. An hour turned into two, and two turned into six, with no such luck. We knew the wait would be long, and we were prepared, but we secretly hoped she'd wake up sooner than later. You never realize how long two weeks are until you count down the days.

An hour ago, at the request of the head nurse, Chase helped Carter back to his room, staying there to keep the grump company while he suffered in limbo down the hall. Since the moment he woke up, he's been in one hell of a mood. I'm sure once Kaycee wakes up and shows him she's okay and doesn't blame him for a damn thing, he'll stop climbing the walls.

> Me: Still nothing yet.

I stare at my phone in the boys only group chat and sigh. They must have passed out down the hall because no one answers. I take a peek at Seger, who passed out on the couch over an hour ago with his arms crossed over his chest and his loud snores filling the room. I shake my head and snort. He complains about my snores and sleep murmurs all the time. He'd grumble and flip me off if he could only see himself now.

Kaycee's parents took off searching for dinner in the cafeteria, promising to return soon with food for us. They begged us to accompany them and eat, but we politely declined. The moment disappointment clouded Mrs. Cole's eyes, I felt terrible, but I can't physically leave this room knowing she will wake soon, and I can't let her be alone. There's a gravitational pull keeping me here, and I want to be the first person she sees when she wakes from her two-week slumber. I can only imagine the confusion she'll feel when she peels her eyes open and realizes she's in the hospital with a tube down her throat and with multiple injuries bruising her body. So, I sit in the chair beside her bed, staring at her like a creep, waiting for any sign she's awake.

Faint yellow and black bruises line her face and body from fighting for her life. My gut churns at the constant reminder of what they did to her. Soon, though, the bruises will fade, and her injuries will heal. We'll be here for her every step of the way

Drifting my finger over her cheek, I trace the faint freckles popping through the bruises. I trace over the tape holding the tube in her mouth and continue the journey down her chin.

"You're going to wake up soon, baby girl," I whisper in a command, hoping to coax her out of her coma. Leaning in, I plant my lips against her cheek and linger for longer than necessary. I ache to feel her in my arms once again. "We've missed you so much. You're our glue." My voice catches when I admit what she is to us, and I close my eyes and count to ten. Tears fall freely down my face, falling to the blanket covering her body, but I can't hold the words back any longer. I'd drop to my knees and beg God to take me instead and bring Kaycee back if I thought it would do me any good. "Without you, we are shattering into pieces. Please wake up. Please come back to us," I beg with all I have, hoping her mind hears my pleas and lets her return to us sooner than later. I know it's silly, but I need her now. I need to know she will wake up and come back to us.

Leaning my forehead down on the bed, I take several deep breaths through my nose and out through my mouth. Two weeks without hearing her voice or seeing her beautiful eyes on us. Two entire weeks without her here with us. I miss her smile. I even miss the way her mind drifts off mid-sentence. I just miss her so damn much that my entire body aches to have her back here with us. Mind. Body. And soul. This whole time, I've kept myself together with safety pins and thin pieces of thread. It was for everyone else's sake that I stayed strong so that they could fall apart. As the clock ticks and the days go by, it's getting harder and harder to keep my tears at bay.

Deep in my heart, I know she'll wake up soon. Once she does, our nightmare won't be over. It'll keep coming back to us repeatedly through dreams and memories. It's pieces of our history we can't erase, much to our dismay. We'd erase our tragedy entirely if it were up to us, only leaving the good times. If only....

I snuggle into the blanket under my cheek and take a deep breath. My mind wanders to dangerous places, but finally, sleep takes hold of me and pulls me under into a dreamless rest of nothingness.

My body jolts awake, awareness coming back to me. A shaky breath rolls through me when the feeling of a small hand runs through the longer strands of my hair, twirling between their fingers. I suck in a breath and slowly lift my head. There, staring back at me, are the eyes of the girl I've been desperate to hold in my arms.

"Kaycee," I whisper, grasping her hand in mine. I run my lips along her knuckles, kissing every inch I can. She gives me a small, tired smile, nodding her head. "I've missed you so damn much," I murmur, resting my forehead against hers.

"I didn't want to wake you," she says through a heavy rasp, making me realize the tube down her throat had disappeared. Jesus, I must have slept through the nurses coming to take them out. I slept through her parents probably celebrating and crying that Kaycee was awake. And all the while, I was laying here, dead to the world in a dreamless sleep, as they worked around me.

"You should have." Tears burn down my cheeks. "Seriously, baby girl, I've been waiting for this moment to see those eyes again." A tired smile blooms across her lips. She runs a finger down my cheek, brushing away my stray tears.

"What happened?" She whispers, imploring me with her curious eyes. She looks at the sling, holding my arm up with quivering lips. "Is Carter okay? Is Seger? Chase?" She asks in rapid fire as worry clogs her raspy throat.

I gulp air, squeezing her hand. "Everyone's okay. A little hurt, but we are all okay. We were so worried about you—" My eyes close on their own as I catch my breath.

"They stabbed me," she whispers in a frantic voice, like it's all coming back to her. Tears pool in her eyes, falling over the edge, and cascade down her puffy, red cheeks.

Wiping away her tears, I nod. "Yeah, but we won," I whisper, kissing the tip of her nose. "Shaw's in jail, and the other two are dead." Her eyes widen at the mention of his name and the fate of the other two.

"Dead? How?" she whispers, face falling with uncertainty.

"That's not important right now," I whisper, running my thumb along her cheek again. "We'll get to that when you're better, I promise. Just know, we've all been waiting here like lost little puppy dogs." She snorts a breath, rolling her eyes.

"My lost little puppy dogs," she says again, wincing at the pain in her throat. Reaching over, I grab her large cup of water and place the straw in her mouth. She hums in approval, wincing when the cool liquid grazes over her swollen throat.

"We'll be any-fucking-thing you want us to be," Seger says, rushing forward towards the bed.

His lips brush against her other temple, and his entire body shakes with the emotions we've kept locked tight. Tears leak out of his eyes, dripping down his chin and onto the covers.

"If I dressed you in kilts with bagpipes?" She teases, setting back to look into his eyes.

"Angel, I'll wear it the proper way. Anything for you," he says through a pained whisper, clasping her other hand into his. He holds onto her like she might slip away again.

"From here on out, we are going to be very protective assholes," I whisper, earning another eye roll.

"You were already protective assholes," she retorts with a tired smile.

And just like that, we are back to how it used to be. It's like she never slept for two weeks, leaving us on the edge of a cliff without air. We've been breathless, sitting on pins and needles, waiting for this moment.

"Where are Chase and Carter?" She asks, narrowing her eyes at us.

"They're in Carter's room. He's just down the hall," I say, nodding my head toward his room.

"Okay," she says, pulling away from us. With shaking hands, she pulls the covers from her body and attempts to sit up with a weakened groan.

"Woah, woah, woah." I stop her momentum, trying to gently lay her back down. "What are you doing?" Ignoring my attempts, she sits back up and reaches into her gown to start removing the wire leads connected to her heart monitor. Fortunately, they muted the monitor earlier, so it doesn't scream when it thinks she has flatlined, but the singular line scrolls across the screen. I rub my temple when she stares at me with those big, pleading eyes, begging me to do as she says. At any second I expect the nurses to barge into the room with the crash cart, screaming to move out of the way. I imagine they monitor every patient at the nurse's station and Kaycee is no exception.

"Take me to them," she demands in a raspy voice and cocks her weak head to the side. Every movement is shaky at best, and at this point, she'd crawl to get to Carter, no matter what.

"Fuck, Angel, you just got out of a coma. I don't think it's a good idea to steal you out of your hospital bed." Seger grumbles, running a hand down his face. "When your parents, brother, and sister come back from coffee and see you fucking missing, they're going to fucking flip and think you're kidnapped again or something." He blows out a breath, shaking his head like he's about to protest, but then he looks at her again. I see the moment his resolve melts away, and he's about to give into her every whim.

She blinks a few times, raising her arms. "Either you carry me to the other two, or I will attempt to walk." Her chin raises in defiance, and we sigh in unison.

"Stubborn fucking woman," Seger groans, looking around again. He points at the door with a determined look in his eyes. "You distract the damn nurses with whatever charm you have, and I'll carry our pretty little princess to the rest of her princes." He points toward the hall, making me huff.

"I have charm, you dick," I mumble, flipping him the bird.

"No, I was born with the charm. You were born with the brains." He snorts at his joke, lifting Kaycee into his arms. They untangle all the other lines, grab her IV bag, and walk toward the exit.

I guess it's time to charm some nurses.

# THIRTY-FOUR

## KAYCEE

This is awkward. Like—really awkward. The need to see Carter and Chase overrides every rational thought. So, here I sit, nestled in Seger's warm arms, carrying my own pee bag. Yeah—my pee bag is still attached to me. The doctors said I wouldn't walk properly until I got into physical therapy, and even then, I'd walk with a walker until I got my strength back. It's something no one talks about after a coma. You can't just go back to everyday life and think it will be normal again. So, here I ride in the arms of my brave chariot, taking me to see my other boyfriends, who do not know I'm awake yet.

I wrinkle my nose, staring down at the clear offending bag in my lap. Make it purple or give it a sweater or something to hide the massive amounts of my urine just sloshing around all willy nilly. Granted, I can't help it. Thanks to my injuries, I needed to go to sleep for two weeks. Despite that, a little discretion never hurt anybody.

I peer up at Seger through my lashes, noting the determination on his tight face. He didn't bat an eye when he scooped me into his arms, retrieved my pee bag like it was a purse, and snuck out into the hall. It must be true love if he can handle my pee bag and a broken girlfriend.

Thanks to my amazing coma vacation, I barely remember

a damn thing about my hospital experience. Needles and me? Yeah, we don't mix. The last time they stuck me, I passed out. Scared the crap out of the helpless techs, so I'm thankful the last memory I have from the nightmare house is Carter's whispered confession. But anything after that? Yeah, it's a black hole in my memories. Half of me thinks I don't want to remember how I got from the decrepit house with a knife sticking out of my stomach to lying in a hospital bed with my family anxiously awaiting my reboot. For now, I'll chalk it up to memory loss and move on. I already have a shit ton of horrible memories floating around in my head from my time in the clutches of the evil bad guys.

I close my eyes, thinking of the happiest confession that came from the lips of the man who swore he'd never say them. *I love you. I'm so fucking sorry I wasn't able to say it, but I've known for a long time.* When the wicked nightmares come, because I know they will, I'll latch onto these words and bleed them dry to get myself through the worst times ahead. I was drowned, beaten, had a fingernail removed, and was stabbed by three psychos hell-bent on making money from my demise. All the while, my boyfriend had to pretend to enjoy my misery while counting down the seconds until he could get me out of there. So, yeah. I will have some mental distress and need a fucking therapist to survive the rest of my life.

No one will utter a damn word about the extent of Carter's injuries. Believe me, I've asked multiple times, and their response is always the same. My mom side-eyed my dad with her lips rolled in and tears on her cheeks. And he squeezed my shoulder with love and told me Carter was fine and in a room down the way. Listen, I may have been in a coma for two weeks, and I may have been left for dead in a disgusting house with assholes who have taunted me for the last few months, but I'm not a fragile doll. I don't need to be coddled and doted on—though it's lovely—I just need some damn answers. And I need them now before I claw someone's eyes out for holding back.

"Why is Carter in the hospital? Did he do something for me?" I mumble, keeping my eyes on Zepp as he stands near the nurse's station with a smirk.

Seger heaves a breath, tightening his fingers on me, and pulls me closer to his rumbling chest. "Angel," he pleads in a soft voice. I almost falter when his warm green eyes stare down at me with concern—almost. But this woman never backs down when it comes to the boys she loves, especially if one of them is in the hospital because of me.

"Seger," I mock through a hiss. "I need to know what you're taking me to." I beg—I fucking beg—because I need to know what we're walking into. Is he in a coma, too? Will he wake up any time soon? The need to know is drowning anything else out, and his safety, Chase's safety, and the twins' safety are at the forefront of my mind, begging me for answers. "I need to know if he's okay," I whisper with burning tears filling my eyes. And it must do the trick because he curses under his breath and rolls his eyes toward the ceiling like I'm way too much for someone who just woke up.

Bingo! One for Kaycee, zero for Seger's secret-keeping ass.

Pursing his lips, indecision crosses his face. He gives in with one last little huff when we stand outside a closed door. "They shot him in the chest four times."

Someone punches me square in the chest, knocking the breaths from my lungs. I suck in a sharp breath, nearly gasping from the news. Colors swirl before my eyes, blending with the tears filling my eyes again and spilling over. Soon, the world is nothing but a blur before my eyes.

"He's okay, Angel. He was damn determined to come back to you, and he did. You won't believe how often he's snuck out of his room to sit with you and forgot his damn boxers. We couldn't keep him down or away. He's fine," he mutters with darting eyes, checking the hallway for any doctors or rogue nurses wandering the halls. Thankfully, it's the middle of the night, and almost all activity has ceased. *But wait, did he say he forgot his damn boxers?*

Tears fall from my eyes when a memory slams into me out of nowhere. A familiar voice rings through my mind repeatedly, letting me know Seger's words are true. Carter snuck out and spoke to me while I rested, and his words came through even though I was fast asleep and healing.

*"It's just you and me, Sweetheart. The others are grabbing dinner. I think your dad finally likes me—all of us." He laughs softly, squeezing my hand in his. The pad of his thumb lightly brushes over the top of my hand. "When we leave here, I'm never leaving your side. Wherever you go, I go. I can run CC Tech from anywhere. I love you, Kaycee Cole." His voice wavers and heavy emotions clog his throat.*

*"I love you, too," I whisper in my mind, wanting to lean into his warmth and reassure him I'm here forever.*

Reality rushes back to me, and the moment between past Carter and me passes in a flash. It's strange to remember whispered words, spoken to someone they assumed couldn't hear because they were down and out. No one tells you what you can listen to, feel, and absorb when you're in a deep coma. Every word. Every breath. Every confession. It's all there in the back of my mind, their sweet whispers of love and encouragement. Their tears spilled when they held my hand, begging me to heal and come back to them.

Seger sighs, pulling me out of the memories flooding back. He adjusts me against him, looking around one last time, and opens the silent door. I swallow hard when the room's darkness swallows us whole once the door shuts and the hallway light evaporates. The moonlight leaks through a crack in the curtain, streaking light on a hospital bed in the center of the room. A large lump lays curled up under blankets. I squint my eyes, trying to get a better view, but I can't break through the shadows engulfing the room.

My soul sags with relief when two distinct, soft snores greet us from within. I smile, relaxing in his arms at the sound of their breaths. Their breaths blow into the air like a melody I haven't listened to in so long. My mind rejoices in their symphony. A heaviness takes my eyelids prisoner, drooping with heavy exhaustion. Since before the Christmas Charity event—hell—before Thanksgiving break, we've slept side-by-side in each other's arms in the warmth of our gigantic bed.

He walks in on his tippy toes, carefully navigating us around the darkness. We come to our first stop in front of my blonde lump, snoring on the tiny loveseat shoved into the corner of the room. His knees curl into his bare chest, barely fitting on the tiny couch built for sitting, not housing a six-foot muscular football player. A blanket lays across his curled-up legs, and a small, flat hospital pillow rests beneath his head. His muscular arms clutch to the pillow, hugging it against his scrunched-up face. A groan slips from between his lips, and his body jerks like he's reliving a nightmare. Bandages stick to his arms and side, reminding me of what my parents told me.

*"Chase is fine, but he has some burns," my mother said grimly. "The house is gone, baby. There was a suspicious fire, and Chase was inside. By some damn miracle, he's not more injured. I think someone was watching over him that night." Tears streamed down her face when she told me in more detail what had happened.*

"Aww! Ain't he precious, Angel?" Chuckles rumble through Seger's chest as we stare down at Chase. His brows scrunch in his sleep, almost as if he detects us hovering above him, but then he turns over, readjusting his position on the couch.

A watery smile crosses my lips as my eyes memorize the curve of his high cheekbones and jaw. His blonde hair is unkempt, sticking up all over his head with grease coating his longer strands, telling me he hasn't been taking care of himself today or yesterday, or possibly the day before that. Tears burn my eyes again when he scrunches his nose, and his softly spoken words come rushing back to me.

*"I miss you so much, Sunshine. You should have seen it. I walked through fire. I shit you not. I have battle scars for you, and I don't regret a thing," Chase whispers beside my bed, clinging to my hand, his lips pressing into every knuckle. "I," he starts in a soft voice, emotions crackling. "I'm not doing okay, Kace. My mind is devouring itself, and it's throwing me into a pit of darkness, and you're not here to lure me out. I'm trying, at least, really trying. Shit. I started talking to a therapist. I think—I think it'll help, and it has a bit. Talking about you, my mom, my dad, and everything in between is helping. So, yeah, that's what's new with me." He kisses my temple one last time, lingering against my skin. Noise from the other boys filters through the room, pulling him away.*

"Has he been okay?" I whisper, continuing to stare at him. Every bone in my body wants to curl up beside him and cuddle, but my body isn't cooperating with me anymore. I try to lift my arm, but the adrenaline must have worn off, and everything is crashing. And all I want to do is go back to bed and sleep for another eight hours to wake up again and be with my family—my boys, my parents, and my siblings.

Seger nods. "He's stronger than I've ever seen him. You'd be so proud of him, Angel. He, his dad, and Ainsley talked to a therapist together. They put him on some new meds and a new schedule. He's been trying so hard these past few weeks, even though he wants to curl into a fucking ball and not exist." My heart swells at the news of Chase and his family getting the mental help they need after this catastrophic bullshit of events. It's bad enough his father, Tate, went to jail and suffered for crimes he didn't commit. But to live after walking through fire, sustaining burns, and battling depression—he's doing so well.

Seger kisses my temple and pulls us away from Chase's sleeping form, bringing me to the other man in my life.

"He's been fucking grumpy lately," Seger murmurs, adjusting his hold on me with a grunt.

I breathe a deep sigh of relief at the sight of Carter sleeping on his side. His arm rests beneath the pillow. Deep even breaths rock through his chest, with the occasional grizzly bear snore escaping from his parted lips. My eyes roam the slope of his nose, which obviously had been broken at some point in his life, and the sharp curve of his jaw dotting with a red-tinted stubble. I suck in a breath, tears burning the backs of my eyes at the multitude of bruises lining his chest. Black, blue, purple, and yellow bruises color the right side of his bare chest. Tears spill over onto my cheeks, and I shake my head in disbelief. How could they? How could they do that to him? My brave Carter took four bullets to the chest, and here he sits—alive and well.

Exhaustion sweeps through me, taking every ounce of energy I have. I slump in Seger's arms, and a yawn forces its way through me. I take a deep breath, snuggling into his warm chest, wanting to stay there forever. The comforting scent of his manly body wash relaxes me more. My eyes close on their own, and my breaths even out.

"Here," Seger mumbles, shifting me onto the bed as the cool hospital sheet scratches my skin. "Lay with him, make his fucking night. Then maybe he won't be such an asshole." He smiles through his entire speech, pulling the discarded sheet at the end of the bed to mine and Carter's chins.

Carter murmurs something in his sleep, snuggling into his pillow. A warm hand reaches for me from under the cover, curling his fingers around mine. A small smile pulls at my lips at the sight of him, and with one last deep breath, my heavy eyes finally shut for good. Seger kisses my forehead, mumbling something about finding a chair to sleep in. His footsteps retreat, and a chair quietly glides across the linoleum. Finally, silence engulfs us, taking me away back into a darkened dreamland full of nightmares, waiting to greet me like an old friend.

# THIRTY-FIVE

## KAYCEE

I SIGH, snuggling into the heat wrapping around me. Warm kisses press into my hair, and hands hold tight to my waist. Another warmth groans behind me, dusting kisses on the back of my neck. Butterflies take flight in my belly at their affections. Sunlight pours in through the windows, erasing the darkness from before.

"You should have fucking woken me up," Carter's gruff voice hisses.

"I thought you'd be less grumpy," Seger whines from across the room with his voice drenched in sleep like he just woke up. A smile burst from my lips, envisioning Seger right now. He's probably leaned back in a chair with his arm over his eyes and his legs spread wide.

"Calm down, Grumpy," Chase murmurs into my hair, pressing himself into my back. "She's here now."

They hold me tight, wrapping their arms and legs around me. I barely have room to wiggle around, but I wouldn't have it any other way. Their warmth is my home, and their hearts are mine. And I am theirs—always and forever.

"I wonder how people in monogamous relationships survive," I mutter. "They never get to enjoy these warm sandwiches. How do they only have one partner? One dick?" I nearly gasp in horror. The feel of their bodies squishing into me feels too good, too warm to want to ever go back to one man. Why have one when I can have four?

Chase snorts into my hair as I process the horror of one dick for life. At least I have variety. Baseball bat, pierced, hearty, orgasm-inducing, and so many more delicious adjectives that would take me way too long to list.

"And she's back," Chase mutters in awe, leaving a lingering kiss on my temple. "I missed your voice, Sunshine. And that random brain of yours." He taps the side of my head with his finger.

"Missed you, too," I say in a small voice, gnawing on my bottom lip. "Are you guys okay?"

"We're fine." Carter swallows hard. "Now," he adds in a whisper.

Opening my eyes, I find his beautiful brown eyes staring at me. Gloss forms over them, filling with tears as one spills over the edge, traveling down his cheek. Leaning in, I kiss it away, letting the droplet wet my lips.

He examines me, fingers softly running down my face. "We are fine," he says with a slight nod, placing his forehead against mine. A deep breath rocks through his chest, and a small tremor forces its way through him.

"You're fine, he's fine, we are all fine," Seger says through a chant. "Now, you two need to heal so that we can leave. This hospital gives me the heebie-jeebies." I peek over at him in a small chair in the corner. He fake shudders with his arms over his chest and his eyes closed, not bothering to look at us.

"What happened to East Point? The others?" I gulp, settling my gaze back to Carter, staring deep into his expressive eyes. "Do we have to go back?" I ask, my breaths coming out in labored pants.

Shit. I can't go back there. I can't manage to walk through those halls knowing those assholes watched and planned everything in a secret house at the back of campus. Fuck. Panic bursts to life inside my chest, tightening my lungs like rubber bands, constricting my airflow. Images of my torture flash through my mind. The fish tank, the beating, the stabbing, and their sneering faces staring down at me. I gasp when two hands grip my cheeks.

"Look at me," Carter demands, holding my face in his palms. "Really fucking look into my eyes," he growls, pressing his nose against mine and forcing me to stare.

"We never have to go back, Sunshine. East Point is done for. The entire place is a crime scene." Chase's fingers brush my skin, working up and down my arm gently. Goosebumps erupt all over my flesh, and their words soothe away some of the panic churning in my gut. My stomach knots at the thought, but I focus on the deep abyss of brown staring at me with concern flashing through them.

"You're never going back there, and we are never leaving your side. Got it?" Carter grits out, demanding my attention.

"Now breathe, Angel." Seger materializes above me, running his fingers through my hair. I nod as the three of them help me count out loud. The more numbers I say, the better my breathing becomes, and finally, air flows freely into my lungs.

My muscles sag in their embrace, finally feeling at ease with the fact East Point is no more. But new anxiety settles in. What will happen when I have to go back home instead of on campus, and they go home, too? I swallow hard, shaking my head. I need to focus on the here and now. I will deal with everything else when the time comes. For all I know, I could be in the hospital for another month. Plus, I don't think the boys would let our relationship fall away because of a three-hour drive.

I jump when the door to the room bursts open and then closes with a bang. Zepp rushes forward, heaving frantic breaths, and panic takes over his eyes. "You have like two seconds before an army of angry nurses rushes in here," Zepp pants, pointing toward the hallway like nurses were hot on his heels. Walking over to the bed, he quickly pecks my forehead in greeting. "Good morning, baby girl," he murmurs, giving me a small smile before we're interrupted.

The door crashes open again, hitting the wall with a thud before a slew of angry nurses with scowls and wagging fingers descend into the room in a flurry.

"You two!" One nurse shouts at the twins, waggling her finger between them. "I should revoke your visiting rights. You kidnapped a patient and moved her. You could have injured her," she hisses through her teeth, and a redness takes over her cheeks. She looks like she's two seconds away from blowing her head off with all the angry steam building up inside of her. I cock my head. Huh, it might come out of her ears like in the cartoons.

I take a deep breath as Chase's warmth disappears. He kisses my temple, moving away from the screaming nurses, and backs away with caution. Carter grunts at my side when the nurses extract me from the bed and place me in a wheelchair, and I look back at his furrowed brows. I know the moment I'm back in my room, they'll have a hard time keeping him in his. The nurses yap on, lecturing me about the dangers of getting out of bed like that, stating that I just woke up from a coma, and I can't pull stunts like that to endanger my well-being. I let them lecture but ignore their angry rants about my boys being menaces to the hospital. They're not menaces, they're simply caring for me and making sure my mental health is a top priority. Sure, I could have seen Chase and Carter when they found out I was awake and rushed to be by my side. But me and patience? Yeah, I don't have any of those. So, screw the nurses and their mean bushy eyebrows.

Once the nurses deem I'm fit, and in perfect condition, they leave me with one warning; If I, for any reason, get out of bed again without permission, they're putting a fall risk monitor on my mattress, and any time I move, a siren will sound. They also threatened to strap me to the bed with restraints and even put it in my damn chart. Talk about overreacting to a situation that doesn't call for that. But I vow to be a good girl, and I stay put, letting my guys come to me.

For the next two weeks, I live in the hospital. The boys stay with me, too, entertaining me when they can. My dad smoothed over the whole "Kaycee got kidnapped by her boyfriends" thing, and they were allowed back in with heavy stipulations. The nurses watch my room like a hawk every night, ensuring I stay put and don't sneak out. But they conveniently turn a blind eye when Carter sneaks in and lays with me until the sun rises, then makes his way back to his room. By the end of the week, on Friday, they released Carter with strict instructions. The nurses almost looked relieved when they discharged him and then frowned again when he stayed by my bedside, day in and day out. When they urged him to leave because visiting hours were over—he flat out refused.

The following Monday, my doctors cleared me for activities. My concussion and brain swelling had gone, but there were some lingering dizzy spells I had to contend with. Other than that, my broken arm from our previous accident was healed entirely and no longer needed a cast, my bruises were fading from my face, and my poor fingernail slowly grew back. Every night Carter kisses my wounds and thanks me for forgiving him—which he didn't need to. He's proving himself, repeatedly, by being here and being present.

After being cleared by the doctors, they put me into physical therapy to relearn to walk, which is surprisingly hard. Who knew laying down for so long could shrink and weaken my muscles so much. It's hard and grueling, but I'm more than determined to strengthen my body back to what it was before the coma. Even the weight comes back as my guys sneak cupcakes and other sweets into my room to appease me.

Before I know it, two weeks pass, and I am finally being discharged. "Are you ready to go home?" My dad asks, steering my wheelchair out the back of the hospital, away from prying eyes. The hum of the crazy news crews hammering questions outside the front of the hospital echoes back here in the quiet, private employee entrance.

I swallow hard. Home—home—not my home at East Point with the boys. My actual home with my parents. It's a few hours away from here, away from the boys who still live in the city. It's near the end of January, so we still have virtual schooling and graduation. Summer and freedom are months away, and we still have responsibilities before we can all be together in one place.

"Yeah," I murmur with reluctance, catching his eye. He gives me a knowing look but says nothing else when I get lost in my thoughts and drown a little.

The twins have to stay in town for their father, whose health is declining at a rapid rate. He's still escaping from the house and wandering their property before the nurse notices or can find him. His dementia is settling in quicker than they had expected, and they want to be there for him since his wife took off with their little brother to who knows where. They've tried to track her down and make her take responsibility for the husband she "loved" so dearly, but they've only been met with divorce papers demanding a twenty million dollar payout. Despite their hate for her, they obliged and sent the money out to her, effectively ending her time in their life.

Chase has to stay with his dad and Ainsley as they navigate a new life together. Tate could get back his company, but his name is still being run through the mud, even with the FBI's support saying he did nothing wrong, and it was all a big scam. Thankfully, his money and assets were returned to him, so they had a place to go and money to help them survive until their next steps.

And Carter? My big grumpy man has rented an apartment in my hometown and vows to be at my side whenever I need him. He says he can run his company from anywhere around the world and that they don't need him in person. So, at least one of my boys will be within walking distance when I need him.

Since becoming an item, the five of us haven't parted from one another for more than a few hours, except for Chase when he went to Louisiana. That twisted my gut and made my anxiety a shitshow until he was back in my arms. I've had them around me for months, by my side, protecting me and loving me. My heroes. My home. My everything. And now I have to function without three of them nearby. My insides twist into knots. God, I hate drastic change, and this one is monumental. It's disrupting everything, but I have to live with it. I have to learn to function without them in arm's reach until we can all go to college together.

The bright afternoon sun greets me when we finally leave through the back doors of the hospital and make our way toward the boys huddling together near their vehicles. Thickening anxiety coats the air, making it impossible to breathe when we approach my boys, who stand in a semi-circle in front of their cars. Their eyes burn holes into the ground but look up at me when we approach.

"Come on, kiddo," my dad murmurs, offering a hand and pulling me onto my shaky legs.

I grunt, leaning entirely on my father, who happily wraps his arms around me. He kisses my head, whispering reassurances about the future. He leans back, leaving me at arm's length, and nods once with a smirk, looking over my shoulder.

Chase barrels into the scene, standing beside us with my new walker in his hands. He places it on the ground as my father steps away, walking back to my mother, who cries into his chest when he embraces her.

Gently, Chase grabs my hands, balancing my weaving body, and guides my hands to the walker handles. "Aw, Sunshine, I seriously think he likes me now. Which is good because when I marry you, he won't protest." He grins, moving slowly with me.

"Marry me, huh?" I ask, looking up at the other three watching us.

Carter stands rigid with his hands in his pockets. Zepp and Seger stand side-by-side in a heated conversation. Seger's eyes light up at my sight, and he slaps his brother on the chest.

"You don't think we've talked about it?" Chase asks, bringing my attention back to his grinning face.

I raise a brow. "You have?"

He snorts at my bewildered look and waves me off. "Of course! From the moment we met you, we knew."

I've always said I'm not the marrying type. I never thought I wanted to be. A life with dogs or cats was what I imagined. But now? Now my future is full of laughs, love, and all four of them.

"This isn't the end," Zepp frowns, cupping my cheeks.

"No one fucking said it was," Seger gripes, elbowing his brother.

"It's just long-distance. It's not like she's moving to Canada or something," Chase says, furrowing his brows.

"Technology is a hell of a thing," Carter murmurs, with fire in his eyes.

"We'll text every day. Hell, we can FaceTime any time you want," Chase adds, nodding his head.

"I still need a fucking tutor. I can't do math without you," Seger says, swallowing hard.

"This isn't the end, you idiots," I mumble, grazing my fingers along Zepp's. "This is only the beginning." Zepp smiles at my declaration, sneaking a small kiss on my lips while watching my father closely.

"To the beginning," Seger whispers, kissing me, too.

"To our best beginning," Chase says with a whoop. He grabs my face, pulling me into him. His tongue dances with mine until a throat-clearing makes him pull away. Redness takes over his cheeks. "Sorry, Mr. C," he says, ducking his head out of view.

Carter's finger edges down my jaw, tracing over stray freckles. "I'll be seeing you soon, Sweetheart," he says, leaning in and brushing his warm lips on my cheek.

"I'll be seeing you, too," I whisper back with a nod.

We all hug one last time, saying our goodbyes for now. The boys jump into their vehicles and go their own ways as I go mine. I take one last look at East Point through the rear window from the backseat of my mother's BMW, watching it flash by like so many times before.

All the car rides. All the laughs and kisses. The sexy time. The mystery, torment, bullying, and closure. I went to East Point for revenge and revenge only. It ate at me every day, and now I can breathe. I finally fucking did it. I found out who murdered Magnolia and spread their names like wildfire until they were dead or thrown in jail. Now, I can relax in the arms of the boys I love and continue with my life.

That's the last time I ever saw the boys. Throughout the school year, the distance became too much. We went our separate ways, never forgetting our time together and...

Jesus, I'm kidding. Seriously? I got you, though, didn't I? That wasn't our end. That was the beginning of the rest of our lives together.

We became even closer throughout the rest of the school year. Even when we were so far away from each other, we found ways to connect and visit. And then, one day, we weren't so far away.

All four of my favorite idiots moved into a tiny two-bedroom apartment together in the downtown area of my hometown. It's a few minutes away from my parent's house. Whether I went to their place or we had dinner at my parent's, we spent every day together. Once summer came, we counted the days until we left for college.

Together. We'll be together. Always.

# THIRTY-SIX

## KAYCEE

**Several Months Later**

"Happy birthday, baby," Seger whispers, wrapping an arm around my shoulders in the sparse front yard of the new home we've rented for our first school year at CaliState. I can't believe we've finally made it to college after everything we've been through. We're stronger than ever, having spent summer together, and we even took a little road trip, just the five of us, to get away from reality.

My lips pop open at the beauty that lies before me, and I still can't believe they did this behind my back. This was not the house we had decided on over the summer. It's beyond my wildest dreams. A massive yellow, Victorian-style home sits in front of me with a beautiful wrap-around porch. I mentally squeal when a three-seater porch swing drifts in the slight breeze of the California wind. The bright sun beats down over our heads, beaming down on the array of beautiful, decorated flower pots littering the porch with bright blooms bursting from them.

"This place is so big," I mumble, my words tumbling out in excitement and awe.

"There's five of us," Carter grumbles, coming up to my

other side, brushing his pinkie against mine, intertwining them.

He peers up at the house, letting his carefree smile tumble free. Ever since his father's death and the downfall of the Apocalypse Society, Carter's been a free man, living his best life. No longer is the threat of prison looming over him; no more orders being barked in his ear by his father. Carter is free, and his smile, attitude, and love prove it. "And," he says, turning toward me. "It's ours, Sweetheart. Happy birthday." he murmurs, pecking my cheek. He smirks at the stupefied expression taking over my face when he stands tall and reaches behind him to present me with the thick paperwork.

"What?" I squeak, flipping through the papers with all our names on them, showcasing we own the home free and clear.

"It's ours, Sunshine! Our first home," Chase says in celebration, running towards the front of the house. He does a weird touchdown dance in celebration, throwing his arms all around, laughing like a buffoon toward the bright blue sky.

"You guys," I whisper, staring back at my parents, who give me a knowing smile, and my mother winks. I stiffen at the scowl across my father's face but see the softness resting in his eyes. He cares about me and cares about them, but ultimately, he wants me to be happy. He knows it resides in this house with them since we had to spill the beans about practically living together at the Maze House.

"For the next four years," Zepp says, spreading his arms wide and presenting the house. "We live here, all together."

"All together!" Seger shouts, throwing a fist into the air.

"College will be one hell of an experience," Chase snorts, running up to me. He hoists me into his arms, winds my legs around his waist, and spins us in circles laughing hysterically. "This is the beginning of our adult lives," he breathes, finally stopping as the world keeps spinning.

"The best is yet to come." I grin back, leaning down to

capture his lips with mine, and we sigh, staying like that for a moment together.

"The best," he whispers, letting my body slip down his body so I'm standing upright against him. "Happy birthday, Sunshine."

"Happy birthday," Zepp says, kissing my cheek but pulls away with wide eyes. "Shit," he murmurs, looking over Chase's shoulder. I furrow my brows, taking a peek, and snort when my father marches toward us with determination in his eyes. My mother tows behind, grabs his arm and whispers words so low I can't hear them. Concern bleeds from her when she releases her hold on him and stands beside us, biting her bottom lip. She shrugs at me when he opens his mouth and growls at the four boys.

"Now, boys," my father grunts, cracking each knuckle with intent. I swear I can hear the guys' balls shrivel into their stomachs when he makes eye contact with all of them. They straighten their backs, swallowing hard, and each of them tracks my father's angry pacing. "I'm trusting you to keep my daughter safe."

"Of course, Sir!" Chase says through his easy-going grin, saluting my damn father like this is a game.

Dad narrows his eyes to slits, looking at Chase and eyes the others, too. Wiping a hand down his face, he sighs, opening his mouth to say more. But my mom steps in front of him, waving a hand.

"You're all such good boys," she cuts in, cooing over them. She hugs them, pinches their cheeks, and fawns all over them like they were her own damn kids. If there's one person who loves them more than me, it's my mom. "I know you'll keep Kaycee in line, and she'll do the same for you. You all have been through so much together, and now, kids, your future awaits." She grins, gesturing toward the house a few yards away with so much happiness bursting out of her I'm sure she could shit rainbows. I snort, picturing my mom pooping rainbows and jetting off into space until they all look at me with varying expressions of laughter and smiles.

I furrow my brows. "What?" I grumble when Seger snickers, leaning over.

"You said the pooping rainbow stuff out loud," he says, giving me a lop-sided grin when he messes up my hair. I scowl, batting his hand away, and he laughs more.

"Did not," I mutter, crossing my arms over my chest.

"You did, Sunshine," Chase says with a smile.

"It's okay, Sweetpea. You know I'm used to it," my mom says with gentle kindness and a cocked head. "Besides, I am filled with happiness today. You guys are going off into the big bad world after so much and...." Tears fill her eyes again, and she looks away, strangling the sob working up her throat.

"Boys," my dad grits out through clenched teeth. "A word?" he gestures to another part of the yard far away from us.

"So he can kill them, and the neighbors won't see," I murmur, shaking my head when the guys stare at me again with wide eyes. "What?" I ask, cocking my head again.

"Get more sleep," Carter grumbles with a huff.

"You're saying things out loud again and scaring your boyfriends into an early grave," Mom coos through a grin, putting her arm around my shoulders.

I sigh when all their eyes remain on me, even as they take a few steps, walking away from us. "They're lambs being led to the slaughter, and my father is the butcher," I murmur, snorting when all their frantic eyes shoot back to me. Mom chuckles beside me, tapping my shoulder a few times until they're out of earshot.

They stand far enough away, and I can't tell what my dad is saying. When I see the boys' wide eyes, stiff backs, and hard swallows, I know he's giving them a stern talking. They nod their heads in return for his whispered words. Chase discreetly wipes sweat from his neck, and Carter turns a dark shade of green. My father's permanent scowl hasn't left his lips since he got here. Ah, now he's waving his finger in their faces with a red face.

Over the summer, the boys and I came up with this plan. We wanted to live together in privacy instead of in the dorms. Since we had dorms at East Point, we didn't need to experience it in college. Except, they didn't tell me they bought the damn thing. They said we were renting some dinky house across from campus. Now, we have this enormous house a few blocks from our classes. My heart flutters, and butterflies bloom in my tummy.

This is *my* forever with the overprotective idiots whom I love.

True to their words, these days they're overprotective assholes to the max. Think of the biggest, most-Alpha, crazy man and multiply it by ten. I'm not exaggerating, either. Some days they drive me nuts, but I know it's all coming from a sincere place. They feel like they failed me eight months ago when the Apocalypse took me, so they flank me everywhere we go, protecting me from all sides. When all five of us go out, they put me in the center of their circle. If anyone so much as side-eyes me, they pounce on the unsuspecting person like unhinged psychos—swoon. It's so romantic how far they go to ensure my safety, even if the poor person on the other end of their glares is innocent. One day, they'll ease up and let me off my imaginary leash, but that day is not today or tomorrow, or probably not next week or year. Hell, they may never relax again—shit.

"Are you ready, Kace?" Mom asks, pulling me out of my thoughts. I must be more tired than I thought because I can't seem to focus on the here and now.

"For what exactly?" I ask, staring up at the vast house and examining every inch of it.

My mom chuckles. "He loves them, you know? I think he's trying to put the fear of God in them, for some reason.

He's having a hard time letting you go." A watery smile passes over her lips, and I know exactly what's coming.

"I know," I whisper as she squeezes my shoulder.

"Just yesterday, I was bringing you into this world, and now here you are, all grown up in college with four doting boyfriends and a house," she says with a hiccup.

"The next four years will be insane," I reply, eyeing the house again, imagining all the shenanigans we'll get up to without parental supervision. Since I'll live here with my guys, I won't have to move back home in the summertime, so this is goodbye for now to my parents, who are excited yet nervous to let me go.

"You five have a lot ahead of you, but those boys, Kace, are loyal as hell to you. I haven't seen loyalty like that since… your father." Tears break, streaming down her cheeks. "Just don't make me a grandmother too quickly." She wrinkles her nose at the same time I do.

"You heard the doctor," I whisper through a myriad of emotions bubbling up my throat.

I never thought I'd want to be a mother, and definitely not right now. I'm way too young and immature to bring life into this world. I want to experience a relationship with the boys and grow together in the future. One day, maybe—we'll have kids. If I can have any, that is. If not, we'll work through it and adopt children who need a home.

"I know what I heard, but miracles happen. In my heart, one day, you'll be a parent," she says with such certainty. I just nod.

"That's not for a long time, Mom. Who's saying they won't get bored with me and want something different?" My insecurities surface and rear their ugly heads for the first time in our relationship.

At East Point, we lived in a happy little bubble. But here? After so much trauma? We are a part of one of the largest universities in the state now. Thousands upon thousands of people attend here. Now, we're thrusting our relationship into the actual world and testing it to the max. Can four boys love one girl and stay faithful to each other? My answer is yes. But we have four years to grow and learn more about each other. We only met a year ago and started this crazy relationship amid the turmoil. I'm confident we can survive anything this university throws at us, but the future is the future. I'll continue to contribute and love the boys as hard as always and grow and become a better girlfriend.

"Mmm," she hums, kissing my hair. "You all are young, yes. There will be women who pursue them and men who pursue you. You can't know for sure, Sweet Pea. Take this one day at a time, okay? You all have four years to figure this out. If it works, it works, but if it doesn't? Then, so be it. It'll break your heart, sure. But look at what you kids have accomplished together. You've overcome what many people wouldn't be able to. Your past makes me confident your father will walk you down the aisle to four men instead of just one. And those men? They're fine gentlemen." She smiles widely, kissing my forehead.

"Thanks, Mom," I choke out. Burying my face in her neck, I force myself to take a big breath, taking my mom's words to heart. Banishing my stupid insecurities into a little box, into the back of my brain, I regain my composure.

The boys and I have cemented our bond in iron. Through thick and thin, murder and mayhem, crazies and cults, we've survived it all. And now, here we are, finally living our long-sought-after new beginning.

# THIRTY-SEVEN

## KAYCEE

"How much fucking stuff did you bring?" Seger gapes at the sea of boxes swamping our large living room, leaving barely any room to walk through it or see the other side. I crane my neck, look up at the towering boxes, and snort. I could probably mountain climb the boxes and touch the hanging chandelier dangling from the ceiling eleven feet above our heads.

Chase scoffs, waving a hand. "Everything, duh."

"Did you empty your whole damn room?" Carter grumbles, eyeing the label on one box with a scowl.

"I think he did," Zepp says, rubbing his chin.

"You're worse than a fucking girl," Seger goads, pushing at his shoulders.

"Shit balls! I like my stuff. Besides, my dad is moving to some secluded villa with Ainsley. He didn't have room for all my shit, either. He didn't even leave a bedroom for me. What if I visit?" He grumbles, running a hand through his shaggy blonde hair, seeming truly offended his father moved to Italy in a villa with his sister in tow.

"Can we fucking hire someone to do this shit?" Seger asks, leaning his head against the wall with his eyes closed, ready to sleep away the rest of the day.

"Spoiled brat," I mutter, eyeing the boxes again. I didn't even bring this much junk.

Well—maybe. I just packed what I thought I'd need for the school year and for the next four years. My parents even gifted us pots, pans, silverware, and anything we would need in the kitchen. Seger's favorite was the Pizza Pizzazz my parents bought us as a housewarming gift.

"Spoiled brat?" Seger asks in a teasing tone, knocking me out of my thoughts. Shit, I hope we have a big bed here somewhere because I'm ready to sleep and ignore everything else, especially Chase's massive amounts of boxes.

Seger snorts, pushing himself off the wall he almost fell asleep against and comes alive with mischief in his eyes. Coming toward me, I see the predator lurking beneath, and I take a step back, feeling like the tiny prey he wants to sink his teeth into. Which, okay, that wouldn't be too bad of an idea, but seriously.

"No, no," I yelp when he throws me over his shoulder, slapping my ass a few times. I will feel those stings on my cheeks for the next week if he keeps that up.

"We'll show you spoiled brat, Angel." He grunts, marching up the steep steps to the house's second floor. We swerve left and right, with the guys behind us laughing when I continually punch Seger in the kidneys, but he doesn't budge. Not even a grunt of a yelp leaves his lips.

Seger slides me down his body, caging me in with his arms. "We've got a little surprise for you, Angel," he whispers, trailing his lips along my jaw, nipping and sucking. A breathy moan squeaks out when I curl my fingers into his shirt, pulling him closer. His body melts with mine, showing me how affected he is by the heated kisses he's leaving behind.

"Save that for the surprise, asshole," Chase says, forcefully pushing his way in between us. He slaps Seger on the shoulder, knocking him out of the way with a grunt. "Come here, Sunshine," he says softly, pulling me into his chest.

"You wouldn't believe what a fucking dump this place was," Carter's gruff voice says from beside me.

"Really?" I ask, looking around at the beauty of this house. It's in pristine condition with wood floors, freshly painted walls, updated light fixtures, and not to mention a fantastic kitchen my mother went cuckoo for, claiming she wanted to host Thanksgiving here instead.

Chase sniggers in my hair, whipping me around. He forces my back to his chest, pressing his palms over my eyes. "This house was once owned by a crazy drug dealer and his army of skanks."

"For fuck's sakes, Elf Ears. It was not. You're making shit up now," Carter grumbles to my left.

"This place was bank-owned, left for dead by the previous owners. The carpet was stained, and the ceilings had water damage from bursting pipes and roof damage. The air conditioning didn't work, nor did the heat," Zepp says, trailing a finger up my arm and leaving goosebumps in its wake.

"We bought this dump at the end of June," Seger muses, pushing what sounds like a door open.

I frown. "That was like two months ago," I huff—secret-keeping bastards. I knew they were up to something and being all sneaky over the summer, but I didn't know why. Well, I guess this is why.

Chase snorts. "But it was for a good cause, Kace. The look on your face when we pulled up was priceless. You thought we would live in some frumpy bungalow that would barely contain us. We bought a house for all of us. There's enough room for your video games in the basement, football practice in the backyard, Carter's insane work, and so much more."

"Parties!" Seger says in a shout full of excitement.

"I live here, too. You can't party all the time," I say, pointing a finger in his direction.

"Nah, Angel, I won't party all the time," he says, laughing

again, letting me know he's ready to live the whole college experience. "Just sometimes," he says with a pout.

"Compromises," Zepp says, thwacking his brother in the back of the head—or what sounds like a thump since my eyes are still covered for some strange reason.

I smile at the first of many compromises I will have to make living in a house full of boys. "Hmm, compromise," I hum, preparing my list. "Put the toilet seat down after you pee. I almost fell into it the other night at your apartment. Falling ass first into cold toilet water isn't fun."

"Deal! If we can have a party every time we win a game." His body heat presses into my front. "I won't bring people here if you don't want them here, Angel." His lips brush against mine. "I'd never make you uncomfortable in your own house. I'll make sure people clean up after themselves. If anyone fucks with you, they're gone. I won't stand for people disrespecting you, ever."

I smile against his lips, my eyes still in the dark from Chase's hands. "That's fine, Seg. This is your house, too. I know we've basically lived together before, but this is a new experience."

"I love you, Kaycee," he whispers against my lips again.

"Yeah, and if these shitheads become too fucking rowdy, you can lock yourself in my office, Sweetheart. It's fucking soundproof for that very reason," Carter says through a sigh.

"A soundproof room, huh?" Chase teases. "You got a dungeon in there, too? Sex toys? Oh, oh! A swing! Have you shitheads seen those swings? We could tie her up and contort her—" Chase yelps, yanking his hands from my eyes. I look at his glaring eyes as he stares holes into Carter's face. "Asshole!" he grits out, rubbing the back of his head. "Shit, that hurt. What was that for?"

"Sex swings? Really, Elf Ears?" Carter asks without any heat behind his words.

"What? People have those! If we can shove a vibrator up

her pussy and chase her around a maze, then we sure as shit can bind her to the ceiling and have some fun. Shit," Chase says passionately, throwing his arms all around.

Carter smirks. "Yeah, maybe you'll actually be invited this fucking time."

Seger snorts. "Fuck, don't remind me. Next, we'll have to plant a hedge maze in the backyard just to play hide and seek," Seger grumbles, moving his hand to the crotch of his jeans and adjusting himself.

Huh—not a bad idea. I'd love to weave through a hedge maze again, especially since the one at East Point was taken out, and the whole campus was shut down. I sneak a peek at the boys as they face-off, getting nose to nose, arguing about sex swings and soundproof rooms. Old habits die hard, I guess. Carter would never admit he loves the guys as much as he loves me, so he fights them—a lot. But it's something you get used to living with four dudes in such tight quarters. As soon as the others venture out and attend classes, and Carter goes back to work, it'll get better.

I know our love isn't perfect or conventional. We'll fight, scream, and yell. Someone will slam doors in each other's faces. One will need to take a walk to cool down, and the other will need to punch to heal their pain. We're five separate souls merging into one. If it weren't hard, then it wouldn't be love. The best things in life are the things you fight for, and we aren't done fighting for each other. This will be a struggle, but I'm not willing to let any of them walk away from this.

"We're in this together," I whisper, taking a step closer toward the surprise they've gotten too distracted from arguing to show me. My eyes widen as I step into the bathroom, if you could even call it that. It's not a bathroom; it's a friggin' spa getaway. "My God."

"Yeah, we kinda hoped you'd be saying that. Or maybe later?" Seger wiggles his eyebrows, wraps his arm around my shoulders, and ushers me into the lavish bathroom straight out of a magazine.

"I guess our night in the hotel hot tub had a lasting impression on you guys." Three large glass walls hang from floor to ceiling around the oversized tub fit for ten people. And I do mean, ten people. It takes up half the large room with its opulence. A stand up shower with beautiful white stone tiles and a large basin sits off in the other corner. Looking like it too could hold ten people or more. And hell–I gape at the amount of sprayers attached to the wall, and the waterfall shower head hanging from the ceiling. My jaw hangs open as my eyes explore the room, taking it all in while they surround me. "It's so gorgeous." My voice hiccups as I hold the happy tears at bay, refusing to let them see my cry again.

"It's a bathroom built for our queen," Zepp whispers directly into my ear.

"This was our last masterpiece," Carter says, taking the space in with a keen eye.

"You guys designed this?" I ask, turning toward my four nodding boys.

"Of course, Angel. Like you said, that hot tub left a long and hard impression on us. How about you?" Seger winks, sliding open the glass to the hot tub. "Wanna take a dip?" He asks, filling the tub with water.

I grin as Seger rips off his shirt, tossing it to the floor with a cocky grin. They have me right where they want me, but you won't hear me complain. My eyes eat up his tattoos and muscles. Before moving here, he and Chase started football practice with their new college team. Working out and hitting the field hard have consumed their daily lives. But that's what they're here for—their scholarships.

Zepp's injury from the shooting kept him from playing football for the school. Instead, his father paid for his education, and I'm glad for it. It brought him here with us, too, along with Carter. He made good on his promise of following me wherever I went. Most of his work will be done in his office, but he will have to go to the headquarters in East Point from time to time.

Before I can answer, Chase picks me up, fully clothed, and heads towards the water. I screech, beating his muscular back, but nothing makes him stop. His body vibrates with laughter as we jump into the filled-up tub. I slap his chest, laughing as the others join us in their boxers. They sure get undressed fast.

"Wait till you see our room!" Chase says with a sparkle in his eye.

"Will I like it?" I ask, snuggling into him and the warmth of the tub. Carter jump-starts the jets, covering us in white bubbles.

"Will I like it? She asks," Zepp sniggers, spreading his arms out on the tub's edge, and closes his eyes. He sighs into the heat of our new tub, and I smile, looking around. It's insane to think this is a part of my new home.

Carter reaches over the edge, pulling a large bottle of champagne out of somewhere. Where the heck did that come from? The popping cork echoes through the bathroom, champagne bubbles fizzing over his fingers.

Holding the fizzing bottle into the air, Carter lets an actual grin slide across his face. I'll never get over seeing his happiness so up close and personal, and I'm thankful he's finally let go. Sure, he's still a grump-bear, but he's my grump-bear, and he's finally happy.

"I've never had a fucking family like this before," he says, looking between all of us. Sincerity rings true in his eyes, the years of hell sliding off his face, giving Carter back his youthful and carefree appearance. "But you fuckheads, and my Sweetheart, this is to you. To our new beginning as a family." He takes a deep breath and chugs a mouthful. "I love you, assholes."

Chase grins. "Shit, yes! I knew this day would come. I knew you loved us, you grumpy ass!" He proclaims, throwing me to the side in favor of throwing his arms around Carter, who doesn't protest. I squeak, landing in Seger's awaiting arms, and glare at Chase.

Chase jumps onto a grumbling Carter, squeezing him into the biggest hug I've ever seen. And much to my surprise, Carter pats Chase's back with a heavy thud, letting him work it out of his system.

"Fucking puppy dog," Carter mumbles, peeling Chase off of him inch by inch, and sets him beside him.

Chase grins, taking the champagne bottle. He gulps several mouthfuls, ending with an exaggerated 'Ahh.' "I love you guys. This year is going to be the best. I may be a second-string quarterback right now, but shit, nothing can beat this. You guys are mine." He smiles. Taking another mouthful of champagne, he passes it to Zepp.

Zepp raises it in the air, toasting us. "We've been through some hard times, and now we move on together." A slow, suggestive smirk crawls across his lush lips. "And to you, baby girl—" He raises the bottle higher. "Here's to you. You brought us all together and strengthened us. To our bright future." He takes a drink.

Seger grabs the champagne bottle and takes a big swig. His Adam's apple bobs with every gulp, making my thighs clench tight at the sight of it. I swear everything he does is sexy as hell, and he knows it by the glint in his moss-green eyes. His fingers grip my hair, pulling my head back with a jerk. The cool tip of the champagne bottle rests on my parted lips and stays there. Seger's fiery breaths brush my hair as he nuzzles into me. The evidence of his intense arousal prods my ass. "You're ours forever, Angel. There's nowhere else for you to go or run to. We're going to show you every fucking day how much we love you. I can't wait to tie you to the bed. We have so much ahead of us, below us, under us..."

I moan into the bottle.

Seger swivels his hips beneath me as the champagne pours into my open mouth. He takes the bottle away, setting it on the tile floor. I snuggle back into him, letting my brain take over.

I try to imagine what life would be like if I hadn't met them. If Magnolia hadn't died, they'd be a passing story to me. If I hadn't made it to East Point, they'd be in the same places they were. Life has a funny way of leading people in the right direction. Destiny intervenes, gripping you by the collar.

My destiny led me here.

To them.

To this place.

It was messy, unconventional, and heartbreaking.

But we made it.

Together.

# EPILOGUE

**KAYCEE**

**Four years later**

No. This can't happen. Not now—or ever—especially not now, damn it! The doctors swore up and down and on some graves that this couldn't happen! Impossible—they spouted. They said, and I quote, *"It would be a miracle if you ever conceived naturally"*—and wouldn't you know, they're full of shit.

I groan, putting a hand on my forehead, and pace the damn bathroom littered with Seger's clothes and probably some ball hair on the sink. Shit, didn't I tell Carter to clean that up last night? Stop trimming your damn junk hairs on the sink, sicko. Men, I tell you what. I need a maid to come in here and keep up with them. Although, Zepp does a pretty good job coming in behind them with a frown and muttered curses. But he's been so busy lately, he hasn't had time.

Shit, what am I going to do? Why did one of them have to have super sperm and cause this? Oh, right. I have four very horny boyfriends and only one of me. It's fine, I'm fine, everything is perfectly okay and fine. Fuck.

Boyfriends.

Crap. Four of them!

How the hell am I supposed to tell them? *Hey, guys, I know it's our senior year at Cal, but guess what? I'm pregnant with a baby.*

Knocked the fuck up.

I'M TWENTY-ONE AND KNOCKED UP. Okay, breathe, you dingbat. You have to breathe for you and this tiny little invader currently housed in your uterus because you and your—as we said before—four horny boyfriends couldn't keep your hands off each other on vacation.

I bite the edge of my fingernails, staring down at the nine tests I took this morning. Yeah, nine, because I couldn't trust just one to tell me whether or not my life was about to change. So, I took one, and then another, and then all of them showed the same word in the window: pregnant.

You see, it all started with a missed period after a delicious vacation to Rome. Where countless fiveways, threesomes, and twin sandwiches happened almost every night. We drank, partied together, swam naked, and fucked like rabbits. It was our celebration before our last year of college. And apparently, we celebrated too long and too hard—pun intended.

Pregnancy wasn't supposed to happen, not for a few years at least, and not like this. I wasn't supposed to be able to conceive because of my injuries. I wasn't supposed to get pregnant at the beginning of our senior year.

What will this mean for Seger and Chase's athletic careers? Seger's speed is a crowd favorite, and Chase has trained hard to become the best quarterback in CaliState history. They both have chances in professional leagues, and here I am….pregnant. Will it hold them back from the NFL? God, I hope not. It's not something I would want to hold them back from.

And Carter? *CC Tech* has contracts with the most classified of organizations. The military, Veritas, covert government projects, you name it. He can't even discuss most of them with me because of security clearance. And I was supposed to work with him there one day—a power couple heading up the world's most elite tech company. Now what?

And Zepp? He's been studying hard as well. Corbin, his father, can't remember us for the most part and stays in a nursing home, getting cared for twenty-four-seven. He no longer escapes into the woods in his birthday suit, simply lives his life in the best place possible.

Corbin's wife, Corey, took off with their little brother when her husband's health took a nosedive. Imagine that. Rumor has it she's holed up on some tropical island, living her best life with some other rich sucker.

Zepp stepped up to the plate, taking charge of his father's recording company, West Records. He makes all the critical decisions, and Seger helps, too. Along with attending college, he has a full-time schedule. Our hands are full, juggling everyone's lives. Why not add an innocent little being to the mix? Or maybe not? Shit, I don't know. If they don't want this and it's not our time, we have other options. I blow out a breath, running through them.

Ugh. My periods have never been regular since the stabbing. Apparently, the knife hit me right in the baby maker, damaging my ovaries—or maybe just one. But obviously, the damage wasn't enough because one sneaky egg and one determined sperm met in the middle and created this little bundle of nerves attached to me.

I run a hand along my stomach in awe as tears spring into my eyes, overriding the panic pulsing through me. There's a life slowly growing inside me, and I don't have anyone to call to talk me off the ledge. Usually, I call Zepp. He's my voice of reason, the man with a plan, and everything in between. But I can't talk to him right now. Not about this. I need someone else sensible, someone else to tell me that I'll be okay. Closing my eyes, I grumble because I know the perfect person to call in this situation, whether it makes it better or worse. I pull out my phone, dialing the one woman I probably shouldn't trust with this information, but I do anyway.

"Hello?" Callie, my sister, asks out of breath. I make an indescribable noise through the phone, halting her following words. "Did you just say what I think you said?!" she shrieks in happiness, spouting off a few more words so loud that I have to pull the phone away from my ear until she settles down.

"Callie," I grumble, setting the phone next to my ear again, hoping she won't screech.

"Oh, my God! This is amazing! The twins and Violet need a new cousin! Gah! They're going to be so excited! And Mom! Have you told Mom? Wait—have you told anyone?" By the time she's done shouting her excitement, she's breathless and panting through the phone.

"I'm currently in the house alone, skipping a class, might I add. But uh, it's nine tests, Callie. They're all positive. And no, I haven't told anyone yet. Should I text them? What the hell should I do?" I whine into the phone, earning me a chuckle in return.

"Deep breaths, Squirt," she says, laughing at me. "I remember when I told Dex, I was fucking terrified. I mean, we'd been together for three years, and I still thought he'd tuck tail and run away."

I frown. "Uh, not helping. There are four of them! God, they're going to flip their shit. This is our senior year! I can't be fat and waddling!" I hiss into the phone, trying to listen to the noises from the rest of the house, and come up empty-handed. They should all be away from home for at least another twenty minutes or more—hopefully more so I can prepare myself for the inevitable meeting.

"Pfft, cool your jets, Kace. I have never in my life seen people have what you five have. You guys are like special little unicorns to each other. They love you so friggin' much, it makes me want to puke sometimes."

I run my hand down my face, pushing off the bathroom counter. "Fair point. But what if they don't want it? He/she? What if we—" I swallow the lump in my throat, reigning in my emotions.

"I think your irrational hormones are already settling in. You're jumping to some wild conclusions. You're the sun to their universe. They literally revolve around you. They bought you a house for your eighteenth birthday. I mean, who does that? Amazing men, that's who! They're going to drop to their damn knees and love you and that baby. God, I hope it's only one," she mutters through a dramatic sigh.

"Fine," I huff. "You actually make sense, sometimes."

She snorts. "Sometimes? I'm older and wiser and—Oh hell no. Owen! Oliver! You had better put those markers down!" I pull the phone from my ear as she hollers some more at her twin boys, who do nothing but cause havoc on everyone and everything around them. Paybacks are a bitch, I guess. Shit. There better not be twins inside of me. I'm so screwed if there are, especially between the possible fathers and me. Fuck, we're in so much shit. I run a hand over my stomach, praying to the little bean inside me that they won't cause too much chaos when the time comes.

"I swear, my twins are demons disguised as tiny humans! They just—Kaycee, they wrote on my walls, and their diapers are MISSING! I swear—" she whines into the phone with a sigh. "I have to make sure they don't write their names in poop. Again. Keep me updated, though, okay? I can't wait to spread the news! K, love you, byeeee!" She sings into the phone with what I can only assume is a giant grin on her lips.

"Calliope," I grit. "Don't tell anyone — not yet, please."

"Pfft, no. That's your job to tell Mom and Dad!" A shuddering breath pushes through her nose.

"Okay. Love you," I whisper, getting the exact words in return.

Setting the phone down on the vanity, I lean against it and

take deep breaths to ground myself. Shit, I should have asked her more questions. What do I do now? I mean—I have to tell the guys. But how? Do I make a big production of it? Or just step up and say, 'Can you pass the potatoes? Oh, by the way, you've all got some mighty strong sperm. I'm pregnant.' When do I need a doctor? Now? Later? Crapppppp.

I lean my head back against the mirror with a hammering heart. Who knew this would be so difficult?

I yelp as the bathroom door bursts open, pounding against the wall with such force that it distracts Seger as he looks at the wall for damage. I bunch the tests in my hands behind my back in a fucking panic and try not to look so obvious when he turns to look at me with his eyebrow raised.

"What the hell, Seger! I could have been pooping or something," I shriek, shifting the tests in my hands again. Yeah, this is smooth, so fucking smooth. Sweat beads on my brow when he cocks his head, examining me from head to toe, and purses his lips.

*Don't be so damn suspicious. Just pee and get out.* I think to myself when Seger steps forward with a swagger in his step.

Please don't let him see them yet. I need time to process this whole pregnancy thing for myself.

He snorts, smirking at me strolling toward the toilet. "Ah, Angel, we know when you do that. The door is always locked, and you watch TikTok for like forty minutes on the loudest volume."

My cheeks heat as I glower at him. "Well, I was alone," I huff, shifting my weight from foot to foot. "I could have left the damn door unlocked or something." I squeeze the massive amounts of tests in my hands, counting down the seconds until he's gone.

Seger snorts at me again, ignoring my sass. "Sorry, Angel Baby. I had to use the facilities. Got the guys downstairs. We are going to watch old games and strategize for the new season. Plus, I had to see what you were up to." He smirks back at me like he knows. God, he fucking knows something. Shit, he always sees through my shenanigans, and this one is way too big for him to see through. I swallow hard when he returns to the longest pee in history, I shift my foot again, and my heart falls into my butt.

One innocent tiny test scuffs to the floor with a loud clatter, and my eyes bulge from my head as I stare at it. So innocent. So life-changing. And it's on the floor, in plain sight. Crapppp. I'm frozen where I stand, limbs trembling. My heart pounds against my ribs, harder than it ever has before. I'm more scared now than I've been since I woke up in the hospital four years ago with no memory of what happened.

*Please don't see it. Please don't see it.*

Yessss! Thankfully, Seger doesn't notice the noise. I quickly stomp on it, scoot it closer, and conceal it under my foot. I leave my foot over it as he strolls my way with that same smirk resting on his lips and narrowed eyes.

"Well, you guys have fun," I squeak, holding my body as still as possible so he goes away without another word.

Play it cool, Kace. You're as cool as a damn cucumber sweating bullets in the middle of summer in the garden. Shit. I'm so not cool right now. Maybe I should tell him I have gas or something, and he'll go away and leave me to my business.

His fingertips run down my jaw, cocking his head to the side. "What are you up to?" he asks, furrowing his brows.

"Nothing," I say as evenly as possible. Okay, not evenly. More squeaky than usual. "I have gas," I hiss out again, shooting his brows up in surprise.

"Right, gas," he says with a slow nod, looking me up and down again. "You seem awfully guilty for someone up to nothing and has gas. Which, by the way, Angel, is okay." Without warning, because the cocky bastard knows me so well, he swoops down and grabs the test from under my foot. I swallow hard when he cocks his head to the side, brings the test close to his eyes, and then backs it away again. His lips pop open when he repeats the process, and then his eyes land on me. "Then what's this?" He breathes like he already knows what the hell it means but wants me to say it. "Is this? Are you?" He stammers, jaw falling completely open this time, and trips over his words.

So much for a grand gesture. I guess it's better than the—pass the potatoes, I'm pregnant—scenario. It's more of the—here's the proof one of you knocked me up—scenario.

I huff, showing him the handful of positive tests. "I think we're going to have a baby." I shrug, trying to play it as cool. But I'm anything but fucking cool. I'm a mess waiting on pins and needles for his reaction. But he's, uh, not moving. Shit—is he breathing? He's a frozen mass of a man, staring down at the tests in my hands with wide eyes and rigid muscles.

I squeak when he crushes me in an embrace, hauling me off the floor. He spins me around and around, forcing the tests from my hands to scatter across the lavish bathroom.

"I'm gonna puke if you don't stop," I grumble into his ear.

"Holy shit," he whispers, placing my ass on the counter. He palms my cheeks, staring down at me with watery eyes. "I'm gonna be a fucking dad?" Relief spears through me at the sincerity of happiness ringing through his words.

I smile with tears burning my eyes. "Yes," I whisper, pecking his lips. "You're going to be a dad. Well—one of four. I guess. How the hell does this work?"

He snorts, throwing his fist in the air. "I'm gonna be a fucking dad!" He shouts in a whoop, pumping his fist a few times.

Tears form in my eyes at his dedication. "You really want this?" I sniffle.

His brows furrow, wiping away the stray tears flowing down my cheeks. "Angel," he whispers, kissing my cheek. "This is all we've ever wanted. You. This house. Our future." The heat from his palm rests against my flat stomach. "Were you scared?"

I nod, resting my forehead against his. "So irrationally scared. It's our senior year, and I didn't want to put a damper on your plans or—" I'm cut off by his hungry lips on mine, devouring my mouth with vigor.

"Don't you for one second think you'd ruin shit. We have enough resources to skip college. We could do anything. Fuck football. Fuck everything. It's you, me, them, and this baby against everyone else," he says, rubbing a hand along my stomach.

"What's going on?" Chase asks through heavy breaths, limping into the bathroom after his few-mile run. Sweat pours down his face, and dear God, he's not wearing his shirt again.

My mouth waters at the sight of him striding further into the room, running a hand through his sweat-soaked blonde hair, and I sigh. I love it when he comes home covered in sweat after running all morning. Damn, maybe this is why I'm currently pregnant with one of their spawns. I'm constantly turned on by the sight of them or their smell, or anything about them. Dang, I'm pitiful, but whatever. I'll continue to be pitiful while running my eyes up and down the delicious tattoos covering his left arm, hiding the tiny scars from his fight against fire. Thankfully, that's all the damage he endured from that horrible night.

"Back from your run already?" I ask in a husky voice, swooning over the way his muscles ripple when he moves.

"Yeah," he says, holding the word out. "What's wrong? What did you do?" Chase asks, pointing his questions to Seger, who immediately frowns.

"Nothing!" he says, shaking his head, smirking that 'Seger smirk,' letting me know he's up to something. Crap. Here we go. "I mean, I may have done something. It's pretty big, or it will be."

Chase's shaggy blonde locks fall into his eyes as he cocks his head. "I feel like you're making a dick joke or something."

He grins with a snort. "But seriously, why are you crying, Sunshine? And wait—don't you have class right now? Shit! What's wrong? You never skip. Did someone say something to you again?" he rambles on, waving his muscular arms.

Again. Yeah—our relationship is sometimes the talk of campus. At least, it was at first. People always had something to say to me. I've been called names and made to feel wrong about my four boyfriends. But at the end of the day, I'm the girl going home with four smoking hot guys, not them. So, ha! Take that, Kristin!

Hmm. Chase bulked up these last four years. I mean, he was strong before, but now Chase is all man. He even has that delicious V leading to his cock with larger biceps and lickable abs. Many cupcakes have made the V journey, followed by my tongue lapping it away. I kind of want to do it again. There should be cupcakes somewhere in this house…

Hmmm. I'd love to ride him or Seger, but I guess that's what got us here in the first place. Too much riding and too little birth control. If I could have just kept in the IUD from before, then everything would have been fine. But after my surgeries and injuries, they recommended oral birth control, instead. Shit. Maybe this is my fault. I should have kept taking it. But when a doctor proclaims you can't procreate, why take the nasty hormones? They make me moody, give me back acne, and I hate taking them. But why now? We've been pretty naughty these last four years. I mean, we've never wrapped it to tap it. Never had to. They told me I couldn't conceive, and now here we are.

Bow-chicka-bow-wow, I need me some dick now. Wetness pools in my panties. Crap. I'm not supposed to get turned on. This is serious. I'm with child!

"Why is she moving her eyebrows like that?" Chase asks, flicking said eyebrows.

"Ow, you brat." I huff, rubbing at the offending spot. "You're not supposed to flick me. I'm fragile."

Chase snorts. "Fragile? You're like the strongest woman I know." His warm lips kiss my eyebrow. "But right now, I'd love a shower before we watch that footage. Those assholes might tear up our living room if we don't get down there," Chase says, taking his running shorts off and throwing them into the hamper.

"So, you're not going to ask what all those are?" Seger asks, pointing toward the nine tests lying around the room.

Chase looks around, noticing the tests. His face scrunches. "Err, what are they?" Picking one up, his face scrunches more, and then he gasps, dropping the test again. "Sunshine!" He shouts, staring at me with big wide eyes.

Seger snorts, nuzzling into my neck. "Get with the program, Benoit! We are gonna be fucking dads."

I sigh into Seger's embrace, watching Chase from across the room.

He bends down, picking up the test he threw. He stares at it, finding more tests on the ground. Looking at them all, he swallows hard. Every emotion Chase feels shows on his tear-stained face.

"Dads?" He whispers through the shock. "Shit, we're going to be dads! Holy shit! How did that happen?"

Seger snorts again. "Do we need to discuss the birds and the bees again?"

Chase frowns, "No! Sunshine—" He marches toward me, cupping my face. "Thank you." He whispers before smashing his lips into mine. "This is the best thing since they approved the taco truck on campus."

"Are you comparing me to a taco truck?" I ask through a smile as he nips my lips.

"Mmhmm. A sexy, delicious, pregnant—PREGNANT! Holy shit, you're pregnant. You're fucking pregnant. 911 the others!" he says, smacking Seger on the chest frantically, panic spearing through his gray eyes.

"You think he's going to be okay?" I snort, watching

Chase dig his phone out of his discarded running shorts. His entire body vibrates with excitement—or he's terrified. Not sure which yet.

"Eh, maybe. Just imagine what it'll be like when you give birth. He might be the one to pass out," Seger says, resting his chin on the top of my head.

"Crap, I have to give birth," I gasp out, imagining the intense pain I'll go through. And all the doctors and nurses staring at my lady bits while I poop out a massive child.

Seger snorts again, nuzzling into my neck. "Mmhmm, and we'll be there every step."

I pat his back with love, feeling his words settle in. The boys wouldn't have left me. They love me, and they want this. Well—two out of four at least.

Chase frowns. "I sent fucking 911 in the group chat, and Grumpy told me to fuck off. What the shit? 911 means emergency. What if this was urgent?"

"He has a big virtual board meeting," I say, tapping my chin. "And Zepp?" I couldn't wait to see the look on his face.

"I dunno, he—"

"What? What? What's wrong?" Zepp asks through a wheeze, barging into the bathroom. His hand squeezes his shirt into his fist, breaths puffing out his chest. It surprises me to see him so sweaty and pale from running.

While he doesn't play football anymore, he still works out with Chase and Seger like he is part of the team. After all these years, he still looks the same with those same assessing eyes and a stoic, serious face to match. His brown hair is longer than Seger's now, almost shaggy and falling into his eyes. Dark circles underline his eyes from the stress of college and running a recording studio.

He eyes every inch of the room, assessing it like usual. Finally, his eyes settle on me, raking up and down my body. Seger kisses my cheek, stepping back to give Zepp room. His eyebrows furrow. "What's going on?"

I lick my lips, taking a deep breath. "Um—I'm pregnant," I say quickly through a breath. The more I say it, the more natural it becomes.

Zepp blinks at me a few times, standing taller. His shoulders roll back, and he assesses me again from head to toe, only stopping his perusal when he makes it to my stomach. "How?" he asks in disbelief.

"Ah, geez, you, too? Do we need to discuss where babies come from?" Seger snarks, earning a middle finger from Zepp. "You put a big D into the little V, and voila! Orgasms and babies!" Seger expands, chuckling as one of them throws a shoe at him. "Ouch, fuckers!" He harrumphs, rubbing his chest.

"You're pregnant?" Zepp whispers, and I nod in confirmation.

"Yes. At least that's what these say." Bending down, I pick up two tests and hand them to him.

He stares down at them with unblinking eyes, reading the results repeatedly. "Zepp?" My breath catches as I say his name, fear brewing deep inside my gut. "Zeppelin?" I question again, lifting his chin so he'll look me in the eye.

If I thought I'd see anger or rejection, I was wrong. Tears flow out of his eyes, and he pulls me close, kissing my cheek. His arms force me against him, wrapping me in a tight hug.

"Too tight," I mutter as he exhales into my hair.

"I love you, Kaycee," he responds, not loosening a muscle. "I love you so much. This is the best news I've heard in a long time. Especially with what the doctor said..." he trails off, and I nod in understanding. "I'll start researching. We need to find the best doctor in the area. You'll need vitamins, monthly appointments, and ultrasounds. We'll look up the best cribs, strollers, and safe proof the house."

I smile into his shoulder as he continues on and on about our baby's safety.

Zepp always has this way of putting me at ease. A giant

comfort. And thank God he has everything under control with his planning. At least one of us does.

I take a deep breath, staring between the three guys. "I need to tell Grumpy."

Seger grins, pulling me from Zepp's embrace. "Good luck, Angel. He's been trapped in his office for like two days. Take him a peace offering or something." He kisses my temple, waltzing out the door and doing a little happy dance.

"Good luck, Sunshine," Chase says, pecking my cheek and getting into the shower.

Zepp takes my hand, and we walk out of the bathroom. "You think he'll be okay with this?" My voice comes out as a whisper. I can't take my eyes off the test sitting in my hand. Despite the positive responses from the other three, Carter feels like the biggest hurdle I have to jump over.

I'm almost positive he'll be happy, but those nagging insecurities rush through my mind. They're stupid—so friggin' stupid. He's been nothing but incredible these last four years. He's come into himself and developed into the man he wanted to be for so long. His father's expectations and blackmailing ways no longer hang over his head like a guillotine. The romance is alive within him, getting me flowers and planning private dinners for the two of us.

"Is that what you thought with us?" Zepp asks, squeezing my hand. His eyes examine mine as I nod. Shame fills me with the stupidity of my thoughts, but sometimes I can't help it.

Girls chased my guys like some sort of conquest: Zepp, Chase, and Seger the most. Carter mainly kept to himself, but girls around town saw him as the bad boy type and batted their lashes at him. He'd pull me closer, purposefully make out with me, slap my ass, and tell them to fuck off.

Of course, the other three boys were oblivious to the flirting right in front of them. But I wasn't. They never took to the girl's advances, blowing them off and telling them straight to their faces they had a girlfriend. And that made me feel all mushy inside. It didn't deter girls, though. Chase and Seger are stars around campus, legends among the football team. So, yeah. I had big insecurities—unfounded, but I couldn't help myself sometimes.

"Ah, yeah, I—" I roll my lips together. "You know how it is up here," I say with a watery smile, tapping the side of my head.

Group counseling and individual therapy have been a part of our lives since our nightmares came true at East Point. We're fundamentally still the same people, but it changed us all. And for me, my change came with roaring insecurities, nightmares, and needing a shit ton of reassurances. I'm still me, but it has chipped my pieces a little. If it weren't for the boys and normalcy, I would have crashed and burned a long time ago.

Zepp's warm lips take over mine, pulling me tightly against him. "I know, Kace. But he'll be thrilled. We are all in this together. Forever. Don't you forget that." He kisses me one last time, slapping me on the ass. "Now, go get him, tiger!"

I snort as he walks away from me, leaving me standing outside Carter's closed office door.

Filling my lungs with a fresh breath, I slowly open the door to his office. When Carter said he had soundproofed the entire room so he could focus, he hadn't lied. You'd never know there were over ten rowdy guys downstairs talking over each other while watching old football footage. Their sound cuts off as soon as I shut his door behind me.

Behind his impressive mahogany desk sits my man. My heart sputters inside my chest as he watches me. Those big brown eyes track my movements when I make my way across the room. He smirks, raising a brow, silently asking me what I'm doing.

I never disrupt his work, and sometimes he's in here for

days at a time working things out. Right now, four other board members from his company talk to him and each other on his computer. I smile, giving a little wave. His head cocks to the side, and I guess it's now or never. I can't hold it in any longer.

I slide the two pregnancy tests toward him, giving him a second to read them. I know the moment it registers in his brain. "Holy fuck!" he yells to the room with an excited whoop, stopping all chatter on the other end.

"Sir?" one voice asks.

"Everything alright?"

"Give me a minute," he says, typing a few things in. He rounds his desk, pouncing on me like a damn predator. Fisting my long hair, he forces me to look at him. "This true?" he breathes with hope sparking to life in the depths of his eyes, bringing a manic grin across his lips.

"Took nine," I whisper, running my hands up his impressively hard chest. I run my fingers over the bars of his nipple piercings, sending a shiver through him. "All say the same."

He grins, pressing his forehead into mine. "Fuck yes," he whispers. "Holy fucking, yes!" His mouth devours mine. His tongue glides against mine, the warm metal of his piercing sending lava throughout my body.

He pulls away, breathless, still holding me close. Our bodies mold together, melting in our embrace. "We finally locked you down for good, didn't we? No running away now, Sweetheart."

I snort, running my finger down his jawline repeatedly. "Who said I was ever going to leave?" I ask, raising a brow. "The moment you fuckers walked into my life, I knew you were it for me."

"I highly doubt that," he whispers through a grin. "I made your life pretty rough at the beginning."

"Yeah, you did," I hum. "Threw me in a dumpster, tried to drown me...."

He cuts me off by kissing me, letting his lips linger. "I love you," he whispers. "To the moon and fucking back a million times. And I hope you never get tired of hearing me say it because, at this point, I'll never stop." I'll never get tired of hearing those words come out of his mouth.

"I love you too, Grumpy."

He chuckles, kissing my cheek. "So a baby, huh?" A huge grin splits his face. "I'm going to make a bet with those fuckers that it carries my fucking DNA. This thing," he cups himself through his jeans, laughing. "It was made for making babies."

I groan, throwing my head back to look at the ceiling. "Noooo, no bets, Grumpy!" I say through exasperation.

He snorts, turning away from me, and ignores my pleas. That's one thing these competitive assholes have picked up over the past four years, bets. Rushing out the door without a second glance, he races toward the stairwell overlooking the living room. "A thousand says it's mine!" He shouts from the top of the stairs into the room full of guys staring at the TV. They continue to watch, ignoring his comment, but he gets the other guys' attention.

"Fuck you, Cunningham! I'll raise your bet to two grand —it's mine!" Seger shouts, slapping a few of his football buddies and getting them to chant, "Two grand it's mine!"

"What is this life?" I groan, slapping a hand to my forehead. I walk next to Carter as he leans over the railing from the second floor and lean against it with a sigh, staring at the men I love below. Each one is spread out on the four couches we've placed in the living room and lounge back, eating snacks.

"This isn't a competition," Zepp remarks with furrowed brows, looking toward the other two. Yes, Zepp, my man of reason. "But if it were, I'd win." He sports a cocky grin, earning a frown from Chase, who throws a damn chicken wing at him.

"A chicken wing?" Zepp curses, jumping to his feet with a frown, staring down at the offending barbeque chicken wing. He huffs at the mess, muttering about them being unruly, messy assholes. He hurries off, gets a cleaner, and douses the BBQ sauce to death.

"Uh, no. I'd win. This cock was made for just that!" Chase says, scrunching his nose in protest while staring down at his junk. He shakes his head. "That kid is mine. I bet three thousand it's mine," Chase says, staring up at me with a grin splitting his face.

"You ready for this, Sweetheart?" Carter asks, throwing his arm over my shoulder and pulling me in, kissing my temple.

"Mmmm," I hum as they continue to up the bet, higher and higher, until it reaches ten grand. "With you all by my side? Yes. I'm ready for anything."

Even a tiny baby that will come out of my small vagina. And hours upon hours of painful labor. I'll make it through anything as long as these boys are by my side because we have already been through so much.

Fire.

Bullets.

Knives.

Hurtful words.

Our love has conquered all, and it will remain that way forever.

# EPILOGUE 2

**KAYCEE**

**Nine Months Later**

Ouch. Pain. Shit.

Not today, little Satan. You stay inside of me. I have one more final test to take, and I'm done with college. So, you little devil spawn, you can't come out yet. Just give me like a day to get my shit sorted!

I rub a hand over my protruding stomach, mentally pleading with my tiny human. Please stay in. And in return, I get a kick. Or maybe it was a punch? Or a contraction. Fuck. I don't know. But it was there, confirming to me my little guy was active. Usually, he's pretty calm and barely moving, but today, he's moved around a lot, pushing through my stomach. He seems unsettled. Maybe that's why he's trying to force his way out because he's out of damn room and wants to meet his mama and papas. Well, we're eager to meet him, too. Just not today.

I check my phone when I waddle through the kitchen and curse at the time. It's eleven-thirty, and if I don't get my round ass to my next class, I'll never make it on time for my exam. And my professor, who is a real asshole, will lock the doors before I can enter. Chase stalks around the kitchen, gathering a sandwich and a small bottle of orange juice, and the moment he sees me, he shoves them into my hands. I immediately drink the orange juice, loving the flavor as it spills over my tongue, and shove the sandwich down my throat. I groan when I lick my fingers, getting every bit into my greedy stomach. Honestly, he could probably make me a few more, and I'd down them in two seconds.

"Eat, drink, and then I'll walk you to class," he says with a grin, kissing my cheek. "And you little fella, be a good little boy so mama can take her last exam in peace." My heart swells when he bends down and talks to my stomach in a soothing voice, rubbing his hand all over it. He grins more when my stomach tightens against his hand, and I hold my breath. "He's really at it today, isn't he?" Chase asks, peering at me with love brewing in his eyes.

"Yeah," I breathe, trying not to let him know what he felt wasn't the baby but a dull ache forming in my lower abdomen like a contraction. A contraction I can't have right now because I have a test I have to take to get my degree. Shit.

Labor lasts over forty-eight hours, right? So, I have plenty of time to take this test, come home, go to the hospital, and have this baby. Yeah, it'll all work out. I just have to make it through.

"Eat the fucking food," Carter barks, marching through the kitchen with a coffee cup in his hand and placing it in the sink.

"Demanding ass bastard," Chase murmurs, kissing my cheek, and steps away to grab his keys. "She already ate, asshole." He sends Carter a scathing look, earning a shrug in response.

Carter smirks when he turns around and cocks his head, checking me up and down with scrutinizing eyes. Every morning it's been the same thing since we passed the thirty-six-week mark a few days ago. He checks to make sure I'm okay and not in labor before he begins his day by locking himself in his office. Now, he keeps his phone on him twenty-four-seven since we're in the final countdown. And apparently, today is the day, or not. I stare down at my stomach and raise a brow. My sister mentioned something like Braxton hicks contractions coming and going before the baby and how she had some. Even my doctor said not to freak out too much. I'm fine. We're totally fine and not in labor.

I shake my head when Carter drops to his knees in front of me in the kitchen and rubs a large hand over my stomach several times. It's almost as if he knows I'm having small contractions here and there and is trying to feel them so he can force me to go to the hospital.

"Kiss for luck," he murmurs to the baby, pressing a long kiss into my stomach.

"Up here, Big Guy," I murmur, pointing to my lips, and he chuckles.

"Kiss for luck for my baby momma," he murmurs against my lips, pulling me hard against him. He groans, slipping his tongue past my parted lips, and his dances with mine.

"No, no," I groan, feeling another tight kick to my stomach. "I have a test, and I can't afford to get pregnancy horny right now." He smirks, holding my face in his hands. I pout when my pussy flutters, and I want him to bend me over the damn kitchen table for more luck before taking my test.

"No sexy time," Chase says, coming up behind me. "She has one more test, and then.."

"We're all done," I groan when Carter takes my bottom lip between his teeth. My eyes roll into my head when his hard-as-steel dick pokes through his basketball shorts and grinds against me. "I'm two seconds away from saying fuck it," I murmur when he chuckles.

"Think of your reward when you get home," Carter whispers against my cheek, pecking it. "Be a good fucking girl and go ace your exam, then when you come home, I'll lay you out and feast on what's mine."

"Jesus Christ, Grumpy. She has to concentrate on her test. Not fucking fantasize about what you're going to do to her," Seger gripes, waltzing into the kitchen. He stretches his arms above his head and yawns. "Morning, Angel, and little dude," Seger rasps, leaning in to kiss me on the cheek. "Good luck and kick some ass," he says, slapping my ass.

I yelp, glaring at him, and he smirks. "Thanks," I murmur, rubbing the blazing spot on my butt.

"Bye, baby girl, good luck," Zepp says breathlessly, waltzing into the kitchen fully dressed. He leans in, gives me a quick kiss before marching up to his bedroom, and gets to work for his father's company.

He's constantly zooming around here in his best clothes and attending virtual meetings with the board members of West Records. Once we're all done here, we're selling the house and moving back to East Point Bluff so Seger and Zepp can run the company in person. Does it make me nervous as hell to return to the town that tried to kill me off? Absolutely. But I'd do anything for these boys, and my therapist has reassured me that I'll be okay.

We've gone through the scenario several times. The bad people who once inhabited East Point are dead or rotting in the deepest, darkest pits of jail, and the town was cleaned up four years after my incident. Even East Point Prep got a facelift, new staff, and new students. It's not a prep school anymore, it's what Dante Van Buren originally envisioned—a place every student could go to learn. So, only the good people remain.

We haven't been back since coming here. I've purposefully kept my head down, ignoring any news about the town, but after this, I have to buck up and face my demons head-on.

East Point Prep shut down for a year or two while Shaw's trial took place. Inevitably, Shaw took a plea deal. Three hundred years to life for several murders and many more crimes. The other townspeople involved in the cover-ups were tried and convicted for their part. The entire town suffered severe backlash for letting something so heinous go on under their noses.

We learned a lot during the trials. Thankfully, they didn't need our testimony in person. Only our statements were used, and we never had to face our nightmares again. Everyone involved went to prison for their crimes, except for Zoe Hart. Veritas would never have come to our rescue if it weren't for her and her efforts to get help.

She confessed Shaw had coerced her, manipulated her, and sexually assaulted her. After hearing her testimony, it was clear she had gotten in over her head. When Zoe joined, she had no idea what the organization would do. They promised her wealth beyond her dreams, and it was something she desperately needed. Despite being a famous rockstar, she went bankrupt and thought they were her salvation. Now, under a new name, Zoe still roams free. She testified against everyone and made powerful enemies. Rumor has it, she's safely studying in Ireland and attending college there under her new name, but we haven't heard a peep from her, not even musically.

I wave to Seger and Carter, who lean against the counters with their shirts off. They're so damn tempting right now. If I weren't in a hurry to get to class, I'd lay my ass on the table and beg them to feast on me—labor or not.

I take Chase's hand and walk out the front door into the beautiful May sun. It beats down on us as a mild wind blows through the trees, blowing my hair, and my muscles loosen. I'm not sure what it is about the spring weather that eases everything inside me, but I love the walk to class from here. Of course, my boys always accompany me whether they have class or not. Everywhere I go, my psychos are on my ass, watching for any sort of danger. I honestly thought I'd get annoyed by their constant stalking ways, but I eventually got used to it. Not to mention how grateful I am to have four loving bodyguards protecting my every move.

Chase and I walk down the sidewalk, enjoying the walk toward campus in silence. He clutches my hand, walking as slow as my waddle will allow. I'll enjoy the day when I can see my feet again. Not to mention I can't wait to shave my legs and my lady bits. Ah, one day, it'll happen.

"How about Axel?" Chase muses, rubbing his chin.

"Axel?" I snort with a shrug.

"Well, we've got Led Zeppelin and Bob Seger. Why not Axel Rose? They're all rock legends," Chase says through a snort. "Or Dash, I've always liked Dashel. Dare? Or Benjamin? Alexander? Shit. Chase Jr? Seger Jr? I could keep going, Sunshine." He grins when we finally make it to the front of campus and start our trek toward the ADM building in the center of the quad.

I wrinkle my nose. "No Jrs. I can't imagine trying to yell at two Segers or two Chases. Or heaven forbid, two Grumpies." I shudder at the thought of having another Grumpy around to yell at.

Chase dramatically throws his hand to his chest with a gasp. "You act like our sweet little guy will be a heathen already. And why would you yell at us? We're perfect little angels." He barks out a laugh when I shake my head and stick my tongue out at him.

"Angels? Right, that's what you're calling yourselves now," I quip, tilting my head. "The name will come to us. Maybe when we see his face, we'll know what he should be called."

"I can't wait, Sunshine," Chase whispers, pulling me to a stop. His palm cups my cheek while the other hand caresses my protruding stomach, rubbing it in circles. "We're all seriously so stoked to be dads. You're giving us the greatest gift we never thought we'd have. We love you… I love you," he murmurs, choking on his words when he leans in to kiss my lips.

"I love you, too. Now, get me to my last class so I can take this test, and then we can have the baby soon," I whisper against his lips, wanting to pull him in for more in the middle of the sidewalk.

"Yeah," he sniffs, "let's get you to class." He grabs my hand again, trying to pull me along to my destination. But my body jolts and my muscles stiffen when another sharp pain tugs at my stomach, this time a little more intense than before.

"You okay?" Chase asks with concern etching onto his face. His lips pop open when he examines my face, and I know exactly what he sees. He sees the pain I'm trying to hide behind my fake smile and nonchalant wave.

I grit my teeth and nod. "I'm fine, just some leg cramps again." I offer him my best smile, keeping the pain of the tightening of my stomach to myself. It'll be hours before I need to worry if it's contractions.

Chase frowns, shifting through his pockets. "Again? Do you want a banana? Water maybe?" His face lightens when he pulls out a whole banana and a small bottle of water and presents them to me with a grin. "Now drink," he demands in a no-nonsense voice.

*Demanding ass boyfriends.*

I frown. "But then I'll have to pee halfway through the two-hour exam," I grumble, snatching the bottle from his hand anyway. "But thank you," I murmur, chugging the small bottle until it's gone, handing it back to him.

His lips tip down when he thrusts the banana in my direction and raises a brow, giving me that no-nonsense look like he'll shove it down my throat if I don't eat it. But that's what got us into this situation in the first place, sticking things in places and producing this hungry beast inside me who wants to eat everything in sight and then throw it up.

"And the banana? It'll help with the cramps. I remember

reading about it online a few weeks ago. Good for your legs and the baby and...." I snatch it out of his hand and peel it open, earning a satisfied grin just to shut him up. Don't get me wrong, they have all been saints since the moment I told them, but sometimes they're too much for me to handle. "Good, Sunshine," he praises, taking my hand, and we start walking in the direction of my exam again while I stuff piece after piece of delicious fruit into my mouth. I'd' never tell him I was already hungry again, and the banana really hit the spot. That would give him too much ego.

When I told them I was pregnant, they went into ultra-protective mode. Zepp researched everything we needed. Baby equipment, what to expect at labor, and throughout the pregnancy. I swear, the man is a walking, talking encyclopedia on babies and birth. Carter stomped after me like a security guard, keeping everyone back with his scowl and growls. Seger and Chase walked me from class to class, eyeing everyone suspiciously. Even the small group of friends I've made got lectured by them here and there about my safety, and I swear I could have smacked them. Stupid, overprotective jackasses---whom I love, of course.

Finally, after a ten-minute walk, we stand in front of the ADM building, meeting up with Chase and Seger's football friend, Alex.

"Hey man," Chase says, leaning in with a grin to do that weird bro hug thing guys do when they clap each other's backs.

Alex grins at him and respectfully nods his head at me. "Hey man," he says back and then smiles at me. "Are you ready for this? I swear I've been studying for like four days straight and haven't retained anything." He shakes his head, wiping at his forehead.

"As ready as I'll ever be," I say with a nod. "See you after class," I murmur, kissing Chase's cheek.

"Good luck, Sunshine. Show that final exam who's boss

and kick some ass. You only have two hours, and then we'll officially be done! And this guy," he whispers, dropping to his knees without care. "Come soon, little man. But not too soon, maybe tomorrow." I run my fingers through his long blonde locks as he kisses my stomach, lingering for half a second. Finally climbing to his feet, he taps the end of my nose. "Be good, Sunshine." I snort when he salutes me, walking down the sidewalk toward a coffee shop on campus. It's the one he always stops at when he walks me to class, and he doesn't have one.

I blow out a breath, rubbing my hands over my enlarged stomach, following Alex through the building to our lecture hall. Everything aches despite the banana Chase shoved down my throat. My back aches, and my feet feel like a thousand knives stabbing me, and not to mention, I'm so fucking exhausted. Being pregnant is a miracle, one I'm happy to be. But I'd like not to pee every five seconds because my little dude is throwing a party against my bladder. Oh, and sleep would be wonderful, too.

The smell of those goldfish crackers makes me hurl. Seger's manly cologne I used to love makes me queasy. I can't walk without farting. And finally, I can't poop. Pregnancy sucks. The only upside? I've been so horny these past nine months. I'm glad I had four guys to keep up with me, and the plus is, they can't knock me up again. So, we've been going at it like rabbits in heat for the past nine months and getting it out of our system.

Ouch. Shit.

I lean against the wall in the hallway leading to my classroom, letting the cold wall cool my overheated forehead. Ragged breaths pour from my nose as pain explodes in my stomach again. My muscles tense, and my belly hardens like a bowling ball, hard and heavy. And so fucking painful. Gah. How do women do this repeatedly? Seriously, this is only one contraction, and I already want to sedate myself. Two more hours and I can go to the hospital. Two more hours, and then this will be over. I just have to survive. And I will.

"Hey. You okay?" Alex asks with concern in his voice.

"I'm good," I say, blowing out a breath, standing tall once the pain subsides. That was the first contraction to slow me down and make me stop.

How long ago was the last one? Shit, I should keep track. I pull my phone out, looking at the time. 12:25. Five minutes to get to my final."Shit, we should go." I nod toward the classroom urgently, and he nods, taking note of the time. His eyes narrow on me as we slowly walk toward the classroom, but he doesn't say anything this time. I'm sure if it continues, he'll be a good friend and text his besties to let them know their girlfriend is in labor.

I swallow hard, walking into the crowded classroom. Students wander around, finding their seats. Their low murmurs flitter through the large classroom. They smile and laugh—some grimace with nerves, including me. No matter how often I've done this, my anxiety still spikes in the middle of a crowded room.

They probably don't pay me any mind, but damn, this anxiety is brutal sometimes. I feel like a beacon for attention between the names I've been called years before and having a huge belly. My anxiety has only gotten worse since East Point. My therapist says I'm doing better, and the more I speak with her and do my exercises, the more I improve. Right now, I'm failing. And okay, it doesn't help that my son is trying to come out when he needs to stay put—two more hours, little man.

I blow out a breath, calming the nerves bursting inside me, and find a seat next to Alex, who stares at me. His eyebrows dip when I carefully lower myself into the seat beside him, and he watches my every move like a hawk. It's almost like having an extra boyfriend when he's around, minus the romantic feelings.

The professor emerges from a side door, scowling at the entire class while making his way to his desk, slams books down, and sinks into his seat. His shiny black dress shoes prop onto his desk. Peering up at the clock, he scowls more and utters one word.

"Begin."

Professor King—dick bag extraordinaire. Brilliant. Brutal. Hardass. Surprisingly young—he's only twenty-eight and in charge of several classes. The dude should probably smile more, though, and maybe he'd lose the wrinkles and the angry scowl. Or perhaps he needs to get laid or something, but I'd rather not think about that right now while I'm diving head first into my exam.

I cringe at 12:55 when another contraction squeezes my stomach into a sharper vice than before. I breathe in and out, gripping the sides of the desk with white knuckles, and praying to God I survive this contraction. Shit. I'm going to die a painful death if these get any worse than this.

Alex catches my eye with a frown, staring between my hands and expression. I offer a shrug, and he looks away. Thirty minutes. Okay. That's not too bad since the last one. It's the three minutes apart contractions I have to worry about. At this rate, I'll be fine.

Totally fine.

I'M NOT FINE. There should be an announcer somewhere narrating my life. Like Samuel L. Jackson or Ron Howard or.. mother fucker!!! AND SHE, IN FACT, ISN'T FINE.

I breathe through my mouth again, clinging to my desk. I'd choke it to death with my white-knuckled grip if it were alive. It's been ninety fucking minutes, and my contractions went from zero to sixty thousand. Fuck. Fuck. I need drugs—lots and lots of drugs to cure the ache in my gut. Jesus, help me! My stomach tightens every three God damn minutes, and I swear I'm about to have a baby in the middle of finals!

FINALS! He's going to just pop out like a damn football and go splat on the ground. Ughhhhh.

"Kace, you don't look good at all," Alex whispers, touching my hand. I grab his fingers and squeeze them to my heart's content. "Oh fuck," he whispers, going pale, and scrambles for something in his pocket. "Holy shit! You're in labor, aren't you?" He hisses frantically, looking around the room.

"Gahhhh!" I throw my head back, taking deep breaths. "Shit, shit, shit!" I groan, tapping my foot against the floor.

My cheeks heat at the stares I'm receiving, but I don't care. Fuck them, and fuck this pain to hell and back. I close my eyes, trying to count inside my head. Go away, pain, shoo! I have two more questions left. Two. If I can make it through that, I'll be golden.

"Miss Cole?" I peek an eye open as the pain subsides for a few minutes, and I can finally breathe. But barely with Professor King looking down at me. His dark eyes take in my appearance, and he raises a brow.

"Yes?" I croak, taking another deep breath.

He sighs. "I take it, it's time?" He asks in a low voice.

"Yes," I say, taking another deep breath. "I have two more questions to go and then, the hospital." I squeak out the last part of my sentence as pain erupts through my abdomen, again taking my voice hostage. Stars swim in my vision, and I swear my eyes cross from the pain exploding through me. I need drugs.

I swear to all things holy, their dicks are never touching me again. They can have each other! No more sexy nights of passion in the hot tub! Gahhhh!! I huff out breaths, tapping my toes on the ground again.

Professor King nods, grabbing my iPad. He taps a few times, scratching at his chin. And then, for the first time in his life, he smiles. "And now you're done. Please exit the classroom, and good luck."

Did douchebag extraordinaire finish my final for me? Whatever. I'm not asking questions, and I'm out. I need the hospital. And my boys. And not in that order.

"Good luck," Alex whispers, shoving his phone back into his pocket.

"Thanks," I croak, giving him an awkward smile and high tail it out of the classroom, as fast as my waddle allows me.

I huff a breath, making it as far as the front door of the entrance before I have to stop and lean against the cool wall. Sweat pours from every surface of my body, and my stomach tightens.

Breathe in and out. In and out. Fucking breathe through it! My God. How do women do this all the time? Like, how? Ugh.

A warm hand glides against my lower back. "I had a bad feeling in my fucking gut. Something nagged me to come and fucking get you," Carter whispers in the softest voice.

"It hurts so bad," I whimper. Tears trail down my cheeks, dripping off my quivering chin. I was so strong for so damn long, now he's here. I can let it go and lean on my support system—the perks of having more than one boyfriend.

"I know," he says softly, rubbing a hand over my tightened stomach. "I know it hurts, Sweetheart, but I think we need to get you into the car and get your sexy ass to the hospital." Thankfully, he keeps his tone calming when he whispers in my ear, and I melt into a puddle. Gripping my hand, he leads me away from the wall and pulls me into his body. His arms immediately wrap around me, securing me in his warm cocoon of support.

"I'm here! I'm fucking—ah," Seger stops before us, bending at the waist, wheezing through his nose. He bends over, recovering with his hands on his knees. Sweat stains every inch of his shirt and hair as he tries to catch his breath to speak again but has difficulty getting the words out.

Carter raises a brow. "Did you run from the fucking house?"

Seger waves his phone around, nodding. "Alex," he gasps. "He texted and said she was in fucking labor."

"Yes, yes, I am. Now, can we please get me to the hospital?" I blow a breath out from between my parted lips, finally coming down from the contraction keeping me captive.

Seger straightens, dusting off his jeans. His brows crinkle, coming to stand in front of me. "We got you, Angel. Don't worry." His voice softens, placing a soft kiss on my forehead.

"Well, we're in luck. I grabbed the damn Suburban to get here." Carter says, dragging me along. And I do mean drag. If it weren't for them, I'd still be against the wall, unable to move.

My feet shuffle on the sidewalk as we make our way toward Carter's Suburban parked not too far away. Seger and Carter each take a hand, ambling beside me, but I can sense the tension bubbling beneath the surface.

"How long?" Seger asks in a soothing but irritated voice, and by the way his hand tightens on mine, he's going to explode.

Ah—and there it is. The tension is about to come to a head when I tell them I've been having contractions since this morning. I bite my lip, contemplating how to answer his questions.

Carter huffs, rolling his eyes toward the sky. "By the look on her face, I'd guess since before her final."

"Damn it, Angel," Seger growls, narrowing his eyes at me.

"It takes like, a full day for a baby to come." I grit my teeth as a fresh wave of pain roars through my stomach and brings us to a halt.

I force lungfuls of air into my lungs as the pain digs in deeper. Dare I say going through labor is more painful than getting stabbed in the stomach. I think I'd rather take that knife again than go through this multiple times. The boys bracket themselves around me, holding me up so my knees don't buckle from beneath me. Pressure builds in my abdomen, ratcheting higher and higher until something explodes, and wetness pours out of me onto the sidewalk. My eyes pop open, and a desperate need to push washes over me. Almost like I need to use the restroom, and from all of Zeppelin's research, I know what it means.

"What?" Carter asks, pulling back to search my face. His palms cup my cheeks, forcing my frantic eyes to look into his. His eyes travel south to the wet sidewalk, and he curses.

"Fuck!" Seger says with urgency, whipping out his phone. "We need to go," I rasp through the pain. "I need to push, Grumpy. Like, it's urgent." His brown eyes widen, and he hoists me into his arms bridal style and takes off down the sidewalk, leaving Seger behind.

"Get the damn hospital bag! It's fucking time!" Seger shouts into the phone, presumably to Zepp, who works at home. He jogs behind us, pulling at his hair with worry lines taking over his features. "Well, swing by; Carter's got the family burb."

A few months ago, Carter went out and bought a top-of-the-line Suburban. Three rows of seats, plenty of room for all of us, and a bunch of kids. Yeah, the guys insist we are doing this again. And again. And again. They want a little army of tiny humans. Hence, the big Suburban we take together—the family car.  But I have news for those assholes….

"Breathe," Carter mumbles into my hair. "You have to keep breathing."

A hoarse cry falls from my lips. My fingers dig into Carter's shoulder, nails biting through his shirt. He pounds the pavement, trying not to jostle me. The cramping pain intensifies in my abdomen again. I throw my head back, screaming to the sky. My agony can be heard throughout campus, causing the birds to lift from the trees. Several students meander on the quad looking at us, but I don't give a shit.

"Just hold on, Sweetheart! We are almost to the car!" Carter says in a panic, running full speed to the car.

"What the shit?" Chase shouts, running down the sidewalk with a small coffee cup in his hand. "Alex just texted me! I ran by the building, but you were already gone." Panic takes over his features, and his face crinkles when he looks at me in Carter's arms.

"Labor. Baby. NOW!" I shout through the pain as they usher me into the backseat and climb in after me. Seger drives, taking off toward the house, and picks up Zepp.

---

I LEAN BACK AGAINST CHASE, huffing and puffing. His hands work up and down my shoulders, kneading knots. I groan, throwing my head back into his shoulder.

"Guys," I say through heavy breaths. Sweat pours down my face, despite the air conditioning flowing steadily through the car. Pain erupts in my stomach again, cramping more and more, and I swear I need to push.

"What's wrong?" Zepp asks frantically, running a hand up my calf. He takes my foot into his lap, massaging my bare arch. "I need to push," I grit out, sucking in harsh breaths.

"P-push?!" Chase stutters, gripping my shoulders from behind. "Shit! Drive faster!" Chase says, banging on the back of the driver's seat.

"Not helping, dickbag! The traffic is bad!" Seger curses, jostling our bodies as he shifts lanes. "How bad?" Carter asks, kneeling at my other foot.

"If I don't push, I'm going to die! Get this fucking baby out of me!" I shout, causing Seger to swerve and jerk the car again. He curses from the front seat, frantically looking around the roads.

Carter and Zepp gape at each other, staring into each other's eyes for longer than needed. But apparently, my words do nothing to make them move until I grunt, shoving my bare foot into the middle of Zepp's chest, gaining his attention. He swallows hard, snatching my ankle with a pale face. Pain erupts in my stomach again, and I'll be fucked if they don't spring into action because the pressure inside bears down more. I'm ten seconds away from having this baby in the car.

"Take my pants off," I growl through gritted teeth, earning nods from the two fumbling idiots who did this to me. Never again will I beg them to take off my pants and do this to me again. I swear this pain will fucking kill me slowly, but not if I murder them first.

"You got this, Sunshine," Chase says in a soothing voice directly in my ear. His strong hands work over my shoulders when the boys yank down my leggings and panties and throw them aside.

"What?" I hiss when Zepp and Carter stare into my vagina like it's the worst thing they've ever seen. They both pale and freeze and fuck, I need them to do something. ANYTHING! "I fucking love you guys so damn much," I wheeze when pain rocks through me, and every muscle in my body tenses up. "But I need you to do something, please," I beg, throwing my head back into Chase's shoulder. He wraps his arm around me and grounds me when the other two finally spring into action.

"Fuck," Carter hisses. "How fucking long has this been happening for?"

"I don't know! Just, just—" I gasp when the pain intensifies, making my entire stomach into a thick rock, and the need to push grows stronger. "I need to push," I grit out, dropping my chin to my chest.

"Push, baby girl! Push now!" Zepp demands, finally jumping into action. The man who always has a fucking plan and who has studied babies for the past nine months in preparation is finally showing me what he's learned.

Leaning forward, he lifts my leg so my foot pushes into his chest, and Carter does the same, giving me leverage to really bear down and push with all my might.

"One, two, three, four," Chase says, grabbing my hand and letting me squeeze tight. "Five, six, seven, eight, nine, and ten," he breaths, nodding his head when I relax, but the contraction doesn't disappear. It only gets longer and harder and more fucking painful. Death! Death is fucking imminent unless I get this baby out of me and into my damn arms.

"Again!" I shout, and Zepp takes over, counting to ten aloud while I push.

"Holy fuck," Carter gasps. "So much brown hair, Sweetheart. He's right there!"

I gasp when Zepp finally reaches ten, and I relax back into Chase with heavy breaths. Sweat slicks every inch of my body as I gasp for air, reveling in the small reprieve from pain until it hits again with a fucking vengeance.

"Shit! Fuck!" Seger curses, slamming a hand into the steering wheel, forcing the car to come to a stop. "Fucking, we just got pulled over." My eyes pop open to a rave of red and blue lights flashing through the car. But I don't have fucking time to listen to a cop tell us we're going too fast or swerving or whatever. I need this child out of me right now!

"Another one!" I gasp out, gritting my teeth as the pain envelops my whole being, and I bear down again, aided by Chase, who holds my hand and lets me squeeze the life out of his fingers.

"No time to waste!" Zepp shouts. "Push, baby girl!" He demands again in a no-nonsense tone, staring down between my legs as the pressure grows more and more.

I push with all my might. My toes curl, and pain roars through my body in massive waves. God, I wish I had that epidural I wanted so bad. This wasn't part of my birth plan!

Zepp had it written to a T. Hospital, epidural, hot showers, and no fucking pain. But here I am, pushing my baby out in the back of our family car in full-blown agony because we had to go on a Roman Holiday and fuck like rabbits. Mark my words... Never. Again.

A scream rips from my throat, and I throw my head back onto Chase's shoulder when the pain notches up to fucking eleventy million. It tears through everything, and I'm on the verge of dying a slow and painful death until I'm not. Everything stops the moment he comes out head first. Somehow, Zepp maneuvers his shoulders through, and all the pain from before stops like it was never there. Panic sets in when I'm greeted by nothing but silence and the stunned faces of all my guys.

"Is he okay?" I ask frantically, trying to lean up and see between my legs. "Why isn't he crying? Zeppelin?" I scream, pushing up to better view the tiny bundle now wrapped in a large, bloodied bath towel.

Zepp gasps, tears falling down his cheeks. "He's perfect."

"Fucking perfect," Carter's voice quivers, wiping the goo from our baby's face.

"Why isn't he fucking crying?" Seger begs, turning in his seat to look back with tears streaming down his cheeks.

"Because he doesn't want to," I whisper, taking the baby from Carter. I lay him on my chest, leaning into Chase for support.

"Oh, baby," I whisper, running a finger through his gooey brown hair. His bright green eyes stare up at me, examining my face—well if he could see. We stare at one another for a solid minute as tears burn my eyes. His lower lip quivers, giving way to a high-pitched wail, filling the car with his desperate cries.

"I'll call an ambulance." We all jump out of our skin at the sound of the officer standing by Seger's open window. His brown eyes glisten with tears, staring at us.

Seger shakes his head. "We were just heading to the hospital, and she--and he—" he swallows hard, pointing toward us with mixed-up expressions.

"I understand, Son. Let's get you to the hospital. Follow me." The officer says in a gravelly voice, wiping the tears from his eyes. He doesn't bother to give us a ticket for whatever traffic violation he pulled us over for. In reality, we probably looked like a drunk, speeding driver and drove unsafely. But we had other things on our minds—especially me.

"Shh, shh, baby," I whisper, wiping a soft towel down his face.

"He's beautiful," Chase chokes out, running a soft finger through his long brown locks, and leans into me. "You did so good, Sunshine. I'm so damn proud of you," he murmurs in my ear. My whole body relaxes into him as we look down at the bundle in my arms.

The officer leads us to the hospital in five minutes flat, staying close to us with his lights on. They take me straight to the maternity ward when we arrive, with the boys hot on my heels. The nurses take the baby, check his weight and run other tests to ensure he's healthy. My nurses set me up in a bed with an IV and vitals and check me over.

My parents showed up thirty minutes after our arrival, doting on the baby and me. My father has tears in his eyes, looking down at my little bundle, cooing at him, and rocking him back and forth. My mother cries, cuddling him and telling him how lucky he has such a big, loving family. When night comes, they kiss us all, leaving us to rest. But before they leave, my mother cries again, staring back at me on the bed. My father practically drags her out of the room by her wrist.

I groan, settling back into the hospital bed. Every inch of my body drowns in exhaustion, weighing down my limbs. "What a friggin day," I grumble, trying to stretch my legs.

"You did so good, Sunshine," Chase says, kissing my forehead.

"I can't believe you had him in the back of our car," Seger says, wiping a hand down his face. "That was insane."

"All because you were in fucking labor and didn't let us know," Carter grumbles, crossing his arms across his chest. He scowls at me, leaning against the wall in his usual grumpy style.

"Hush, I'm too tired to hear you bitch at me, Grumpy," I mumble with heavy eyes.

The entire day's events weigh heavily on my shoulders. From the moment the contractions started and I didn't realize, to the moment I did realize my son was coming, and finally having him in the back of the car. But, it's the little moments like these that leave big impressions on my memories, and I'll forever have a story to tell our son. Our son. How strange to think that we've come this far from where we started. From friends, to enemies, to intimate lovers. We went from high school sweethearts to college students, and finally we're parents.

"Yeah, Grumpy, leave her be," Chase chastises with a taunting smile pulling at his lips. I can tell he wants to antagonize him more and rile him up, because that's what Chase loves to do these days, but he holds his tongue when he looks back at me with love in his eyes. "You're tired, Sunshine," he says, cocking his head to the side.

"Yeah, tired of your fucking face," Carter quips, coming to my side. I sigh when his fingers run through my ratty hair, careful not to pull at the tangles. Everything in my body says sleep, but there's a nagging in the back of my mind, reminding me my precious bundle still hasn't returned from all his tests. And Zepp is missing, too.

"When's he coming back?" I ask, peeking an eye open to look at Carter. His entire body tightens, and his hand stops its motion through my hair. He swallows hard, suspiciously darting his eyes to Chase on my other side.

I turn my head in time to see Chase waving his arms around, making a cutting motion across his throat. I narrow my eyes. "Where is the baby?" I nearly growl, threatening to bring out mama bear.

"He's coming back, Angel. Zepp's down there with him right now. They had to run an additional test--on something-- uh, they're fine! Don't worry," Seger says, waving a hand with his eyes closed as he lounges on the couch half-asleep. Yeah, don't worry, he says. But there's something weird going on between the three of them, and I'll get it out of them.

"What about his name? Have we decided on that yet?" Chase asks, glaring at the other two.

"Why do I feel like you're all up to something?" I frown, looking between the three of them, and they all shrug, looking away as innocently as possible. Yeah, definitely up to something. But what? I have no friggin clue. I'm way too tired to figure out their weird eyebrow conversations and arm waves. Too much to decipher with too low of energy. They could be planning to tuck tail—highly unlikely, I know—and I'd let them because I'm too tired to deal with them. Of course, I'd track their assess down, lock them in my basement, and never let them go again. So, yeah. No running from Kaycee, Sirs.

"We're not up to anything," Carter says, soothing my wet hair behind my ear. " I promise." Oh, promise my ass. I know those looks. Those sliding eyes and guilty faces. It's the same looks I've been seeing for the past five years.

I sigh, "I have a name in mind, one we didn't talk about. What about—" my mouth snaps shut at the sight of Zeppelin walking in with our baby bundled in his arms. And relief slams into me. Not that I thought my baby had run away, but after carrying him for nine months, it's strange to be away from him. I just want to hold him in my arms and snuggle him forever.

Zepp smiles down at him, running a finger down his plump cheeks. "He's been so good," Zepp murmurs with tears in his eyes. "They had to check some things, and I swear he didn't make a peep." My heart swells at the sight of them, and all the hormones rush forward.

Tears gather in my eyes when I look at the little face we created. We went from something so unexpected to something so full of pure joy–it completes us. This is our family. Our future.

Tears leak out of my eyes as he places our baby in my arms, and I feel the name deep in my bones calling to me. It feels so right, and I can't help but blurt it. "Roman," I whisper, lifting my eyes to the guys. They crowd my bed, widening their eyes. "Roman Weston--"

"Cole," Zepp says. "He takes your last name." The others nod in agreement without a fight.

"Really? You don't want to do the DNA and have it as one of yours?" They shake their heads, eyeing each other. Oh yeah, they're up to something. But what could it be?

"I do like the Weston part," Seger says with a smug grin. "West-on, uh-huh, it's fuc--freaking perfect."

"Good save, dickbag," Chase mutters, swiftly covering his mouth.

"We are really going to have to watch ourselves. Babies pick up on words fast." Zepp says, messing with Roman's blanket.

I smile down at my bundle. His bright green eyes stare up at me, exploring my face. And then his lip quivers again, exploding into a loud cry.

"Fuck! He's got some lungs on him," Carter says, covering his ears. "Fix him!" He says, waving a hand and scrunching his nose.

"What's wrong with him?" Chase asks, leaning down,

wrinkling his nose. "Does he need a change? Hungry?" Roman continues to wail as I set him down on the bed between my sprawled-out legs. Unraveling his blanket, his arms and legs kick out in stiff movements, jerking around with every cry. His tiny fists clench together, and I stop everything and freeze. My brain freezes, reading the four words printed on his onesie. Something I never thought I'd be capable of doing or want to do. I never expected one husband, let alone four.

'Will you marry us?'

I run a finger down his little onesie, tears filling my eyes. "Seriously?" I ask, tracing the four words printed on it.

"Yes," Zepp says, pulling a ring box out of his pocket. Flipping it open, he reveals a simple engagement ring. One large diamond sits surrounded by four smaller ones, representing our love for one another.

"What do you say, Angel?" Seger asks, dropping to his knee.

"Will you marry us?" Carter asks, dropping to his knee. One by one, they each drop to their knees, reaching out to me with glossy eyes.

"You planned this?" I sniffle. Roman grabs onto my finger with an iron grip, wailing more like he's urging me to say yes so he can latch onto my breast and finally eat.

"Of course, Sunshine," Chase whispers, bringing my left hand in the air. "We love you so much, and we never want to let you go."

"We want to make you ours," Zepp says, slipping the ring onto my finger. It glitters in the light, sending my heart into a frenzy.

"Forever," Seger nods. "And always, Angel Baby."

Tears fall, and I nod. "Yes, oh my God, yes! I'll marry all of you." Someone pulls me into a hug, letting me cry into their neck, while someone else takes the baby and soothes his cries with hushed words of love.

After their proposal, I stare at the ring while feeding Roman. This is my life. My baby. My boys. And a massive wedding ring on my finger.

---

A FEW DAYS after Roman is born, we are discharged and in perfect health. We got back to our house and settled in, trying to get used to caring for a baby. Roman proves to be a quiet baby. He cries for milk and when he needs a change, but other than that, he doesn't make a peep.

Zeppelin plays guitar in his room every night, soothing him to sleep with a quiet melody. Every morning Carter takes Roman into his office, holding him tight while working. Seger and Chase take turns getting up every night with him, helping me feed him, and caring for him. They never take their duties lightly, coming to fatherhood the best way they know how.

---

"ALRIGHT, fuckers! The results are in! Who's ready to pay up!" Seger shouts, strolling into the living room with an envelope in his hand.

"They're in? Already?" I ask, leaning back into Carter's embrace. His arm settles under mine, helping me hold Roman up as he feeds.

"I can't wait to be a thousand dollars richer!" Carter says in a low voice full of humor.

"You'll come to learn your daddies are idiots," I coo at Roman through a grin, earning a scoff from Chase.

"Alright, alright! Tell us who the daddy is." Chase says, pausing Netflix. He leans forward with a serious expression, resting his elbows on his knees, and his chin rests in his hand.

"You know you're all his dads, right? This doesn't change

anything." I look around the room, and they nod in confirmation.

"It was just for health reasons so that Rome can have a detailed history for the future," Zepp says, rubbing his hands together with a small smirk.

"And we were really fucking curious," Carter says from what I can only assume is a big grin. "So get fucking on with it!"

"Fine, fine," Seger says with a smug grin. "But you better be ready to hand over my money because that kid has my DNA running through him."

As Seger rips into the envelope, we all wait on pins and needles. Pulling out five papers, he shifts through them with raised eyebrows. Finally, he snorts in disbelief, barking out a laugh.

"Well, I'll be damned!" He grins more, shaking his head.

"Spill it!" Chase shouts, jumping to his feet.

"Well, it looks like my DNA does run through the kid's DNA, just not exactly mine," Seger says, handing the paper over to Zepp.

Zepp stiffens, tears filling his eyes. "Wow," he whispers. "Holy fuck," his eyes lock on Roman, suckling his breakfast. "He's mine."

"Congrats, bro, you contributed to our spawn," Seger says, shoving Zepp's shoulder. He comes and claims the spot next to Carter and me, peering down at Roman's face. "With his DNA mixed with yours, how much do you want to bet he's a boy genius?" Seger grins, pecking Roman's forehead.

Zepp snorts, "Well, we'll show him the ropes."

"He'll be an expert Angel Warrior player by the time he's ten," I whisper, watching his lips move on my nipple, pulling milk into his mouth.

Seger scowls. "I have to get to a higher level, or my kid will be better than me. Good thing they added more levels."

An evil grin spreads across his face. "I'll be better than you soon," he says, rubbing his hands together.

I frown. "No! You can't play without me. That's not fair." He grins, flicking my nose.

"Sorry, Angel! I can't hear you over the sound of my level going up!" He says, running off towards the basement with a pep in his step as he marches down the stairs, and the sound of the video game loading blares through the house.

"Bastard," I mumble, setting back into Carter.

"Want me to kick his ass?" he asks, kissing my cheek.

"Nah. He's so far behind, I could take a month break and he'd still be behind me." I snort, closing my eyes, snuggling into Carter's warmth.

"Sleep," Carter whispers. "I know it was a long night."

"We've got him, Sunshine. What's the point of four dads if we don't treat you like a queen?"

"Mmmkay," I mumble, letting the darkness of sleep take me over.

---

AFTER SEVERAL MONTHS, we made our big move and sold the house we started our life in. We built a place on the outskirts of East Point Bluff, with acres upon acres of land and no neighbors in sight. Security gates sit at the edge of our driveway and continue around our entire property, helping me feel safe in the town that almost killed me. For the first few weeks, I refused to leave the property without one of the boys by my side, but as time went on, I moved on, too. Through therapy and healing, we made a home in the place we ran far away from.

When Roman was nine months old, the boys and I got married on the beach. Surrounded by our excited families, we officially said 'I Do.' The boys surprised me at the end of the ceremony, pulling out paperwork with grins on their faces and bouncing on their toes.

"We wanted to share a last name, and since we are marrying you...."

"We're the fucking hyphenated Coles now." Seger whooped, pulling me into his arms.

After conquering numerous obstacles and surviving near-death experiences, we made it. We made it to the future, and we couldn't be happier.

# BONUS EPILOGUE

## SEGER

**Seven Years Later**

"Dead Records?" I ask, scrunching my nose. Looking up the worn letters line the top of the storefront and then to the neighborhood around us.

Jesus. I've seen my fair share of neighborhoods since we started this whole thing, but this one is the worst. Cracked sidewalks. Buildings falling apart.

"That's what her neighbor said," Zepp says, rubbing his chin and no doubt, inspecting everything. "Said she lived here now after her mom—" A large lump jumps down his throat, and he looks away, no doubt reliving the pain of losing our mother. You're never the fucking same after your mother takes her last breath.

"Yeah, I get it, man," I say, blowing out a breath. "Maybe up there?" I ask, pointing toward the upper windows overlooking the worn out street we're standing on.

My skin crawls with unease at the neighboring buildings and the people walking around. Don't get me wrong, I'm not one to fucking judge. But this entire town is a shit hole filled to the fucking brim with violence and crime. Even walking to our sister's sketchy ass ex-apartment made me uneasy as hell. I'm no stuck up prick, but I've always grown up in affluent places. But this town? This place? It's fucking shady as shit, and I can't wait to climb back onto our private plane and get the fuckity fuck out of here. Call me an over privileged asshole all you want, but this place is up to no good.

"I hope so," Zepp mumbles, eyeing the foot traffic on the opposite side of the road.

"This is such a fucking mess," I mutter. "If the old man had fucking money set aside for everyone then why didn't he just fucking give it to them."

"Maybe he forgot?" Zepp asks, shaking his head. "Those last few years, he didn't even recognize us or the kids or Kaycee."

"Right. Well, his fucking lawyer could have said something before now. Now we have to fucking traipse the globe looking for our long-lost siblings and presenting them with a fucking wad of cash when we have other shit to worry about," I say, blowing out a fucking breath.

This entire year since my dad fucking finally croaked has been a whirlwind of fucked up revelations. First his lawyer informs us that we have fourteen fucking siblings to track down and offer their inheritance to them in person, per our fathers request. Apparently, he'd been setting money aside for each of them all this time. Before we thought he was a deadbeat who abandoned his children for more pieces of ass. But now? Fuck, I don't know. He probably knew the quality of woman he was attracted to and didn't want the gold diggers taking all the fucking money when he inevitably fucked off and cheated on them or she left. Maybe he did it to protect all the kids.

"Well, she's the last one. You remember her, right?" He asks, raising a brow.

I snort. "Dad had so many women in and out of the house at so many fucking times in our lives, I don't remember shit," I groan, running my fingers over my brow. "I'm just glad she's the last one. This has been such a fucking stressful year." I shake my head and check my phone again.

"He kicked River and her mom Stella out because she talked to a repair guy over the phone. He thought she was cheating on him and didn't give her a chance to explain herself. I vaguely remember them leaving with the clothes on their back and nothing else. A week later, Dad was with someone else," Zepp mutters, and when I peek up from my phone, he runs a hand down his face, displaying his frustrations.

My brows furrow when I think that far back. Fuck. River was maybe two when that happened, and we were seven. I vaguely remember Stella begging for my dad to change his mind, and that she just wanted the damn dishwasher fixed to make life easier. Closing my eyes, I think back to her loving words, the last words she ever spoke to us. She was one of the good moms who had come through.

Fuck. My phone beeps again, and my heart races. I know exactly who's texting me, and I can't help the smile on my face. My poor wife has been stuck home with Chase, three boys, and a pregnant belly for the last week. Carter's been working his ass off finalizing contracts and doing other Veritas bullshit.

> Angel: I know you're checking in, but I'm fine.

> Angel: Well maybe not fine..... I think the boys need....less sugar.

> Me: Snort. Are they running up the walls?

> Angel: Axel and Dash ate the dog food, and Rome is....refusing to wear clothes again...

> Me: And my little angel? She okay? No contractions? We'll be home right after this!

> Angel: Kicking like a kickboxer...

> Me: that's my fucking girl.

> Angel: She's definitely taking after you \*\*kissy face\*\*.

I beam at the prospect of finally holding my baby girl in my arms. My own little angel in the making. With each kid, we've DNA tested for health concerns, and so it's on their records as they grow up. And with each kid, it wasn't mine biologically. Sure, I fucking love Roman, our oldest, Axel and Dash, our fraternal twins, who by the way, have two separate fathers. But—

"Come on, man. One last sister to deliver money to," Zepp says, knocking me out of my thoughts. "Then we can go back home. We have so much work to do," he says through an overwhelmed sigh.

> Me: Love ya, Angel! See you after a while.

"That's an understatement," I mumble, shaking my head.

Zepp's been the head of our dad's record company empire since our senior year of college. He ran himself ragged trying to balance school, the company, and our family. Soon after we graduated and moved back to East Point, I stepped up and became his partner with the company. And now, we run it together. West Records was once our father's, and now, it's ours. We've kept the same shit going on, but we've improved the label with new bands. Battle of the Bands at our newest club, The KC Club. Where we can display all our new favorite bands and showcase their talents to the population.

"Let's fucking do this," I grumble, marching toward the front door of the record store, and waltz inside.

A little bell rings above my head, followed by another

when Zepp finally steps through. It's a quaint little store, filled to the brim with new and old records.

"Welcome to Dead Records, if you need anything my name is River. Just let me know." I stiffen at her worn out voice, turning to get a glimpse of the little sister who was ripped away from us in the blink of an eye.

Every time I come face to face with them, it's like looking at myself in the mirror. No matter the hair color or the shape of the face, or the color of their skin, the eyes are always the same. It seems to be what our father handed down to each and every one of us—moss-green eyes.

She sits behind a large L-shape counter with a glass front and wooden top. Old, valuable records sit in the protected case on stands. Magazines, old cassette tapes, and CDs line the countertop in tip-top shape. Jesus. This is like a fucking perfectly kept monument to what music used to be.

Her long brown hair, much like the color of ours, is pulled up into a messy bun on the top of her head. One earbud sits in her right ear with an open laptop resting beside her as someone's face, much like a professor's, appears on the screen.

"You're River Blue West?" Zepp asks in a fucking clinical way, making her eyes snap up to us.

River frowns and scrunches her nose in disgust, taking out her earbud.

"Whoever you are," she says, cocking her to the side and examining us with a calculating eye. "I'm not interested. You assholes keep coming to me thinking I can get you whatever it is you think, but that's not how it works. I am a West. As in, one of over a dozen, and I'm not the West that can get you fucking famous." She shakes her head, going to put her earbud back in, but stalls when Zepp opens his big fucking mouth.

"I'm Zeppelin, and this is Seger, we're —"

"My fucking brother. Yup! I've heard that one before" She

says, narrowing her eyes and scoffs, waving a hand. "It's funny, last I checked my billionaire brothers were living it up in California and signing douchebags like Whispered Words, to their label. Not coming to bumbfuck nowhere, Illinois. It's almost laughable. You scammers will do anything to get a buck. But newsflash, dickweeds—I'm as broke as an unfunny joke." She scrunches her nose again, and I can't fucking help myself.

I break out in a deep laugh, putting my hands on my knees, and wheezing. "You're definitely a fucking West. Shit."

"You done?" She asks, looking at me like I'm the weirdest person she's ever met. "There's a clinic down the street if you need it. It shouldn't be too crowded right now."

"A clinic?" Zepp asks, rearing back.

"For his obvious drug addiction," she says with the wave of her hand again at my crazy outburst, which causes me to bark out another laugh.

"Here, here, fuck," I wheeze, digging into my wallet and throwing my license at her. She catches it with ease from her seated position and furrows her brows. "See? I'm Seger fucking West. The real fucking deal." I turn to Zepp with a gigantic grin and murmur, "I think she and Kace would get along fucking fine."

Zepp side-eyes me with a snort and steps up to the counter and flips open his wallet. Her jaw drops, and our shit falls to the counter.

"The fuck you doing here? Listen, the shit I said about Dad, I....." I hold up a hand, stopping her before she says more.

"Dad was the biggest fucking cock on the planet when he was alive…"

"We're not here to discuss a dead man's shortcomings. We're here to discuss your inheritance," Zepp says, gaining her complete and utter attention.

She swallows hard and shakes her head. "I don't want his

fucking money. I don't want anything from the piece of shit. He kicked me and Ma out without anything but the clothes on our backs. Ma dragged us back here, and we've lived on food stamps and the medical card for fucking years. I don't need a damn dime from Corbin West," she hisses, jumping to her feet. "I've done fucking fine without him."

I swallow hard at her swollen stomach, protruding from a long band shirt and small shorts when she stands behind the counter, earning me a frown.

"What? You've never seen a pregnant woman before?" She chides, narrowing her eyes at me with so much suspicion I could choke on it. This girl will be a hard fucking nut to crack, but I have a feeling once we have her trust, we'll be bonded for life.

I snort, running a hand down my face. "Sure I have. It's just fucking uncanny, you're as far along as our wife. Twenty-eight weeks, right?" I eye her up and down as her hand flies to her stomach, and her nose scrunches.

"Um, yeah," she says quieter than she was before, nibbling on the bottom of her lip.

"Do you have time for lunch?" Zepp asks, gesturing toward a diner across the street.

She licks her lips when a loud rumble erupts from her stomach, and she hangs her head.

"Now that you know we're really your brothers, we have some shit we'd like to discuss with you. And I think you want to hear it." I lick my lips when she finally meets my eyes, and I see the indecision resting in their depths. She's fighting with herself and losing the mental battle to push us away.

"Let's get some burgers, fries, and hell—a milkshake. We really do have things to discuss with you. Big things," Zepp tacks on with a convincing voice.

She licks her lips again and finally sighs. "Fine. Class was fucking boring today, anyway. Who cares about the history of business bullshit. Take me to lunch, but don't expect me to take a damn handout," she gripes, shutting her computer down, and closing it. She picks up a small backpack style purse and flings it over her shoulder, before grabbing a set of keys off the counter.

Looking down at my spunky ass sister, I fight the smile trying to take over my lips. Yeah, she's definitely a fucking West with her hard head and fucking stubborn ways. But we'll wear her down and gift her the fucking dream of a lifetime.

---

"Hold the Weiner," she says, putting a finger in the air. Her entire body trembles, and her mouth hangs open. "Twenty million dollars? Shut the front door," she gasps, slumping in the bench as the waitress drops off her strawberry milkshake and mounds of food. "I just...I can't...he just..." she stutters, shoving a handful of fries into her mouth and moans.

"Twenty million is just the tip of the iceberg, River. More will be deposited, according to our father's lawyer. He left money for each of you..."

"Each of us?" She asks, slurping her milkshake in a few gulps. "You've met...."

"All fucking fourteen of the West children, yeah. We've been down that road, and you, dear sister, are the last damn one," I mumble, shoving my cheeseburger into my mouth. "Fuck. Nothing beats a quaint little diner's burger," I moan around my food, taking another bite.

"Animal," Zepp grumbles, taking an itty bitty bite of his burger like the gentleman he thinks he is.

My ears perk up as a song blares over the speakers, and a familiar singer's voice washes over me. I swear that Kieran Knight has a way with his raspy voice to fucking draw you in and get his claws in you.

Normally, owners don't mix in with their talent, letting the agents handle everything, and only intervening when money is involved. But that's what sets West Records apart from everyone else. We're front and center for our Battle of the Bands, and we intermingle with the people who trust us to thrust their careers.

"Is this?" Zepp asks, tilting his head.

"Fucking right it is. They're hella fucking talented, and I can't believe they came out of nowhere," I say with a grin, turning back to our sister.

Her face pales and moisture pools above her lip. A mist takes over the depths of her green eyes, and her breath shudders. Her hand rubs the length of her stomach. A silent alarm flips in the back of my mind at her glazed over expression, alerting me to something....odd.

"Whispered Words," she mutters, her once shocked face shifting to rage. A vein pounds in her reddened forehead, and her lips twist into an angry scowl.

"Uh, yeah. That's them. They won our battle of the bands like seven months ago and have taken the world by storm. They're absolutely…"

"Absolute fuck heads," she hisses, clenching her teeth.

I hold up a hand. "Um….I feel like I'm missing something," I mutter, side-eyeing my brother with confusion.

"I'll sign the papers for the money," she says, taking a deep breath, but steely determination settles on her shoulders.

"Okay, cool," Zepp says, reaching down for the manila envelope he brought inside, hoping she'd take the inheritance to help her.

"On one stipulation," she grinds out, looking over the papers.

"What's that?" I ask.

"I want a job at West Records. I want to intern. I want to become a band manager," she says, nodding vigorously as she looks over the papers. "I have experience managing bands from the area. So, in return, I'll sign the papers if you give me a job. I'll move out to California and start as soon as possible."

"I...Umm..." I look at Zepp who scratches his chin.

"To become a manager is a hefty undertaking. You'd have to intern at the bottom and get the feel for it. A bachelor's in Music Management is a necessity at West Records. We want the best of the best, but you're family. And if you want a job..."

"I'll start at the bottom. I'll sort fucking mail. I want this..." she says again with a snarl, taking another gulp of milkshake to calm herself down.

"But why? You could take your inheritance and never work another day in your life. Why would you want to?"

She rubs her stomach again, looking out the window with that same distant look forming over her eyes, like she's trapped inside a memory, and she can't break free.

"I'm getting my business degree right now and working through summer programs to obtain it ASAP. I can change my major to music business. I'll put in the work. Anything to make those assholes pay for what they did to me." She frowns slightly, shaking herself out of her thoughts.

"Who?" Zepp asks, furrowing his brows.

"They promised they'd take me with them. They promised....they loved me." A slight hiccup escapes from her trembling lips, but she looks away, refusing to let us see her break. "They promised me everything, and I believed every lie they told." She swallows hard, vigorously wiping away the tears falling down her cheeks. "They left me, and they left her," she whispers, pointing to her pregnant stomach.

I blow out a breath, filled with so much fucking confusion. "Who?"

She stares out the window again, letting the emotions take hold. "Whispered Words promised me the world, and then they turned their back on me."

**WANT TO GO BACK TO THE BEGINNING AND FIND OUT WHAT WHISPERED WORDS DID TO RIVER? PREORDER BITTER NOTES HERE AND FIND OUT!**

# CONNECT WITH ALY

Made in the USA
Las Vegas, NV
20 February 2025

18447599R00351